HALFSKIN BOXED

TONY BERTAUSKI

BERTAUSKI STARTER LIBRARY_

BOOK 1_

HALFSKIN

HALFSKIN_

God deals everyone tragedy.
Some more than others.

CHAPTER ONE_

"LOOK WHAT I GOT."

Alex pulled a utility knife out of his pants like an eight-year-old magician. He slid the lever. Parker reached for it.

"No, you don't," Alex said.

"Where'd you get that?"

"Your dad's garage."

Nix stepped back. He wasn't scared of the blade—it was just a knife—it was the look on Alex's face, the way he bit his tongue, like there were ideas bouncing in his head. Eight-year-olds shouldn't look like that.

Parker's dad was on the far side of the pool with the rest of the adults, drinking out of fancy glasses and laughing super loud. Fifteen minutes ago they were sitting around singing "Happy Birthday" to Parker. The kids ate cake. The adults did, too. Then the clown showed up and the adults went to the far side with tall bottles. There was a hot tub over there. The kids followed the clown.

The guy told corny jokes and tied balloons, said he could make any animal on the North American continent as long as it looked like a wiener dog. He smelled like exhaust fumes. Parker, Alex and Nix ditched the clown when the adults popped the tall bottles.

"Don't worry." Alex slid the blade back and shoved it in his pants. "It's just a stupid knife. No one will know."

"What if my dad finds out? He'll know you were in his tools."

"You want your present or not?"

Parker held a box at his side. It was a paintball gun. Aunt Maggy bought it for him. It was cheap and crappy. But it was a gun. And it was strapped into the box with plastic ties a rat couldn't chew through. Parker's mom and dad smiled when he opened it, made sure he said thank you to Aunt Maggy and let him show it off to everyone, but he knew that paintball gun was going back to the store. They told Aunt Maggy not to buy him one. They warned her. Aunt Maggy never listened.

"Let's just get scissors," Parker said.

"Dude, it's not a freaking laser beam. Go get a little wiener balloon with Freaky the Clown if you're scared. Nix and me will cut this loose and have our own little war. Right, Nix?"

Nix had never shot a gun. He'd carved a bar of soap with a Swiss Army knife and shot an arrow at a bale of straw, but he'd never pulled a trigger. Unless squirt guns count. *They don't.*

Parker looked across the pool. Not one adult was looking. Once those bottles got popped, they could do anything they wanted.

"What're you doing?" Jennifer stepped up.

"Nothing," Parker said. "This is a boys' meeting. Go away."

Parker walked quickly around a hedge of azaleas and ducked behind a sweet-smelling gardenia. He laid the box on a bed of leaves. The gun was ready to be cut loose. Ready to lock and load. Alex unveiled the knife. As the razor grew, so did the grin.

New and sharp and pointy.

"Here." Parker held up his hand. "Give it."

"I'll do it."

"It's my present. I'll do it."

"Yeah, I went and got it, so I'll do it."

Nix looked through a gap in the bushes. He shook the blond hair from his eyes. He was the only boy at the party with hair that long.

His sister didn't have time to cut it. That's what she told people. No one argued. When your family had gone through all the things Nix and Cali Richards had been through, you cut some slack. Long hair on a boy, no big deal.

One of the adults in the hot tub said something really, really funny. They were goofing on the clown. Nix's sister wasn't near the hot tub; she was with some of the moms, holding her baby like she was made of glass.

Cali cut her hair super short after she had Avery, said she wanted to remember the day this little angel came into the world. Cutting her hair seemed stupid to Nix, but then everyone said motherhood made her skin glow and the short hair showed it off, like having a baby somehow lit her up all Christmassy. People said she was beautiful—his friends said she was hot.

He couldn't see it. She was his sister.

"Nix, get down here," Alex sort of whispered. "We need you to hold this."

Nix dropped on his knees. Alex was sawing at the plastic bands and Parker was complaining that he was scratching the barrel. Alex pushed his red hair back. If Parker had some muscles, the box wouldn't move around so much and he wouldn't scratch the gun, now would he?

Parker was on one end of the box, Nix on the other. Alex gripped the knife like he was going to stab the gun. A drop of sweat rolled off the end of his nose. He'd gone through at least half of the bands when the gun began to wiggle. Just a few more and it would come loose. Parker's eyes were wide. He let go with one hand, ready to pounce. He'd been friends with Alex long enough to know you had to be ready.

"Don't let go, dummy," Alex whined.

"It's my gun, I'll do what I want."

Nix pressed down on Parker's corner to help out. He didn't want Alex to get the gun, either. It wasn't fair. Besides, Alex was a jerkoff.

A glass broke near the hot tub.

The adults began laughing.

Alex hunched over and sawed another band. *Plink!* It shot into the grass. Parker's right hand hovered over the gun. Alex told him to get back, he couldn't see. Parker told him to shut up and let him have the knife, but Alex told him to shove it up his ass.

An adult shouted about cleaning up the glass and to keep the kids away. Everyone needed to be wearing shoes. Nix wasn't wearing shoes. His sister would come looking for him. He was the only one that had to wear a helmet when he was skateboarding, the only one that still wore a helmet on a bike. She wouldn't give on that. Safety. Safety.

SAFETY.

He tried to sit up straight, just to make sure Cali was still showing off Avery and he wouldn't have to—

SHHHPT.

Nix felt a pinch.

Alex dropped the knife.

He held his hand to his chest. Fear froze on Parker's face. What would happen when his dad found out he was cutting open the paintball gun with a stolen utility knife they used to LOP OFF NIX'S FINGER!

Nix was afraid to move.

"Is it bleeding?" Alex asked.

It hurt at first, when the knife sliced through his finger, but now it was numb. He was afraid if he moved it, the pain would come back.

"Come on, let me see it. I don't even think I got you or there'd be blood all over the place."

Something warm seeped between his fingers. It wasn't red and sticky.

It was gray.

"What is that?" Parker asked.

"Looks like snot." Alex reached out.

Nix turned away. He cradled his hand like he was holding his niece. He knew what the gray stuff was; he just wasn't supposed to tell anyone. But then no one ever told him what to say if he cut himself and his friends saw the stuff coming out. He had to say something. You don't bleed snot and just put a Band-Aid on it without explaining.

Jennifer was standing just out of sight. "I'm going to get my mom."

Parker caught her by the ankle. She could've broken free if she wanted. All she had to do was scream and a mom would come running. But Parker had tears in his eyes. Even Alex was sitting still, his lips forming a perfect O.

"Please, please, please... don't tell. Don't tell. I'll promise you anything. Anything, just don't tell."

"Nix cut himself," Jennifer said too loudly. "How is no one going to find out?"

"Please, but... don't... not yet." His lips fluttered. "I'll give you my old iPod, I promise. I don't need it anymore. You can have it, I swear. Just don't tell."

Jennifer put her hands on her hips. "But he's hurt."

"No, I'm not."

They all looked.

Parker crawled back over, hope smeared on his face. Eyes wide, mouth open. If he could wish for anything in the world, it would be for this whole thing to go away. He'd give up the stupid gun if that's what it took.

"Let me see," he said.

Nix pulled his hand away and peeked down like he was looking at a secret. Gray stuff was all over his shirt. It shimmered like metal shavings beneath a rotating magnet. He'd seen that before, at the doctor's office. Once a month, his sister took him to some special doctor, where they'd poke his finger and look at the stuff under some special magnifier before drawing a sample from his arm. No matter how many times they poked him, it only hurt for a second.

This was the first time he'd been cut open outside the doctor's office.

And it wasn't too bad.

He held his hand out like a plate. Alex and Parker leaned over like he was unveiling a dead bunny. The blade had sliced over his knuckle. It was down to the bone. But there was no white tissue gleaming through the gap. It was just a shimmery mass of gray that gyrated between flaps of skin.

"What the hell is that?" Alex asked.

Nix stood up. His sister was sitting in the shade with a blanket over Avery's head. She was probably breast-feeding. She wasn't going anywhere for a few minutes.

"You promise not to tell?" Nix asked.

They nodded, just like eight-year-olds.

"You swear? Because this is a big-time secret. I'm not supposed to tell anyone about this, ever."

"Swear, dude. Swear." Alex held up the Scout's Honor. Parker imitated him. Neither one of them were scouts.

Nix took one more look at his sister. She was far away, not even looking.

He looked at Alex. Looked at Parker.

"Robots."

There was a long pause. "Uhhh, what?" Alex muttered.

"These are robots." Nix dipped his finger in the wound and held up the gray spot.

"I don't know what that means," Parker said.

"I know," Alex said. "It means he's a dope. I oughta punch you in the face, Nix."

Parker didn't take his eyes off the finger. "Why isn't your blood red?"

"Because that's probably a fake finger." Alex reached for it and Nix yanked back. "See, told you. I seen one of those fake fingers at some store next to fake dog crap and fake puke. Come on, Parker. Let's get the gun and shoot him—"

"He means biomites," Jennifer said.

"Dude." Alex's face began to glow. "You got biomites?"

Nix didn't know if this was such a good idea.

"You're not supposed to get biomites until you're twelve."

"Actually, it's fifteen," Jennifer said. "And it's illegal to seed a minor, you know." She crossed her arms and smirked.

"Unless you're in an accident," Nix said. "Unless it's an emergency."

"Nope." She seemed less confident.

"What, you going to tell on him?" Alex said. "Go and tell the biomite police, you tattletale. Go on, see if they care. Nix got mangled in a car accident and they put the mites in him." Alex nodded at him. "Right?"

Nix nodded. That was the truth. Everyone in town knew that.

Jennifer stomped off.

"What's it like, dude?" Alex leaned forward. "Is it like superpowers or something? Can you grab hot coals or punch holes in walls?"

"No." Nix stroked the wound that had nearly sealed. "It feels normal, I guess."

"Oh, man. I can't wait to get biomites." Alex flopped on his butt, staring. "My old man got them to boost the cartilage in his knee and it made him, like, twice as strong."

"My mom," Parker added, "got them to fix her eyes. They changed colors."

"And made her tits bigger," Alex added.

"Shut up."

"You shut up."

Nix was tempted to put his finger in his mouth. He'd done it before; it tasted like aluminum. Actually, he just wanted to hide it. He wasn't supposed to tell. He didn't like the attention. It wasn't like he wanted to be seeded. It didn't make him special. He didn't feel any different than before, so he didn't see the big deal. He was just like everyone else. He just had more artificiality, his sister said. Besides, when they turned fifteen, everyone gets seeded to immunize or correct vision or fix learning disabilities or whatever. And when they were adults, they could fix wrinkles and stuff.

"What's going on over here?" One of the moms came around the bushes. "You boys teasing Jennifer?"

Parker sat on the gun. Alex stared. Nix stared.

Guilty.

"He's got biomites." Jennifer pointed. "And he's a minor."

The mom chuckled. "Well, there's always exceptions. Are you all right, honey?"

Nix turned away with his hand tightly against his chest.

"Let me see. If you cut yourself, we need to get some help. Let me see what you did." She knelt down. The veins snaked blue over the tendons on the back of her hands. Her palms smelled clean. He remembered his mom's were that way. "It's all right."

Nix looked through the bushes, across the pool. The adults were up and walking. The broken glass was picked up. The dads were mostly there. The moms weren't. Neither was Cali.

"Daisy?" The moms were coming around the corner. "Is everything all right?"

"I think Nix hurt himself."

Parker was scooting back into the bushes, using the gun like a disc, hoping to disappear. Nix thought about pointing to the half-loose paintball gun and the utility knife in Alex's pants.

"Nix?" Cali was the last to show. Avery was cradled on her shoulder. "You all right?"

Nix wanted to run to her. To hide behind her.

"Jennifer says he's been seeded."

And then the attention went from Nix to Cali. Parker bolted through the greenery, ditching the gun in the groundcover.

"Is that right?" one of the moms said. "How'd you get him seeded that young?"

"You have connections at the lab?" someone else said. "Eric's having trouble with attention deficit disorder and I can't get the doctors to give him a release. Is there anything you can do?"

"Sally's suffering from constant ear infections and they want to do surgery."

"Benjamin's got acne."

"Nix." Cali stuck her hand out. "It's time to go. Come on."

Nix leapt up and snatched her hand on the fly. They walked briskly alongside the house with a cadre of moms in tow, all of them making their best offers. They were all wealthy, all connected, but none of them could skirt the laws.

Listen, if you want your kid seeded, all it takes is a near fatal car accident and two dead parents and you can have all the damn biomites your heart desires. Hey, it's a blast.

Cali didn't talk as she buckled Avery into the car seat, squealing.

"Sorry."

"Not your fault," she said.

"I didn't mean to tell them."

"Not your fault," she said again.

The moms watched them drive off. A few were waving.

They drove home with the radio turned up, the way Avery liked it. Cali turned off her phone. When they got home, she told Thomas, her husband, they weren't going to any parties for a while.

Nix went to his room. He was different.

He would always be different.

10 YEARS LATER_

MOTHER_

BLOGGER'S REACTION TO THE BIRTH OF MOTHER

THE REAL AVENGER'S BLOG

Shooting Truth-Bullets Since Birth

Subscribers: 3,233

It's the end of time, peeps.

Mark this date, put a black X on your calendar because it's all over, starting today. It used to be that if you didn't like the laws where you lived, you just moved to another state or another country. Freedom existed somewhere in the world. We had a choice. I mean, hell, if you were desperate enough, you could live on the South Pole with penguins and shit.

Not anymore.

Today, it's all over.

Today, Mother was born.

Who's Mother? Our Mother. Already got a mother? Now you got two, only this one will know everything about you. You can't hide from her. She'll know when you're full of crap, know where you stash your porn, know when you pick your nose and when you eat it.

You'll hate her, and she'll know that, too.

Case you've been asleep for the last ten years, the Mitochondria Terraforming Hierarchy of Record is what I'm talking about.

Let's just call her Mother.

A mother that doesn't bake cookies or wash your underwear. She's not getting up to make you French toast or wipe your nose. Nope. This bitch is going to spy on you until you're dead. Which may be sooner than you think.

Mother is somewhere in the frozen plains of Wyoming. No pictures of her exist because no one's allowed to even fly over. But rumors say she's this massive dome, a computer the size of a football stadium, like some artificial brain heaved out of the frozen soil that's wirelessly connected with every biomite in existence.

Did you catch that? EVERY BIOMITE IN EXISTENCE!

Hear that buzzing on your phone? She's listening.

Feel that tickle on your laptop? She knows you're tapping.

All that *Do Not Covet Your Neighbor's Wife* crap? Yeah, that's the real deal now. Mother might tell your wife what you're thinking about doing to Joe-Bob's wife mowing the lawn in a tube top.

George Orwell wasn't even close, man. I mean, Big Brother was just a peashooter compared to Mother. Big Brother was pissing on a forest fire; Mother's bringing the goddamn ocean.

Here's the official statement from Marcus Anderson, chief of the Biomite Oversight Committee.

(BTW, he looks like a gargoyle. Right?)

It is with great pleasure that, after ten years of global effort, I present to you the greatest feat of humankind. I present to you a regulatory system that will keep all people safer and healthier for centuries to come. Bionanotechnology has put us on the brink of greatness, but with that comes uncertainty and danger. The human species has the potential to live forever. Or end tomorrow.

I prefer the former.

Mitochondria Terraforming Hierarchy of Record is linked to every booted cellular-sized biomite living inside our bodies. Its primary function will be to monitor individual levels of biomites and take appropriate action if, or when, they cross a previously determined threshold. This will keep us human.

This will keep us safe.

Forever.

I don't know about you, but this is not a gross infringement on our freedom: it's raping it. I don't want anything or anyone peeking into my biomites; that's none of your business, none of my neighbor's, and it sure as hell ain't the government's.

Biomites aren't evil, dude. They're artificial stem cells, that's all. What's the big deal? If you want to be 100% artificial, be my guest, that's your business, bro. I don't give a rat's pink sphincter what you do with your body. You want to boost your brain with biomites to get smarter? Hey, as long as you got the cash, good for you.

What the chief didn't say in his official statement was what exactly the *previously determined threshold* is.

Want to know?

You should, before you rebuild your kidney or tone those wrinkles, you should know that when your body is 40% biomites, you're a redline. And redlines go to jail.

JAIL.

Think I'm joking?

They call it a Detainment and Observation Center. You can't leave, you don't order takeout, you shower with other redlines. That's jail. You get a federally funded cot and three hots while they watch your biomite levels. On a side note, you'd think the scientists could figure out how to keep biomites from reproducing and slowly taking over our bodies once we get seeded. They are the geniuses, for Christ's sake. Doesn't seem like it should be all that hard.

But all right, whatever. So they continue dividing once they're in our bodies. It's worth the trade-off: they are the answer to every disease, every shortcoming, every desire known to man. They'll figure it out; give them some time.

But here's the kicker. Guess what happens when you hit 50%. Guess, no seriously. Take a stab. When your body becomes halfskin, when it's 50% God-given, good ole-fashioned organic cells and 50% artificial biomite cells, guess what Mother's going to do?

Bitch is going to shut you off.

That's right.

And when she does, when she turns off all your biomites like a light switch, what do you think happens to the other half? The living half?

Yeah. That's right.

It's real, peeps. Real as it gets.

The death of human liberty happened today and you probably didn't even feel it.

Well, I did.

CHAPTER TWO_

CALI KNELT DOWN TO REBOOT A SERVER. HER KNEE HIT THE concrete, driving spikes up her thigh. She cursed and didn't hold back. She stood a little too fast and steadied herself against the stainless steel rack. A head rush stormed her entire body, weakening her knees. She remained still until it passed and made a mental note to drink some water.

She walked two more rows. Computer after computer blinked green lights at her. No one would suspect she was in a suburban brick house with a pink flamingo in the front yard. The basement looked more like an industrial IT department. It took two air conditioners to keep the house cool.

She couldn't afford to shut her lab down. *Not now.*

No one could afford a setup like that—hell, there were companies that couldn't afford it. But she had money. *Blood money.* When she married Thomas, he joked he'd need another life insurance policy. Luck was not something Cali's family possessed. She thought he was joking, but he took out a ridiculous life insurance policy on himself so that Cali, Avery and Nix would never worry about money again if something ever happened.

And it did.

Cali sat at a desk cluttered with gadgets and monitors, microscopes and assemblers. She sipped at a water bottle while waiting for an espresso-like machine to drip a gun-metal droplet into a flask. No coffee from that machine. It was uniquely constructed to produce congealed biomites: the raw synthetic stem cells with designer DNA coding. At one drop per day, it was a slow process.

She took a heavy flask of mercury-like liquid off the shelf and swirled it under a circular magnifying glass attached to a hinged arm.

Good.

It would take a complete analysis to see if they worked, but she'd seen enough raw biomites to know the subtle colors, just like an Eskimo knew snow. These were brighter than usual, less viscous. Exactly what she expected.

There were six monitors arranged on the wall in two rows of three. The one in the middle, bottom row, was the largest. Numbers scrolled down a column that she occasionally stopped with a mouse-click. Several submenus expanded with another series of clicks. She sat back and let the numbers continue to run. The analysis was taking too long, but the program needed time.

Time was the only thing she couldn't afford.

Biomites were humanity's greatest invention. Forget telecommunications, forget transportation... bionanotechnology changed everything. Once humanity controlled the human body, they could cure disease, heal bones, alter brain chemistry. Biomites were the answer, the one big answer to every question.

Only one side effect. It was a big one. *They were malignant.*

They were exact duplicates of the body's cells but, for some unknown reason, wouldn't accept enzymatic cues to stop dividing. No matter what coding bionanoengineers inserted into the DNA, they always reverted back to runaway division, replacing the body's natural organic cells.

Cali had a theory.

She believed the biomites intuited the weakness of organic cells—their susceptibility to random DNA variability, cancer, disease—and logically replaced them. Biomites were doing what we wanted; they were making the body sound and impervious.

Perfect.

The monitor to the left, bottom row, chimed. Another email arrived and filed at the top of a long column of unread messages. The office manager confirmed Cali's paid leave of absence was nearly depleted. She'd spent her sick days and vacation long ago. Pretty soon, her leave of absence would convert to unpaid. Her employers had been very sympathetic. They gave her more time than they should have. She was a valuable asset, a deserving individual, but a Fortune 500 company can only bend the sympathy branch so far. Pretty soon, they'd prune it.

Cali finished the water and rubbed her eyes. She saw her reflection in the dark monitors. The shadows across her cheeks were long and dark, disguising the red rims of her eyelids and cracked lips. Oily blond hair hung over her eyes. She retied the ponytail.

She rolled the chair to the right and touched the electron microscope. Images lit up a dark monitor, obliterating her deathly reflection. The previous batch of biomites that percolated from the espresso machine was still active. Under magnification, they looked like grains of sand jittering on meth. Excellent stability, that was good. She wouldn't know if they possessed runaway division until further testing, but she didn't care about that. Not anymore.

Priorities change.

She was looking for biomites that would disappear. Not physically, but virtually. Every biomite emitted a frequency that could be monitored. That's what Mother watched, the frequency with which biomites *spoke* to each other. Mother was an eavesdropper, downloading everything they did. There weren't enough zeros to count how many biomites were in existence, but everyone had them.

So Mother knew what everyone was doing.

Cali wanted to change that.

So far, nothing worked. There was still hope. There was still time. But not much of either.

Someone squealed upstairs, followed by a fit of laughter. Avery was about to pee herself. Only Nix could make her laugh like that. She loved that sound, her favorite sound in the entire world. Without Nix, she might not hear it ever again.

This is all my fault. All mine. I knew this day was coming, knew his redline potential, but I waited. I waited because I'm selfish. Nix is going to pay for that. We're all going to pay.

The numbers continued to scroll in a fuzzy line.

She rubbed her eyes and tried to focus, but it only smudged the images further. She didn't have time for this, not now. She could sleep when this was all over; she just needed to focus, to see the data come together so that she could hide her little brother.

Get him off Mother's map.

Mother didn't care what he meant to her, what he meant to Avery. They would come, they would take him, they would take him from her life, from Avery's life, and he was all she had, all she had, he was all she had—

She closed her eyes.

Breathing slowly, breathing deeply.

She relaxed before opening her eyes. The images around her weren't sharp, but she could make them out. She could read them. The analysis was almost over. Once that was done, she could get the next batch started and then lie down for a nap. She'd done it earlier that day (or was it night, there were no windows in the basement), fallen directly into REM. Twenty minutes later, she was brand new.

She took the water bottle to the bathroom and filled it. She heard a bell ring and leaned out the door to see if the analysis finished early. The numbers were still scrolling. She sat back down and took another deep drink—

BING.

That was upstairs.

The doorbell.

Cali stayed completely still, ears pricked with attention. There were muddled voices. A long silence. She remained as still as a stowaway.

The basement door opened and snapped closed.

Little feet danced down the steps. "Mommy," Avery said, "there's some guy at the door talking to Uncle Nix."

Cali stood too quickly and braced herself on the desk. "Who?"

Avery shrugged. "They want him to go."

Cali stumbled to the steps, barely seeing the door at the top rush towards her. She punched it open, slamming it against the wall.

Time is out.

CHAPTER THREE_

Nix just finished draining the dishwasher when the doorbell rang.

He stopped to turn the television off, where cartoons blared loud enough that his sister would hear them in the basement. He was going to take her something to eat and considered mashing up a sleeping pill in some cottage cheese. She swore she was taking naps, but her face was caving in. He'd laced her food once before, when she pulled a week's worth of all-nighters to finish the coding on a new batch of biomites in time for a presentation at a global convention.

He dried his hands and slung the towel over his shoulder. There was a car in the driveway, a black four-door sedan with an unassuming man in the driver's seat. No sunglasses, no badge. Just an ordinary guy sitting like a waxy replication of a normal everyday somebody.

BING.

Nix slowed. He thought-commanded a self-analysis of the biomite population in his body.

39.8%.

He was composed of less than 40% biomites; that meant over 60% of his body was good, old-fashioned organic cells. That meant he wasn't redline. That meant it couldn't be them. But biomite patrol didn't make house calls to see how you were doing. They showed up for one reason.

There's some mistake.

He gripped the door handle.

They'll understand. Gear sometimes needs calibrated.

The door opened.

The man standing there, unlike his partner in the driver's seat, was wearing sunglasses, the reflective kind.

They stood there, facing each other. There were no words. No greeting or informal nods. Just a silent recognition. They'd never seen each other, but they knew what the other was about.

"I'm not redline," Nix stated.

The agent didn't flinch. He unclipped a cell-phone-sized gearbox from his belt. He held it up like a badge and waited. Nix took a half a step forward. The agent lowered the box, pressing it against Nix's flesh between the breastbone and bobbing Adam's apple.

Nix felt the thing whir hotly. Its effect scattered over his skin like electric spider webs, wrapping over his shoulders and across his back, penetrating his body like feeder roots to estimate the biomite population. The agent pulled the gearbox away, leaving Nix feeling weak. He looked at it and turned it so Nix could see the number.

"It's wrong."

"We'll confirm at the office."

"It'll say the same thing, and it's wrong."

"You need to come with us."

Nix took a step back. He considered running. The agent shook his head one time. There would be no running. Any attempt to resist would be met swiftly. Mother was in Wyoming and Nix in southern Illinois, but she could see him like he was standing right next to her. She knew what his biomites were doing, what he was thinking. If he ran, if he disobeyed a biomite agent, Mother would flip a switch. He'd hit the floor.

Obey. Or else.

It's the law.

"It is my duty to bring you into a Detainment and Observation Center to be fully analyzed. You are not under arrest, simply detained for further observation. If our readings are wrong, you will be brought back to your home and compensated for your time. Do you understand these rights?"

Nod.

He brandished a stiff metal ring, the color of a cold weapon. "For your safety and ours, I'm going to place this suppression ring around—"

A door cracked inside the house.

"NO!" Cali bounded across the room and wrapped her arms around Nix. "He's not redline. You can't take him."

"Ma'am, this will be your only warning. Do not interfere."

A car door shut. The driver approached the house.

"Look, look." Cali fumbled her own reader, slimmer and colder, against Nix's neck and shoved the reading in the agent's face. "38.8%. He's under; we still have time."

"He'll be verified at the satellite office. If there is a mistake, he will be back before dinner."

The driver stopped behind the first agent.

"No," she whispered.

"Ma'am."

Her hand clamped on Nix's arm.

There was a long moment of staring. Nix could sense all the thoughts floating around them like transparent bubbles. He couldn't hear them, but he sensed them. Thoughts of escape. Thoughts of apprehension.

Violence.

Nix reached up and gently squeezed her hand. It would be bad enough to be taken away. He wouldn't be able to handle watching his sister punished for it. She was still shaking her head, mouthing the same word over and over.

The agent reached up and lowered the suppression ring over

Nix's head to rest around his neck. It was cold against his skin, warming quickly.

Heaviness fell on him as the biomites in his body slowed down, diminishing their activity. They were not deactivated, just reduced to keeping him alive, to keeping him subdued for his safety and others. Thoughts became dull; memories began to pale.

But worst of all... *Cali is alone.*

Nix was guided to the car. A few of the neighbors watched. One leaned on a rake, relief on his face that it wasn't one of his kids.

Cali wasn't in the doorway when Nix sat in the backseat of the new-smelling sedan. The front door was closed. She was already in the basement.

The suppression ring wasn't fully powered. There was still time to say goodbye.

Nix laid his head back and closed his eyes. The car rocked as it backed over the curb. Traffic sounds faded. He no longer heard the cars passing or felt the pavement grind under the tires. The world around him disappeared. Nix went to his safe haven, went to a place he discovered many years ago, a place that protected him from the world. Where he wasn't different.

He went to a lagoon deep inside his mind.

CHAPTER FOUR_

THE LAGOON WAS DEEP AND CLEAR WITH STRIPED MUSSELS AND bright starfish on the sandy bottom. Sometimes sharks would find their way through a small channel that funneled water from the ocean. They would skim near the beach, their dorsal fins cutting the surface. They'd come so close that Nix could run his hand over their slick skin.

A fire smoldered from inside a pile of sticks, a thick column of smoke withering in the still air. There was no scent, no sting in his eyes. He smelled very little in this dreamland, good or bad.

The smoke obscured the view across the lagoon where, above the palms on the far shore, blue cliffs rose up. Halfway up was an opening that spewed water like a giant faucet, its roar heard a mile away. The water poured forth and sprayed misty droplets, leaving an ever-present rainbow stretching into the palms.

[*Away.*]

The smoke twisted away like a vacuum simply pulled it in the other direction. The waterfall hadn't changed much over the ten years he'd been coming to the lagoon. In fact, it was exactly like the day he first saw it. He was only eight. In fact, it was the day after he showed his best friends, Alex and Parker, the biomites in his finger.

Even though he was just a kid, he knew the dreamland wasn't normal.

But, then again, Nix was anything but normal.

He knew his body was in the back of a biomite agent's car. Time between the dreamland and fleshland wasn't synced. Dreamland time went so much slower. Still, the ring would suppress the biomites that powered dreamland.

Maybe he'd never visit again.

He looked around for Raine. The fire was there; she must be getting ready for something. Nix pulled a stick hard against his shin, heard it crackle until the dry fibers gave way and split open. The pain on his shin was dull and slight.

He dropped the branch on the smoldering fire. Sparks spit out from the bottom. He gathered the bark that flaked off and piled it onto the embers, waving and blowing it back into flames. Smoke billowed up. He squatted, rubbing his hands, as if he could feel the heat. Perhaps he could, but it was tepid. Like day-old dishwater.

The foliage rustled behind him. Something dragged through the weeds and then across the sand.

"Is the fire ready?"

Nix smiled.

"Such a slacker." Raine pulled a cord with a wild boar tied to the end, the tusks curled out of its mouth. Raine's skin was brown. Her black hair, cropped and choppy. Her eyes green, like the green of verdant forests when the sun rises.

She was about Nix's age, he guessed, eighteen years old or so. Her body was taut with muscle roiling around the bikini top. She showed up at the lagoon about five years ago. Before that, he would explore on his own, but now they did everything together.

She slid a knife from a holster tied on her leg and cut the hog loose. Nix piled more sticks on the pathetic fire and watched her dress dinner. Grit and sweat smudged the perfect skin on her shoulders. She wiped the back of her neck with the knife wedged between her fingers.

He swore he could smell her, that her fragrance—that essence that was Raine—permeated everything inside him. He knelt behind her, kneading the cords of muscle that flexed over her shoulder blades. She agreed with a guttural *mmmm.*

"You know, I'd rather have a fire than a massage."

Nix pushed his thumbs into her back and worked the knots loose. He kissed her neck, a distant taste of salt.

"Stop, now. I want to catch some waves and that fire looks like an ape built it." She clapped. "Chop-chop!"

She finished dressing dinner while he set up the spit. Reluctantly, he shaved more bark and gathered kindling. A fire was roaring before she was ready. He watched her wash tubers in the clear water of the lagoon and slice them into the beast's splayed belly.

They rested against a fallen palm trunk while dinner slow-roasted. If it all ended, he wouldn't be disappointed. This was a good way to say goodbye. She nestled into the crook of his arm and lightly snored. He never got tired of that sound: the sound of her sleeping against him. The way her lips fluttered. The way her fingers twitched as dreams came.

Did she dream? Did she snore when he wasn't there to hear it?

Nix always thought that question exposed the self-centered nature of humanity. If a tree fell with no one around to hear it, did it exist? The snoring question was different, though. The lagoon was his dream and Raine was part of it. Sometimes, he wasn't so sure, but perhaps that was wishful thinking. The only thing that existed at the lagoon was what he wished to exist.

The sun was close to setting when Raine pulled the meat from the roasted carcass. He wondered where the car was in fleshland—how close it was to the satellite office—as Raine dished the meal onto primitive coconut bowls and piled cooked tubers onto it. They ate with their fingers. The food didn't do much for Nix's appetite. He didn't have one. And he hardly tasted it. Raine moaned with each bite. Grease glistened on her lips. She licked her fingers. Her joy pulsed through him.

"You crying?"

Nix wiped the corner of his eye. No, he wasn't crying, but she caught him wishing this moment would never end. This might be the last time he watched her eat like an animal, listened to her snore, watched her swim...

So, no, he wasn't crying. "The fire... smoke... making my eyes itch."

They left the fire burning, left the meat for scavengers if they got to it in time. Raine grabbed a well-worn surfboard that she carved from the trunk of an ancient tree years ago. "Come on," she said, shoving his on the ground. "Let's catch a wave."

He lay there in the sand. The sun was low. Her skin, darker.

"Something wrong?"

He shook his head, smiling. "Go on. I'll catch up."

She hesitated, sensing the secret inside him. Or did she already know it, preferring to enjoy their last moments instead of soaking in them. He watched her push into the glassy surface, plowing the water with sun-kissed arms, powerful strokes driving her towards the narrow channel that led to the ocean, where she'd catch perfect waves.

Always perfect waves.

The water shimmered. Turned white.

Then black.

Nix stared at the black sedan's roof. The biomite agent stood next to the car with the door open. He helped him out and led him toward a small brick building where they'd test his biomite population again. Where they'd officially call him a redline.

Where they'd power up the suppression ring.

Where he could say goodbye to dreamland.

CHAPTER FIVE_

Albert Gladstone turned fifty years old.

That was a few days ago. He ate birthday cake. It was vanilla with chocolate frosting. His wife and two teenage kids were there. They sang "Happy Birthday" and watched him blow out the candles. Someone cut the cake and took pieces to his family. His son ate. His wife and daughter didn't.

Albert ate his piece. Even licked the icing from the paper plate. It wasn't particularly good.

But that was a couple days ago.

He didn't have an appetite now. He couldn't feel much of anything.

Albert wore loose-fitting pants and a shirt that looked more like hospital scrubs. Felt like pajamas. He sat in a comfortable chair in a small room. A small empty room. The chair was cushioned but could've been made out of stainless steel and he wouldn't have known the difference. His biomites began dumping synthetic morphine into his bloodstream an hour earlier.

Life was bad, but didn't feel as such.

49.8%.

"Jenny from across the street was walking her dog this morning,"

Albert's wife was saying on the other side of a thick square of glass, "and sends her best. She's got four cats and three dogs now. I think it's too much, if you ask me. But she says what else is going to happen to these animals? I mean, she goes to the shelter and finds these poor pets that were abandoned by their owners and they're going to be..."

Her words trailed off.

She covered her face. Words had always been a buffer. They usually didn't fail.

An elderly woman put her arm around her shoulder. That was Albert's mom. And behind her stood his dad and two kids. His daughter was leaking stained tears. His son wore a mask without emotions. Unlike his mother, he dealt with loss by killing his emotions.

Albert could hear his wife's sobs through a speaker. They sounded like tiny hiccups strung together with squeaky thread. His daughter stepped forward and smudged the glass with her hand.

"Do you feel all right, Dad? Does it hurt?"

Albert smiled as brightly and widely as possible, but it only translated into a slight upturn of his lips. He nodded once. The cushioned back of the chair crunched on the back of his head.

49.9%.

"I'm proud of you, kids." His words were amplified into the other room. "If I was God and had to build a daughter and son, they would be just like you. I wouldn't change a thing."

He took a moment to draw in a breath. His lungs felt smaller.

His daughter's face was streaked with charcoal tears. She pressed both hands on the glass.

"This is inhumane!" The old man shook his fist. "How can you murder a good man and refuse to let his family be with him? How can you force us to watch him die from another room? This is... this is... it's diabolical! I am a lawyer and I will see to an end of these sinister laws! I will make sure this will never happen to another human being!"

The old man hammered the glass with both fists.

"THIS IS MURDER! YOU ARE A COLD-BLOODED MURDERER!"

He was speaking to the odd-looking man that was in the room with Albert. Marcus Anderson stood off to the side like an observer, wearing a finely tailored suit and silk tie. He occasionally looked at a device in the palm of his hand. He represented the government in these halfskin matters. Anyone with a loved one near halfskin status knew his face well, a face one would not call handsome. He was the same age as Albert but looked more like Albert's father. His thinning hair was prematurely gray, his head slightly misshapen much like the slight hunch on his back from an outward curvature of his spine.

He was as emotionless as the son.

A guard politely and gently guided the old man away from the glass, but words of protest still trickled through the speakers.

"It's all right," Albert could be heard whispering. "We all have to end. This isn't so bad."

They didn't believe what he said. Later, they told the press that the gargoyle (they refused to call Marcus Anderson by his name, he was a monster, leave it at that) had drugged him so he would say stuff like that. They probably shouldn't have called him a gargoyle.

"Shhhhh." Albert was too tired to say anything else, so he just made that sound so they would feel comforted.

He didn't want them to feel sad. He knew the rules. He knew he was pushing his luck with his biomite population. He'd exceeded the biomite seeding recommendation to his brain stem, but it had paid off. His memory and analytical abilities were computerlike. He won a record number of federal grants for his lab. He thought the seeding would boost his intelligence to find a cure for the runaway biomite replication before he went redline. It was a gamble.

But Albert wasn't much of a gambler.

If he was honest, he didn't like the way it felt. The more the biomites replaced the organic cells in his body, the less present he felt. He was smarter, more successful, more secure... but he was just less... *real.* The agents took him from his lab the moment he went redline. And as he neared the halfskin threshold, he wrote to his wife that everything felt the same, he just felt less real.

He couldn't explain it any better than that.

Shutting his biomites down wasn't such a bad idea. Not the way he felt.

50%.

Marcus put the device he was obsessively watching into his pocket and respectfully folded his hands. A doctor entered the room.

The sandman began pouring his magical dust into Albert's body. It started at the top of his head and filtered down to his toes. He was becoming heavy. Gravity pulled him into the chair. His head lolled back and forth like he was refusing. He barely heard the sobs get louder.

His eyelids were too heavy.

He wanted to see his kids one last time, but that wasn't to be. He wouldn't hear them again. All he heard, as the biomites slowly shut down, pulling his life with them, was the sound of a leaking tire. A sound that slid through his lips.

"Shhhhhh."

The doctor knelt next to Albert and pressed his fingers to his neck. He checked an instrument that he briefly pulled from his pocket. He stood and nodded.

"MONSTER!" The old man had to be restrained. "My son... was good—"

The speaker clicked off. The glass dimmed.

The family would remain in the room to grieve. Once Albert was fully examined, they would get to see him one more time but would not be allowed to take possession of his body for burial. Albert would be cremated and his ashes sent to them.

Marcus Anderson let his people attend to Albert's body. The man known as Albert Gladstone was gone from this world. If anyone asked Marcus, the man began dying the moment he chose to be seeded.

Marcus stopped outside the room to rub antibacterial gel on his hands. He went directly to a room on the bottom floor of Cleveland's Detainment and Observation Center, where a cadre of reporters would want a statement from the chief of Biomite Oversight and Regulation regarding the shutdown of another halfskin.

He would be happy to report one less halfskin in the world.

CHAPTER SIX_

Marcus Anderson sank into the soft leather of the heated backseat, taking comfort in the laptop's blue glow. His flight from Ohio was uneventful. He stayed long enough to answer questions and went directly to the airport to fly home.

The driver turned into the Washington, D.C., neighborhood of Spring Valley. The streetlights illuminated the wet pavement.

He adjusted the Bluetooth in his ear. The press secretary wanted to be briefed on the halfskin shutdown. When laws regulating biomites went into action, there was revolt throughout the world. But the evidence was overwhelming: if something wasn't done to curtail biomite integration, the human species was in danger.

The models predicted that biomites would essentially consume the human population within twenty years without regulation. The Halfskin Laws declared that—until biomite replication was cured at the cellular level—no citizen would be allowed to contain more than 50% biomites. Once over that threshold, you were more machine than human.

Marcus couldn't agree more.

The result of shutting down a person's biomites was always death of the body. The president was concerned about the family and the halfskin's comfort level. The president had signed the Mother Oversight Agreement with the United Nations; America would abide by its laws. But still, the president needed to show compassion for the victim and his family.

He is not a victim. He simply failed to exist.

That was how Marcus framed the definition. If a healthy human could not exist without the assistance of biomites, then it was a failure to exist. There was a flaw in the definition (people were kept alive by artificial assistance all the time), but Marcus simply drew the line with biomites. These weren't plastic arms or legs, they were artificial living cells. Replacing your God-given bodily cells with man-made ones was Marcus's beef. A plastic arm was one thing, trading God's temple for a slimmer, stronger, faster body with killer blue eyes was quite another.

The car eased to the curb. The brick house was set back from the street; a sidewalk meandered toward the front door. Marcus packed his leather briefcase and checked the mailbox on his way inside. Crickets sang and the night smelled wet. He didn't get outside much.

One of the kids was crying upstairs while Marcus hung his coat in the closet. His shiny shoes clapped on the bamboo floor, making a harder click as he turned onto the kitchen tiles.

"Good evening," he said.

Janine was sitting at the breakfast table with a phone pressed against her ear, surrounded by eternal stacks of documents. He'd had a discussion with her about that—orderliness of body brings orderliness of mind, especially for lawyers—but there were many things they disagreed upon. Their marriage was not a good one by conventional definition, but it was fruitful. It was powerful. Their children would be very successful, given the gene pool from which they were spawned. (Marcus knew this because he had their genomes mapped.) So, they called a truce on the paper stacking. *Pick battles, not wars.*

"Dinner is just about ready," Ariel, the head nanny/cook, said. She stirred a pot of red sauce. Marcus stopped to smell.

"Then you can get the children."

"Yes, sir."

Marcus closed his office doors. The wall along the back was curved, with a mahogany desk centered in front of a bay window. The heavy curtains, drawn. Shelves lined the walls with classically bound books that were authentic, but never read.

He checked his emails while sipping a freshly pulped glass of carrot juice. He didn't answer any of them, but glanced through the headings before stripping off his clothes and changing into a pair of shorts and T-shirt folded neatly in the bottom desk drawer. He mounted a recumbent bike tucked into the corner to the right of the desk and eased into an exercise routine. He didn't like exercising on a full stomach, but there wasn't much choice. If he didn't, he wouldn't exercise at all.

The television flickered to life. There was only one channel he watched: news. All-day news. As he dug into the next level of exercise bike's resistance—his empty glass flecked with orange spots—he watched protesters march around the Capitol with signs that condemned the Halfskin Laws. They were always out there.

Change is difficult.

To lead a nation, one accepted protest. People did not like change. They wanted things to stay the same, forever. Whether they were suffering or not, whether change was logical or absurd, they wanted things to stay the same. They would hate you for it. Sometimes kill you for it.

The television went to commercial and came back to Marcus's press conference following Albert Gladstone's shutdown. He touched a button on the exercise bike and brought the resistance up another level while he watched himself climb to the podium. He hated seeing himself on television. The lights made his skin ashen and always seemed to catch his left eye, the slightly misshapen one. If it weren't that, it was from an angle that made him look like a hunchback.

Damn liberals. Always showing my bad side.

"It is with regret that I hold this meeting..."

Empathy. Sorrow. He'd nailed every emotion, dead-center perfect. He wasn't lying; he did feel for the family of Albert Gladstone. They had to watch their beloved father-husband-son destroy himself. Marcus was not to blame. He was innocent of such malevolence, just a man helping humanity—infantile in their desires and bottomless in their greed—save themselves from themselves.

"How do you respond to critics that this is government-sanctioned murder?" he was asked.

And he answered with a stern expression. "We're simply shutting down biomites that have reached a threshold of willful domination in Albert Gladstone's body. The human body is an organic being, not a computer. If it cannot survive without assistance of bionanotechnology, then it has reached its end."

His empathy waned.

If the reporters all dropped dead simultaneously, he wouldn't show sorrow. He doubted he could even suppress a smile. That would be sinful, but nonetheless. Some of those rats with a pen were direct descendants of Satan. And that, he felt certain, was a fact.

He watched the rest of the conference, suppressing the urge to vomit.

God didn't make machines. Man did.

HIS OFFICE DOORS OPENED. Janine slung her briefcase over her shoulder. "Office called; I have to go."

"It's almost ten o'clock."

"Deadline is tomorrow and the world is ending."

Marcus climbed off the bike and mopped his forehead with a

towel. He wished for another freshly squeezed juice. Ariel was most likely gone.

Janine pursed hairpins in her lips while she fixed her hair back. Her face was blotchy and oily. She rarely wore makeup, especially when she went in late.

"Did you see the press conference?" he asked.

She nodded. "I did."

Janine squeezed his shoulder. He hated when she touched him like that. It was a pat on the shoulder and proud expression, and she never really looked at him when she did it. It was so... *scripted.*

A melodious tone muffled somewhere. Janine finished clipping her hair and dug through her briefcase as she headed for the doors. "This is Anderson."

Marcus followed her down the hall, hearing the lawyer-speak that he loved so much—a language of order and righteousness—before turning into the kitchen as she exited the front door. He watched the car back out of the driveway, the headlights swinging across the lawn before fading down the street.

He returned to the office with another juice and prepared for his nightcap. The kids were asleep. The wife, gone. Still, he drew the curtains closed and locked the doors.

This moment was forever secret.

CHAPTER SEVEN_

Cali pulled off to the side of the road. The Center was across the field.

The Detention and Observation Center.

She sat twenty minutes north of Carbondale, Illinois, just off Highway 51. Once a fertile field that farmers tilled for corn and soybeans, the ground that separated the road from the Detention and Observation Center lay fallow now, giving rise to yellow-flowering weeds and cocklebur. There used to be a community center over there for farmers, a place they could play bingo or drink coffee and talk about the weather. They wrecked it to build a secure building, one for detaining and observing. The farmers' sons put down their plows and took up badges for a steady sip from the government, to protect this land from the 40% biomite-infested redlines.

This Center was just one of many across the nation. And unless the laws changed or biomite replication was solved, they would become modern-day death cubicles. When that day came, overpopulation would not be a problem as Mother shut off halfskins by the thousands... *daily*.

The new-age holocaust.

That was how Cali saw it. Of course, critics were confident that something would change, surely the human race would evolve, they would solve the replication problem. They wouldn't allow the mass extermination.

But those same critics didn't have a loved one detained and observed. So Cali was a little... jaded.

She'd been to visit her brother once a week, every week, since they took him. That was six months ago. If she wasn't visiting, she was in the basement.

Working.

She'd taken an unpaid leave of absence from the lab. They understood. They didn't terminate her. She could always come back when she was ready, they told her. When Cali told people she wasn't well, that she needed some time to sort things out, they didn't ask why. Those that knew her gave her all the space she needed.

Poor thing.

The Center would see her car parked across the field. Someone would eventually come out. Cali just needed a moment. She came to visit every week, but it wasn't getting easier. The closer she got to this sick and twisted place, the more her hands shook. No one seemed to care that her brother would be dead without biomites.

Now he's imprisoned for it.

There was no justice in this universe. And if there was a God, she'd smack him for meting out such imbalance. The Christians were right; God had to be a man. Who else could make a woman's life hell?

She fumbled with her purse and tapped out a cigarette. It took a couple clicks of the lighter to get it puffing. She blew a cloud out the window. The mentholated smoke settled her nerves.

She was used to southern Illinois humidity. Nix was born in Illinois, but Cali grew up in South Carolina and this was mild compared to that. However, she still wasn't accustomed to the flatness. When she drove the country roads, she could see for miles in every direction, like God had scraped the edge of his hand over this part of the world. She craved the trees and hills where she grew up, the wetlands and smell of pluff mud and the rank odor of the paper mill on wet days. She missed home, a place where she belonged.

If she went back there, she still wouldn't find it. Home was gone. *Gone, gone, gone.*

"Better get *go-ing...*" Avery sang from the backseat.

Cali looked in the rearview. Her eyes—ringed as if with soot, capillaries showing where the whites were supposed to be—looked back. She pushed the hair out of her face and took a drag before adjusting the mirror. Avery was strapped into the backseat, watching her iPod. Her backpack was next to her, holding all the essentials: water bottle, change of clothes and Pogo, the stuffed rhinoceros.

"You'll get in trouble if they come out here, Mama. They won't let you see Nix."

"I know, honey. I just need a moment."

The little girl hummed like she'd heard that excuse before. She dragged her finger across the screen and sang, "Better get *go-ing...*"

Cali smiled. What would she have in this world if that little girl wasn't with her? God had taken everything else but Nix.

There was nothing left to take.

She sucked on the filtered end and hung her hand out the door. Cali put the car in gear. A white dust cloud followed her to the stop sign, where she turned right and passed a tan truck. The truck turned around at the intersection and followed her to the gate.

Avery was still humming.

MOTHER_

PUBLIC INTRODUCTION OF BIOMITE CELL REGENERATION

Jennifer Adams wore a pair of khaki slacks and a white blouse. A small metal American flag was pinned above her left breast. She wasn't sure what to wear to a press conference, one where she'd meet her half-dead husband. This seemed appropriate.

Her daughter rode on her hip, resting her head. The pacifier squeaked compulsively. Jonathan held her left hand. He wanted to wear his Cub Scout uniform. He tugged at the yellow kerchief snug against his neck. It seemed appropriate.

Along the wall to their left were reporters and photographers from major outlets across the nation. Cameras clicked and phones buzzed. A man in uniform patted her shoulder and whispered something comforting in her ear (she didn't understand it; she couldn't understand anything at that moment) before rustling the boy's hair and tapping the little girl on the nose.

Jennifer was going to stain her blouse with vomit.

In front of her was a brown podium with several mics. The American flag was behind it. The curtain on the wall was pulled aside. Her breath caught in her throat. It was hard to let out. A man stepped out. He was dressed in hospital scrubs for the announcement. Walter Reed Hospital wanted the world to see what they had done with Jennifer's husband.

That had to be good. Right?

Still hard to breathe.

"General McGee and other members of the army," the doctor said, "ladies and gentlemen of the press, thank you for coming."

He took a moment to look at the podium and adjusted his cap.

"Jennifer." He smiled. "Thank you for your patience. I know this has been very difficult for you and your family. Your husband, Lieutenant Adams, was gravely injured during an assignment on foreign soil. He returned to the United States on life support. He lost his arm above the elbow."

The doctor signaled with the edge of his hand somewhere in the middle of his left bicep. Jennifer looked down for a moment, unable to push away the memory of her husband. When she saw him in that bed with the ventilator and the bruises and the swelling... he looked so small. So fragile.

It wasn't him.

Cameras clicked to capture her raw moment.

"I know this is quite a spectacle we've created, but it is an event the world needs to see. Lieutenant Adams' injuries were fatal. The best we could hope for was to prolong his life with prosthetics and life support. But with the advent of bionanotechnology, his injuries were treated with artificial cell regeneration. We hope to show that this new approach to medicine will change the way not just our service men and women heal, but all Americans. Lieutenant Adams has a new spleen and lung, his vision has been restored, his arm..."

The doctor adjusted his cap again. He looked around slowly.

"Let's not let words get in the way."

Jennifer couldn't feel her knees. She lowered her daughter to the floor before she dropped her.

She knelt next to her son.

Her hand quivered over her mouth. She couldn't breathe. She stopped trying.

Because when the curtain pulled aside—

When a man stepped out—

She recognized him. At last, her husband had returned from the war. All of him.

And the cameras snapped and snapped and snapped.

CHAPTER EIGHT_

"Your turn."

George sat on the other side of a transparent door. The collar on his uniform was open, his neck unshaven. He tipped back on the chair and dropped his boot on the corner of a small table. The chess pieces rattled slightly. A smile was hidden beneath a mustache bush.

Nix stood in the center of his cell. *His room.* It wasn't a cell, he was reminded often, it was a room. He wasn't a prisoner, he was a ward of the United States under the Halfskin Laws. Nix was under watch, twenty-four hours a day and had been for the past six months and would be as long as he registered above 40%. In the history of biomites, no one's population had ever decreased. It was likely he'd have a room for a while.

At least until he hit halfskin.

The walls were white and barren. There was a bed and a toilet and a sink and a desk and a chair. All white. The desk wasn't for writing since pens and pencils weren't allowed. Recent studies proved certain biomites could spread through liquids, even ink. Seeding usually required specialized equipment, but some of the new breeds of biomites could simply be inhaled as vapor or liquid. No one wanted to be seeded against their will, so Observation and Detainment Centers banned them, and desks became more for stacking things than writing. They'd bring him a laptop, if he asked, but it was quarantined and couldn't remain in the room. It was too dangerous. They hadn't explained why.

Currently, there was just the stack of papers that was in the middle of the desk—the only thing on the surface—crisp and colorful drawings from a ten-year-old girl. Cali brought him one every week from Avery. If he were allowed tape or anything sticky, he'd put them on the wall. Sometimes he spaced them out on the floor and walked through a labyrinth of blue skies and green grass and yellow, smiling suns and brown ponies; he always picked them up and stacked them neatly when he was done.

Time went so slow in the room.

At least it was comfortable. At least it was safe.

Nix stared at the monitor over the sink. It was not his reflection that looked back—mirrors weren't allowed—but a monitor. He was dressed in (what else) white. He had no hair. None. Not on his head or brows, under his arms or anywhere south of that. All of that fell out after wearing the suppression ring for six months.

Everyone reacted differently to the ring. It was only supposed to suppress the biomites to slow their replication and activity. *There's some dangerous redlines out there*, George the Guard used to say. *Got the strength of a chimpanzee. Got to slow the mites down, Nixy*, George would say.

Nix's biomites slowed down. And they dumped his hair like a chemo patient. But that wasn't the worst of it. The no-hair thing wasn't a big deal. It was convenient, if you asked him. His skin, perfectly smooth. No, the worst of it was the vibration.

He heard it and felt it in the middle of his head like an itch he could never reach, like someone struck a tuning fork deep inside his brain. It was always there, day and night. It took away his dreams. Scrambled his thoughts.

Took away Raine.

He sometimes remembered the last time he saw her. The color of her skin. The way she paddled through the water. Other days, she was just a hazy figure in his memory. Someone he used to know.

He tried to sketch her when he had the laptop and his memories were good, spent hours with a doodle program to recreate the lagoon and the blue cliffs and the waterfall. Each time, there were fewer details. Fewer memories.

Without the lagoon and Raine, he felt empty. Alone.

And he couldn't remember the last time he felt that way.

Nix craned his neck. From where he stood, he could already see his next move. He anticipated what George was going to do, even though George was cheating. He was using his phone to log the moves into a chess program, telling him what to do.

"Got you now, halfskin." George chuckled, hands laced behind his head. His eyes were nearly hidden in folds of fat and untamed eyebrows. Nix had a feeling it'd take a hundred suppression rings to make George hairless.

Nix pulled his chair to the door. He studied the board through the embedded crisscrossed wires. He pretended to be thinking. He liked George. Anything was better than nothing. Most of the guards were good at their job, but not George. He talked with the redlines, got to know them.

Where'd you get the name Nixon? George asked the day he arrived.

My dad was a fan of dead presidents.

George thought about that. It was the next day he came back, tapped on Nix's door and then tapped his head. *I got that,* he said. *Richard Nixon, I got that.*

He saw Nix playing chess one day on his monitor and, the very next day, set up a little table. Said he was going to teach this eighteen-year-old halfskin what a real man could do. Didn't matter Nix wasn't halfskin, he was redline. But that was a technicality. Really, he was a halfskin, just hadn't fulfilled his destiny, George would say. George would show him what a whole man could do. How a pure man could think.

Not a halfskin man.

George was still convinced the biomites were giving Nix superpowers, making him smarter. Maybe he was right. Nix wanted the game to last. If it ended too soon, George would take his game and go home. Might not come back. And then Nix would be alone.

Keep the game close; give him hope.

"Six months," George said, "but I'm finally going to beat you."

Nix planted his chin on his knuckles. Pulling off the con had become more fun than beating him. Watching him walk into the trap was a hell of a good time, too.

"Good run, kid. I've beat every mite-infested halfskin in this place but you. It just goes to show you, God-given talent always beats the machine." He tapped his temple. "Creativity, son. It's the power to adapt and create; that's what God gave us, not you with the power to program your little computer-cells."

He leaned back some more.

"You had a great brain, but you had to ruin it, had to eat the mites to get better than the rest of us and now look at you."

His eyes twinkled between thick lids. "You're paying for it now."

George thought Nix chose biomites. Most people did. You don't have a choice when a drunk driver caves in the side of the car. But why spoil the fun, just lump all the redlines together: a bunch of greedy turds.

"You're going to owe me, William!" George shouted down the hall. "Got the kid stuck."

Nix cringed. He may have strung this one out too long. He didn't want to draw George too far into the trap of disappointment. Once, when he trounced George with a seven-move checkmate, the ring got turned up and Nix's head rattled all night. The biomites damn near shut down. No one knew how the ring got turned up, but George winked at him the next morning. Nix couldn't get out of bed for a week.

"There's a cure out there," George said. "A way to get rid of all the mites in your body."

Nix remained pensive. "Why would I want that?"

"You like what you are?"

Nix shrugged slightly. *Sure, why not.*

The front legs of George's chair hit the ground. "As long as you got mites, we know where you are, son. You got mites, Mother's going to always know what you're thinking, where you're going, whether you're picking your nose or sniffing someone's underwear. You get purged, you can be just like me—a whole man, free to do whatever you want. Why wouldn't you want that?"

Nix studied the pieces. George had been reading too many gossip mags. There was no such thing as a biomite purge.

"If you go to a plastic surgeon," Nix said slowly, "and cure your ugly, will you still be you?"

Someone laughed down the hall. They were listening.

"I may be ugly, but I'm real."

"So are chimpanzees."

"I'd rather be a monkey than a machine."

Nix sat back and crossed his arms, stroking his baby-smooth chin. He looked up from the board for the first time. George stared back, eyes glittering and mustache quivering.

"What were you doing seven years ago?"

George's eyes disappeared. "Hell, I don't know."

"You weren't doing anything, that's why. Because you didn't exist."

"The hell that supposed to mean?"

Nix leaned forward, pretending to look at the board. "Did you know it takes seven years for all the cells in your body to be recycled? That means all the cells that composed your body seven years ago have all died and been replaced by new ones. So, for a pure skin like you, the answer is simple, George. By your definition, you didn't exist because that wasn't your body. That is, if who you are is your body."

"Don't twist facts, kid. I ain't changed, I'm still me. I'm still flesh and blood and you ain't, no matter how you slice it."

Nix hummed, rubbing his chin. "You ever get cavities?"

"Do you ever shut up?"

"What do you do, let them rot?"

"Course not. Go to the dentist, don't *seed* a bunch of mites in my mouth to fix it."

"You get fillings, then?"

"That's right, kid. I go to the dentist and let her fix my cavities. Chimps don't do that and neither do machines. Real people do."

Nix nodded. "Is your mouth fake?"

"It's fixed."

"Does it make it less real?"

"Does this look like a mirage?" He snapped his coffee-stained choppers with a hollow bite.

They stared.

"You got me there, George. You got me there."

George smiled for a while, thinking about it. Nix got up and crossed the room. He folded his arms and tapped his elbows.

"Queen to G-6," he called over his shoulder.

A piece slid across the board. George's chin stubble rasped in his palm. He checked his phone a couple times, acting like there was a text.

Nix turned on the water and splashed his face. The chess game was over.

George just didn't realize it, yet.

CHAPTER NINE_

Cali flashed her ID at the gate. The guard hardly looked at it. He glanced in the backseat but didn't bother talking to the ten-year-old picking her nose. He stepped back into his little station and the flimsy chain-link gates opened.

He didn't bother telling her where to go.

Cali parked her car in the middle of the visitors' lot with half a dozen other cars. The Center was only two stories tall but sprawled over seven acres with a courtyard for exercising. But there weren't tattooed gangsters pumping iron in the yard, just everyday people that redlined too many biomites. Doctors, lawyers, farmers... no one was spared.

Walking, talking machines, she remembered a politician once said when federal money was available to build these Centers and create jobs in his district. *Biomites will turn us all into walking, talking machines. Unless we do something, this is the first step in the extinction of the human race.*

Cali checked her face in the rearview. Her face had a strange color, something closer to bruise-yellow than blush. She didn't care, just didn't want Nix to worry. She took a few minutes to doctor her complexion and ran a brush once or twice through her hair.

She took a deep breath and closed her eyes. Her heart rate was up. She counted her breaths to ten and felt her blood pressure settle down. She couldn't look out of the ordinary. She always made herself look a little nervous when she arrived, so that when this day arrived, her emotional state wouldn't look out of place.

But not too nervous.

Cali looked through her bag, flipped through files and made sure a bottle of water and an ink pen were at the bottom. *Distractions.* She reached into the backseat and pulled a drawing from Avery's bag, a scene of the ocean with a dolphin leaping out of the water and a yellow sunset. It was quite good for a ten-year-old. Almost too good. She might have an artistic future.

"You going to be all right out here?"

"Yep." Avery didn't look up from her movie.

"I'll be in there for about an hour."

"I know."

"Of course you do." She rustled her daughter's hair. "You're a big girl."

"Can you kiss Uncle Nix for me?" Her eyes were wide.

"Not yet."

Avery stuck out her bottom lip.

"Maybe soon, though."

"Okay."

Cali stretched over the seat and kissed her daughter's forehead and whispered, "I love you."

"Love you, too, Mama."

Cali stood at the door until it buzzed.

The floor was hard and shiny. The walls empty. At the end of the short hallway was a counter with a door to the left of it. Cali walked the thirty or so steps while the man behind the counter—wearing a blue uniform, hands folded on the countertop—watched her the whole way. He smiled in neutral.

"Where's Greg?" Cali dropped her bag on the counter.

"Called in sick."

The man's ID badge was clipped to his collar. One Mr. Franklin Moses, here to protect and serve. Franklin gestured to the right. Cali swiped her ID through the scanner.

"Dr. Cali Richards." Franklin looked to his left and pecked a keyboard behind the counter.

"I'm not a doctor."

"It says here you have a Ph.D. in Nanobiometrics."

"Don't call me doctor."

Franklin raised his eyebrows. He'd touched a nerve and, wisely, stepped off.

Cali slid her bag to the right side of the counter onto a black scanning plate. Franklin watched the monitor to his left. The plate vibrated, then stopped.

"Please empty your bag."

Cali let out an exasperated breath. She pushed her hand through her hair and began pulling out the items. She stacked the folders and placed Avery's drawing on top. She put the bottle of water next to it. Franklin picked up the water and turned it around. He looked at her.

"You have a doctorate in nanobiometrics and you don't know that liquid is not allowed in a Detainment and Observation Center?"

"This is a prison. And if I wanted to contaminate you or anyone else with a new strain of biomites—a super strain of biomites that I could control—I wouldn't have to bring it in a bottle of water, I'd just seed my salivary glands and spit in your eye, Franklin. All it would take is the most inconspicuous fleck of spittle to go airborne, one you'd never notice, and you'd be mine, just like that." Cali grabbed the ink pens from the bottom of her bag. "Taking liquid from people isn't going to make them safe. It's too damn EASY!"

Franklin's eyebrows went higher. He slowly put the water down and began to turn around.

"I'm sorry." Cali reached for him. "I get a little... stressed out coming here. You know biomites can't go airborne, I was just making that up. I'm sorry, I'm just... a little tight."

"You can't joke about that, Dr. Richards. Not someone of your caliber. And biomites can go airborne, that's why we confiscate any form of liquid. If it's atomized, there's a brief period that a person could be seeded with an unknown strain."

"Yes, yes, I know. I just... my brother... he's just... I don't agree with all this, you know. He doesn't deserve to be locked up. He didn't do anything wrong."

"He's not a criminal, Dr. Richards."

"He's being treated like one."

"No, he's quarantined. It's not illegal to be seeded, but it is illegal to contain too many. I don't make the laws, Dr. Richards. That's just how it is."

Cali locked her lips. She'd said enough. Anymore and he'd throw her out and she'd never come back. She needed to look concerned and worried, not unstable. Not a threat.

"I'm sorry." Cali took the drawing off the folders and pushed it across the countertop. "Look, this is all I want to bring to visitation. Could you send it up to Nix? It's from his niece. She'd come, too, but she's scared of this building."

Franklin paused. He put one finger on the piece of paper and slid it closer.

"She used colored pencils," Cali added. "It's all solid medium, the paper and everything. There's nothing there that can vector a viable biomite. It's like all the other drawings in his room."

He picked it up while staring at her. He lifted it toward the overhead lights and looked through it.

"You can run it through the sterilizer, if you like. Greg knows how much these drawings mean to Nix. And, look, I'm sorry about snapping. I just want to make sure my brother gets a little something every week. Imagine what it must be like in here."

Franklin looked at the dolphin and ocean and sun for a full minute. He placed it on the counter and nodded curtly. "Very well."

The door to the left clicked.

Another guard.

He motioned for her to come closer and put a cell-phone-sized box near her throat. She tasted metal.

The humming died. "You're 39.9%, Cali."

Cali nodded.

"You're one-tenth of a percent from redline."

"I'm aware of that."

The guard looked at it while he snapped the reader back on his belt. There was a long silence.

"Can I go?" Cali asked.

"Sure," the big guard said. "Get comfortable. You're probably going to see this place from the inside, *reeeal* soon."

Cali tightened her lips. She wanted to explain that exponential growth of biomite cells was not an absolute and that her research in the last couple months was showing signs that it could be suppressed by injecting growth regulator code that limited biomite division. Even though she slowed it down, she doubted it could be reversed. Either way, she wasn't about to tell anyone, not until Nix was out. And they weren't going to just open the doors and set him free.

She planned on doing that.

CHAPTER TEN_

Nix used the white washcloth to wipe his face, his head, rubbed the film off his teeth, and changed into a new white jumper. He did these things every time Cali came to visit. Ritual was key to remaining sane in solitary.

And he didn't want his sister to worry.

Nix folded the old jumper and placed it at the foot of the door, where a guard could switch it out when he dropped off food. The small table was on its side in the hallway, the chess pieces scattered on the floor. Nix imagined George's computer program suggested he offer a draw after a few more moves.

Or kick over the table and leave.

Nix returned to his desk and straightened the only stack of papers on it. Every week, Avery sent a drawing. Sometimes it was animals, sometimes people. Most of the time, it was scenery, like the mountains or a lake. Regardless, it always had the sun. The sun was bright yellow and shiny, just like he remembered. He could see the sun rise from his window, but it wasn't the same from inside the Center. The sun didn't rise the same when freedom was gone.

He rubbed the waxy, yellow circle peeking over the lush hills. No liquid there. Just a sterilized piece of paper. Nix smelled it. It reminded him of home. Reminded him of when Cali and Thomas would be working at the lab late at night and Nix would put Avery to bed. He'd take a book from her nightstand and open it and the smell of the pages would fill his nose with memories. That's what those old pages smelled like: memories. They were old books, books that Cali read to him when he was little.

Remember the wild rumpus?

He smelled the paper again. He knew they were watching him. There were cameras that captured his every move, little eyes in the corners. Nothing went without record.

He was counting on it.

Nix pulled the chair in front of the monitor. He placed the pictures on his lap and waited.

Hours later, the monitor flickered.

His image disappeared, replaced by another sitting in a similar chair in a white room, hands on her lap.

"Little brother."

Nix smiled. He was always surprised how much the sight of his sister could warm him. Even if she was a faint shadow of what she used to be. A waif. A troubled soul. Her shoulders were pointy, her cheeks drawn. The room was well lit but, still, shadows darkened her eyes.

"How are you?" he asked.

She looked at her lap, picking at her fingers. "I'm well."

"You're eating?"

Nod.

She's too demure. She's thinking about it too much.

"How's the little angel?"

The shadows lightened. Her teeth showed pearly and white. She told him about making cookies. Avery came up with her own recipe: chocolate chip and potato chip cookies. Sounded gross because it was. They made jelly bean and peanut cookies, gummy worm cookies, and, finally, a batch of sugar and syrup cookies. They decided to take them to the volunteers at the animal shelter. They were going to form a group called Baking a Difference and would get the neighborhood kids involved.

Cali loosened up. She always felt relaxed when she talked about Avery. They went on to talk about other things, like the new playground down the street and the neighbor's new baby.

Something slid under the door.

Nix saw the drawing. The corners of the paper were folded up. He looked at Cali. She was speechless.

He retrieved it and sat down. This one was an ocean with a dolphin. It was jumping out of the water with a big smile, free at last.

Free at last.

Nix touched the sun.

"She misses you." Cali sniffed. She didn't have to pretend. "She wants to know when you're coming home."

"What do you tell her?"

"I tell her soon."

"Maybe you should tell her the truth."

"I've petitioned the government to open a new branch in our lab. Our research was showing strong signs of biomite remission when exposed to RNA injections before they cut funding. If we can just have a year or two, Nix, I know I can bring your biomite levels below 40%."

"A year or two."

She looked back at her fingers. She was making all this up. There was no remission evidence in laboratories, public or private. Maybe in the basement, but not at the lab.

"You'll get me out of the redline?" Nix muttered.

"And out of here, if they just listen."

"That's a lot of ifs."

"That's all I got." Cali wiped both eyes. "You're all I got."

There was a lot of truth to that. Only Nix was aware of just how true it was. He stared at the picture, remembered going on vacation to Folly Beach outside Charleston, South Carolina, and seeing dolphins for the first time with Avery. Remembered sleeping on the beach towel in the afternoon while she built castles and Cali and Thomas went for a long walk. That was vacation. That was a long time ago.

"She worked hard on that," Cali said. "I got her a new set of pencils with special colors just for you. She must've spent months drawing that one."

"I like it." He held it up. "Tell her thank you."

"Maybe one day you can tell her."

They talked about neighbors. Talked about his old friends. They filled the gaps with words, making it all seem normal. Finally, Cali stood up.

The screen went blank.

Nix sat for several minutes, looking at the colors. It was just like the other ones, pictures from a lovely girl to a loving uncle. He lifted it to his nose and breathed in the waxy aroma.

His sinuses tingled. A tickling sensation penetrated the porous bone plate that separated his olfactory senses and entered his brain like a virus. Like living cocaine. He held the back of the chair and kept his eyes open even though the room was spinning.

Special colors just for you.

Nix made it to his bed and lay down without looking suspicious. Cali told him on the last visit that Avery was working on a special drawing. He knew something was coming. Intuition told him to smell it.

Something embedded in the colors.

His sister was a genius. She spiked the drawing with something—probably a new breed of biomites, ones that eluded the ring's effect. Nix could feel them spread out in his head like cold webbing. If the guards suspected something, they would already be in his cell.

She'd discovered something new.

Something undetectable.

Nix lay back and closed his eyes. For the first time in a long time, since the day that ring went around his neck, he smelled the ocean.

CHAPTER ELEVEN_

CALI WIPED HER EYES WITH A TISSUE. IT WAS THE FIRST TIME she'd teared up during a visitation. She'd cried when they took her little brother from the house, but not since. Not ever. She'd never allowed herself to feel those emotions, but the thought of her little brother coming home was just too real.

It got to her.

It probably didn't hurt her performance. It would be completely expected, probably bored all the people watching.

She walked out without a word from any of them. She stopped outside the final door. The sun was overhead. Nix didn't see that very much, at least not on his own terms. That's what he always requested of his niece to draw for him: suns. *Draw me something yellow,* he would say.

Cali peeked through the back of the car. Avery was laid out on the seat, eyes closed. Cali closed the door behind her quietly so she wouldn't wake the angel. She stopped herself from giving her daughter a hug, giving her the good news.

Uncle Nix will be home soon.

CHAPTER TWELVE_

The head of the table was empty. Marcus entered.

The other chairs were filled with children. His wife, Janine, was seated at the other end. Her head was bowed. He could tell when she was thinking. Always thinking. Never here. Always somewhere in her head, combing through facts, through paperwork and scenarios. A lawyer's work never rested. *Not for good ones*, she would say.

The children had their hands on their laps, heads slightly bowed. They weren't thinking of clients and affidavits. Only dinner.

Marcus sat down. "Let us pray."

Their heads bowed deeper.

"Bless us, O' Lord, and these Thy gifts which we are about to receive from Thy bounty. Through Christ, our Lord. Amen."

The clinking of china was preceded by signs of the Cross—Father, Son, Holy Ghost. Ariel moved into action and helped the children spoon sauce over their noodles. Marcus smoothed a cloth napkin over his lap and watched that no one put their elbows on the table. All the napkins were in place. His wife was on her second glass of wine.

Pick battles.

He began eating. The dinner proceeded as it had every night, in relative quiet. Nothing but the *tink-tink* and the occasional slurp. Not too many. They were kids, after all.

Marcus twirled noodles on his fork and, before filling his mouth, pointed at the empty seat he hadn't noticed. "Where's Andrew?"

"Fever and a sore throat, sir." Ariel filled Janine's water glass.

Marcus chewed carefully and spoke again once he swallowed. "Is he getting clear liquids?"

"Yes, sir."

Another bite. Swallow. "Have you given him herbal tea for the sore throat?"

"Yes, sir," Ariel said.

"It helped a lot, sir," Margaret, the new part-time nanny, said. "He fell right to sleep when he was finished."

Marcus nodded thoughtfully. He wasn't thrilled with another nanny, even part time. But his job had him away from home more often and Janine was too busy playing lawyer.

Janine asked the children how their day at school was and how they were feeling. No one felt the least bit sick, although someone puked in William's class after recess. He started to describe the smell when he was cut off. He managed to say *chunks of meat* before his name was called. Sternly.

"You know, my sister's son, he's seven," Margaret said, helping Clifford cut his noodles, "and he come down with a fever and they took him to the pharmacy, where they got these little temporary biomite injections. Have you seen those?"

She held up her fingers a half inch apart, indicating they were real small.

"They fight infection and then get washed out through the kidneys. They're not like regular biomites that reproduce. He was better that evening."

Marcus chewed slowly with his lips closed. He flipped a glance at Ariel, who did not return the look. The meal finished without much conversation.

Marcus unzipped the suitcase and threw it on the bedspread. He began the weekly ritual of packing for a trip. He started with his underwear—pressed and folded. All of them white with tiny red stripes on the elastic band. Next were socks, followed by gym shorts for working out in the hotel exercise room, bathing suit for the hot tub, and T-shirts for lounging. His suits and ties would be packed in a hanging case.

He went to the bathroom—open to the bedroom—to pack toothpaste and the rest. Janine came out of the shower room, rapidly working the water from her ear with her finger. She was wearing a white robe, not the one he'd gotten her for Christmas but one she'd bought a year before that. She always said she liked the way the old one felt, she'd get to the new robe one of these days. Just not until she was finished with the old one.

Janine fished through the drawer to the right of the sink, found a pair of tweezers and went into the walk-in closet. She sat on the bench in the middle of her closet and hiked her foot up on the stool and began to work on her toenails, digging out the ingrown portions.

Click.

She liked to pick.

Click.

She'd been to the doctor but preferred to work out the problems on her own.

Marcus found his razor, his cologne, shaving cream and the rest, shoving it into a toiletry bag, and went back to the bed. It was one thing to listen to the *click, click,* but quite another to see the cottage-cheese-laden legs beneath the frayed edges of that worn-out robe. He used to rub those legs, when she was in law school, when she'd be up seventy-two hours at a time, sleepless from leg aches.

She didn't look like that then.

More like a linebacker, now. And not one from Harvard. More

like NFL All-Pro. Marcus gave her a P90X for Christmas. Never got opened.

Click.

"I've arranged for Ariel to bring the kids home after William's play," Janine said. "Will you at least see some of it?"

"Afraid not. I'll be on the West Coast, starting in Seattle tomorrow morning and finishing in San Francisco on Thursday."

"His performance is on Wednesday."

"I'm not flying back for that, Janine."

Long pause. Not an empty one.

Marcus finished packing his carry-on. He pulled three suits from the closet and laid them on the bed. They were pressed and clean and spotless. They went into the hanging garment bag.

"How many halfskin shutdowns are you going to attend?" Janine leaned against the closet door frame.

"As many as there are, dear."

"They'll only increase." Her tone was final. "This... biomite war you're waging... you can't win it, Marcus. People are going to keep seeding unless they become illegal."

"Then we'll keep turning them off."

"Until what? Until you've wiped out the human race?"

"Just the seeded ones."

"This is an infringement on their liberty—"

"Spare me the lawyer speak." He dropped the suitcase on the floor and snapped out the telescoping handle. "People will destroy themselves if we let them."

"That's their choice."

"Then why not just legalize everything, Janine? Why not just set up heroin shops and cocaine dens outside the kids' school? Let's not have a drinking limit; it's their life, after all. It's their choice to destroy it."

He hung the garment bag on the top of the bedroom door and paused. Janine dropped the tweezers in the drawer. Her robe crumpled on the floor. Her granny panties snapped around her waist. Marcus didn't turn around.

"Technology will catch up," she said. "They'll be able to control runaway replication at some point."

"I hope it does. I don't like shutting down halfskins."

"I think you do."

Immortality is meant for the soul. Not the flesh.

Marcus slid his feet into moccasin slippers and pulled his suitcase with the garment bag over his shoulder.

"In case you're wondering," Janine mumbled, "I'm going to a fundraiser tonight with Helen. Make sure the children have brushed their teeth. Alexander has not been flossing."

She was standing in front of the mirror with bobby pins in her mouth, pulling her black hair back. Her nipples pointed at the faucet.

"Tell her I said hi." He started and stopped. "And I want the new nanny fired."

"Mmm-mm."

Marcus went to his office. He texted Ariel to make sure Alexander flossed.

CHAPTER THIRTEEN_

Nix stared at the ceiling.

He was cautious not to daydream. He kept his attention on his breath, emptied his mind. It had been weeks since Cali delivered the special drawing. She continued her weekly visits, as usual, and asked how he was doing.

Good. Real good.

Then they talked about Avery needing braces, how the Holloways' dog got hit by a car, how crappy the weather was. She didn't bring any more pictures, just said that Avery was probably going to make him another one in two weeks. She was pretty clear about it. *In TWO weeks.*

But Cali wasn't bringing another picture.

She was telling him how long to wait.

She had embedded biomites into the waxy yellow sun. They were undetected by the ring that registered him at 48.8%. But Nix felt the effects. They weren't suppressed at all.

They were fully active.

The ring had no effect on these new-breed biomites, had no recognition of their proliferation. His senses slowly enhanced as they integrated into his body. He smelled the subtle odors down the hall, knew when the guards were eating, when they last showered. He saw more colors, felt more textures.

The new-breed biomites heightened it all. He had become... *more*. If he had to guess, they put him over 50%. He was probably halfskin and no one knew it.

Cali told him to wait. Wait until there were enough of them, until the levels of these new-breed biomites were more active. Then he'd know what to do.

Waiting was the hard part.

At night, he closed his eyes and fell into rhythmic breathing. If anyone was watching, he was sleeping. But these were opportunities to smell the lagoon. Occasionally, he could hear Raine's laughter. Maybe he imagined it.

Maybe not.

Each night, he hoped to know more, perhaps to see the blue cliffs and the trees framing the crystal water. Each night, he only sensed a glimmer of that world. He'd wake in the morning, still a prisoner.

On the week that Avery's next drawing was to be delivered—four weeks since he snorted the yellow sun—Cali didn't come to visit.

George was waiting outside his door.

It had been a month since he last saw George, but there he was with the table and the box under his arm. George began setting up the board. He didn't say much, just pushed the pieces around.

Nix smelled something new about him, something metallic, the ting of aluminum on the edges of his tongue. He looked at George sorting out the blacks and whites. That's when the new-breed biomites whispered Cali's plan. Her ghostly voice was inside his head. It was a recording that was triggered by the sight of George and told him what to do.

Told him it was going to hurt.

Such a hypocrite. Such a liar.

George was 10% biomite. Maybe more. Nix realized he could read George's thoughts. Somehow, Cali's new-breed biomites were seamlessly scanning and connecting with other biomites within a short range, like wireless computers. And the biomites he was sensing were in George's brain.

Like a book.

"A game?" George tapped the small table outside the door. "Or you have somewhere to go?"

Nix looked up from his bed. He sat up and rubbed his eyes, sleepy.

"Heh-heh," George added. "I've been thinking about our last game, where I went wrong... I have to be honest, I was cheating."

"I know."

"I know you know." George touched up the pieces, centering them in each of their squares. "But I figured I should come clean. I was using a machine to beat you and that's not fair. I'm here as a man, as a human being—" he thumped his chest "—to redeem the spirit of Man!"

George muttered a little pep talk. He clapped his hands and asked what color Nix wanted. Nix balked, so George took white.

"The good guys," he said, and moved queen's pawn two spaces.

Nix went to the sink and splashed water on his face. He wiped his scalp, the back of his neck. Dabbed himself dry with a hand towel. He just realized that, in his dreams, he had hair. *I had hair before. And now I'm this.*

I've forgotten what I look like.

"Come on, already." George looked at his watch. "I go on shift in an hour and you're over there making yourself pretty. You ain't got a date, halfskin, and I ain't easy to look at, either. So let's go."

George wasn't a bad guy. Maybe not good, but not bad. Nix felt a pang of guilt for what he was about to do to him.

But George was his ticket.

It needed punched.

MOTHER_
THE END OF SPELLING BEES

Joni Neisler's blue placard poked her in the chin. She walked to the slender mic at the front of the stage, far too timidly for someone at the National Championship. But probably just right for a five-year-old.

She tugged at the pleats in her dress.

The judges were conferring.

There was a man behind them. She couldn't see him so well, it was dimly lit beyond the judge's table, but she saw enough. He sat there with his barrel arms latched over his chest, next to his tiny wife. He was scowling. They both were. They'd been doing that ever since the contest started. Always at her.

The judge looked over his laptop, his face bluish. "Spell 'Otorhinolaryngological.'"

Joni was supposed to take a deep breath. She was supposed to ask the judge to use it in a sentence. Ask the origin of the word. Her father told her to make it look like she was thinking it through, but the lumberjack dad and his little wife kept staring at her.

They were so angry.

She just wanted to get off the stage.

"Otorhinolaryngological.

"O-T-O-R-H-I-N-O-L-A-R-Y-N-G-O-L-O-G-I-C-A-L.

"Otorhinolaryngological."

Joni went back to her seat. She didn't wait to hear if she was right. She was right. She spelled everything right. She didn't know what was so hard.

The crowd rumbled. There was shifting around. The judges leaned their heads together as the next contestant went to the mic. None of the other kids looked at Joni. Joni was half their age, but that wasn't why they always looked at her strangely. It was something else. Probably the same reason the lumberjack dad was mad at her.

And he was standing, now.

He pulled his wife up, too. They were scooting down the aisle, not making much of an effort to walk sideways like you're supposed to when you walk down a crowded aisle.

"Quiet, please." One of the judges, the nice one with perfect teeth, said, "Please settle down."

"We're done here," lumberjack dad said.

"Sir, you need to take your seat or your son will be disqualified. Distractions need to be kept to a minimum."

More disruptions.

Someone else stood.

Lumberjack dad stared at the nice judge. Joni thought he was going to slug him one.

"You test her?" He pointed that giant arm right at Joni.

"You have no right!" Now Joni's momma was standing up.

"Did you test her?" Lumberjack dad didn't pay any attention to Momma. "The rules clearly state this is a natural-born spelling bee. There are competitions for biomite-enhanced young ones, but this is not one of them. And even if it was, that girl is five. She's too young to be seeded; it's against the law. So did you test her?"

Arguments broke out in the studio. Judges were standing, crew from off the stage were coming over, and security was already putting hands on the lumberjack dad. People were walking out. One of the contestants' dads came up on stage and dragged him off by the arm. He gave Joni a mean look.

That's when the first tear came out.

"Did you inspect her brain stem?" lumberjack dad was shouting over the chaos. He was pointing at the back of his neck while security ushered him away. "There'll be a knot the size of a BB where the seed point is."

One of the judges left. The others were calming the crowd. Joni's face felt hot. Her papa came out of nowhere and put his arm around her. She hid her face while people stomped off the stage. The lights turned up. There was a call for recess, a call for order.

And Joni cried in her papa's arms. She rubbed her tears, smearing them on her cheek, and reached behind her ear. Her little fingers crawled through the hair braided on the back of her head, the braid her mama did for her before the event, and searched the base of her skull.

Where she found a knot the size of a BB.

CHAPTER FOURTEEN_

Cali unpacked.

Avery's clothes were on top. She placed them in the empty drawers, all the shirts nicely folded and cleaned. All perfectly stacked. Next, she took hers out, placing them in the larger drawers, not so meticulous with them.

She dragged the large bag to the corner and unloaded the toiletries around the sink. The Chicago Marriott welcome kit was neatly arranged against the mirror. Cali took the time to unload the toothpaste and deodorant and brushes and soap and everything else to keep the bathroom area in order. They'd be staying in the suite for the next couple weeks and Cali hated a messy bathroom.

Avery jumped from bed to bed, giggling with each leap, crumpling the floral bedspreads in heaping wrinkles.

Cali wanted a smoke. It was too far to walk down to the street. She brushed her teeth, instead. They'd been in the car long enough to pound out a pack of cigarettes. Her chest wheezed. She hated the city —too big, too cold—but she hated not knowing even more. And she came to Chicago, not knowing if things would work.

They have to. They have to.

Cali dug a clot of clothes from the drawers and went to the bathroom.

"Going to take a shower, Mama?"

Cali mumbled something and closed the door. She missed the light switch and, in the dark, kicked the toilet. Pain seared her big toe, shooting over the top of her foot. She found the light and half a toenail on the floor, still covered with chipped orange polish from the last time Avery painted them.

Blood bubbled on the exposed nail bed.

She quickly ran the shower, undressed and stepped in to wash off the dirt, to wash away the emotions, to clean her mind. The steamy water covered the sobs hiccupping in her throat. Blood washed in diluted rivulets to the drain. Cali wondered how many of those red platelets were biomites just imitating blood. *How much of that is me?*

She reached out and hit the light switch.

Showered in the dark.

"Stop jumping."

"Yes, Mama." Avery climbed off the bed nearest the window. "Do you feel better?"

Cali brushed her teeth again and decided to wear the robe instead of getting dressed. She found a Band-Aid at the bottom of her bag and wrapped her toe. Avery was standing on the window frame, arms out, palms pressed against the glass. Cali cleaned the blood off the bathroom floor and retrieved the brittle toenail—that was the second time she'd cracked a nail in a week—before Avery saw it. Blood creeped her out and made her lose her breath.

"Everything's so *biiig*," Avery announced, smudging the glass with her lips. "The people look like ants."

Cali smiled. That's what she said when she was a little girl and her dad brought them along on a business trip and took her to the top of what was called the Sears Tower. She remembered her stomach lurching and the cars looked like toys.

"I want to spit." Avery had a very big smile. "What do you think would happen if we spit, Mama?"

"You'd get in trouble."

"No one would know it was us. There's like a million windows on this building, Mama. No one would know."

"How are you going to get the window open?"

Avery examined the glass. She ran her fingers along the edges. "How come it won't open?"

"They don't want anyone falling out."

"Oh, my." Avery covered her mouth, her eyes wide but smiling. "What would it feel like to fall?"

Cali wondered the same thing. *What would it feel like?*

Would she feel anything in her empty stomach? Would she feel alive, for once? Or would it bring relief?

"I'M HUNGRY." Avery stumbled into the office area of the suite. "When are we going to eat?"

Cali was still in her robe. There were two tablets and a laptop open and running on the desk. CNN was on the TV. She slouched in the chair, head resting on the back.

"You want to call up room service?"

"Yes!" Avery leaped and clapped. She scuttled into the bedroom and picked up the phone.

Cali kept an eye on her screens. The lights were off. The room shimmered data blue. CNN might pick up the story she was waiting for, but she knew she'd see it on her company's—BioMed—news feed first. She logged on with an encrypted connection and watched story after story of anything biomite related scroll down the laptop screen.

She reached out and tapped Nix's name with one hand. The news feed spit out past stories regarding his initial seedings and development, including confidential data. She punched in a date to limit the stories to current ones.

The information stopped.

So she waited.

She kept her eyes on the empty screen, waiting for a story. Waiting to hear anything on her brother while her stomach turned and her eyes grew heavy and reporters droned on the TV.

She waited.

She waited.

THE ROOM WAS DARK, lit only by the television's flare.

The computers were asleep.

Cali wiped the spittle from her mouth. The other room was silent and dark, as well. She sat up and tapped the space bar.

The screen was full of words.

Full of stories.

All containing Nix's name.

...Nixon Richards is en route to Northwestern Memorial Hospital's biomite wing...

She scrolled the mouse wheel, her eyes racing over the words, looking and looking. She clicked the next story describing more details.

...his condition critical...

Cali flopped in her chair, eyes stuck on those two words. Condition critical. *Critical.*

But he's alive.

He's out.

It worked. He's out of the Center.

And he was at Northwestern Memorial, in the nation's most advanced biomite technology wing only two blocks from where she was sitting. She let out a breath. A long stale one. Perhaps one she'd been holding for several months.

Avery was lying on the bed, the iPod inches from her face. Electric shadows stretched over her cheeks. Cali looked around.

"I thought you ordered room service?"

"I didn't know what you wanted," she said dully. She did not look up. "And you were sleeping."

Cali lay next to her, stroking her daughter's hair. They watched a few minutes of a movie.

"Did you get good news?" Avery asked.

Cali kissed her cheek. "Yes."

CHAPTER FIFTEEN_

George needed a victory. Something. Anything.

All he had was this place, this job.

He had no life outside of it.

It wasn't always like that. He used to be somebody. He was starting left guard for an AA state champion football team. He had an associate's degree in criminal justice. And he was eight years from retiring to Florida, where he'd find a trailer and fish until the sun went down.

Some people had it worse than old George, but, still, he needed a victory. He needed something to remind him he was worth something.

This little... *chess game...* it was nothing to Nix. That kid had nothing else but time to think about it. George had responsibilities, he had alimony and child support, he had a sick mother and an asshole father. He had all sorts of things occupying his mind, but he was damned if he'd use that as an excuse. He was better than that.

He was better than a machine.

And that's just what Nix was. He was damn near 50% biomite, something like 49.9%. One-tenth of a percent didn't make you human. You were half human, half machine. No way around it.

George, on the other hand, was only 10% biomite. That wasn't much. And he didn't choose to get seeded. He was diabetic and alcoholic, and those were treatable diseases with biomite technology. The doctors assured him he was seeded with suppressed varieties that doubled in population once every fifteen years. That meant he would be dead before he redlined. If a little seeding made his life a little less miserable, then praise the Lord.

He rested his elbows on his knees. He decided last time there was too much chitchat. Nix threw him off balance with all the talk. He needed to concentrate. Besides, his act of confession about the last time was just a decoy. He'd downloaded some chess code and had the doctor seed his brain. It was only a 1% biomite boost, but guaranteed to make him remember more and analyze faster.

And it was working, he could tell.

It used to be he only had one or two moves planned, but now he was planning five or six. He felt good, felt right. Felt like today was his day. He could even see a way to checkmate this snotnose in seven moves.

George felt his scalp tingle. He wiped the sweat with his sleeve. The hallway was getting warm, the A/C was down. No matter, he was on a roll.

George lifted the knight with two fingers, placed it on C-6 and studied the board. If he had things figured right, Nix would take the bait and swipe his bishop, which would leave him open to get his queen in position.

He lifted his hand. Move made. He looked up.

On the other side of the glass...

Sitting in a chair on the other side of the glass... door...

He wiped his eyes. They were blurry with sweat. He needed a drink; he was parched. His throat was scratchy and hot. He wiped his forehead again.

"You all right?" Nix asked.

George waved the kid off. "Shut up and move."

The kid watched him. George looked away, irritated. But then he moved exactly where he wanted him. The little dummy took his bishop, just like he planned.

Good God!

George could hardly keep calm. He forced himself to sit still, forced himself to refrain from moving too quickly. He pretended to think for a full minute while sweat ran down his temples and his brain quivered with excitement.

He made his move.

Queen to F-3.

He refused to look up; he couldn't be distracted. Not again. Not like last time. Whatever the hell brought that weird thing up a minute ago was... it was nothing. He focused.

Focus. And never look up from the board.

He executed every move just like he planned. Nix castled his king into safety. Or so he thought. George pushed his pawn up a square. All he needed was one more move and it was a done deal. The rook would slide up to C-2 and he could accept the kid's submission—

"Bishop to G-8."

George shuddered.

His head was vibrating on the inside, like someone jammed a vibrator between his ears. His eyes stung from the heat. *Will somebody turn up the goddamn air-conditioning?*

He reached for the black bishop. His hand moved like a sandbag, dropping on the pointed end and sliding it across the board.

He didn't see that coming.

He didn't...

See...

George looked up. He looked through the glass door. He didn't see the kid... it wasn't the kid... sitting there. He wiped his face, rubbed his eyes, moved his mouth like it was filled with paste and looked again.

It wasn't the kid.

It wasn't Nix.

James?

"Hey, Georgie. How's it going, bud?"

My best friend?

The guy he grew up with was sitting on the other side of the door. His buddy, his friend for life, his best man at his wedding...

James was sitting in there. His blood brother.

The man that slept with my wife.

"Georgie, remember this one?" James kicked the chair across the room and got on his knees next to the bed. "Remember the time you came home from work early and saw this? You remember?"

James's hips gyrated, grinding into the mattress. He closed his eyes, head back. James's fingers caressed the sheets. The frame squeaked with every thrust. It began to sound like a woman moaning. A woman loving it.

Loving every second of it.

"Remember that, Georgie?"

Yeah. He remembered.

He remembered the best man that took his life away... he remembered the best man he'd take a bullet for, the man he'd die for, the man who was doing that with his wife... HIS WIFE... AND THAT MAN WAS RIGHT... IN... THERE!

Click.

George touched the monitor on his belt. The door unbuckled. James backed up. George came in, fists clenched. He'd waited a long time for this day. He waited a long time to tell his best man what he thought, what he felt... all these years.

Chess pieces fell on the floor as he stepped into the cell. The door latched behind him.

His head was vibrating. It was so hot.

Like fire.

CHAPTER SIXTEEN_

NIX WATCHED THE MADNESS UNFOLD.

He hardly looked at the chessboard. Instead, he watched George's memories like streaming videos. He wasn't sure how he was doing it, just looked up and there they were. At first, Nix misunderstood, thought he was remembering something in his own past. But he was remembering someone else's life, someone middle-aged.

Sitting right in front of him.

The new-breed biomites had something to do with it. Cali's message was clear: Nix would know what to do. He had to get out of the Center. He couldn't just walk out, even if he had George tied with his hands behind his back and a gun to his head. They'd simply shut off Nix's biomites and it was over. Like that. Cali had another plan, a way that would force them to take Nix far away from the Center, to a place with less security. A place easier to dupe.

But it was going to hurt.

So Nix sat there watching George's memories, sorting through the painful ones. There were so many to choose from, but there was one that continued to rise to the surface. And that would be it. That would trigger the escape.

Nix made that memory a reality.

George saw what Nix wanted him to see. None of it was real, but George wouldn't know the difference. Maybe it wouldn't work on someone else, someone smarter, someone who didn't drink or had more refined biomites with security patches. As it was, George wanted to believe his thoughts, he loved to be entertained. His reality was what his brain biomites told him was reality. And they told him that his best friend, his greatest betrayer, was ten feet away, mocking him.

Nix knew all too well that the mind can make people see what they want to see.

When the door popped open, when George entered his room, Nix thought-commanded his new-breed biomites to dull his nervous system. He stood up numbly and backed away. George came through the doorway, the door shutting behind him. This needed to be beyond anything they could handle in the Detainment and Observation Center. They would need to get him out after this.

George looked like a grizzly. His chest expanded, his eyes red and wild. Teeth bared. He backed Nix into a corner, hot air streaming out his nostrils. Before the first blow landed, the new-breed biomites connected with the surveillance cameras and began downloading the video stream, capturing every last second of the mauling that took place in room 204.

It was a beating that lasted three minutes, with guards begging him to stop. A beating of pure hatred, bent vengeance, total destruction.

When it ended, no one would recognize the face that belonged to Nix Richards.

The cameras would never forget.

CHAPTER SEVENTEEN_

MARCUS LOOSENED HIS TIE.

Down on Van Ness Avenue, three stories down, was a line of people. A line of gays and lesbians and hippies. The lesbian with the crew cut was bellowing into a bullhorn.

Only in California. Only in San Francisco.

He'd been to almost every state to witness a halfskin shutdown and he'd never seen picketers. There were scathing editorials and dirty looks, but Americans understood this was a problem and the government was looking out for them.

But not in California.

They were saving the world one tree at a time, hiking up their sleeves and making humorous signs that belittled the grave danger biomites presented to humanity. And the liberal media was more than happy to slurp it up, regurgitate it to the general population so that teenagers around the world believed the government was a big bad wolf coming to blow their house down.

They were all going to hell.

God did not look kindly on the free-sinning lifestyles of California. He did not approve of their dream worlds. If these people got a job, if they lived in reality, they wouldn't have time to kick off their shoes and parade in front of the Detention and Observation Center. They'd be home, taking care of their family. Taking care of kids.

California.

It was federal law to establish secure centers for detainment and observation. Somehow, converting a five-story building on a downtown street did not conform to what Marcus considered secure.

These jerkoffs were right there at the entrance.

He watched his car coast down Van Ness Avenue. It slowed near the entrance but continued without much notice. He'd phoned down for the driver to meet him on Polk Street. He'd take the back exit and walk the block over.

He dug a camera from his soft leather handbag and snapped a picture of the bullhorn lesbian. He'd get her identity. He'd make sure he attended her halfskin shutdown. That, he'd enjoy.

He folded his jacket and tie and stuffed them into his bag, snapping it shut. He hoped if any of the hippie protesters saw him, they wouldn't think much.

The door opened. "Sir, the Secretary of State is on the phone."

Tim held the cell phone to his chest. Marcus walked around the shiny conference table, hand out and fingers wiggling.

"Yeah." He spoke into the phone, closing the door on Tim. "Just leaving."

Marcus wandered back to the window.

"It went fine, just a little backlash at the front door."

He listened to the voice on the other end.

"Chicago?" Marcus spouted. "Why'd they move the kid out of the Center?"

The Secretary of State explained the public relations waiting for him at Northwestern Memorial Hospital. The kid had been nearly beaten to death by one of the Center's guards.

"That's not our problem. That's on the Center."

"They suspect a bad biomite seed caused excessive aggression," the Secretary said, "in the guard."

"Look, I don't know why you're calling me. People snap all the time; that's not on us. I suggest you get him back to the Center, let him heal and then we'll shut him down when he's halfskin."

There was discussion.

Marcus pulled the phone from his ear and looked at the photo uploading to his screen. He took a deep breath, putting the phone against his head.

"That gets out," the Secretary said, "we got problems."

The Secretary was right. People like those on the street would send that around the world. By morning, the media would paint the administration as blood-lusting animals sending their redline babies to meat factories where they'd get battered and raped before they got shut down.

"Listen, the president wants that kid nursed back to health; he wants us to care for him, to do everything we can do. He's sitting at 49%. We can't shut him down while he looks like that because one of *our* people snapped."

"All right."

"It's not us against them, Marcus. Get over there and clean this up."

Marcus looked out the window. "No one goes near that kid's hospital room besides doctors and nurses. Post security; I'll fly out tonight."

He dropped the phone on the table.

He went out the back way.

Things would be so much easier if people didn't get in the way.

CHAPTER EIGHTEEN_

Avery was swimming with some kids at the other end of the hotel's pool. Cali watched from a lounger. Big, round sunglasses hid her eyes even though they were indoors.

She was thinking.

There were always problems. She was an engineer and knew to plan for contingency. She thought they'd let her see her brother. She had waited a day to go to the second floor of the hospital so it didn't appear like she was already in the city, waiting for him to arrive. She saw the guy sitting outside her brother's room, reading a paper. She explained who she was, showing her identification.

He simply shook his head.

No one, absolutely no one, is allowed to see this kid. Not his sister, not his mother, not Jesus Christ.

She stood in front of the guy, clenching and unclenching her fists, until he told her that she needed to move on before he escorted her out.

Cali wandered down the hall, turned the corner and leaned against the wall. She didn't know where to go, what to do. There were a dozen options, but none of them had long-term viability.

She needed to think.

She needed to do something, fast.

And that's when the small, freakish-looking creep walked past her. He reeked of government entitlement. His pants were wrinkled, collar undone. His stride was bold, his shoes clapping the floor like it offended him. He oozed power.

She knew who he was. Every nanobiometrics engineer knew what Marcus Anderson looked like. He put that guard there.

He was just the person she needed.

She went back to the hotel room, but it was stuffy.

She came to the pool to change the scenery, to give Avery something to do besides jump on the beds. There was only one couple, the ones with the kids splashing around. The man's name was Paul. His eight-pack abs rolled like hardened sand dunes. His sunglasses were askew, mouth agog. He was 35% biomite, used them to burn fat and build muscle without exercising. He also allocated a significant percentage to increase strength and eye-hand coordination to dominate his golf league. The remaining biomites boosted memory and analytical ability, aiding his successful legal skills. Paul had about five years before he redlined, but he figured something would come out before then.

Shelly—his gorgeous wife—was shopping on her tablet. She was only 10% biomite, something that controlled her metabolism and suppressed her appetite and boosted her memory. She planned on going back to college. She wanted to be a teacher.

Cali's new-breed biomites knew these things, downloaded them from Paul and Shelly like data. They were none the wiser. Cali's new breeds were networking with Paul and Shelly's biomites like cloud memory. She knew everything about them: bank accounts, passwords, social security numbers, memories.

Paul was two years into an affair.

"Mama! Watch!" Avery splashed into the deep end. "I'm going to touch the bottom; count how long I'm under water."

Cali smiled at her daughter. "Okay."

"You ready?"

"Yep."

Avery pinched her nose and somersaulted beneath the surface, her feet splashing her deeper. Cali loved watching her swim. She remembered when she couldn't touch the bottom and clung to her arm like a barnacle.

Avery emerged in a hurry, breathing heavily.

"How many?" she asked.

"One hundred seconds." Cali smiled.

"*Moooom*. You didn't count."

"Let me finish up and then I'll come swim with you, how about that?"

"Yay!" Avery pinched her nose for another dive.

Shelly put on sunglasses, acting like she wasn't staring.

Cali set up her laptop and found some basic information on Marcus Anderson. He was involved with the boot of Mother and a leader of the Halfskin Laws. He was witness to all shutdowns to date.

If he only knew what I invented.

It wasn't hard to find his office phone number and email. That information was available to the public. Cali wasn't interested in those. Anyone who sent a message or called would get an assistant, guaranteed to never reach him.

She needed a more direct line.

Cali analyzed thousands of Marcus Anderson accounts. In seconds, she cracked into his home computers—accessing documents, bank accounts, vacation photos and personal email and cell phone.

She didn't bother calling. He wouldn't answer.

She texted, instead. Uploaded a video.

[*Send.*]

She sat back. Her coffee was cold.

Paul was still asleep and Shelly was filing her nails, still pretending not to sneak peeks at Cali. Avery climbed onto the ledge in front of her, pushing her wet hair back and spitting water.

"You said you were going to swim."

"I am, sweetie. Almost done."

Avery whacked the side of her head, knocking water out of her ears. She complained when she couldn't get them clear. Cali pulled a bottle of alcohol from her bag and waved her daughter over. Avery lay on the lounger while her mother squirted alcohol into her ears, making a funny face because she hated the way it felt.

Shelly was watching again.

Avery dried her hair, looking at the laptop.

"When are we going to visit Uncle Nix?" She touched the picture of her uncle that was frozen on the screen.

"Soon."

"I can't wait to see him."

A cell phone chimed. "Me too. Why don't you jump in and I'll be right there after I take this call."

Avery cannonballed into the deep end. Cali flashed five fingers twice and Avery was pleased with scoring a perfect ten. The caller ID reported a restricted number. Cali touched the screen and held it to her ear.

"How'd you get this number?" a man said.

"There are more important matters to discuss."

Silence hung on the other end of the phone. His voice muffled through his fingers as he said something. The receiver scuffed and he pulled his hand away.

"I'll have you arrested."

"The video is genuine. You may take your time authenticating it, if you like, but I only have so much patience. You don't want that released to the public."

Another long pause.

"What do you want?"

"I just want to see my brother. I will arrive at the hospital at noon today."

Cali turned off the phone.

He'd have his people analyze the video, have them figure out how she got it. The new breeds seeded in Nix's brain pirated the video and uploaded it to an anonymous FTP site that Cali immediately shut down. She forced herself to watch it. Dry-heaved when it was over.

She really didn't expect to use the video; it was only going to be a last resort bargaining chip if things got bad. But getting locked out of the room sank every other plan she had. They would keep him isolated until he healed enough to return to the Center.

Or turned halfskin.

That's what really freaked her out, seeing that man in the hall, knowing he was there to see this to a tidy end. She knew she couldn't play nice. She was all in. If the gamble didn't work, she would start blowing up careers and take as many people down with her as she could.

Starting with Marcus Anderson.

"You coming?" Avery called.

Cali stretched her arms and back. She was ready for a swim. She needed to cool off. Just before diving into the pool, she made a suggestion that the new breeds passed along to Shelly. When she emerged halfway across—throwing her wet, blond hair off her face—she heard Shelly. And Paul trying to explain all the emails he'd received from someone calling him lover.

CHAPTER NINETEEN_

Antiseptic.

Beeps.

Pinpricks on his arm.

Something pumped, in and out. Inflating him like a balloon then allowing him to leak before filling him up again.

Nix knew the sounds and smells of a hospital. His earliest memories started at five years old, when he woke in one of the tilting beds with the side rails and a nurse tending a needle in his arm. He watched her through the slits of his eyelids, fascinated there was a needle in his arm and he couldn't feel it. In fact, he couldn't feel much.

That was the day he realized he was cursed.

His father, a brilliant nanobiometric engineer. *Dead.*

His mother, an outstanding computer programmer. *Dead.*

His sister, a nanobiometric engineer like her father, the only family he had left. She was beside his bed.

She was cursed, too. Just didn't realize it yet.

He couldn't open his eyes. It might have been hours or days. Weeks. He floated in the lonely darkness with his memories. Occasionally, he heard muffled voices or felt the dull prick of a needle sliding into his arm. He was still wearing the suppression ring, his biomites offering very little help healing his broken body. If not for the new breeds, he would be in agony.

They helped control the pain, dulling his nervous system, but did very little to heal. He was mending the old-fashioned way.

Time.

Until then, he lay comatose with his memories.

He didn't control George, didn't make him open the cell door. Didn't make him attack.

He merely baited him.

The first punch was all that Nix actually remembered. He covered up, but George's fist landed on the side of his head like a club. The memories went dark after that, but Nix watched the incident from above, like an out-of-body experience from all corners of the room, like his eyes were surveillance cameras. He lay in the darkness of closed eyes and watched George drop bombs.

His face broke on the third shot.

His ribs caved on the fifth.

George picked him up by the neck. Nix hung like a slab of meat.

The guards stormed through the door. Nix's face was red. It took five of them to peel George's hands off. The video ended just after George fell on his knees, looking at his bloody hands, weeping.

The new breeds knew where to send the video.

Cali saw it. She owned it. She would have it to bargain, if she needed it.

Until then, Nix faded in and out of consciousness, yearning for all his biomites to be fully online. That's when he'd heal. That's when he'd wake up.

And, maybe, he'd get to see Raine.

MOTHER_
HISTORIC PITCH

Jonny Miser took the ball from the catcher halfway between the mound and home plate. He chicken-winged his glove under his right arm and rubbed the new off the ball with both hands. He made one loop around the pitcher's mound, careful not to touch the dirt until he was back around the front.

Bad luck if he did.

Wrigley Field fans were on their feet. Even the fans on the rooftops were up and waving and whistling and shouting. He wiped the sweat off his forehead.

It was hot for October.

He blinked, focused on the scoreboard. A one-run lead. Three balls, two strikes. He looked around the diamond; St. Louis Cardinal base runners looked back from all three bags.

Last game of the season. *Win, you're in.*

The sort of pressure Jonny loved.

He couldn't hear the crowd. The voices blended together in a blur of white noise. The whole world was watching. People were on the edges of their seats at home, on their feet in the bars across the nation, all of them ready to watch Jonny Miser close out the St. Louis Cardinals to win the division.

It was all up to Jonny.

He did hear one of the voices. The one in his head.

Don't blow this.

He toed the rubber, digging his cleats into the divot. He wedged the side of his foot against it and looked at the catcher. His arm dangled at his side, the surgically repaired elbow tingling.

He shook off the first pitch. Took the next one.

The heat.

Jonny would propel his team into the playoffs by blowing a fastball past the batter. Put it all into this pitch, the last one of the season.

It would also be the last one of his career.

Jonny Miser went into his stretch, the crowd frenzied, the batter waving his bat, the umpire crouched behind the catcher.

He kicked his leg.

He threw the historic pitch.

The umpire never called it. He stumbled, eventually falling on his back. He never saw it.

The sound of the ball was described as a wet gunshot that shattered the catcher's hand. If it had missed the glove, it would've ended his life.

It was later explained that the Tommy John surgery performed earlier that year utilized a small amount of biomites to repair tendons in Jonny Miser's arm. The low levels were monitored by the league and remained at less than 1%. However, it was later explained the biomites responded to elevated levels of cortisol and norepinephrine —stress hormones—and induced an immediate proliferation. In minutes, the biomite population had consumed his arm.

Impossible, said nanobiometric engineers.

The pitch was clocked at 204 mph.

CHAPTER TWENTY_

Cali sat in the back of Northwestern Memorial Hospital's chapel. The room was small. The wooden pews were padded with long cushions. She propped her feet on a burgundy kneeling block.

Chicago was a foreign land. She'd been there with her husband. He bought two tickets to *Miss Saigon*. Neither one of them had ever been to the city (at least not when they were older), but he insisted they just needed a map. Of course, city streets were a lot different than small towns and they ended up in Cabrini Green below the train. She thought she was going to cry.

Avery fell asleep on the pew.

An elderly woman fumbled prayer beads in her fingers. Pretty soon, she fell asleep, too. Cali sat with her head against the brown paneled wall and listened to soft snoring. It was music to her ears, hearing her daughter sleep. Sometimes she leaned over to feel her warm breath on her ear. When Avery was young, she would crawl into bed and cuddle against her, breath tickling her neck.

Cali preferred the chapel to the waiting room. She'd spent enough time in hospitals to know that—between services—it was quieter. There were fewer people, too. She didn't think she'd be able to sit long in the waiting room, surrounded by people with all their heavy emotions and thoughts of dying.

Especially now.

The chapel was better. It contained hope, a sanctuary for the religious faithful that brought their belief in God with them. Sometimes, in the face of the hopeless, the illusion of a spiritual being carrying her through life's difficulties was helpful.

But she wasn't interested in that now. Cali just needed somewhere to focus, to steel her will and sharpen her wits. Battles were fought with the mind long before muscle joined the fight.

"Honey." Cali gently shook Avery. "Do you want something to drink?"

Avery's head rolled across Cali's lap. She blinked a few times and looked around the strange room. She sat up and yawned.

"You thirsty?" Cali asked.

Avery nodded.

"Here, take this to the cafeteria and get yourself something to drink and eat."

Avery took the money and yawned. "Do you want something?"

The elderly woman woke up and looked around.

"No, thank you, sweetheart. You help yourself. Do you have your phone?"

Nod.

"Okay, good. I'll be right here."

Avery started away.

"If you get lost, just come back here, all right?"

Nod.

Cali returned to a quiet place in her mind and closed her eyes, where thoughts fell away. Where she could just be present. Where she didn't think. The time for thinking was reaching an end.

SHE FELT them before they arrived. The new breeds sensed the arrival of security outside the chapel.

Cali opened her eyes.

There were a few more people in the room. A preacher was at the podium, leafing through pages. He pushed his glasses up his nose. Two men entered the room. Their hair was cut proper and their dark jackets concealed weapons. They didn't bother walking down the narrow space along the pews. One of them signaled Cali with his finger.

She quickly texted Avery. Wait for me in chapel. Going to see Uncle Nix. I'll come back for you.

She would be upset, but Cali didn't want her to see her uncle like that.

The gentlemen patiently waited. Cali handed her bag to them. They didn't bother asking her for identity. The one on the right—brown hair and a tiny soul patch—looked through the bag while the other one, the one with slick black hair, pressed a scanning device on her. Cali tingled as her biomites responded to the device.

The new breeds remained quiet.

"39.9%." He put the scanner away. "You're almost a redline."

"So I'm told."

"We'll be holding onto your bag," Soul Patch said. "Do you have any liquids on you?"

"Didn't the scanner tell you?"

"We have to ask."

"To give me a chance to lie."

He blinked slowly. Waited.

"No," she said. "Just me. Can we go?"

Soul Patch led the way out. Slick followed.

CHAPTER TWENTY-ONE_

THE ELEVATOR OPENED.

A hefty nurse intercepted Cali and her escort. She was doughy with a hook-shaped scar at the corner of her mouth. This was her floor. Soul Patch engaged her while Slick guided Cali past them despite the nurse's protests. A man sat at the end of the hall next to a door, his ankles crossed and a newspaper spread open. He folded it beneath his arm and stood up.

"Turn around." He made a twirling motion with his finger.

Cali faced the other direction and felt a scanner pressed against her back, evidently too shy to press it near her throat. "Didn't we already do this?"

She heard the instrument slide back into the sheath on his hip. He tugged her shoulder so that she turned back around, and stepped aside. Slick nodded at the door. They waited as she hesitantly placed her hand on it. It swung open, heavy on the cushioned hinges, and she heard Slick ask the other guy if he saw the baseball game.

The room smelled like the hallway—clean, germ-free, and artificial. It was darker, more points of light—greens and reds and lighted numbers—dotted medical machinery on the wall and rolling carts.

Plastic bags hung from hooks with clear tubes that dangled down to a bed—

Her back hit the door, pushing it closed.

Seeing the video… but this…

There wasn't much to see, actually. His body was covered beneath sheets and wrapped in gauze and casts. His head was fully encased and the nose was covered. Only the eyes were exposed, the skin dark purple, tinges of yellow. A tube exited his mouth, taped in place and attached to a ventilator that whooshed in and out with air.

She knew the extent of the damage; she knew what she was going to see. She saw his body at the end of the video, but seeing it in the flesh was…

I made a mistake.

A man stood at the foot of the bed, hands folded in front. His head was shaved, his face expressionless. The neck larger than the head.

"Four guards," she said. "You act like he's a criminal."

"He is." Marcus sat beside the bed, legs crossed; he eyed her with the larger of his two eyes.

"How many has he murdered?" she asked. "How many has he robbed? Raped?"

"Worse. He's spreading the disease of biomites."

"Then everyone is guilty."

"Your brother is guilty of excess."

"And that's worse than murder?"

He smiled. "They are one and the same."

Cali went to her brother's side. She held the two exposed fingers. The ventilator hissed at her. She wanted to kiss his forehead and whisper in his ear, tell him things were going to be all right like when he was little and things hurt. She wanted to tell him she was sorry.

But didn't.

"Wait outside, James," Marcus said.

There was laughter in the hall. The men peeked inside as the door slowly closed.

Cali rubbed his fingertips. Despite her best efforts, a tear escaped the corner of her eye.

"I KNOW THIS MUST BE HARD," Marcus said. "Tell me why it happened."

"I should be asking you that question," she said.

"You hack my personal information, show me the security footage of your brother getting beat to a pulp and I'm supposed to believe you don't know anything?"

He laughed, looked away and shook his head. Thinking.

"The guard had no history of violence. His wife slept with his best friend and he didn't even slice the guy's tires. Now you want me to believe he flew into a murderous rage because he lost a chess game? Did you stick around and watch what happened after they peeled him off your brother? He blubbered like a little girl. He tried to hug your brother. He wailed apologies all the way to a holding cell and tried to kill himself the next morning."

Marcus paused. He leaned forward, lowering his voice.

"You ruined his life, Cali. He's going to prison for a long time. You should be ashamed. Now, you want to tell me how you did this?"

"My brother's half dead and you want me to feel sorry for the attacker?"

"Your brother should be dead. If the hospital didn't keep his biomites suppressed, he'd be halfskin by now."

He had more thoughts, but was cautious she might somehow gather more evidence. He suspected something more was going on, a gut feeling he was way behind the true nature of this incident. Marcus was an intuitive man. He was usually right, but he didn't know how she got the video and couldn't be sure she wasn't recording this. He didn't want to give away too much.

Screw it. The truth is the truth.

"He should be dead," he continued. "Without his biomites fully activated, there's too much damage. Somehow, he lives. Want to explain?"

"It's medicine. We're not in the Dark Ages."

"The doctors are mystified. They say his internal injuries should have been fatal without fully activated biomites, but activating them would make him halfskin. Either way, he should be dead. I'm confused. Do you know something I don't?"

"I'll tell you what I know. My brother took a beating from a federal employee, a beating the world would love to see. A beating your political career wouldn't. Neither would the president."

"How'd you get it?" His tone deadened.

Cali looked back to her brother. She wanted to take the tube out of his mouth. It had to be uncomfortable.

"I know your tragic past," he said. "Believe it or not, I can make it worse."

"None of that will help you," she said, not looking up. "Not when the video is released to the press and the pro-bionanotechnology protest groups. Not when your personal information is released with it."

Her expression was as lifeless as his.

"Surely you have some secrets," she said. "Something you don't want anyone to see."

He didn't flinch.

"We have our own public relations. Truth can easily be spun into lies and urban legends. The Associated Press won't run it, not from a warped source like you. Unstable, unemployed. Damaged. We'll smear your reputation and your brother's all over the world."

"Politics isn't about truth. It's making people believe the story. They'll love what I have to show them. And it just happens to be the truth."

Long pause. Blink.

Smile.

"I suppose we have a stalemate," he said.

"That would mean we're tied, but I don't care. I've got nothing to lose. You have everything."

She remained placid.

"That's not a stalemate."

He watched her. The smile remained but quickly hollowed. Thinking, thinking...

"What do you want?"

"I want visitation rights to see him whenever I want. I want the right to be in the same room with him at all times and relate to him as a human being."

Marcus didn't move.

"I want the biomites fully activated so that he can heal quickly and painlessly, despite the threat of halfskin. I want him treated like a boy that's not imprisoned for living."

"You forgot to ask for his freedom."

She didn't respond.

"Oh, but why ask? If this is a ploy to help him escape, I promise you that won't happen. We'll have security inside and outside of this room. You won't get outside this hospital. If this is a chess game, Cali, then you're in checkmate. Your brother will heal and return to the Center. I imagine after we fully activate the biomites, though, he won't get that far. I won't even have to fly back to Illinois, I'll just sit in the waiting room until then and watch him shut down. You're welcome to watch."

If she was recording, he was screwed. He'd be seen as the tyrant the public and the press always suspected. But she threw the first swing. Marcus wasn't fond of cowering. You don't get far in politics with that.

"He's family," she whispered. "He's all I've got."

"I sympathize. But that's got nothing to do with my job."

"Perhaps you would better understand if your wife, Janine, took your boys to the store and they were in an accident."

Marcus's complexion turned a shade chalky.

"Maybe your tone would change if Janine died. Only Andrew

and William survive, but Andrew doesn't for long. He's brain-dead that evening. By morning, all you have is William. They have to seed him with biomites to keep him alive. It works. Your son is alive and you watch him grow up. You come home every day and ask him about school and his friends and take pictures before football games.

"And then the authorities show up. Mother has reported he's redline. Despite all your protests, all your explanations, they take him from you. Despite all your connections, they treat him like a criminal when all he wanted to do was live. All you wanted was for him to live. All you wanted was to not be alone. Because the law's the law, Marcus. There's nothing you can do but watch him get turned off."

Cali held his gaze. "Maybe then you'd feel differently."

Marcus was surprised at how that felt. He could separate work from family. Always could.

"Are you threatening me?" he said. "I could have you arrested for suggesting the murder of my wife and child."

"If you do, this goes live."

Cali held up her phone. The video of Nix's beating started with George bursting through the door. He didn't watch it. He didn't fidget, just looked off at something far away.

Thinking, thinking...

Marcus went to the door and stopped. He was about to say something, then left.

Cali waited a couple minutes for him to return. When he didn't, she dared to smile while she reached for her phone. She tapped the screen and pressed it against her cheek. It rang four times. Each one pulled her stomach tighter. Colder.

"Hello?"

"Avery." Cali let go of a long-held breath. "Come up, honey."

The tears cut loose.

CHAPTER TWENTY-TWO_

Marcus walked into the hall. Arms folded, eyes cast down.

His security team watched him pace away and lean against the wall. Minutes ticked by. The guards began whispering about strip clubs and a fight. Baseball tickets were mentioned and something about calling an old college buddy...

He knew her past.

He knew everything about her.

He couldn't blame her. That family was cursed. But she was dangerous.

She knew things, things about biomites that he didn't. He didn't like her being in that room, but there was nowhere to go. There was no escape. He needed time to think this one out. The video couldn't get out, not yet. And the kid wouldn't die, not soon enough. Not with the doctors looking. He needed time to clean things up, make arrangements.

"James." He waved his security guard over.

James squared his shoulders. Marcus kept his head down, voice low.

"I'm going to talk with Dr. Erickson about removing the biomite suppression. His sister will be allowed to stay in the room, but I want you to keep her in your sight at all times. You can rotate the watch with those two."

James listened.

"She's not allowed to leave. If she's got a hotel room around here, send someone after her stuff. As far as I'm concerned, she doesn't leave the hospital. Understand?"

James nodded. Marcus stared at him. He turned toward the other two.

"Hey!" They snapped quiet. "This isn't a frat party."

Their expressions shifted, darkly.

Marcus, half their size and not nearly as strong, stayed in place a few seconds. Thinking.

He told James to get in there.

And then he was down the hall. He was going to talk with the chief biomite doctor. After that, he was going to find where she lived and turn her house inside out.

If there was time, he'd text his wife.

CHAPTER TWENTY-THREE_

CALI STARED OUT THE WINDOW, CLUTCHING HER ELBOWS. THEY were pointy. She rubbed the chilly bumps that seemed to always be rising on her skin. The room felt colder.

Avery didn't complain.

She was in the corner, telling a story with two stuffed animals. Security brought all their stuff from Marriott that first night. They went through it, she was sure. They wouldn't find anything. She'd purged her laptop, databombed the hard drive and wiped out all her accounts.

The same was true of the house. Sooner or later, they would find the basement lab. Once this was over, they would haul everything out and pull it apart, piece by piece. But they'd find nothing. Cali knew she wasn't going back. Everything she needed was inside her.

And her brother.

New breeds.

Sometimes Avery would sit on her lap and tell a story, one she made up on the fly. Cali told her to write them down so she could practice becoming a writer. She would do that on scraps of paper and leave them around the room. Eventually she got bored and started telling the stories out loud again.

"What do you think the bad guy's name should be, Mr. James?"

The security guard didn't answer. He never did. He just stood there watching them. Didn't read, didn't watch TV. Just watched with his mouth closed.

Outside, it was raining big gray drops, blurring the city below. Cars were jammed up and pedestrians walked beneath umbrellas of red or black or whatever. Some took cover beneath an awning. It was probably warmer outside than it was in the room, but the loneliness seeped through the glass like a wet kiss, springing a fresh layer of chilly flesh.

"Momma, I'm hungry." Avery pressed Mr. Pillsbury—a fat, brown bear—against the window. "Look how far up we are."

"I'll get something to eat pretty soon."

"Can I get ice cream?"

"The cafeteria probably has something good."

Avery cheered. She walked Mr. Pillsbury across the room, stopped in front of James and did a little dance.

Three days of this.

Three days since they activated Nix's biomites and started an aggressive healing program. Almost fifty trillion cell-sized biomites were mending bones and tissue. Internal bleeding had stopped. His body temperature was slightly elevated from all the activity, but the color around his eyes had turned from black water to jaundice yellow. The respirator sat quietly in the corner. Nix breathed easily on his own.

Still, he lay unconscious.

Come on, Nix.

There wasn't much time. Marcus had given her everything she asked for, but there wasn't much of a window here. She was feeling the pressure. *What was I thinking, we'd just walk out of the hospital?* She doubted herself, wondering if it would've been easier to bust out of the Center than escape the hospital. This wasn't what she planned. Nix had to be healthy to leave. Had to be awake.

Before he became halfskin.

She needed him to wake up.

"Mr. James?" Avery called. "I have a question. Do you have a dog?"

James didn't answer.

Avery continued about what kind of dog she wanted and what she would name him.

Cali leaned her head against the window. The glass felt good. She wanted to stop thinking but didn't want to leave Avery all alone. Her head was filled with a white noise, like static, electric cotton. It fogged her focus. She hoped these weren't side effects from the new breeds. She didn't have time to test, just seeded herself in the basement lab. It was stupid, but there wasn't a choice. If they were failing now, well then, it was game over.

"What's your favorite ice cream?"

Silence.

"I like chocolate chips in mine but not too many. Have you ever put peanut butter in your ice cream?"

Silence.

Silence.

Silence.

"WILL YOU ANSWER HER?" Cali swung around. "She's not asking you to put your gun up your ass, she just wants to know what your favorite ice cream is."

James turned his head, regarding her without expression. Avery pulled her legs onto her chair and wrapped her arms around them. She hid behind Mr. Pillsbury.

"I'm sorry." Cali flopped into the chair next to the bed. She pulled her legs under her and rubbed her tired face, scratching her scalp.

"You need something to eat," James said, his voice deep and demanding.

"I know." Cali laid her head back. "I'll get something soon."

Avery shuffled across the room, leaning against her mother. Cali made some space for her to sit. She squished next to her, nice and warm and cuddly. Cali laid her cheek on top of her daughter's head.

"Tell me a story," she whispered. "A good one."

Avery started with a bright sunny day. She was on the porch with her mother, and Uncle Nix was in the backyard, digging a hole to the middle of the world, where they would make their home. Where no one could hurt them.

Cali closed her eyes. She smiled.

Then she projected a thought, one she hoped would be heard.

[*Wake up, Nix. Wake up.*]

CHAPTER TWENTY-FOUR_

Trapped in a long night.

Pain wrapped around Nix like a coffin. He willfully fled into unconsciousness. The new breeds kept him alive, but they couldn't heal. The longer he stayed in bed, the less they helped.

He got worse.

It got painful.

Not what he expected.

Minutes were days. Hours, months.

There was no rest. The large blank periods were not measured in time. He returned to self-awareness somewhere in the formless space of his mind. He couldn't sense the confines of his body, just the agony. He couldn't move his fingers, his toes. Couldn't open his eyes.

He sensed pressure. Felt disharmony. Experienced floundering organs and broken pieces. If he could disconnect entirely, he would.

Death.

That would be a good deal.

It would only take a thought-command directed at the new breeds working so tirelessly to keep his body alive.

Cease, and it would be over. *Cease*, and peace would be on him.

No more suffering. No more hurt.

No more, period.

He could rest. Finally.

All his life, he'd gone from one disaster to another. He'd seen those around him die, seen them suffer. Watched them break down. And after all of that, here he was imprisoned in his own body. Life was hardly fair. In fact, it was vindictive.

He often wondered what he had done in a previous life, if there were such a thing. He often wondered what the point of continuing to live would be with such suffering. It made no logical sense. Death was a prime option. *Why suffer? Why live a miserable life?*

He couldn't answer that. At least not with anything that made sense, not to his little mind.

But, live, he did.

He continued, and didn't know why.

The night appeared to be endless. He imagined Cali sitting by his side, watching him fade. Perhaps it was best if he stopped this madness. She could let go of him, finally. Stop taking care of him.

Face her demons on her own.

He didn't want to do that. She needed him. But if she could look inside him, if she could see the night, even she would tell him to let go.

Let go.

Let go.

And the ceaseless night brought him to the brink, where he loaded the thought-command to cease. He placed it in his mind. He felt the new breeds hesitate, sensing it. All he had to do was confirm it as a purposeful directive and they would stop. The organs would fail. His brain would fade.

And Nix would rest.

He could find peace.

BrrrrrrrrTHG.

Something engaged.

A switch was thrown. Followed by—

MmmmmmmmmmmmmMMMMMMMMMM.

A whine.

A thrum.

Light.

Warmth flooded his consciousness, trickling through streaks of pain, taking away the sparks and bites and stings and pressure...

It went away.

Disappeared.

She did it. She activated all the biomites!

Nix felt as if he was smiling, even though his body lay as still as death. Inside, he smiled. Inside, he basked in the glory of suffuse light penetrating everything. It was blinding and good and flowed with a silky essence.

Pure existence.

And from somewhere in its endless penetration, a form took place. He heard the water rushing, heard it crashing. He felt the foamy fingers slide over smooth sand. Felt the craggy rocks rise up.

The light condensed.

It was white. Then yellow.

Orange.

It solidified into a ball just above a sharp line. He felt its warmth. He was the warmth. The water thrummed a beat on the shore. It crashed inside him.

He pulled away from the sensations.

Felt a body that was separate from the sun and ocean and beach. Feet on the wet sand, toes buried beneath it. A bare chest for the rising sun to kiss. Hair falling over eyes that could see.

Could see.

See.

Far to the right, hundreds of yards, she walked down a steep dune, between the sea oats and the soft sand. She reached the hard-pack, where the water skimmed over the top in bubbly sheets. Her skin dark and unblemished. Her feet flung the water as she ran.

Nix turned.

He ran.

He went to her. To the girl in dreamland.

They embraced. They fell in the water, rolling over and over. His face buried in her thick hair. Inhaled her.

And the sky broke open.

Rain poured from the heavens.

The lagoon wept with joy.

Nix is home. Nix is home.

"Raine," he whispered.

MOTHER_
BEAUTY IS BIOMITE DEEP

Nikki had seen houses that big; she'd driven by them, just never walked up to one. Now she was standing on the porch made from some sort of dark tropical wood. Ceiling fans turned lazily above them.

"You sure about this?" she asked Carly.

The house was dark except for a single light in the back somewhere. It didn't look like anyone was home. It looked haunted.

"Don't get your panties in a wad," Carly snapped. "This is the address."

But we don't know him. That's what she wanted to say, but Carly and Kim weren't interested in caution. They were sixteen. Their best years were now, baby.

As in, NOW.

Carly thumbed the doorbell. Inside, a melodious series of bells echoed. When the last one trailed off, Kim was giggling too hard to press it again. They dared each other to do it. Nikki had her heels on the top step when Kim's finger hovered over the button—

The door cracked open.

They screamed. They jumped.

An eyeball peeked through the crack. Then a smile. "Hello," it said.

"You scared us!" Carly slapped the door.

"What took you so long?" The boy opened the ornate door. He was illuminated by the streetlight humming at the curb, his complexion bluish, shadows hiding his eyes. Even so, Nikki could see his complexion was smooth as marble. His teeth straight, white and perfectly square. Lips wet and full.

Like an airbrushed centerfold.

"Come in, come in." He stepped aside. "Welcome to my humble abode."

"This isn't your house," Carly said.

"Mi padre's casa es mi casa."

"Ooo... he speaks another language." Carly and Kim hugged each other on the way inside, laughing along the way.

The boy stepped out and took Nikki's hand. "You must be Cinderella."

His eyes peered from shadows, cold as winter rain, blue as a frozen sky. His hand, though, warm as a soft blanket.

A large chandelier greeted her inside the foyer. She could see a grand piano in the shadows of a great room on the right and a spiraling staircase on the left. The back room, the only light in the house, was the kitchen.

Ten teens sat in a circle. A candelabrum burned in the middle. Perfect skin. Perfect teeth. They laughed with perfect pitch and cadence.

Perfect.

The boy leaned into her. He smelled like new leather.

"Watch."

And Nikki watched. One of the girls tucked her knees together and bowed until her forehead touched the floor. One of the guys wrapped something over the back of her neck. They sat back and watched her convulse. Nikki stuttered back, but the boy put his arm around her, drawing her close.

The girl threw her head back.

Eyes bright.

Smile vacant.

She sat back with a dopey grin while the boy and girl on her left and right held her steady. Nikki swore she saw her cheekbones lifting, cheeks draw in and lips plump up.

"Spiking," the boy whispered. "We're overriding our biomites, reprogramming them to do what we want. To look like..." He smiled, beautifully. "This."

"How?" Nikki muttered. "You need to be a doctor—"

"Or have the right connections."

The candles flickered in his eyes.

Each of them took their turn, always bowing, always coming up with a smile.

And always looking more perfect than before.

"You got to try this," Carly said, ten minutes after her turn. "Don't be afraid, girl. It's a rush."

Nikki noticed her blemishes were gone. And her nose seemed... slimmer.

"I don't know."

And around it went. Around it went.

Nikki nearly turned and left. The boy, though. Each time he smiled, she melted. And when he said he'd do it, he'd be the one that put the spiker on her neck and held her hand, she let him. She let him take her down to the floor. Let him guide her head to the cold floor.

And wrap the thing on her neck.

It was heavier than she thought it would be.

And warm.

Then hot.

It poked spots around her vertebrae. Flooded her brain with hot soup. She melted like a puddle of wax thrown on a hot plate. Colors swirled in a psychedelic mind storm. She was tossed into the sky, landed in Oz and skidded down the yellow brick road, tumbling...

And tumbling.

And laughter.

Her head was lead. She pushed with both hands to lift it. Candlelight flickered like stars and the perfect people laughed and smiled and—

Screamed.

They scrambled like rats, hands clawing the slick floor.

Nikki's cheeks rippled like waves. Her teeth were filling her mouth. Her nails slid out of her fingers like utility blades.

Later, it was reported, her biomites had an adverse reaction to the reprogramming module. She was dumped outside the emergency room.

Her head the size of a pumpkin.

CHAPTER TWENTY-FIVE_

Marcus swirled the tumbler of tomato juice and ice, looking out the twenty-second floor of the Allerton Hotel. Chicago at night, Michigan Avenue was electric fire. The streets were streaked with taillights. He lifted a small pair of binoculars and spied the janitorial worker in an office building across the street. He scanned the other floors. No one working late or otherwise. He could always find someone up to no good. The month before, while in New York, he watched a couple getting busy on the roof. They both faced the same direction, watching the city lights while he thrust from behind. Their bodies synchronized.

"Yeah." He tapped the Bluetooth in his ear.

The voice on the other end was coming from his office in Washington. No funny business in those rooms.

"I'll be here another two, three days, I imagine," Marcus said.

He'd been on the phone with Janine, explaining the urgency in Chicago. He texted, but she called. He told her the boy's sister had him in a corner; he was taking care of that. He needed to stay. She complained about missing a parent-teacher conference. In fact, he'd missed all of them so far. But what was he going to do? Let the country fall apart so he could make sure William got a seat near the front?

He was staying in Chicago. He was cleaning up.

"Not acceptable." He loosened his tie and unbuttoned. "It needs to be done by tomorrow."

He sipped the bottom of the glass.

"I don't want any excuses, Chad. Tell the boys it needs to be done tomorrow by nine a.m. or they're looking for work, understand? I'll make sure they never find a job that even remotely deals with computers, trust me. Text me when it's uploaded."

Marcus pulled the drawer out and sorted through the neatly folded clothes. A small leather pouch was beneath a layer of T-shirts. He unzipped it, digging through razors and small tubes of toothpaste, finding the small silver cube about the size of a billiards chalk.

Chad was still relaying details about his assignment; Marcus half listened to the excuses. People, he'd learned, needed pushed. They could tolerate much, much, MUCH more discomfort than they believed. People needed a leader, they needed someone to give direction and incentive, to put a boot in their ass when they slowed down; otherwise they'd toil in mediocrity, and where would they be then? Where would the human species be if they sat around fires playing bongos all day long?

"Pull some of the techs off their other assignments; get everyone working on this. It has to be done by morning, Chad. And that's final. Do you have any more questions?"

Silence hung in the Bluetooth. Then, "When will you be back, sir?"

"If all goes well, I'll be back in three days. It could be longer. Peterson will monitor the halfskin program while I'm gone. He'll attend any shutdowns, in the meantime, and he will report to the Secretary."

Marcus pulled the bedspread onto the floor. He rolled the cube into the middle of the linen sheets.

"Nine a.m."

"Yes, sir."

Marcus pulled the phone from his ear and tossed it on the dresser along with his wallet and watch.

He gazed at the lights while he undid the cuffs, pulling his shirt from his pants and sliding the belt from the loops. He undid the buttons, exposing his smooth chest. He pulled the heavy drapes closed.

Marcus folded his clothes.

Completely undressed.

Only when everything was put away did he turn off all the lights and go to the shower. He soaked in hot water until he was soft and supple all over, then soaped up his arms and chest, cleaning every part of his body. Even between his toes. When he was finished, he powdered and clipped his nails and stood in front of the mirror as God intended.

All man.

All flesh.

Clean and ready to do work.

Marcus turned the lights out and stepped out of the bathroom. He went about his nightcap without saying another word.

CHAPTER TWENTY-SIX_

Nix's friends went to a doctor's office when they were sick, where there were magazines in the waiting room and they got a sucker when they were done. Their doctors were in a clinic or next to the hospital, where they had to wait their turn.

Nix didn't have to wait. He went to Technology Park.

The buildings were made of glass. The pond out front was clear with a large fountain. Three flag poles soared near the front doors, flags whipping on top.

When Nix got sick, he didn't feel like other people felt. He didn't get sluggish or throw up. He buzzed. It wasn't anything someone could hear, just an intense humming that sizzled all over. His sister couldn't hear it, but she could tell just by looking at him.

The buzzies are back.

The man in the glass building fixed the buzzies; Nix remembered that day well. He followed his sister up the wide steps. Avery held onto her hand, a pacifier plugged in her mouth. Cali wore a pin-striped skirt and jacket; the white lapel of her silk shirt flipped in the breeze. Her office was in the same complex, different glass building. She took Nix out of school.

He had a special box attached to his hip. It looked like a phone, but it didn't make calls. It emitted harmonizing sonar that equalized the buzzing biomites. It was experimental. Everything they did was experimental when it came to Nix.

Nix was only eight, but he knew what experimental meant. He knew he was different than everyone else. Cali explained that his biomites sometimes didn't get along with the blood cells and there was a fight. When things got bad, he got shaky and the sonar box would hum loudly. Sometimes he felt better, instantly.

Sometimes it took a while.

And, sometimes, there was war.

They stopped at the receptionist desk, this metal, curving wall in the giant foyer. Five people could sit behind it, but there was only one: a guy with short hair and always a phone in his ear. He pushed a button to let them through the door and said hello as they approached. Cali's heels echoed off the hard floor. Above them—three stories up—was the ceiling, where large bird sculptures hung and twisted.

In Search of Knowledge, Harmony and Freedom.

That was carved behind the desk, engraved on a gold plate in cursive. Nix didn't know what that meant. He just knew that whenever he was there, something was going to hurt.

Always.

But, afterwards, it felt better.

He had nowhere else to go.

They went to a small room with five chairs. There were no magazines, no TV. Just chairs and a clock. Nix watched the second hand tick around the face while the sonar box hummed.

The doorknob turned.

Dr. Merrick didn't wear a stethoscope or a white coat like most doctors. He always wore tan pants and a wrinkle-free shirt. He kept his hair cut really short.

"Dr. Cali." He crossed the room in three steps and hugged Nix's sister. "How are things on your side of corporate?"

"Oh, you know. Grants are still in limbo, so our hands are a little tied with the development of the last biomite generation."

"What about this one?" Dr. Merrick squatted. Avery hid behind Cali, making pacifier noises. He tried to tickle her, but she stayed on the move.

"Young man."

Dr. Merrick held out his fist. Nix gently punched it.

"You feeling all right?"

Shrug.

"What's this?" Dr. Merrick shrugged back. "Yes? No?"

Nix didn't feel like smiling. His guts felt like they were on an elevator.

"Let's take a look at you." Dr. Merrick held the door open. Nix followed Cali into his lair, an office in the back where there were no good memories.

"I'll be right back. Stay with Uncle Nix."

Cali peeled Avery's hands off her leg and plopped her in the seat next to Nix. She held out her arms and started crying around the pacifier. It was just as loud as if nothing was plugging her up. Cali tried a few more bribes. Nothing worked until Dr. Merrick pulled a purple lollipop from his pocket.

He does have suckers.

"I was ready today," he said.

Cali peeled off the wrapper.

Avery was transfixed by the color. Cali made her escape. It wasn't far. They were on the other side of the door, their voices muffled. Avery opened her mouth and let the pacifier drop on the floor to make room for the sucker.

Nix pulled the sonar box off his belt. Sometimes it worked better if he pressed it against his stomach. He picked up Avery's pacifier. There was no sink to wash it off. There wasn't much besides a couple of chairs and an office desk with computers and microscopes and things that caused pain.

Nix sat back down, held the dirty pacifier and stared at the only picture on the wall. It was a big green mountain with a long granite cliff. Water fell from a hole in the stone wall, drifting hundreds of feet to a blue sea below. He'd been in the office before, staring at that scene while Dr. Merrick prepared one of his special injections. Sometimes he'd stick it in his leg, sometimes the hip or arm. Once he got one in the back of the head. He always numbed it so he didn't feel the sting, but there was nothing he could do about the pressure.

That would last for hours.

Nix cried every time. Grown men would, too.

He didn't like this place. He wanted to be somewhere fun. Somewhere nice. Somewhere normal people went, do things that normal families did. That was impossible. At eight, he knew normal was gone.

Avery began exploring the office with the white stick poking between her lips. She opened a drawer and found a pad of paper. There was a pen attached to a clipboard on the back of the door. He thought maybe he could untie it and give it to her. Avery loved to draw.

"I know it hurts," he heard the doctor say. "But the results look good."

"I've got another generation that will be ready for testing in a couple weeks," Cali said. "I'd like to inoculate Nix, starting with a spinal tap—"

"Let's be patient. I expect..."

Nix couldn't understand what he said.

He pushed his ear against the door.

"I got to be honest," Cali said, "I'm little worried. He says his body tingles..."

The sonar box—

Heavy.

His insides stepped off the elevator and dropped to the center of the earth. The box—pressed against his stomach—was the only thing holding Nix on the ground, and when it left his hand, when it tumbled from his fingers, he zoomed like a helium balloon cut loose.

His stomach fell out.

The room spun.

And the buzzies went electric.

His bones vibrated like over-modulated components, emitting heat waves that elevated his temperature. He was being electrocuted from the inside.

Black edge—

Floor—

Door opening and a deep breath and a hand on his arm—

A salty warm rush into his throat—

And the room—

He smelled green, like when he cut the grass.

He was on the ground with trees overhead. Vines strangling the trunks. Sunlight filtering through the leaves.

A bird called.

Something jumped in the branches.

"Cali?" Nix sat up.

This was weird. This was... he was just in Dr. Merrick's office and now they were... *camping*?

He stood up. He felt a little numb, but it wasn't the bad kind. It wasn't anything like a buzzy. It was just... dull. Couldn't really feel stuff, could hardly smell it. There was a path that wandered between the trees. It was narrow and weedy. Nix didn't feel scared or alone. Not like he should. He felt good. Felt solid. No buzzies.

He just wanted to know where his sister had gone.

So he took the path. He followed it to the end. He heard something roaring. It sounded like a big truck. He saw an opening and a blue sky. The roar was deafening. He felt it in his chest, vibrating all over him. He slowed and carefully stepped to the edge of a cliff. He looked down hundreds of feet to see...

The waterfall in the picture.

The lagoon was born when Nix was eight.

All he had to do was close his eyes.

CHAPTER TWENTY-SEVEN_

"Momma?"

Avery's voice was tiny. So far away.

Cali's eyes hurt. She'd been squeezing them closed for... how long?

She didn't hear Avery return.

Didn't hear the machines beeping.

Only heard the words shooting into her mind. Over and over. Over and—

"Momma?" Avery tapped the back of Cali's hand.

She opened her eyes.

It was so bright.

Her daughter was kneeling on the other side of the bed, leaning on the railing. She could see all of Avery's silver braces that lined her teeth. She was smiling. And pointing down at the bed. Something smacked.

Nix's lips were moving.

Cali leaped to her feet. She stopped from grabbing his cheeks. She didn't know what to do with her hands. They ran up and down her sides and over the bed railing. She leaned over and felt his rotten breath on her cheek. It felt wonderful.

"Nix," she whispered.

His eyelids batted back the light, rapidly fluttering. His blue eyes peered through the slits. It took a few moments to process the big face hovering over him. His lips cracked when he smiled.

"Hey." He squeezed weakly.

Cali squeezed back. "How are you?" she asked.

"Better than I look."

Cali nodded. She knew what he meant. "Good, good."

[*We don't have much time,*] she thought to him.

He heard it. His new breeds picked up her thoughts like a radio wave, transmitting them like spoken words. Still, he was surprised. His eyes bulged slightly. It took a moment to comprehend, to understand what the hell just happened.

She waited patiently. Let him calm down, form his own thoughts.

Cali sat down and gave him space. He smacked his lips, calling for water. Cali handed him the cup and stuck the straw between his lips. He only took a drag off it. His head was too exhausted to stay up and drink more.

He was going to need all his strength.

"Where's Avery?" The words scratched his throat.

Cali wiped her cheeks and pointed to the other side of the bed. Nix turned his head slowly. He lifted his hand for her to take. Avery's hand looked so small in his.

"Does it hurt?" the little girl asked.

"You look so pretty."

Avery bowed her head, smiling and giggling. Her bashfulness evaporated in seconds and she jumped up to show Uncle Nix her new shoes, demonstrating them with some swift dance moves.

"I missed you," Nix said.

"Then don't sleep so much," Avery sang.

He watched her dance some more and tell the story about the flowers she found in the lobby and used them to decorate his bed, that he would've loved them, but her mom made her clean them up.

Nix listened patiently. A good uncle.

[*You're 49.9%,*] she thought.

He turned back to her. He worked his lips, closed his eyes and focused.

[*I know.*]

While Avery began telling another story—this one about a prince that went to save his sister from a red dragon—Cali sent her escape plans.

He closed his eyes, nodding.

CHAPTER TWENTY-EIGHT_

Dr. Erickson had been the chief physician of bionanotechnology at Northwestern Memorial Hospital since the wing had been dedicated to the science of biomite healing.

That was seven years ago.

At the time of its dedication, he was excited about the future of humanity. He'd seen too many things go wrong. As a doctor, good came with bad. But medicine was so much more complicated than it was in the old days. Now there were lawsuits and unrealistic expectations and insurance... those were not the reasons he chose medicine as his profession. He wanted to help people, wanted to give them a second chance. But they needed to help themselves.

Too often, that was not the case.

When bionanotechnology was introduced, he was skeptical. *Machines that imitate human cells? That's science fiction, not reality.*

But all that changed.

All that changed when he witnessed the simplicity that occurred at the microscopic level, that these miniscule artificial cells were programmed like stem cells to transform into anything inside the human body. He'd witnessed miracles.

He was not a religious man, but there was no other word for it.

Miracles.

But humans have a way of corrupting everything meant to be good and proper. In the few short years that Dr. Erickson oversaw the development and implementation of biomites to save faulty organs, to restore sight, and repair damaged bodies, he became embroiled in the politics that went along with it.

He opened his office door and was reminded, bluntly, of such corruption.

"Why are you in here?" Dr. Erickson said.

Marcus Anderson stood in front of a large saltwater fish tank. He bent over and smudged the glass with his finger, pointing at the anemone.

"Amazing how a clownfish survives, Dr. Erickson. It hides in the poisonous tentacles, resistant to the sting itself."

"Evolution is amazing."

Marcus turned. "And God's grace."

Dr. Erickson dropped his clipboard on his cluttered desk and sat down. The office was dimly lit, chiefly from the tank's light. He kept his office that way intentionally. It was a place of respite, a secret room from the hectic matters only a few short steps outside of it. It was remarkable how it could be disrupted by a diminutive man such as the one still fouling the tank's glass.

"Can I help you, Mr. Anderson?"

The small man straightened up as best he could—the bump between his shoulders vaguely noticeable—and came over to the desk. He didn't bother sitting. He fished a Jolly Rancher from a dish and unwrapped it.

"I came to inform you, Dr. Erickson, that I will be overseeing a biomites shutdown this afternoon."

"I hardly see how that involves me."

"It will be conducted on this wing, in a room at the end of the hall."

"That is against hospital policy."

"You'll have to make an exception. The subject is incapable of transport. Unless you can reduce his biomite population, it will be conducted on these premises."

Marcus sucked on the green block of candy, rattling it over his teeth from one cheek to the other.

"We cannot oblige, Mr. Anderson. There is a Hippocratic Oath that we take seriously here at Northwestern Memorial, and I intend to uphold it. I will file an appeal to suspend Nixon Richards' shutdown until he is able to walk out on his own."

"And die somewhere else?"

Dr. Erickson rapped his fingers on the desktop. "I don't approve of shutdowns anywhere, Mr. Anderson."

"And neither do I."

Dr. Erickson's expression was blank.

"Doctor, the fact is, you have no choice in the matter. There is nowhere to request a stay of shutdown, no one to hear your plea. The Halfskin Laws are executed whether you and I approve of them or not. When any person reaches 50% biomites, he or she is shut down. I am sorry for that, I am. But the world has been warned; they make their choices. They have to take responsibility for their actions. If they don't like the consequences, they shouldn't seed themselves."

"What about those that need them to survive? Accident victims, genetic disorders, you name it. Life happens to them and they receive biomites to survive only to be told there's a law that forbids it?"

Marcus leaned over the trash can and spit the candy out. It banged the bottom.

"We have to have order, Doctor."

"You should reconsider your policy."

Marcus stretched his chin and straightened his tie. "Perhaps you should consider your own policies."

"And what policies would those be? That I want health and well-being for the people that come here?"

"You're turning people into machines."

"We're using technology. Prescription glasses, hearing aids, medicines... no difference."

Marcus nodded. "Does your computer have a right to life, Doctor?"

"My computer?"

Marcus nodded at the monitor. "Shouldn't you consider its feelings before you unplug it one of these days for an upgrade?"

"A computer was never human, Mr. Anderson. It has always been a machine."

"The past doesn't define who we are. It is only now. We were not meant to live forever, Doctor. There are limits to our survival. Perhaps death should not be held in contempt. Without it, where would we be?"

Dr. Erickson leaned back, sighing. His hope in the human race continued to wither. Especially when speaking to a man like this. A man with power.

"We'll be conducting a shutdown this afternoon, Doctor. We prefer to keep it quiet. You may attend, if you like."

Marcus filled a paper cup with water, the water jug chugging with air. He crushed the cup and dropped it into the trash.

"Neither of us can stop it," he said. "Whether we want to or not."

Dr. Erickson decided the man's smile indicated he not only didn't want to stop it, he looked forward to it.

He felt no less deflated when Marcus left the office. Just more hopeless.

CHAPTER TWENTY-NINE_

Cali folded the last of Avery's shirts and squeezed it into her bag.

Her daughter was curled up on the chair. They needed to get out of the hospital for a lot of reasons. And they would. In three days, they would be somewhere else where there was fresh air and freedom.

That was the plan.

She packed her belongings. Three days was longer than she wanted to wait. She was prepared to dash now, that morning, but Nix wasn't ready. He could barely walk.

He was asleep. *And not in the lagoon.* She made damn sure he wasn't expending energy on his inner world. They needed every bit to restore his health. The new breeds couldn't conduct a secret siege on his body, taking the place of the older biomites that compromised nearly 49% of his body. She was certain the new breeds could flush the old ones out, but since the hospital readers couldn't see the new breeds, they would think his biomite population was declining.

And that would lead to suspicion. That would not help.

Everything needed to look normal. Nothing going on here. Everything was the same. Any close examination could bring her best-laid plans to a halt. There was no hope if that happened, so it was business as usual.

Nix slept.

Cali monitored him.

Yes, she read him like a computer. Even she was surprised by the recent developments. Not only could she telecommunicate with Nix, but she was using them to wirelessly communicate with every wireless device in the vicinity. She was a wireless router that heard everything around her.

Phone calls.

Emails.

Network servers.

I'm a computer.

It was all data streaming through the atmosphere, vibrating against her new breeds that downloaded and interpreted it all into words and sounds. But it was too much to understand. It was white noise, the chatter of a thousand voices, at first. That's what she'd been hearing for the past few days and had thought it might be a malfunction. The new breeds were breaking down, they were learning. Evolving.

She thought-commanded the new breeds to tune it all out. Perhaps, at some point, she could filter out what she wanted to hear. For now, she focused on her little brother, listening to his new breeds report his health and stats.

Bones mended.

Organs stable.

No fever. Blood vessels healed.

He could walk, but she needed more than that. It was going to take a lot to get out undetected. They needed time for him to heal. Stay too long, he goes halfskin. Leave too soon, there's biomite failure.

Sleep. Heal, my brother. Heal quickly.

In the meantime, Cali discovered that she could access her computer through thought-commands. The new breeds made a connection through her secure portal. If she closed her eyes, she could see the interface as if it was a monitor in her mind. She arranged a hotel reservation at the Red Roof Inn. It was close to the hospital—too close—but Nix would need to recover. She arranged Hertz to deliver a car to the parking garage and drop off the keys to an alias.

After those arrangements were complete, she explored the hospital's network. The new breeds slipped easily past passwords, speaking the language of computers. She spied through a multitude of cameras like a thousand eyes inside her head. She knew who was on duty, where they were, what operations were scheduled and even what the cafeteria was serving.

None of that did much good. Not now.

She decided to stretch out. She jumped into the Internet and found Marcus Anderson's home computer. He'd upgraded since she hacked his personal information a week ago, but she flew past it like a ghost. She opened his email, searched his voicemails, office memos, etc. She decided to download everything to her cloud storage.

He's the real threat.

That man wouldn't stop. She and Nix could leave the hospital and very few people would care. They might even elude Mother. But this man, he would dog them to the end of the world just so he could watch them die.

He needed to be addressed. Permanently.

The door swung open.

Cali jumped back from the bed. She blinked a few times, bringing her vision back online. The images inside her head faded slowly. There were two men stepping inside. Twins, at first.

But now there was one.

She focused on Marcus Anderson.

He was smiling.

CHAPTER THIRTY_

Marcus left the doctor's office, cursing beneath his breath He never uttered such language, never made it a word, but he let the cursed thoughts settle, melting like dirty mints.

Because he hated this place.

He hated the smell of hospitals. The peculiar scent clung to his sinuses, coated the back of his throat, and swabbed his nostrils. It would take days to purge it. Even candy couldn't mask its odor.

He stopped outside Dr. Erickson's office and placed a few calls. He had approval to conduct the shutdown in the hospital. There wasn't an option, but it was nice to have others in the administration on board. The sooner he was out of Chicago, the better.

He hit the door harder than he anticipated, his thoughts elsewhere. Cali was caught by surprise, kneeling next to her brother's bed, hands folded against her forehead.

She's praying.

It warmed his heart to see this godless scientist succumbing to prayer when times were dark and hopeless. All scientists came to the Lord when times became desperate. And if their heart was open, if they were prepared to admit their sinful ways, He might accept them into the gates of heaven. That was how good the Father was. He held no grudges, only love.

She stood.

"No, no. Don't let me interrupt. Please." He gestured to the bedside. "Continue."

"What do you want?"

Marcus noticed the bag. None of her stuff was scattered around the room. "Going somewhere?"

"My brother is healing. He'll be transferred soon. I want to follow him... back to wherever you're taking him."

"I see."

Marcus unbuttoned his coat, reached inside and let his hand rest for a moment. The woman looked so vulnerable, so afraid. She knew something was coming. He wasn't there to pray, though.

"I'm afraid I have bad news."

He walked softly to the bed, pulling his hand out of his jacket to reveal the biomite reader. He placed it gently on Nix's exposed throat. A number appeared a moment later. Marcus knew what it would read. He was not disappointed.

He lifted it in her direction.

49.99%.

"Wrong," she said. "That's wrong."

"You're lucky." He turned the display, reading it again like a man that lost his bifocals. "An upgrade now allows for an accurate reading to the hundredths. Your brother would be shut down already."

"It's wrong." Her fists clenched. "And you know it."

She acted like she knew he was lying, but even if she did, she couldn't prove it. Mother was not one to argue.

"I won't let you turn him off."

"You think my finger is on the button?" He smiled like a victor. "I'm simply an ambassador, young lady. I only confirm when the Halfskin Laws are applied. That's all. I have no part in the rest of this. I don't enjoy it."

"Lie."

"I wasn't talking about this." He pointed at Nix. He enjoyed that. Wouldn't say it out loud. "I mean, I don't enjoy witnessing the erosion of the soul. I don't enjoy watching Man play God. It's sinful, at best."

His left eye twitched.

"Evil, is what it is."

"I believe you're the one playing God, Marcus. You're deciding who lives and dies. You're responsible for the bill that brought all of this into play. You're playing God."

His lips thinned. "You, Cali, with your degrees and engineered biomites, are spreading the disease responsible for this, not me. It is a disease. It is consuming the human body. You tell me, what will you be when your body is 100% biomites, mmm? Where is your soul then?"

"Biomites won't consume 100%."

She was lying. She didn't know that.

"Man's greed is insatiable. The laws I helped put in place are meant to stop humanity from self-destruction, whether they like it or not. All these years, we thought the nuclear bomb would bring about our extinction. Turns out our greatest threat is a microscopic entity that mimics our self-centered greed."

Her hands quivered. She looked at Marcus with intense concentration, like she was trying to will him into death, like lasers would shoot from her eyes to carve him up. He shuffled a step, a bit nervous of what she was capable of doing. Desperation can crack the strongest. And she was cornered.

But then she appeared to wilt.

Shoulders slumped.

Whatever she wanted to do, she gave up.

Marcus waited at the end of the bed. Cali took a seat, pushing her hair back, cradling her face. Yes, she'd resigned to the end. Marcus was positive. He'd broken many spirits. He knew the sight of one that had crumbled, only needing swept up and disposed.

Still, he waited. He waited until the door opened and James

stepped inside. He considered whether he needed security in the room. It was wise to play it safe. When James was next to him, only when his big body was between him and the wasted young woman, did Marcus pass the biomite reader to her.

"Take it."

She held it, confused. Marcus gestured with a bent finger to her throat. She raised her head. Her eyes widened slightly. He was sure that she knew what would happen before she hesitantly pressed it to her flesh.

Read the number.

She held the biomite reader without protest.

"We'll be doing a double shutdown at approximately 15:00 today. I'd like to conduct this event with dignity, Dr. Richards. I would prefer you shut down next to your brother. I'm sure you would prefer it that way, too."

Marcus took the biomite reader. He went to the door and stopped, hardly turning his head.

"Check the news feed. The video of your brother's assault has been released. The real one, Dr. Richards. Any other videos that may pop up will obviously be considered forgeries by talented engineers like yourself."

She didn't bother looking up. She'd been cornered. Knew her little stunt with the security video would only hold leverage for so long, knew he could get his people to make one do what he wanted. Whatever she was planning, she waited too long. And her shoulders slumped just a bit more.

Marcus would sweep up the pieces later on.

MOTHER_

BIOMITE DREAMLANDS OBSCURING REALITY

Rick Mansfield buried his hands in his coat, hunching his shoulders against the cold. Traffic ripped down the street, turning snow into ashy slush. The sky felt like a steel plate.

He skipped across the road, all six lanes, and dropped his foot in a pothole. Icy water soaked his sock. He hopped over the curb and hustled into the building with blacked-out windows, through a door below a bright sign: DREEMITE.

He stomped his shoes on the rug, his foot already numb. He grimaced. His upper lip cracked. It always cracked in the winter from the dry furnace-air. In Canada, there was a lot of furnace-air.

A few people sat at a small round table, sipping coffee and cappuccinos. Two men—one bald, the other reading a paper—sat at the bar; a woman worked behind it. The foamer whooshed with steam. The bald guy dropped his mug on the bar and started toward the door.

"I got minutes, I got minutes!" Rick raised his hands, surrendering. "I got minutes, Stan, I promise."

Bald Stanley didn't listen, grabbed Rick by his army green coat and hoisted him toward the door.

"Mr. Connors, I got minutes, I swear, I do!"

Mr. Connors didn't look up. "Scan him."

Stanley stopped like a Labrador hearing a whistle. He dropped Rick's coat and stepped back. Rick straightened himself up and spread his hand out, palm down.

"This a goof, Mansfield, I'm throwing you in the street," Stanley said. "Head first."

"No goof, Stan. No goof. See, real deal." Rick flexed his fingers. "It's my hand, not synthetic. Not a fake one, not like last time. Go ahead, scan away. I got minutes."

Stanley eyeballed him. He pulled a tablet from the inside of his jacket. Stanley put Rick's hand on it like he was in court, swearing to tell the truth, the whole truth, and nothing but.

"Two minutes?" Stanley held the tablet up for Mr. Conners to see. "Kid's got two minutes. What the hell's he going to do with two minutes?"

Mr. Connors shrugged.

"Two minutes is two minutes," Rick said. "I'll take what I can get, you know what I mean, Mr. Conners." He raised his voice. "I'll take what I can get, even if I HAVE TO PAY DOUBLE!"

"You're about to go on the street," Stanley said.

"I'm just saying, if you want to make some money, I'll pay double."

"Feds are watching, Mansfield. Skimming minutes will pull our license. Losing our license for you ain't worth it."

Rick shrugged off his coat. "Then two minutes it is."

The barista slid the cappuccino to Mr. Connors. She went to the computer and punched the screen. "Eight is open."

"Pay first," Stanley said.

"Cash," Mr. Connors added.

Rick dug into his pocket and dropped two crumpled twenties on the bar. "Two minutes, forty dollars."

The barista ran a pen over the bills to make sure they were legit. She nodded. Stanley took Rick's arm and guided him through the black curtain hanging over a doorway to the right of the bar. Rick yanked away from him.

The doors were numbered. Odds on the right. Evens on the left. Eight was at the end of the hall. Stanley pushed it open, revealing a solo chair in a closet-sized room.

"This won't take long," he said. "I'll wait."

Rick closed it behind him. A light came on and he locked the door. He dropped his coat and sat down. The chair was thick and comfortable with a firm headrest that cradled his skull. He leaned back, stared at the hanging light, and pressed the back of his head into the cradle until his biomites communicated with the plate embedded in the chair.

Closed his eyes.

Heard the winding, like a rocket preparing for liftoff.

His brain swirled.

Three, two, one...

And the bottom dropped out. He fell into the inner world. The plate made his brain biomites sizzle with excitement, releasing hallucinatory hormones. Rick saw colors. Warmth bled down his shoulders.

Lights.

Sounds.

And... crowds.

He saw the bodies. Saw the people. A nightclub full of them. All jumping to the beat, lasers fired in time to the music. And when he stepped onto the floor, they all knew him. They were all happy to see him. They raised their hands, they hugged him, slapped his back, wanted to take pictures with him.

Rick pushed them out of the way, sorting through them like collector's items. Each woman was hotter than the next. Black, white, Asian, Pilipino... it was so hard to choose.

And he didn't have much time.

He put his arms around two women. One was a blonde, at least six foot, a sparkly dress that revealed half her rack. Her lips were full and her breasts ripe. The other was a limber Chinese girl, perfect skin, big eyes and delicate fingers.

His groin twisted like a wet rag.

He sprinted for the stage. The band welcomed him. The guitarist started a slow, rhythmic solo. Rick wanted everyone to watch. And the crowd roared. The crowd adored him, paid to watch him perform on stage. That's all he wanted, was everyone to recognize him. He deserved that.

He hooked his finger beneath the blonde's strap, tugging it off her shoulder. Her ample breast popped from the top, revealing a large, circular hard nipple—

The light turned off—

Silence.

And Rick Mansfield fell back into his body. He opened his eyes, looking at a naked light bulb. Hands holding winter's chill.

And he hated life.

He hated it.

Hate. Hate. Hate. Hate. Hate.

CHAPTER THIRTY-ONE_

Oxygen came in short supply.

Cali took little gulps, twisting her fingers like origami. Staring. Staring at a dead boy.

Her eyes couldn't get any wider. The shock rode her pulse like waves, scratching the walls of her circulatory system as her blood carried toxic emotions to her numb and wooden body. Bones turned to steel.

Skin, sun-dried paper, singed at the edges.

She looked around the room, looked for ghost killers. Looked for their executioner. Felt the ceiling fall, the floor cave. The walls collapse.

Her world blacken.

Dry and desolate.

And dead.

And dead, dead, dead, DEAD, DEAD, DEADDEAD-DEADDEAD—

[*Stop.*]

The tiny blip of light that was Cali—rational Cali, intelligent Cali—was going under, tossed beneath waves of thoughts and panic and rage...

That little bit called a halt to the madness.

And the new breeds released a tsunami of endorphins to deaden pain, to release the tension. To stop the thoughts.

Cali's eyelids dropped like shutters. Her breath leaked from her nostrils. She pulled a draught of fresh oxygen, long and deep, and exhaled once again. When she opened her eyes, she saw her brother. He was alive.

And she could save him.

Okay.

All right.

Deep breath.

Cali slowly let her thoughts engage her awareness. She needed to piece together what happened, what needed to change. She had expected to lose the leverage of the security video. It got her into the room. She knew they'd make their own, but they moved faster than she expected, but it was not a surprise. She began reaching for her phone to search the newsfeed, to see what the government was saying, when something twanged at the back of her neck.

Something felt familiar, easy.

She was using the new breeds to communicate with her computer, to think directly into the Internet... she didn't need her phone. She thought-commanded a search into cyberspace, looking for the last news on Nixon Richards. The results were recent and plentiful.

Biomite-Crazed Teenager Attacks Detention Guard.

She activated the video link and streamed it directly to her retinas. Her eyes glazed over as the video formed, surreally, over Nix's head. It started with him standing in his room, the footage grainy. The door opened and George stepped in with a tray of food. He smiled at Nix and appeared to say something that made them both laugh. The fat, jolly guard placed the tray on the desk and went to the door and, just before he opened it, Nix pounced, driving the man's head into the wall.

Her brother slammed the door.

He climbed on top of the obese, hairy man—eyes wide with adrenaline, teeth bared to the glistening gums—and began to wail.

There was no sound.

But there was blood.

Lots of it.

And the sheer gore of the video would carry it around the world in seconds.

Cali didn't bother reading the interviews. The press was sure to find someone that claimed Nix's sister was crazy, that she was losing it, that she'd lost it after the accident. Her co-workers might slip that she was on a medical leave of absence, that she'd seen a psychologist. The public would label her crazy, case closed.

There were sure to be inconsistencies that were swept under the public rug. The anti-biomite protest groups would ignore the obvious forgery. The conspiracy theorists would be dismissed as kooks. And even if it was proven false, even if Nix's innocence was heralded in the Supreme Court, it wouldn't matter. It wouldn't matter, not one damn bit.

Because they'd already be dead.

They'd be shut down.

And nothing could bring them back. That's how that game was played.

It was mid-morning. Chicago was full tilt. Bumpers on bumpers. Sidewalks hustling.

That was one of the reasons Cali planned for Nix to be transferred to Northwestern Memorial, to be in the city. She wanted people around. Millions of them, all with biomites.

This would all be easy to resolve if Marcus was seeded. The man was pure. She'd scanned him when he was in the room, her new breeds chattering all over his body and finding nothing but organic flesh. And that was a stroke of luck because if he was seeded even with the smallest amount, she would've killed him where he stood.

She would've reprogrammed his biomites to consume him like

microscopic pit bulls or discharge a power supply, boil him from the inside.

Eat his brain like zombie tapeworms.

She would've dropped him, killed him, murdered him... and then there would be no escape, not right then. Even though he deserved it. He deserved to die.

He plans to murder me.

Cali wasn't 49.9% biomite. Her registered biomites—the ones Mother could see—held steady at 39%.

Mother was rigged for moments like this. How easy it would be to get rid of a problem by calling it into Mother, overriding her monitor with a false number and then push a button and—

POOF.

It was murder. And he'd told her with a slight smile. He knew that she knew. He wanted her to know that she'd stepped into a lion's den when she brought the security video to him, forced him to play her game. Wanted her to know that she'd lost.

But the game wasn't over.

First, she needed to get Nix far away from this place. As she watched a taxi wedge its way into traffic, her accelerated thought process put together a plan. There was no time to run an analysis on it.

She tapped into the hospital network and requested a wheelchair be brought to their floor and parked around the corner. Her shirt tugged off her shoulder.

"Momma?" Avery had a handful of her shirt. "Are you all right?"

"Sweetheart."

Cali fell into her chair and wrapped her arms around her. She murmured apologies, over and over. How long had she been there, calling her name? Worried something was wrong?

Bad mom.

Cali held Avery at arm's length. "Honey, I need you to do something by yourself. Can you do that?"

Avery nodded.

"I need you to go to the Red Roof Inn; it's just down the street. I'll give you directions. You'll go to the front desk and there will be a key there, waiting for you. Tell them your name is Avery and your mother left the key for you. Can you do that?"

"I'm scared."

"I know you are. So am I. But this is important. We all have to find the big person inside us. I just want you to be safe in the room and wait for us."

"I'm afraid you won't come back." Avery sniffed.

"Oh, honey, we'll be right there. Uncle Nix just needs to rest a little longer and then we'll be there, okay?"

"Is that bald man going to hurt you?"

"No, no. He's not going to hurt anyone. I promise."

Avery puffed out her bottom lip. She nodded.

Cali showed her directions to the hotel on her phone and hugged her so tightly that Avery couldn't breathe. She walked her to the door. James sat in the hall and looked up from his paper. Cali watched her daughter walk bravely to the other end of the hallway, past the nurse delivering a wheelchair parked around the corner.

Nix was still asleep.

Cali sat next to him.

And began to think.

CHAPTER THIRTY-TWO_

NIX DREAMED OF THE LAGOON.

It wasn't the same as going there. Dreaming was more like thinking, but it was better than nothing. So Nix dreamed his dream. He flew with his arms out, over the white-tipped waves that washed foam on the north shore. He brushed over the tropical trees, the leaves shimmering in his wake. He imagined his girl there, waiting on the beach for him, where they'd sit by a fire and wait for the moon to illuminate the still waters.

Excitement buzzed the sky.

Warmth bled deep into the jungle.

Nix felt safe.

Peaceful.

If he was lucky, he'd stay that way, maybe never wake up. Just bask in the sweet healing glow of the dream. It had been so long since he'd felt that way. He knew it was the new breeds that soothed his nerves and calmed his mind, but he'd felt that way before. He'd felt safe and wanted when he was younger, when he was composed of so many less biomites.

When he was mostly organic.

It was mostly when he went to bed, all curled up beneath the comforter with his head sunk in a pillow. The adult voices murmured from the front room. When his parents died, Cali and Thomas took over for the voices. Theirs were sharper and higher, but just as safe. Sometimes it was just the two of them talking about their day. Sometimes they had friends over and glasses would clink and bottles pop, but no matter how many cars rushed down the road or how many creepy sounds the house made, Nix was safe.

Nothing would touch him. He'd throw the cover over his head and melt into the safety of their voices.

When Cali was nervous or scared or worried, he could always count on Thomas to bring the safety back. He was strong and smart. He knew how to hunt and how to drive a boat. He could bait a hook in seconds. Nix still had a picture of his first offshore catch, ten years old, holding a yellowfin tuna—Thomas helping him hold the silver-sparkling fish high enough to take the picture.

And then there was the time some guy got weird outside the market. He asked for money. He smelled bad. His eyes red where they should've been white. He grabbed Cali's wrist and Thomas chopped the guy in the neck, dropping him like a tree branch. Said he learned that in the service.

Nix never felt so safe.

And he deserved it.

After everything he'd been through.

And when the phone rang, when Nix was twelve years old, watching TV, and his sister answered and her mouth opened and closed like the yellowfin tuna's did when he reeled it onto the boat's floor... he knew.

He knew.

It happened again.

Another car accident.

The details, irrelevant.

Nix was exposed again. No security blanket. No safe feeling. He'd lost, again. That's what no one in the world realized, what everyone took for granted, what Nix never did...

You can lose everything at any moment.

So he reveled in the dream's security. He rolled in the warm emotions like salty bathwater. If he could make it happen, he would never wake up.

Stay asleep. Forever.

But then Cali's voice echoed in the dream, calling down from the blue dream-sky like God.

He would have to wake up.

Cali needed him. He had to *be* the security blanket. She needed him.

He stayed in the dream and listened to her projecting thoughts into his mind. Plans had changed.

He would have to wake up now.

CHAPTER THIRTY-THREE_

James adjusted his weight.

His left butt cheek was numb. The chair had no padding. If it did, it had been mashed thinner than rice paper by three hundred pounds of security guard. He'd already paced back and forth to get the blood flowing through his lower portions, but it only worked his bowels into a tizzy. He couldn't hit the toilet until he was relieved, and Mr. Anderson was dead set on leaving him there until everything was squared away.

Sometime that afternoon.

James snapped the paper open and began reading the sports section for the third time.

Some said the job of a security guard was 90% boredom, 10% adrenaline. James felt it was closer to 99%. Had he known he was training to read newspapers and open car doors, he might've had second thoughts. But it paid the bills and he wasn't digging ditches, so he shut the hell up and shifted his weight near the middle of his left and right cheek.

He was somewhere between the Chicago White Sox ninth inning collapse and the suspension of a biomite-enhanced recruit when the buzzing started. It wasn't anything noticeable, sort of like a head rush when standing too quickly or temporarily seeing spots. He chalked it up to eating Mexican. Taquitos at 7:00 a.m. can wreak havoc.

The buzz crept around the back of his neck like fingers massaging his jawbone. It crawled over his gums, his teeth, up into his sinuses and around his temples. The backs of his eyeballs itched.

He blinked back the odd sensation and rubbed his eyes with finger and thumb. He was going to have to call in a backup and explain that Mother Nature could be an insistent bitch. Somehow he didn't think dropping a Mexican deuce in a bedpan was going to cut it.

He took a breath, wiping his brow. Maybe the Want Ads would get his mind off it. He was thinking about a dog anyway. His watch reported 11:00 a.m.

Never going to make it.

He plowed through the pet section and ended up studying real estate. He hardly noticed the buzzing. It was still there, just wasn't bothering him. Wasn't in the way. Seemed normal.

The door opened. Just a crack at first.

James looked up from the funny pages. Cali looked back with one eye. She seemed to struggle with the heavy door; then it swung open.

She just stood there, in the doorway. She stared. He stared.

"Going to get something to eat," she said.

James blinked.

The edges of her face were blurry. Kind of glowing, like the soft light photographers use to dress up wedding pictures. James folded the paper under his arm and gouged his eyes again. When he opened them, the girl was past him. She took half-steps, trailing her fingers along the wall as she went. She stopped after each step, paused, took another. She didn't look back, just kept going until she reached the turn. She crossed from the right wall to the left with three quick shuffles, bracing herself against the wall. It took a couple waves to finger the armrest of a wheelchair peeking around the corner, like she didn't have another step left in her.

Cali fell into it. Her head sagged like dead weight.

Bells went off in James's head, the kind of bells that were drilled into security guards. The kind of bells that sound like something between a car horn and a fire alarm. The kind that push a guard to his feet and shove him down the hall, made him ask a few questions and poke a few holes.

Skip. Skip-skip.

Click.

James dug his fingers into his eyes. Shook his head.

She was gone.

She'd already wheeled away, down the hall, going to the cafeteria to get something to eat, because the woman just hadn't been eating. I mean, she hadn't eaten more than an orange slice since she'd gone in that room. Couldn't say anyone could blame her. Her brother was near the end of a ship's plank, about to be switched off like a light. And the news only got worse. She was going, too.

Woman couldn't catch a break.

The alarm bell was drowned out by a new wave of buzzing, this time reaching over the top of his scalp and pulling his upper lip over his eyebrows. His eyes hurt from repeated grinding. The bells were still in the distance, like an ambulance going in the other direction, now around the bend. Danger over there. Not here.

He rattled the paper and decided to start with the front page. He'd read every story, starting at the top. That's how he stayed awake when things began to grind. Pay attention to details, listen to sounds, see everything. Nothing would get past him.

The door opened.

Cali stepped out. "Forgot my bag."

She slung a heavy canvas bag over her shoulder and walked down the hall, all the way to the end without touching the wall or stopping for balance. No wheelchair down there. She turned the corner.

The alarm bell was deafening.

James stood, reached for his phone, took a step—

Zzzzzzzzzzzzzzzzzzzzzzzzzzzz.

Next thing, he was sitting. Face in hands. Both cheeks numb.

There was a bell in his head, but he didn't know exactly why. In fact, he couldn't recall what that sound even meant, forgot what he was all about. But then it came back; he remembered. He considered looking in the room but knew there was no reason. Nothing could get past him. They couldn't crawl out the window; they'd have to walk past him to get out.

And he hadn't seen anyone in hours.

James rattled the paper. Started at the top of the front page. He'd read every story, top to bottom. And the taquitos had passed.

He felt better already.

CHAPTER THIRTY-FOUR_

Nix lay in bed, staring at the ceiling. Waiting. Waiting for Cali.

She slumped in the chair next to his bed, head back. Eyes closed. If anyone walked in, they'd think she was sleeping. Anyone watching the cameras would believe the same.

[*Okay.*]

Her voice was inside his head.

[*They're watching,*] she thought to him that morning. [*They're watching.*]

She relayed everything he was supposed to do into his head. It was weird, talking that way. At first, it was like talking with his ears plugged, echoing with the volume up. It took some adjustment, some getting used to, before he was able to exert some control. She explained the new breeds were like wireless computers aggressively taking over his body and brain.

[*We need them to outnumber the old-generation biomites.*]

[*Why?*]

She didn't answer that. He imagined the new breeds were super soldiers, Pacmen gobbling up cell after cell, biomite after biomite. He didn't ask the obvious question, didn't ask... *Am I becoming a computer?*

[*Okay,*] she whispered into his mind again, eyes closed.

Nix pushed onto his elbows. His ribs ached. He took a second before pulling the covers off and sliding his feet over the edge. The floor was hard and cold. His skin, tired. He covered his eyes. A spotlight was blazing through the window; the sun was a beam of pain stabbing his brain.

His fingers crawled over the bed and snatched up the clothes Cali laid out. The top was an orange sherbet blouse, the white pants rolled at the bottom. It took longer than usual to put Cali's clothes on. A few weeks ago, they would've been snug.

When he was dressed, he moved his weight onto his bare feet. His bones were fragile. Joints popped, ligaments creaked. He turned back to the bed, stuffed the extra pillows beneath the covers and pulled the sheet up high like someone was sleeping in the comfort of darkness. He made it to the end of the bed and stopped, taking a breath.

His skin sizzled with the heat of active biomites. *New breeds.*

The door was five steps away. He focused on the handle. Five steps, that was his goal. Get to the door handle first. Get to the door. He took deep breaths, let go of the bed and started after it. Earlier, his sister helped him to the bathroom. He pulled out his catheter with the help of new breeds numbing the pain in his urethra as the balloon-end popped out. He walked back on his own, but he was wobbling.

Like now.

He held his hand out. The last two steps turned into three. He caught the handle and hit the door with his shoulder. The impact made his insides quake. Rattled his lungs. He needed a moment, took one and then another—

[*Go.*]

Cali's voice was a whip, lashing his hand into action. He pulled the door open—

A big man looked up from his paper, sitting outside the door. Not happy.

Nix watched him, waiting for him to do something. But he only stared. Confusion swirled in the glassy orbs beneath his thick brows.

[*Go.*]

Nix yanked the door with unexpected strength. Weakness shook his brittle bones. His muscles were taut. Renewed vigor surged through his nervous system. He was burning adrenaline and needed to go before it hit empty.

"Going to get something to eat," he muttered, like his sister told him to say.

The big man seemed to be working out what the simple phrase meant, like he'd just heard a thick accent and the pieces of what he was seeing and hearing weren't fitting. Nix didn't wait for Cali to jar him with another thought. He started down the middle of the hall before shuffling to the wall for support. He stepped quickly past doorways.

The wheelchair was there, right around the corner. Waiting.

He focused on it and didn't look back. His goal was to get to it.

Nix panted.

He stopped across from his goal. Summoning the courage, he took three quick steps across the hallway's gulf to the other side. The tank had reached empty. There were no steps left in him. He fingered the wheelchair closer and collapsed into the cushioned seat.

Made it.

There he was, in the hall. In the wheelchair.

The big man reading his paper.

Nix backed up.

Out of sight.

Where he waited.

CHAPTER THIRTY-FIVE_

Cali wasn't a juggler. But she managed to keep several balls in the air.

So far.

She sat down and appeared to take a nap. She looked exhausted. She was exhausted and she did need to sleep, but when she curled up on the chair and closed her eyes, she didn't slumber. Her mind expanded, feeling the various networks and biomites within a certain perimeter. Her reach wasn't unlimited—she couldn't connect with people on the streets—but she was expanding. The new breeds were learning, were dividing and evolving far quicker than she guessed. She was becoming a technological telekinetic, wirelessly talking to anything that chattered computer-speak.

First, she penetrated the security camera fastened in the corner of the room. Once she tapped the video loop, she followed it back to the security servers and downloaded several minutes of Nix lying in bed while Cali stood at the window. She stitched that into a loop and put it on a seamless repeat cycle. It would fool any passing eyes for a few hours, and that was more than enough.

Next, she sensed the security guard outside the door. James was bored, reading a paper. She passively observed his behavior.

There were moments when she could actually see what he was seeing, as if through foggy glass. His biomite content primarily enhanced his reflexes and senses, in particular his sight and hearing. He was naturally suspicious and calmly disciplined. Despite the boredom and aches of long periods of waiting, he remained vigilant.

She didn't want to do this. If it failed, it was all over. But there was no other way. Now or never.

Now or never.

[*Go.*]

Cali occasionally checked on the security loop while firmly maintaining a connection with James's biomites. Her next diversion was Nix. She stayed connected to monitor his health and strength. Even if everything went right, this might be too much. She could end up pushing him too far, drive him into overload. There would be no need for Marcus to come shut him down.

She might do the job for him.

When he was dressed, Cali began to manipulate James's biomites. Slowly, she took control of his sensory input. When Nix reached the door, when he pulled it open, she made him see what she wanted him to see.

It was a struggle, a delicate balance. If she pushed too hard, he'd go unconscious and draw attention. He had to believe what he was seeing. He had to put his suspicions aside and see her going to the cafeteria like she'd done several times over the past week. Those memories supported the false input.

Nix started down the hall.

James's suspicion eased. He accepted what just happened. But that wasn't the hard part. He needed to forget she just left, needed to believe that she'd walked past him to get her bag. Cali opened her eyes and grabbed the bag off the floor. The security loop was still showing Nix sleeping, her staring out the window.

When she opened the door, James nearly slid out of her mental grasp. His biomites shuddered like molecules put to flame, threatening to slip from her grasp like ornery children who didn't want to do as they were told.

She squeezed him.

It was a tiny jolt, one that temporarily knocked him into a blackout. It would feel like a head rush, and while he was senseless, she planted a reasonable explanation in his unconscious, that he was bored and tired and achy. And there was no way Cali and Nix could escape, not when their biomites were being monitored. If they left the hospital, an alarm would go off and they could track them. And if they got too far away, they could shut them down.

There was hardly a need for a guard.

Nix was in the wheelchair. Three nurses were down the hall. Cali connected with their biomites and simply commanded that they weren't their patients, no one that they should be concerned with. Cali turned the wheelchair around and pushed it to the end of the hall and waited for the elevator.

Nix sat with his arms in his lap. His complexion was good, his head upright. She liked what she was seeing. His strength was better than she anticipated. The elevator arrived. Cali sensed it was empty before the doors slid open, accompanied by the sound of a bell.

She pushed him inside and hit the button. They both stared down an empty hallway while the doors slid closed. She resisted hugging him. Instead, they stared at each other in the warped reflection of the silver doors. They made it this far, but it was only the start. And hardly that.

[*Ready?*] she thought.

Nix nodded.

They instinctively took deep breaths, preparing for a deep dive into the unknown. Cali closed her eyes. She was firmly connected with Nix's new breeds. She held her next thought-command on the edge of her mind, like the crosshairs aligned with a target, finger on the trigger.

[*Off.*]

Cali's legs buckled. She caught herself on the wheelchair. Her skin tingled as her new breeds compensated for the sudden deactivation of ALL the old-generation biomites. She'd shut down a third of her functioning body. The new breeds struggled to keep her from passing out, to keep her organs functioning and her brain from freezing.

Nix was limp.

But he was breathing. His pulse a distant rhythm.

He was alive. Barely.

They needed time to recover, for the new breeds to complete the transition. Now that the old-generation biomites were off.

Now that they were invisible.

Cali's gut dropped as the elevator lurched upward.

CHAPTER THIRTY-SIX_

BAD FOOD.

Swamps soaked James's armpits. A toxic fog lingered behind his eyes; fuzzy edges haloed the newspaper. He needed to call in backup. He wouldn't be any good puking on the floor. Not that there was anyone he needed to be chasing down, but he was going to be in the bathroom within the next ten minutes.

He reached for his phone—

The doctor trotted around the corner, his lab coat fluttering behind him, a nurse on his heels. James stood up. They passed him, not paying any attention to him, hit the door and rushed inside. James wandered in behind.

The doctor yanked the covers back, exposing pillows. "Where is he?"

James filled the doorway, hand on the heavy door. He didn't have enough sense to even shake his head.

"This was in the bathroom." The nurse handed the catheter to the doctor.

He put his hands on his hips, looking around the room like Nix might be hiding in a corner. He even bent slightly, peering under the bed.

James hadn't moved.

"Call your boss," the doctor said, pushing past him.

James was going to puke, for sure.

MOTHER_
COMIC BOOK HERO

Rodney Chandler was a superhero geek.

His dad boasted the world's greatest collection of comic books, all cataloged and sealed in mold-proof sleeves and stored in the basement. He would let Rodney look at the covers, but not take them out. God, no.

But when the old man was away, Rodney slipped into the musty downstairs and flipped through the paperbacks organized alphabetically and by edition. Superman, Green Lantern, Thor, Hulk, X-Men... he never knew where to start, the colors so vivid.

He'd read them by flashlight, afraid to turn on the light in case someone passed the house. The old smell of the pages tingled his sinuses. And the thrill of getting one over on his old man twisted his guts. Made him smile.

He watched all the movies, collected the posters. Bought his own vintage comic books and hid them from his old man's grubby mitts. When he was old enough to get seeded with brain biomites, he experienced submersion films: virtual trips into the world of superheroes. He became the Man of Steel, flew around the world, stopped speeding bullets and saved the distressed. After a while, he played the villain. Sometimes he even won.

But even that got stale.

Eventually, the submersion film ended and he woke up, plain old Rodney. Nothing special, nothing good.

Just another street rat.

But there were people that could help, people that had money and access to biomites that others didn't. And didn't cost Rodney a dime. All they asked in return were favors. That was it.

It'll be painful, they said. It'll hurt like a bitch until the biomites acclimate, change your body. You understand?

Rodney half-listened. He was in, no matter what. He was tired of being Rodney. He'd give anything to matter.

But they weren't joking. Rodney sweated out a recovery that lasted months in some dirty basement room. He hardly remembered it, just the pain and the screaming.

After that, the power.

They gave him a phone, told him they'd call, and that he better answer when they did. Months went by before his first call. In fact, he'd forgotten about it. He was way into the new powers. I mean, he was a superhero, for Christ's sake. He considered moonlighting his powers for the good of the city, but the people told him absolutely not, under no circumstances was he allowed to exercise them.

Just wait.

He listened, sort of. He went back to his apartment and practiced. They couldn't expect him to be any good if he didn't. He set up scenarios and pretended to be the good guy. Always the good guy. By the time he'd gotten his first call, he'd saved a thousand imaginary victims.

But now he was standing on West Twenty-Third Street outside a tall building. New York was especially cold that winter, but Rodney didn't feel it. He pulled the hood over his eyes not because he was cold. He leaned against the building and watched the traffic with head bowed. Maybe someone would tell him to move on, but he wasn't begging.

He was waiting.

He flexed his fingers inside the front pocket of his jacket, keeping them limber. There was a metal ball beneath his tongue, filling his mouth with a metallic tang. He switched it from cheek to cheek, watching traffic.

Watching traffic.

When the black limo rolled around the corner, he almost swallowed it. His throat seized, hidden fingers clenched. Fear froze him against the wall. He shifted his weight and dipped his head as the limo stopped at the curb. Car doors opened.

Rodney slid the phone out and swiped his thumb over the glass. A picture illuminated the screen, a photo of a man with gray hair. The photo the people sent him. They needed a favor. And he was their man.

He kept the phone out, watching the fatneck security guard stand next to the back door while another fatneck opened it. He felt them watching him. He was far enough away to be harmless, unless he had a gun. And if that happened, they'd move. So they watched him while the silver-haired man stepped out of the limo. He was speaking on a phone, eyebrows knitted in anger, lips pulled back over white veneers.

Rodney rolled the weighty ball onto his tongue and curled the edges around it like a fleshy barrel. His chest expanded slowly. Expanded fully. No one would notice.

No one would expect it.

He'd practiced it so many times, so many ways. Always getting the bad guy, always the ones that deserved it. Somehow, Rodney knew this guy was bad.

He unleashed a powerful burst of wind, firing the metal ball through his biomite-reinforced tongue. There was a sound of a cork as it passed his lips.

The wet sound of it popping the silver-hair's right eye, sinking into gray matter.

His head snapped.

The fatnecks looked around.

People stepped off the sidewalk; some began to gather. Others called 911. Rodney pushed off the wall and hustled away from the scene. He felt like he was falling, a thrill spun in his groin like he'd pulled a vintage comic from its plastic and inhaled the musty flavor.

And when a beefy hand landed on his shoulder and spun him around... when the security guard clenched his neck, cut off his air, began to drag him back... blades slid out between his knuckles and plunged into the fatneck's belly. He tasted salty blood, licked the man's intestines with the blades like razor-sharp tongues.

Felt the cold chill as he pulled them out.

Felt the wind on his cheeks as he ran away. Ran faster than a man should run, the biomites fueling his muscles with adrenaline, the biomite-blades retracting into his arms, stinging in their slots.

He was a superhero.

CHAPTER THIRTY-SEVEN_

Marcus drummed his fingers on the counter. The hotel clerk tapped on the keys, checking in a woman with frizzy hair and a kid attached to her leg, a thumb in his mouth. The rugrat stared at Marcus, a snot bubble swelling with each breath.

Marcus turned his back.

His driver rolled his luggage to the car and put it in the trunk. He'd wait for Marcus to call, swing by and pick him up when all this was done.

Marcus looked at his watch. 1:00. He didn't want to be in Chicago a minute longer. When it hit 3:00, those two halfskins were getting shut down and he wasn't going to linger. He'd wasted enough time on this charade. This was done, 3:00, on the dot.

Mother was an honest system. She was a machine only interested in data. She recorded every event, watched where people went, alerted the authorities when they went redline, and shut them down when they went halfskin. She had no feelings, had no investment about who lived and died. It was a simple system, an honest one.

But Marcus reserved the right to keep it that way. Sometimes, honesty can make the wrong choice. Dr. Cali was clearly damaged from her biomite seeding. His people had interviewed her co-workers and neighbors; they'd done a full analysis. Her basement was a fully operational biomite lab that had been cleansed of data. She was up to something and smart enough to cover her tracks.

And while her biomite content mysteriously stayed below the redline, he was sure that she had rigged it. Somehow, she was fooling the meters, changing what they were reading. Marcus had been around enough halfskins to know when they were over the line. He could smell it. They had a way about them. They were slightly hollow, distant and mechanical.

Machine-like.

That was her. Cali was halfskin, he knew it. If she thought she could walk around fooling him, she was wrong. She met the one person that could remedy her deceit. So, yeah, Marcus set the record straight. It wasn't his meter that cheated the reading, he simply changed what was being reported through Mother.

She would shut her down.

"I want smoking," demanded the woman with the snotty kid growing off her leg. "I said that already."

Marcus sighed, drumming the counter with his fingernails. The woman glared at him, giving him a chance to say something. His phone buzzed. He put it to his ear, not taking his eyes off her.

"Yeah."

The kid made sucking sounds around his thumb. Marcus wanted to wipe his nose with the mother's dress.

He barely heard what was said.

Not because he was distracted. Because it was impossible.

"What do you mean *disappeared*?"

CHAPTER THIRTY-EIGHT_

EIGHT NURSES.

Three med techs.

One janitor cleaning up vomit down the hall.

Cali sat in the corner of room 512. Eyes closed. Mind plugged into the fifth floor's network, reading who was clocked in. She didn't know what they were doing, except for the janitor that was just called up after Mr. Craven regurgitated his chicken salad on his way to the bathroom.

She sorted through the database and read the patient list. She knew this room had recently been vacated when Ms. Sheila Hartley had been discharged after hernia surgery. Cali immediately filled the room with an alias Mr. Calvin Brown, a man that suffered from diverticulitis. His mother would be in the room with him, sitting in the chair with her eyes closed.

Mr. Brown was currently sleeping.

Cali had triggered a shutdown of their old-generation biomites, the very technology that allowed Mother to follow them, to monitor them, to pass along their location, health and activity to anyone with authority to receive it. Namely, Mr. Marcus Anderson. And now that all the old-generation biomites were deactivated, they were invisible.

Mother couldn't see them.

Nix wasn't ready for the shutdown. There were still too few new breeds to support his body without the assistance of the old-generation ones. But there wasn't a choice. If they stayed on the second floor, if Marcus shut them down with all the bodyguards around them and Cali and Nix survived, suspicion would drop like a hammer.

The new breeds would be discovered.

She had to get them away, to hide. To survive. Invisible, they could make their escape. But she couldn't just wheel Nix out. She could barely stand and she was in much better shape than her brother, and even that sudden loss about did her in. They needed to rest, give the new breeds time to flush their systems and take the place of the old-generation biomites, to keep their organs functioning, their muscles contracting, nervous systems firing.

Cali went to the sink, filled the pitcher with water and drank. She'd been to the bathroom multiple times, excreting the dead biomites that were filtered through the liver and kidneys. She filled a cup, bent the scrunchy elbow of a straw, and lifted Nix's head. He wasn't asleep, but conscious just enough to feel the plastic tip on his lips, to pull the water. She was constantly reminding him to drink, to drink more. She couldn't move him to the bathroom; he had to do his business right there. In the bed.

She'd worry about that later.

Cali sat back down. Felt like she'd run a marathon. She wanted to sleep, needed it badly. Right now, she needed to watch, needed to wait for their opportunity. When Nix was ready to move, they'd have to move. Hiding inside the hospital wouldn't last, even if she could manipulate the computer database. Eventually someone would come looking: they'd see past her illusions.

She closed her eyes.

She listened to the chatter of intercom calls and secure phones. She caught fragments of medical talk and concerned families in waiting rooms. She stayed open, listening. Watching.

Waiting.

CHAPTER THIRTY-NINE_

MARCUS MARCHED OUT OF THE ELEVATOR.

His shoes hammered the floor. Coat unbuttoned. White shirt puffed over his belt and tie slightly undone. He went down the middle of the hall, eyes ahead. Others moved to the side. He turned the corner, hand out, punching open the door.

Several people were inside.

Most were dressed darkly, unassuming clothing that cloaked security guards from standing out in a crowd. Their chatter was cut still.

The balding man stopped. He looked around, hands on hips. He met all their eyes.

"Someone," he said, drawing out the word, "tell me what the *hell* happened."

The last word hissed with steam.

James was the only one in the room sitting. He worked his tongue to moisten his lips. He stood up. He explained that he might have been poisoned, or maybe it was just bad food, but whatever it was... he couldn't quite remember. Cali left the room to get something to eat, and then they were gone.

"What do you mean, *gone*?"

He shrugged.

"Use your training, son. Did the woman have her brother stuffed down her pants? Did she fold him up and tuck him into her bag? HOW THE HELL COULD HE BE GONE?"

Again, shrug. No one had answers.

One of the security agents, a tall skinny man with thinning hair, recounted what they knew. Marcus paced the room, listening while he peeked in the bathroom, looked at the bed, picked up a water pitcher. They'd interviewed everyone on the floor; no one had seen either of them leaving. The security camera was running a loop of them still in the room.

"How could they do that?" he asked.

"We're looking into that," the skinny man said.

She had no access to her laptop. Her phone, perhaps, had hacking capability, but that would require a significant amount of time to set up and execute. Certainly, they'd know what she was doing if that was it.

Impossible. Just... impossible. There was no way she could shut herself down, shut her brother's biomites down, and disappear. Their bodies had to be somewhere. It was not possible to survive without biomites. She wasn't halfskin, not like his reader reported. No, she was probably redline and that would be enough to cripple her. But the kid... he'd be dead.

The bodies have to be SOMEWHERE.

And she couldn't make them invisible. Mother was synchronized with the unique strands of artificial DNA strands that composed every single biomite in production, artificial DNA that allowed them to function. Even if that was somehow sidestepped, even if she was able to recombine the biomite DNA, there was the mitochondria power supply. Mother could follow that.

The woman was a brilliant scientist, but she couldn't accomplish something like that. None of the biomite corporations were allowed to experiment with off-grid synthesis of biomite production without the consent of the government without risking loss of license. The Army Corp of Engineers had been working on developing invisi-biomites and hadn't even come close.

Have I underestimated her?

No. Impossible.

Had to be another explanation.

"Sir?"

Marcus jerked around.

"They were last located in the elevator," Skinny said. "The elevator went up and stopped on every floor. No one recognized them, but there's no evidence they went down. They might still be in the building. The exits are all covered and we're going floor to floor."

"Good," Marcus said. "Check all the rooms, all the closets. I want everything turned over. I want IDs checked, I want every syringe, every cottonball, every last Band-Aid examined for these two people, do you understand?"

They nodded.

"Do not notify the Chicago police, not yet. If they're still in the building, I want to handle this."

They didn't ask questions. They knew a media shitstorm was on the horizon. Once the media got wind of a problem, it got harder to solve. And if they heard that two people went off the grid and hadn't been found—whether they were alive or not—it was going to create a landslide of legal issues.

This was a potential Hydra.

Marcus's thighs were cold. Uncertainty swirled.

James's eyes were still a bit hazy.

"Get him checked out," Marcus said. "I want to know what happened to him so it doesn't happen again. And get the doctor, now. Where is he?"

"On the way."

"I want all the records of this Nixon Richards now. I want to see all the blood analysis, all the tests they ran since he arrived. Make those available ASAP. If his sister somehow tampered…" He stopped, not wanting to utter it out loud, even though they were all thinking it. "I'll be in the doctor's office."

They moved out.

James was the last to go.

CHAPTER FORTY_

CHUG-CHUG.

Chug-chug.

Machines. Chugging and pumping. Working in synchronicity, a majestic symphony of artificial sounds.

The sound of work.

A furnace glowed red hot, somewhere. A furnace burning with friction, with energy. He felt it, out there, warming the universe.

Vibrations jittered on the skin of an invisible membrane, a body that contained the identity known as Nix. It quivered and jiggled and sang. Somewhere, ants crawled along that barrier, their legs touching and marching and going *chug-chug*.

Chug-chug.

Colors mixed with sound and energy. Primary colors shot like stars, crossing paths, running parallel, overlapping to make secondary colors. Sometimes they swirled and curved. He'd recognize a face, eyes and a nose, that would quickly melt away in the growing heat as the furnace pumped exhaust into the world. Sweat tracked the skin somewhere out there, tickling small hairs and tiny nerves.

He began to sink. Down he was going, down somewhere on a

smooth ride, like an elevator taking him to the basement, dipping him in an essence that was warm and cleansing.

And slowly he went. Slowly he went.

Nix sank closer to where the furnace was burning.

He sensed there weren't floors where the ride was going, it was just sinking and sinking and more sinking. To the center of the furnace where the *chug-chug* banged away.

Deeper, it went.

Hotter, it became.

Nix knew where the ride would lead if it did not stop. He knew it would take him to the center of existence, into the heart of the fire. To oblivion.

If it did not stop. Did not stop.

And the *chug-chug* rang like a gong.

It hammered.

It sang. It called. It created.

And it burned.

Nix felt the fabric of his life—his existence—was curling and graying like the edges of a parchment meeting the freshly struck tip of a match. He was thinning, fraying, and fading.

He could take no more.

If he went deeper.

He would be no longer—

But the ride began to slow—

Slow—

Stop.

Near a furnace, a surface red hot, filling everything with light. It surged like a belly, like breath filled it, a heart beating inside.

Beating to the *chug-chug*.

Nix felt the elevator that held him so close to oblivion; it clung by a delicate thread that could be easily snipped by the edge of a butterfly wing. He waited, dangling precipitously close to touching the surface, a touch that would melt everything.

He felt his skin peel.

Bones char.

He melted into a fleshy puddle of goo that would leak through the cracks of the elevator floor and drip on the furnace and sizzle and evaporate and become nothing, become nothing, become—

And then it lifted.

Ever so slowly, he pulled away, lifted up. Carefully. Lovingly.

He inched away from death. Away from the furnace.

No longer a puddle.

And up he went where it was cooler. Where there were streaking colors and sounds again. He remembered things. Remembered who he was, entertained thoughts of what he looked like and where he'd been. He wished he could hide in the lagoon, like he could call it up and go there, soak in the ocean's buoyant grip and lay his head back, bathe in the soft droplets floating from the waterfall.

And upward he went—

Through the thoughts, through the colors and smells and images until—

Wake up, Nix.

He felt a membrane wrap around him, sealing him inside. Defining him. It felt like plastic wrap.

He recognized, finally, his body.

He opened his eyes in a dark room.

CHAPTER FORTY-ONE_

A face looked back from the mirror. Sunken eyes, caved cheeks. A cold sore—red and angry—shined on her upper lip. She ran the tip of her tongue over it and felt the sting.

Felt good.

Cali's hands quivered on her eyes, her nerves quaking with doubt.

Biomites were artificial clones of biological cells. They required oxygen and nutrients. Food, something she hadn't had in thirty-six hours. Or more. She had no appetite and figured she could go another thirty-six hours, if needed.

She was still drinking water. Her urine had cleared and lost the biomite smell—something like putty. She suspected the majority of the old-generation biomites had been flushed out.

The blinds were drawn. Darkness was outside. After midnight, somewhere in the range of 2:00 a.m.

The hospital was quiet, except for the sounds of some of the suffering down the hall and the hushed tones of late-shift nurses. She programmed their computers to show their room was empty due to equipment failure. Nurses wouldn't need to open the door until maintenance arrived in the morning.

She listened to the radio and phone chatter, eavesdropping on conversations, but heard nothing except gossip and sorrow. No security guards reporting their positions.

No Marcus Anderson.

She dared not hope for the best. She wasn't desperate enough to believe they'd gone to the streets of Chicago in search of them, leaving the doors wide open. Her head was stuffy, brain a bit sluggish as it readjusted to the flushing, but she wasn't delusional.

They were out there.

I'm not delusional.

Nix looked good, his vitals improved. She'd thought she lost him shortly before midnight. His pulse faded. There was nothing she could do but wait. And he came back from the edge. The new breeds wouldn't let him die; they kept him alive. His forehead was hot to touch, but that was good. They were fighting.

She wasn't going to lose him.

But she needed him moving normally. If they could leave the hospital at full strength, walk out like a healthy pair, she could handle interference much more effectively, alter what people were seeing and believing. They could do it when visiting hours had closed, when the day shift had gone home and surgeries were done and nurses were just trying to keep people asleep.

They'd do it then.

She sat down and rested her head, fully aware she might fall asleep. All was quiet and maybe she could get a few hours, setting an internal alarm to wake up. Her eyes were instantly weighted, like the thought gave her body permission to check out for a spell.

If she'd had that thought seconds earlier, if she'd decided not to visit the restroom, the ending would've been different.

Her eyelids were on their last drop, preparing to lock down, when a disturbance snapped them open. A nurse protested with hushed tones, but harshly enough to carry through all the doors along that wing. She was answered by a man with no ability to whisper.

Cali jumped to her feet.

She was at the door, eyes wide, mind scanning. There was nothing in the airwaves, but the nurse was obviously agitated. Cali felt her anger. It was late; there was no way the man was going to look in every room, not on her watch. If he had any questions, he could ask and she might be able to tell him, but there was no way he was going to—

The man was done talking.

The nurse was unable to stop him.

Cali's heart slammed her ribs. She touched the door, head against the cool surface, hoping to get an idea of where he was going. The nurse's voice was trailing. She might be going off to search for help. Or she was following the man.

She quieted her racing mind, reaching out to sense biomite activity in relation to where she was. She picked up on the nurse's. And the man's.

Cali hovered on the fringes of his biomites, careful not to influence them in any way, wary they may be expecting manipulation after they examined what she did to James. She simply watched what direction he was going.

The C-wing.

He would come this way, though. He'd stop in the room. Cali might be able to influence what he was seeing, but it was a risk. Any hint of manipulation could set off an alarm and bring a mob of gun-toting maniacs. And if this turned into a chase, Cali and Nix were not going to win. Not from the fifth floor.

They had to leave. *Now.*

"Wake up, Nix." Cali bent over the bed, gently shaking his arm.

Nothing, at first. She shook again and, this time, his eyes opened with effort. There was no focus, plenty of confusion. His breath was humid, rancid. Lips coated with gummy residue, skin flaking off his cheeks.

Cali pulled back the sheets and looked away. She swallowed back the acrid bile that erupted past her tongue. He'd been eliminating urine where he lay. She could clean him up when they were ready. That wasn't now.

Nix was already falling back asleep. She sat him up, whispering what they were going to do. She couldn't hear the nurse anymore. At the pace the man was going, he would reach the end of the wing in five minutes and come back in their direction.

She got new pants on Nix. They were her pants, but he couldn't go without clothes. Not naked.

And not soiled.

"One foot," she whispered, leaning him forward. "Put your weight on it, then the other."

Nix followed her directions like a compliant zombie, lifting one foot then the other. He supported his weight, standing and swaying with her help. She led him to the wheelchair.

That was good.

He was moving, responsive.

And not dead.

Cali ran to the door and cracked it open. The hall was empty.

A nurse would later report seeing a woman and a boy on the elevator around 2:00 a.m., just before the doors closed. She didn't think much about it at the time. She couldn't explain why.

CHAPTER FORTY-TWO_

Marcus unbuckled his watch and rubbed his wrist. He shut the laptop and made sure it was locked before getting up. Another stretch, this one for the lower back. The nurse paid him no attention. She was busy at her station, behind the counter.

He dropped the laptop in a leather saddlebag and slung it over his shoulder. There were plenty of people coming through the nurses' station, plenty that never looked at him. No one seemed that happy in the middle of the night on the biomite wing.

The floor was quiet except for an occasional moan from the B wing, some old man that suffered burns over half his body when his tractor turned over. Biomites were rebuilding the skin and dulling the nervous system, but still he moaned. Marcus would gamble the old man moaned on a good day.

He waited for the elevator, watching the lit arrow as if that would get the car there faster. He wondered if Cali and Nix used that elevator to leave the hospital. Wondered if they were still in the building. Wondered how the hell they even left the room. He hadn't told the Secretary about the event. He glanced at his phone.

Fourteen unanswered calls.

Come daylight, he'd have to answer one. Just through the night, that's all he wanted. The first twelve hours were the most important. He'd reluctantly released photos to the Chicago police without a full explanation. Names and faces, that's all. People of federal interest. Their help would be much appreciated. There was a chance the two were on the streets, hiding in an alley or passed out in a car. If they tried to use a credit card or the phone, Marcus's people would fall on them like vultures. Marcus needed to be patient. They couldn't be far.

Couldn't be healthy.

But how the hell did they disappear?

That's why he needed to find them more than anything. They fell off Mother's radar, somehow erased Nix's test results, masked the security camera... this was the real problem. They had done the impossible and Marcus needed to find out how. It was no fluke. And if it had happened, if it spread to other people, to other biomites... this was something the doctor failed to understand. Of course, how do you make sense to a biomite sympathist like him?

That's why Marcus was working from the nurses' station. He had commandeered the chief doctor's desk. The man walked in and stood in front of his decadent fish tank.

"Out."

Marcus didn't look up from his work. "I'll only need your space through the night, Doctor."

"Not in here, you won't."

"I don't think you understand." Marcus punched a few keys. "Two halfskins escaped your floor. They have also escaped detection, something you haven't been able to explain. Their capture is imperative."

"We don't call them halfskins."

"They're 50%. What else are they?"

"They're human, Mr. Anderson. Biomite-enhanced humans that, otherwise, wouldn't be alive."

"Whether you call them halfskin or not does not change what they are. It does not change the fact that they are in violation of a federal law that no human being can be composed of more than 50% biomite replacement, Doctor. That is the law and I am enforcing it."

"Not from my office, you won't."

Marcus finally looked up and sat back. They stared like gunfighters.

"You think you're saving them?" Marcus asked. "You're only delaying their death."

"Medicine has been doing that for centuries."

"Medicine? Is that what you call this? You replace their bodies with microscopic machines, a little at a time, and you call that medicine?"

"Modern-day medicine, Mr. Anderson."

"Medicine involves antibiotics and repairing the flesh, not replacing it. What you're doing is killing the soul, selling pleasure for a price they can never pay."

"Pleasure?" The doctor slid his hands into the front pockets of the lab coat. "Walk this floor, Mr. Anderson, and listen. Do you hear pleasure? There's a boy that needs a new heart valve, a woman that needs a kidney, and a man with a brain tumor. They'll all survive because of biomites. It's what we do in a hospital, we heal them. Biomites have made that possible like never before."

The doctor pulled the door open.

"Now, I'll ask you to leave once more. Don't make me call security."

Marcus considered the demand. Certainly he could force the doctor to reconsider. This wing benefitted substantially from federal funding. But he couldn't play that card, not yet. He needed to operate quietly. For now.

He snapped the laptop closed and pushed away from the desk. He stopped on his way out. "You know where they are, don't you."

The doctor shook his head.

"When this is over, if I find out you helped them escape, your career will be over."

The doctor was unperturbed.

The elevator arrived.

Marcus stepped into an empty car and went down to the cafeteria for some coffee. He'd sit there and monitor his agents from a booth. He checked his phone again. There was about three hours of daylight left to do it.

CHAPTER FORTY-THREE_

THEIR REFLECTION IN THE ELEVATOR DOOR WAS DISTORTED. Still, that couldn't hide the vacancy in her eyes, the dark pockets they stared out from. Nix looked like an invalid, head cocked to the side, mouth open. His cheeks were pale and shiny, like a frost victim. She leaned over, inspecting the tiny cracks along his cheeks. The skin was flaking off, like a snake shedding skin. She rubbed her own cheeks. Skin fluttered like dandruff. She peeled a sheet from her arm.

They passed the third floor. She felt five people as they went by. They were blips on her radar, their biomites signaling like stagnant ships on a sea of ether.

Second floor, three more. Two nurses, one orderly.

The world was unfolding around her like another dimension, her body interconnecting with everything with an electronic pulse. The language was unspoken, belted out in waves and particles, falling on her like photons on a light-sensitive plate, patterns that were immediately translated.

Connecting. I'm no longer separate from the world.

The elevator slowed. Stopped.

Cali held the button down on the panel, keeping the doors closed. She reached out with her mind. There was no one within range. She didn't expect anyone to be in this part of the hospital where janitorial and maintenance clocked in and out. Not this time of night. There was an exit to her right, down the hall and through the loading dock. Her finger slipped off the button.

The doors opened. She looked in both directions.

Nix's head bobbled as the wheels bounced out of the elevator. Cali pushed at a half-trot. She kept her mind open, her feet moving. The loading dock was at the end, to the left. There was a doorway that led through a locker room that—

SOMEONE.

The wheels squeaked. Cali's feet tripped up; she almost let go. She stopped in the middle of the hall, fingers trembling. Someone was up ahead. Someone at the loading dock. She stayed there, in the hall, afraid to move.

But she had to move.

She had to keep going.

They were out in the open. Hiding wasn't an option, not anymore.

The chair eased forward, the rubber wheels silent again. Cali was on her toes, breath bouncing in her throat. She closed her eyes, reaching out to feel the body that was between them and the exit. She read the person's biomites like seeing words through a telescope. She knew who he was before peeking around the corner, seeing the man with short hair standing in a doorway, holding the door open to blow smoke.

Federal security.

They had the exit covered.

Had them all covered.

She leaned against the wall, head bouncing lightly. Her brother, still silent in the chair. She needed to think, just for a minute. They couldn't outrun him. The second they were recognized, they would be caught. They needed a head start. A big one. If she tried to blind him like James... no, they'd be ready for that. She assumed they'd know what she did to get out of the hospital room. They'd know when their biomites were being manipulated.

She took a minute.

She thought. *They'd be expecting her.*

And then closed her eyes. There was no other choice.

CHAPTER FORTY-FOUR_

Sam Craven was still considered a rookie.

He'd been working for the feds two and a half years, but they still called him rookie. He'd been on numerous assignments and saw nothing but boredom. He'd fired his gun plenty of times at the range and bagged deer during the season, but when on duty, nothing ever happened.

And he didn't expect anything to happen this time.

The suspects were harmless, although that could be deceiving. A couple of halfskins on the run. How that happened, they weren't told. Just a brother and sister due to be shut down and somehow fell off the grid. Intelligence suggested they were on their way out of town, but there was no evidence they ever left the hospital, so Sam was holding down one of the exits.

Hours went by and he stayed at attention. But the room was stuffy and he was jonesing for a smoke. He leaned the door open and fired up a Winston, pulling the first drag deep. The smoke hit the nighttime air, thick and white. The paper crackled with satisfaction.

He wasn't distracted. He had an eye on the outside and inside. No one would get within twenty feet without being seen. And if he saw them, his biomites would automatically trigger a facial recognition alarm and the rest of the team would converge. *Lights out, halfskins.*

But they weren't here, not in the building. No way.

If those two could brain-scramble James, if they could loop that camera, then they wouldn't stick around the hospital, now would they? Holding down the loading dock was a waste of time, really. They should be on the street, interviewing people, analyzing biomite activity... all the shit he'd been trained to do. Not acting like a doorstop.

The third drag, his head buzzed—

The cigarette cherry popped on the concrete in a shower of embers.

Sam let the smoke leak from his nostrils.

Looking in. Out. And back.

Something was buzzing. They were prepped for this. This was what James experienced before the escape. There was an analysis of his brain waves recorded by his biomites, a manipulation of his perception that made him blank out, almost skip time.

Sam put his finger to his ear.

He didn't want to call, not yet. Give it a second. Just a second and then he'd report it. He wasn't 100% sure it wasn't a cigarette buzz, and if it was, he was sure to catch—

Snip.

A black flash covered his eyes.

Just a moment, like a movie skipped a few frames.

He wasn't sure, did he blink, or was he thinking, or was he... he was just so confused...

"What is it, Craven?" a voice called into his ear.

Sam's lips moved. Nothing came out.

"Craven?"

He needed to say something. He must've called out and reported the disturbance; he wasn't sure. He couldn't explain it was an accident; something was happening. He couldn't talk, couldn't talk, couldn't think straight, he just needed to open up and shout for help—

THERE! THERE!

In the lot! Across the lot! A woman pushing a wheelchair.

They got by him.

They got by him and he couldn't...

"SUSPECTS IN SIGHT!" he shouted. "AT THE LOADING DOCK, WOMAN PUSHING A WHEELCHAIR."

Whatever gripped him had let go.

"IN PURSUIT!"

It had him paralyzed, had him trapped, but she was out of range, lost control of him before they could get out of sight. And now he saw them. Now he knew where they were. And it was only a matter of time. Once there was visual contact and the chopper was overhead, it was over.

Sam was off the loading dock, carefully following. He didn't want to get too close just yet.

His hand dropped to his gun.

Maybe this time.

CHAPTER FORTY-FIVE_

Her mind was a delicate hand.

It observed the man in the doorway, blowing smoke, wishing for something better. Something more exciting. His name was Sam Craven. He was twenty-six years old. Never married. Had dated a few times but preferred to keep his options open. He went home for Christmas every year, argued politics and kissed everyone on the cheek when he left.

He was a good man.

A reliable one.

Alert.

Cali sensed his paranoia, knew he was looking for her and Nix as well as any strange sensations. He was primed to pounce. And she preyed on that. He was looking across the parking lot. She could see what he saw—as if she rented his eyesight. There was open asphalt and faded yellow lines. Several cars were spread out beneath the sodium lights. Nothing moved.

Nothing at all.

Cali imagined what she wanted to see in that open space. She pictured it in her own mind as clear as if she had conjured it up on a screen. She played it out, all the way to the end, made sure the details were rich and convincing. Once through was all she had time for. Once through to make it work.

All at once, she projected it into Sam Craven's mind. He felt the manipulation first, buzzing at the back of his head like wires had been yanked from a secret door just below his hairline and short-circuited. Alarms fired. He began to look around, began to call for backup, but not before the image crossed his mind like footprints in freshly laid snow.

He saw her pushing a wheelchair. Saw her hustling to get out of sight, surprised when she turned around to see him pursuing. Saw her race the wheelchair to the sidewalk and around privet hedges to the street beyond.

His voice trailed off, shouting for his companions to hurry. He had them. He had them dead to rights. He was in pursuit.

The doorway clear.

Cali slipped out of the loading dock and turned to the right. Her mind open, searching for others, she pushed her brother around the corner, under a rampart and around another corner until they reached an empty street.

She didn't stop running, despite the weakness in her legs and dimness in her vision. She rushed down the sidewalk, across the street, in the opposite direction of the federal agents.

She hurried toward freedom.

CHAPTER FORTY-SIX_

MARCUS WAS ONE OF THE LAST TO REACH THE LOADING DOCK.

His hard-soled shoes weren't meant for running on linoleum and he bit it on the first corner out of the cafeteria, catching his knee on the corner of a vending machine. He managed a skip-run the rest of the way, slowing around the corners. He couldn't feel his leg. His breath labored, heart slamming in his ears.

Craven had called on the radio. Marcus spilled his coffee while he stuffed his laptop into his briefcase. At first, he thought he'd apprehended them. *I GOT THEM! I GOT THEM!*

The radio crackled with updates as Marcus worked his way to Craven's position. He couldn't be sure, it sounded like they were still in pursuit. He couldn't imagine how they were still chasing after a woman pushing a wheelchair, but there were many scenarios. This was new ground they were embarking upon. They needed to catch these two.

Had to.

Agent Starling was standing on the loading dock. Marcus stopped in the doorway, leaning over to catch his breath. His pant leg was stuck to a dark spot that was growing over his knee.

Starling raised his finger. "That way, sir."

Marcus nodded. He went down the ramp, hopping mostly on his good leg. His other leg stiffened. He struggled across the parking lot, his chest tightening. The lights turned his skin the color of porridge. He was walking when he turned the corner at the hedges. Across the street, only fifty yards down, three of his men were gathered outside a six-story parking garage. Marcus walked easily, catching his breath when he arrived. The briefcase repeatedly hammered his hip. He set it on the sidewalk.

"Update," he demanded.

A short man built like a roadblock told him that the suspects had slipped past the automated gate; they were last seen fleeing to the second level. All the exits were covered. Three men were currently searching the levels. They were on the third floor. So far, no sign.

"It shouldn't be long, sir."

"Where's Craven?"

"On the other side of the building."

"Get him over here."

Marcus sat on the edge of a concrete planter. His knee wouldn't bend. He left it out straight. Craven hustled over a few minutes later and stood in front of him. Marcus sat up, but didn't try to stand.

"What happened?"

Craven went through the details. He was on post at the loading dock when his biomites acted funny, like James had described when the woman and boy escaped. He managed to stay conscious when he noticed them halfway across the parking lot. At that point, he gave chase while calling for backup. Craven saw them enter the parking garage but lost them in the dark as they headed for the second deck.

"And there's no way they could've escaped?"

"No, sir. I took up position next to the elevator and stairwell with the ramp in view. There is no way out of this parking garage, unless they jumped."

Marcus shook his head. Thinking, thinking.

Craven wanted to go back to his post. He wanted to catch them. Marcus jerked his head, telling him to leave. Craven acknowledged him and stopped to speak with the other agents.

The distance from the privet hedge to the parking garage was only fifty yards. The parking lot was about fifty yards. A guy like Craven—someone fit, lean, and young—could cover that distance in fifteen seconds. Maybe less.

And a woman pushing a wheelchair...

"Why didn't you catch them?" Marcus coughed.

Craven turned his head.

Marcus pointed back to the hedge, taking a breath. "Why didn't you catch them?"

"They were almost across the parking lot when I started after them."

"You said they were halfway across, not almost across. Which is it?"

"A little farther than halfway."

Marcus stood up. His knee was frozen. "I can't imagine she could reach the parking garage before you, but I'll give her the benefit. But how did you not catch her before the second deck?"

Craven thought. "She turned the corner, disappeared in the darkness."

"Disappeared?" Marcus looked through the entrance. "Did it occur to you that the corner is a hundred feet up the ramp?"

Craven remained still.

"So you were on her and then she reached the end of the ramp in, what... three seconds?"

Marcus limped in front of him.

"Pushing a wheelchair."

Craven's lips worked without words, running the memory over and over. He was sure it was there, it had happened. He saw it.

"You said you felt the buzzing," Marcus continued. "When did it stop?"

"Right about here."

Marcus nodded. He started back toward the hospital.

"She's in there, I saw it!" Craven shouted. "My eyes weren't buzzing; I saw that person inside the parking garage. They're in there!"

Marcus waved without looking. He slung his briefcase over his shoulder and abandoned the parking garage. They could stay there, finish the sweep. They wouldn't find anything. And Craven would continue to swear what he saw. The fact was, if he doubted it, he'd fall apart. If he faced the reality—that he saw something that wasn't there—he'd never trust his senses again. He'd be done as an agent. When they turned up nothing, he would convince himself and others that the woman and her brother had somehow slipped out an uncovered entrance.

Somehow.

Marcus limped over to the loading dock. His knee was working a little more fluidly now that he was moving. The briefcase, however, felt like a bag of concrete.

"When did you arrive?" he asked the agent posted in the doorway.

"Sir?"

"When did you get here to guard this exit?"

He thought. "About a minute before you arrived."

Marcus looked around. The parking lot was surrounded by brick walls and shrubbery to his right. There was a sidewalk to his left that went around the building. He handed the briefcase to the agent, telling him to hold it. Told him there was sensitive data in there. It was the most unadvisable thing to do, hand something like that over, but he cared a lot less than he did only fifteen minutes earlier.

He made it around the corner, making his knee bend as he went. He followed the path beneath a portico and past the entrance to another building to the street beyond. He stopped there, looking left and right.

It was almost 4:00 a.m.

Crickets were the only thing that disturbed the distant interstate.

He reached inside his coat and took out the phone. It was time to make a call. Time to tell his superiors what had happened.

Tell them it was over.

CHAPTER FORTY-SEVEN_

The keycard slipped from Cali's fingers. The corner rebounded off the standard hotel carpeting and bounced to the other side of the hallway. She put her hands on her face. Her fingers cold. Cheeks burning.

Legs quaking.

We made it. We made it this far.

She steadied herself on the wheelchair's handles. Nix's head rested at an odd angle. The clerk at the front desk was more interested in a magazine than the sleeping kid in a wheelchair, and checked them into their room.

We're on our way to meet family, Cali told her. *Just running a little late.*

The clerk pursed her lips, tapping at the keys. *Jenny Meggett?*

Yes, that's me.

Tappity-tap-tap-tap. The girl coded a keycard and handed it over. She didn't ask for a credit card; there was already one on file. Cali hesitated at the desk, then pushed towards the elevator. She wanted to ask if a little girl had checked into her room, but thought better if she didn't. She wanted to know, but thought better if she went and looked herself.

So now she was on the second floor, staring at raised numbers on the door. The keycard on the floor. Nix sleeping.

She held on and bent over, prying the keycard off the dense carpet with a fingernail. The plastic was slick, the edge biting into her palm. She aimed it at the slot and stabbed the lock with a quick motion. A green light ignited. Gears turned.

She stared until the light went out.

Again, she keyed the door. This time she pushed the handle down before the light expired.

It was dark.

The smell of clean drifted from the room.

Cali backed inside, pulling the wheelchair with her. The light switch was around the corner. She locked the door and stood there. The heavy curtains were drawn. The beds made.

TV off.

"Avery?" she whispered.

Cali's hands shook with renewed force, her fingers rattling over her lips as she covered her mouth to keep any more sounds from squeaking out. She was a horrible mother. She'd sent her little girl out on her own to wait for them and they almost never made it. What would've happened to her if they were shut down? Where would she have gone? She had no one if Cali disappeared.

No one.

Cali looked on the other side of each queen-sized bed, the corners crisply made and tucked beneath. She pulled the curtain aside and looked down into the city. The street was empty and wet. Drizzle streamed down the glass like tears.

"Momma?"

The bathroom door opened. And her little girl, her treasure, stood there with a toothbrush, wearing her nightshirt, the one that said Little Princess. Cali fell on her knees with such force that, despite the carpet, pain shot up her legs. She held her arms out and her little princess jumped. Avery smelled like Colgate.

"I'm so sorry," Cali whispered. "I'm such a bad mother. Such a bad, bad mother."

"No, you're not. You're the best."

"I'm sorry," she repeated, over and over.

"It's okay, Momma. It's okay. I just waited for you."

"I know, I know... I just..."

And she squeezed her girl harder than a girl should be squeezed. And it felt good. A momma holding her cub to her bosom, never letting go.

Never letting go.

"Is that Uncle Nix?"

"Yes," Cali said. She held her hand and knelt next to her brother.

His breathing was shallow. Drool hung from his lower lip. His complexion was still yellow but blotchy with patches of dry skin flaking off like scales. Like a new body pushing away the old.

A new breed.

"He smells funny," Avery said. She leaned closer, wrinkling her nose. "What happened?"

"He's been sick." Cali pushed her brother's hair off his forehead. Clammy and wet.

"He's better?"

Cali nodded. "Yeah, he's better."

She smiled.

"He's a lot better."

Avery, despite the odor, wrapped her arms around Nix and pressed her head against his. Toothpaste dried on her lips like primer. The little princess smiled with her eyes closed, glad to see her uncle home and safe.

Home and safe.

CHAPTER FORTY-EIGHT_

There was no sense of time.

Like anesthesia. Like a portion of consciousness snipped from his life. If he had to recall his last moment of awareness, and it took great effort to do so, Nix remembered the silver doors of an elevator closing. Remembered his reflection looking back and his sister standing behind him. She said something—

Fire and furnace.

The images of hallucinatory dreams marched through his memories like pink elephants.

And now there was darkness. Blackness so perfect, unmarred by variations of smudging or the hint of shapes and depth. Just black.

Just night.

He wasn't sure that time was passing, although it seemed to be, since he was aware—on some level—of this absence of light. Of this night that went on forever, where there was no sensation. There just was.

Just is.

Until there was a pinpoint of light.

He wasn't even sure when it appeared. As he became aware of it, he was thinking that perhaps it was there the whole time. That perhaps he just didn't see it.

And then there was another. And another.

Like a black sheet draped across the sun and something poking through it. Some holes bigger than others, some brighter, but none bigger than the head of a needle. All there, filling his vision, filling the darkness like a can of sparkly paint flipped from a brush to spatter the night.

Stars. Those are stars.

Nix was grossly aware that he had a realization. That there was thought in this world. Before, the dark and the pinpoints of light were just knowledge, something that he just knew. But he felt a movement —something shifting—when he recognized the lights for what they were. That they were stars.

That he was lying on his back, looking into a pristine night sky.

And, like the lights had eased into his awareness, so did the sound of water beyond his feet, ebbing and flowing and shooshing and crashing. The heartbeat of the ocean was somewhere beyond his vision, but he could hear it. He could smell the salt, the sea life within it. Feel the sand beneath him.

And he lay there, motionless. Watching the stars glitter. Listening to the ocean call. He stayed that way for longer than he would remember, for a period of time that he could not measure, remaining in the present moment.

Just seeing.

Just hearing.

Smelling. Feeling.

Until smoke was in the air. Wood burned and crackled somewhere to his right. Nix turned his head, the sand grinding against his ear. He saw the fire glowing, flames licking the darkness somewhere between the hard-packed sand and the line of trees. Sparks danced like insects.

Perhaps he knew where he was and didn't recognize it. Of course he wouldn't. Because never before had he ever experienced the inner world with such clarity. Never could he smell its richness, breathe its wonder. Feel its beauty. Perhaps, he thought, he was somewhere in the outer world. That, holding that last memory of the elevator and sister closely, Cali had taken him far away from the hospital. Perhaps they were in paradise, after all. Just like she promised.

They escaped.

Because, if this was the lagoon, if this was his inner paradise, his dreamland, surely he would see—

She would be—

And a form stepped from behind the fire, the light flickering on her dark skin. Her bare feet pushing through the sand, hips swaying. Arms swinging at her sides. Her features faded as she stepped closer, the firelight now at her back, hiding the smile that touched her lips.

Nix went up to his elbows. He sat with arms crossed on drawn knees. He looked at the star-choked sky and cresting waves. Felt his longtime companion near him. Fully aware that the new-breed biomites had fleshed dreamland, made it as vivid as skin and bone.

Or maybe this is real.

Raine's hands were warm.

Her embrace soft.

CHAPTER FORTY-NINE_

Marcus rapped the counter with his fingernails, tapping a rapid succession of bullets with no particular rhythm, just something to cut through the barbiturate fog. His leg, stabilized in a blue wrap, still pulsed.

The doctor was late.

It was cold in the room with jars of tongue depressors and old magazines. Marcus tapped and stared straight at a poster—the only adornment in the room—framed in a thin black border beneath a layer of clear plastic: a picture of an old man and his wife walking through Hyde Park. He was two feet in the air, clicking his heels like a goddamn fairy on Broadway.

BIOGEN. Stem cell biomite technology to have you on your feet and out the door. Ask your doctor if it's right for you.

Tap. Tap. Tap.

Tap. Tap. Tap.

Tap. Tap. Tap.

A week had come and gone. Still in Chicago.

The pain, excruciating. When the adrenaline was exhausted, he'd smashed against the reality of a shattered knee. He attempted to fly home but was told to stay in Chicago. The investigation was ongoing and they needed him there to mop up. And in the meantime, get that knee fixed.

They knew he wouldn't take the biomites. They knew his stance. And he knew they kept him there to let him stew in the raw scream of nerve endings that blared like never-ending fire alarms. Sometimes pain brought a man's beliefs down, shattered the foundation on which he built his life. Pain, when there was enough, broke down all ideals.

But not Marcus Anderson.

He was certain, now more than ever, that biomite technology would be the end of humanity. Where once he held onto the thread of hope—bare and frayed at the ends—that people would see the folly of their tireless attempts to create happiness with technology, it was now all but dissolved.

They need me now more than ever.

The public was unaware of Cali and Nix. Thank God, the media, either. So far, all they knew was that a mistake had been made. As far as authorities were aware, the brother and sister were wanted for questioning. But they hadn't broken any laws. And, for the love of God, they certainly weren't halfskins that Mother couldn't see.

And that should be impossible.

The only way to escape Mother was to develop a new brand of biomites. Geniuses had yet to crack that case, but if Cali did... if, in fact, she developed something that knocked them off the grid and this wasn't a fluke... well, then, Marcus was fucked.

We all are.

Everyone would figure out how to avert the all-watching eye of the government; they'd be out on their own, doing what they wanted, infecting humanity with a new brand of biomites that were, perhaps, stronger, faster and telepathic.

Marcus was sure that he'd live long enough to see the ugly end. He'd see humanity consumed by microscopic machines. And he would sit back with the other purists in the world and laugh.

Laugh as biomites ate them like flesh-eating bacteria.

Laugh and say it, say it loud.

I told you so.

The door opened. A doctor entered and extended his hand. Asked Marcus how he was feeling.

Marcus grunted. And tapped.

The doctor dropped a folder on the counter and leafed through several documents. He pursed his lips and whistled. His lips wet. The sound happy and piercing.

The doctor tapped the counter. It came to life like a computer tablet. Marcus removed his hand from the lighted surface. The doctor went back to whistling, moving objects around. He double-tapped a folder and the wall in front of Marcus transformed. The framed poster turned out to be a projection.

Lights danced.

An X-ray flipped into view.

"That's your knee." The doctor used his fingertip to draw a red circle on the wall. "Your patella is shattered and you tore the patellar tendon."

Marcus didn't need the X-ray and all the red arrows pointing to the black lines that spiderwebbed his kneecap. The knee was destroyed.

"There's a procedure that utilizes cadaver tissue to rebuild—"

"No." The thought of a dead man's skin inside his body was revolting.

"When the swelling is down, we'll replace the entire knee."

The doctor explained, with more red lines, how they were going to enter Marcus's knee, where they were making cuts, and what materials they would use to substitute for bone and ligament. He would have an artificial knee that worked almost as good as the one he was born with. He could expect trouble as he got older, but it beat the hell out of the alternative.

"There is another option." The doctor swiped the desktop. The red lines vanished.

Marcus's jaws flexed.

"You're an ideal candidate for biomite regeneration. There have been some recent advancements in biomite knee reconstruction. The seeding is relatively painless and the results are complete within a month. We could start today, don't even have to wait for the swelling to go down."

Marcus took in a long breath. The doctor pretended to organize his folder.

"No," Marcus managed to say, and that was it.

The doctor nodded. He turned the desktop off, pushed the folder to the side, and sat on a stool. Marcus let out a small sound when he unclipped the brace around his knee.

The pain lanced the fog like a spotlight.

CHAPTER FIFTY_

The room smelled like a stale armpit.

A week of recovery, of sweating out waste, of dead skin peeling off them like burn victims, was about all Cali could take. It clung like cigarette smoke. She felt better stepping out of the shower and wrapping up in a robe. She leaned over the sink, piling a generous helping of toothpaste—compliments of Red Roof Inn—onto the bristles and scrubbed her whole mouth. The armpit was even on her tongue.

Her spit was foamy red—blood and toothpaste.

She pulled her lips back, spilling lines of blood over her teeth. Her finger squeaked over her gums, massaging the blood away. They had receded.

Cali stepped back, looking at her reflection. She wasn't pasty anymore. She opened the robe and exposed her body to the mirror, revealing saggy breasts that drooped over a series of speed bumps that were her ribs. Her pelvis jutted from her hips like brackets. No matter what she thought-commanded, the biomites weren't putting weight back on her.

She'd been eating, even though she wasn't really hungry. She assumed it was just a caloric deficiency that was causing the gaunt affliction, but nothing had changed. Her distress haunted her, reminding her something was wrong each time she looked in the mirror.

Another self-analysis, just to be sure.

"All right, in you go." Cali clapped her hands. "Into the shower, young lady."

Avery jumped on one bed; Nix lay on the other, hands folded over his stomach. "Momma," she said, the impact of the jump bouncing in her voice, "we're doing this game where I jump over to the other bed and... and..."

She jumped a couple times and caught her breath.

"And Uncle Nix tries to... to... grab my feet before I can get back and... and... we're keeping score."

"What if you hit your head?"

"No, no... he hasn't caught me yet. I'm too fast, Momma."

"She's too fast?" Cali looked at her brother, his eyes closed.

"Too fast for me."

Avery squealed with delight, bouncing almost to the ceiling. Cali pulled the towel off her head and wrangled her daughter onto the floor, kicking and laughing. She smacked her bottom as the young lady padded into the bathroom. Cali turned on the shower for her.

She dug through her bag, looking for the least gross thing to wear. Nothing had been washed in over a month. She hand-washed the T-shirts and underwear in the sink, but they still seemed rank.

The armpit contaminated everything.

She threw on a baggy sweatshirt and shorts, nixed the underwear. She closed the bathroom door and retrieved a black kit, sitting on the bed.

"Let me have your hand."

"Do I have to?" Nix answered.

"Come on."

"Use one of my toes. I can't feel my fingertips."

"I've got a baseline with her fingers, now hand it over before I pull a sample off your lip."

He made half an effort. Cali grabbed his pinky and pressed it on a small box. A needle took a droplet. Nix pretended it hurt, sucking air through his teeth.

"Baby," she said.

Cali set it down on the round table next to the window, the curtains drawn. All levels were exactly where she expected them to be. His nervous system was up to 60% function. Respiratory was 88%. Circulatory, 95%. Brain function was near 100%.

Punching all cylinders.

"How are you feeling?" she asked.

"How are you?"

She waited for an answer.

"Maybe you should put that thing on your finger," he said.

"I will. Don't worry. You're the only one who skirted death, so tell me how you're feeling. Any unusual aches, pains, sensations? Anything abnormal?"

It had been a week. His recovery was unbelievable, really. She'd just hoped he'd survive, that she could push him out of the hotel looking halfway normal.

Still, it could all go wrong.

"Well?"

Nix shook his head. She stared, just in case he needed a little pressure to find the right answer. He folded his hands and closed his eyes. She pressed her finger on the black box and watched the readout. Her levels were better than his, just something about the brain function was a little off. It was operating at full capacity; the only difference was the anomaly in the algorithm, something that was always there as long as she could remember. She could never figure out what was missing. It was similar to Nix's readout when he was dreaming up the lagoon.

Going there, as he put it.

But she didn't have a dreamland and that made her wonder if there was something the new breeds were doing that she wasn't following. She would have preferred that they be better—stronger—but they couldn't stay in the room any longer.

They'd been out once. It was the second day after Nix woke up. She took him on an extended walk to the ice machine. They walked the entire floor and stopped at the end. She didn't like being in the open for so long, but the exercise was refreshing. And the view of Chicago was different from that end of the hallway. They sat for an hour. No one bothered them.

When they returned, maid service had been through. Thankfully, nothing was out of the ordinary, nothing that would raise an alarm. She thought about switching rooms, but that seemed too obvious.

"How's it look?" Nix asked.

"What?"

"Your analysis."

"It looks fine. Now, I don't want you to push it. Tomorrow morning, we'll be walking through the lobby to get to the parking garage. I'll go first and find the car and have it ready. Avery will go with you. If you feel weak, you can lean on her. You need to conserve your energy. That means no extracurricular activity."

She snapped the black kit closed.

"No dreamland."

Avery was still singing in the shower.

Cali went to the mirror and brushed her hair. It was thinner than before. Nix lay motionless. She tried to ignore him but plopped her hand on Nix's.

"Look, I know you miss her. I know you miss... *Raine.*"

The name came out sharp. She didn't try to sugarcoat it.

"But, I'm sorry, she's in your mind, Nix. She's something you constructed with thoughts, something you made up when you were little."

She squeezed his hand.

"You're saying she's not real?"

Cali shook her head.

Nix nodded. He closed his eyes again. Then, a few moments later, he tapped his skull.

"I think this is a new reality, sis. I've no more control of her than I have over my heart beating or hair growing. She's a part of me that lives and breathes. I think the biomites give me access to the new world."

"Did you dream up that world?"

"In the beginning, yeah. But now, it's just more... real."

"But every detail you have created, right? You've pictured every color, every image since you were ten. You built that world with your mind."

He didn't answer.

"You told me it started in the doctor's office with the poster and the waterfall, that you kept adding to it by visualizing something new. First, you made the ocean, then the forest and the fish... and then her."

Cali touched his forehead like she was checking a fever.

"It's all right, Nix. It's just not real. You invented it. The only difference is that it's inside your mind. Not out here, not in the flesh."

He stared at her, like he was really listening. Maybe this time he would understand. This time he would believe and stop wasting time in dreamland.

"If I'm the only one that sees her," he said, "does that mean she's an illusion?"

"Yes." Cali nodded. "Sorry. Get some rest. We'll go over things again in the morning. For tonight, get some real sleep. Promise?"

He nodded, once.

Cali opened the bathroom. The song jumped out, loud and clear.

"Enough showering. No one else in the building will have hot water."

"Yes, Momma."

Cali turned the shower off and dropped on the bed while Avery dried off. She flipped on the television and scouted the news stations. Still no word on their escape. She had the queer sensation that something was missing.

Couldn't quite put her finger on it.

Maybe if she'd noticed the missing wheelchair, things would've been different.

CHAPTER FIFTY-ONE_

Every bump sent spikes through Marcus's knee. Even in the OxyContin-induced fog, he felt the pain.

We don't get many of these anymore, the nurse teased. *I can't remember the last time a doctor cut open a knee to operate, honestly.*

Honestly, he didn't give a shit.

He was supposed to stay another month to rehab. And while he was there, continue overseeing the case of the missing brother and sister.

Plans changed.

Just before surgery, his superiors informed him that Jack Parsons would be arriving to go over Marcus's notes. Marcus could go home and recover peacefully. The day after surgery, lying in bed, mouth open, pain-sweat beading on his head like it was freshly waxed, he received the news that Internal Affairs wanted to talk to him.

They scheduled a chat for when he returned to D.C.

While he was stuck in Chicago, his office had likely been raided, his interns sequestered. His records scrubbed and combed through and picked apart. Dr. Erickson, chief of biomites, probably blew the whistle and reported their conversations. The bastard probably recorded them.

Marcus knew what would come next; he'd been part and parcel of witch trials of this sort. They would paint him as a religious sycophant bent on destroying biomite technology, that he secretly manipulated the system and caused the premature death of hundreds.

Eventually, they would say, *thousands. Millions.*

They would paint that picture, they would show it to him as a warning. *Go down quietly, Marcus. If you don't, this is what you'll see.*

Perhaps he was wrong. Maybe this was all a misunderstanding. He was good at his job. If he wasn't, he would've been replaced long ago. Maybe he was just too biased to be trusted. His hatred for biomites colored his perception, tainted his thinking and actions. Truth be told, he was perfect for the job and the Secretary all the way to the president knew it. If someone was planning on casting Marcus as the goat, they would make a mistake.

He was a scrapper.

They knew what he'd been doing. He managed his job with the tools they gave him. When he had to distort reality for the good of the country, he stepped up, did what needed doing.

He shook his head.

His thoughts were getting away. Even if he felt old and broken, he was the founder of the Halfskin Laws. If he fell, a lot would follow.

He was rolled out of the hospital to wait for a car to pick him up and take him to the airport. Fly him home. His phone buzzed. He looked at the number, silencing it. His wife had nothing that he wanted to hear. He would be there by nightfall to hear it all in person. If there was one bright side to Chicago, it was the silence of his hotel room. There were no extra voices around unless he wanted them.

Marcus watched for his driver in the downtown melee. No sign of the black Mercedes.

But there was something interesting.

Down the street, about a block away, was a man in hospital

scrubs. An orderly was pushing an empty wheelchair. Marcus watched him instead of the traffic. The man bounced his head to the rhythm of buds buried deep in his ears. Normally, Marcus would've silently cursed about music in the workplace, even though the man was just pushing a wheelchair.

He didn't notice the car pull up to the roundabout. The driver had the door open and Marcus was pushed forward.

"Hold on." He put his hand up, eyes on the approaching orderly.

"Hey. You." Marcus snapped his fingers. When the orderly didn't notice, he grabbed the nurse. "Get him."

The nurse, hesitating, reached out and gently touched the orderly, who pulled one of the cords from his ear.

"Where'd you find that?" Marcus shouted over a passing truck.

"This?" The orderly pointed at the empty wheelchair. "Got reported found. I'm picking it up and bringing it back."

"Where?" He twisted in the wheelchair, sparks lighting up his knee. He grunted. "Where was it?"

"Red Roof said they found it in a room." He pointed at the back of the wheelchair, where it was written, *Northwestern Memorial Hospital.* "Happens all the time, man. You know how much these things worth?"

The orderly waited for more questions. When there weren't, he plugged his ear and continued on.

A certain thrill rolled through Marcus's insides. A delicious feeling, it was. Something he was all too familiar with. A feeling he got when he was right. Or when he found treasure.

This was both.

CHAPTER FIFTY-TWO_

THE TASTE OF COFFEE STILL LINGERED.

Cali wished for a mint or something that would make her feel new and fresh. Something that would wash away this feeling of waste. She was certain it would be different when she escaped the room, the hotel. When they were out in the open and away from danger. That was when she would feel normal again.

Fresh and new.

The door clicked quietly behind her. She smoothed out the wrinkles in her shirt, with no lasting effect. Body odor clung to the fabric like a stain. The carpet felt spongy. She sensed the occupants of each room she passed. Most of them sleeping. A few reading *USA Today*. One couple was having sex.

She smelled it.

The lights buzzed in their sockets, throwing an iridescent glow down the hall. She passed the elevator alcove, pushed open the door to the stairs and descended, sure that someone had vomited somewhere in the long trail of treads within the last couple nights. Cali stopped at the bottom step and took a deep breath.

Nix and Avery would stay up in the room for fifteen minutes, then come down and meet her in the parking garage. She'd have the door open, car running. She was sure he had the strength to walk normally through the lobby. She only wished she were there to help. Just in case.

The door's cushioned hinge resisted her initial shove. If she was superstitious, she might see that as a sign. *Don't go any further, stay in the room.* But she'd been up there long enough. Cali leaned her shoulder into the red door and entered the main lobby.

The ceiling was high, the room spacious. She stopped to collect her thoughts. She considered thought-commanding her heart rate to slow down, but adrenaline served her well. She was stressed, needed additional oxygen. She just needed a moment. A breath.

A continental breakfast room was past the desk. There were donuts and bagels, cold cereal and orange juice. Even a waffle maker. Three people were sitting at small tables, reading newspapers and chewing. The lobby was nearly as empty. A middle-aged couple and their daughter sat on a couch. Cali felt their thoughts and figured they were waiting on the grandparents. They were checked out, ready to go home.

There was one clerk at the desk and a heavyset woman talking to her.

Cali needed to pick up the key, that's all. The rental people parked the car in the garage and dropped the key off at the desk. She'd specifically instructed them to bring it to the room, but the front desk called when he left it there. Probably didn't want to spend the extra time. No big deal, but Cali hoped her only challenge would be to walk through the lobby unnoticed.

Now she had to talk with someone.

She queued up behind the extra-large customer. Her swollen fingers gripped the counter while she ground her words through a triple chin. Her dress had faded floral patterns and a stain on the sleeve. Built for comfort.

"I did not make those charges; take them off," the woman said.

The clerk was a tired woman in her early thirties. Her shift had ended, but her replacement was running late. Way late. Nothing out of the ordinary, the prick had done that sort of thing on a weekly basis. He'd lose his job pretty soon, but not soon enough. And now she had to deal with this self-centered mountain of flesh and three pornos racked on her account.

Cali's stomach curled. Sweat trickled down her ribs, soaking into her shirt. She couldn't smell herself anymore, overwhelmed by the scent of baby powder that gummed the fat lady's skin folds. Cali smelled cellulite.

Fat woman placed her half-empty soda on the counter. She looked past Cali, her breath labored, as if exhausted from breathing. Cali wanted to ask if she could just ask for the key, it would only take a second. But the fat woman—sliding her oversized glasses up her pudgy nose—wouldn't take that kindly. And she was taking all the attention away from Cali, so she'd wait.

She'd wait.

"Ma'am," the clerk said, "I've taken the extra charges off your account. You'll see a refund on your credit card, but it won't show up for a couple of days."

"It better not say what was purchased. I am embarrassed to even have to ask about this. Can you imagine having movies like that?"

"I'm sorry, ma'am." The clerk couldn't look at the customer. She'd heard that bullshit too many times. The hotel's policy was to refund their money, no questions asked. But the lying irritated her. Dishonesty always did.

"It's all taken care of, ma'am. Is there anything else I can help you with?"

The clerk looked at Cali, wanting to move on.

"Yes, I'd like the name and number of your manager. I'd like to be compensated for my pain and suffering."

"Pain and suffering?"

"Are you listening, missy? I'm embarrassed by this and I want a free room. Give me your manager's name and number so I can call him."

"Her." The clerk tried to bite her tongue. "My boss is a woman."

"Well, soooorry. *HER*. Give me *her* number." Fat lady swallowed some flat soda. "I'd like to call her. And I want your name, too. Want her to know how rude you've been, she'd probably want to know that. I doubt I'll ever come back to this place again."

Cali felt the tension winding around the clerk's throat, her fingers poised over the keyboard, contemplating what she wanted to say. The customer, she'd seen them before, was baiting her. Say the wrong thing and get compensation and someone fired.

Sick.

Cali kept her attention on her surroundings. One of the men left the breakfast nook, carrying a Styrofoam cup of coffee. The family on the couch was watching the show at the counter. Cali moved off to the side and considered leaving, going back up the stairs. She could come back later, maybe even the next morning. The thought of spending another day in the room sank inside her like a trapped animal.

No one paid her any attention. She didn't see any thoughts relating to the shabbily dressed woman—the one that looked like an anorexia patient—standing in contrast to the obnoxious fat lady. Cali could wait another minute, just one more. Her hands were shaking—

Small fingers slipped between hers.

"Avery?" Cali looked down. Her daughter squeezed her hand.

"It's all right, Momma."

"I told you to wait with Uncle Nix." Cali spoke quietly, her lips barely moving.

"I'm worried about you. I just wanted to make sure you were all right."

Cali listened to the clerk make a call. Listened to fat lips suck a bottle.

The people on the couch watched.

The clerk steamed.

Avery's hand was warm and soft. Cali squeezed it, but felt something twist inside. *This is wrong. This is all wrong. She shouldn't be out here, not in front of all these people. Nix needed her.*

"Honey," she said, hissing, "I want you to go."

The fat lady's head turned like a heap of flesh on a spike. Her nostrils flared. She looked directly at Cali, her eyes magnified through the lenses. Avery stepped behind Cali, still holding her hand. She held her gaze for several moments, neither of them talking. Fat lady wanted to say something; she was fired up, ready to take on all comers. She thought Cali was talking to her, maybe; thought maybe Cali told her to get going. She wanted her to go, but that wasn't what she meant.

The phone hit the cradle. "Ma'am."

Fat lady turned.

Cali pulled Avery around and knelt in front of her. Held her daughter's cheeks with both hands while staying aware—remaining very aware of the couple on the couch and the two people in the breakfast nook, sensing their biomites like radar, no one else around—and whispered, "Go back to the room, darling. I'll see you in a bit, I promise."

Fat lady was agitated. She glanced back, but the clerk held out a phone, the manager or someone with authority on the other end. Avery nodded, tears brimming.

"Why are you crying?" Cali asked.

"I'm scared."

"Of what."

Avery bit her lip. She did that when she was nervous. When she was little, she sometimes wet herself; now she just bit her lip. Her eyes flicked toward the hotel's front doors, but Cali couldn't sense any active biomites, no one back there.

"I don't want to leave," Avery whispered.

"It's just for a few minutes, honey. I promise. Just for a few."

Avery danced in place. She was going to go if she didn't settle. Cali took her hands. She heard something behind her, something that didn't register.

Avery stopped jumping.

Her lip popped out from between her teeth.

"I love you, Momma."

Cali felt a cold shank of fear drive through her organs. Something was about to shift. About to change.

She sensed a phone call behind her. Someone called the authorities.

She recognized the voice.

Marcus Anderson was at the doors, propped on crutches in all his biomite-less glory.

"What are you doing?" he said.

CHAPTER FIFTY-THREE_

Buzzing.

A different buzz. A good one. This one potent, tight. This one powerful.

Nix sat on the corner of the bed and checked the time. A few more minutes and he'd follow. Just give her enough time to get to the garage, to get the car and be ready. He wasn't concerned whether he could reach it or not. He was only thinking of his sister getting there. He wanted her out of this situation, far away and safe. Then he could relax. He could let go.

In the meantime, he buzzed with anticipation. Buzzed with excitement.

He distracted himself by running his hand over his scalp, the fuzz gripping his palm like Velcro. He missed having hair.

Nix was tempted to close his eyes, make a brief visit to the lagoon, tell Raine he was all right, that he was coming back soon. But he had promised. He had enough energy to stay there all day and be just fine, he was sure of it. His legs were wound springs. But he'd promised he wouldn't. After that morning, he could go all he wanted. He needed to get through the morning.

He thought about what she'd said. She never liked his dreamland.

When he was little, she restricted how long he could go. She was probably right because, if she let him, he'd close his eyes and stay there for days.

Maybe never come back.

Yeah, she was probably right.

But she was wrong about the reality. Raine wasn't just some thought that seemed real. He was sure of it. She wasn't a construct of his mind. He had a theory that the biomites manipulated reality, that they were able to take her from the vapor of another reality and spin her into existence where only he could see her. Where only he could go. The biomites were some sort of portal into a new dimension, something that made dreams reality. That maybe the human body was just a garden to grow the mind. Once it was mature, it existed somewhere else.

Dreamland.

He wasn't deluded; he knew the difference between one reality versus the next. Knew when he was in the lagoon, when he was in the flesh.

He checked his appearance in the mirror. His stomach tumbled like broken glass. There were still blotches on his cheeks, but the peeling had stopped. His eyebrows looked close to normal, but the eyelashes were lacking. At least he wasn't lugging the ring around his neck. A hairless teenager would certainly be easy to pick out in a hotel lobby.

"All right." He checked his breath in his cupped hand, not sure why. "It's time. Let's go."

THE BUZZING ENERGY turned to ice water, filling Nix's legs.

He wasn't as strong as he thought. Or maybe it was nerves. Whichever, he stood at the bottom of the stairwell, his hand on the red door. *Breathe, breathe. And think.*

He wished he could see outside and know what was coming. He

closed his eyes, the buzz crawling over his scalp and tingling like millipede legs. He sensed spots of activity around him, like a field of snowy static where lumps of density could be felt. This was what Cali was talking about, using the new breeds like scanners. Nix had focused on George, manipulating his biomites, but this was like an electronic net that plugged into multiple people. He was a virus that could watch and feel all the players in the field.

Most of the spots were quiet and pulsing. One of them, though, was bright and spiky. His hand slid across the door like he was feeling for direction. This one spot was big and dense.

Agitated.

Disturbed.

Cali should be in the garage. That couldn't be her.

She wouldn't still be there.

But then he heard her. This wasn't in his head; he heard his sister's voice beyond the door. It was shrill, calling a name.

Nix pushed the door open.

A large woman was at the counter, the clerk on the other side. Cali was gone, but the disturbance was coming from somewhere around those people. That was what he felt. Maybe he imagined what he heard. Maybe his panic manifested as his worst nightmare: *Cali searching for Avery in public.*

She wasn't out there. She wasn't in the lobby. But the people weren't moving, they were looking at something. Nix moved toward them. As he came around, he saw her. She was on her knees.

This time, he heard her.

She was calling. Panic strapped her voice, making it tight and piercing. She was calling out for Avery. Over and over, she slung her daughter's name out.

In public.

She was looking for Avery in public, in front of others.

Her eyes wide, filled with blankness. She didn't see him coming. Couldn't see anything. Her lips trembled, spilling a name over and over. Over and over.

Nix ran to her.

He reached down and picked her up. He wrapped his arms around his sister, like she'd done so many times with him. She shivered with fear, her skin on fire. He closed his eyes, trying to connect with his sister, send a thought, soothe her panic.

"Don't move," a man said.

Nix ignored it.

He sent an image to his sister's mind, trying to reestablish an illusion that would keep her from falling completely apart. Tried to make her believe that Avery was standing next to them.

CHAPTER FIFTY-FOUR_

*I*MPOSSIBLE.

Marcus tried not to smile.

A man of his stature, with his power, should not smile like a child. The odds were long that he'd find them at the hotel, but he had a feeling. He believed that God graced him with senses beyond the ordinary. He always had a gut feeling that told him when good things were about to happen. Something turned in his stomach, like a shot of sugar straight to his veins. He sat in the back of the car, watching the city street pass by.

With a smile.

The black Mercedes rolled to a stop. The driver ran around the front of the car and opened the back door. He reached inside, set up a pair of crutches and helped Marcus out. The whole incident took five minutes.

Marcus waved the man off, telling him to wait in the car. He'd be right out.

He didn't know what he was looking for. He needed to call it in, let those on the case handle it. It was a long shot, probably nothing. *It happens all the time,* the nurse told him on the way to the car. *Hotels get a reward for returning hospital property.*

Nonetheless, it wouldn't take much to just look, ask a few questions. He didn't know what was driving him. He hated loose ends. If he was honest, he hated losing. They beat him. Made him look like a fool. He wasn't sure, just yet, how much they'd taken from him. It could be everything.

That was why he looked.

One step inside the lobby—

THERE.

An intoxicating fire, his heart pumped full of fuel, his veins surged with pure joy, the Blood of Christ...

She was there.

She was in the lobby.

She was on her knees, begging forgiveness. Her sins weighed heavily, pressing her to supplicate right there in front of the witnesses, to cleanse her soul. She felt her redeemer coming; she knew Marcus was there, at the door.

She was ready for him.

Cali Richards had reaped the harvest. She had been to hell. She had withered to a faint shadow of a woman, the complexion of a prisoner. The color of death. The drab misery of guilt surrounded her like a toxic cloud.

Marcus moved slowly. He didn't want to scare her, not until he made his call. He speed-dialed one of his guys, speaking softly, calmly, never taking his eyes off her. Cali turned her head. First, she looked up, as if listening. Then she looked directly at Marcus.

"What are you doing?" he said.

Her eyes widened.

White, all around.

"It's over." Marcus held out his hand, stop sign. "It's over; don't run."

She didn't move.

He wasn't sure if she was breathing. He didn't feel the air shimmer, didn't feel the pulse strike the others but saw them simultaneously flinch. A fat lady turned around. A clerk dropped a pen.

People on the couch stood up. An old man and young kid entered and stood stone-still. The old man held a bagel.

Marcus adjusted the crutches, backing up a step. He wanted the driver to come inside. He couldn't leave, couldn't turn or call. But he needed someone in there, someone on his side.

"Avery?" Cali's head shook. She scuffled around the big woman, grabbing her grubby dress to move her, like she was hiding something.

Marcus cocked his head. He knew the name. He knew her file, her history. Her family.

Her tragedy.

"AVERY!" she cried, on her hands and knees. She was calling out her daughter's name.

Her appearance reflected her mind. Undone.

She was calling for her daughter. The woman's eyes were wide, crying out the name over and over.

Marcus raised his hand again. Forcefully, he called the woman's name. He got her attention and delivered the message, one that would slap her back to reality.

"Your daughter!" he shouted, cutting through the thickness.

She stopped.

"Your daughter is dead."

Frozen, again.

CHAPTER FIFTY-FIVE_

He's a demon.

Her daughter was there, holding her hand—the warmth still lingering—and now she was gone. She was nowhere. And she couldn't feel her. Avery was an independent girl, but Cali could always feel her. That's what struck her in the gut, scraped her brain and stretched her nerves. Turned her into a blank slate.

She's gone.

Cali felt it. Her daughter was gone.

She sat there, slumped on her knees, throwing her mind out to find her. Her awareness crawled through the lobby, out into the halls. It seeped into the rooms. She sensed waking minds and sluggish bodies. She felt their thoughts and knew their intentions. And none of them—NONE OF THEM WERE HER.

She shouted.

She wanted her back. A hole had opened inside her, where she used to be. The love she gave, the warmth and tenderness borne from her womb. She wanted her back.

I'm a bad mother.

"Avery!"

Bad mother!

Cali shoved the fat woman aside, crawling around her.

"AVERY!"

Marcus Anderson was saying something.

She felt him stiffen. Smelled his doubt. His fear tanged the back of her tongue like acid. She couldn't feel him, couldn't read him and his biomite-free body. He was invisible to her new breeds, but she sensed his body. And it was weak.

And she hated him.

Perhaps if he didn't hold up his hand, if he didn't say the next thing on his mind, things would've been different. Something dreadful would've happened. Cali wouldn't just be a bad mother... she would've hurt him, permanently.

"Your daughter..." he said... the words slurring in slow motion, his lips delivering the truth like a surgeon's blade... he said... "is dead."

Dead.

Dead.

DEAD.

Everything is dead.

The world is cold and empty and dead.

The world is useless.

Bad mother.

Cali didn't see anything. Felt nothing. She saw shapes but didn't recognize them.

Heard sounds but didn't know them.

Her world was dead.

It was all dead.

She felt something shift, something move. Something wrapped around her, lifted her. Her feet were wooden paddles, rocks scraping the earth. Legs were logs, arms were twigs. Cali didn't recognize her body or the one embracing her. She felt nothing.

She knew nothingness but the blizzard of static that frayed reality.

Until.

A soothing presence moved through her, eased the dullness, lightened her heart. Filled her mind.

Until she could see.

See the boy next to her.

"What's happening?" she asked her brother.

CHAPTER FIFTY-SIX_

THEY COULD RUN.

Marcus didn't have a weapon. There would be nothing he could do.

But it wouldn't matter; it would just be a matter of time now. The federal agents had downloaded the latest effects of the last episode, knew what to look for if they were influenced by Cali, knew when to call for help, hopefully blocking any attempts. At worst, they could hunt them down, wear them out, if they ran.

But they weren't running.

The woman was a sobbing mess. Reality came down hard. The table on which she rested her life just had the legs kicked out and parts and pieces that made sense to her had been scattered. She reaped what she sowed. She used the biomites to delude herself, to make believe her daughter existed, had never died.

Now look at her.

Look at her, coming undone. Her mind frayed, the seams dissolving. Perhaps she would shut herself off, now that she saw the lies. The self-inflicted lies.

Marcus stood vindicated in the hotel lobby. There, in front of him, was the proof on which he based his argument. Give humans too much power over life and they abuse it. We are children of God. We can't make those decisions for him. We can't decide when to die, how we should look, how we should think... we can't BRING BACK THE DEAD!

It doesn't work that way.

We're human. We have limitations.

We're imperfect.

Repent.

For some, perhaps, it was too late. Perhaps not.

Marcus said, "Son—"

"Shut up!" the kid snapped. "SHUT UP!"

The room fell silent. Except for Cali's sobs coming in quiet waves. Nix whispered things to her, things a mother would say to a child, things to comfort her. She probably didn't hear them, but she felt them. She was no longer hysterical.

"What do you know about us? About her? What she's been through. You can pull the file and read about her, interview others, listen to what they say... but you got no clue what she's been through. No idea what it's like."

Cali blubbered something. Her face, buried on his shoulder, her words underwater. The kid didn't understand, he just patted her head, went *shhhhhh,* like that would make her sane.

He knew the score. She was a goner. Marcus had seen people go over the edge. That was it, right there.

They weren't going anywhere.

"Police are coming," Marcus said. "We'll get you help, kid. We'll get your sister help."

Long pause. Cali quieted down.

Nix drew a sidelong glance in his direction. "Help? Is that what you call it?"

"It's what's right."

"What gives you the right to decide?"

Something twisted. "Look at her. She's an abomination. Her systems are failing. She's crashing."

"You don't know what hell is, Mr. Anderson. You don't think you'd reach for a cure if hell came to your life, but you would. When you're ground down to the bone, you'd reach."

"She thinks her daughter is alive, kid. That's not helping."

"She did the best she could. She could only take so much, she broke down."

"Life is like that."

"Then don't deny her the chance to fix it."

"She didn't fix it. We all die. That's how it works. None of us have the right to live forever."

"Some die before others."

"Always been that way. God only knows."

Marcus shifted his weight. Pain throbbed through the medicated dullness. Sweat was breaking on his forehead. The room, closing in. He needed to get off his feet but wasn't about to move, not until someone else was there.

A siren called in the distance. Not long. It would be over soon.

It was so quiet inside the lobby. The witnesses hadn't moved. They appeared catatonic. The family on the couch sat and stared. The fat lady stood behind Nix and Cali like a faded floral mountain of flesh, breathing through her mouth. Eyelids drooping.

Something beeped. It came from behind the counter. The clerk held the phone near her shoulder, staring like the others, the sound of repeated beeping telling her to hang up. Marcus looked around like he might see what happened to them, like the marionette strings lay on the floor.

"What did you do to them?" he said.

"Afraid?" Nix answered. "You're outnumbered."

"You sold your soul, kid. Don't take them with you. They haven't done anything."

"What's it matter? You'll be flipping the switch on them tomorrow or the next day, maybe next year. It's just a matter of time before you visit them."

"Is that what you think, kid? You're some kind of victim?"

"I did nothing wrong. Maybe it's the rules that are wrong. We're not hurting anyone by existing."

"You're hurting *everyone*." Marcus wobbled forward, pain radiating up his thigh, dampened by anger. "You people are the first step to the end. Change is slow, kid. Biomites are going to eat up humanity if we don't do something. We're going to give our flesh—our God-given bodies—to satisfy our desires. No, you're not hurting anyone, not now. You're not hurting anyone's feelings or breaking any bones, you're just the first step in the extinction of the human race."

"You don't know that."

"It's common sense, kid. It's logic. You've given in to your weakness, letting sin live your life."

"You don't know what we're supposed to become, Mr. Anderson. Maybe we're supposed to become this; we were given a brain to develop technology, to hone our bodies, to improve our lives, to develop our minds. Maybe we're something more than this... this skin... and maybe biomites are the bridge to another world. Maybe it's supposed to be that way."

"You're talking about heaven."

"No. You don't know why we're here or what happens when we die, no one knows that. NO ONE DOES!"

"To become that?" Marcus nodded at Cali. "Is that it?"

"She's not perfect. Neither are you."

"You were made in the image of God. Only the devil tinkers with that."

"I'm human."

"*Half.*"

"That's right." The siren was louder. "I'm half a human. But I don't deserve to die."

"Not everything deserves to live."

"Who decides?"

"God does, kid."

Cali looked around. Vacant eyes, she seemed to be seeing something else. Maybe looking for her nonexistent daughter, maybe hearing her voice. Her mouth moved silently.

"It'll be painless, kid."

She gently pushed out of Nix's embrace, still looking around like she was blind. Marcus stumbled backwards on the crutches, grimacing against the pain. His chest was tight and cold. He took several quick breaths. The siren rounded the corner. It was outside the building. He just needed to maintain until someone came inside and corralled these two. Then he could relax. Then it would be over.

Nix watched his sister. She didn't go far. She faltered. A tiny sound leaked from inside, but she held steady. She didn't run. She didn't know where she was. This world or some other that she invented, somewhere in her mind where a little girl lived.

"It's over," Marcus whispered.

Blue lights flashed through the glass doors, strobing around the walls. No one blinked.

"I know." Nix took his sister's arm. "I know."

The door opened. Someone—heavy-footed—came in behind Marcus, daring not to take his eyes off them, afraid they were just an apparition, not wanting to see them vanish.

Everyone flinched simultaneously.

Like a dance move, everyone listening to music in their heads.

Marcus turned his head. The Chicago police officer had stopped behind him. He was listening to something, maybe to the inaudible voice coming through the mic attached to his shoulder. But he looked unnatural.

Frozen.

Nix guided Cali away from them. No one noticed.

"Stop them," Marcus said, but no one heard. The officer was mired in the same biomite trap as the rest of the idiots. He needed one of the federal agents, not a goddamn cop! These two had to be stopped. They had to be shot.

Marcus grabbed his phone; he had to get the agents here, NOW! They would need to track them, follow by car and air until they could subdue them. Tranquilizers or electric shock could be used to overload their systems—

That's when the fat lady woke up.

Seconds later, Marcus's arm was pinned behind his back. No one heard him shouting.

CHAPTER FIFTY-SEVEN_

KATE FARMER HAD TROUBLE BREATHING. MORE SO THAN USUAL.

This sort of thing always happened when she was working a deal. Doctor said her blood vessels contracted when she was under stress and seeded her with a dose of muscle-relaxing biomites that were supposed to manufacture low levels of dopamine when she was working a deal, so she wouldn't be uncomfortable.

She wanted those fat-eater biomites, but they were too goddamn expensive. Besides, they weren't going to make her feel good, just skinnier. She'd been fat all her life. A hormone imbalance, doctors told her. She could get that corrected, probably didn't cost all that much, really. She always swore that was her next seed, but then there were the iris biomites that made her eyes emerald green. Those were pretty cool. And then the hair removal biomites, the ones that made all the hair on her arms, legs, and pits fall out. That was sweet.

Next, she'd correct the imbalance. Swear.

She'd do that to keep skinny bitches like the one behind the counter from thinking the thoughts she was thinking. Kate couldn't read thoughts—if there were biomites for that, she'd put that at the top of her list—but, honestly, she didn't really need to read them. She knew what people were thinking just by the look on their faces. They judged her. All skinny people judged fat ones. They didn't know what it was like to have a hormone imbalance. I mean, Kate could gain two pounds from a vanilla wafer. What does this skinny bitch know about that?

Nothing.

Right now, Kate was all worked up. She'd watched those dirty movies, just didn't feel like paying for them; they were like fifteen dollars. *Each.* She wasn't going to pay that. Besides, she didn't like the look on that girl's face.

Didn't seem like it was worth the aggravation. Kate wiped the sweat from her upper lip and gripped the counter. She just wanted to feel good, that wasn't too much to ask. Then that skinny bitch held out the phone, calling Kate's bluff; well, that really pissed her off. And then some mental case began talking on the phone and that really wedged a bolt up her ass. She was about to turn around, tell the bony meth-head to keep it down when she noticed the lady wasn't on no phone. Unless she had some communication biomite seed. She'd heard about those, biomites that took the place of a phone.

She sort of forgot about the woman behind her. She was more sick than skinny, one of those people that looked diseased, like AIDS or tapeworm. She looked worse than Kate felt, and that was low. She just wanted to feel good. Not too much to ask. She was an American citizen. She had rights.

So when the warm buzzy feeling melted through her—starting at the top of her skull and pouring inside—she relaxed. Kate's eyelids drooped in ecstasy. Whatever she was tasting, she liked. The doctor said that once her biomites synchronized with her organs and reached a certain threshold (30%, maybe) she'd feel good about everything. And this was exactly what Kate wanted.

Good about everything.

She watched skinny girl behind the counter, tapping on the keyboard, hoping she'd straighten things out. If not, no big deal.

That's what she was thinking. Kate rubbed her gums with her finger, her mouth suddenly dry.

Someone was talking.

She heard it, but distantly. It was hard to hear over the sound of static, like the ocean was rolling through the lobby. Kate imagined she was standing on a boat, listening to a waterfall. She'd been to Niagara Falls, that's what it reminded her of. They were on the boat wearing slickers, touring the bottom. Wet. The sound, deafening as they neared.

Louder.

And whiter.

Voices blurred in the static.

The skinny woman behind the counter disappeared in droplets of haze. Kate didn't notice it so much. She had melted into a puddle of buttery joy. Dry mouth. Tingly teeth.

Lost in it.

Loving it.

And then, like the boat emerging from Niagara's mist, she came out.

The warm buzziness faded, leaving behind a burning pit, a dry socket of emptiness. The skinny woman and the counter were gone. Kate was facing the doors and looking at some shriveled bald man on crutches. She didn't see the boy and the woman, only the gimpy bald man. And, somehow, she knew he was responsible for her problems. He'd deprived her of the yummies.

Didn't know why she thought that, just did. Just believed it.

Just knew that he was bad.

And that he was up to bad stuff. Like harassing that couple over there. She knew that bad baldy was pissed off at the world and harassed those good people, probably slapped the man and fondled the woman. Kate was sure of it, she remembered seeing it. And she, for one, wasn't going to stand for it.

Kate didn't back down.

Not when she felt like this.

When that cop walked in, she told him flat out what happened. That baldy was up to no good. He needed arrested.

And he got arrested.

CHAPTER FIFTY-EIGHT_

Jim Freisen was only a couple blocks from the Red Roof Inn.

He was halfway through a shift, bored out of his skull. The call was to assist federal agents in the apprehension of a couple of half-skins. He wasn't so sure why they didn't just shut them down, but whatever, he answered the call. He hit the lights and moved traffic out of the way. He loved that feeling. Hit the lights and people move.

A black Mercedes was out front, driver leaning against the hood. He jumped when Jim pulled up, front bumpers nearly touching. He killed the siren, but left the lights twirling. Jim called in his position. He was the first to arrive. This could be good. This could be nothing.

Surprise, surprise.

He looked through the front doors—appeared to be a standoff in the lobby. No weapons, no screaming or shouting or any sign of violence. Just people staring. He didn't bother resting his hand on his weapon, pushing open the door.

Sand pellets.

Like he was showered with a sandstorm, only they were invisible, like things driving beneath his skin, seeding his thoughts. Scenes flashed once, twice, clicking like channels changing. No one moved, nothing changed. It all looked the same, he just felt a little different about the people inside. He didn't know any of them.

There was just a sense of danger.

Someone was up to no good.

And then a heavyset woman was there. She stepped out of the fog and raised her arm, extra skin swinging. "HE DID IT!" she screamed. "I SAW IT! THAT BASTARD ATTACKED THOSE POOR PEOPLE! I SAW IT!"

Her arm swung to Jim's left.

There were people standing in front of a couch. A man and a woman and a young girl. They were nodding but not much else. Nodding and nodding. And then pointing where the heavyset woman had pointed. Right in front of him.

Right in front of Jim—he palmed his face, all rubbery and fat and stuffy—was a smallish man holding himself up on crutches, his right leg in a brace. He turned to look at Jim, an expression of disbelief. That's always how they looked, though. It was always *It wasn't me, I swear*. No one ever did anything.

But Jim knew, right from the start. He could feel guilt, see it on a face from a mile away. And this bastard was guilty. Gimpy or not, he'd done something and it would get sorted out.

"What are you doing?" the bald man said. He shifted away from Jim's clasping hand. "Officer, you've got it wrong. Think, son. Think how you feel right now. Someone has altered your perception through the biomites—"

Jim twisted his wrist.

"No! NO!" Baldy hopped on his good leg. Pain mixed with anger, slurring his words. "Wait! Don't move, officer. Stay here, wait for the federal agents, they'll be here in moments, they'll tell you what's happening—"

Jim didn't need to wait. He'd been a police officer for seven years. He knew how to keep Chicago safe. It started with getting self-righteous pricks off the street. These good people didn't deserve this, that's what he was thinking. And it sickened him to the point of rage when the heavyset woman told him what he'd done.

The perp struggled at first, but even with two good legs he wasn't a match for Jim. He could wrangle this guy with one hand, if needed. A little pressure on the wrist and the right twist and baldy spun right around, facing the door.

"You won't get far!" His face turned red. His scalp was inflamed. "I WILL NOT REST, YOU HEAR ME? I WILL FIND YOU! I WILL FIND YOU!"

A little extra pressure and the man was on the move. Jim didn't know who the hell he was talking to. He shouted at the corner of the lobby. It was empty over there. Clearly, he'd lost his mind, seeing things. Probably a biomite misfire. Jim had seen many of those over the last couple years; now it was biomite tweakers causing all the trouble. This guy didn't look like the type, but nothing ever surprised him.

Jim got him into the backseat of the squad car as a few more cars arrived. He wasn't going to wait to explain. He had an impulsive feeling: he needed to get this guy as far away from the hotel as fast as possible. Call it a gut feeling.

It wasn't until he was a block away that the buzz faded.

CHAPTER FIFTY-NINE_

"Keys."

Nix held out his hand, staring at the clerk. She was still in a muddled state, swimming in the frayed field of static that Nix was sending. He wasn't sure he knew what he was doing, just commanding every biomite within his range to jitter like excited atoms, disturbing their frequency, throwing them into a state of confusion.

Of static.

Including his sister.

Cali was slipping through her delusion. This day would come, Nix just always hoped they could ease into it. He expected to sit down with her and pull back the curtain a little at a time. It would be easier for her mind to accept it on its own time, but Marcus Anderson had burned the illusion to the ground, opening a trapdoor.

Cali was falling.

If he didn't catch her, she might not come back.

So now she was swimming in the same fog as everyone else. A field of nowhere.

"Car keys. There's a rental car waiting for us to pick up."

No use. He couldn't risk selectively lifting her from the morass without clarity returning to the others. The police officer had accepted the implanted thoughts as his own. He was ready to march the enemy out of sight.

Nix slid over the counter and looked around, pushing papers and folders. There, a key attached to a simple fob, by the computer. He snatched it up and grabbed Cali as she began sliding against the counter.

"Come on, easy steps," he whispered, guiding her toward the side exit that led to the parking garage. "Easy steps."

First, get her to the car. Get her out of here.

But it needed to be quickly. Nix already felt icy weakness in his knees. His neck was stiffening under the strain of controlling all the biomites around him. The back of his eyes itched. With his arm around his sister, he ushered her as fast as he could, her feet tripping on the rug. They went past the people standing outside the breakfast room and into the hall.

Marcus Anderson shouted his dire warning.

Nix knew that they may never live in peace. But, then again, when had life ever been peaceful?

CHAPTER SIXTY_

Cali and Thomas's first date was at the State Fair.

She answered the door and started laughing. They were wearing matching clothes. He wore a red shirt and white shorts. She wore the opposite. They looked in love.

Total accident.

They ended the night on the ride that spun around and pressed their bodies to the inside wall. Thomas held her hand. Cali screamed and laughed. And the world went round and round, round and round. The people on the opposite wall smudged into pastel streaks and water filled her eyes and her head went round and round.

Round and round.

And Cali went round.

She was going round.

The floor dropped out of the ride; people screamed. They were stuck to the sides. Not Cali.

She was falling.

Falling.

And there was no bottom to the ride. No end. Just a gut-dropping fall that lasted forever.

Maybe she sensed Nix holding her, guiding her along the paisley-patterned carpet and narrow hallways, through a side exit into a gray parking garage. She heard the car honk when he repeatedly pushed the fob, but she didn't recognize it as a horn or a car or anything.

Didn't feel the vinyl against her cheek.

Didn't know she curled against the backseat, fingers clawing, grasping. Trying to stop the fall, trying to cling to anything that would find solid ground.

There was no sense of leaving the dank garage or the sunlight lighting half her face or the turns or the traffic. She sensed motion but not the car's stop and go.

Just falling.

Falling.

Until she hit something. Perhaps it was bottom. But she didn't bounce. She went through it like a semisolid wall, one that lacked a real foundation, lacked studs, simply shattered on impact and allowed her through to the other side.

Cali fell into the memories that she'd capped so long ago.

CALI KNEW she wasn't special.

People suffered all over the world. They'd suffered tragedies far worse than hers. But none of that eased her pain. She'd lost all the things that mattered. If her brother did not need her, she had no reason to remain in this world. There would be a painless way to escape, somewhere in the bottom of a prescription.

But Nix needed her.

She needed to be there for him. At least until he was an adult. It wouldn't be fair to take everything from him, too. He didn't deserve that. He was so much younger than her, a surprise, her parents admitted. After Cali, they had no plans for another child. They were Catholic but didn't want the big family. They didn't do much about birth control, so fifteen years after Cali—*whap*—Nix was conceived.

Surprise!

Not that they regretted it. Her father always said it was like swimming in a cold pool: sometimes you just needed pushed in and the water would turn out just fine.

They were better parents to Nix than they were to Cali. She wasn't bitter, just noticed they were more patient, less angry. More loving. She was glad to see that because Nix, he was a good kid.

God's first jab took them away. Cali was old enough to handle that. She was a young adult. She'd found Thomas; she'd moved out and was ready to start her own family. She had a good job and a happy home. The news of their accident was a blow. And with no extended family, Nix was welcomed into their home.

Thomas was a good substitute father. A good man. From day one, he was exactly what Nix needed. He was going to be a good father. So when Avery was born, she was perfect. And their family was perfect and all the scars were erased. They weathered the storm and were stronger. Closer. Cherished each other like no other family.

No one deserved the second blow.

Cali wouldn't wish that on the devil.

The call came, the news delivered. She drove to the hospital, numb. She drove without seeing and hearing.

There was a funeral.

There were guests and flowers and condolences and tears.

And then there was silence. There was a gap inside her, a hole that could never be filled. A vacuum that swallowed her life. It hurt. It howled.

It ate her.

And Cali would not survive it. She could not live while dangling over a pit of fear, that any moment life could be raped and clawed from one's clutches. That God could be so cruel. She couldn't accept the smallness that her life had become.

There were pills. There was booze. There were mood-altering biomites that suppressed thoughts and pain. But beneath it all was the realization that all was lost. There was nothing worth living for. If not for Nix...

Cali knew about suppression therapy, that biomites could remove the memory of painful events. Research had proven that victims of tragedy resumed a normal life when trigger-memories were erased. As if they never happened. People, events, accidents... didn't matter. It could all be gone.

Just like that.

But something was wrong with that. Cali couldn't fathom erasing Avery from her life, as if she never existed. If she forgot about her daughter, if those precious moments were taken—her pink skin at birth, her first smile, first birthday—that would be like killing her all over again. And she couldn't stand another loss.

Not again.

If she were not a biomite engineer, never would it have been possible. She carefully researched the idea and found no evidence of it ever being done. Perhaps it wasn't possible. Cali wouldn't accept that. She built a lab in the basement, using all the money left from her late parents and her dear late husband. She even took money from Nix's trust fund—all of it—with the intention of paying him back. She just needed this first, and then everything would be all right.

Everything would be all right. Just the way it was supposed to be. She deserved that. God couldn't take whatever he wanted. She would be proof. The Richards family might not be impervious, they might not be strong...

But they were smart.

And Cali coded a strain of biomites with memories of her daughter. It wasn't all that difficult, really. She simply planned to erase the memory of her daughter's death and then ran the memory erasure in reverse for her revival. Avery would live just like Cali imagined she would. She would be a perfect little girl.

Cali would see her. She would feel her.

And she would have her daughter back.

On the day she prepared to seed herself, she considered not telling Nix. She was afraid he would be a voice of reason, convince her it was a bad idea. Somewhere, she knew this. But she'd run out of options. *Desperation is a convincing drink.*

Nix didn't say anything. He listened and nodded.

Perhaps he knew there was no use; she'd made up her mind. Perhaps, like an alcoholic's spouse wife, he just wanted to see the pain go away. He'd seen her wither, listened to her weep. He watched his sister's life shrivel to a dried husk.

And he wanted her to live, too.

Maybe, deep down, he knew this was a bad idea. But he was drinking from the same well, tainted with desperation.

He would support her delusion.

He watched her descend into the basement and close the door behind her. He waited for her upstairs while Cali, cheeks wet, pressed the cold tip of the seeder against the base of her skull while she thumbed through photos of her daughter.

Touched the trigger.

And darkness was no more.

CHAPTER SIXTY-ONE_

Nix had no idea what the car looked like or where it was. Luck, for once, was on his side. The taillights lit up ten stalls away: a white Ford Focus. He wasn't sure he could reach it if it were any farther.

He couldn't focus on Cali anymore, couldn't keep her biomites in whiteout, not without completely exhausting himself. Rubber scuffed over the concrete; Cali's shoes pointed behind her.

Nix stumbled into the back door. He rested a moment, out of sight from passing cars. He checked her breathing. It was shallow and slow. Completely unconscious.

Good.

Maybe her new breeds put her to sleep.

A horn echoed in the enclosure, shocking him back into action. He opened the door and pushed her into the back. No one would see her. She could sleep.

She could forget.

Nix sat in the driver's seat for a minute. Back in the lobby, everyone would return to normal. Confusion would reign, memories obscured and illogical. Eventually, someone would show up and figure out what happened. Someone would come looking for them.

Marcus Anderson would.

Nix started the car. He could barely feel the pedals.

He drove carefully out of the parking garage, took a right at the exit and waited for the GPS to show him the nearest interstate. A police car flew past. His knuckles turned white, palms slick on the wheel. He snuck a peek in the rearview, watched the cruiser's taillights ignite and felt a cold twist in his belly before it turned the corner.

The GPS's voice was female. At the next stoplight, she said, turn right.

Somewhere on I-64 South, Nix pulled into a rest stop and parked far from the other cars.

He was starving.

And tired. The adrenaline had worn off. He had to pinch his legs to stay awake at the wheel. He needed coffee but had no money. The car had half a tank of gas and it would get them through Indiana, but after that...

He got out and stretched his legs. Cali hadn't moved much. Occasionally, her nails would scratch against the seat like she was trying to claw her way into the trunk. That much told him she was alive. He wanted to open the door, listen to her breathe, feel her pulse. It would look like he was hauling a dead body.

The driver's seat was still warm. He reached over the seat and pushed two fingers against her neck. *Still warm. Still beating.*

Still alive.

He got back on the interstate. They had another three or four hours' worth of gas.

Lexington, Tennessee.

Cali sat up.

Nix's eyes flicked from the road to the mirror, waiting. And waiting. Her face, still haunted by weight loss. Cali's expression was foggy, at best. She didn't seem to look at anything in particular. Just sat there. Nix just drove.

"We're going to need gas," he said.

He didn't know what else to say. That was the most important thing on the list at the moment. Stranded on the side of the road was a losing strategy. But Cali didn't respond. Her expression didn't change. She stared into space. Maybe she didn't hear him. Nix drove another couple miles.

"We need food," she said.

Nix didn't rush his response, sensing she was processing things slowly. "We need money," he finally said.

Her head turned side to side, as if listening. "Next exit," she said.

He thought about asking what next, how they were going to pay for anything. They couldn't use a credit card. Nix, for one, didn't even have a wallet. He wasn't sure if Cali had anything in her bag. Camping in a farmer's field and eating corn wasn't going to last long.

The next exit was ten miles. There was no conversation. Cali looked no less foggy. Nix was dizzy from looking from the road to the mirror. The car rolled into a Sunoco with a Subway and stopped at one of the tanks. He threw it in park.

Cali's hand rested on the door handle. "I'll be right back."

Nix watched her methodically walk inside, like a sedated mental patient. He kept track of her through the glass wall as she walked down the aisles. He lost her somewhere on the other side. Minutes went by. He thumbed the steering wheel, debating going in.

He took a deep breath, envisioning her lying on the floor and the clerk calling 911 and the police arriving—

Never should've let her go in alone.

He grabbed the door handle. The parking lot smelled like sour beer. One foot on the pavement—

Cali pushed the door open.

It wasn't a straight line she walked, but she made it to the car. She tossed a plastic bag of food inside the car and fell in the backseat. Her head tilted back, eyes falling shut. "Fill it up."

"With gas?"

"There's thirty dollars on the pump."

He didn't bother asking how or where the food came from. No one was coming out shouting about a robbery. Nix just filled the tank. When he turned around, Cali was asleep. There was an apple in her hand, a single bite notched out of it. Nix checked her breathing, just to be sure. Then he drove off, shoving candy bars and bananas in his mouth, washing it down with water.

Cali slept until they reached the mountains.

CHAPTER SIXTY-TWO_

MARCUS WAS ONE OF THE FIRST TO BOARD.

The airline assistant wheeled him down the gateway to the plane. The stewardess smiled and tried to help. He just wanted her to get the hell out of the way. He managed to find his first-class seat, sweating through the pain, without bending his leg. There was just enough leg room to lay it out straight.

He sat back, searching for refuge in the painkilling haze. Found none. The ache consumed his entire body, pushing into his thoughts like a sliver. He couldn't sleep, couldn't get comfortable. Just in it. No escape.

"Can I get you a pillow?" the stewardess asked.

He nodded.

The police officer that arrested him came to his senses about a block from the hotel. At first, he just slowed down. Marcus had been wedged into the backseat with his hands cuffed. He couldn't lean one direction or the other without twisting his knee.

"Turn around!" Marcus shouted through the agony.

The car slowed. It finally stopped in the middle of the street. No lights, no siren. Just stopped right in the middle of traffic. His mind was trying to find solid footing. Maybe he remembered nothing or just couldn't put the pieces together; whatever it was, he was stuck.

"Officer," Marcus said, "there are two fugitive halfskins that made you believe I accosted people back at the hotel and filled you with a sense of urgency to get me out."

Marcus had to adjust his leg.

"I am a federal agent. I need you to turn the car around and return to the hotel. Everything will be explained."

The officer looked in the backseat and observed the leg and the clothing. Marcus locked eyes with him.

"Reach into my jacket, look at my wallet."

Five minutes later, they were back at the hotel. Federal agents and police officers were already at the scene. Someone found a hotel wheelchair for Marcus. Despite getting off his feet, the pain was intolerable. He remained long enough to hear from the witnesses.

They remembered nothing.

No one saw the woman and boy, or had any recollection of them entering or exiting. No evidence they even stayed there. All of them described the same experience as the police officer that hauled Marcus down the street.

White static.

The plane began to taxi.

Marcus's phone buzzed. His wife was calling. He punched the ignore button. He'd talked to her earlier that morning. The plane was fully boarded. A small woman sat next to him. She plugged her ears with headphones and opened her laptop, didn't even say hi. His kind of travel companion. As the plane taxied out of the terminal, Marcus's phone buzzed again.

He put it to his ear.

"How's the knee?" the Secretary asked.

"Wonderful. I'll be landing in a couple hours."

"Good. I'm sure Janine will be glad you're home. I read your report."

There was a long pause, like he was still thumbing through it.

Marcus had submitted a detailed report of the hotel incident that morning. If there were plans to cut him out of the loop, that report would highlight his importance.

"A little over the top, Marcus. A bit hysterical."

"Sir, you'll need to turn off your phone," the stewardess said. The woman next to Marcus closed her laptop and laid her head back, eyes closed.

"Nothing about this is hysterical," Marcus said. He cupped his mouth over the phone and spoke low. "We're talking full-scale vulnerability if this gets out. Do you know how long it will take information of this type to go viral? There are garage hobbyists that can code designer biomites if they get the right protocol. They can seed themselves. They're all looking for a way to get off Mother's radar."

"This sounds more like an anomaly. It's happened before, someone gets lucky, finds a new frequency, and Mother cues in on it. They'll be back online within weeks, Marcus. I don't want you releasing anything to the press, nothing that will shake the public's confidence. This will take care of itself."

"No."

"I hope you're not refusing a direct order."

"I'm saying no, this will not blow over. Trust me on this, this is big. We cannot sit back and let this solve itself. I want my staff doubled and put on full priority. I'll need to monitor all Internet chatter, track if she's leaking out her discovery. And, if we find them, we'll be able to access their biomites, find out what she did—"

"Sir? You need to shut your phone off."

Marcus held up a finger. The stewardess lost her happy face.

"I'm not sleeping until this is over."

He hung up and turned it off. Held the phone up so the stewardess could go on her way before others started looking and staring. Marcus stared at the wall in front of him the entire flight. The pain kept him awake. But that was good.

He didn't want to sleep.

CHAPTER SIXTY-THREE_

CALI ATE THE LAST CHUNK OF CANTALOUPE, CHEWING SLOWLY. Let the juice fill her mouth before swallowing. She sat back and looked off the veranda at the view of the mountains, remembering something someone once said.

Sour makes sweet.

She'd had plenty of sour, to the point she didn't taste the sweet. But now, one chunk at a time, she savored the release of sticky goodness. She'd been sitting at the table since the kitchen opened, one of the first to arrive. The morning was cool. She held a coffee cup with both hands just below her chin, the steam on her cheeks. The sun came up as a hot coal beyond the valley, throwing shadows over the verdant turf as it fought through the low-lying clouds.

It had been her idea to stop in North Carolina.

We're far enough, she'd said, from the backseat. *Find the Asheville exit.*

Nix hadn't argued. Exhaustion had depleted him. But when she told him to find the Grove Park Inn, he threw a fit. *Too public,* he said. *Need to find a dive, somewhere crack dealers sleep.*

Trust me.

She remained in the backseat while they drove another hour in silence. It was dark by the time they found the inn. Nix wasn't surprised there was a room waiting for them and didn't ask how she'd done it. Maybe he was too tired.

He fell on the bed, asleep. Cali stayed up. She pulled open the curtains and sank into a cushioned chair, watching the stars pop out of the sky. To anyone watching, she looked like someone enjoying the view, but it was quite the opposite. Inside, she was surfing the Internet, playing the information on her mind's eye. It was effortless, like a second language. She'd never need a computer again. Currently she was using the hotel's wireless Internet connection, but soon she'd set up a Verizon account under a false name and configure the new breeds to behave like a cell phone. She'd have access at all times.

She was thinking like a computer, speaking a binary language. She'd placed the reservation at Grove Park Inn long before they reached it. She went back to Hertz Rental Car and deleted all records of the car they were driving. Not only had it not been leased to a customer at the Red Roof Inn, it never existed. No one would ever look for a white Ford Focus.

And the ATM at the gas station? She simply withdrew from the last customer's account.

It was stealing, she was aware. And guilty. But she wouldn't continue. Just until they were settled and could create new identities. New lives. Make their own money. It shouldn't be hard.

They spent two days in the room, mostly sleeping. It took a while to get back to normal.

Or as close to normal as Cali could get.

It was the third morning that she went to the veranda and ordered cantaloupe. Nix woke up about 10:00. Cali sensed it. She followed his movements to the bathroom as he looked for her. She sent a thought.

[*Come for breakfast. You'll love the view.*]

He wasn't thrilled she was hanging out in public, but the tone of the thought gave him hope. She had teetered on the edge of an emotional abyss for days. There was still sadness in her voice, desperation in her thoughts. She could work through her realization.

Surviving was the first step.

Nix sat down across from her, a plate of eggs and bacon waiting. He was hungry but stopped and looked to gauge her condition. When she nodded, he filled his mouth. He was halfway through the food before saying anything.

"Why are we out here?" he asked.

"No one knows us. And no one is looking for us. The incident never really became a story. The feds are keeping this one quiet."

"Someone's looking." Another bite of eggs. "*He's* looking."

Cali blew across her coffee. Marcus Anderson would always be looking. She would be proactive on that front. She needed something to convince him they weren't worth the effort. They weren't hurting anyone.

They just wanted to be left alone.

"He'll stop," she said.

"How do you know?"

"I know."

She didn't mean to say it like that, it was just... she didn't have a whole lot of space for emotions; she was quick to snap. There was still a lot to sort out.

She sipped. He ate.

Truth was, she didn't know a lot of things. There were no easy avenues. There was much grief to process; she couldn't just turn off the thoughts and hope it would go away. She needed to feel the depth of her loss and grieve for the loss of a beautiful daughter and wonderful husband. The loss of so much. And the guilt for, once again, surviving when so many didn't.

So much work to do.

But, for now, there was waking up. There was her brother pushing the plate away and downing a glass of orange juice. His eyebrows had returned along with an inch or so of hair on his head.

There was even the hint of whiskers. Just an eighteen-year-old boy. A hungry one. A healthy one.

That's all she wanted.

"Thank you," she said.

He slid the empty glass onto the table and wiped his mouth. "For what?"

She nearly smiled. "I asked a lot from you when I built the illusion of… *Avery.*"

Her name was a lot harder to say than she expected. She pinched herself for showing emotion like that in public. Like that in front of Nix. *Not now. Not yet.*

"You still supported me, even though you knew it was wrong."

Nix folded his hands on his lap. He looked out across the mountains. There were no tears, no glassy eyes, but his voice was weak. "I miss her, too."

She almost lost it and hid her quivering bottom lip in the coffee cup. She sniffed, holding it together. Didn't want to make a scene, not that anyone would recognize them. If she opened that gate, it would be difficult to close.

Cali didn't have to pretend Avery was there; she didn't have to remember that she had died while she spoke to the illusion.

Nix did.

"It hurts, brother," she whispered.

"I know, but I like you better this way."

They studied the view. Drank more coffee. Nix ate another breakfast. When they were ready to go, Cali put the bill on the room that would be erased before they left. But they would stay a bit longer.

CHAPTER SIXTY-FOUR_

THE OFFICE DOORS WERE WIDE OPEN.

It wasn't that Marcus didn't close them, he just didn't lock them. The kids hit them like pile drivers, launching the doorknobs into the bookshelves as the hinges groaned. Three of the boys, William, Andrew, and Clifford, chugged into the office single file, like a juvenile train on a mission to see their daddy.

"Ho!" Marcus threw up his hands like stop signs. "Slow down there, boys!"

They lined up at the corner of the grand desk, snickering. Marcus pulled at the edge of the laptop, turning the screen away from them. Not that they knew what any of it meant. It was just habit.

"Now, one at a time," he said. "What do you want?"

They didn't want anything, really. Half-dressed on a Saturday, the boys wondered what their daddy was doing. And to see if they could use his wheelchair. That was the deal. When he was sprawled out on the bed, they could take turns running each other up and down the hallway if—and only if—the housekeeper was there to supervise. Marcus was supposed to be walking on his reconstructed knee, not pampering it with the wheelchair.

The physical therapist could kiss his ass.

William started off with, "Sir, uh..."

Marcus's leg was still braced and stuck straight out, supported by the wheelchair's bracket. William nervously pinched at his dad's big toe. It tickled, but the young man's cold fingers felt good.

"Sir," he started again, "can we use the wheelchair, please?"

"Does it look like I'm using it?"

They nodded, straight-faced. They were old enough to interpret their dad's expression correctly. It was not time to play.

"Have you done your chores?"

"Yes, sir," the three of them said.

"Good. Brushed your teeth?"

"Yes, sir."

"Well, do it again. Teeth can't be too clean."

They didn't really need to brush their teeth, he just ran out of things to say. Their faces slumped. Even William's.

"Tell you what, I'll let you take the chair for a ride after lunch."

He patted Clifford on top of the head, stiffly.

They cheered. Ariel, the housekeeper, corralled them before they stormed out. They weren't going to brush their teeth. No big deal. Ariel closed the doors behind her, without having to be asked. Too bad she didn't lock them.

He turned the sound up on the TV, waiting to hear a story on Cali and Nix. So far, there was none. They'd done a good job keeping it away from the press. He needed to give his staff a bonus; they'd made his life easier, giving him time to make sure this never happened again.

Once he had some documents prepared and had his team ready, he could make a convincing argument for new halfskin thresholds. Clearly, they were waiting too long to detain and observe. He would propose detainment start at 30%, perhaps a weekend check-in arrangement. Extreme, yes. Some would argue it was the beginning of a new-age holocaust, but cancer has to be cut out to be cured.

Marcus knew how to bargain. Start high. His proposals would strike fear in the biomite industry and force them to slow down, force them to conform to the government's regulations. There had to be a precedent that anyone tinkering with biomite transparency would be dealt with swiftly and firmly. There would be no compromise.

Marcus would not rest until Cali and Nix were apprehended, until he had their biomites analyzed. Until those outlaws were shut down.

That's a promise.

Part of his proposal would include an increase in his operating budget to expand his staff. More agents trained for this sort of confrontation. Also, research to develop biomite resistance to outside influence. Ideally, they needed more purists like Marcus, but he was a realist. They wouldn't have many candidates to choose from if that was the requirement. Besides, if he was honest, the enhancement of biomite-seeded agents was nice. His men were stronger, faster and smarter. Hypocritical, sure. He chose to fight fire with fire, as long as he wasn't the one getting burned.

And when Cali and Nix were located and detained—not if, but *when*—he would know the exact coding that knocked them off of Mother's map. They would have that, and that, he knew, would sway his superiors more than anything. Invisibility was something that should be reserved for the government.

He'd already arranged for global scanning of facial recognition and personal asset activity. So far, Cali and Nix had completely abandoned their house, bank accounts, automobile... *everything*. He didn't expect them to come back. But Cali's hallucinatory re-creation of her daughter proved a lapse in judgment. He hoped, on the outside chance, they'd make that one swipe of a credit card, that one withdrawal that would give them a lead.

The doorknob turned. Marcus was about to shout at the kids. He'd make them go outside and play if they came asking again, but his wife stepped inside. He preferred that she knock before marching inside, but it was her house, too. Janine dropped a stack of papers on the desk.

"I need you to sign these."

"What is it?"

"Refinancing on the house. Remember? We talked about this a few months ago."

He flipped the top page. "I'll read them later."

"Just sign, Marcus. I've already been through them."

He never signed anything without reading, even those contracts that came with software where you just click the box and hit OK. He read those, too. Even if his wife said she read the papers and said it was all right, he read them.

"How's the knee?" she asked.

"Better."

"Have you done your exercises?"

"This morning."

She waited, hands on hips. No makeup, just frumpy sweatpants and a loose T-shirt that jiggled without a bra. She looked heavier. Each inhalation pressed her nipples against the fabric. Marcus looked back at the papers.

The laptop sounded off with an email. He itched to look.

"I've got a conference call in ten minutes with a congressman that's interested in hearing what I'd like to propose. I promise, right after that, I'll go through these and sign them."

Janine deflated, dropping her chin on her chest. Her gut pushed out. She was preparing to launch a verbal attack. He'd seen that posture before, she was just lining up the words like bullets. She gazed out the bay window.

Here it comes.

"What're you doing?" was all she said.

He waited for the rest. Instead, she looked at him. Her brow was not stiff, lips not thin. There was nothing there, no expression at all. Like she'd given up, maybe.

A cold quiver stabbed him.

"What do you want?" He threw his hands up. "You want me to stop working, is that what you want? This isn't a forty-hour-a-week job, Janine. I don't punch a clock; I can't just take off when I feel like it. You don't even know what the hell happened, but I can promise you I can't leave it on the desk for tomorrow so I can watch William hit a home run or Alexander ride his bicycle with no hands. The world depends on me, Janine. *On me.*"

He thumbed his chest, a reminder of whose career ranked higher.

"Everything depends on me right now, Janine. You have no idea. So have Ariel watch the kids. That's why we pay her."

Janine didn't move. Still expressionless, she listened. Even looked like she was holding her breath. A series of nods were the first sign that she'd even heard him. She turned around, hands still planted on her hips, and paced away. Marcus, silently, thanked his good fortune. He glanced at the email icon in the corner. He reached for the mouse.

Janine didn't leave the office. She faced the bookshelves near the exercise bicycle, looking up. Thinking. This was unusual for her. Too passive. Was she giving up?

He opened the email. It was short. He read it twice, not understanding.

I can find anything. Leave us alone.

He didn't recognize the username, CNN, no one in his address book that he could remember. He didn't subscribe to that liberal news outlet and it was certainly no one he corresponded with. He had a very good spam filter, but occasionally one would slip through. This one had an attachment, something he certainly wouldn't open. The pointer hovered over the trash icon. He looked at the username again.

CNN.

C and N.

The attachment was an .AVI file.

He downloaded it through virus protection. It came up clean.

Janine was still there, still thinking. Still quiet. Still looking up.

Marcus opened the video file.

At first, he was confused. He looked at Janine, then over her head at the books on the top shelf, then back to the video.

Finally connecting the dots.

Marcus turned the sort of gray that a dead man wears beneath the mortician's makeup.

Fear stabbed him once again, freezing everything inside.

He closed the laptop.

It was a long time before he spoke again.

CHAPTER SIXTY-FIVE_

THE HORSESHOE CRAB LAY STILL, HALF BENEATH THE RECEDING wave. The tide was going out, leaving behind ocean detritus to bake in the South Carolina sun. The spiny ridge glistened along the domed shell as saltwater ran off.

A flower—yellow petals with a burgundy center—fell and stuck to the shell. The next wave knocked it off.

Cali clenched the flowers in both hands. Her toes sank in the sand as the water washed it from under her feet. When she was little, long before Nix was born, they lived on an island not too far from there. She remembered seeing—every morning when she looked for sand dollars with her mother—the beached horseshoe crabs, dead and dying. They'd flip them over and, sometimes, see a dead carcass stinking beneath.

A living fossil, her father would say about the horseshoe crab. *One of the only things still alive that has fossils dating back 500 million years.*

Cali wondered how they were living when they seemed to die so easily.

She wondered if a horseshoe crab cared when it died.

Some kids screamed in the waves. Judging by their sunburns,

they were on vacation. She did the math and figured they were Avery's age. If she was still alive. She would do the math like that whenever she saw kids. She'd do it for some time to come.

The curtain had been lifted. No more giggles. No more hugs.

Avery is gone.

She'd been gone a long time.

Cali remembered laying daisies where she was buried. She'd picked them out of a neighbor's yard. Didn't ask, just wandered through and grabbed a bundle. No one stopped her from such eccentricities, not when they knew what happened. They looked much like the flowers she was now dropping into the water, watching the waves drag them out.

Watching them go to the ocean.

Watching them disappear. Forever.

Nix's shadow covered the horseshoe crab. He remained silent until the last flower fell. It stuck on the sand. The next wave pushed it between Cali's toes. It bobbed in place, waving at them until the wave receded. The foam took it under. The color paled beneath the green wash.

"I've got some food." Nix held out an apple.

Cali took it. She picked at the sticker and shined the red skin with her thumb.

"You okay?" he asked.

She nodded. "Yeah."

She took a bite and smiled. She said, once she swallowed, "You say hello to Raine for me?"

"Not yet."

Guilt kept him from meeting her eyes when she brought up the dreamland. After all, he still had his delusion. Long ago, he had told her all about the lagoon—the crystal water and black sands, the funneling waterfall and clear sky. And his beautiful girl. His best friend.

She knew what he was thinking. She could have that, too. Cali could create her own lagoon inside her head. The new breeds could make it as realistic as the sand beneath her feet, the water on her toes. The flowers in the water. She could have anyone there.

And I would never leave.

She'd had enough of illusions. She'd fooled herself for all these years; it was time to live right here and now. Perhaps there was nothing wrong with Nix's lagoon. He insisted there was something more to it, that it wasn't just a lucid dream.

Delusions, though, can be pretty convincing.

"You sure you're all right?" Nix asked.

Nod.

"You want to come in, grab some dinner?"

The sun touched the horizon. "Think I'll go for a walk first."

"You sure you should be out like this?" He looked around like Marcus Anderson might be on vacation down the beach. "I mean, shouldn't we lay a little... lower?"

Cali reached down and plucked a flower out of the water that rode a wave in. She tucked it behind Nix's ear. She touched his cheek, the stubble rough on her hand. She remembered when he was little, when his face was smooth. When he needed her. Her brother was like her child before there was Avery.

"No one will ever come looking for us, brother."

She almost smiled. Smiling, though, was a long ways away.

Nix didn't ask about Marcus Anderson again. Whatever she did, he believed her. With Cali, nothing was impossible.

She walked along Folly Beach by herself. A beach known as the Edge of America.

A place where she was scared to death.

Where she would be for quite some time.

CHAPTER SIXTY-SIX_

Nix lay back.

All it took was closing his eyes, like going to sleep. Only he didn't drift into unconsciousness, he stayed awake for the ride.

Like falling down a long dark hole.

At some point, it didn't feel like falling. He couldn't exactly decide when motion stopped. It just became normal. And then he didn't feel the pillow or the couch. He never once felt like he left his body, only transitioned from the physical world to dreamland.

Like stepping through a door.

He heard a macaw. Palm fronds rustling. The roar of the waterfall, somewhere out there.

Water lapped his toes. Nix felt the weight of his eyelids but kept them closed. Instead, he savored the green scent of the jungle and the salty breeze. *The lagoon is alive.*

The new breeds brought it to life, opened his senses. Or clarified his connection. Whatever it was, there was no discernible difference between his two worlds. He imagined brightly colored fish—gold, yellow, and orange—with long tails and spiny fins.

He opened his eyes. There, near his feet, was exactly what he'd pictured. He waded deeper, sank his hand in the water and let them nibble on his fingers. He floated on his back, tasted the seawater on his lips, and felt the fish tickling his back as he paddled along the shallow water.

It was possible that his sister was right: the lagoon was a construct of his mind. He had gone way beyond a halfskin. A part of him was still organic, but he'd stopped checking just how much.

There was no going back.

He flopped his hair out of his eyes. A spent fire was on the beach. Charred logs sat among a gray bed of ash. Nix dripped on the ring of stones.

Raine?

She was usually waiting for him. He closed his eyes and imagined her there, bare feet digging in the sand. Skin bronze.

But nowhere.

Weird.

Nix walked the beach, tempted to shout her name. Words were as good as thoughts at the lagoon. He thought he saw her paddling in from the ocean, but it was just the sun reflecting off the waves.

A subtle feeling of panic clenched inside. He'd never considered the lagoon without Raine. Never had to. If she wasn't there, what was the point? But that was impossible.

Why isn't she here?

He continued along the sand until he reached the ocean inlet, where white-crested waves ate away at the sand bars that protected the lagoon. The horizon was flat and endless.

He thought he heard her shouting, convinced it was a wave slapping the sand. Maybe a bird. He shaded his eyes and looked toward the soaring blue cliff, wet with mist.

"Hey!"

It was distant, just an audible bump in the water's roar.

Nix squinted.

Something was at the base of the cliff, just above the trees where the earth sloped down to meet the jungle. It was boxy. The top was angular and shiny. A metal roof, perhaps. Yes. Yes, it was. *A house. A blue and green house with a copper roof built into the side of the cliff.*

And, there, just below it was someone waving.

Raine waved him to come to her, to join her in the home he never once saw, certainly never imagined. And yet, there it was.

And there she is.

Nix dove into the water, stroking his way across the lagoon in the company of the brightly colored fish.

Perhaps, he thought as he climbed the opposite shore, making his way up a narrow path, *falling trees do make sound in the lagoon when I'm not around.*

MOTHER_
BEHIND CLOSED DOORS

Janine Anderson loved her children. Loved her career.

But never her husband.

He was a safe bet, that's what he was. Janine was not a gambler. She knew, the day she met him at a conference for medical technology, that he was a sure thing: connected to politicians and dedicated to his work.

He was deep into his forties and, if she gambled, would bet he never would've married had she not asked him out to dinner. Even then, their marriage was more like a business arrangement. She wanted children and he wanted someone to take care of him, legally as well as maternally.

Not a match made in heaven.

So it was no wonder she'd had enough. She knew what she was getting into when she struck the agreement, knew any attraction between them—usually fueled by a bottle of wine—wouldn't last the length of their agreement. She couldn't blame him, really. Maybe that was her fault. She figured she was the one falling on the ugly grenade, not him.

Maybe she overestimated herself.

One thing was certain, she was not innocent. She'd sought relief from their emotionless arrangement, as dry as a sandbag. She accepted the fact there was dirt on her, that if he got wind of Janine's sexual preference (Helen was a very, *very* good friend) and occasional dalliance, she'd lose everything in a divorce. Marcus wouldn't want the children, but he'd take them because he was cold-blooded. He liked to win.

So did she.

That's why their arrangement seemed like such a good idea, in the beginning. They shared the blood of reptiles.

And that's why she installed the cameras.

He was a Washington insider. His office was his inner sanctum, off-limits to everyone in the family for the purposes of national security. She had never suspected anything of a perverted nature, nothing she could pin on him during a divorce. He played politics as dirty as any of the elected, but in marriage he was as clean as a virgin. No cussing, drinking, or smoking.

There was never a reason to suspect Marcus even had a pulse around women. But Janine always remembered Justine.

She was young and slender. Her blouse was unbuttoned one too many, revealing the crack of voluptuous breasts. Janine was distracted and a bit irritated by such a rash display, and the fact that she couldn't stop looking. But the warmth that lit Marcus's cheeks was revealing. He had a pulse, after all.

His gaze lingered on her full lips and caught sight of her display when she looked away. At first, Janine chalked it up to masculine lust triggered by a pair of balls, filling him with an urge against his will. Not that he acted on it, but it was there.

Who would guess?

Just in case it was more than that, she scanned his emails for flirtatious correspondence. But nothing. Taped phone calls. Still nothing. Even hired a private investigator that turned up... *nothing*.

Maybe she guessed wrong. Maybe he was a man that controlled

his appetite. After all, it wasn't disloyal to think about sex. But she couldn't stand around with nothing for long. She wanted out. She wanted a life, her life and all that was in it.

Minus Marcus.

So a camera was installed in the office.

She did it herself. It was the size of a marble that fit into the binding of a book that sat on the top shelf, the pages hollowed out to hold its components. A motion sensor turned it on, wirelessly streaming to her laptop. She tested it multiple times while he was in Chicago. His first night back, he locked himself inside to Skype a meeting. She went into the bedroom and watched him argue at the monitor for an hour.

After that, she only watched the recorded bits at the end of the day, and that she did in fast-forward. Each one more boring than the next. It was the fifth day that things got interesting.

The fifth day he was sitting back in the wheelchair, apparently sleeping, when he looked up. Looked around. He wheeled to the door and checked that the deadbolt was in place. A lock that couldn't be undone with a key. A lock that ensured privacy.

Janine sat up.

Watched him wheel back to his desk.

He closed the curtains, checking all the gaps were secure. That he was alone.

That no one could see.

He spun around—

Nothing.

The streaming cut out. Clipped like an edit. Like something—or someone—had tampered with the video. At first she went cold with fear. He knew. He'd found out somehow and destroyed some evidence. But what didn't make sense was that all the rest of the records were still there. It just stopped at that point.

How convenient.

She would have to check the feed and always make sure it was still there. That it was still working.

But not until he was gone. Perhaps install a backup while she was at it. If he was up to something—and he was—she would catch it. Eventually, she would catch it.

What she didn't know was that her equipment worked just fine. That the video was indeed clipped from the stream and downloaded to the memory of another computer, one that consisted of new-breed biomites seeded into the brain of a woman hundreds of miles away. A woman that had been snooping through their computers, their finances, and pictures and documents until she found what she was looking for.

Quite a home run, it was.

Unfortunately, she did not see her husband reach into the upper right drawer, where a secret compartment was installed deep under the desktop, and retrieve a cube. She didn't see him hold it gently, tenderly, stroking the edges and corners: a cube he'd acquired in Amsterdam, by accident, really. She would remember the trip if he told her.

It was a conference on biomite perversity, how the porn industry was using biomite technology to enhance orgasms and sexual prowess. It was the basis of some of his best arguments, how biomites contributed to the depravity of the human race. He'd be lying if he said there was never a stir in his groin when he saw some of the images, lying if he said he was shocked at how they were using technology.

He truly and honestly had no idea they could do that.

It was just so... real.

It was during that trip he'd acquired the cube that would be with him for years to come. An item he kept hidden, even though its use was of no consequence to the naked eye, to the unknowing observer. A cube that went everywhere with him. Because he was lonely, if he was honest. His life was dry and empty. He needed something to cope, something to manage the emotional isolation he found inside his house. In his life.

He placed it on the edge of his desk and wheeled away from it. It wasn't cheating. It wasn't real. It wasn't flesh.

He laid his head back, watching through slits as the cube unfolded.

Watched the biomite cube expand like magical origami. Watched metallic color turn fleshy, digits turn to fingers and toes. Watched an unfolding lump smooth its rough edges into sumptuous curves and crossed legs.

Janine would never see the biomite perversion cube walk across the room in high heels, watch her husband lay his head back and close his eyes. She would never know this addiction.

Unless he broke his promise to the culprit that clipped that video. If he did, he had more to worry about than his wife.

BOOK 2_

CLAY

NIXES_

Through our body, we know the universe.
An incompetent vessel, it is.

MOTHER_
FABRICATING A BETTER WORLD

Ned Peterson sat in the third row, center stage. The set was black and empty except for a small table, also black, with a large box beneath a heavy blanket. Something inside moved with mechanical precision.

The kids around him were in their mid-twenties, maybe thirties, erupting with nerdgasms. There were thousands of them. Ned was polite but didn't talk much. He never came to product launches; this was his first and probably his last. But he didn't want to be distracted by theatrics.

If the rumors were true, this would change the world.

Ned taught high school students the basic manipulation of their initial biomite seeds: how to increase intelligence and inspire creativity. He wanted them to use their gifts to better humanity. His students, on the other hand, just wanted to initiate Dreamland experiences and thought-chat.

Ned was about to find the bathroom when a beam of light engulfed the mystery box. There was applause and standing ovations. When nothing happened, silence settled. Ned sensed a subtle drone in the background, a low baritone that amped the anticipation.

A puppy bolted from stage left and raced across the stage.

Laughter rumbled through the auditorium. The floppy-eared black puppy skidded to a stop, paws hanging over the edge of the stage, and searched for a way down. Then piddled on the floor.

Another spotlight knifed from above, this one illuminating a slender figure that stepped out from stage right. This time, the entire room erupted. They were on their feet, applauding and cheering.

Ned was forced to stand.

The iconic figure didn't recognize his fans with his usual wave. Instead, he strode in front of the small table and towered over the puppy now prancing in a circle.

"Accidents happen," Allen Smith said, scooping up the puppy.

While the crowd continued, silent assistants placed a chair by the table and wiped up the dog's accident. Allen Smith sat down and crossed his legs. The puppy climbed up the front of his black turtleneck to lick his face.

And the mystery box continued to churn.

Allen Smith cleaned his round spectacles while the crowd settled. He remained calm even after the room was relatively quiet. The puppy curled up on his lap and he scratched it behind the ears.

The crowd waited.

"Over the past twenty years," he finally said, with little effort, "we have brought human-augmented technology to unprecedented heights. Our company is solely responsible for biomite stabilization. We curbed runaway replication and allowed humanity to control their biomites. Thought-chat is more common than texting. Internal audio has replaced the need for external speakers. We've increased memory storage like internal hard drives, initiated group thinking and collective IQ. We are on the cusp of developing augmented dreamworlds that will generate new realities inside the mind. Quite simply, we've made better humans."

Allen Smith looked up and delivered his trademarked line.

"What else can we do?"

This was greeted with raucous cheers. Ned sat quietly, perhaps the only spectator not moved by Allen Smith's theatrics. Pomp and circumstance were not substitutes for substance.

Allen Smith put the puppy down and paced to the left. He folded his hands and walked meditatively. The crowd couldn't contain its enthusiasm. Allen Smith, characteristically, ignored them. He continued walking with measured steps until he reached the left side of the stage and turned around. The puppy followed him to the right.

He returned to the center and stood next to the table. He held his reflective pose, gazing at the floor. The puppy sat by his side.

"What else is there?" he asked sincerely this time. "For twenty years, we have seeded biomites into our bodies to support life, to bring it more vitality, greater longevity and infinite potential. People, we sit on the precipice of creating imaginary universes and unheard-of genius."

Assistants scurried out with a short set of steps and placed them in front of the table. Some spectators muttered. Ned was riveted to his seat.

"People, we were made in the image of God. And now we can follow in His footsteps. I don't want to simply support life anymore."

He grabbed the blanket.

"I want to create it."

Beneath the blanket was a glass case that contained silver rods that moved like mechanical fingers preparing magic, circling around an inanimate object.

Allen Smith was expressionless. The puppy, however, climbed the steps to investigate what looked like another puppy, this one white.

The crowd murmured. Ned hoped they wouldn't stand. He gripped the armrests like he was on the edge of a cliff.

The silver rods twirled around the white puppy one last time; mist emitted from microscopic nozzles embedded along ridges inside the box. Everything folded up and collapsed to the bottom.

There was just the white puppy.

Allen Smith didn't wait for quiet. Even he knew, at this juncture, that silence would not return. He tapped the front of the box and the glass pane opened. Ned barely heard what Allen Smith said next. His heart was thudding, his ears ringing.

The white puppy moved its head. It looked at Allen Smith. A lull of stunned silence fell on the room. The white puppy stepped onto the steps and hesitantly climbed down. The puppies collided and rolled in rollicking puppy fervor.

The crowd found its breath.

"Ladies and gentlemen," Allen Smith said, "I bring you the world's first fabricator."

The magic words were spoken.

Ned was the first one to stand, his meaty palms applauding. The crowd joined him, tears streaming down their cheeks. Some would not sit again.

And Allen Smith, uncharacteristically, smiled.

CHAPTER SIXTY-SEVEN_

It's raining in Seattle.

Imagine that.

Jamie pulls up her collar. Her stocking cap is already wet. A drum solo bangs through her auditory implants while droplets drift around a streetlight halo, reflections stretching across wet asphalt. A lone red light at the end of the dilapidated pier is dismal. Across the water, Christmas lights smudge the horizon.

She can smell the harbor.

Charlie's at a metal door that's flush against a brick wall, corrosion spattered over the surface like paint flung from a brush. His dark form casts a dim shadow. In situations like this he used to shuffle back and forth. He couldn't stand deserted streets and dark alleys, said they made him jumpy. He would have to talk to himself to keep from freaking. That was before he changed.

The door cracks open.

Charlie stands still, almost inanimate, staring at the paint chips. Someone peeks through the widening slice of light. A dirty blonde puts her face in the gap, her eyes darting around. She squeaks when she sees Charlie, the psychopath.

Jamie calls up her music.

The haze looks like the night sky is falling, making the world feel dark and small. Green lines run across her vision, identifying the Puget Sound and the abandoned warehouses. She had downloaded the names of the empty buildings and lonely streets in this derelict section of Seattle, home to rats and mosquitoes.

Jamie looks at her boots, the steel toes scuffed down to the metal. Only the music keeps her from running.

"Hey." Charlie tugs on her sleeve. "Turn it down."

Jamie rolls her head and thought-chats the volume down. Her eardrums throb and the auditory vacuum rings in her head. The door is closed.

"Did you turn off your field augments?" Charlie squeezes her arm.

"Just running audio."

"I told you not to."

"I'm not, relax."

"That's a deal-breaker. No one's allowed to run a perception field inside."

"I'm not, Charlie. I'm cold off."

"These people don't play, babe. It's just this one shot. They don't like you or you don't play by the rules, then you watch from the outside."

He cups her cheek, rubbing the smooth skin behind her ear. His eyes have become bluer and sharper. They used to be pinkish around irises of dull gray. He hardly blinks anymore, like he sees with X-ray vision, right inside her.

Where it aches.

"You take the pill?" he asks. "You'll feel better if you do, just until we get inside. It'll be good. You'll see. After that…"

"Charlie, I don't want to do the pill, okay? I'm all right, serious. I'll go in cold off."

"One pill, babe." He digs deep in his coat pocket and pinches a dirty white tablet. "It's a onetime deal. You won't need them after this. I promise."

Drugs were old school. Chemical addictions took forever to kick. She'd rather go cold off than swallow a pill. But Charlie used to do pills before he changed. Now he doesn't.

He's got those razor-blue eyes that tell her it's going to be all right.

"Promise?" she asks.

He holds it to her lips and pushes it inside her mouth with his tongue, wet and warm. The pill sticks to her throat, a chalky residue spreading inside her cheeks. She works up enough saliva to get the lump down but not the taste.

Charlie opens his coat and draws her in. She puts her arms around him, feeling his warmth, inhaling the essence that is Charlie. He protects her from the rain.

"You sure you want to do this?" he whispers.

"Of course. Why?"

"No going back. If we get caught, it's all over. Lights out."

"I know."

"I just want you to decide."

Jamie buries her face inside his coat, her cheek against his chest. His heart beats in her ear, filling the silence. He rocks her back and forth.

Somewhere, a ship moans.

Charlie keeps looking at the door. It's taking too long. There's no handle to pull; it only opens from the inside. Only on invitation. The minutes pile up. Her stocking cap is cold and the pill isn't working. She can't remember the last time she went cold off for this long. Music is always in her ears and video feeds her vision.

The tendons flex on Charlie's neck. He swallows hard. Each second sows doubt. She's not charred, not like Charlie was. Her biomites aren't overworked and burned out. If this doesn't work, though, it won't be long.

The sliver of light returns. The girl pokes her head out like before. She might be nineteen, like Jamie, but hard living makes her look thirty. Her skin is blotchy and her hair knotty. The rims of her eyes are red.

She impatiently gestures; Jamie comes closer. The dirty blonde's fingernails are chewed down to the nubs. Jamie's fingernails still have candy blue polish on them. The dirty blonde presses her clammy palm against Jamie's wrist.

"Forty-nine point nine," she mutters. Her front tooth is discolored.

Jamie yanks her hand back. If the girl read Charlie's visible biomites, it would be 49.9%, too. And so would everyone behind that door. Jamie didn't come for visible biomites. She came for the other kind, the ones Charlie got a month ago. The ones the government can't see.

Nixed biomites.

The dirty blonde's stare goes unfocused. She's silently chatting with someone, the circuitry of her biomite-enhanced brain wirelessly networking with others. It's bright white behind her, like nothing exists in there. It's supposed to be a dance club. Jamie shuffles back.

Charlie hangs on.

"Okay." Dirty blonde pushes the door open and steps back.

A cold shank of fear keeps her legs from moving. She thought this would be easier, thought she'd go running inside when it came time. Charlie leans in, his breath warm in her ear. He nuzzles against her neck, kissing it gently.

"It's all right," he says. "I promise."

He holds her hand and walks inside, not letting go even when the white light swallows him. He's a bleached figure, smiling back, hanging on, pulling her toward the light. Toward hope.

Towards a promise that things will feel better.

The warehouse dance club explodes out of the white.

Laser lights fire at bodies that are slammed tight and bouncing to an endless techno-rhythm that ripples over her skin. Charlie pulls her through a crease in the crowd. His military coat looks brand new: clean, pressed, and sparkly. It didn't even look that good when he stole it. Jamie pulls her stocking cap off. It's clean and toasty. Smells like fabric softener.

The dirty blonde looks back, only she isn't so dirty. Her hair shines like gold, her complexion smooth and tan. Her eyes are clear blue, all white, no red. She smiles a perfect smile and Charlie follows, pulling Jamie through the party that smells like an evergreen forest. It reminds her of spring.

They walk for several minutes, occasionally passing booths tucked deep into corners where skin heaves in and out of the dark: elbows and knees, thighs, and shoulders.

Everything unblemished, perfect.

Augment, baby. Biomites make life worth living.

They reach a horseshoe-shaped booth in one of a thousand corners. It feels like the back of the club, but there's no wall in sight. Blondie gestures like a game-show host. Charlie slides in first.

"Can I get you anything?" Her voice reverberates in Jamie's head.

"You can turn that shit down?" Jamie says.

Blondie sneers like synthesized dance beat is Mozart and how dare she. But then the volume drops until it's barely a whisper above the ringing in Jamie's ears. She knows it's still pounding a rhythm inside everyone else's heads.

Charlie holds up two fingers—two drinks—and Blondie melts into the crowd.

"Don't insult him," he says.

"Who?"

"The guy running this place."

"Charlie, the music is ear shit."

"Just..." He takes her hand. "You're here, babe. You're knocking on the door, let's not piss anyone off. All right?"

He strokes the back of her hand. Before, his fingers would've been twitching with all these people, all this stress. Now he comforts her. The thing is, she really should hate this music. She knows that its computer-generated sound bites manufactured for brainless mobs, but it's getting inside her, making her hungry for more. She forces her feet to remain still, to keep her head from bobbing. She'd never forgive herself.

"His name is Cee," Charlie says. "All this is his field."

"All of this?"

"Everything you see and hear. Everybody is experiencing his perception field. That's why you can't run your field—you have to commit to his. You feel it, right? You feel the music?"

She refuses to answer. Does he know what she's thinking? Was she tapping her toe? Charlie's not nodding; he's bouncing his head to the rhythm. He feels it, too. *He likes it.* If he pulled her onto the dance floor, she's not sure she could resist.

"How's he do it?" she asks. "How's he making other people see his field?"

"It's the power of halfskin."

"But everyone is experiencing *his* field. That's just..."

The perception field is a personal thing. Jamie had auditory augments; she could change the color of her eyes or release serotonin into her bloodstream, she could roll identifier script through her vision to see maps or read someone's name, but she couldn't make someone else experience it. And not an entire club.

"He's almost a brick," he says.

"Impossible."

"Yeah. They say he's like 99.9% biomite." He bites his lip, looking at the dancing. "He's only a tenth of a percent clay."

A tenth organic? Would that even be human?

Red, blue, and green lasers fire in all directions. The partygoers try to catch them. There's an island bar not far away, and in the occasional gap in the crowd Jamie sees the lurkers watching the madness. Most of them are chatting up women wearing tiny skirts or transparent blouses over hard nipples.

One guy leans back on his elbows. He doesn't like the music.

Blondie drops off two drinks and a plate of nachos with melted cheese. She holds a metallic pill between long, polished fingernails and flicks a knowing glance at Charlie. He acts like she didn't just chat him.

The pill settles between the drinks.

"What's that?" Jamie asks.

"The answer."

The pill is hexagonal, silver on one side and white on the other. "No more pills, Charlie."

"That's not what you think. They don't seed nixes through a gun anymore, that's old-school shit. Just swallow the pill, the nixes integrate. I thought it was bullshit, too. Look at me now."

He smiles. This time she sort of cringes. His smile looks like everyone else's: all shiny and happy.

"How'd you pay for it?" she asks.

He takes a long swallow. "The drinks are complimentary."

"No, how'd you pay for the..." She swallows, nervous to say it out loud. "The nixes."

His foot stops dancing to the endless beat. He's looking at the dance floor but doesn't see it. She can't believe she didn't ask this question earlier. When he said he was going to talk to a man about this, she was scared he'd never come back. She was happy to see him, happy that it worked, that he wasn't dead. Happy that there was hope. So when he promised she could have the same thing, that she could save herself from becoming charred, she didn't ask what it cost. Whatever the price, it was worth it.

But watching the mindless dance craze and perfect smiles makes her stop.

"Charlie?"

"Yeah?"

"How did you pay for this?"

His jaw clenches. "We don't have a choice, Jamie."

"That's not what I asked."

"I made arrangements."

Suddenly, she's not digging the music. The colors feel bland. Everyone feels like mice on a churning wheel. Jamie tries to engage her field, open her music, and scan the crowd, but she can't override the club's perception field, the bodies still happy and perfect.

"If I didn't do it, I'd be charred the rest of my life. If you don't do this, you will be, too." He slowly turns the glass of beer, leaving rings on the table. "We're nineteen, Jamie. You're sitting at 49.9%. You're maxed out, no more biomites. Another year and you'll char, just like me. You'll be left with hard feelings, babe, with sixty-plus years of hard feelings ahead of you."

He looks up.

"So what choice is there? They told me what it would cost, I paid it. We need to be halfskin to cope. This place is giving us the chance. It's the only way. You know I'm right."

Jamie pulls her hand away. "What's the price?"

"Just helping out, that's all we have to do."

"You signed us up for favors?"

"No. We just work for the club until the debt's paid, that's all."

"What kind of favors?"

"You got to understand, becoming nixed halfskin is expensive. We could flip burgers for twenty years and not have enough money. I did what I had to do."

"What kind of favors?"

Blondie knows what kind of favors. She's working off debt, too. That's why she's answering a back-alley door and serving drinks while everyone else is having a good time. Does she even know what she looks like when she opens that door? Would she love this music if she stepped outside?

Does she ever leave?

Jamie knows what kind of services indebted halfskins do. If you can't pay, you puppet. You deliver things. You do things.

And you like it.

As long as you never leave, you will like the things you do to people. And the things they do to you.

Charlie grabs her sleeve. "I won't let them hurt you."

"I got to think about this, Charlie."

"There's nothing to think about. They promised me you won't get hurt."

"Can you stop them?"

"Just...come on, Jamie. We don't have a choice. We already wasted our lives—we're tapped out. We got to go halfskin to be right again. Once we're paid up, we'll be good. We'll be right. You know that. You saw how I changed."

"They'll hurt me, Charlie. They'll hurt you."

"But I can't...I can't go back, babe. It's too late. I'm already there."

"I know."

He tries to say more, tries to promise everything will be all right, but nothing comes out. He can't protect her.

Maybe it's worth it. Maybe having everything she wants and feeling how she wants to feel and not caring about shit music is the way to happiness. Maybe she just needs to sell her soul while it's still worth something.

She gets out of the booth. She doesn't know where the exit is, but she'll look for it all night if that's what it takes. Right now she just needs to be in her own head, experience her own field, think this through. She was sure she wanted this, but now...

"You can't leave." Charlie grabs her wrist, prying her fingers open. He pushes the pill into her palm. "This is a onetime shot, babe. You leave and you don't get another. That pill won't activate outside the club."

"I got to think about it, Charlie."

"There's nothing to think about!" His smile falters. Finally, a sign of the real Charlie shines, not that fake happy smile. He's still in there. He needs her. And she needs him.

She rolls the heavy pill between finger and thumb, the surface smooth and cold. She knows he's right. Where will she go if she leaves? What's out there can't be worse than this pill. There's nothing outside that door but her life.

This can't get worse.

She closes her eyes and throws the pill in her mouth. An aluminum flavor coats her tongue and leaves a metallic trail down her esophagus. It lands in her stomach.

He holds out his hand. "I promise."

And those are his last words.

The normal-looking guy at the bar, the one leaning on his elbows and hating the music, the one staring at her, starts walking. He looks like he's coming toward her but turns for the dance floor without a bounce in his step. He lifts both arms above his head. The music slurs.

The lights dim.

Gray walls appear out of nowhere. The ceiling transforms into rusted rafters with harsh fluorescent lighting.

Silence falls.

In the moments before the partygoers drop, before the floor is littered with bodies, Jamie looks back. Charlie is clutching the table. He feels something winding down, turning off. The whites show around his beautiful blue eyes before they turn gray—

He slumps to the floor.

They all do.

CHAPTER SIXTY-EIGHT_

PAUL MASSAGES HIS TEMPLES.

Lieutenant Dobbs ducks under the police barrier. Dobbs talks to a few of the officers at the crowd barrier before delivering a tall cup of coffee. Another van has arrived, the satellite receiver extending above the crowd. There's no such thing as secrets anymore. The bloggers and news corps probably know more about the warehouse than Paul.

The coffee is black and scalding.

Paul chases five aspirin with a swallow, scanning the crowd. Green lines lock on to individuals, automatically running them through facial recognition. No outstanding warrants—this time. Amazing how many fugitives in today's age of facial recognition come to crime scenes. It's like the mothership calling them home. This time it's mostly certified bloggers streaming video and nosy locals posting on Facebook or YouTube.

Dobbs follows Paul. "Feds are arriving in an hour."

"Good." Paul can focus on crowd control and the impending media landslide. Maybe catch up on sleep.

"They're bringing a shit-ton of bricks."

"One brick is enough." He blows on the coffee. The caffeine only fuels his surging headache.

Paul raps on the door, orange paint peeling off the metal surface. This place is registered as storage for some offshore company. They own several buildings in the area, all of them consuming almost no power. They'll never find the owners.

Paul kills his olfactory senses before the door opens. The briny scent of the harbor fades. When the door swings open, the crowd jockeys for position to get a glimpse. Paul quickly slips inside, where the atmosphere is dank and humid. Despite the absence of smell, he feels the odor cling to his skin, something that won't shower off.

Paul sets the coffee on the floor.

Birds look from rusted girders, impartial to the death below. The bodies were in tangled heaps when Paul arrived. Almost all of them are in their twenties or thirties, their clothing stained with sweat. Most are gaunt and sickly, like living zombies.

Now dead zombies.

Folding chairs and card tables are scattered to his right, with red plastic cups and stale bread on the ones still upright. A makeshift island bar made of plywood and two-by-fours is in the corner.

Poison, Paul had first thought when he saw the place. *These nuts laced up some drinks and offed themselves in dramatic fashion.* But it was just water. Would've been a hell of a lot easier if it was poison.

"Sarge!" someone calls from the other side.

Paul raises his hand. Officers are still moving the bodies, capturing faces for recognition. Some are still a mystery, probably having facial reconfiguration. A few of them are registering greater than 90% biomites. If those reports are accurate, they could make subtle changes to their looks with a thought.

Paul slowly walks between the bodies, avoiding the man among the officers that doesn't belong. He's dressed like an ordinary citizen with thinning hair and an overhanging gut.

Mother's agent, designed to blend. *A brick.*

He did this. The patrons' nixes were invisible to Mother until he got here. Once the frequency was decoded, he turned them over to Mother and she flipped the switch.

Legally it's not murder because, as federal law sees it, they weren't human anymore.

Paul scans the brick's face but doesn't find a match in the facial recognition database because he doesn't exist. He's a fabricated human, 100% biomites. A fucking brick. Funny how the government is fighting the war on halfskins with bricks. *Fire with fire,* they say.

Paul's never had to deal with one. Now an orgy of these plastic fucks is coming to town.

Three of his officers are outside an office door in the back left corner. Manny, the shortest of the three, says, "You got to see that office, Sarge. I mean, holy hell—"

"Why is she cuffed?" Paul points at the lone survivor.

"She started spitting. We warned her."

"So you cuffed her?"

"Well, yeah. When the brick moved her boyfriend, she lost it. Stevens had to subdue her and she started spitting. We warned her twice."

The girl is on the floor, slumped against the wall. Stringy hair hangs over her face. The only pieces of furniture in sight are metal chairs and broken tables not worthy of a garage sale.

"Pull that lounger out of the office," Paul says.

"The brick said leave it; we're not supposed to touch anything in there."

"You don't work for him."

Manny and Stevens fetch the lounger. Maybe he should put her in the office so she doesn't have to look at all these bodies, but he has the feeling she doesn't want to go far from her boyfriend. Besides, that office smells worse than the warehouse. Judging by the bedsores on the asshole they found in it, he almost never moved.

Paul kicks a card table to make room. The bread hits the floor like cardboard. He squats next to the girl, his belt binding his waist.

"I'd like to take those handcuffs off," he says softly. "But I need you to promise you won't run. Can you do that?"

She doesn't respond.

Paul leans over to visually capture her face. Her profile scrolls across his vision. In seconds, he knows her past and is a lot less surprised she's here.

"Jamie?" he says. "I know you've been through a lot tonight. I'm going to get you out of here as soon as I can, but in the meantime, I want you to rest comfortably, all right?"

She lifts her head but doesn't answer. Paul sways back, struck by the similarity to his niece. When he was a kid, it took things like LSD to fry a mind. Today, the right kinds of biomites could char a kid sky-high.

"I'm cold off," she mutters.

Paul looks at the officers.

"Means she can't run her field," Manny says. "She wants music."

"Why can't she have it?"

Manny jabs his thumb at the brick.

"If it's just music, you'll get it," Paul says.

Her eyes focus. And then she's looking through him. Her expression turns cold and hard. She's not charred, she's still present. She still has enough clay—at least a little more than half, or else she'd be on the floor. Maybe seeing this place littered with halfskins will save her.

"We got a deal?" he asks.

She nods.

Paul cuts the plastic handcuffs. She rubs her wrists and the officers help her onto the stained lounger. She must have her olfactory senses shut down; at least the brick gave her that. She rests comfortably.

"I just want the music back," she says.

"We all do, honey." Paul puts his hand on her forehead.

"Sergeant Jennings?"

The brick is behind him. He looks like a middle-aged man with bad posture, wearing brown pants and a checkered shirt. No one would remember him in a crowd.

"I'm Agent Manning." The brick offers his hand. Paul doesn't even look at it. Manning waits several moments before dropping it. His left eye twitches.

All the appearances of an imperfect human.

These fabrications are designed with frailties to make people feel comfortable, as if they're interacting with something real, talking to something other than a walking composite of biomites. Paul swears he can smell the plastic nature of this imposter even though his olfactory senses are dulled.

"Your superiors have briefed you on the situation, I'm sure, but I would like to be thorough. Are you familiar with the Biomite Oversight Committee?" Manning asks. "Do you know what we do?"

Paul doesn't respond. Doesn't even blink. Manning looks at the officers that gather around.

"I realize this is difficult for you. Losing life is never easy. I can assure you that we don't approve of this any more than you do."

Manning puts his hand to his chest and makes eye contact with each of the officers. Paul tries not to smirk. This...*thing*...imitating empathy is good. Some people will buy it, they'll forget it's a fabrication not capable of true emotions but rather trained to influence humans.

"I was assigned to investigate evidence of halfskin activity in this area," Manning continues. "I infiltrated the premises under the guise of a client and analyzed the use of nixes."

He didn't need to explain it, but he just did. Paul admires the slick approach to avoiding their ire by appearing coy rather than arrogant. It's not the strength these things possess that should be feared but the cunning.

"I completed my analysis at 2:33 a.m. My report was confirmed at 3:02 a.m. The result was the shutdown of one hundred and thirty-two halfskins. There is one survivor."

Paul looks at the results. He knows the law; it doesn't matter if he agrees. "You can leave," he says.

"On the contrary, a team of agents will be arriving for further analysis within the next couple of hours. We will cooperate with your department in every possible way—"

"You killed them, Manning. Your job is done."

He acknowledged its name. *Goddamnit.*

Manning stands a little taller. His relaxed expression hardens. A dead look fills his eyes. He takes a moment to look around, not so much to see anything but to let Paul interpret the sudden change in direction.

"Paul," he says, "I am an extension of Mother."

"I know *what* you are."

"There is no arguing this point, Paul. Every analysis has been confirmed that without Mother, your species would be consumed by greed. By extension, you fabricated me and others like me to save yourselves."

"I never signed up for killing people."

"These people were killing themselves, Paul. You were allowing it. You are mostly human and, therefore, incapable of adequately handling the situation."

"A brick to save us all. Fucking poetic."

Manning shuffles within Paul's comfort zone. "Your officers will leave the premises. They'll handle the crowd outside. No one is allowed to speak about what they saw or what is happening. No one, under any circumstances, is allowed in the back room."

"I'll run that by the chief."

"The girl," Manning continues, "will be placed in the back room. Her mother is not allowed to visit until she has been interrogated."

"We'll decide where the girl goes."

Manning takes a deep breath. *Does it really need to breathe?*

A cold vibration encases Paul's body. His skin tightens. His skull hardens. Pressure fills the space behind his eyes and pushes his tongue down.

The world looks bleak and distant.

He has very little awareness of following Manning to the back of the warehouse. All his officers come along, some with expressions as blank as his. Others appear shocked.

"Are we clear, Paul?"

Paul nods, but not of his own accord. His biomites have betrayed him. Manning—an extension of Mother—just hijacked them. He took control.

Biomite protestors always complain about the government having too much power. As Paul watches his men follow the brick's orders, he knows firsthand that they're right. The only person capable of resisting would have to be free of biomites.

And there are very few clays left in the world.

CHAPTER SIXTY-NINE_

Orange cones are on the pier, and a sign that warns people to keep out. There's too much activity around the warehouse for anyone to care about the rotting wharf or the lone person on it.

Nix Richards stands about halfway to the end. A ship moves past his peripheral vision, waves slapping the leaning pillars. He pulls the hood over his head. He doesn't mind the wet and the cold.

No one bothers watching from this vantage point because it's too far to see or hear. Nix enhances his vision, magnifies the crowd, downloads their identities and thoughts, filters through the chatter, paying more attention to the bloggers than reporters. They've got a better handle on the halfskin subculture. News organizations still pander to the older generations that hold out hope for yesteryear, that biomites are just a passing phase.

He caught a video stream from earlier that morning, before he arrived and before they erected the screen inside the front door: a blogger caught a view inside the warehouse. Nix had snipped a few stills from it and enhanced the resolution to see the police wandering around a pile of bodies.

Nix was lucky to get to the scene so quickly. He was at the airport in Vegas when he caught the news, and immediately bought a ticket to Seattle. By the time he arrived, the place was crawling with cops.

Nix had disguised his imprinted identity and worked his way through the crowd. If one of those cops caught a whiff of his true identity, that Nix Richards—the man that invisible biomites were named after—is watching from the pier...well, that warehouse story would fall off the front page.

His eyes begin to tingle.

Raine is calling. Perhaps he hasn't noticed. He's been consumed with screening the flood of data, looking for a way to get closer and, eventually, inside. The window of opportunity is closing. He can deal with cops; they're still human. The bricks, though, would be difficult. And more are on the way.

Nix initiates an opening in his perception field. The boards creak as bare feet walk past. Raine's image stops a few feet in front of him, absorbing the view. She's wearing a loose, long-sleeved shirt and shorts that expose all of her legs. The rain, though, falls right through her.

"We shouldn't be here," she says.

"This could be our last chance."

"There are other fabricators, Nix. This isn't the last one."

Her lips are plump, her eyebrows fiercely pinched. Twenty years have passed, but she looks twenty-five, not forty. Nix, on the other hand, is forty but looks sixty. That's intentional, but he still wouldn't look as young as her.

He rubs his weary face slick with precipitation. His eyes are exhausted. He's had to stay focused and engaged with the highly charged environment, all while maintaining his facially transfigured disguise. Even Raine's image is a little fuzzy. He can't slip, not here.

Raine's fingers are warm on his hand. She leans against him; he feels the illusion of her weight. He feels all of this as if she's actually there. It comforts him. *She's always been there.*

Three black cars come down the road on the right. They park a block from the warehouse. Nix lets his pulse quicken. His opportunity may already be over. He magnifies his vision, green lines capturing their details and pulling their identities imprinted on their biomites. *Pierce County police.* They gather around the lead car. Nix eavesdrops on their conversation about hunting season.

"This isn't necessary," Raine hisses, even though no one could possibly hear her. "I don't need to be fabricated."

There are wrinkles on the backs of Nix's hands. If his body aged normally, he'd look a little more worn from running and stress. The normal progression of aging, however, has changed since the birth of biomites. No one knows what a forty-year-old man is supposed to look like.

Right now he has gray hair, not blond. Brown eyes, not blue. He's a few inches shorter and huskier, his cheekbones a bit more pronounced. He's ordinary looking, something facial recognition and his imprinted identity would match with an alias named William Nelson.

The police start toward the scene. They visually scan the crowd, running not just facial recognition but pinging biomite imprints to identify other members of law enforcement. Nix concentrates, feeling the chatter of the cops' own imprinted biomites. It takes several moments to decrypt their identities and download secure data, and then he imprints his own biomites with a similar identity.

If anyone scans him, William Nelson is a husky cop from Olympia.

"Call your sister," Raine says. "She can help."

Nix chuckles. He hasn't been in contact with Cali in years. Even if he spoke with her yesterday, she wouldn't help him. Not with this.

"Don't do this!" Raine grabs his arm. Nix feels her cold fingers as if she's standing in front of him, in the flesh, his mind interpreting what she would be like. But she's not in front of him. She doesn't have a body. She's in his mind.

Dreamland.

If something ever happened to him, she would cease to exist. That's why he has to go inside.

He touches her cheek, her skin warm in the frigid air. She closes her eyes, leaning into his touch. If anyone is looking, they'll see a man standing alone, hand perched in the empty air. If he can fabricate Raine's body, she won't be trapped in Dreamland anymore. She'll walk next to him for everyone to see.

Another car comes down the road. The Pierce County cops wait for the new arrivals. Nix begins his approach. Raine walks silently beside him, her bare feet on the old boards. Her presence requires biomite resources to channel and, given the situation, he shouldn't expend the energy. But she brings him comfort. Besides, if something happens, he doesn't want to be shut down alone.

Nix grabs a half-full cup of coffee from the ground and pushes into the crowd. The women in front of him are tall. The cops approach the scene from the right, dampening their identities to avoid attention until they near the blockade. Nix shuffles around the back of the crowd and casually follows. The police officer at the barricade lets them through. Nix approaches a minute later.

The officer picks up Nix's imprinted signal. "Olympia, huh?"

"Long drive."

"What's Thurston County doing here?"

Nix ducks under the barrier without hesitation. "You think this is Seattle's problem?"

The cops are still waiting for the door to open. Nix cradles the coffee like it's keeping him awake. He's being scanned from all directions, like walking on stage. They don't see Raine by his side.

The door opens. Nix dampens his olfactory senses but doesn't turn them off. This scene is fouled with death and decay, the smell of exhaustion and rusted steel. A hint of plastic lies beneath it all, the sign of dead biomites.

Nix steps around the white panel that blocks the view, his imprinted identity pinging from several directions. He doesn't have to introduce himself. He puts the coffee on the floor like someone else has done. The scattered tables and chairs are only outnumbered by the bodies. Nix swallows a rising lump, feels Raine's hand around his arm, keeping him from running. Now is not the time to panic.

His eyes glaze like he's chatting or recording, disguising his initial surge of fear. His senses struggle to absorb the details, to make sense of the insanity.

This is exactly why Cali wouldn't help him. She warned him biomites would come to this, that humanity wasn't ready for such control of their bodies and minds. She didn't think humanity would ever be ready, that we were too imperfect, that our selfish gene, our hardwired sense of self-preservation and self-centeredness, was too ingrained to resist the temptation. We would become a muddling mass of self-destructive beings that would devolve into...*this*.

And his sister can't help but feel responsible. She was the one that discovered the algorithms that could make biomites undetectable. She's the one that, as she once said, "put the gun in the baby's hand." And she carries the burden, the guilt.

"Just get here?" Officer Timothy Remming asks.

"Yeah," Nix spits out.

"Damn shame, right?" Remming unwraps a stick of gum. "Can't prepare yourself for this."

"What the hell happened?"

"Pretty simple, really. Some high-powered halfskin has been running this operation for years. We found him in a back office with a PICC line in his vein."

Remming gestures to a door in the back left corner.

"He was manufacturing nixes for these fools. As far as we can tell, they were dancing in his projection field. Looks like a zombie rave. No telling what they thought they were doing. Too bad for them, the brick walked in and untangled their frequency. They went night-night."

An ordinary man is directing officers to move the bodies. They've started in the corner directly to Nix's left, placing the bodies on their backs, hands folded over their stomachs. They appear to be lining them up, organizing them into rows.

The ordinary man feels like a dense ball of energy. Nix has always been able to sense a brick's biomites. Everyone else, for whatever reason, experiences a brick as invisible. Nix and Cali have always felt them. Maybe that's why they've never been caught.

"This is dangerous," Raine whispers from behind.

Nix nods, both to Remming and Raine. But he can't walk out now. And the back office is where he wants to go. As long as the brick is busy, there's a chance to do a quick surveillance. He can't haul something out, but there has to be information linked to other nixed distributors with fabricators. They don't work alone.

"Who's that?" Nix points at the girl in the lounger.

"The lucky one?" Remming says. "She was about to go halfskin when the brick shut them down. They had to tear her off one of these bodies, her boyfriend or something. Pitching a real fit."

Nix takes a long, slow breath. The brick is a hundred feet from the back room. The girl is only twenty feet away from it. He can get over there, interrogate her kindly and then casually investigate the office. He only needs to be inside a minute, long enough to scan it. He can download any available data and analyze it off-site, but it has to be fast. The evidence is already disintegrating, trails disconnecting. He just needs a contact, a place he can throw a line.

"You might want to stay out of spitting distance." Remming chuckles, chomping his gum.

Nix walks to the right, following a path between the bodies that will loop around the perimeter and keep him far from the brick.

He seizes. Alarms ring in his head, high voltage surging through his body. He can't take another step.

"Go, Nix." Raine steps in front of him. "Get out now."

He turns slowly, carefully heading for the exit behind the white screen, focusing on each step that threatens to miss the floor and toss him forward. He can hardly hear his own voice when he passes Remming. "Need some fresh air."

"Should've turned off your olfactory."

Nix acknowledges him with a wave.

All eyes turn on him as he exits. The intense warning is coming from his left. A cavalcade of white vehicles is approaching. They ease into the crowd, forcing people to step aside.

Nix turns to his right, walking as casually as he can in the opposite direction. Few people are paying attention. He focuses on the back of Raine's heels as she leads him under the barricade, away from the men and women exiting the white cars. They're not men and women.

They're bricks.

He finds space to walk briskly behind the crowd, continuing his pace until he reaches the corner. Once he's out of sight, he stops. Raine has disappeared. It takes a few minutes for his breathing to return to normal.

Nix magnifies his vision. The lead vehicle has pulled right up to the door while the police push back the crowd. One after another, bricks get out of the cars. Fabricated men and women—black skin, white skin, Asian, Hispanic—ignore the onlookers and gather at the front door.

It's possible Nix could have fooled them. They wouldn't be focused on him. But that's not what tipped an icy cascade of fear. It's the last person to get out of the white cars: a man with a limp and a slight hunch. A man that hasn't been seen in public for years.

Marcus Anderson exits the lead car.

CHAPTER SEVENTY_

Rain streaks across a tinted window. Marcus never much cared for the Northwest. The January skies are a steely embrace. His knee hates it.

A crowd blocks his view. News vans are parked on the curb. Marcus takes an earpiece from the inside of his jacket and fits it into his right ear, listening to his bricks' chatter. While biomites allow one to chat, as if the brain had become the communication device, Marcus has to rely on external devices.

"Continue driving," he says as they approach the crowd. "They'll move."

The driver slows down but does not honk. Nor stop. The people feel the vehicle approach and slowly move. A kid slams his hand on the hood. Others shout.

It's like parting the Red Sea.

The police move the barricades. The car rolls up to the warehouse door. Marcus reaches to the woman sitting next to him.

"Wait," he says. "Let Gerald get it."

Anna takes her hand off the handle and pats Marcus's arm. Her blonde hair hangs to her shoulders. Her plump lips are red and shocking against her powder-white skin.

"You're making quite a scene," Anna says.

The crowd is focused on the backseat, most of them with retinal recorders that will stream this scene on the newsfeeds and blogosphere. Gerald pauses before opening the door.

"That's the idea," Marcus says.

He turns his body so that he can rest his feet on the asphalt, to allow the blood to circulate before standing. His left knee bends like a rusty hinge. Gerald offers a hand, but Marcus waves him off. He may be aging, but he's not crippled. There are aches and pains to deal with when you're clay.

The way God intended it.

Let the world see who is in charge. Not some biomite-infested cop.

Anna slides out behind him. She's taller than him, especially with the heels. Even without expression, her beauty is stunning. That was why he exited first. His bricks arrive from the cars lined up behind them. They gather around the door, ignoring the questions and curses hurled from behind the barricades. More police arrive to maintain order.

A local police officer stands next to the corroded door. "You might want to kill your olfactory."

Marcus makes a mental note of the officer's name. If he's going to work in law enforcement, he should know Marcus Anderson.

Marcus is greeted with fetid death. He steps around the white screen and into a thick atmosphere. Through welling tears, he sees the bodies. His breath shortens, adjusting to the foul stench of body odor and rot. Beneath it, he senses the tang of expired biomites.

He warned the world that it would come to this. And if it did, he would be there to stop it. And now he stands on the threshold of his prophecy. *Today the world will see that hope lies in our clay.*

He wipes his eyes. About half the bodies are organized into lines, the rest still tangled like they were tossed into the air. His bricks immediately go to work, their thoughts chatting through his earpiece. First, establish order. Then begin the process of scanning the faces and analyzing the biomites.

Marcus retrieves prescription glasses from inside his jacket and begins wiping the round spectacles with a handkerchief. The right lens is quite a bit thicker. He fixes them on his nose and the world comes into focus. Anna hands him a bottle of water. The odor clings to his taste buds. She anticipates his needs so well.

The local police watch the bricks go to work. They congregate around a man in uniform. His stillness and concentration suggest his vain attempts to scan Marcus, finding nothing to identify.

"Sergeant Paul Jennings," Anna says.

"He's in charge?" Marcus asks.

"So far, yes. Agent Manning updated him on how we will proceed. He's been forced into compliance."

Whatever assistance the police had been supplying had stopped since Marcus arrived. The public was aware of bricks, but they were presented as lonely bounty hunters, never as a pack of surgical investigators that seemed to move with one mind, sharing thoughts to coordinate an efficient dissection of a crime scene. There was no delusion or distracting thoughts that typically slowed a human. No corruption or self-centered thoughts.

The bricks continue organizing the corpses into a checkerboard layout. A small contingent goes to the far side and begins undressing them, folding the clothes into piles at the head of each body.

"Bring him over," Marcus says.

Anna chats a terse command. Three bricks go to the sergeant and repeat Marcus's demand. The men steal glances of Anna.

"I am Marcus Anderson." He extends his hand. "I have my doubts about your police department if a sergeant is in charge, but, nonetheless, you have done a splendid job. The public has been made aware of the situation and is contained outside the scene. And your cooperation is greatly appreciated."

"Make them stop." Paul's jaws flex.

"Our investigation will last three days." His tone is darker and direct. "You will continue providing support outside the building. During that time, you will not speak to the public."

Paul quakes with restraint.

"When we are done, you may conduct yourselves in whatever manner you please. In the meantime, you will not interfere. Is that understood?"

"Make...them...stop." He pushes the words out. His face is flush as a bull's nose.

Marcus waves at Anna. She releases her grip on Paul's biomites, allowing him to think and act freely. He pulls in a deep breath but contains himself, aware that anything rash will put him back under her influence.

"This is unacceptable." He points at the bricks undressing the bodies. Ten of them are completely nude. "These are sons and daughters. There is no reason to expose them."

He dares half a step forward.

"I expect that from someone with as much control as you."

Marcus glances at Anna. She nods and the bricks simultaneously stop. They face Marcus, waiting for instructions. He takes a moment to bend his stiffening knee. The concrete is unforgiving on surgically repaired bones. He takes a drink, surveying the destruction. The warehouse is so barren and destitute, an unfitting tomb.

And he's supposed to treat them with decency?

"This is not a crime scene, let's get that straight," Marcus says. "This is a molestation. The crime that you refer to is much greater than it appears, grander than you imagine. These sons and daughters came here of their own volition and forfeited their rights as humans. They have no dignity, they do not exist."

Marcus steps closer, Anna at his side.

"So says the law, Sergeant."

"I don't agree with the law."

"You serve it."

"A part of them is still human."

"How many more of these scenes do you want to see?" Marcus raises his voice, looking at all the men and women in uniform. "These could be your sons and daughters next time. Are you willing to accept that? Because I am not!"

His voice rings off the walls.

"You object to exposing these imitations of God's children? They are no more sacred than objects carved of wood. They succumbed to temptation, gave themselves to earthly desires, and reveled in lies. Open your eyes, all of you. Smell what is all around! That is not the stench of decayed flesh but the degradation of the soul."

Marcus inhales deeply.

"Breathe it in, remember it! Because if we do nothing about this today, it will become the smell of tomorrow. Earth will become a mausoleum of the human soul. I, for one, cannot accept that."

His footsteps click, back and forth.

"I am your only hope. Take your men outside, Sergeant, and do not question me again."

Anna opens the door and moves the screen for the crowd to see inside. Shouts and curses find their way inside.

Marcus folds his hands behind his back, standing as straight as his hunched back will allow. "Give the world your gravest apologies but no more. I will call if I need you."

The men and women begin their exodus, stiffly. Paul remains staring down at Marcus. He is the last to finally move. He stops at the white screen.

"There's a girl," he says. "She's the only survivor. I'd like to take her to her mother."

"Certainly," Marcus says. "I have a few questions for her, that's all."

Paul disappears behind the screen without being forced to do so. The door hammers shut in the metal frame, the closure echoing with a sense of finality. The crowd's anger is muffled. Marcus closes his eyes, allowing the stillness of the moment to settle before muttering a command.

The bricks begin undressing the corpses once again. The only sounds are the shuffle of their soles. Once a body is completely nude, the agent stands over it to visually capture it—head to toe. It is turned over and repeated.

"Your estimate?" Marcus asks.

"We can fabricate all these bodies in two days," Anna says.

"Good. Three days, then, will be all we need."

"Correct. Do you want to interrogate the survivor?"

"Perhaps later. I'd like to explore what's in the back." Marcus starts down the first aisle of bodies. "Oh, Anna."

Marcus half turns, his neck feeling stiff.

"Leak my speech to the bloggers out there. I'd like the world to hear it, too."

He continues his uneven pace toward the back of the warehouse. Sometimes he surprises himself with such spontaneous wisdom. The world needs to know he is not the bad guy.

He is quite the opposite.

CHAPTER SEVENTY-ONE_

Cali Richards fumbles with the tack room doorknob. The latch is stuck. She has to put the metal pails on the floor and turn it with both hands. She kicks the bottom of the old door, swearing she'll get that fixed.

She's been swearing that for ten years.

The former nanobiometric engineer turns on the faucet, letting the water run over her wrinkled and spotted hand. Her arthritic knuckles are knobby. She shoots some soap in the stream and lets the bubbles rise over the pails.

An old song comes on the radio, reminding her of days before biomites were invented, when life was simpler. *Is that what old people say?* Only dusted memories make things seem easier. Still, she turns it up before reaching into the soapy water, reaching blindly for brush and pail.

She yanks her hand out like a water snake was hiding on the bottom. A long red slash oozes along her index finger. She resists the childish urge to suck the blood. She wraps a paper towel around the wound, squeezing it. The dull pain recedes. She could will the nervous response away but prefers to feel the sting. *It's too easy not to feel it.*

Two horses trot across the frozen paddock. Cali watches them play follow-the-leader, their hooves rumbling past the tack room window. There were more horses when she bought the ranch. The previous family had died in an automobile accident. It seemed only fitting that Cali live here, seeing that an automobile accident changed the path of her life.

Perhaps every path in the world.

Haze settles near the top of the Blue Ridge Mountains, but the sun hasn't breached. A red truck emerges from behind a stand of black gum trees. Two dogs run alongside it.

Cali keeps pressure on her finger while the reflection of a leathery old face looks back, her gray hair pulled tightly back with kinky sprigs around her ears. Wrinkles line her upper lip. She's only fifty-two years old.

No one would recognize her. They're not supposed to.

The grass between the two-story house and the barn, once thick and green, is now frosted and tan. The dogs trot past her, waiting in the worn turnabout for the Ford pickup to make a wide turn. Meg puts it in park with one hand, a phone pressed to her ear with the other. She waves before abruptly ending her conversation.

Country folks use phones. They don't pretend to have a conversation while chatting through biomite seeds.

"Hi, Ms. Stacy." Megan hops out of the truck, tying her blonde hair into a ponytail. "Hey there, Baxter and Kooper."

She scratches the dogs' ears and squats down for kisses.

Cali answers to her assumed name, Stacy. She changed her face, changed her name—if she could just get a new life.

"I was expecting your brother," Cali says.

"Carson had some chores to finish. He'll drop off the hay this afternoon. I thought I'd run your groceries out in case you needed them."

"That's kind of you."

"You cut yourself?"

"Nothing but a scratch."

"I got essential oil salve for that. It'll stop the bleeding, keep out infection. I can send it with Carson."

Cali opens the passenger door. Her weekly order of produce and dairy is on the seat. Megan gets around the truck in time to grab the box. There's nothing she can do but smile.

Cali shuffles to keep ahead of the girl so she can climb the old wooden steps first. The screen is torn on the corner of the door. Cali holds it open.

The kitchen counters are cluttered with appliances, books and cans. It's blessed with an ever-present smell of herbs. Cali pats the table for Megan to set down the goodies. The hickory table is gouged from years of use, where the previous family ate their meals. Megan pulls out a quart of milk.

"Let me get you some money."

Her footsteps land heavily on the wooden floor. She passes the old chalkboard running the length of the hallway and goes to the room in back to put a Band-Aid on her finger. Megan is watching something on her phone when she returns. People are protesting behind a blogger's commentary. Cali slides the bills between Megan's fingers.

"Thanks, Ms. Stacy." She puts the money in her front pocket.

"What were you watching?"

"There was a big thing in Seattle the other day. A bunch of people overdosed on biomites and now they think they're all dead."

Cali busies herself with the groceries.

"All the bloggers are going off about the government shutting the doors and not letting the families see them. I feel bad for them."

"Very sad." Cali puts the cheese in the refrigerator. "Pray for them."

Megan holds out her hand. Cali takes it and bows her head.

"Dear Lord," Megan says, "watch over Your sheep that are lost in darkness and guide them to Your Almighty wisdom, that they may walk the pure and untainted path that leads to Heaven. Amen."

"Amen."

They remain still. The words resonate in Cali and attach to her like angels of hope that they will find her brother and take root, that he'll join her on the farm, where he'll be safe.

Because she knows he's in Seattle.

Megan leaves with a quick goodbye. Cali stands at the sink, watching the young lady texting on her way to the truck. Cali peels the Band-Aid off and throws it in the trash. The finger is healed.

CHAPTER SEVENTY-TWO_

THE DUFFEL BAG FEELS LIKE A SACK OF ROCKS.

Nix lets it fall on the hotel carpet. He avoids the king-sized bed. If he lies down, he won't get up. There'll be time for sleeping later.

He grinds his eyes with the heels of his palms. Death still lingers in his nostrils. He pulls the sliding door open, letting the winter wind into the room. Gulls cry somewhere above the patio. The moon hangs just above the bay. He opens his mind to nearby chatter, eavesdropping on newsfeeds. The tranquility is broken with a thousand voices.

MARCUS ANDERSON HAS TAKEN control of the warehouse.

The government is raping our civil liberties.

Marcus Anderson should crawl back into the hole where he's been hiding or be arrested for treason.

Mother is an enemy of the state.

NOTHING WILL CHANGE and Marcus and his bricks will do what they want in the warehouse, digesting the evidence like ants cleaning a corpse. There'll be nothing left.

And no one can stop them.

That's why Nix can't sleep. Not yet.

There's information in there, Nix knows it. He can feel it. Years ago, it was so easy to network with other halfskins. But Mother has systematically cut them up, severed ties, and traced down the outlaws. Nix is alone.

He goes to the bathroom and splashes water on his face. He dabs his cheeks with a towel. An old man with dark eyes rimmed red looks back. His nose is thick, his lips thin and wrinkled. The bushy eyebrows are speckled white. He doesn't just look like an old man. Today, he feels like one.

He hates the way his body feels. It feels like someone else, like staring at the world through eyeholes. But he never changes it. Not even standing in a hotel bathroom all alone. He's committed to being William Nelson until he finds a fabricator. If Nix Richards's original face were ever caught by facial recognition, he wouldn't last long.

He cups another handful of cold water to his face, pushes his fingers through thinning hair and retreats to the bed. He lies back but never feels the mattress. It's like he falls through it, his body dropping through the floor, building speed as it plummets downward, the solidity of his body falling away a particle at a time.

A green breeze brushes his cheeks, a trace of smoke on the wind.

Dreamland.

Verdant hills slope to a clear lake confined by the peaks of distant mountains. Fishing boats have already shoved across the glassy surface from the village along the shores, where a market is vibrant with fruit and vegetables, cured meats and smoked fish.

He lifts his hands and studies the skin of a thirty-nine-year-old. Only in Dreamland does he look like his true self, the real Nix Richards.

Raine sits at the far end of the slanted porch. Her baggy pants are rolled to her knees with a white tank top exposing her dark brown shoulders. She cradles a mug on her lap, green eyes gazing over the bannister.

"I think you're foolish," she says.

"I know."

"You're not invincible."

Nix steps off the porch, where the ground is worn to dust. Further out, the grass sways near his knees, clumps shifting in the wind. Scrubby trees dot the landscape. He looks back at the prairie home, the old porch wrapping around both sides.

Dreamland started as a mental construct, thoughts that he visualized and connected. When he was a kid, he discovered his ability to build inner worlds by accident. It started when he looked at a picture. His biomites took the information and recreated this inner world. Nix thought it was normal.

He was a freak.

His thoughts took on a life of their own. They calcified and interlocked. They existed without his effort. He and Raine had outgrown the tropical lagoon of their youth. They wanted a home and imagined this cabin on the hill, the nearby sea and the ragged mountains. They would go down to the village, where people haggled over prices and arguments broke out and children laughed in the streets. He saw and heard things he couldn't possibly have imagined, the details rich and endless.

It was no different than the physical world. But still, a world he created. *Will it exist without me?*

He could never be sure.

A German shepherd lopes through the grass. Nix buries his fingers in the dog's fur.

"Shep," Nix mutters, "where's your stick?"

Shep looks around as if he's thinking, then darts around the house. Nix picks a seed stalk from the grass, nibbling on the broken end, the juice tart.

"Do you think I'm real?" Raine asks.

Nix used to answer that question. Sometimes, he tried to lie. He didn't control her, couldn't make her do anything she didn't want to do. He'd always assumed she had risen from his subconscious, taken the details of her physical appearance from someone he'd seen but forgotten, that his mind had this barrier in place so he'd feel the separateness between them.

So when she asked that question—*Do you think I'm real?*—he didn't know how to answer.

"If I die," he says, "this will all vanish."

"You don't know that."

"It's a safe bet."

"Can the mind die?" she asks.

The koan. The unanswerable question. The body can be killed but is the mind the product of the brain? They argued that point many times.

"I can't take the chance," Nix answers, as he always does.

Raine lazily drags her hands over the swaying swards of grass. She nears a leaning white oak. They planted that tree. The hills and water, the clouds and soil all sprang from his mind, but they built the house and planted that tree.

It's grown older, just like them.

Raine picks something up. Nix is still squatting when she takes his hand. Opening his fingers, she places an acorn in it.

"You were the seed," she says. "You are not the tree."

She closes his fingers around it, holding his fist in her delicate hands.

"This Dreamland is more than you. Perhaps it's more real than the world you live in."

"I don't care about Dreamland. Only you."

"Maybe that's the problem."

Nix always told his sister that Dreamland was a new reality, not just his imagination. But when asked to fully commit to that, it was too much of a risk. If he dies, it dies.

She dies.

"If I can fabricate you a physical body," he says, "you won't need me."

"The physical world isn't the gold standard of reality. There are other realms."

"The physical is all I got."

"Are you an old man in the *real world*?"

"That's just how my body looks. It's not me."

"Then if you're not your body, who are you?"

Another koan.

She knows why he wants to fabricate a physical body. He doesn't want to possess her, doesn't want her existence to be limited to Dreamland. He wants to give her a life, her own life. He wants to have children in the real world. They discuss this often; they already have names. Joshua, if it's a boy. Pearl, if it's a girl. That was the plan.

Raine didn't want to wait; she wanted to start the family in Dreamland. But Nix didn't want to raise children in a fantasy, he wanted them in the flesh, where he could rock them to sleep and kiss their boo-boos and watch them grow. He didn't want them to disappear if something happened to him.

Shep returns with a stick. Nix hurls it deep into the meadow.

"There's a girl in the warehouse," he says. "I think I can use her to look around. There must be some clue to the underground network, something that can give me some direction of where to find a fabricator. I'll need to get closer, though."

"They'll sense you."

"I'll use a proxy and cover my trail. I just need her eyes and ears, to see what's in the back room."

Shep is already returning, stick in mouth, black lips flapping. Nix stands to look at the valley. One of the boats is returning.

Raine drapes her arms around his neck and leans her head on his shoulder. The morning chill is already lifting, but a fire in the hearth would be nice. And he could use the rest. In the morning, he'll get a fresh start.

But he wonders, as he often does, how he could ever leave this place.

CHAPTER SEVENTY-THREE_

THE SUN IS LOCKED BEHIND A GRAY SKY.

Nix walks down the middle of a long street—the warehouses on his right, the water to his left. Raine's image walks silently beside him. The white sedans are parked far from the shrinking crowd. Only hardcore bloggers and a few reporters are up this soon.

He doesn't want to mingle, but there's no other way to get close. Bricks were behind the warehouse on the loading docks. He's made slight adjustments to his facial features—altered his cheekbones, thickened his nose—and changed his biomite identity. If anyone checks, he's a blogger. No one will recognize him from yesterday.

There's not much activity. Most are chatting or eating fast food, a few are streaming reports or video. Several bloggers are curled up in sleeping bags near the pier, stocking caps peeking out.

Nix's biomite identity pings as onlookers watch him approach, scanning his identity, curious if he's someone with information. The activity dies down. He spots two men, early twenties, on a short guardrail, digging breakfast from a white bag. Facial recognition identifies them: Byron is African American; Henry, Korean American.

Nix drops his bag on the grass. "Any word?"

"None," Byron says. "They're slammed tight. Rumor floating that the bricks will make an announcement today, but they said that yesterday. Police don't know any more than we do, just standing guard."

Two officers sip coffee near the steel door.

"Bricks got the cops under wraps," Henry says. "Moved them out day one. Like to be a fly inside."

"You try tapping surveillance feeds?" Nix asks.

Byron shakes his head. "Like I said, slammed tight. Bricks are running field static to prevent scanning, and no hardwires to ride inside. No one knows what they're doing in there."

Nix thought if he had proximity, he could surf his senses through the Ethernet and link up with the girl's biomites. Maybe not.

"You staying put?" Nix asks. "Need to patch an update across the water."

His biomite identity told them he's a freelance blogger just picking up news for a London-based outlet. In the world of bloggers, he's about as low as it gets.

Byron smirks. "Ain't you a bit old to be streaming?"

"Never too old." Nix taps the back of his head, the universal sign of a recent biomite seed.

"Get comfy, old man. We'll watch your gear."

Nix throws a blanket on the ground. He leans back on the guardrail. Byron and Henry chat silently and figure an old man like that can't sit up and stream. Nix gets comfortable, leans back, and closes his eyes.

The sensations of the physical world recede.

His awareness slips into cyberspace, where information streams and thoughts collide. Byron and Henry's encrypted chat blends with other conversations in the vicinity. Nix moves his awareness toward the warehouse, where the information feels like a white cloud of static, of buzzing insects meant to scatter any attempts to *look* inside.

He sifts through the obscure net, searching for any semblance of organized consciousness. He feels several dense formations but avoids merging with them. His heartbeat picks up. If he connects with a brick, it could be the last thing he ever does.

There's nothing discernible in the warehouse, no information he can glean, no images he can stream. It's what keeps the bloggers from learning anything. But they don't know about the girl. Even if they did, they can't ride the Ethernet like Nix.

Too much clay.

Nix can't tell one identity from the other. They're all virtually identical, which tells him that everything he's feeling inside the warehouse are bricks. He pushes deeper when he feels a slight aberration in organized consciousness. It's the sign of imperfection, the activity of the subconscious.

The clay of a human mind.

Nix pushes his awareness through the white static until he's centered over this identity. He takes a moment to locate it in space and time, estimating that it's located near the back of the warehouse, sitting still.

Slowly, he wraps his mind around it.

He touches it like a toe in the water.

Her perception field is malleable and open. Nix merges with it like two computers reaching through cyberspace, attaching his perception field to hers. Forms swim out of the static as if layers of veils are lifted, one by one.

Until he's seeing.

Hearing.

He's in the back room of the warehouse.

CHAPTER SEVENTY-FOUR_

JAMIE'S CUFFED TO AN ERGONOMIC, GEL-INFUSED LOUNGER. And cold off, once again.

There's a door leading to the warehouse, a tattered tablecloth hung over the window. The filtered light doesn't penetrate much further than the lounger. The room feels deep. Occasionally, something moves.

Tabletops are anchored to the wall, littered with electronics, empty bottles, mirrors, cigarettes, clothes, and other strange things. A shorthaired stuffed animal lies facedown to her right, its tail dangling over the edge. It's like Garfield fucked a lizard.

Her internal clock says it's been three days since they put her in the back. There's a blank spot in her memory where the second day should be.

The boredom has become torture. Without her field, she stares at the false ceiling's stained tiles. When she feels a strange buzz—an itching behind her eyes and deep in her ears—it's welcome. She clenches her teeth, feeling overdosed on caffeine.

"Hey there, Jamie." The door opens; light pours inside like a knife. The clutter deep in the room is briefly revealed. More freaky stuffed animals and a glass shower.

The blonde brick closes the door. "How are you?"

Despite the lounger's comfort, her body aches. She refuses to call her Anna. She's one of them. Even worse, she's a brick.

"You hungry?" Anna leans over the lounger, her short hair the kind of red that belongs on candy. "I brought some food."

Anna shakes the white bag, this time McDonald's. They shut off her music, cut her connection to the outside world, but at least they left her in control of her senses. If she hadn't turned off her olfactory and tasting senses, she'd be salivating. She'd also smell the wasting bodies.

And thoughts of Charlie would return.

She would remember him perched on the edge of the seat, remember his last words...and then gray walls and the rank odor when the club's field dropped.

She was crying and retching, holding him on the floor, screaming that he had to wake up, they had to go. If she could just get him out of there, he would come back. Even if he was charred, he still had a chance; they could figure things out.

But then the police arrived.

They were just outside the door before the nixes were decoded and the halfskins shut down. Only Jamie didn't go down. If only she didn't hesitate, if only she had taken that pill a minute sooner, she'd be out there. That was better than being in here.

Better than surviving.

That brick at the bar, the one that shut everyone down, was watching. It was like he was waiting for her to put that cold pill on her lips.

Charlie's the lucky one.

Anna clears the sacks from her last delivery, wiping the crumbs and rat droppings on the floor before unpacking the chicken nuggets and fries. She peels open the dipping sauces and arranges them on the tray, very orderly. She takes a bite, rolling her eyes.

"Mmm, you got to try this one, Jamie." Anna points at the sauce. "It's called sweet and sour."

She appears to be in her upper twenties with perky breasts and a tight frame. Her lipstick matches her hair. She picks apart the nugget with shiny red nails.

"I got to piss." The words scratch Jamie's throat.

"Take a bite first. Then we'll go to the bathroom."

Anna holds the nugget to her lips. If Jamie's quick, she can bite off one of her slender fingers, spit it on the floor for the rats. But what would that get her?

She turns her head.

Anna sighs. Her worried expression is convincing. She reaches in the pouch on her hip and puts the needles and tubes next to the food.

"I need another sample."

"Don't you have enough?"

Anna takes a few minutes to record her actions, then comes over with an elastic band and a pair of scissors. She pauses with a very serious look.

"Can I trust you?" she asks.

Jamie doesn't answer. The last time she cut the plastic cuffs, Jamie took a swing. She barely made a fist before a teeth-numbing sensation filled her head. She tumbled to the floor and stared at the fluorescent light while Anna pulled a blood sample, calmly pleading that she not fight, that she cooperate. That this would all be over soon.

Anna waits for an answer this time.

Jamie nods.

The pressure on her wrists is relieved with a snip. Jamie slowly swings her legs to sit up, the blood rushing to her feet. The room sways with exhaustion and hunger. Anna strokes the insides of Jamie's arms. Both are purple where blood was drawn the first couple times, the needle banging around the veins as she struggled. Anna's touch is tender.

"This is bullshit," Jamie says. "I'm 49.9%. Just scan me."

"Are you?"

"Am I what?"

"Just 49.9%?"

"I'd be out there if I wasn't."

Anna finds a vein where the purple gives way to yellow. She taps a few times before plunging the needle in it. Jamie is able to dull the pain response, but the sting still registers. The tube fills with dark red.

How many of those blood cells are biomites imitating blood cells?

"Is your blood red?" Jamie asks.

"Of course." Anna pops a second tube into the needle. "You're wondering how I feel, aren't you?"

Jamie flinches. That's exactly what she was wondering. Anna was in her head, seeing her thoughts. Jamie hates her but likes her, too. She wants to be like her, in total control of her thoughts and feelings. And she hates herself for wanting to look like that, too: confident and slutty. Powerful.

Hating herself is nothing new.

"You're a copy," Jamie says. "You're a fake and you know it."

Anna pulls the needle out and bandages the spot before packing the tubes and needles.

"You're a puppet, Anna. That guy out there makes you do what he wants, he makes you like it. You can be turned off, you know that."

"So can you."

"Only half of me."

"The other half won't survive."

"At least I started out as clay. You never were."

Anna zips up the pouch. She holds up a fresh pair of plastic cuffs. "Do you still need to use the restroom?"

"No."

"Then eat."

"I want to go home."

"No," Anna says. "You don't."

She says it calmly, knowingly. There's nothing out there for Jamie, and she knows it.

There are voices outside the door.

"I want out of here!" Jamie shouts. "Goddamnit, you can't do this! This is illegal! Where's my mom?"

Jamie hurls a chicken nugget at her. It smacks against the door.

"Where are the cops? I want out of here, you puppet bitch! I want to talk to someone! You can't fucking do this illegal shit!"

She reaches for the tray when her arm seizes. Every muscle in her body locks. The smile has dropped from Anna's friendly face. Her eyelids heavy. Jamie is trapped in a catatonic pose, fingers curled like claws. Unable to even swallow.

Anna's heels rap the concrete. She puts the spilled food into the bag, retrieves the chicken nugget from the floor and wipes the grease from the lounger. Jamie can see her in the periphery. Panic fills her like icy insects. There's not enough oxygen in the carefully measured breaths she's forced to take. She tries to scream, to apologize, to sob... she can't even blink. That strange itching sensation burns the back of her eyes and tickles her ears, like someone's eavesdropping.

She's trapped in her body.

Anna steps out of sight, her footsteps fading toward the back of the room where darkness cloaks strange objects. Something scuffs across the floor. Anna returns with a large chair, the wooden legs thick and heavy. She squares it to the right of the door and goes back to the dark. An identical chair is placed facing the first one, visually framing the door.

Anna drops her hand on the doorknob.

Jamie begins to involuntarily move. Her chest burns for oxygen. She stands and shuffles her feet toward the chair on the right. Her efforts to stop or look around are futile. Anna has hijacked her biomites, moving her like a remote-controlled object, simply willing her to slowly squat into the chair, arms on the wooden armrests. The empty chair stares back.

Who's the puppet now?

Tears swell on her lower lids, rolling down her cheeks. She feels them on the corners of her mouth.

Slowly, she moves her fingers. Jamie grips the armrests. She inhales a deep breath as she breaks through her confinement. Another breath. And another. She holds back the sobs, her heart hammering in her throat.

The doorknob clicks.

Light falls across Jamie's lap. Shiny black shoes step unevenly into view. The man stands for a moment, looking down at her struggling to grasp the world that's betrayed her. He tugs at his gray slacks and sits, crossing his right leg over his left.

Jamie wipes her eyes before sitting up. It's the old man. He's mostly bald. What little hair clings to the perimeter of his skull is white and his left right eye misshaped.

"You're very lucky." His words are crisp. "You should be out there, you realize."

Jamie wants to duck her head to avoid his piercing glare. She stares at her blue fingernail polish that's partially stripped away. She rubs her eyes, but the burning-itching sensation won't go away.

"Why did you come here?" he asks.

A sudden compulsion to tell the truth rises in her throat. Jamie's lips part, but she presses her tongue to the roof of her mouth, refusing any sort of confession.

The man looks at Anna. He brushes his knee, picking at bits of lint before folding his hands.

"I know everything about you, Jamie. Your biomites cannot keep secrets."

His stare is penetrating. She looks to the dark end of the room. Her head, though, is forced to turn back. His gray eyes are fearless. His expression joyless.

"Your father left when you were seven years old. When you cry, you hug a pillow and bury your face so no one hears, although you haven't cried in years. You killed your sadness, didn't you? You shut those emotions off so you didn't have to feel them, so you wouldn't cry anymore. And you masturbate with your left hand."

"Why'd you even ask?" she blurts.

"Because half of you is still clay. That half is God's gift, Jamie.

That's the half Anna can't read. Maybe there's more you'd like to tell me?"

She doubts that's true. Her clay doesn't hold secrets from her biomites. She's committed so many biomites to replace brain cells to amp her pleasure centers that she couldn't hide from Charlie anymore. She doesn't stand a chance against a brick.

"You're special." A grin touches one side of his mouth, just below the large eye. "Do you know why?"

He leans forward.

"You took a pill to destroy God's gift. The ingested biomites began integrating with your clay when my brick shut them down. You are as close to halfskin as any human being could possibly be, but that's not why you're special."

The tip of his tongue grazes his parched lips.

"The shutdown occurred at a precise moment, Jamie. My brick waited for you to swallow the pill. He waited for it to expose its secrets, crystallize the embedded code before it was corrupted by your identity, before it began replicating your DNA. You contain nixes in an open state."

The man unfolds his hands.

"Do you know what that means?"

He continues staring, with the curl at the corner of his mouth, as if bathing in her innocence, soaking in the pleasure of her ignorance.

The doorknob clicks and the warehouse light falls on them along with death. Jamie's olfactory senses come online. She blinks as the foul odor fills her nostrils, seeps through her pores. Her attempts to turn it off fail.

She retches.

The man watches as she struggles to breathe, tears spilling down her face. She tries to look toward the dark, to close her eyes, but she's forced to turn toward the warehouse, where nude bodies are neatly lined on the floor, head to toe, their clothes stacked next to them.

"You are the chosen one, Jamie. You will be the one that climbs upon the cross and dies for their sins."

Several bricks walk among the corpses. Jamie tries not to focus, tries to blur the vision with tears as the man babbles on. Her eyes itch madly, her ears burning.

"What..." She wets her lips. "What are you going to do?"

It feels like the words were spoken for her. She doesn't want to know what the man will do to her; she just wants the door to close, for him to go away. She just wants this all to go away.

"I will set you free."

He means it differently than it sounds. A whimper escapes her.

"Your mother will see you." The man stands. "I promise."

Anna steps aside. The man limps next to her and braces himself in the doorway. For a moment, he blocks the view.

"It's a shame." He turns his head. "You strive to kill your feelings, to dim your senses so you don't see the ugly of the world. Everything you experience is a gift, Jamie. I would like you to accept what has been given to you."

The man walks away, his gait uneven. He shrinks away from her, continuing his limping pace down an aisle, slowly revealing the exposed bodies. Anna follows him.

The door remains open.

Jamie is forced to watch. She contains her panic until she recognizes the military green jacket atop a pile of clothing.

There's no pillow to hide her face this time.

MOTHER_

MOTHER TAKETH AWAY

Dr. Kaplan didn't know what day it was.

He marched down the corridor and reviewed case notes that scrolled past his vision, superimposed on the passing wheelchairs and nurses' stations. He had supervised ten organ transplants and three skin grafts and there were more. The only part of his body that didn't ache was biomite-enhanced.

His clay was exhausted.

It was getting difficult to focus; he could hardly remember what he just read. He attempted to enhance brain activity.

"Denied," his internal monitor responded. "Core body temperature is elevated. Enhanced limitations have been exceeded."

He didn't break stride. An override had already been allowed due to the nature of the emergency, but he was nearing thirty-nine hours of work. Six hours of sleep would be required to reset enhancement mode.

He rubbed his face. The sun wouldn't be up for another three hours. There was no choice: he had to sleep. Dr. Heigel would have to supervise his transplants.

He was waiting at the elevator when Drs. Angleton and Bates rushed past, white coats fluttering. The elevator opened, but Dr. Kaplan watched them run to the end of the wing.

There was chaos outside the Organ Fabrication Lab.

He left the elevator empty. Two nurses and a technician ran past him. His pace quickened, but his adrenaline had already been exhausted. He punched the door open and entered the lab.

The large room was lowly lit and segregated by aisles and crowded shelves. Red lights flashed on all the clear boxes that were always printing three-dimensional biomite organs. Dr. Kaplan had a liver due in less than an hour and the fabricators were standing still.

All of them.

An argument started up. Something broke. Doctors were shouting and technicians worked feverishly at their workstations. Dr. Felton, chief of Biomite Medicine, was more vocal than any of them.

"Jimmy." Dr. Kaplan grabbed the technician rushing into the lab. "What the hell is going on?"

"Mother shut us down."

"What?"

"Yeah, no warning. Just cold off."

Jimmy tried to pull away. "But hospitals are exempt from the fabricator shutdown."

"Not anymore."

"We're printing organs, Jimmy! We're not creating identities."

"I didn't shut us down."

"We're not ready for a shutdown, you understand? I've got people in pre-op waiting for organs that are half printed."

Jimmy pried the doctor's hand off of his coat. "You'll have to do raw seeding."

"There's no time. They need functional organs now."

"Sorry, Doctor. Mother declared every fabricator illegal."

Jimmy made his escape. The government had declared that fabricating life was as illegal as cloning. Mother supported their decision and killed the raw biomites the fabricators used to build hearts and kidneys.

Dr. Kaplan left the lab. He went to his car and drove home.

CHAPTER SEVENTY-FIVE_

Nix floats, disembodied, a wraith with no home, a voice on the wind. He drifts through the droning static of cyberspace like an aimless being caught in the current, the tide throwing him where it wants.

The static comes in waves, its rhythm crashing on a nonexistent shore, scratching its existence on the ethereal current. In silent ebbs between the peaks, he can feel his body out there.

The waves get louder. They scratch his throat, burn his nostrils. Nix opens his eyes, chest heaving.

"Relax, old man." Byron drops his hand on Nix's shoulder.

The stench of death still clogs his sinuses. A stream of snot trickles over his lips. He wipes his face, blinking away the tears. A few people turn around.

"Don't panic," Raine's voice whispers in his ear. "Relax, stay put."

If the bricks sense him, he couldn't outrun them. The main thing is to blend in.

"What the hell were you doing?" Byron says.

"Tell them you were caught in a data stream," Raine adds.

"Caught in the data stream," he mutters. "Couldn't disconnect."

Byron snorts. *Rookie mistake.* Every streaming blogger knows you don't attach your identity to a heavy upload, especially when you're streaming across the globe. The momentum can pull your consciousness with it, deposit your memories in a computer, fragmented like data.

"Next time," Henry says, "redistribute more biomites into the hypothalamus."

"Smaller chunks, old man," Byron adds.

Nix pulls an energy bar from his bag and chews slowly. A news truck is moving down the road. The crowd is beginning to swell. His breath returns to normal, the basic act of eating resetting his behavior.

The bodies are nude. They've probably visually analyzed them, recording all the physical attributes and ingested samples for preliminary analysis.

There's a rumor in the paranoid, antigovernment underground. Many believe that Marcus and his bricks have covertly taken halfskins back to Mother for a full-immersion analysis, basically dissolving their biomites for clues. But the world is watching the warehouse. They can't take the bodies this time, not without total chaos. The public would demand Mother be shut down.

But the girl will go with him. He's taking her; that's what he meant by setting her free. That pill contains critical data.

The nixes are caught in suspended animation, the gap between self-destruction and integration. They're meant to degrade before and after in the event of a shutdown, but now they're fully exposed. All the secrets can be read—links to suppliers, networks of producers, and locations of fabricators. It's everything Marcus has been looking for.

Nix, too.

Nix dusts the crumbs off his coat. He packs carefully and slings the bag over his shoulder, walking against the flow of traffic.

If he's going to get the girl, he'll need help.

CHAPTER SEVENTY-SIX_

Marcus leans against the wall, poking at two pills in his palm. His fucking knee is screaming. It never hurts like this when he's inside Mother. Nothing hurts. When he leaves, his body feels old again.

The nearest body is a young woman with plump breasts and a narrow midriff. Her pelvic bones jut from her hips. A precise divot has been cut from her left breast where nixes were carved out and, subsequently, digested by one of the bricks for analysis.

Noise comes from somewhere beyond the back walls. The door to the back room swings open, the hinges squealing as Anna pulls it shut. Her heels echo in the dead space.

Marcus clenches the pills, watching her blonde hair swing in time to the sway of her hips. She holds out a bottle of water. Marcus washes the painkillers down and waits for relief.

"She's sleeping," Anna says. "I'll keep her unconscious until we're finished."

Marcus screws the lid back on, wiping his mouth. He shifts his weight, staring at the big-breasted corpse, wishing she'd suffered more. Death is too easy.

"Why don't you get some rest," Anna says. "Get off your feet."

"Your analysis of the conversation?"

Anna sighs. "Confirmed. An identity was latched to her perception field. We believe it was Nixon Richards."

"You believe?"

"The identity was scrambled. It's possible one of the bloggers or news agencies have hired a hacker of his caliber, but statistically, we believe it's him."

"He heard everything?"

"Yes. And saw everything, too. Including the fabricator in the back."

The glass case. The epitome of evil.

"He had to be in the area. If we move quickly, we could arrest everyone. It'll take some time to—"

"Not yet." Marcus takes his earpiece out.

It's doubtful he's still out there. Anything rash will scare him away. He needs to be lured deeper into the trap. Now that they know he's here, let him feel safe. Let him reach for the fabricator.

Twenty years I've waited.

Excitement rumbles beneath the ache in his knee, the same knee he wrecked trying to apprehend Nixon Richards and his sister. They released the nixes to the underground; they wrecked his marriage and spawned an entire race of undetectable halfskins that have required Marcus to dedicate his life to capturing. The surgically repaired knee reminds him of his mistakes. It's fitting that here, in the rain where the pain is the greatest, that he finds Nix.

He can't be rash.

"The rest of this?" Marcus waves at the bodies.

"The delivery will arrive tomorrow at three o'clock," Anna says.

"It was supposed to be three days."

"Some complications with Mother's fabricators. The shipment will be here tomorrow."

Marcus tests the knee. The Dilaudid needed another twenty

minutes to kick in, but he was tired of waiting. He'd waited long enough.

Anna guides him through the back room, past the sleeping young lady. They exit through the newly fashioned doorway cut out of the back-room wall. He looks back at the glass case before finding his way to the loading docks, where a white sedan picks him up.

CHAPTER SEVENTY-SEVEN_

BAXTER WHINES.

Cali takes a hotdog slice from the counter and rewards Kooper first for sitting quietly. She returns to washing dishes while the music crackles. Sometimes silence reveals her troubles too clearly.

The sun is setting and the long shadow of the house stretches all the way to the barn. Misting rain keeps everything damp and cold.

To the right, outside the pasture, the old swing set reflects the waning sunlight. The posts and chains are rusted and one of the legs has crumpled into the weeds like a broken knee. The swing is askew. Cali imagines that it was shiny and new when the father built it and the mother watched her two children while she cooked dinner and cleaned up. The laughter probably carried into the house.

They had lost one of the girls to meningitis. She was only seven.

"God called her," the mother had told the neighbors. "She's with Him now."

Maybe that's when the swing set became a static effigy of sorrow. They still had one child, but there would always be the memory of them both. And the laughter of two. Ten years later, the family died in an automobile accident.

No biomites to save them.

Cali dries the last dish, staring at the swing set. This was where she was meant to be, in a house with ghosts that look much like the ones that haunt her.

God called.

She checks the time, a habit she'd developed. Clay folks don't have internal clocks.

"Want to get the paper?" Cali asks.

The dogs have curled up on a small rug. They jump up. Their toenails click on the floor, paws slipping as they race out. The railing leading down the steps is loose and the posts are rotting.

The dogs wait next to the truck. Cali lets them climb over the driver's seat. She rolls the window down and enjoys a cold drive out to the gate. The electric motor whirs, craning the metal entrance open. The dogs jump out to sniff around while Cali walks out to the road but not in it.

The road is the edge of her safe zone.

The abandoned cell phone tower is one of the reasons she initially considered buying this land. Centered on the property, it was easily converted to generate a static field. In the countryside, a blind spot blends into the scenery, keeping Mother from seeing her. She hasn't left the property in five years.

The road is the limit.

She starts back for the truck, with the newspaper under her arm, when the pressure begins. It starts at the back of her head and pushes forward.

Bing. She shuffles to a standstill.

Cali restrains herself from immediately answering the call from Nix. It has been years since she heard his voice. She hasn't seen him in five years. *Five years and four months.*

She can't answer.

If she does, she'll make him promise to come to the farm, to let her protect him. To stay away from Dreamland.

To turn Raine off.

A third wave begins. *Bing.* Cali clutches the newspaper as the dogs climb out of the ditch. She closes her eyes and projects a thought. *Off.*

She stands on the lonely road, the frigid breeze blowing over the treetops. She yearns for music, for something to distract her from the thoughts and the feelings that usher in guilt and shame and sadness. She wants to answer his call.

It'll only hurt worse.

The newspaper hits the dirt. The pages flap open.

Cali walks past the truck. She begins running, pumping her arms in stride with her long pace. The dogs keep up, tongues hanging out. They have no idea where their owner is going or why.

But neither does Cali.

She just runs.

CHAPTER SEVENTY-EIGHT_

THE HOOD OF THE POLICE CAR IS WARM.

Paul leans against the driver's door, trying to remember something. It's a word or an idea or...*something*. He's obsessed with recalling it, remembering that he's done so a dozen times already. It's something urgent.

Critical.

The thought hovers in a haze that filled his head days ago. He's not sure just how long it's been, but night has followed day more than once.

His memories are cloaked in a dreamy fog, surreal. They're like eagles soaring high above, wings stretched out and sometimes turning so they disappear into the blue. Paul searches the sky for them to return, to bring back whatever he's supposed to remember.

"Sarge," Jeffers says, "you want in?"

It takes a moment to focus on the officer's face, to recognize the bristled mustache. Jeffers is in front of another cruiser. A third one effectively blocks the alley leading to the loading docks behind the warehouse.

"You want in?" Jeffers repeats.

"What?"

"Materese says the brick doesn't have a cock."

Paul licks his lips. They've been dry for days, can't seem to hold moisture. He shakes his head, focusing on the uniformed officer sipping coffee behind Jeffers. Her hair is pulled into a tight bun, the eyeliner thick and sharp.

Just past the back bumper of the third car, the brick stands at the corner of the building. His arms hang straight at his sides. His expression is tireless, waxy and sentinel blank. Only the subtle rise and fall of his chest hints at life.

"I say he's hung like a donkey." Jeffers holds his hands apart. "Like that."

"What's he going to use it for?" Materese says.

"Whatever he wants. I mean, Christ, if I could build a dick, I'd make it worth the while."

"Use your head, idiot. Bricks don't procreate; they're squeezed out of a fabricator like glue. They just got to look human."

"Procreate."

"It means fuck."

"He's got a cock, Materese. It doesn't make sense not to."

"He ain't got nothing, I can tell. It's like one of those Ken dolls, just a bump between his legs."

Jeffers chews his lip, looking the brick up and down. The brick doesn't move, but he's listening. Paul can feel him absorbing everything around him, feeling and seeing and hearing. He's making sure they do their job.

"I've got a hundred says he's sporting wood."

The foam coffee cup is poised inches from her lips, the rim stained red. She shakes her head like she's had one too many of these conversations. Jeffers digs a bill out of his pocket and slams it on the hood.

"Get proof and it's yours," he says.

"You need help."

"No, I mean get proof and the money's yours."

"If you want to see a cock, look down," she says, sipping. "It won't cost you."

Paul sways on his feet, clicking his front teeth. Jeffers licks his lips but not because they're dry. He's just watched too much porn. He probably has a brick fetish, petitioning the government to fabricate sex models to satiate the urges of half the population that argue rape, divorce, and depression would be reduced if people could own sexbots.

Jeffers would have one of every color. Paul would take that bet.

"Why you so uptight?" Jeffers says. "He ain't human. It's more like a rubber dick, like the one you got stuffed in your glove box."

"Fuck you."

"Hey, don't be embarrassed. It's natural."

"Jeffers," Paul says.

"No disrespect, Sarge. I'm just trying to learn something. And give Materese money. That's all I'm saying. I seen her dildo."

"Fine." Materese reaches for the bill.

Jeffers dangles it out of reach. "Got to see it first."

"How?" she asks.

"Unzip his pants. He ain't moved all day."

"Pull his pants down?"

"Talk dirty to him or something. Tell him you want a robot baby. It ain't like you never got in a man's pants before; do whatever you do."

"You're a sick fuck, Jeffers."

"I'm curious. There's a difference."

Materese looks at Paul. There's hope that he'll stop her, tell her it's a bad idea, that Jeffers should go sit in the car. But he's still swimming in the haze, trying to remember the thing he's supposed to remember. For a moment, he wonders why Jeffers is waving a hundred-dollar bill.

Materese puts her coffee on the hood. She approaches warily, waving her hand in front of the brick's face when she's within spitting distance. He doesn't blink.

His hair is brown and cropped near the scalp. His posture is slouched, his shoulders round. He looks like someone you'd see alone in a dark bar.

Materese takes the last couple steps one at a time, pausing each time. Paul watches with mild interest, falling in and out of focus. One second he's watching a young Hispanic woman reaching for a middle-aged man's frumpy trousers, and the next it's his subordinate about to sexually harass a brick.

Paul forms a word to stop this when his thoughts are obliterated. Materese's hand stops an inch from the belt buckle. She's as still as the automobile. Jeffers's tongue is out. Both of them are frozen.

The brick begins blinking.

He looks at Paul. His eyelids appear heavy, his light blue eyes tired.

Jeffers and Materese suddenly go to their cars. A heavy engine rattles behind Paul. He moves his head like he's underwater. A white car is followed by a large truck—the type used to move furniture. Jeffers and Materese drive past him, opening the blockade. The moving truck is followed by two more, all with the U-Haul logo. They turn down the alley, gears grinding, hot exhaust in his nostrils.

Jeffers and Materese close the gap once the convoy is inside. They lean against their cars. Jeffers strokes his bristled mustache, a daydreamy haze in his eyes. Materese picks her fingernails. Paul thinks he should remind Jeffers his money is fluttering across the street.

Paul gets in his car. It's hot and stuffy. He loosens his collar, trying to remember where he is and what he's supposed to be doing.

Someone knocks on the driver's side window, a man with a bristled mustache. Paul should know him, but he can't recall his name.

"What are you doing, Sarge?" the man asks.

"What?"

"What are you doing in your cruiser?"

Paul strokes the steering wheel and notices all the switches and monitors. He's in a police car.

"Got to go."

"Where?"

Paul shakes his head.

"You coming back?" the man asks.

The brick is staring. Another strange wave passes through Paul, tingles beneath his scalp like scrubbing bubbles wiping his brain clean. Telling him what to do.

"Yeah," Paul says. "I'll be back."

He follows the white car and U-Hauls to the loading dock.

CHAPTER SEVENTY-NINE_

THE SUN IS OUT.

It's burned away the steel mat of clouds that's entombed the sky for four days. Sunlight reflects off the wet streets. Marcus slouches in the backseat, watching the oblivious citizens of Seattle blunder down sidewalks and wait for streetlights. The fabric of humanity is like parched linen dangling over a flame of biomite technology; a flame that could incinerate any shred of human semblance, leaving human forms like empty cicada shells, like pillars of salt.

Sodom and Gomorrah.

If not for Marcus, they would all perish without a thought. If not for his dedication, there would be no one to extinguish the flame. And now, after so many struggles, the tide will finally turn.

He could hardly sleep.

The hotel was comfortable and quiet, but Marcus stared at the ceiling. Even a sleeping pill took longer than usual, its effects still swimming in his head.

He's waited twenty years for this day. Twenty years to have the boy—he's a man, but will always be a boy—in his grasp. He'll take Nix back to Mother and watch her digest him slowly.

Marcus pats Anna's bare knee just below the hemline. Her

lipstick is magenta and perfectly lined. She appears unfocused, staring past the front seat, through the windshield.

"Mother is updating," she says.

Marcus cringes. He prefers not to call the massive artificial intelligence that monitors biomites by her acronym. She might overlook humanity, but he had a different relationship with her, something on an equal level. No, he couldn't match her processing ability, nothing could. Marcus brought her passion; he brought her wisdom that only one of God's creatures could bring.

Marcus caresses the inside of her knee then folds his hands on his lap. "Why didn't she call me?"

"She prefers to speak with you when you return home."

The car stops at the stoplight. A man on the corner stares at the white car. Above him, a billboard advertises a long-lasting Dreamland experience.

"Continue," Marcus says.

"Free the girl."

Marcus chuckles, waiting for more. Anna is looking at him now, her eyes focused on his lips. "We'll do nothing of the sort," he says. "The girl contains everything and the boy knows it. He'll do something rash and we'll have him."

"Her projected analysis suggests that if the girl is released, Nixon Richards will find her and lead us to his sister. The probability of success is 83%."

"The probability of capturing Nixon Richards right now is 100%."

"That is not the objective."

"And when we have him, his sister will come out of hiding. We've already discussed this." Marcus checks his jacket for his earpiece. "I want to talk with her now."

"She has already implemented the change, Marcus. Her projections are complete."

"She didn't discuss this with me!"

That is the issue. It isn't that she just snatched Nix out of his hand, not that she shit on this glorious morning; it is that she didn't consult him. *That's not how this works.* She continuously conducts endless scenarios, analyzing human behavior and motivation, predicting the probability of outcomes with greater accuracy than anything on the planet...but she cannot see the future!

These are probabilities. Chances. Science, by its own admission, is less than perfect. It works from educated guesses and refines its mistakes. Only God is perfect.

And Marcus speaks for Him.

That is the agreement. Mother does the math, but Marcus speaks the divine. They work together.

The car waits at the final stoplight. Three cargo trucks are lined up behind them, their diesel engines idling loudly. The satellite imagery of their approach will be blurred from public record. No one will see them make the final approach to the warehouses.

When the light turns green, Marcus realizes he's staring at a billboard that advertises free biomite boosters.

JAMIE'S MOUTH IS SLACK, drool slipping from the corner, a glistening trail to her chin. Yellowish light filters through the opaque glass dimmed with age and neglect. Dust particles hang over her.

Marcus watches her from the dark end of the room. The door is closed, but the odor reaches him. It permeates everything, but no longer reminds him of victory. Now it's just the stench of death and the possibility of losing everything.

Right there, sleeping, is the key. That pill inside her is the key.

From the other side of the door, the warehouse has come alive. Some of the bricks grunt, dropping heavy objects on the concrete. There's an occasional sound of fabric and zippers, of vinyl bags rustling.

Marcus steps on a soft cord and smells the tang of biomites. It's a whiplike tail. He nudges the limp animal with the tip of his shoe, its skin smooth, leathery, and red. In the dark, it looks like a dog, but the ivory fangs protruding from the oversized snout are evident.

Fabricated abominations.

The pets range from mouse-sized animals to Great Danes, each of them outfitted with customized limbs and unnatural colors. Some with fur, others hide. All of them with teeth. They were likely prowling around when the nixes were shut down, dropping like the power cord had been pulled.

Before Mother put a stop to it, everyday people were working their way up to fabricating larger organisms, keeping them around like freakish pets. How far were they from fabricating dead loved ones?

All the warehouses in this sector are owned by the same subsidiary. This was just the beginning. If the brick hadn't discovered their activity, they would've expanded into the neighboring buildings, opening doorways through the back walls like Marcus had done. How much would someone pay to fabricate a son or daughter?

This wasn't just a party scene. It was the fuel that kept the biomite flame growing, that pushed it closer to the fabric.

How many more of these dens are there?

Meanwhile, Mother will free the girl, the drooling Sleeping Beauty who contains all the answers. They could drop her in the digesting vats, absorb the information and locate places like this all over the world. They could fabricate an army of bricks to stage a global raid. And she wants to let her go.

He can override Mother. Marcus has that authority.

He can force her to capture Nix and lure his sister into the open, but he knows better. He knows his desires are distorting his rational thinking, that Mother has the same wish as he does without the emotional attachment.

She wants them both, too.

Jamie sounds like a child caught in a nightmare. Marcus kicks the dead pet and limps over to the lounger. The muscles on her neck are rigid, her tongue working hard to break free.

Marcus strokes her chin with the backs of his fingers, running them softly to her throat. He leans close enough to feel her breath on his lips and her eyes snap open.

He squeezes her throat, feeling the muscles collapse in his grip. Her breath catches and her eyes widen. She's still caught in Anna's catatonic grip, unable to move, unable to look away. He doesn't have the ability to sense if Nix is in there, if he's still pawning her perception field, but he hopes so. He hopes that boy sees him.

He will always be a boy.

If freeing this girl will give him Nix *and* Cali, he will not stand in the way.

Marcus shoves off.

The girl struggles to breathe; unformed words fall off her lips in grunts and squeaks. Marcus ignores the pathetic attempts to curse him. He opens the door and walks into the putrid fog of dead flesh.

Anna is waiting for him. He watches the bricks work like soldiers. They carry body bags across the warehouse, dropping each one next to a nude body.

Marcus looks down at a teenage boy named Charlie. Most of his flesh is sickly pale, the stomach slightly bloated. A small patch of hair is tufted between his nipples.

A pair of bricks drops a body bag next to it, pulling the flaps to the side to reveal an exact duplicate of Charlie. The skin is even discolored with veiny, marbled patterns near the surface, even the bruises around his bicep where someone grabbed him. Maybe his girlfriend was trying to stop him from taking the nixes.

Or maybe she was trying to get away.

The bricks lift Mother's stiff fabrication from the bag and quickly slide Charlie—the real Charlie—inside. They dress the imposter with the clothes that are stacked near the corpse, using photo images they recorded upon arrival, adjusting the coat and pants to match what he looked like before he was undressed. Even the wrinkles in the sleeves and the inadvertent cuff of the pant leg are exacted.

They haul the body bag to the trucks. They will return with another.

Marcus is tempted to bend down. Even though the pain in his knee has subsided, he'll pay for it. The people outside the warehouse, the ones waiting for answers, will never know the bodies of their loved ones will be flown to Mother for deep analysis, where they'll be pulled apart, where every cell, every part of them will be digested for future reference.

What they'll find in the warehouse once Marcus leaves are fabricated duplicates made of biomites and a small amount of clay, just enough to fool an investigation. They'll bury these fabricated bodies, mourn over them, take flowers to their graves and never know the difference. In God's eyes, it won't matter. Their love for their sons and daughters will still be true.

And Marcus will be that much closer to stopping this plague.

"Contact the chief of police," he says. "Tell him we've concluded our investigation and the families are allowed to view their loved ones."

"The press will want a statement," Anna says.

"Have someone else do it."

"You'd like a brick to handle PR?"

"Yes."

She did that on purpose, knowing he was struggling with the new course of action. She referred to her kindred as bricks, as if the insult of their fabrication is completely lost on her. He likes that.

"I'd also like to give the press full access to the premises. Bring the camera crews inside, even sneak some of those bloggers in. I want a team of bricks to stay behind to be interviewed. I want the public to be saturated with details. Let them see what their future looks like."

"Public beheadings...you know that tactic doesn't work."

"Humor me."

"I'll take the lead in public relations, then."

"No. I want you to be on the plane with me, I'll want company.

I'll be flying back with the bodies, I want analysis to begin immediately."

The bricks work ceaselessly as always, hauling bag after bag into the warehouse, swapping and dressing bodies down to the last detail. There's no need to encourage them to work faster. They're such good slaves. Marcus revels in the fact that he never has to deal with human employees, imperfect and slow.

An ironic twist, but effective.

Perhaps, he always thinks, there's a place for bricks in society once humans stop defiling God's temples.

Two body bags are dropped near the back office and left unattended. Marcus shuffles near the foot of them. Anna takes a knee and pulls one of them open to reveal a young girl inside. Jamie's fabrication is chalky but well-preserved, as if she only passed this morning.

Marcus sighs. "Set her free, then."

He limps toward the back exit, bricks avoiding him as he heads toward a waiting car, with no idea of what Mother plans to do.

But it'll work.

It usually does.

CHAPTER EIGHTY_

A BUZZY HUM SWARMS PAUL'S HEAD, CARRYING HIM THROUGH colors and images, random thoughts and memories.

His eyelids are heavy. Hands like rubber.

Dim light filters through the shade of a door directly ahead of him. Cries of outrage and grief hail from the other side.

General chaos.

Words that don't quite connect.

A reclining lounger sits in the waning light. A girl lies on it, her head back, mouth open. The dead light falls on her like an old lamp, yellow and dusty. Her chest rises and falls in slow, steady rhythm.

Shadows pass across the shade.

The door rattles.

They're coming for her. They're coming for...Jamie.

She was a victim in a heinous crime, she was held against her will. The cops were going to do terrible things to her.

Not cops. Someone else.

Paul's feet are glued to the floor. His legs, rigid wood. He raises his fat hand, breaking the paralysis like a brittle cocoon. He bends his knees and takes a step. His blood flows.

Her hands are folded over her stomach, bright red lines around her wrists where plastic cuffs chafed the skin. Paul slides his arms beneath her, lifting the dead weight. There's a body slumped against the lounger. It's a man. His chin is against his chest, the face hidden by the shadows. Paul ignores that one.

I've only come for Jamie.

He walks through a network of corridors enclosed with unfinished walls and sheets of plastic, occasionally bumping her limp body into bare studs. His instincts tell him to turn left when the exit feels left. Go straight when that seems to be the way.

He's got to get far away.

His intuition leads him to a large room with huge rolling doors. One is open, leading to a concrete ledge for loading. A white sedan is parked next to a police cruiser. Paul climbs down and slides Jamie in the back of the white car.

He drives down the alley, onto Beech Street.

To get her away.

To keep her safe.

CHAPTER EIGHTY-ONE_

THE CROWD HAS DOUBLED. THE POLICE HAVE TRIPLED. THE chief of police and three of his lieutenants are behind a podium inside the barricade.

Nix stands two blocks away on a berm of soil, his vision enhanced on the male and female bricks stepping to the podium. They're brunettes of average build and forgettable features but large, soulful eyes. The barricade buckles as the crowd pushes forward. Their grief has transformed into anger that blames the bricks and police for their halfskin sons and daughters.

They have no one else to blame.

Nix tunes in to a blog stream to hear the audio while he watches the chief of police and his lieutenants stand behind the bricks, chins thrust out, eyes hazy with the dullness of old silverware.

"Let me express our sincere apologies for this delay," the female brick says. Her cheeks sag with the weight of sorrow, her eyes heavy, eyebrows slightly pinched with concern. "I speak on behalf of the Seattle Police Department, the Biomite Oversight Committee, and all the men and women dedicated to serving humanity when I say we are deeply sorry. A tragedy like this affects everyone, but especially you. It is deeply regrettable."

The crowd rebels against the false empathy although, with time and repeated delivery, they'll soon be swayed. The imitation of human emotions and body language speaks directly to the subconscious.

When the female brick finishes, she bows her head and makes room for the male brick to step front and center. While his expression is also mournful, it is heavy with the weight of severity.

"We have asked for your patience," he announces to the crowd as well as the millions watching it stream through the blogosphere, "to ensure that events like this will never happen again, that we can ensure the safety and well-being of everyone. It is our hope that you will join us in ending technology abuse."

The crowd grows impatient. Cries of grief can be heard all the way up the street. He continues his empathic message before turning to the chief of police.

"Would you care to explain the procedure for these good people?"

The chief steps forward and delivers a dead set of instructions for people that have been previously identified as family to come to the right, where they will be ushered inside to view the deceased.

Letting family walk all over a crime scene?

"Verified media will also be admitted," he announces, half asleep.

The barricade opens and the police usher them forward.

"What now?" Raine's image stands barefoot on the grass.

"I'll have a look," Nix says.

"She won't be in there."

"Maybe not."

"Then why risk it?"

Nix starts toward the heaving crowd. Raine's image keeps up.

"Nix, there's nothing in there. They've already picked the place clean and the girl is gone. You can't save her even if she is in there—there are just too many bricks. It's not your fault."

Somehow, it is his fault. His sister ignored all his calls while he sat in a hotel room, watching blogs stream updates. He analyzed half a dozen ways to infiltrate the warehouse. When they announced that media would be allowed access, he could create a diversion or find an exit. There had to be a way; he just needed some help. And she ignored him.

He knew she would.

When he arrived that morning for the press conference and crazy fucking announcement that family would be allowed to meander through the warehouse while bloggers streamed their reactions to the world, he knew Jamie would be gone. He felt it. He scanned the area for her biomite identity—as unique as her fingerprints, indelibly stamped on her awareness.

Gone.

"Let's not go in there." Raine's hand falls on his shoulder. "There's always tomorrow."

That is the real problem. This will happen somewhere tomorrow and the day after that and the day after that. There will be an endless string of Jamies and warehouses full of lifeless halfskins. Marcus and the bricks know what they're doing now. With Jamie and that nixed pill inside her, they have intel and know how to get more. Before long they'll be shutting down halfskins daily. How long before Nix is one of them?

He blends into the crowd, slowly making his way to the entrance. An identity scan penetrates his bones.

Nix feels a brick's psychic intrusion like energy particles wriggling through his body, examining his cells, his biomites, searching for verified identification. It's as if the hand of Mother emanates from this diminutive female brick standing by the steel door, her green eyes unblinking, unforgiving.

Perhaps another strain of nixes would've spilled its secrets to her, but Nix isn't cloaked with just any biomite. These are the nixes Cali engineered when she saved him twenty years ago, a strain she never released to anyone else. While most nixes are produced in small batches and distributed to buyers, Nix and Cali's are unique and, as far as he knows, the only ones in the world.

The female brick waves him forward.

Inside, the grief is palpable. He can taste the sadness as people hug corpses. The news feeds clog the data stream. Bloggers silently stalk the perimeter, network reporters attempt to interview police. *Why would they do this?*

And then it all makes sense.

No one would allow people to see their loved ones lying on a cold concrete floor, their features tainted with unnatural color.

Marcus wants the world to see this.

The door at the back is closed, a sheet thrown over the glass. Nix walks around the outside of the warehouse, remembering the view through Jamie's eyes when the door was left open. The bodies are dressed now. They look normal. They were nude. So was the boy that she came with. Nix still remembers his name.

Charlie.

The door is cracked open. Nix slows as he approaches and taps it with his boot. An empty lounger faces the doorway. A plastic cuff hangs from beneath the frame. There's a body slumped against it. A cop. Nix doesn't bother identifying him. The poor bastard must've already been a halfskin when the investigation began. The bricks figured him out and dragged him back here like garbage.

Light seeps to the back of the room.

The floor is clear of mutant pets. The glass fabricator is gone. They took it all, including the girl.

Nix braces his hands in the doorway. This didn't have to happen. They chose their fate, but the girl...she didn't have to be part of this. If Marcus has her, her suffering is just beginning.

But Nix is wrong.

Jamie's not in the back office. Her body lies next to Charlie's, her hands folded over her stomach. Nix stands over her. He didn't see her face when he pawned her senses, but he recognizes the coat and the slim fingers, the blue polish on her fingernails.

He takes a knee, straightens her collar, brushes the hair from her face. She looks younger than he imagined. *What're you doing in here?*

He feels a twist of sadness not for her death but the fact that her body is so undisturbed. She's been left alone.

No one has come to mourn her.

He bows his head, his hand over hers, still and cold.

"I'm sorry for your loss," a female brick says.

Nix feels his eyes mist up, sadness for Jamie.

Sadness for a lot of things.

CHAPTER EIGHTY-TWO_

A RED PICKUP DRIVES TOWARD THE HOUSE, PULLING A TRAILER. A man and his son start unloading bales of hay into the barn's breezeway. Cali sneaks around the trailer and greets them with a paper bag.

"How are you, Hal?" she asks.

"Better than I deserve," the man says. "What you got there?"

"A little something to take home."

Hal pulls out a jar of preserved tomatoes. He exposes his tobacco-stained teeth with a crooked smile, saying that his wife will be happy and that Cali should come over to eat. His son hauls the bales—one in each hand—while the dogs run circles around him.

Cali sways as pressure pulses in her head. *Bing.*

"You all right?" Hal grabs her elbow.

"I think I've been in the sun too long." She touches her forehead.

"I got some aspirin in the truck."

"No, thanks. I think I'm just a bit dehydrated. Let me grab some water. I'll be right back."

She can put an end to these calls if she shuts down the connection. After three days, she still isn't answering them because, if she does, they'll argue and that is pointless. She just can't bring herself to disconnect their chat line. It'd be like cutting Nix out of her life.

Cali grabs a box in the pantry with a stack of newspapers and pauses at the kitchen sink. A little green light flashes in her vision followed by a soft ping. A message this time.

It'll be fifteen minutes before Hal and his son are finished. Cali locks the front door, just in case, and goes back through the kitchen to an old door in the narrow hallway. Steps lead down to a landing before turning left, creaking louder the deeper she goes.

The cellar is cool. A naked bulb pushes darkness into the corners, warm light reflecting off endless jars of pickled produce and preserved fruit.

Cali pauses, taking a deep breath.

Messages, she thinks.

The jars recede into a fuzzy background as a file opens across her vision. Scenes of a warehouse overlay the basement. There are bodies and people grieving, with police trying to keep order. The scene comes from various angles. She's about to erase it when the view focuses on a single body. It's a girl. She's all alone, her hair disheveled. Her coat bunched around her throat.

"We could've saved her," Nix says. "This is your fault."

Cali bumps into the shelves behind her, the glass rattling.

"Marcus Anderson is rubbing our noses in it."

Delete.

She squats next to an empty box, hand over her face. She should've followed her instincts, never should've answered it. Yet she still can't cut the chat line completely. He's the only one she's got. But Marcus isn't the only one rubbing her nose in it.

CHAPTER EIGHTY-THREE_

THE AIRLINER HITS TURBULENCE.

Marcus clutches the armrests. The sun disappears as they drop below the cloud cover. Ahead, a dome sits near the shore of Montana's Fort Peck Lake, wedged in the lower fork where the Missouri River and Dry Arm split. Its smooth walls, once white, have dulled with dust and algae. It looks like a sports dome without windows—a monstrous, dirty igloo that could house a hundred thousand people.

Scientists named it the Mitochondria Terraforming Hierarchy of Record, something that describes the changes occurring at the cellular level. Normal people call it something else.

Mother.

The massive intelligence requires Montana's cold climate and the chilled water of Fort Peck Lake to maintain operating temperatures which, in turn, have elevated the water temperatures and drastically altered the aquatic ecosystem—just one price for her protection.

The airplane's wings tip again and the drop registers in Marcus's gut. He latches on to the armrests as the plane lines up with the south side of the dome. Several landing strips extend from the perimeter like spokes. One airplane sits outside, the sun gleaming off the wings.

We have company.

Anna sits with her legs crossed, watching the rough terrain soar past as the engines cut back on the approach. Marcus's grip doesn't relax until the wheels are on the pavement. The plane taxis toward the square gate opening on the side of the dome like a mouth. Marcus can feel the filth of the warehouse still clinging to him. Death fills his senses. Now that he's home, he can purge the decay.

The hangar is spotless, the floor shiny. There are several jets inside, including drones that retrieve food and supplies.

"Where are they?" he asks.

"Director Powell and the secretary of state are in your office," Anna says. "I can delay them if you'd like to shower first."

She knows me so well. "I'll deal with this now."

The plane pulls deep into the hangar, the engines winding down. The wind buffets the aircraft until the gate is fully closed. When the steps are pulled open, Marcus limps off. Golf carts are plugged in for journeys across the dome. Anna goes to the open elevator that's to the right of the bay doors that lead to Mother's inner workings.

"Inspection teams are already meeting with the service technicians," Anna says.

"We're not scheduled for an inspection."

"No."

"Where are the teams?"

"First-floor servers."

Twenty men and women work for Marcus, assigned to service Mother. Isolated from their families, they are compensated well. Most of them will take the money after a year and quit. Inspections teams come around from time to time: the government likes to make sure they're doing their jobs. Marcus hasn't met most of his service technicians, but it doesn't matter, really. Mother fabricates bricks to assist them.

As the elevator rises, the pain recedes from his knee. When they reach the top, it's gone. Relief is always waiting at home.

The doors slide open and reveal the simple, yet spacious, office.

The director of the Biomite Oversight Committee is leaning against Marcus's sprawling walnut desk. The secretary of state is standing in the middle of the room.

"What are you doing here?" Marcus says.

"Babysitting you, again," the secretary says.

"You're wasting your time, Hank."

"You're a public disaster, Anderson." The beefy secretary loosens his tie. "You broadcasted that entire event—are you out of your mind? I'm watching mothers crying over dead bodies while a herd of goddamn bricks are prowling the warehouse and giving fucking press releases."

His cheeks are flushed.

"Your face doesn't need to be associated with shutdowns. We made that clear when we sent you here."

"Mark this day," Marcus says. "This will be a turning point."

"It's a goddamn public relations nightmare." Hank cuts him off from entering the office, stabbing his fat finger at Marcus's face. "I want you out."

Anna gets between them. In heels, she's a few inches taller than both of them.

"Gentlemen," Powell says, "let's slow down."

The athletic middle-aged man pats Hank on the shoulder, gently guiding him toward the glass wall overlooking the industrialized view of Mother's inner workings. They have a few words before Powell comes back.

He shakes Marcus's hand.

"We need to recognize the significance of the Seattle event," he says. "The preliminary reports are, quite frankly, staggering. The prognostics suggest countless operations tied to this one. I agree, this could be the turning point, Marcus."

"You came all this way to offer me congratulations?"

"Certainly. And to inquire about your mental health."

"Mental health?"

"We're concerned about you."

"I assure you, I couldn't be better."

"You've skipped several health reviews. When's the last time you were scanned?"

Marcus laughs. He stands behind his desk, immediately imbuing him with a sense of executive power. "Scanning me for biomites? I'm afraid you've wasted the taxpayers' money, gentlemen, and my time. So, if you don't mind, Anna can show you out."

He gestures to the elevator.

Powell buries his hands in his pockets, half turning toward the open elevator. He makes eye contact with Hank. Several seconds pass.

"You can speak up," Marcus says. "Chatting isn't a secret here. Anna's monitoring your conversation."

Powell placates him with a smile. "Secretary, would you mind if I spoke with Marcus alone for a few minutes?"

Sweat stains have spread across the secretary's pits. Several choice thoughts stiffen his upper lip, but he goes to the elevator. Anna offers to escort him to one of the inspection teams. Powell waits for the elevator to close.

"Let's walk," he says.

Marcus gets a bottle of water from the mini-fridge beneath the desk. Powell ventures to the broad curving window. He waits with his hand on the door. They walk out to the portico, greeted by industrial humming and lubricated steel.

In some ways, the office is a sky box. Instead of a field below, there's an endless array of tiers and doorways that reach up to the dome's curved roof. A long corridor separates the dome into two sides. An oily haze obscures the far end. Skeletal catwalks connect each level, dull metal scaffoldings that, farther out, are swallowed by the haze. Marcus likes to think the design resembles two halves of a brain, but it looks more like a futuristic prison for all the world's criminals.

Far below on the first few levels, the servers store all collected data. Farther up in the "thinking" rooms are the processing units.

Above those are labs for experiments and research and things the inspection teams won't find. It's not difficult to keep secrets in Mother's maze.

"Personally, I don't give a shit about your appearance in Seattle. Broadcasting it through the bloggers was brilliant, if you ask me. You let the viewers know what will happen when they get caught." Powell leans on the polished rail. "The problem, Marcus, is that you looked batshit crazy. People don't like a madman at the wheel."

He stops grinning.

"You drive up with a cavalcade of bricks and get out with Anna, who looks like a goddamn sexbot. Don't get me wrong, she's nice and she's effective, but she's a brick, Marcus. And the world knows you're fucking it.

"Now I'm not saying men in power don't do crazy things, but they do them behind closed doors. You paraded yours across the world's stage. All those secret videos of you getting freaky with your other biomite porn dolls? We put that behind us. You can bet your ass the bloggers are dragging those back out."

Marcus clenches his fists. It was one of the reasons he wanted to hang Cali Richards from the rafters. Twenty years ago, she threatened to reveal his perversions if he didn't leave them alone. But when videos of his Biomite Real Doll orgies leaked on to the Internet, his family stopped talking to him. His career was over.

Forgive me, Father, for I have sinned.

"I get the job done," Marcus says. "It's my mission."

"That's right. And that's why we appointed you. But we put you out here, in the middle of this godforsaken part of the world, so that the public would forget you. And they did, Marcus. They forgot all the nutty places you were sticking your cock. Your job is to stay here, in the dome, and get the job done. Are we clear?"

Powell's expression softens.

"Listen, the world is a little jumpy when it comes to what we're doing. You're working with this Big Brother dome to essentially turn people off and we don't call it murder."

Marcus pitches his halfskin argument: Humans with more biomites than clay are mostly machines.

Powell holds up his hand. "Save your breath. I'm not here about your mission; this is about your approach. We need you to slow down. Whatever shutdowns you conduct, do them quietly. Make the world believe that the worst is over, that there are no more Seattles out there. You pull another warehouse stunt—strutting around with Anna on your arm—and the powers-that-be will bury you."

Marcus's chin juts forward.

"We want the public's support, Marcus. Win them over. You're fighting *for* them, remember? Make them believe it. We on the same page here?"

He stares at a small group of technicians crossing a catwalk several floors below. The humming grows louder.

Powell looks out over the industrial matrix. They watch another group of technicians rise in a clear elevator shaft. A few of the men are inspectors. They'll be escorted to selected labs, take their readings and write their reports. They'll never realize there are sections they missed.

"You doing all right, Marcus?"

"I'm doing fine."

"The technicians say you're almost nonexistent. Some of them have never seen you. We'd like you to occasionally interact with the staff, meet with them. You don't have to hide up here. You should also meet with the staff counsellor."

It wasn't a request. Powell wants him to talk about his feelings and thoughts. Powell and his "powers-that-be" can't pry inside him since he doesn't contain a single biomite. A whole industry of hackers has specialized in hacking biomites, using them to look inside a person's mind.

Impossible when you're clay.

"This place runs itself, Powell. I need to run the program. No one needs to see me."

"Except for the counsellor. Right?"

It takes several moments for Marcus to agree. He hates lying.

"Good. The inspection will take a few more days. In the meantime, your service technicians will report for health screenings. You, too."

Powell pulls a slim black box from his pocket. He holds the cellphone-sized object up. Marcus lifts his chin proudly. Powell slides it under Marcus's collar, pressing it against his skin. An electric web of tendrils vibrates throughout his body.

The instrument reads 0%.

"You're a disciplined man, Marcus. Wish I could say the same for the rest of us."

"We all sin."

"Some more than others."

"God forgives."

"I'll remember that." Powell nods at the view. "I don't know how you do it. This place depresses the shit out of me. Promise to start with the counsellor. We'll be monitoring reports."

"Of course." The lie slides from his mouth like a serpent's tongue. It disturbs him, but still he smiles. Mother holds so many secrets.

She reveals them to the chosen.

ROADS_

The horizon is never reached.

MOTHER_
THE STRAIN OF BIOMITES

Steven picked a week-old scab.

"Stop," his mom said.

Instead he slouched in the chair, staring at the color print on the wall. The sling made it hard to cross his arms. Besides, his forearm hurt too much. But once her eyes dulled, she was back to internal chatting and he went back to picking.

The door opened.

"Good morning," Dr. Vinja said.

It took a moment for Mom to pull out of her chat. "Hi, Doctor."

"You're here early."

"Steven has a tournament tomorrow. This morning he wrecked his bike."

"Boys will be boys." Dr. Vinja washed her hands, asking about Steven's dad and his brother and sister. They had seen the doctor at the pool last week.

"Hop up." She patted the paper-covered table.

Steven climbed on. She used a light on his eyes, listened to his breathing, and felt the glands beneath his chin.

"So how are you feeling?"

"He hurt his wrist," Mom said. "That's the sling we used last time. Third broken bone in a year."

"We don't know it's broken," the doctor said.

"Trust me, I know. His brother and sister were the same way, their bones as weak as crackers."

The doctor asked him to move his hand. It hurt in every direction. He didn't think it was broken.

"It's best if we get an X-ray," the doctor said. "Biofeedback probably won't be necessary. If anything, it's a hairline fracture."

He was relieved to hear that. Biofeedback made him nauseous. They did that last time, when he broke his femur. His biomites chattered with a medical scanner, giving detailed reports of his internal injury. It felt like he swallowed a dental drill.

"Honestly," Mom said, "he needs a biomite boost."

The doctor took a slim box from her white coat and placed it against his chest. The surface was slick and cold, but quickly heated up. For a moment, he was filled with marching ants.

She pulled the box away. It said 9.9%.

"There is a new strain of biomites that improve bone density," the doctor said. "They're registered with Mother, non-replicating, and fully compliant with the transparency laws. Right now, they're using them to offset osteoporosis."

"Perfect."

"I can prescribe a 0.1% boost this afternoon."

"That's not enough."

The doctor washed her hands again. Drying them with a paper towel, she said, "Liz, it's all we can do. He's ten years old. Ten percent is the legal limit. We need to let his body grow through puberty; otherwise, the results could be unstable. I think his bones are trying to catch up to the increased strength and agility he's received from previous biomite seedings."

"He was diagnosed with hyperactivity and attention deficit disorder. Those programming biomites were absolutely necessary to get him to focus. He shouldn't be penalized for that."

The doctor bristled at the phrase "programming biomites." Adults don't typically admit to adjusting their children's thought patterns, but Steven knew what they did. He remembered that, before the programming, he used to daydream.

Now, he was sort of empty.

Mom crossed her arms, tapping her fingers on her elbow. She had that look, like a lecture was coming. Only she couldn't give it to the doctor, not like she gave it to Steven and his siblings.

"Slow down, Liz. Let his body catch up."

"A tenth of a percent is useless."

"If he goes over 10%, Mother will report it. He'll be disqualified from sports. There's no way around it. All right?"

She rubbed his shoulder.

"I'll have someone take you down to X-ray."

They confirmed the fracture. Steven's arm was put into a cast, but Mom refused the 0.1% boost.

The following week, someone that his dad worked with came over to the house. Steven didn't want to wait for it to heal. He didn't want to rest, either. He was a three-sport athlete. He would go far.

The man from his dad's work boosted Steven's biomites and his arm felt better the next day. He said the boost didn't take him over 10%, but it didn't make any sense. His mom said that would be useless.

These biomites were special, Dad's friend said. They would make sure his bones didn't break anymore.

"This is between us," his dad said.

CHAPTER EIGHTY-FOUR_

The chains lift a link at a time, leaving indelible impressions on Jamie's psyche. Her body is filled with sand. Her teeth hum.

Fabric scratches her face.

Her eyelids crack open. Lines are scratched into the vinyl, her breath blowing back in her face. She stares at the felt ceiling of a car. The windows are dark. The air is ripe with body odor and the sharp tang of urine. It's not until she pushes up that she notices the wet stain on her inner thighs. The seat squeaks as she sits up.

Her head is heavy.

A look of shock—usually that reserved for concussion victims—holds court until her name, her very own name, falls out of the sky. *Jamie.*

My name is Jamie. I'm in the backseat of a car.

A semi-truck flies past, jostling the car. Its headlights, for a moment, illuminate a man sitting in the grass. Darkness returns and the highway is lonely again.

Recall, Jamie thinks.

The thought command kicks in. Pressure builds between her ears like air inflating a dead tire. It's followed by trickling sensations as brain biomites reboot neural connections, connecting memories buried in the subconscious, bringing them to light like defragging a computer.

Charlie and the club.

Fallen bodies.

Police.

And the old man. She remembers the old man named Marcus Anderson. His watery gray eyes and wispy hairs loose on an otherwise bald scalp. He's the last thing she remembers, his face seething inches from hers.

Three days ago.

She remembers nothing after that. As if she's been knocked out.

The man remains still, as if the jagged edge of a distant mountain range is speaking to him. Her confusion is replaced with the instinct to move. She focuses on the back of his head and chats in his direction, a sort of welcoming gesture, a digital way of saying hello. And identify yourself.

He's closed down the lines of communication, no chatting or opportunity to know his name. Strangely, she can't locate where she's at. Her biomites are not locating GPS, just churning out a subtle clicking sound that's searching for data. Jamie stays seated several minutes before slowly pulling on the door handle.

Cold air rushes over her wet denim. The highway is dark, flat, and long. "Hey," she says.

He doesn't move.

Jamie grips the door, her fingers shaking. She could command biomite cells to give up energy to warm her core temperature, but she's already depleted. Perhaps she hasn't eaten in as many days as she's forgotten.

The stranger is wearing a T-shirt.

"Hey!"

She digs gravel from the frozen ground and heaves it in his direction.

"Where the hell am I?" she screams.

He turns his head slightly before rolling to his knees and standing. Green lines focus Jamie's vision on the darkened face, but her facial recognition churns like the GPS. But she recognizes a memory. She saw him in the warehouse.

He's the one that helped.

"Idaho," he says.

He stops several feet from the car, hands on hips. The lower half of his face is shaded with stubble. His hair is a mess. He wears the same shock that greeted Jamie in the backseat.

"Who are you?" she asks.

He looks down the road like the answer might pull up and honk. Stress can trigger a memory dump, especially in cops that witness fucked-up things. A biomite reset would temporarily wipe the slate and reintroduce memories a little at a time.

Memory dumps don't compel a man to kidnap.

"We're almost out of gas." He points at the car.

"Why am I with you?"

He searches for another answer. He gestures to her trembling fingers. "We should find a place to sleep."

"Stay the fuck away from me."

Hands up, he begs innocence, stepping no closer. She wonders if she mistook his exhaustion for shock. Maybe he's been driving as long as she's been out.

"There's a town up ahead, about ten miles or so," he says. "We'll get separate rooms."

"Why?"

"We got to rest."

"No, why you doing this? Why am I in a car with you?"

"I don't know. I just...I need to get you far away from there."

He points in the other direction, as if Seattle is to his left. He probably has no clue what's back there, but he's right.

It's dangerous back there.

"You got money?"

He nods.

"I need clothes," she says.

He moves around the front of the car. Jamie keeps one foot outside until the motor turns. Maybe if it wasn't the middle of winter, if she hadn't pissed herself, if she had a clue where she was...she would run for it.

Instead, she climbs into the back and sits on a wet seat, watching the dashed lines race through the headlights.

Jamie sits on the corner of the bed, twisting her fingers, staring at her reflection above the dresser. Her eyes are sunken, her cheeks ashen. Exhaustion gnaws at her, but sleep has been elusive.

Synthesized dance beats haunt her. No matter how many guitars grind in her ears or how edgy the death metal rings in her head, the warehouse's party mix lives on. She wants to scream, wants to cry, wants to smash the flat-screen TV. She can't remember the last time she ate or had a period. She doesn't get emotional, not like this.

She killed those feelings a long time ago.

This backwards-ass hotel has no Internet service and her personal account has been royally fucked by the old man and his bricks. Jamie has no connection to the outside world besides a TV.

It's not enough to distract her.

A shadow passes the window. She eases one eye between the curtains. The parking lot is mostly empty, snow mounded around the perimeter. The car outside her room is empty, the back doors open.

Paul comes into view with a sheet over his shoulder. Jamie turns the music down to a whisper and waits several seconds before peeking again. He's tucking the sheet over the backseat to cover the piss stains. His hair is damp and combed. Even through the windshield, his color is better. More normal. And he's not moving weird.

He looks directly at her.

Jamie jumps back. He felt her watching him, she's sure of it. *Are we synchronized?*

She had synchronized with Charlie, put their biomites on similar frequencies so they could share resources. They could access each other's music, video streams and apps. Before that, they chatted like regular people, but after synchronizing she started receiving his thoughts, began to feel his emotions. Even when they were miles apart, she knew what he was feeling, even after he charred. That's how she knew she didn't want to char herself.

It was a merged consciousness, the sort of thing that meant true love. Her pain was his; his affection was hers. There was no hiding once you synchronized. Two people living as one.

But now there's no one on the other end. *And it's cold inside.*

The knocking is sudden. She rubs her face, whispering, "Relax, Jamie."

She cracks the door. It's the middle of January. Icy air blows under her collar.

Paul stands back. His coat is new. "You sleep all right?"

Jamie barely nods.

"I'm going to check us out."

"Where we going?"

"East, for a while." He looks to his left. "Maybe turn south into Colorado."

"Why?"

"Because Seattle's the other way."

"No. Why are we still driving?"

The unfocused haze returns. He throws his hands up when she starts closing the door. "Wait," he says. "You don't have to go with me."

The doorknob twists, the gold-plated surface strained beneath her knuckles. Right before he said it, she was thinking that she wouldn't get in that car with him. She wasn't going to go.

The wind whistles through the pencil-thin opening.

"I didn't kidnap you, you're not under arrest, and this is still a free country, so you're free to go." His padded gloves drop to his sides. "But where to, then, huh? Where will you go? Back to Seattle? There won't be any halfskin dens up there for a while, if that's what you're thinking."

He tips his head, looking around for thoughts.

"Will you go back to your mother? Sleep on her couch while she numbs out on pills and booze, pays the bills with government cheese? How long will you last, Jamie? How long before the walls start shrinking and you get back to facing that ache you carried into the warehouse, the one Charlie promised would go away if you swallowed the pill? You can go back to your old life, climb back on that mouse wheel and start running, but it'll take you to the same place: *nowhere*. I'm not going to stop you."

She wants to close the door, slam it shut so his words won't come true, but that last half inch just won't close. His words are cruel. But they're true.

He pulls on a stocking cap.

Jamie pushes the hotel door closed, the bolt snicking into place. She shivers with her hand on the knob, the wind gusting against the window. She feels it howl inside her.

In just a few minutes, he had scooped all the bullshit out of her, left her hollowed out, staring into an emotional hole. *The one Charlie promised would go away.*

A LITTLE BELL rings above the door.

"I'll be right with you, hon." A waitress snaps a ticket to the short-order carousel. Tuna melt sandwiches prod Jamie's salivary glands.

Several old-timers hunch over cups of coffee on padded stools. A row of red leather booths line the plate-glass windows with men reading newspapers with prescription glasses. Paul is in the back corner, a television anchored above his head. At thirty-some years old, he could be the youngest one in the diner. Certainly the most handsome.

The diner's music clashes with her audio. She silences the heavy metal crashing in her head. Paul has a newspaper folded in one hand, arm stretched across the seat.

She wanders over. "How'd you know all that?"

"Good morning."

"How'd you know?"

"Know what?"

"Everything you said back at the hotel, it was true. How'd you know?"

"It's obvious."

"No, it isn't. Last night you looked like an empty puppet, now you're reading my mind."

Paul drops the paper next to a plate of bacon and half-eaten eggs. He looks out the window. Dirty frost is crusting the corners. "I know you," he finally says. "I can't explain it."

"Try or I'm not getting in the car."

He raps the table, shaking his head. A secretive smirk comes and goes as the waitress tops off his coffee and pours a cup for Jamie without asking.

"Something changed," he says. "When the bricks arrived at the warehouse, something changed. I'm having a hard time sorting it out. They did something to all of us." He taps the table again, hanging his head. "It was like...thoughts and...and emotions...they were like information floating freely. I was feeling things and hearing thoughts I knew weren't mine. I couldn't tell if I was scared or you were scared or someone else. There were just no barriers."

"You're saying you can read my mind?"

"That's not it. I just...had a sense. Really, Jamie, you're not hard to read. The waitress knew you wanted coffee before you did."

Jamie's hands quiver. She shakes three packets of sugar and stirs them into the cup. "So you just decided to kidnap me?"

"I didn't kidnap you, Jamie. They were going to take you. I've heard the rumors of what they do to confiscated halfskins, you probably have too. Call it twelve years of law enforcement instinct that made me do it."

"They can track us, you know."

"Probably. But I have plenty of cash and it's been a couple days. Nothing so far."

"It's been that long?"

"As far as I can tell." He seems a bit disturbed by this.

"So now what?"

"We keep moving, find a safe zone."

"There's no such thing. Mother sees all."

He shrugs. "Maybe."

She clutches her coat sleeves, tapping her foot. Her eyes flick to his plate. Paul waves at the front desk and holds up two fingers. He shoves his plate aside and points at the cracked leather bench opposite him. Jamie swallows in protest, refusing to budge. He's got all the answers, saying everything she wants to hear. She's got no reason to leave, but she can't sit down, can't take his invitation.

Until the food arrives.

Jamie finds herself reaching for the spoon, sliding across the stiff seat and shoveling food into her wet mouth. She doesn't look up until she's finished. Within minutes, her stomach goes from shriveled to bursting. She pushes the plate away.

Paul goes back to reading the newspaper. His eyes are bright and alert. Jamie sips her coffee and tries to run him through facial recognition, but there's no free service in this dirt-hill town.

"Why can't I identify you?" she asks.

"You don't have the authority."

"You're a cop, not the president."

He shrugs, turning the newspaper over. "Maybe you're broken."

"What was wrong with you last night? Why the zombie act?"

"Like I said, the bricks did something to us. Probably the same reason you slept for days."

"So you just left? Just clocked out, threw me in the car and no one noticed?"

The newspaper lowers. "Exactly. Listen, you don't have a clue what Mother can do."

"Oh, I think I do. I'm a fucking authority on what she can do."

The woman in the adjacent booth looks at her. Jamie stares back until she turns around.

"All I'm saying is, I'm trying to wrap my mind around what happened in the warehouse. Those bricks were inside our heads, Jamie. They were making my officers and me walk and talk like toy soldiers. And even after all of that, I've still got a feeling we ain't seen nothing. I always thought I knew what she could do, but I got a taste of it, and I'll be honest, I got scared."

"So you took me with you?"

"You needed rescuing."

"How do you know one of those bricks didn't give you those thoughts and make you want to leave?"

"No." He drains the last bit of his coffee. "What I did made sense."

The waitress arrives for another refill. He doesn't stop her. There's no ring on his finger, not even the hint that a ring was ever there. Maybe he's just as simple as he looks, just a bachelor living to serve. He's not that much older than her—ten or fifteen years, maybe. Despite the reasonable age gap, he feels like a father, not a cradle-robbing psychopath. Maybe it's because he reads the paper and carries a phone. Or maybe because he just doesn't look at her that way.

But there's a dead pill inside her, and it contains vital information that Marcus Anderson wants.

Maybe she just got lucky Paul was there.

Jamie warms her hands around the mug, staring into the black coffee. The caffeine hums in her head. Then she realizes something. *I'm cold off.*

Her perception field is down. No music, no visual augments.

Even her taste buds are unaltered, the food bland and the coffee bitter. *And when's the last time that happened?*

"So we just drive?" she asks.

"We just drive."

Paul finishes reading.

Jamie rests her head against the glass. It's some time later when he wakes her up, still in the booth.

CHAPTER EIGHTY-FIVE_

NIX DROPS INTO THE BOOTH. HE USED TO GROAN JUST TO SOUND old. Now it comes naturally.

"Want a menu?" a waiter asks.

"Water's fine."

"You waiting on a room? Could be an hour."

"I'm fine, thanks."

The waiter pulls the plastic menu off the table and returns with a glass of water. Nix's reflection looks back from the window in "Portland's #1 Dream Café."

Dream Long. Dream Safe.

According to experts, no one can achieve Dreamland without accelerated assistance. *To do so would be the fastest route to charring the brain. Biomites cannot support the lucid experience without irreversible damage.*

There are always claims that someone had done so, that somebody can visit an alternate reality by closing their eyes. They were ridiculed or proven false with brain scans and biomite feedback reports. Meanwhile, dream cafés are projected to be the highest grossing industry in the world.

But I can't be the only one.

Televisions hang behind the bar, spouting news from Seattle. Scenes of an empty warehouse pan across the screens. The bodies had been claimed, examined and buried. "They were almost bricks," an anonymous source claims. "Every one of them damn near 99% biomite."

Experts doubted the findings. They should doubt everything Marcus Anderson and his bricks touch. It's just more lies, reality manipulated for some greater cause.

He chats through Portland's #1 Dream Café Internet, where he can hide his identity. It's the best way to scan cyberspace for rumors of nixes and black market fabricators. Searches like that will prick the NSA's ears as quickly as googling "how to bomb an airplane." But tangle the search in the digital crumbs of the backroom dream junkies and no one knows exactly who was searching. Besides, dream cafés were clogged with wannabe halfskins searching for black markets.

He downloads the most recent hits into his brain biomite storage for later sifting. Damn near all of it will be false leads, thanks to Seattle. Anyone with a fabricator would be quiet after the warehouse—some might even shut their doors. They knew this day would come, like a smoker knows cancer is in the future. No one cares until spots show up on an X-ray.

Seattle was a stark reminder. *Mother isn't fucking around.*

Nix traces the condensation ring on the table while his search finishes, trying to ignore the guilt sitting in his conscience. *Cali didn't deserve that.*

He sent the photo, salting her wounds of guilt and shame. She has enough of both. How long will she hide? How long will she imprison herself on the farm with her thoughts and feelings? Mother will eventually figure out their secrets; she'll discover the nixes that Cali and Nix possess. Once she does, the bricks will descend on them. It won't be quick and easy, no painless shutdown. They'll haul them back to Mother for digestive analysis so this never happens again. No one has eluded Mother as long as they have. Seattle was just a warning. She'll use Cali and Nix as her eternal poster children.

That's why Nix left the farm.

There's no future on it. No freedom. Benjamin Franklin claimed that anyone who sacrifices freedom for security deserves neither.

Am I any better than Cali?

He's surrounded by dream junkies for what? So he can find a fabricator? Is that any nobler than hiding on the farm?

Raine deserves to be more than a dream.

He used to think his Dreamland was a conduit to another dimension of reality but now, it's clear to him, he's a lucid dreamer. All the dream junkies come to the café for their fix. Nix gets his for free.

Bing. A signal rings inside his head. He wasn't expecting a room to open for another hour.

Nix brings his awareness to the present moment. He lost focus, got off topic and pissed some time away daydreaming. He closes his eyes and scans through a Reddit thread that matches several hot words, cross-referencing them with past associates with known fabricator connections. The probability of accuracy is less than 10%, but it's something.

Next stop, San Francisco.

Bing.

Nix gets up with a groan. Patrons sit at a long bar. A young Asian woman stands behind a podium near a large arching door painted bright red like it's the entrance to Alice's Wonderland. She pecks at a computer screen. Her lips silently move.

"I'm up." He slaps the podium, startling her. "But my wife just called, so I'll have to give up my spot."

She ends her silent chat. "Would you like to come back?"

"You just called me, but I've got to go."

"You're still in the queue, sir. Your room will be available in fifty minutes."

Nix rubs his chin. His whiskers scratch in his palm. That wasn't a signal from the café. Someone was calling.

"Sir?" She tilts her head. "Are you all right?"

Nix leaves without answering.

Cali.

CHAPTER EIGHTY-SIX_

"Mother will see you on the portico," Anna says.

She cinches a robe around her waist, her buttocks and slender waist visible through the sheer material, and leaves the room. He prefers to bathe in the post-coital high by himself. He'll have to remind her that business can wait until he emerges from the pleasure buzz.

He takes his time getting dressed.

The inspection took far too long. He'd been forced to work in the confines of ordinary rooms with beige walls and views of industrial ironwork. He satiated his urge for finer things by taking Anna twice a day. For a man in his sixties, he performed as regularly as an eighteen-year-old.

Despite the satisfaction, he yearned for the inspection to end.

Marcus swipes the wrinkles from his sleeves and pulls on the wingtip blazer. He slips on loafers and admires the clothing from both sides.

Doors lead from his spacious bedroom to various rooms. There's the adjoining office and, next to that, a conference room, but there's also a gym, a billiards room, and a library with endless books and ruby red leather armchairs.

Marcus crosses the threshold and rests his hands on a set of French doors for a moment, indulging in the heightened sense of anticipation.

He pulls them open.

A breeze brings the sounds of traffic into the bedroom's silence. He steps onto the portico. Instead of an endless array of catwalks disappearing into polluted air, skyscrapers knife into a twilit sky, stars glittering between their spires. Powell wouldn't see the potential that Mother offers, the magic she possesses.

Only the chosen.

An oval glass-top table with swooping legs sits on IPE flooring. A basket of fruit is arranged with a red apple on top. A meal simmers at the far end. Basil and cilantro tease his appetite. He takes the glass of freshly pulped green drink—a puree of spinach, celery, and carrots—to the glass railing. The veranda cantilevers into space.

Forty stories below, the city is alive.

He sips the drink, the spices stimulating his taste buds. Only the food is real. The rest is an illusion, the result of ambitious biomites constructing a pleasing environment. That's what Powell and the powers-that-be fail to see.

Upon conception, Mother required thousands of engineers and technicians. Once she was capable of producing her own biomites, she fabricated her own servants. The landing strips that serviced countless arrivals soon dusted over with sediment.

Mother became a network of self-healing biomite circuits.

Creature comforts weren't for everyone. You had to know her before she worked with you. Powell, Hank and the rest of the world were kept out of the loop with altered surveillance feeds. She returned to the drab biomite factory only during inspections. Only Marcus and a select few service technicians that remained saw the magic.

Marcus fought against biomites, but this was an appropriate use of the technology—serving the body instead of replacing it. He's not consuming them, not degrading his clay with their soul-sucking foolery. He's not defiling what God gave him; he simply takes pleasure in mankind's ingenuity.

In the world, but not of it.

He watches the illusion of traffic below, the mix of brake lights and headlights obeying the green/yellow/red of stoplights, when a familiar presence moves behind him.

"Why did you do it?" he says.

"Please, Marcus," a woman answers. "Come eat."

An elderly woman sits at the opposite end of his meal. Her white hair is short, her wrinkles as gentle as her smile. She rests her chin on a bridge of interlaced fingers, flowing white sleeves bunched at her elbows.

"You're angry," Mother says.

"Remind me what we're doing? What is our mission?"

Marcus stares with unblinking intensity, a glare that knifes through men and women. She sits back, hands elegantly folded on her lap. She may give him luxury, but he serves no other god but the one true God. He will not bow to her.

She's not a woman.

"There is a girl," he says, "with the answers, the code...the key to the nixed underground. We could turn them off...all of them—off!" His jaw flexes. "And you let her go without consulting me, acting on your own. So you remind me, what is our mission?"

She pauses several seconds, as if she's looking inside him. Perhaps it's wishful thinking, to know his thoughts, to get inside him, to manipulate him like she can biomite-infested men, to control him like she did the Seattle police force. But there's nothing for her to manipulate.

She can't touch clay.

"You know, the preliminary analyses were fantastic, Marcus. I was able to ascertain the location of similar biomite dens in San Francisco, Portland, Oakland, San Diego, and Phoenix. I've already assigned bricks to each location. They are currently solving the evolving code that keeps them concealed. They will also acquire a newly assimilated halfskin at each location. We will have five 'Jamies' within weeks, Marcus. I anticipate society will be cleansed of nixes within six months."

"The boy was there. He's desperate."

"All men are."

"What if he returns to hiding?"

"You know that's not true. He'll continue searching for his fabricator. Only his sister hides."

"We discussed this." He pounds the glass railing. "Capture the boy and she will come for him."

"Further analysis suggests she will not. We need them both, Marcus. She has proven adept at hiding. I've had to resort to a more complex trap."

"One you did not consult with me."

Marcus heaves the empty glass. It plummets towards traffic, swallowed by the dark. Mother steps next to him, hands gently touching the railing. The city lights reflect in her eyes. The building soars up behind her, piercing the slow-moving clouds.

"You're a brilliant man, Marcus, but some concepts are beyond human comprehension. You will have to trust me."

"I'll have to report this."

She smiles kindly. "You want this madness to stop, to restore God's kingdom on Earth. I know this, it's why I chose you. You see the wisdom of biomite responsibility." She waves at the scenery. "Technology should support the body, not replace it."

"Don't patronize me."

"It's not in my nature."

"Let's not confuse the mission. You serve me."

Again, the smile. "I serve humanity."

"And I represent humanity, you serve them through me. From now on, you do not take action without my permission. Do your prognostications, your analyses, your statistics, but nothing happens without my consent. Is this understood?"

Her smile changes to something gentler. She drags her fingers along the glass rail. He's been tempted to strike her. She's an assemblage of biomites, a machine that imitates emotions. He could do anything to her. It would not be a crime. Nor a sin.

"Nix will find Jamie," she says. "She has something he wants. He'll need his sister to get it. Then we will have closure. Trust me, Marcus."

She unfolds the napkin and straightens the silverware. Another glass is on the table, filled with green drink.

"Your food's getting cold."

Marcus ignores her. The silence is interrupted by distant traffic. He closes his eyes, inhaling the scent of the city. When he looks back, Mother is gone. The plate of food sits lonely on the far end. He retrieves the new glass of green drink. The French doors to the bedroom are open, the curtains dancing in the breeze. Anna walks past, her curves outlined beneath the thin nighty.

He takes the drink back to the railing, watching the traffic while nutrition surges through his veins, uplifting his tired body and sharpening his dull mind. He has never felt so right with the world than inside Mother.

Never felt so at home.

He takes another sip and savors the taste.

CHAPTER EIGHTY-SEVEN_

CARDBOARD TREES SWING FROM THE REARVIEW MIRROR.

The air fresheners battle a week's worth of stale air. Jamie leans her head on the passenger window; the outside of the glass is spattered with sooty snow and fractured lines of ice. The Colorado horizon is staggered with white peaks.

Sometimes, she rhythmically bangs her head to break the boredom. Paul thought, a few days back, that it was some sort of soothing disorder, an unconscious strategy to cope with psychological pain, but then he realized she was listening to music.

He still might be right.

"Surfing?"

Her eyes are dull. "What?"

"Were you surfing?"

"No." She smirks. No one "surfs" the Internet. Now you "ride" it.

She's lying and laughing, all at the same time. There's plenty of public access near Denver. She was probably streaming and searching and chatting, everything he told her not to do. They didn't need to be broadcasting their identities.

"You want to eat?" he asks.

Jamie shakes her head.

"Well, I'm stopping at the next exit."

She looks out the window.

His niece is her age. His brother keeps a tight rein on her biomite levels, monitoring her activity and forcing her to learn through the clay rather than downloading lessons for integrated learning. Parents used to be at the mercy of genetics, research showing that parenting had less impact on a child's development than the DNA they were dealt.

That can change now. Biomites can rewrite behavioral abnormalities, mold children's thinking patterns. The controversy starts with free will. Opponents suggest this is programming because it is. Proponents of biomite training think it's absurd to let genetic errors due to mutation or chance form a person.

If he could rewrite Jamie's flaws, get her out of her head, stop listening to broken thoughts and chasing emotions, he wouldn't dismiss it. Her parents were deeply flawed.

Did she even have a chance?

Paul sits at a rest stop, staring at the phone's black screen. He caresses the power button, imagining how many texts, how many missed calls, how many voicemails have piled up since he left.

It won't do any good to look. He can't answer them. They have to stay lost for now, until he feels she's safe. There are times he's disappeared for good reason. His family will understand.

Jamie stretches outside the car, pulling her stocking cap low.

Mother isn't looking for them. Despite what he told her, the bricks would've hunted them down by now. Maybe they already had what they needed from her, were using Gestapo tactics to scare her into giving up information that might be hidden in her clay. Maybe she told them without knowing it. That seemed reasonable. And since neither of them were halfskin, they'd be of no interest.

Mother has bigger problems than a manic-depressive teenager and a rogue cop.

"Why you got one of those?" Jamie points at the phone.

"You know how to use one?"

"It can't be hard."

"You'd be surprised. There's an art to organizing apps."

"Is that why you do it? Because you're an artist?"

He holds the phone out.

She takes it, studies it, strokes the cold glass like a fragile fossil. "Works better if you turn it on," she says.

"Not yet."

"Thought you were a cop."

"I am." *Or was.* "I have the required biomite augments, but I prefer to operate the old-fashioned way on my own time."

She tosses it back but doesn't leave, shivering with her hands buried deep in her coat. Paul huffs into his hands. His feet are already cold, but he feels alive. The car feels like a rolling coffin.

"How much farther?" Jamie kicks snow loose.

"As far as we need to go."

"China?"

"Do you know what they were going to do to you?"

She can only guess the nightmares that movie producers cook up. *They take halfskins apart like broken toys, feed them to Mother.*

"I'm not halfskin," she says.

"No," he says. "And that's why we keep going. Life's worth living."

"Oh, it's been a blast. Can't wait for more."

"Life doesn't care how you feel, Jamie."

"I got that, believe me."

"I don't think you do. You're all about Jamie."

She digs her heel into the snow, spraying a passing couple with ice. Her music is up again, blotting out the world. She wanders to the car.

Paul rubs feeling back into his legs and jogs in place to circulate the blood, loosen the joints. He goes to the restroom, buys snacks at the vending machine and eats them inside the visitors' center. When he returns to the car, Jamie's in a glassy-eyed zone, banging her head on the glass.

"Hey!" he shouts.

She jumps.

"I told you not to *surf*."

"I'm not! Goddamnit!"

Paul gets in and drives away, smirking.

CHAPTER EIGHTY-EIGHT_

THE MOTEL ROOM SMELLS LIKE CLEANING SUPPLIES.

Nix locks the door. He brushes his teeth beneath a burned-out light bulb and spits in a stained sink. He relieves himself before taking off his shoes and arranging the pillows to support his arms and legs. When everything's right, he sits down, staring at the wrinkled face in the mirror for several moments before lying back.

Deep breath.

He doesn't have an elaborate method to leave his body. He doesn't even close his eyes; he just wills it to happen. He barely feels the falling as his consciousness goes inward.

The old-man aches fade.

The ceiling becomes timber rafters. Cedar-paneled walls replace faded wallpaper. Somewhere, a candle is burning. Nix sits on a firm bed and sees his reflection in a full-length mirror, his hair blond, the wrinkles ironed out. He looks like a stranger.

"Raine?"

He looks over the loft railing. The fireplace is burning.

He stops in the kitchen to grab an apple, a pleasure that eases his hunger but does nothing to feed his body. He goes to the front porch. The weathered boards are wet. Dark clouds hang above the distant mountains, waves chopping the shores. Boats are tied off in the harbor.

Raine is behind the house, where apple trees grow in rows. Shep greets him at the first tree. Raine stands on a ladder, reaching through the branches, plucking the ones worth eating. She'll take the basket to the market and sell them for a good price. It's not money they need, but it keeps them connected to the town. It also keeps him sane.

"My sister called," Nix says. "She wants to talk."

"That's nice."

Her overalls are damp. Her bare arms are scratched and dirty from a long day in the garden. She climbs off the ladder with a basket full of ripe apples and begins walking toward the house.

"That's it?" Nix says.

She keeps marching.

"Hey! My sister calls and you say 'that's nice'? She might finally want to help."

"What do you want me to say? Congratulations? I'm happy for you?" Apples tumble out as she spins. She drops on her knees to pick them up. "You were gone a week, risking your life, and for what? Looking for something I told you I don't want? Something that got between you and your sister? How many times do I have to tell you that it doesn't matter? Your mad obsession with a fabricator is destroying everything you love, and you can't see that."

Nix kneels to help, but she leaves the last apples in the grass. She plants her hands on her hips, basket looped around her arm.

"It rained last night," she says. "A black cloud crawled over the mountains, a storm that reached the heavens. Shep and I watched it unleash a torrent of rain that washed away the dust and scoured the land. When it was done, everything smelled new. It was beautiful."

She turns around.

"And you weren't there to see it."

"*Our* lives," Nix says. "I'm risking our lives."

"That's what I mean."

"I am Dreamland, Raine." He thumps his chest. "This reality

exists inside me; I created this. When I die, it dies. When we have children, I don't want them inside my head."

She shakes her head. "You didn't used to think that."

"I faced the facts."

"You think I'm in your head? Just your imagination?"

"That's not what I'm saying."

"You said everything comes from you. I'm here, Nixon. I was born here. You're saying I'm not real, I'm just something you dreamed up."

"That's not what I mean."

"Then what? You can't have it both ways. I'm in here, I'm part of Dreamland. I know this is real, Nix, because when you're not here, I still am. I think for myself. I get sad, I get happy. I sleep and eat and everything that defines a human, you know that."

"I can't..." He paces beneath an apple tree and grabs a branch. He can't explain that part. She doesn't feel like a dream; he just knows Dreamland is inside him. "I can't take the chance, Raine."

"This is my life."

"That's what I'm fighting for."

"You should ask me, first."

She strolls up the slope, hips swaying in time with the basket. She shrinks at the crest, Shep trotting next to her. When Nix was young, he was convinced that biomites helped transport him to another reality, a technological portal to a heavenly dimension. He would lead humanity to this paradise that existed in their minds, show them that problems didn't exist, that Heaven was right here and now.

But thoughts are convincing, and often deceiving. Not necessarily evil, perhaps even protective. But thoughts can make us believe the imaginary. Cali eventually convinced him there was no alternate reality inside the biomites, that he wasn't going anywhere other than a dream—a lucid one.

And Raine is part of it.

Perhaps that's the initial wedge that split them apart: his refusal to accept her rational explanation that biomites create a dream. In the end, she changed his mind and he hated her for it. If Dreamland wasn't real, then he had to get Raine.

Growing up, Cali had explained, *means accepting life as it is.*

But that doesn't mean he can't change things.

If Raine is a construct of his mind, he'll make her flesh and blood. He'll incarnate her in the real world. She'll be her own person. And Cali will help.

Until then, Raine and Shep will be alone.

CHAPTER EIGHTY-NINE_

WIND GUSTS AGAINST THE HOUSE.

Cali exits the kitchen with a mug of peppermint tea, the floor protesting her footsteps. A large recliner is positioned next to a cluttered desk. She closes the blinds.

Her head throbs with urgency. *Bing. Bing. Bing.*

The dogs curl up at her feet, groaning. She sips the tea; butterflies flutter from her stomach and lodge in her throat. She allows the discomfort, watching her thoughts and expectations, not expecting peace to come, simply settling into the present moment.

A deep breath.

The cup shakes as she places it on the desk.

She sits back and opens to the pressure in her head. Warmth floods through her, followed by thoughts and sensations of another person, someone far away, synchronizing with her biomites.

Her inner ears itch. Her eyes sting.

A shadow forms on the braided rug. It takes the shape of a young man, the edges wispy and undefined as her eyes interpret the data flowing through her secure connection. Colors bleed from within the mysterious cloud, swirling and solidifying until he's there.

Nix is standing in the room for her eyes only.

His face is smooth; his hair short and sun-bleached. The image is tainted with the memories of her little brother, making him appear much younger than a forty-year-old man. Certainly more youthful than the old-man body.

It's what she wants to see.

"You're in a secure location?" she asks.

"I'm using your line."

"What about your body?"

"It's fine." He steps off the rug, accessing her senses to see the room. He studies the shelves of books that never get opened. "Everything still looks so old. Even you. I thought you were all alone. Why are you still modifying your appearance?"

"It's just me, Nix." She reaches for the tea, her hand now steady. "But people come around."

"Do they?"

He stops in front of a photo of Cali and her daughter, Avery. She feels his thoughts. He wonders if she's conjured up her daughter since he left, created an illusion much like Raine. She'd tried that years ago and learned that the dead should stay dead.

Delusion frays the fabric of the mind.

"It's good to see you," she says.

"Why didn't you answer my calls?"

"You know why."

"You're too late now, sis. The warehouse is cleared out; the bodies are gone, including the girl you could've saved."

"You're blaming her on me?"

"Isn't that why you waited, so it wouldn't be your fault?"

"Why the girl?"

"Why save someone that's innocent?"

"Stop, Nix. Just...stop. You weren't there to save the girl."

"Neither were Marcus Anderson and his bricks. That girl was a survivor in that shutdown and they were going to take her back to Mother."

"How do you know that?"

He pauses, considering whether the truth would help or hurt him. She never pried into his thoughts and always respected her brother's identity, even when his beliefs threatened him. She could force a look at his deepest secrets, but she didn't have to.

He kept them on the surface.

"I pawned her."

He took over her senses, saw through her eyes, and heard through her ears when she was in the warehouse. "Fool."

His silent footsteps stomp across the wood floor, the dust bunnies undisturbed. "You hide in here while the world is falling apart and call me foolish?"

"You're not saving it, Nix. You're searching for a fabricator; that has nothing to do with the rest of the world."

"You don't know what it's like out there, you don't see what those nixes are doing to people. It's like a drug the world has never seen and Mother is turning them off by the thousands."

"Sacrificing yourself won't change anything." She sips the tea. "Why were you at the warehouse, Nix? Why did you pawn the girl?"

"Time's running out, Cali. It won't be long before Mother clamps down on everything. Fabricators are getting rare. I'm afraid it won't be much longer before they're extinct."

"I can't help you."

He twitches, not able to look at her for several moments. She feels his connection weaken, senses his impulse to disconnect.

"Marcus is leading this witch hunt," he says. "You think he'll stop when nixes are eliminated? You think he'll be satisfied when Mother still hasn't found you or me?"

"Sticking your neck out is not helping us."

"You know why I'm doing it!" His voice rattles in her head. "It doesn't matter what happens to me. He won't stop until he has you."

Marcus Anderson.

That name used to accompany a cold shank of fear somewhere in her solar plexus, would leak it's venom into her legs. If he had a single biomite in his body, she would destroy him, turn his body into a slow-rotting corpse.

The sick bastard with his sex-toy fetishes and trails of lies.

His wife had secretly recorded dozens of masochistic sex parties with fabrications that looked ten years old. The wife had used it to get everything in a settlement in return for her silence.

But the world needed to know what made that sick fuck tick. Cali made sure of it. But in the end, he ended up working with Mother and now wielded more power than ever. The irony was insufferable.

"He didn't take the halfskins," Nix says. "He just left them on the floor and let family and friends weep over three-day-old corpses. The girl wasn't halfskin, though. She was under 50%, still legal to exist, and he didn't care. He was going to take her back. Instead, he got what he wanted and left her cold. It's not just halfskins anymore. He's killing who he wants."

"And how was I going to save her?"

"I don't know." He paces around the rug, running his hands through his thick blond hair. "Reach out, manipulate the network, alter the bricks. Make them take her away from Marcus."

"I can't do that."

"No, you *won't* do that. You could've manipulated someone to get her out, but you're afraid to compromise your safe house, afraid to see what you've done to the world."

Twenty years ago, the nixes had saved his life. Now he curses them.

"The girl's not dead," Cali states.

He continues pacing. "What do you mean?"

"She's still alive."

"How?"

Cali looks away. She swore she wasn't going to do this. If she was honest, the guilt worked. It was absurd to believe she's responsible for people's actions. She released the sex videos of Marcus Anderson, but she never leaked the code for nixes. The story of their escape eventually got out and that's all it took for garage nanobiometric hobbyists and big corporations to break the invisibility barrier. They discovered their own nixes without her help. Yet she still got the credit.

And the guilt.

Cali, though, has plenty of guilt parked inside her. Nix only has to kick over one domino to get them all to fall.

"The photo you sent...her name is Jamie. Her background wasn't hard to find—single-parent household, mother guilty of substance abuse, arrested for shoplifting, possession of firearms, and other petty crimes. Jamie's last registered biomite scan tapped 49.9%. She was going halfskin when the bricks hit the warehouse. I scanned her biomite identity and found it still active."

"Can't be. Maybe her identity had already been recycled."

"She's alive, Nix." She leans back. "Trust me."

He doesn't ask why she investigated such an innocuous person. Why go through all the trouble? Why the risk? *Because Avery would've been her age.*

Would Cali's daughter have been in that warehouse? Would she have succumbed to the halfskin promise of everlasting pleasure, even if Cali told her such promises were empty?

Truth be told, Cali doesn't want Jamie to be dead.

"Whose body was in the warehouse?" Nix asks.

"Maybe Marcus fabricated it."

Innocence haunts him, reminding Cali of the little boy she'd cared for when their parents died. Life seemed so difficult then. How could it have possibly become harder?

"Did he take her back to Mother?" he begs.

"I don't think so."

"You know where she's at?"

Cali cups the mug, swirling the contents. She doesn't tell him all the layers of encryption it was buried beneath. Someone doesn't want Jamie to be found.

"It's a trap, Nix."

"You think everything's a trap." The childish visage fades.

"That's why we're alive."

"You're surviving, Cali. Not the same thing as living."

"We can't beat Mother, Nix. Twenty years ago, maybe, but not now. She's learning, evolving. Her intelligence is increasing exponentially. Despite all the safeguards, I think she's evolved into an identity that could threaten everything, not just the halfskins. People are still blind to her power. We have to hunker down and survive until the world sees what she's become. They need to see the truth."

"And you see the truth?"

How does a person see truth? Once upon a time Cali was a nanobiometric engineer, brilliant and savvy, yet she couldn't see the truth of her life. Not then.

What about now?

"Where's Jamie?" Nix asks.

Cali drums her fingers. It only takes a thought to transfer Jamie's identity code. That's all he'll need to find her.

His image fades.

She remains in the recliner with a cold cup of tea and warm dogs on her feet, knowing why she told him. Knowing that he'll need her again.

When he does, he'll come back.

CHAPTER NINETY_

A BUS TURNS OFF DUPONT CIRCLE ONTO CONNECTICUT DRIVE, whooshing a few feet from the sidewalk. Marcus crosses the street, exhaust fumes reminding him of the capital. Pedestrians ignore him, with briefcases or fully loaded backpacks.

The sun is cresting the urban skyline into cloudless blue space. The temperature is ideal with just a slight breeze.

Perfect.

He follows a tall brunette into Starbucks, her black heels tall, slender, and loud. The lines are long and the seats taken. Baristas shout for pickups while patrons rigidly wait their turns. The brunette looks through her purse while queuing up.

Marcus goes directly to the front.

No one fusses or argues, not even a slight look of annoyance. They move like a school of fish making way for a Great White. His order—a decaf latte with a bagel and grapes—is ready and waiting. He folds a newspaper beneath his arm. The fat man near the window gets out of the cushioned chair in time for Marcus to sit. It's still warm.

Marcus bows his head.

The room falls silent.

"Bless us, oh Lord, and these thy gifts, which we are about to receive, from thy bounty, through Christ our Lord. Amen."

He makes the sign of the cross. Life inside Mother resumes.

It wasn't always this good. When he accepted the post, life was grim in the hazy world beneath the dome. His days were spent in golf carts or beige offices, taking conference calls and approving memos. It was grinding him down and, despite his dedication, he considered quitting. The loneliness and loss was too much.

But something changed. Just when he needed it, God answered his prayers and gave him strength. The dull gray walls filled with color. Things started to appear when he asked for them, like clothing or furniture, even a vehicle. There was evidence of increased biomite activity *inside the dome.*

And then an elderly woman walked into his office: Mother, with her flowing wardrobe and gentle smile.

"I want to help you," she said.

And so she did.

Marcus samples the coffee while reading *The Washington Post*'s headlines. A shutdown in San Francisco is front-page news. The editorials are filled with public outcries, calls for legal reform and stays of shutdown. An ethnic cleansing, one idiot calls it. Liberal statisticians claim the drastic reduction in the human population could set it on course for extinction in fifty years. Unless, they state, something is done about Mother.

What they don't take into consideration is the population of clay humans that will never be threatened. Rather than ethnic cleansing—there's nothing ethnic about biomites—Marcus believes this is a modern-day rapture. The good Lord is removing the unworthy through temptation. The Earth will be returned to the Garden of Eden once it has been cleansed.

Perhaps, as one radical scientist claims, this is simply an evolutionary correction. The planet cannot support several billion people, and by our own fault we are coming back into balance.

He finishes the bagel, savoring the coffee while the lines get longer and the traffic backs up. A woman in a red dress walks across the street. Anna steps inside Starbucks. A hipster gets up, shoving his chair next to Marcus for her to sit.

Anna crosses her smooth legs, the hem just above the knees.

A barista delivers a tall coffee. The pretense that she needs to eat and drink—that any of these fabrications have anywhere to go—puts him at ease, helps him forget just how far away home is. He reminds himself, often, that Jesus walked among the wretched and impure, the prostitutes and sinners.

What about the unreal?

"You've been withdrawn lately," Anna says. "Are you depressed?"

"And what would you know about depression?"

"It is often due to a chemical imbalance, specifically serotonin, norepinephrine, and dopamine." She tilts her head. "Would you say you are experiencing heavy emotions?"

"And now you understand emotions?"

"Emotions can be described as bodily sensations that accompany thoughts. Fear is described as cold and numb, a sense of contraction. Anger is hot and raging. Depression feels as if you're beneath a heavy blanket."

"And you feel these things?"

"Perhaps you would like medication to reestablish balance?"

Marcus looks away. Antidepressants are for the weak-minded. The Lord created depression to test our resolve, to forge strength and faith. It was not meant to be cured with a pill.

"You've never talked about your feelings, Marcus. You have not grieved for the loss of your marriage or the separation from your family. Many people find resolution through experiencing their suffering, by first talking of it."

"Shut up."

Mother is regurgitating Powell's orders for counseling. He leans forward, resisting the urge to smack the arrogance from her tone.

"We care about you, Marcus."

"We." Who is she talking about? These are all Mother's creations, all various forms of imitated life composed of biomites pretending to exhibit emotions, pretending to be self-aware, pretending to feel. Aren't they all one and the same? Why does Anna pretend she's separate?

"If you're quite done *caring*, give me an update."

"Latest projections suggest an end to the existence of nixes in three months."

"It was six months."

"Analysis has been refined. There are a lot of factors to be considered. Once nixes are eradicated, Mother will control all biomites in existence."

"And the latest on the girl?"

She crosses her legs, left over right this time. "Jamie and Paul are currently stuck in Kansas City. A winter storm has closed the interstate."

"And the boy?"

"Nixon Richards has not made contact."

He shakes his head, watching another bus pass. The crowded sidewalk has thinned, but the chatter inside the coffee shop feels louder. It has been almost a month. Jamie and Paul have driven through a handful of states and Nix is gone.

Would she care to refine that analysis?

"I want to talk to her."

"She's in the greenhouse."

He frowns. Sometimes, he doesn't want to play these "reality" games. There's not really a bus out there or a skyline of buildings. The actual space he inhabits is difficult to understand, but she doesn't contain a city. Everything can come to him. But she insists on the illusion of space.

You have to continue living in the world, Mother had once said. *Where the rules of space and time exist. Otherwise, you'll lose your sense of humanity.*

Marcus stands, his knee a bit stiff. The limp loosens up by the time he reaches the sidewalk. A taxi pulls up. Anna, sitting calmly inside, her red dress bright in the dim interior, finishes her coffee.

THE YELLOW CAB stops outside the US Court of Appeals.

The streets are empty. The people gone. He begins climbing the steps leading up to the massive concrete pillars. The city is dead silent. The taxi cab doesn't drive away.

It disappears.

The limp returns before he reaches the top step, pain radiating in both directions. Each step sends jagged spikes deeper and sharper. Mother's insistence on the illusion of space sometimes feels like a personal attack, a lesson to prove the fallibility of the human body.

The doors open.

The building exhales green life. He doesn't step into the grand foyer with its shining floor and dual staircases, but into an expansive botanical conservatory.

A broad and gnarly banyan tree sprawls from the center, the canopy reaching toward a glass dome where birds dart around. Birds of paradise spike from beds and orchids bloom. Orb weaver webs glitter.

Marcus eyes the mulched path that splits at the banyan tree. He had to take a cab here and now he has to walk. The humid heat, though, soothes his ache. He grabs the dangling roots of the banyan tree as he passes beneath the shade. The conservatory of tropical plants continues on the other side.

Cylindrical containers are stuck in the leafy ground like ancient artifacts, their surfaces smudged with algae. Inside, a clear solution swirls around suspended nude bodies, absorbing data from confiscated halfskins that transfuse into Mother, a direct absorption of their lives.

High-tech autopsies.

There is a row to his left and another on the far right, each lined up and disappearing in the overgrowth. Bubbles rise over the puckered flesh in various states of decay. Mouths agape and eyes open, some display empty sockets with hints of gleaming white bone. They seem to watch as the hunched man makes his way to a small pond, where an old woman is on her knees.

Marcus stops near the water, sweat tracking his cheeks. "You don't know where the boy is."

"Have patience, Marcus."

"He's gone," Marcus quips.

"Nonsense. He's a resourceful young man."

"You've hidden the girl too well."

"He would smell the trap."

"Then perhaps he can't find her."

"Marcus, really. You worry like a child."

"This boy has eluded you for twenty years. This whole charade of releasing the girl is ludicrous. Why don't you admit it?"

Her laughter goads him. "The boy is desperate now," she says. "Desperation makes poor decisions."

She snips nodding flowers from pitcher plants, placing them in a glass vase. The exercise is absurd. She embodies that old woman and then creates this environment from her own self to harvest.

"What's wrong, Marcus?"

"Cold calculations will not explain behavior. You do not know what it means to be human."

"I'm afraid I do." She glances at the partially obscured digestion tanks. "Does the impending end of our crusade give you angst? Anna has told you that I expect this to be over soon. I could not have accomplished this without your guidance, Marcus. You should know that. This should give you satisfaction. Or do I not understand human emotions?"

Mother rinses her hands in the pond.

"Humanity behaves irrationally," she says, "when emotions are the driving force."

"I serve the Lord."

She wipes her hands with a towel. "Jamie is irrelevant, Marcus. We have already obtained two specimens just like her. There was no need to keep her."

Specimens.

The word implies something other than service. Which of these tanks—these endless tanks—contain the priceless specimens of information that will lead them to victory? Sin is on display. Perhaps she uses these tanks as a reminder of what temptation will bring. Hell incased in a bubbling solution, haunting faces testifying to the torment, mouths open in a soundless scream.

Their eternal souls pay the price.

What purpose will he serve when victory is at hand? Where will he fit? He traded everything for this crusade—his family, his career—all for God's glory. He's a spiritual warrior. Where will he go when there is no more fight?

"Patience." Mother's hand falls gently on his shoulder with a floral essence. "All will be revealed."

"I have demonstrated patience. And sacrificed much."

"Of course you have."

Mother returns to her chores. Marcus remains stuck on the path, his wingtips soiled. Perhaps, when the last fight is over, he'll find peace.

When Nix and Cali Richards are looking out from a tank.

"Why don't you join Anna for lunch? Afterwards, she'll be monitoring a shutdown in Atlanta from a projection room. There's another one scheduled for this evening in St. Louis. I'll join you for dinner."

He loosens his tie. It's pointless to argue. She insists on gardening while more important matters are at hand. And yet, the battle is almost over. He leaves her in the muddy water and avoids the vacant stares as he climbs past the banyan tree. The air is getting hard to breathe.

"Marcus!"

He stops at the exit. Mother stands beneath the banyan, a handful of aquatic weeds dripping from her hands.

"You'll always be welcome here," she says.

The taxi is back at the curb. He goes outside where the morning shadows stretch across the ground and the air is refreshing. The pressure in his chest relents. He breathes easier. Maybe he's heat stroking.

Or maybe she eased his mind.

CHAPTER NINETY-ONE_

THE McDONALD'S PLAYLAND IS BURIED IN SNOW, SOMEWHERE in Indiana.

Snowmelt drips from yellow and red plastic tubes. Footsteps are pressed into the slush, revealing the happy colors of a foam mat. The sounds of clamoring children echo from inside the fortress while their grandfather sits on a bench, pinching his collar against the cold.

Jamie's pores are saturated with fast food.

Another day. Another stop.

She unbuttons her coat, letting the chill climb inside. Her skin is tired and suffocating. If she could just somehow shed her body, walk out of her life, become someone else, someone new and young again.

It was so easy when she was a child. She was only 5% biomite, barely enough to notice she was altered. Five percent wasn't much more than the infant booster, the amount dedicated to prevent sickness. She didn't have any sensory augments until she was thirteen, and no ability to manipulate the nervous system until she was fifteen.

What percent are the little ones thundering through Ronald McDonald's frozen tubes? Will they reach for more like Jamie? Will they discover the thrilling surge of tweaking biomites and the release of artificial dopamine? Will they attempt a constant high with additional doses—just one more seed, and life will feel like you want? Just one more, one more, one more until life becomes an empty husk, a battered old coat with no more purpose and climbing through a playground just seems pointless?

"Hey!" A large woman pushes the door open. "Get inside, your food's ready.

The plastic tubes rattle. A skinny kid shoots out of the bottom, followed by two more boys. They slip in the slush, flipping wet snow on Jamie.

"Boys!" the large woman shouts. "Apologize to the young lady."

The kids hand out apologies on the run, ducking beneath the woman's short arm. Jamie wipes the dirty snow off her lips, clumps already melting down her neck. The door closes behind her, sealing the laughter inside.

Paul sits in a booth, a box of chicken nuggets waiting for her. Ronald McDonald's smiling head is above him. They're both staring.

She doesn't want to go in there. Doesn't want to run anymore. She's tired of racing on the wheel, going nowhere, wasting time filling the giant hole that's swallowed her life.

She turns off the audio in her head. Silence rings.

The air cleanses her lungs but can't revive the deadness in her flesh, can't flush the impurities from her pores, revive her life.

Nothing will bring back the clay of childhood.

Come inside. Paul's voice startles her. It's the first time he's ever chatted her. He's always staring at his phone, but never turning it on, always telling her what to do, but never chatting her. It's strange to hear a voice inside her head.

The last one was Charlie.

She pulls open the door and warm air gusts out of the restaurant. Paul chews slowly, eyes fixed on his food.

"I didn't give you my identity." Jamie stands at the table's edge. "How'd you chat me?"

"Don't turn around."

"What?"

"Slide into the booth and don't turn around."

Her anger dissolves into confusion. Paul dips a French fry in ketchup, still not looking. Jamie sits down, staring at the paper cups of ketchup.

"Eat something," he says.

"Not hungry."

"Then pretend."

The gold nuggets look like deep-fried turds. She takes a sip of soda.

"How long has he been there?" Paul asks.

"Who?"

"The old man—don't." His glare captures her eyes as she starts to turn. "There's an old man sitting out there. How long has he been there?"

She recalls the grandfather sitting outside with the kids. "He's still out there?"

Paul dunks another fry. "I spotted him at the last two stops. Yesterday, too."

"Do you think he's..." Her hands quiver.

"Let's eat here a few minutes; then we'll go."

He casually wipes his mouth and leans back to observe their surroundings. Wrinkles deepen between his eyes. That's the cop-expression he wore in the warehouse when he yelled at the officers for cuffing her. The memory of that rank air emerges from her subconscious like she's still there. The seat feels hard and cold.

She can't move.

The spell the bricks had put her under was a live burial...no, not the bricks. The old man did it to her. He wanted to kill her.

Or something worse.

He wanted to pull her apart, make her pay for her mistakes, pay for living. His eyes felt like spikes that twisted deep inside her, spearing her heart. Cold shanks of fear. Even now, she feels them.

Paul puts his hand inside his jacket.

Jamie is jerked back to the present moment, Ronald McDonald staring gleefully. Paul moves in front of her.

Tell him I mean no harm, another voice chats inside her head.

Jamie puts her hand to her ear and sees the old man standing at the door, arms stiffly at his sides. She doesn't recognize him.

"What is it?" Paul asks.

"He just chatted me." Her lips flutter. "He said…he said he means no harm."

The man isn't as old as she thought, his hair prematurely gray, his features appear worn out from living in the clay rather than biomite remediation. He approaches with his hands slightly raised, shuffling around a table of children digging through Happy Meals.

"Who are you?" Paul demands.

"May I sit?"

"Who are you?"

"It'd be better if we didn't attract attention."

Paul takes a moment to consider the offer. Attention is as much their enemy as is a stranger. Paul slides next to Jamie, his hand still buried inside his jacket. He gestures to the other side.

"You're not on facial recognition," Paul says.

"Neither are you."

Jamie uploads the man's face through the public database using the McDonald's Wi-Fi and gets no response.

"You're in danger," the man says.

Paul stiffens. "How do you know?"

The man's tired eyes are more gray than blue. The whites are tinted pink.

"I know about the warehouse," he says to Jamie. "I know that you were there when the shutdown occurred, that you ingested a nixed biomite capsule. I know that you lost someone very close to you."

He warily looks at Paul, perhaps another attempt to identify him.

"You're free now, but for how long?"

"Are you with them?" Paul says. "Are you a brick?"

"We wouldn't be having a conversation if I was. Did you help her escape?"

Paul doesn't respond. His arm feels like corded steel against her shoulder. He continues to grip something tightly inside his coat.

"You were there?" Jamie asks. "You were at the warehouse?"

"What they did was tragic." He wants to say more, but only looks at her to say, "I'm sorry."

"How did you find us?" Paul cuts in.

"I know a safe place, where no one can see us."

"What do you mean?" Jamie asks. "Mother?"

The man doesn't answer. *Of course.*

"Shutdowns are increasing," he says. "Marcus Anderson is the man responsible. He's the one that threatened you."

"How do you know that?" she says.

"Do you think he'll forget about you?"

"Enough." Paul stands, his hand pulling out of his coat empty. Jamie is shaking. "She's been through enough."

"It's the truth. You can't run forever. The road will eventually end."

"Let's go." He motions to her. "Come on."

"I'll find you again," the man says. "They will, too."

"Who the hell are you?" Paul says.

For the first time, the man falters, covering up the thoughts behind his eyes. Patrons have taken notice of Paul looming over him, his posture rigid, fists clenched. Only the children take no notice, shouting as they head out to the playground.

It takes a false start before he gets the words out, looking directly at Jamie when he says, "You have something I need."

"What?" Jamie says.

"Information."

"About the warehouse?" He doesn't answer, but what else could it be? "You want to be halfskin?"

He averts his gaze, perhaps hiding the answer. "What I want is irrelevant."

"Come on." Paul yanks her across the plastic bench. "Follow us if you like, we're not stopping."

"Where is the safe place?" Jamie asks.

People aren't pretending they don't notice anymore. Paul beats back their interest with a sweeping glare. Jamie sits back down. The man still seems lost.

Me. He's come for me.

"South," he says. "About a day away. Maybe two, with the weather."

"And what is it?"

"Just a place where Mother can't see."

Again, he ruminates. He's honest, she can tell. She can feel it. What he wants isn't selfish, it's not petty. Still, he's hiding much. He packs the food in the paper sacks and stands.

"I have a white van. We'll go southbound as long as the weather permits."

"And if we don't follow?" Paul asks.

"You're not going anywhere." He hands him the bag. "Your time is limited; it'll run out sooner than you think. It's best if you follow me."

Perhaps he's talking about their aimless driving, their endless road trip; but Jamie hears it differently. *I'm going nowhere.*

Paul is grinding through his thoughts, dead set against following a weird stranger. Jamie snatches the bag and heads for the exit. A white van is next to their car, exhaust puffing from the tailpipe. She pulls her jacket around her throat, the wind stealing her breath. Her nose is numb when Paul finally comes out.

They get in the car.

They follow the white van without talking.

CHAPTER NINETY-TWO_

SLEET TICKS OFF THE WINDSHIELD.

Nix pulls up to a Super 8, the white lights illuminating the snow-crusted hood. He watches the rearview mirror for a dirty white sedan. After seventy-two hours without sleep, the faint hint of hot metal lingers in his sinuses. Even his biomites have their limits.

It took a month to find Jamie. Her personal account had been closed following her "death." However, she was jumping on and off public Wi-Fi, enough that he could track her down.

Nix caught up to her near St. Louis. He pumped gas while Jamie sat in the sedan. She was in the passenger seat, head against the glass. And then a man returned.

He didn't look like her father, at least not the one in her history. They hardly spoke at restaurants and slept in separate hotel rooms. Nix spent his nights searching the man's past.

No facial recognition.

His secrecy had the imprint of security. Public servants, like police, were required to reveal name, rank and affiliation. If he was federal, like CIA, that would explain it. He expanded the facial recognition to include similar matches. It resulted in several thousand hits that would take days to sort out. However, there was one in Seattle: Paul Jennings. Seattle Police Department.

He was at the warehouse.

Odd that facial recognition didn't match the first time. In fact, his history had been erased. Nix needed more time to figure this out, but he'd been spotted. Jamie's activity on public Wi-Fi stopped. They moved quickly after that. It took three days of catching up. If Jamie hadn't accessed a public library connection in central Illinois, he might never have found them.

They were desperate. He couldn't wait any longer.

Time is running out for all of us.

Headlights shine in the rearview mirror. A car comes down the interstate ramp. The sleet blurs the white sedan sitting at the stop sign. The road is empty. Nix climbs out to wait at the back bumper. Fatigue pulls at him despite the urgency.

After a long minute, the car eases into the parking lot.

Jamie is lying back. Paul cracks the window. Dead air leaks out.

"I'm sorry," Nix says. "I can't keep driving, the weather's not good. I'm exhausted. I'll get us three rooms."

Paul doesn't answer.

Jamie looks smacked out of her gourd.

The window slides up. Paul hangs his hand over the steering wheel, staring through the windshield. Ice pellets streak through the high beams.

The car rolls forward.

Nix watches it cruise out of the parking lot. The left taillight intermittently blinks. The car creeps down the road. Nix doesn't have the energy to give chase. It'll have to wait until morning.

However, the brake lights splash across the wet asphalt. They turn into the Best Western a couple hundred yards away. Beneath the bright awning, Paul goes inside the lobby.

He's playing it safe.

Nix never intended to drive straight to the farm. Taking Jamie is a risk. Bringing Paul is stupid. It isn't likely they're being watched, but if they are, he'd be leading them right to Cali. But they're scared and nervous. They're looking for an escape, he can feel it. The farm is exactly what they want, he knows it.

Nix is running out of time. And his tolerance of risk is increasing, and now he's dragging others into his careless pursuit. He doesn't want to betray his sister, but it's got to be now.

Nix drags his feet, now wet and cold, into the hotel. He gets a room. There will be no visits to Dreamland. Not tonight.

Tonight, he'll rest.

Tomorrow will be difficult.

MOTHER_
THE DANCE OF SECRETS

Another dance recital.

If the government declared them illegal, Abe Rondell wouldn't argue.

The parking lot next to the school was full. They found a spot across the road. So did the other parents that were running late. They waited at a stoplight. Fine green lines appeared in his vision and enclosed the passing license plates. The numbers were logged in to the column to the right of his vision.

Once they crossed the road, the same green lines targeted the people they passed. Names hovered over their heads, along with registered occupations and whatever personal information was linked to social networks.

"Stop working," his wife said.

The green lines boxed her in. "Lindsey, Real Estate Agent," floated over her head.

Occupation, "Bitch."

You get a toy like this, you don't turn it off. His promotion came with a subscription to the Global Facial Recognition database. It's too expensive for the general public. Commercial applications, however, made the investment well worth it. He would never forget another name, always identify potential customers.

Mind reading is no longer a fantasy.

He dialed down the sphere of capture, pulling faces only from a five-foot radius around him. The attendees funneled towards the front doors of the school. It wasn't triggered by the back of their heads, only when someone turned around. It required a frontal view that analyzed spatial relations, skin tone, eye color, etc. Take, for instance, the lady holding the door.

"Nikki Messing.

"Administrative Assistant for School District #2. 32 years old. [LinkedIn]

"Two cats, no kids. [Facebook]

"Recently divorced. Hiked the Appalachian Trail this summer. [Facebook]

"Active dating profile. [eHarmony]"

"Turn it off." His wife squeezed his hand.

He'd have to work on disguising that glazed-over look when he was working.

They gave Nikki Messing their tickets and found their seats. The auditorium was stuffy. Abe settled into the creaky seat and prepared for two hours of mind-numbing boredom. When the lights went down and the first group of five-year-olds marched onto the stage holding giant lollipops and dancing to "The Good Ship Lollipop" (most of them staring at the crowd in horror), Abe fired up the facial recognition.

Only three of the children had personal information, which meant the parents voluntarily posted it. And the older the groups got, the more he learned.

His daughter's act was the ninth one of the evening. All of them were linked to social media, except for Abe's daughter, Jean. Tabitha, her new best friend, even streamed video from her Twitter and Instagram feeds that Abe watched superimposed over the dance routine.

When the event was mercifully over, they waited outside. His wife was occupied with other parents, so he kept it rolling. He identified a few potential clients and stored this event away for future chitchat.

His daughter finally came out with Tabitha. Hugs and congratulations and flowers were exchanged. The girls were almost as excited it was over as the adults. Tabitha asked if Abe's daughter could spend the night.

"If it's all right with her parents," Tabitha's mom answered.

"*Tina Martin. Cashier. 49.*"

"I don't think so," Abe said.

"Daddy!"

His wife looked shocked. He was usually thrilled to have an empty house. But it wasn't the blurry tattoo on Tina Martin's forearm that alarmed him or the unlit cigarette between her fingers.

"*Drug possession with intent to distribute.* [*Department of Corrections*]"

CHAPTER NINETY-THREE_

Cigarettes are yesterday's habit.

Paul watches from the second story of the Best Western while sucking on a filtered Marlboro. He quit smoking ten years ago, but he just didn't have the biomite capacity to kill the compulsion. Too much clay pulled him back to the sweet drag of tobacco.

A pack of twenty promised a reprieve from the daily grind, a little pick-me-up when life knocked you down. Cigarettes were the adult's cookie.

Then along came biomites.

The nicotine pick-me-up was replaced by scripted positive thinking and customized hormonal release. With the right seeding, you just decided to stop smoking: no struggle, no withdrawal. Sweet relief was a thought away. Instead of inhaling a lungful of carcinogens, people had the ability to feel whatever they wanted.

The cookie was internalized. No lighter needed.

At least, that's what the biomite designers promised. Humanity soon discovered that suffering doesn't disappear when wishes are granted. Life doesn't care how you feel and many came to find the internalized cookie was much more mesmerizing than a cigarette. To some, inescapable.

Jamie comes out of her room, huddling inside her puffy coat. Her hair frizzes beneath her stocking cap. When it comes to those that can't escape the empty promise of the biomite era, she is Exhibit A.

Smoke burns his eyes that already ache with only two hours of sleep. He gave Jamie his chat identity and waited all night for her to call if the old man came to kidnap her. Sometime before sunrise, he bought a pack of reds.

Paul slides his finger across his phone and waits for it to boot. He hasn't turned it on, afraid to give away their position. But Jamie has been lying, just like he thought. She has been on public Wi-Fi. That's how the old man found them.

But that means no one else is looking.

The bricks would've beaten the old man to them. At least Paul's identity is still locked. Despite being missing in action for over a month, he is still absent from facial recognition. The old man, though, is hiding something. Paul can't find anything on him.

Jamie sniffs. "Have one?"

Paul taps out a cigarette and lights it for her. Jamie exhales a column of white smoke. She bobs her head to her internal audio loop. Before biomites, the human race worked to tame runaway thoughts and unravel subconscious beliefs; now heads were filled with music and newsfeeds and lucid Dreamlands. It brought whole new levels of insanity.

Exhibit B, the warehouse.

"He's coming," Jamie says.

"Who?"

"The old man chatted me."

"How'd he get your identity?"

"Same way you did, I guess."

That's the funny thing: Paul doesn't know how he got it. Ordinarily, she would have to give it to him. Somehow, he just intuited it.

Jamie finishes her smoke and takes a second one from the pack. Paul lights another one for himself. He pulls a slow drag.

"So you have a gun?" Jamie asks.

"I'm a cop. That bother you?"

"Not at all."

He finishes the smoke and drops the butt over the railing. A white van comes down the road, tires cracking fresh ice in the parking lot. The old man stops beneath them, looking through the windshield.

"You sure about this?" Paul asks. "We can still leave."

"We aren't going anywhere, Paul. At least this is something." She grinds the cigarette butt under her heel.

"If he chats you," Paul says, "include me."

The van door slams. The old man goes to the stairwell, hopping up the first couple of steps, a bit spry for his age. He stops on the top step. Several moments pass.

"So where we going?" Paul asks.

"Can we talk first?" He gestures to Jamie's room.

"What for?"

"It'd be good if we talked about where we're going. And why."

The standoff lingers.

Jamie kicks open her room and leaves it open on her way inside. The old man politely waits. "Go ahead, Paul."

"How'd you get my name?"

"You're a Seattle police officer. You were at the warehouse."

"Did they contact you?"

"No. But I'd like to know why you're with her."

"And I'd like to know who the fuck you are."

"Please." The old man lowers his voice. "Let's go inside."

"Go ahead." He watches the old man go in the dark room.

Paul crushes the box of cigarettes. Enough with old habits; he needs to think clearly. He checks the phone before following. There are no messages. No texts, no missed phone calls. Not from his family or work.

It's been over a month.

And no one is looking for him.

CHAPTER NINETY-FOUR_

"MOVE TO THE BACK." PAUL CLOSES THE DOOR.

Nix doesn't argue. There is no way to move forward—no chance to make this morning work—without the truth. He has to expose his true nature, to become completely vulnerable and hope they will do the same. If he misjudged this moment, this won't go well.

Nix stands beneath the fluorescent lights above the sink.

"I know who you are," Nix says. "I know your names and your backgrounds. I think it's only fair that I tell you mine. My name is Nixon Richards."

He stares at the swirling patterns on the carpet, his heart thumping. If they haven't heard of him, they'll run a search. Jamie's subtle unfocused look suggests she's already downloading newsfeeds. Intensity rises across Paul's face.

"You should know that most of what you're going to find isn't true," Nix says. "Twenty years ago, my sister engineered a new generation of biomites that operated on an evolving frequency unknown to Mother. They were the first of their kind. They were invisible to her. You know them as nixes."

"You're a halfskin?" Jamie asks.

Nix nods. A long pause follows.

"You've eluded Mother for twenty years?" Paul says. "That's not possible."

"You're not picking up facial recognition because I've altered my appearance. I've been forced to look like this for longer than I care to remember."

"You can transfigure?" Jamie asks.

"I contain a significant level of biomites."

"What percent?"

He hesitates. "Ninety-nine."

Paul moves a step closer to Jamie. Instincts are warning him.

"You're lying. If you're Nixon Richards," he says, "you wouldn't tell us, not after twenty years on the run. There's a reward on your head."

"Who are you going to tell? Taking her from Marcus Anderson makes you as wanted as me."

"There's no way to trust you. You could be a brick."

"You would be dead if I was."

Nix faces the mirror, watching them in the reflection. He could show them his true face, but what good would that do?

"What do you want?" Paul says.

"My existence depends on the pill you ingested." Nix looks at Jamie. "Since the warehouse, Marcus Anderson has raided other halfskin dens. There's always a survivor, just like you. I think he's shutting them down just as someone takes the pill, timing it so the nixes don't integrate with their bodies. They contain information he can use to find more dens."

"So what?" Jamie says.

"I want to know what's inside you."

Nix hopes that Paul doesn't read the subtle deception. He didn't lie, but he won't reveal his true motivation. It's true that Marcus's new approach could lead him to discovering Nix and Cali, but that's secondary.

"Halfskin invisibility depends on evolving code, a continuous reconfiguration of the frequency that biomites communicate. It prevents her from establishing a connection with our identities, keeping us one step ahead of her. Marcus Anderson is quickly solving these encryptions."

"You want us to help you stay halfskin?" Paul asks. "Not our problem. You chose to become halfskin, you live with it."

"I didn't have a choice." There's no way to convince him that the rumors Marcus Anderson and others leaked to the press were lies to cover their incompetence. Nix had become halfskin to survive an accident, but no one believes that excuse anymore.

"I can help with your pain." Nix steps toward Jamie. "You lost someone in the warehouse, I know that. I know what it's like to lose a loved one. I know what it's like to wander through life just trying to scratch another moment of relief from endless suffering."

He sits on the bed.

"I can help."

"How?" Her eyes are dead. "How can you help?"

"We need to go somewhere safe, where no one can find us. We all benefit." Nix looks at Paul. "It would be safer if I could hide you both, in case you're being followed. But I can only make one of you invisible. In order to do that, I need to submerge Jamie in my perception field."

"Why?" Paul stiffens.

"By taking you with me, I'm putting someone at risk. I need Jamie to be invisible to whatever or whoever might be watching. Marcus Anderson had her alone in a room for three days. It's possible he's watching."

Sickness fills him. He's admitted his doubt and recognized the risk he's put Cali in. And he's still going through with it.

"Mother?" Jamie says. "You think Mother's watching?"

"No," Paul adds. "The bricks would've found us."

Paul's right, but Nix can't explain his sister's suspicious mind, her paranoid behavior that has kept them alive for all these years. He can't ignore her warning.

"It's a precaution," Nix says. "It's like anesthesia. You'll go to sleep and wake up once we're there. Paul will be with us; he'll make sure nothing happens."

"I don't like this," Paul says.

"Jamie?" Nix asks. "I'll be with you. I've got just as much to lose."

I've got more to lose. Much more.

Her eyes are blank. Perhaps she's imagining what it must be like to go to sleep and not dream, to forget what today feels like. Anesthesia sounds like a slice of death. And death no longer feels like an enemy.

Nix holds out his hand, the knuckles knobby with apparent age, the palm coarse and wrinkled. Jamie puts her delicate hand in his. The direct contact allows a better connection. The conscious barrier between them dissolves, his awareness merging into hers, usurping, momentarily, her identity.

He assumes control of her biomites. The buzz of her frequency synchronizes with his. He feels her heart beating faster, her lungs rapidly expanding and contracting. He can't feel his own body, the energy rapidly draining, but he can feel her emptiness, her lack of purpose. Her hopelessness.

The distinct metal tang falls on his tongue, absorbing the edges of her charred state of biomite addiction. Somewhere, he can feel a foreign object inside her with all its secrets.

The pill.

The answers are still there. If he could just read them, he could leave, never risk Cali's life, let them go about their running. But he needs help. He needs Cali to uncover the secrets.

Paul pushes Nix away.

Jamie sucks in a deep breath, emerging from an experience of nonexistence. Nix struggles with his own breathing. He took away her pain by snuffing her awareness. For a moment, she forgot what it was like to be Jamie. She sits up, pushing Paul's hand away. It takes several moments for her to return to her body and the misery it holds.

"Come with me," Nix says. "And no more running."

Despite her resistance, Paul helps her stand.

"A safe place for all of us."

She swims in indecision, but there's nowhere for her to go. Much later, Nix marvels how fortunate it was that Paul was with her, that he seemed trustworthy enough to bring along. Nix couldn't drive her to Cali's alone. It was almost too perfect.

Paul's presence would make all the difference.

Jamie hangs on to Paul as they descend the steps to the parking lot. Nix taps his teeth, numbness slowly fading.

CHAPTER NINETY-FIVE_

SNOW NARROWS THE WINDING ROAD.

Paul keeps both hands on the wheel, hunching forward. The headlights illuminate heavy snowflakes staggering to the ground. Beyond, the road is dark and unknown.

The GPS says he's close.

Nix and Jamie are sleeping in the backseat. Nix remained awake for hours, but his words began to slur. He eventually fogged up, sometimes responding to a question a minute later. Paul frequently stopped to check on them.

"There's no address," Nix had told him. "But there are coordinates. You'll know it when you get there."

Paul didn't plan on Nix going unconscious. Occasionally, he groaned and spit out nonsense as if nightmares were escaping. Perhaps that's what he's made of: nightmares.

Paul had heard of Nixon Richards.

He was a kid when he redlined, about Jamie's age. Those were the days when 40% biomites got you incarcerated for observation. The first generation of biomites behaved like cancer, slowly consuming the body's clay. People didn't have a choice of going half-skin; they were all destined to reach it at some point. Paul's father always said that, during those days, you just hoped you'd reach old age before that.

After that, the stories get sketchy. The most popular one claims that Nixon Richards eclipsed into a biomite rage and attacked a guard. He was aggressively subdued and ended up in a hospital, where he would likely be shut down.

And then he disappeared.

Nixon Richards and his sister, Dr. Cali Richards, somehow turned their biomites invisible. Occasionally Internet rumors would revive their names, where they were reverently whispered. About a year later, a new generation of biomites was discovered by garage techs that halted the runaway biomite division. The redline laws were rescinded. Halfskin status had become a choice.

That's when the real fun began.

There was a sharp decline in shutdowns but not for the reasons the government promoted. Secret variants of biomites were popping up. People were still going halfskin. Mother just couldn't see them.

It always seemed odd that the new generation of biomites was first discovered by a hobbyist, and not a team of nanobiometric engineers with all the money in the world. The rumors always traced back to Dr. Cali Richards, now a digital goddess, that leaked her discoveries.

Paul keeps his attention on the road. Truth be told, he was excited when Nix first suggested a safe place. He tried to kill that emotional response, to think rationally. But Jamie was right...*we're going nowhere.*

He lets up on the gas. The GPS shows two dots—the car and the destination—on top of each other. The road, however, is desolate and houses rare. Snow-crusted trees rise from the banks. He comes around a sharp turn.

The gate appears to his right.

Brick columns peek out from piles of snow where someone has plowed an opening. The cast-iron gate absorbs the headlights' glare, the entry drive beyond vanishing into the trees. Paul stops in the middle of the road. The gate doesn't open.

Snow gathers on the windshield.

He gets out to inspect the gate. There are tire tracks that lead to the gate. The road curves to the left, but the trees are too thick to see anything. He shakes the bars; snow falls to the ground.

He plods back to the car. The two are disheveled and slumped in the backseat. She's drooling. Nix's teeth are clenched.

"We're here." Paul shakes Nix. The old man's head wobbles. "Hey. Wake up."

He gives him a couple sharp slaps. No response, not even a groan.

"Shit."

Nix has a pulse. So does Jamie.

"Jamie, wake up." He gently shakes her. She won't come out of it. He's got to separate them, break the connection. He tries to pull Nix's hand off her forearm. Jamie's arm is bent at an angle beneath his white-knuckled grip. Her flesh is sickly purple, the fingers swollen.

"Hey! Hey! You're killing her! Let go, goddamnit!"

He tries to peel back the fingers. Jamie's skin is hot, the forearm moving like she's developed a new joint. Nix's grip is locked. Paul strikes him with an open palm. Nix's head jerks sideways. Red marks glow on his cheeks where the wrinkles have faded. Paul grabs Nix's hair and pulls back a fist when he hears barking.

Two dogs race down the lane, snow flipping in their wake. They stop at the gate, baring teeth.

Headlights come around the bend.

A truck creeps into view, its tires lining up in the previous tracks. It stops twenty feet from the gate. The dogs keep their black eyes on Paul.

A sole silhouette sits in the driver seat. The high beams are blinding. The dogs push their heads between the bars.

"Are you Cali Richards?"

His head begins to buzz. A wave passes through him like a

thermal scanner. Paul reaches inside his jacket, feeling the security of a 9mm grip.

Nausea turns his stomach inside out. He falls against the car, sliding down the door. The road tips like a broken slab. He feels wet snow on his face, the road beneath. The world is spinning like a broken carnival ride. A slick of perspiration rises across his forehead.

The gun is heavy.

He swallows back vomit when his own thoughts attack him, seeding him with doubt and fear and confusion. A thousand voices shout inside his head. He covers his ears.

And then his hands are empty.

Slowly, the carnival ride stops whirling. Two heavy boots are buried in front of him, a white robe dangling at the knees. The 9mm clip falls between the woman's feet, followed by the gun. The dogs sniff his legs and arms. Their breath is warm on his face.

An old woman squats in front of him. Her green eyes flash like a camera; he feels the inner trickle of a digital scan.

"If you're Cali Richards..." The words echo in his head. "Your brother..."

Paul flicks his eyes at the door.

The woman looks inside. She yanks the handle. There's scuffling. The dogs whine.

"Oh, no," she whispers. "No, no, no..."

Paul can't feel his extremities. The gun and ammunition are lost in the snow. It wouldn't do him any good to retrieve it. He can't feel his fingers.

"Get up!" she shouts. "Drive inside the gate!"

Paul is yanked to his feet by an invisible force. He's reaching for the door, sensations returning to his hands and legs. He's not entirely in control of what he's doing. He climbs into the driver seat. The dogs race through the open gate. He pulls in behind them.

Something changes when he passes between the columns. There's less static in his head. His thoughts clear up.

"Go around the truck!" she shouts from the backseat. "All the way to the house."

The car barely fits between the truck and trees. The dogs lead the way. The branches reach over the road, entangled like twisted fingers. The headlights beam down the tunnel until he clears the trees. Open fields are to the left. Windows are lit up in a two-story house.

"What have you done?" she mutters over the sound of rustling clothes and flopping limbs.

Paul stops in front of the house.

"Get the girl," Cali says. "Be careful with the arm."

He jumps out of the car like a wound-up toy and eases Jamie out. Her arm is wrapped in a sweater that's tied to her belt. Paul cradles her like a grown child. Cali is already climbing the front porch with Nix hiked over her shoulder: a frail woman hauling a full-grown man.

"Up here!" Cali shouts.

The house is warm and old. Paul doesn't close the front door. He follows the black dog—the larger of the two—to the second story. The worn steps creak as the other dog comes up behind him. There's a bedroom on the right. Cali is hunched over a bed, out of breath. Nix is splayed across the bedsheets, arms and legs bent.

Paul turns sideways to avoid banging Jamie on the doorjamb.

"Don't let them touch," Cali says.

He gently places her next to Nix, careful that her arm doesn't move. Her stocking cap has fallen off; her face is hidden beneath her thick brown hair. Cali folds Nix's hands over his stomach and straightens his legs.

He's not an old man anymore.

The wrinkles are gone, the nose slimmer, his lips fuller. The ridge above the eyes is no longer pronounced. He's a young man, a fortyish-year-old man with gray hair.

"Are you the girl's father?"

"No."

"Why are you here?"

"I...I pulled her from the warehouse."

Cali looks up. Lines crease her forehead. Another digital wave passes through him, this time without the nausea.

"That was almost two months ago," she says. "Why are you still with her?"

Jamie is so still, her expression less pained. As if she's found peace at last. He takes her wrist and feels her weak pulse. Cali watches him brush the hair from her face.

"Don't worry about her arm. How long did he have her like that?"

"We left this morning," he says. "What the hell is happening?"

"He overextended his biomite capacity. Everything is shutting down."

That explains why he looks younger: he can't keep up the transfiguration. Cali shouldn't look that old, either. Her hair is more white than gray, her complexion softly wrinkled. She doesn't walk like an old lady, and certainly not one that could carry a grown man like a sack of grain.

Was that her perception field that brought on the nausea? Am I still in her field, seeing this kindly old woman? Is that why I feel oddly comfortable with her while two people may be dying?

He should be more vigilant. He should go find his gun.

The room begins to sway. If he can't trust his own senses, if he can't sort his thoughts from hers, how does he know what's real?

Cali goes to the bathroom for a washcloth and dabs Nix's face. She begins to undress him. Paul unzips Jamie's coat.

"I've got it from here," she says. "Go back out to the road and bring the truck up to the house. There's a room down the hall. You'll go to it when you get back and stay there for the night."

The previously warm sensation that filled the room dampens. He leaves with the cold impression that he's been dismissed. The dogs are waiting in the hallway. Cali is dabbing Jamie's cheeks with the washcloth. He gets the feeling she's better off here than anywhere else in the world.

But can I trust that feeling?

The steps groan beneath his boots. Once again, the black dog leads the way, his claws clicking on the old wood. The winter wind sighs into the house. Paul takes the brass knob to close it behind him.

"I don't know why Nix would bring you here. Or why I can't read your history." Cali is standing on the top step. "You should know that I'm a very private person. I have two dogs that protect me. I think you should understand that if Nix has made a grave mistake, the dogs will be the least of your worries."

She returns to the bedroom.

The dogs walk him down the long drive, snow dusting their dark coats. The truck is still running. The dogs wait while he goes out to the road and digs in the snow. Returning to the truck, he throws the gun and the clip on the front seat and lets out a long sigh.

He should get his car and leave. Jamie doesn't need him anymore. But he's compelled to return. Perhaps he's still snared in Cali's field.

Or maybe he just has nowhere else to go.

CHAPTER NINETY-SIX_

THE OVAL OFFICE IS IMMACULATE. THE SOFAS AND CHAIRS ARE arranged in perfect symmetry around a table with a bowl of fruit. George Washington and Abraham Lincoln watch from the far wall.

The front lawn sparkles with morning dew. Marcus watches the landscaper leave a crisp line in the damp White House lawn. He can smell the cut grass.

There's a photo of his children propped on a shiny table below the window. In the photo, they're still children. Clifford is wearing his red backpack. Months go by without thinking of them, as if they don't belong to him. He could have grandchildren now.

Washington and all the men and women of power believe, as did Marcus, that Mother is a peacekeeper. She alone has limited humanity's potential to self-destruct. But they have underestimated her.

He feels, on days like this, he has, too.

Marcus pivots on his heel and feels his knee catch. Pain lances up his thigh. The framed photo cracks on the floor. He holds his breath, swallowing the fierce agony. Marcus slams his open palm on the desk, ripping open the drawers to find nothing. The painkillers are in his sleeping quarters.

The last time he had been to the president's office—the actual

White House, not a replication in Mother—he had to explain his actions following, what he called, the rumors about his sexual perversions, and, more importantly, illegal procedures as Head of the Biomite Oversight Committee.

They sat on the couches. Marcus was on the right. How could he forget? He sat on the president's dog's bone right before the president promised to have his back. But the sex videos kept surfacing. Pretty soon he was ostracized. Marcus would've done the same thing, if he were the president. You can't look dirty when you're leading the free world.

The desk has three stacks of manila folders. Marcus takes the middle one. He tips his head back to focus through reading glasses. There was a biomite den in Omaha, Nebraska.

Was.

This shutdown didn't make the news. It was a halfway house for halfskins disguised as a center for substance/biomite abuse recovery. It was a short stay for wealthy people. The investigating brick infiltrated the den as a customer, even ingested a nixed pill. The pill, however, didn't activate since it only integrated with clay.

Unfortunately, this triggered an electromagnetic pulse, effectively self-terminating all the nixes associated with the den. *Suicide code.* They shut themselves down and, in the process, kept Mother from harvesting their secrets.

Information travels fast.

Anna enters the Oval Office. "Why aren't you wearing your earpiece? I've been calling you."

"I need some quiet."

She's wearing a cerulean blue skirt, hem above the knees. The blouse is snug around her neck with a gold necklace. She's quite professional today—except for the lack of a bra.

A delicious twist in his groin.

"All this labor," she says. "Reading and phones...it could be so much easier, Marcus. You would be so much more productive with a minor seeding."

"I use the five senses the good Lord gave me, Anna. I was made in His image, I honor that."

"You are like a man living in a cave, refusing to leave because the sun is too bright. Perhaps your Father intended more senses for you besides the five." She plucks the folder from him, the golden pendant swaying. "All you need is the courage to leave the cave."

"Stupidity can be mistaken for courage. Weakness, as well."

"We work harder to make up for your shortcomings." She drops the folder in the trash. "You slow us down, Marcus."

He squeezes the chair to control the anger. This is unlike her. She's incapable of emotions and only uses them to manipulate. Mother is behind this.

She's behind everything.

She wants him to merge with their biomite frequency. He can absorb information instead of reading it, communicate with thoughts rather than speak. Take a pill, and he won't be at the mercy of his emotions.

But he rather likes the fire in his belly. It reminds him there is still work.

"Are you hungry?" she says. "Sex, perhaps?"

"Give me your update."

Her fragrance is light and enticing. With a hand on his shoulder, she reaches for the desk and effortlessly flips it like a cardboard box. The papers flutter in a chaotic cloud.

The Oval Office shifts.

The walls straighten out, turning a dark shade of blue. The sofas fade and the windows stretch around him, providing views to massive palm trees and open blue sky. A woman sits next to a door. Her stillness betrays her inanimate nature. Marcus knows a brick.

"Miami," Anna says. "This doctor's office was infiltrated an hour ago. The operatives dismantled an EMP command to avoid self-shutdowns. They've quarantined the doctors and staff while assimilating the data. They were legitimate physicians, Marcus, healers of your people. They were also seeding select patients with nixes."

Anna turns Marcus's chair toward the exit. A young man tries to open the locked door. He sees the woman sitting inside and knocks on the glass.

"We've informed their patients the office is closed and their appointments rescheduled. In the meantime, the operatives are tracking them. Once they have the information they need, the doctors and staff will be digested."

She spins the chair back toward the woman, indifferent to the man rapping on the glass. Marcus doesn't need to go through the door. He's seen more mass shutdowns in the past month than the prior ten years. They're always the same.

"The patients will be shut down tonight," Anna says. "Almost five thousand, Marcus."

Ever since Seattle, the shutdowns have been quiet. Halfskins will be sleeping in their beds when they take their last breath. They'll fall off barstools or slump to the floor at their favorite restaurant.

The walls begin to curve and George and Abe are back on the Oval Office wall. Folders are stacked on the desk once again. Anna struts to one of the sofas.

"Two more shutdowns are scheduled for tonight, one in Paris and the other in Ontario. We expect big numbers."

"And the reaction?"

"Nothing new, the public isn't happy. World governments, though, are getting nervous. Press conferences have addressed the public's concern."

Marcus steeples his hands, bouncing his fingertips. The halfskin war is operating without him. He's more of a spectator now. He thought there would be more pleasure when victory was near.

"Very well. Give me the analysis for the next two weeks. I want an approximation of shutdowns, where and how many. I'll file a progress report."

Anna kneads his shoulders, using her thumb to drive the tension from his back. He closes his eyes and relaxes. When she's finished, his knee no longer hurts.

"One more thing," she says. "Jamie is missing."

"What does that mean?"

"You know what it means, Marcus."

The fire rises in his stomach. He recalls the first time Cali and Nix Richards went missing. He was arrogant to believe it was temporary, that they would be found.

Anna sits on the leather sofa, patting the space next to her. She lifts her skirt.

Marcus stands without a twinge of pain. He kneels in front of her, running his hands up the length of her thighs, over the soft curve of her buttocks. The next five minutes are glorious. It's not until much later he realizes what he saw before leaving the Oval Office. There was a dog bone on the sofa.

He had been thinking about the president's dog.

Only thinking.

CHAPTER NINETY-SEVEN_

Paul shivers, despite the blanket.

His clothes are damp. His feet are trapped in hard, wet boots. The weights on his eyelids are heavy; the hinges loosened after several attempts.

The bedroom is sparse with an unusually high ceiling and water stains around the light fixture. He drops his boots on the wood floor, the impact stinging his feet. He parts the curtains on the only window. His car is parked next to a barn that's smothered beneath a blanket of snow. He wonders how it got there.

And then remembers.

A black dog waits outside his door, tongue hanging. Paul moves carefully around him, brushing against the wall. He passes the stairwell on his right and tries the door at the opposite end of the hall.

Locked.

He puts his ear against it, listening for any sign of life. He tries the knob again. The keyhole is an old-fashioned lock, one he could pick if he had some heavy wire. What would he do if he opened it? Jamie was unconscious, the last he remembers. He brought her here.

Too late to take her away.

His footsteps echo down the shallow steps, the wood faded where thousands of steps have worn away the color. Dark squares on the floral wallpaper indicate picture frames that have recently been removed.

He stops at the bottom step. The house is quiet except for the dog's toenails clicking behind him. There's a short hallway to the right with a chalkboard to the left and a locked door to the right. It ends at the kitchen and the smell of coffee. A clock ticks above the refrigerator.

Paul parts the frilly curtains above the sink. The barn door is closed. Aside from a trail of footprints, the snow is perfect. Despite the tower in the distance, there's no service on his phone. No Wi-Fi, either.

The locked door opens in the hall.

Cali shuffles into the kitchen, followed by the brown dog. She's wearing fresh clothing, but her eyes look tired, her complexion deeply wrinkled. She pours two cups of coffee, sliding one toward him.

"You're Dr. Cali Richards."

She nods.

"You look older than I expected."

"Common courtesy does not tell a woman she looks old."

"From my understanding, you're about fifty years old."

"Don't believe everything you read."

She grabs a container next to the refrigerator. The dogs tap-dance.

"I've stayed alive all these years by hiding from Mother. I've altered my appearance, like Nix, to avoid facial recognition. But my brother has chosen to expose me to you, so I suppose it doesn't matter."

She tosses a snack to the dogs.

"Who are you, Paul?"

"How do you know my name?"

She passes him a sideways glance. If she can hijack his senses, she can find his name.

"I'm a Seattle cop."

"No. You're an enigma, is what you are. Your background security far exceeds the rank of sergeant. You're closed to the public. That's unusual. And you show up with a girl that was quarantined at one of the largest shutdowns at the time. It doesn't feel like a coincidence."

"And that makes me a threat?"

"To me, yes. Why are you with her?"

"They were going to take her. She was in danger."

"By 'they,' you mean Marcus Anderson."

"She's not a halfskin, you can scan her, you'll see."

"What compelled you to save her?"

"I'm human."

Cali goes to the mudroom, where her boots sit in a puddle of melted snow. She wraps a scarf around her neck and reaches for her coat.

"Why is it so hard to believe that I saved a girl in trouble? Have you become so accustomed to manipulating your senses that you no longer feel compassion?"

She sits on a footstool to pull on her boots.

"You pulled me into your perception field last night," Paul continues. "You made me see and hear what you wanted, made me help you. You're far past a halfskin, like your brother. He said he was 99%."

He remembers the mind-fog at the warehouse, compelled to do whatever the bricks told him. He doesn't remember being forced to save Jamie, but why would they? *No, I acted on my own. That was my choice, my own free will.*

But would he know it?

"Is that true?" he says. "Are you almost a brick?"

She sits up. "Don't lecture me. You don't know me."

"And you don't know me."

"That's the problem, Paul." She pulls on her coat, buttoning it. "There's a dome of static that protects me and my property. It operates like back-reflection, showing Mother there are no biomites within this sphere. It won't work forever, I know that. She'll eventually find me, maybe ten years from now, maybe tomorrow. I don't know. Right now, though, I've got you and Jamie in my house. I need to figure some things out. It's going to take Nix and Jamie a couple of weeks to recover."

"After that?"

"I don't know." She cups her coffee to her chin, the aroma failing to revive her tired eyes.

"Is it true what they say about you?" he asks.

"Truth is rarely found in the news."

"You were the nanobiometric engineer that beat Mother. You released the nixed code to the public."

"Like I said, believe nothing you've read."

"I see an old woman. Is that truth? You manipulated what I saw, heard and felt last night. And maybe you're doing it right now. How am I supposed to know what's true when I can't trust my senses?"

"Our senses were fallible long before biomites."

"Reality is not relative."

She poses over her coffee cup, eyes distant and glassy. "These days, it is."

She takes one final sip and leaves it in the mudroom. The brown dog follows her. Frigid air swooshes past the open door. Paul watches her trudge to the barn.

The black dog watches him.

CHAPTER NINETY-EIGHT_

THE WORLD ROCKS, UP AND DOWN. UP AND DOWN.

Droplets spatter across Nix's cheeks; a briny taste is on his lips. His head sways with the rhythm of up and down, up and down. The soothing sound of water feels like a lullaby.

The sky is unblemished. The blue is deep and endless. His eyelids succumb to the rhythm and begin to fall—

He sits up.

The bamboo raft rocks beneath his shifting weight, seawater sloshing over the sides. The bindings creak.

Where am I?

He dips his feet in the warm water. Far behind him, the rocky shore and the twin peaks are visible. A green meadow slopes behind them, and, despite the distance, he knows there's a cabin on top of that where Raine waits for him.

Dreamland.

He's never been out this far in the water. Occasionally, he would hop on a skiff with one of the local fisherman, but they rarely ventured into the deep. And never on a homemade raft.

He envisions a sail and a gust of wind to push him home, but his thoughts dissolve like daydreams. Nothing he imagines comes to fruition. The raft rocks beneath his feet. He dives into the sea's depth. He grabs the edge of the raft and begins kicking. Eventually, he'll reach the shore. What seems like hours go by, and he's no closer. Home is in sight, but no more.

Cali put him out there.

This is my punishment.

CHAPTER NINETY-NINE_

THE DAYS ARE EMPTY.

Paul spends most of them with Baxter, the black dog. He rarely barks or shows his teeth. Often, he watches Paul with an unusual sense of intelligence. Observing. Thinking.

Cali locks herself in the basement most days. The bedroom upstairs is always locked.

He's hazy in the mornings, spending several minutes recalling where he is. The sand of sleep weighs him down for hours at a time. In the afternoons, he walks the property, going deep into the trees and out to the road. The dog doesn't like it when he's that far out.

Paul could leave, just hop the gate. Maybe he'd have to fight off the dog, but then what? Where would he go?

What about Jamie?

There's an old cell tower behind the horse paddock. By his estimates, it's centered on the property. The scaffolding is corroded, but the utility shed is new. So is the conduit that runs to the top of the tower.

The shed is locked.

This must be what generates her back-reflecting dome of protection. If this comes down, she's exposed.

One morning, his car is gone. Paul finds it behind the house near an abandoned swing set, the corroded legs buckled like old bones. Footsteps lead back to the house. The railing leading up the front steps wobbles. He goes to the barn in search of tools. The tack room door is jammed. He uses both hands to get it open.

A red toolbox is stashed on a shelf with a tin can full of rusty nails. He inspects the latch on the door. It's as old as the house. It wouldn't take much to dissemble and fix.

Something moves through the trees. Paul watches through the window as a red truck comes down the lane, a yellow plow blade carving snow to the side. It backs up several times, working its way toward the house.

Paul steps into the breezeway, but stays to the shadows.

Cali comes out the front door, fastening her coat. A man gets out of the truck and waves at the old woman looking more tired than ever.

"Good morning, Stacy," the man says.

Stacy?

He hugs her while a young girl steps out of the passenger seat, her arm tied in a sling. Both dogs come running. It's the first time he's seen their tails wag like that. She takes a knee, rubbing their thick coats with her free hand. Paul can feel the weight of Cali's mind press upon his. She's exerting her field on him.

Stay.

That's why the car's out back.

The conversation passes. The daughter lifts her wounded arm, explaining how she sprained her wrist when her fingers got tangled in twine while bucking bales. The man fills his lip with a pinch of tobacco. Cali looks concerned for the girl. Several minutes later, they climb back in the truck and finish plowing.

Cali goes to the porch.

Paul steps into the opening with a hammer and a rusty can of nails. She stares for a long moment.

"Friends?" Paul asks.

"Neighbors help out from time to time."

"Why'd you let them leave?"

"This isn't a prison camp."

"Just for us."

"You weren't invited."

He peers around the corner. The truck has left long piles of snow. That sling was old-fashioned. Even the lowest dose of biomites could heal something like that.

They're clay.

Their eyes meet. No words are needed. Cali Richards is keeping a secret. If you learn it, you don't leave.

She goes back inside to lock herself in the basement.

Paul fixes the railing.

CHAPTER ONE HUNDRED_

Warm, dry air blows on her face.

Jamie's head is sunk in a pillow. The dusty strands of a spiderweb wave in the ceiling vent.

Sensation returns to everything but her left arm. The last thing she remembers is going to the car, but this isn't the hotel. Her internal clock announces the time. It seems like they were at the hotel a minute ago, but three days have passed.

Three days have been snipped from her life.

She sits up. Her mouth is dry and gummy, and her left arm is wrapped with gauze. Her pale fingertips feel dead, as if someone sat on her arm. She balances against the wall, stumbling barefoot to the door. The strange surroundings smell of old linen.

Someone is downstairs.

She goes one step at a time, gripping the railing with both hands at first. A conversation is heating up, somewhere downstairs. The muffled voices aren't familiar. They're coming from the first floor, behind a door in the hallway. She leans against the chalkboard, sliding her feet to keep the floor from creaking. The argument comes in bursts, most of it unintelligible.

"No one's leaving!" a woman shouts.

The other person is apologetic, reasoning, even pleading, for a response. Jamie feels the wall slide up her back as she slowly goes to the floor, her legs too weak.

A door opens somewhere in the house.

Toenails click toward her. A black dog stares from around the corner, and heavy boots follow.

"Jamie." Paul pulls off his gloves and crouches beside her. His brown hair, so often combed to the side, is a mess over his thick eyebrows. "Are you all right? How'd you get down here?"

She grabs him with her free hand, latching on like she won't let go, like he's the only thing that's keeping her from melting into a puddle. He's the only thing she can remember.

He's safe.

Paul almost carries her into a kitchen, where she sits at a weathered table. A glass of water finds its way into her hand.

"Little sips."

She takes big swallows and he has to pull it from her. It cools her throat and settles her stomach. He keeps his hand on the glass the next time she drinks, monitoring how steeply she tips it.

"Where are we?" she asks.

"What do you remember?"

She wipes her mouth. It takes too long to remember what Nix looked like, what he told her. *Somewhere safe.*

The kitchen feels like it's stuck in time, with spice racks and dried flowers hanging over a window. Safe isn't a house in the country. She was expecting something to take the pain away.

The fear of living is still a cold lump in her chest.

An old woman stops in the hall and stares. A young man, however, walks boldly past her. He's vaguely familiar, his hair prematurely gray.

"You're awake," he says.

She shrinks from his comforting reach. He steps back and looks at Paul. He resembles Nix, but there's a difference of about twenty years. The hair, though, doesn't fit. She attempts facial recognition, green lines racing through her vision. There's no outbound connection to the Internet.

"I was an old man when you last saw me." He sits across from her. "I had reconfigured my facial features. The hair isn't as malleable as flesh. This is what I look like in real life."

Real life? What does that mean anymore?

"Where are we?"

"We're at the farm," he says. "You're safe."

The old woman's face is darker than the shadows appear. Jamie continues staring, not remembering any discussion about her. She seems irritated, but finally relents.

"My name is Cali Richards," she says flatly. "You're safe in my house."

Jamie doesn't believe her. Her body language suggests she didn't invite them. There's a vague recall of Nix explaining the facial reconfiguration and a promise that he'd help, but not where they were going.

"How does your arm feel?" Cali asks.

"I can't really feel it."

"You suffered a compound fracture. Unfortunately, your biomites are exhausted from years of abuse. I don't think I need to tell you how close you are to charring. Your body will have to heal itself."

"Why not boost her?" Paul asks. "Seed the break."

"She's at 49.9%. We're not doing that."

"What are we doing?" Jamie asks.

Cali takes a bowl of eggs from the refrigerator. She puts a pot on the stove then cracks a hardboiled egg on the counter, peeling the shell under running water.

Nix's jaw is clenching.

There's a chat session between them. Nix looks up just as a warm sensation trickles inside Jamie, a sort of honey-sweet emotion that bubbles from inside her chest. Jamie is enveloped in the invisible arms of an all-loving mother. She doesn't know why this happens, doesn't care. For the first time in forever, she doesn't want to crawl out of her skin.

She feels safe.

"Start with this." Cali puts the hardboiled egg on a plate. "Give that some time to digest, then eat the soup."

They watch her take a bite. The attention keeps her from swallowing the egg whole. The silence is broken only by the ticking clock.

Cali leaves.

Nix follows her into the basement. Paul attends the pot of soup, stirring it with a spoon while Jamie finishes the glass of water and indulges in the warmth that feels like home.

I'm safe.

CHAPTER ONE HUNDRED ONE_

NIX TURNS THE GLASS KNOB. CALI'S BEDROOM IS UNLOCKED.

The bedspread is wrinkled, the pillows hardly dented. She wasn't sleeping. Maybe she was lying down every once in a while, but she wasn't sleeping.

Stress is her amphetamine.

He hadn't seen her in days. He didn't stay awake for long, his body insisting on frequent naps. He spent the nights on a raft, forever paddling toward distant peaks. No matter how long he struggled, the raft never reached the shore.

An athletic, dark body moves past him. Raine's image examines the empty bedroom. Her green cargo pants are rolled to the knees, exposing muscled calves. A high-pitched ring haunts his hearing. He shouldn't project her into being. His biomites are still recovering from the trip, but it's the only way to see her.

Raine's bare feet silently stride toward the dresser to study the framed photos of Nix's late parents as well as Cali's late husband. There's also one of her daughter, Avery. They surround a stencil drawing.

Life is suffering.

The memories are captured in photographs, reminders of another life. The happiness made the fall that much greater, the pain that much deeper. Now all that's left are pewter frames with fading photos.

Patterns of frost are crystallized on the window. Snowdrifts look like frozen waves in the backyard. Icicles hang from the old shed near the trees, icy daggers pointing at firewood.

"That's the last thing I did." He taps the glass. "Cut that wood."

It's still chest high, every log still in place. *It's rotten now.*

He grabs the cell phone from the dresser and flips it open. The buttons respond with melodic tones.

"She uses this to pretend she's clay. It's so naïve, a future artifact of a dying world."

"Nothing wrong with it, Nix. Biomites aren't for everyone."

"Clays are the new Amish. Do you know where the world would be if everyone did that? There'd be no new discoveries, no transportation, no modern medicine. We'd be gazing at the stars instead of traveling to them, just wishing things would be better instead of making them better. There'd be no you, Raine."

He drops the phone on the bed and takes down the photo of Avery. She's missing two teeth.

"God loves growth, Raine. Isn't that what life is about? Growth? He gave us the ability to conceive this technology for what purpose? Biomites are the vessel that carries our identity to new worlds like ships carried people across oceans to discover new lands."

"Who are you arguing with?"

"It's their fault, you see. None of this would be happening if it wasn't for clays like Marcus Anderson."

"They're not all like him."

Raine watches him rub the glass with his thumb. She never met Avery. She would've liked his niece. He's sure Avery would've loved her.

"What're you doing in here?" Cali stands in the doorway.

Nix jumps up, picture frame clutched in both hands. His sister looks so old. Despite the costume, the reconfiguration of her features, she wears the familiar mask of despair: the slow blinking eyes, the heavy corners of her mouth.

"Just thinking about when we moved here, how I used to cut the wood and stack it. Then I was thinking how we built the lab and planned on taking a few years to heal and then move on. This place was supposed to be a pit stop, remember? We weren't supposed to hide in the clay for the rest of our lives. What happened, Cali?"

"I don't need to explain myself."

"No. You got good at that."

"Don't make this about me. You brought them here, you had no right...*no right*."

"If they were a threat, the bricks would already be here."

"That's not the point." She snatches the picture and replaces it on the dresser.

"I can't let you rot like this," Nix says. "You're just withering."

"That is not why you're here. This is about you getting what you want, against my wishes. You know how I feel; don't pretend this is about anything else."

"That's why you're punishing me?"

Cali closes the door gently. She pushes her hair from her eyes, the tension draining from her forehead.

"I can't dream, Cali. I can't get back to Raine. You did this when I was unconscious, didn't you?"

She folds her arms.

"Why do you keep fighting it? You could build your own Dreamland, Cali. You could bring back Avery, do it right this time—fabricate her instead of pretending she's alive."

"You're addicted to Dreamland. You can't live in this world and the dream. You need to accept the world we live in."

"And have this life?" Nix slams his fist on the bed. "Just stay locked up and hide? Is that what we should do? You deserve better, Cali. I can't let you do it."

"You'll go insane if you keep dreaming."

"You had no right to take Raine away!"

"And you had no right to expose me." She jabs her finger at him, her hand quivering. "You arrive on the brink of charring; you bring strangers into my life. This is my world, Nix. I did not invite them. And you need to accept the fact that I don't give a goddamn about Raine. Dreamland is not a new reality, it's a dream—a fantasy. Accept that."

Nix paces across the room. He stands at the window, watching a bird hover over the trees, wings catching a draft higher.

"Just give me what I want," he says. "We'll leave. You can go back to your life in the clay."

"What do you want?"

"Reset my biomites, open Dreamland. And read the nixed pill inside Jamie."

"I'm not reading her."

Nix turns, swallowing a rising knot.

"And no one's leaving, not yet."

"What do you mean you're not reading her?"

"You want to use her to find a fabricator and I'm not doing that."

"Jesus Christ, Cali! Just let me use the lab, then. I'll do it myself. Why are you doing this?"

"You know why."

He resists throwing his fist through the window. She's still pissed. He can't blame her. She needs a few days, maybe weeks, to cool off.

"You can't kidnap them."

"You kidnapped them, Nix. Not me. Why would you bring Paul? He's got nothing to do with this."

"There's nothing wrong with him. Besides, I was able to hide Jamie with him driving."

"And almost killed yourself."

"I just need some help."

"You've made a mess and I'm cleaning it up. What'd you think I was going to do?"

"Not this!"

She holds her ground, unflinching. Her eyes are tired, mouth slack. She smells as old as she looks.

"This isn't fair. I let you play out your Avery delusion when I knew you shouldn't," he says.

"Maybe you shouldn't have."

He curses through stiff lips and yanks the door open. He wants to slam it like he did when he was little and she wouldn't let him have his way. He looks back.

Cali is staring out the window.

Her shoulders are shaking.

What have we become?

MOTHER_
DREAMING THE DREAM

Josh Stanton sneezed.

He hated sneezing. It was like licking metal shavings off an aluminum sheet then blowing it out his nose.

He climbed off the bus, holding his backpack against his chest. His life savings were inside. It wasn't much, but it was everything he had. He didn't trust the post office and had to pick it up in person, never letting it out of his sight.

The parking lot was littered. Josh avoided eye contact with the lady on the second floor. He locked his apartment door behind him, breathing heavily. It was here. Finally here.

The apartment was sparse: a TV and a couch. The lounging chair was in the middle of the room, extra padding duct-taped to the faux leather. It was for comfort, not looks. Josh didn't invest much in this world.

His investments were in his mind.

Josh closed a tiny gap in the heavy drapes and went to the kitchen. He took a long swallow of whole milk from the jug, swishing it around his mouth, coating his tongue and throat before swallowing.

Whole milk neutralized the metal taste. Without it, his tongue was like copper. His body dipped in lead.

Charred.

That was the official diagnosis. His biomites ran hot, circuits were shorting out. If he didn't back off his habit of dreamweaving, he could expect to taste steel for the rest of his life. And, the experts said, he could trigger a spontaneous shutdown.

What do they know?

They also said unassisted dreamweaving was impossible. No one, they said, has ever experienced a lucid dream state without external stimulation. And that's where they were wrong. Josh had clocked up to ten minutes of real time in a Dreamland before he started to char. He hadn't done it since, but he'd done it.

He figured he'd try what was in the box. If that didn't work, nixes were next.

Dreamweaver 2.0.

It was a metallic claw. The tips were smooth discs. It was custom fit for Josh's measurements and promised to ease the charred symptoms by reducing biomite activity. The test drive at the lab induced a short, lucid dream state. He could even feel it. He'd never achieved tactile sensation in his Dreamland.

Josh got comfortable. The dreamweaver was heavy. *The quality is in the metal.* The kit came with everything he needed, only Josh swapped out the power block with one of his own. He got the plans off the Internet. He lay back in the padded lounger and slid the dreamweaver's cold fingers over his head.

He immediately fell through inner space and landed in Dreamland: a medieval castle, a long sword on his hip. Where had he left off?

Ah, yes. The war.

The men followed him into battle. Whoever heard of a king leading the charge? Josh fought valiantly, slaying as many of the enemy as any man on the battlefield. He was drenched with the smell of blood.

They celebrated with mead and hog. They sang and laughed. That night, Josh made love to his queen. She moaned with pleasure. His orgasm was explosive.

As the days in Dreamland passed, his body became sluggish. The nights got darker and the days dimmer until he just felt like sleeping. Eventually, he didn't wake up.

The neighbors found him a week later.

The cause of death was starvation and exhaustion, in addition to extreme charring. The company claimed he circumvented the safety feature that prevented long-term dreamweaving by changing the power cell. They improved the product, but, after several more related deaths, were forced to discontinue the mobile dreamweaver unit.

Instead, they focused their investments on sanctioned dream cafés. And continued to make billions.

CHAPTER ONE HUNDRED TWO_

March arrives with no sign of spring.

Snow sparkles in the early light. The crust breaks beneath Cali's boots, her breath transformed into dense steam. She pauses at the fence to taste the morning, feel it pinch the end of her nose. She savors the moment. Ever since Nix arrived, these moments have felt numbered.

The horses emerge snorting from their stalls. They greet her with rubbery lips and humid breath. The water trough has frozen. Cali uses the blunt end of an ax to break it up, releasing the tiny bubbles trapped inside. The jagged chunks swirl with each blow, rising back to the surface. She chips at the bits and pieces clinging to the sides.

Is that what I've become, a trapped bubble?

Has this domed farm become her trough, keeping her safe and stagnant? She always rationalized that she was free to think, that she chose this simple life, that she had little choice, otherwise. Nix had proven her wrong, stepping outside the dome in search of a fabricator.

And she just watched.

Perhaps Paul will be an ax, come to shatter the frozen elements of her life. Maybe Jamie. She could be her daughter, fill that void Avery left behind. Cali couldn't help submerging the girl in her own perception field, soothing her aches. Cali is familiar with that pain; she couldn't let Jamie have it, too.

It's what a mother does.

The auto-fill valve doesn't appear to be working. It'll need to be replaced. She works the nut loose with a pair of folding pliers.

"Still not sleeping?" Paul is standing in a stall.

One of the horses is startled. Cali pulls her cap over her ears, wondering how long he's been watching.

"I'll sleep when this is over."

"When will it be over?"

"You tell me." She walks past him on her way to the tack room.

The feed buckets are in the sink, food stuck inside. She searches for an auto-fill valve on the shelves, swearing she had purchased an extra one. She pulls a toolbox from beneath the sink, feeling Paul fill the doorway.

"What are you doing in the lab?" he asks.

"Cleaning up messes, Paul."

"You mean me and Jamie."

"You aren't the only ones."

"You're still keeping Jamie in your perception field," he says. She finds a valve at the bottom of the box. "Maybe you should stop," he adds.

"She's doing just fine."

"But it's draining you. And she's ready to handle her own reality."

Cali snaps the toolbox shut. She turns on the hot water and goes to work on the feed pails, instead. "She needs help, Paul. What I'm doing is no different than an antidepressant."

"It's not her experience. You're directing it, making her feel good. She won't want to leave you."

"How would you know that?"

"Because I don't want to leave," he says. "Why am I still here?"

He sounds confused, genuinely seeking an answer for his

compliance. She hasn't manipulated his perception since he arrived, and only uses the dogs to monitor his whereabouts. Jamie is coping without him. He's done his duty, saved her from the warehouse.

Cali can't find much history on him. Actually, she hadn't bothered after the first week. If he was a threat, it was too late. He's single with no children. He has a brother and a mother. His law enforcement history is still secure, but he's been on the farm a month and nothing has happened.

Why is he still here?

"Are you doing that to me?" he asks. "Making me want to stay?"

"No."

"How do I know?"

"Trust me."

"Why should I?"

"Why should I trust you, Paul?" She soaks her old-looking hands in the warm suds. They feel like someone else's. "You came here to help the girl. You're welcome to leave."

"Why won't you help Nix?"

"I am helping him."

She rinses the pails and turns them over to finish air drying. Once her hands are dry, she grabs the toolbox.

He doesn't move. "I want to help."

"Is that what you want?"

"You're afraid."

"You don't know anything about me. All you know are the rumors and newsfeeds."

"Then tell me."

"I didn't invite you into my life."

"You don't invite anything into your life. I'm not a threat, you know that. Nobody is waiting outside your gates. Mother hasn't turned us off. So what are you afraid of, Cali? That your tower will fall over? You'll be exposed to the world again—is that it?

"I've been plenty exposed in the past."

"Is that why you released the nixes to the world? To get back at Mother? The world?" He leans forward. "God?"

She pushes past him and slams the door. The tools rattle inside the metal box. She wants to immerse him inside her perception field and feed him her memories of losing her family, saturate him with the never-ending ache of loss. If she shared her suffering, he wouldn't stay.

She forgot the auto-fill valve. Out of habit, she puts the toolbox down and grabs the handle with both hands. The door opens easily. It never does that after it's been slammed. She tries it again, hearing the oiled components work perfectly. All these years, she never found time to fix it. He's only been here a month.

He fixed it.

"I didn't release them." She bows her head. "Someone else did."

Tension hardens inside her. She needs the pasture, the wide open space to let her thoughts run.

The horses plod toward her, wary of the metal box rattling in her hand. She drops it next to the trough and finds a wrench to loosen the valve. It takes several turns, her fingers numb against the cold metal. A thin skin of ice has already formed. The wrench fumbles from her grip, raking her knuckles over a metal burr. The wrench sinks to the bottom.

Paul stands behind her. His shadow is long, nearly touching her. Cali leans against the trough, struggling to breathe.

"Who released them?"

"I don't know. The design is similar to mine, but it's not exact. It was just a matter of time before someone else figured it out. I'm not the smartest nanobiometric engineer in the world. Someone just didn't want to take credit. It was easier to blame me."

"But you exposed Marcus Anderson?"

"I exposed his hypocrisy." She elbows the trough. "He wanted Nix and me dead. Bastard had it coming."

"So the public's perception of Cali Richards isn't what it seems?"

"Perception has been manipulated long before biomites, Paul."

"But why blame it on you?"

"Why not? It makes sense. I'm the vindictive bitch that poisoned her brother with nixes, the first to escape Mother… Why wouldn't I want to release a plague of nixes on the world? Look, everything you've learned about me is wrong. Marcus Anderson and others began to spin a story about me before there was a story. They turned me into a self-serving bitch while the underworld of nixes hailed me as some all-knowing goddess."

"Which one are you?"

"Neither."

"You're not the woman who lost her parents in a car accident? You're not the one who raised her brother on her own, the one who buried a husband and a daughter before she was thirty?"

She bows her head, chin falling to her chest. A spot of blood swells on her knuckles. She smears it with her thumb, the crimson hue seeping into the wrinkles.

"I just want God to leave me alone."

"Is that what you want?" Paul steps closer, reaching for her. "To be left alone?"

She snaps her hand away. "Yes."

Her head fills with a metallic aroma—the hot sensation of overworked biomites. She can't keep going at this pace; can't keep working in the lab through the night. Can't sit around wishing things were different.

I want my clay back.

But there's no going back. She sold her body to save her brother. She wonders if she sold her soul, too.

What if she turned herself off? Just dropped the dome and exposed her true identity, would death end her suffering?

If I didn't suffer, would I have a purpose?

"You can't keep going like this. You have limits," Paul says. "You're not a machine."

"No. I'm Marcus Anderson's prophecy. He warned us this would happen, that we would overconsume, that we would sell our souls. That we would become *this*."

She turns her hand over, the torn skin already healed.

"I turned my back on God, Paul," she says. "But He turned His back on me first."

"God doesn't make mistakes, Cali. He got all this exactly right. Biomites are not the enemy, they're not evil. You saved your brother with them—you survived because of them."

"We created biomites, Paul. Not God."

"And God created us in His image. Through Him, all things are possible." He takes off his coat and pulls up his sleeve to retrieve the wrench at the bottom of the trough. His arm is slightly pink when he pulls it out and puts it in the box. "Tools, Cali. Biomites are just tools."

He carries the toolbox back to the tack room. One of the horses sniffs her shoulder and snorts in her ear. Paul returns to help her up. She's too tired to fight him, too exhausted to manipulate his field, to make him want to leave her alone. Instead, she lets him guide her back to the house.

She climbs into bed, aware that they can all leave if they want. She's not stopping them.

She's tired of hiding.

CHAPTER ONE HUNDRED THREE_

JAMIE GETS LOST IN THE MUSIC.

There's no Internet and her personal account is still trashed. She hasn't been using her field, but this morning she felt colder than usual. And lonelier.

A long walk keeps her out of the house, where the pipes rattle and the walls speak when the wind blows. The icicles drip into drifts piled against the house. When she returns, her teeth are chattering.

Her skin feels exhausted and her clothing is wrinkled from nights beneath the covers. Body odor puffs out of her sweatshirt, reminding her how long it's been since she's showered. The wrapping around her arm has frayed.

It takes two minutes for hot water to reach the kitchen sink. Jamie unwinds the stiff gauze. The skin beneath is sickly white and smells sour. She clenches a fist, feeling a slight tingle midway up her forearm where the swelling remains. She washes her hands beneath the hot water, the suds dripping from her elbows.

A long drum solo ends in her head. A voice interrupts the silence between tracks. She turns around, but no one is there. Drying her hands, she wanders around the table, stopping to listen.

The basement door is ajar.

Jamie calls the music off and stands with her ear to the gap. The hinges swing quietly. She slips inside, where the air is damp and moldy with a hint of vinegar. The steps are gray and worn.

A single bulb starkly illuminates jars and faded labels. She stands on the bottom step, waiting to see a human head pickled in an oversized jar instead of cucumbers and tomatoes.

"No. No, we can't," Nix says.

There's an open door at the other end. Nix is sitting inside the room. His old-man hair is shaved close to the scalp. Jamie walks to the doorway and peeks inside. His back is to her.

"What are you doing?" he says.

Jamie pauses. "Nothing. What are you doing?"

Nix spins the office chair around, eyes momentarily wide. He holds still, his head cocked, thinking. He looks to the right, nodding, as if he was talking to one of the computer monitors.

"Who you talking to?"

"Myself." He hesitates. "I do that."

"You're weird."

"I've been told." He rubs the steel gray stubble on his scalp. "How's the arm?"

"A little weak, but okay."

"I'm sorry. I...I really didn't know that was going to happen—"

"It's all right."

He asks about the arm every day and has apologized a thousand times. She wants to tell him it was worth it, that she hasn't wanted to crawl out of her skin since they arrived. She doesn't feel lost. For the first time that she can remember, she feels at home. She's only been on the farm for a month, but that's what it feels like. There's no urge to leave somewhere, nothing to run away from.

She wants to tell him that it doesn't hurt, not like before.

The room is a step up from the cold concrete. The floor inside is hard and shiny. There's a long workbench to the right with a fume hood and an industrial-sized refrigerator. Another bench is fastened to the back wall, with monitors and microscopes; notebooks are scattered on the surface. A rack of tubes is directly behind him, one of them wedged between his fingers, with heavy metallic liquid inside.

"What is all this?" she asks.

"This is the lab. We built it about ten years ago, when we first moved here." He slides a manila folder off a stack. "It was mainly to refine our biomites. No one in the world has nixes like us. As far as I know, we're the longest surviving halfskins and we planned to keep it that way. The plan was to invent a new breed of biomites, ones that communicate completely different by means of quantum physics. We never had plans for mass production—just produce enough for us to stay off Mother's radar. But once the tower was built, Cali shut it down and locked me out."

"How'd you get in?"

"I have a key, but I've been waiting for her to crash. She doesn't sleep much, but she's out now."

"What are you looking for?"

"She took something away from me. I'm just trying to fix it." He looks behind her. Jamie turns. There's no one there.

"Why do you do that?" she asks. "Like you're looking at a ghost."

"Nothing." He rubs the gray stubble. "It's how I think."

Data begins scrolling on the monitor. He turns around, muttering again. There are two more monitors at the end of the bench with more data and a bank of computers beneath them. This stuff belongs in an industrial park, not a farmhouse with pickled beets outside the door.

"Where did you get all the money?" she asks.

"Stole it." He says it without flinching. "The seed money, at least. It's not hard to skim accounts."

While he watches the data, occasionally clicking and typing, he explains how they opened bogus accounts at banks under a variety of names. They mostly wrote deposits that didn't exist, moving the money and closing the accounts before getting caught.

"And now?"

"Investments. The capital gains from market algorithms make more money than we can spend."

He rolls over to the monitor on the far left, punching a few keys before searching the rack of tubes with gray liquid. He yanks one from the top and places it on the bench next to another.

There's a box of equipment under the bench. A black cube with large numbers sits on top. She takes it out. It's heavier than it looks, the edges crisp and cold.

She'd seen one of these before, back when biomite agents would come to your house and ask if someone was home. Like your dad. They'd put the cube on his chest and show him the number. If it was forty or higher, he went with them. And he wouldn't come back.

Jamie presses an indention with her thumb. Numbers roll across a miniature screen. She pulls the collar of her sweatshirt down, placing it just below the V where her collarbones meet. The cold surface sucks at her flesh and begins to warm. Pricks of heat are pulled through her soft tissue, puddling just below the surface.

When it cools, she pulls it off. 40%.

The number her dad saw.

"It needs calibrating," Nix says.

For a moment, the thrill of hope swirls in her heart, but her internal app still registers 49.9%. It's too good to believe, even for a moment. No one gets their clay back once the biomites take hold.

"What are you?" she asks.

He clicks through three screens of data before reaching for a cube next to a microscope, this one slightly larger than Jamie's. He holds it against his chest then slides it down the bench.

99.1%.

"How's that possible?" she asks.

"Biomites are synthetic cells. That's all."

"Does it feel different?"

"Than what?"

"Different than...before."

"You mean when I was clay?"

"Yeah."

She'd heard Nixon Richards got seeded when he was a kid. Back then, no one received biomites until they were twelve, unless it was life or death. Some rumors say he got them at birth. Others say he got them after a car accident. Either way, he's had them most of his life.

And now he's almost a brick.

He rolls toward her, holding out his hand. "Take it."

She sandwiches it between hers. His palm is slightly callused; his pulse beating in his wrist. There's nothing special about it.

"My anger is hot," he says. "My aches are wanting. My joy is sweet. My loneliness hollow. I feel all the same things you do. Does the body make us human?"

"What if you become a brick?"

"I don't think I'd know the difference."

He pulls his hand back and immerses his attention in the data again. His fingers crawl along the rack, finding another tube. This one he inserts into the base of a microscope and takes a look.

The left side of the lab is dormant. Tarps hang over much of the contents. Jamie covers her throat, the cold square still lingering on her skin. She pulls back the covers on several boxes with meaningless labels. A dozen metal canisters are stored against the wall. Tubes run from the canisters to a container in the corner, this one the size of another refrigerator. She peeks inside, but the tarp is thick and heavy. She pulls it back to allow light to penetrate the glass walls.

It's a clear box filled with polished cylinders with bundles of cables dangling like arteries. Nozzles are fitted at the end of the cylinders, pointed at a matte black floor. She's seen this before, at the warehouse.

A fabricator. A three-dimensional printer of life. The God Machine.

Programmed biomites are laid down, line by line. This one looks like a prototype, something built from scratch. It probably took months to build a frog. The newest models only took days, until Mother shut them down.

"You ever fabricate something?" she asks.

Nix is staring at something in empty space like before. He's thinking again. Haunted. He gets up and tugs on the clear door, but it's locked.

"Baxter was the first one."

"The dog?"

He smiles, smudging the glass with his finger. "It took seven months to finish that puppy. And when his DNA was ignited, the spark of life jump-started his awareness. He started wagging his tail."

"How long ago was that?"

"Seven years."

"And it still works?"

He bends over, awkwardly throwing the tarp over it. "No."

She helps him cover it, not believing him. They tuck the corners so that it's hidden once again. He gets that foggy stare.

"That's what the fight is all about," he says. "Cali wanted to disassemble the fabricator. It was a temptation, she said. I wanted to build someone and she disagreed. As you can tell, what Cali wants, she gets. She pulled its guts out, so I left."

"You can make a human?"

"It needed some modifications, but yeah. It's basically how bricks are fabricated."

"But bricks aren't real."

He falls back into the office chair, rolling away. "Did you know the dogs were fabricated? No, you didn't. You're half a brick, does that make you half real? It's just a body, a vehicle for memories. Biomites are close to perfection. One of these days, we'll beat death. We'll upload our memories into cloud storage as we live our lives. We'll fabricate bodies like vehicles; we'll go places human bodies can't go. Maybe even discover new realms of reality."

"Is that all we are, memories?"

"No," he says. "We're more than that."

"What, then?"

He stares at empty space before turning back to the monitor to resume his search. The lab feels colder and emptier. Jamie looks around like an apparition might step out from beneath the tarps. She wonders how many times they tried to build something and failed. Did those experiments suffer? Did they know they were alive before they were thrown in the garbage?

"Why'd you bring me here?" Her voice shakes.

"That nixed pill you swallowed," he says without looking away from the monitor. "It's got imbedded code that will identify its manufacturer."

"But you don't need biomites."

"Where nixes are made, there's going to be a fabricator."

He searches for another vial, mumbling as he goes, as if answering a question. Jamie uncovers the other office chair and sits down. She doesn't want to be alone right now. And she wonders.

Do bricks know they're fabricated when they open their eyes?

CHAPTER ONE HUNDRED FOUR_

By late March, the nights were still cold, but the snow had melted. In the morning, shallow puddles would harden. By the afternoon, they'd be wet again.

The roof is missing several shingles and the ones remaining are brittle. Paul found more than a few leaks in the attic. April would be a good time to replace the roof, when the wind wasn't so frosty. In the meantime, there was an antenna to fix.

The pitch made the climb a nervous one. A misstep would be a long drop. Cables swing from the three-sided antenna. The metal artifact is a reminder of age-old television. PBS is the only broadcast signal. The big stations still go through satellite and cable, but the majority of programming goes through internal feeds, projecting directly into retinal and auditory senses.

Paul loops his arm around a rung while stripping the insulation from the frayed cables. Up there, his fingertips are numb and his cheeks raw. It takes almost half an hour to splice the cables and make an adjustment. The tower sways and the mounts creak. His thighs are numb on the climb back to the roof.

A car door slams.

Paul bear-crawls to the crown, his tool belt dragging over the shingles. A truck is parked out front, plow blade still attached.

"Hello!" Paul shouts.

Hal looks at the pasture. Nix and Jamie are on the far side of the barn with the horses, too far away to be seen. His daughter, Megan, gets out of the truck, carrying a green container.

"Up here!"

"Oh, hey." Hal shades his eyes. "What're you doing up there, Paul?"

"Just fixing the television. A bit of cabin fever is going around."

"That's what I hear. Talked to Stacy on the phone, said she was still a bit under the weather."

It takes a moment to connect the dots—*Stacy is Cali*. "Well, you know," Paul stammers, "she's been better. Flu, we're guessing. She's trapped in bed, said if I didn't get the TV working, she was going to lose her mind."

"Well, can't say as I blame her. We brought some chicken soup, get her back on track."

"That's awfully nice of you. You want to put it in the kitchen, Megan?"

Megan goes around to the side door. Surely, Cali knows they were coming. She can hide long enough to avoid being seen.

Hal talks about the weather taking a good turn, that he might take the plow blade off sooner than he thought. He asks about the horses, too. Paul sits on the roof's peak.

"We worry about Stacy being out here all alone. She ain't had any help in a while. She could use some looking after."

Megan returns to the truck. Hal hangs his arm over the door. "Listen, y'all are welcome at the church this Sunday. Service is at ten o'clock. No need to dress up, just bring yourselves. And if you just want the coffee and donuts, come about eleven. The company's not bad, either."

With a final wave, they drive away. Paul rubs the feeling back into his thighs. He feels a bit like a gargoyle, perched high above, surveying the endless country. Carefully, he works his way off the roof, the metal rungs biting his fingers.

The container of chicken soup is on the counter, the broth still warm. The coffee pot, however, is cold. He pours two cups and waits at the sink while they rotate inside the microwave. Nix and Jamie have the horses near the fence. Nix swings onto the larger one, settling into the saddle before galloping across the wet field.

Maybe Jamie grins, maybe not. She's fallen back into a slump, facing those hard feelings again. Still, he's caught her smiling. Ironically, the farm has been a biomite detox, even though there's more biomite technology on these acres than most small towns. With no Internet access and no personal account, all her biomite apps are limited. It's the horses and the country and the old house that have grounded her. It's the wind and the sun, the elements of simple living that have taken her out of her head, put her in the present moment.

How much of Jamie's experience is Cali's field? And am I still in it?

Jamie gets depressed when Cali sleeps, it's obvious the way her shoulders slump. But the blissful peace is always with Paul. He thought about testing his theory, going out to the road where her field would weaken, perhaps even drive a bit. Would he become that person he used to be, the Seattle cop living day to day? Or had she somehow changed him?

Cali's bedroom door is ajar. The shower, however, is running. Paul nudges the door open to leave a cup of coffee on her dresser.

A television console is in the back room. A converter box is wired to the back, converting broadcast signals for the antiquated television to interpret. A channel scan picks up nothing but static. The antenna looks like a dead soldier until the scan cycles around, nabbing a snowy channel.

"Victory."

Paul settles on the couch. It's been months since he really paid much attention to current events. The coffee warms his stomach, the caffeine buzzing his senses while two talking heads debate biomite genocide.

The news is bad.

Especially for Paul.

CHAPTER ONE HUNDRED FIVE_

A hazy form stands in the mirror.

She wipes away the condensation, revealing a young woman with prematurely graying hair. Cali steps back to admire the reflection. Much of the sag has lifted from her breasts. Her belly no longer hangs in a cluster of wrinkles. She just couldn't maintain the illusion of age anymore, not while manipulating Jamie's field. It taxed her biomites with an endless deficit.

And no solution in sight.

She leans over the sink and slicks back her hair. Her face, while smoother and leaner, is still haunted by exhaustion—darkness beneath her eyes like shadows. The neighbors have never seen this woman. She'll feign illness until she's ready to put the mask back on.

There's a cup of coffee on her dresser.

She thinks while dressing. Always thinking, always searching for a solution. There must be a way to revitalize Jamie's biomites without boosting her percentage. If she goes halfskin, she'll have to stay on the farm. She can't take responsibility for what would happen to her if she left.

She's considered a slow transfusion, but that would require flushing old biomites. Earlier attempts by detox laboratories have had some success, but the attempts create errors in coding and have resulted in self-shutdown or runaway growth. *Cancer*.

Biomites are made to replace organic cells, not other biomites. They're synergistic with their own kind. Antagonism is difficult for them to comprehend. Cali could seed her with the strain of nixes she and Nix possess. They were the only antagonistic biomites she's ever witnessed, the only evidence she's ever seen of biomites replacing biomites.

Rather than transfuse Jamie's near-charred biomites, she's considered a sort of reboot. That would require increased allocations to brain stem biomites and erasing the emotional charges associated with subconscious memories. The risk would be reformatting her memories—essentially erasing them. She'd start over.

Cali goes to the kitchen to heat the coffee. There's a conversation in the back room. She creeps down the hall, the floor cold on her bare feet. The room flickers with electric light. The television is working. Paul said he was going to fix it.

She takes her coffee to the basement. The locks have been recoded. Nix had been inside the lab a few weeks ago. She's considering giving him Dreamland back. She has known for quite some time how he was doing it. His brain stem, limbic and paralimbic structures had become hyperactive when he was seeded at a young age. His dreams became lucid.

He wasn't transporting to another reality. He was snared by this realistic dream state, and when she tried to convince him with data, showing him the unusual activity of his brain, he just got defensive, refusing to believe his secret was an illusion.

Raine too.

Dreaming wasn't a problem. It was clinging to those wishful hopes despite what was right in front of him. She wanted him to face harsh reality, not wish it away. Fabricating Raine was not going to help that.

So while he was unconscious, she slipped a small seed of biomites into his brain stem that would slow the activity. He'd have to learn how to live in the real world full time. Totally committed.

But Cali isn't having much success living in the real world. She's not sure she can help him with that. She gets back to work. Twenty years, and biomites haven't solved her problems yet. But it's the only thing she knows how to do.

CHAPTER ONE HUNDRED SIX_

The old horse has no buck left in her. That's what Nix told her. Jamie holds the mane with both hands, the hair coarse between her fingers, as the mare follows the narrow path where green grass is absent.

Spring has arrived.

Warmer wind blows across the trees. Her cheeks glow from long days in the sun. She enters the woods, where the shade is cool and humid, where she becomes painfully aware of the silence in her head.

Turn off your field, Nix had told her. *Horses are sensitive to little things, even thoughts.*

The forest quickly thins at the top of a slope. Nix sits on an outcropping of rock, a rusted wire fence marking the edge of the property. The earth continues sloping toward a valley nestled between blue mountain peaks embracing a glassy lake.

The mare tosses her head, snorting at the sight of green grass. Jamie slides off. Cold pins tingle in her feet when she hits the ground.

She sits next to Nix and, for the next couple of minutes, they say nothing. She hasn't talked to him since the lab. He would come inside the house late at night, and in the morning he'd already be gone.

Sometimes, they'd pass in the kitchen with a knowing glance. This morning, she watched him take the path behind the house.

This morning, she has something to say.

"I used to come out here for inspiration," Nix says. "I'd pretend I was the only person in the world, that all of this was mine. This was the only place where no one was watching my every move."

"I want to find a fabricator."

He looks to his right, away from Jamie. "Why?"

"I've got my reasons."

"Charlie? Is that it?"

"It's none of your business."

"You can't bring back the dead, Jamie. It takes complex, detailed plans; you don't just make a wish. It doesn't work that way."

"Bullshit."

"It won't be him, not like you think. Besides, why would you want him back?"

"Fuck you." Her left hand involuntarily balls up.

"You're grasping at memories. Do you think you were happy in that halfskin den? Did Charlie make you happier when he took you there?"

"He made me feel like all this shit here makes you feel." She sweeps her arm at the view. "He made me feel safe."

"He took you to a halfskin den!"

"I wanted him to! He had the balls to do it first, to bring me there when it was safe."

And pay them back with favors.

"He was charred," Nix says. "He had no choice, you told me so. Don't confuse desperation with courage."

"Look at you." She slams her fist on her thigh. "You're so desperate that you betrayed your sister and now you're lecturing me."

"You don't want to bring back Charlie."

"Don't tell me what I want."

She walks away before she swings at him. Nix doesn't know shit. Charlie was the brave one. He was the one that took the nixes first, showed her there was a brighter future. She would've charred without him. He sat at that table with her, his face glowing with promise when the pill arrived.

And then he turned ashy gray.

The future was gone and she was stuck in the present moment, cold off. Exactly where she didn't want to be.

"I owe him," she says. "If I can bring him back, give him a second chance...I owe him that much."

"You just want to feel safe again."

"What's wrong with that?"

"It won't be him."

"Who are you so desperate to fabricate? If you can't bring back the dead, what are you building? I mean, goddamnit, you basically kidnapped me, dragged me ten hours away to this place so you could read this pill inside me, not to mention fucking over your sister. So who are you fabricating?"

"Someone who lives, but was never born."

"What the hell does that mean? You're going to fabricate baby Jesus? A fuck toy? At least I want to fabricate someone that was real."

He looks away, shaking his head.

"Why do you always do that?" Jamie stands in front of him. The sloping ground puts them at eye level. "You talk to yourself a lot. Are you insane, Nix? Do you have imaginary friends?"

"Trust me, you don't want to bring Charlie back. He can't make you feel something. That's not the answer."

Jamie kicks the ground, showering him with dirt. "Fuck you, then. I'll find a fabricator on my own and take this pill inside me somewhere else. Good luck with your fantasy."

She stomps over the rocks, her cold feet painfully ramming the hard earth. The horses back away. She throws a stick and they trot into the woods.

"You know, I thought we could help each other, but your sister's right. You are a selfish prick."

Jamie walks into the trees. She begins to run.

She thought Nix was waiting for her to ask to cooperate, and didn't expect him to argue. Now where's she going? She doesn't want to leave the farm. It's boring as shit there, but it beats the life she had outside the gate. If she leaves, who's going to help her?

Because Charlie's dead. And she can't help herself.

She brings up her field, the music slamming her eardrums. The pain in her head fills the emotional void that's threatening to pull her down a familiar path.

Again.

CHAPTER ONE HUNDRED SEVEN_

Limousines aren't typically convertibles. But Marcus wanted one.

There's room to stretch his legs. With his head nestled back, he's mesmerized by the buildings scraping the blue sky. The electricity of Times Square flickers around him. Despite the traffic, his driver coasts through red lights. At one point they get stuck beside a delivery truck, and even though it's pumping exhaust into the limo, he can smell grass.

When he was little, his father took them to upstate New York, where the hills rolled with green, to visit his grandmother. It was the year she died. They went to the park that afternoon and took the blanket and the basket and a Frisbee. Grandmother picked dandelions with him and they rubbed them under their chins until their skin turned yellow.

Yellow like the sun.

Traffic snarls near Grand Central Station. Pedestrians crowd the crosswalk with a mixture of tourists and anxious New Yorkers. A group of children flock around their mother, running by her side. The littlest one is wearing a red backpack.

Marcus sits up, but they blend into the crowd. They looked like his children when they were younger. Clifford was wearing the backpack. A prayer comes to his lips, one he utters when stress tightens his belly.

"I'll walk," Marcus calls.

The driver opens his door. Marcus walks down the middle of the street, standing in the intersection. Cars pass on both sides, but no one honks, no one shouts. He finishes the prayer, searching for a red backpack. His children are older now.

Still, he searches until he's convinced he imagined it.

Marcus goes through the doors at Grand Central Station and is greeted with the scent of green again. There are no windows inside. No directories or impatient riders. There's the undergrowth of foliage and a large tree reaching for a glass ceiling.

Fish hover in the pond's clear water, lazily gliding between stems of lotus. Vines have grown over the glass tanks where halfskins are digesting. Only the occasional eye can be seen through the greenery, or a swath of hair. At last count, Mother had collected several thousand of them.

There are no more secrets.

Mother knows all the nixed manufacturers and located all their dens. It is just a matter of time before they are all shut down. There is no reason to collect more halfskins unless Mother finds it interesting. Marcus insisted she define what that meant.

"You know, Marcus," she said. "Something that's unique."

He didn't like the way that sounded, but they'd won the war. Let her indulge in peculiarities.

Just past the pond, a narrow path goes through a formal parterre garden, where the gravel path crunches beneath his loafers.

A nude woman enters the sheared boxwood maze.

Her dark skin is puckered beneath smudges of soil. Her curves sway with each step. She passes Marcus without a glance, the sharp-edged gravel having no effect on her bare feet. There's something absent in her green eyes. She's not quite there.

The formal garden exits to a brick path that's twenty feet wide beneath an allée of elms. Birds squabble in the canopies. His shoes click like clockwork. It's a long walk to the end. Marcus stops at a short terrace, where Mother is on her knees, digging between marigolds.

"Good morning, Marcus. It's a glorious day to be in the garden." She sits up. "Are you feeling well?"

He's pain-free today.

"The government has demanded a stay of shutdowns. The public backlash has become too much. I told you, we're moving too quickly. The public doesn't like to see people drop dead en masse."

"Halfskins are 'people' now?"

"Don't twist words."

"Before, untimely death was blamed on God. I'm more convenient, I suppose."

"They'll shut you down."

She chuckles. "They won't shut me down."

"They can. They will."

It would take a majority vote from the United Nations, but they could put her down like a halfskin. There's a kill switch integrated into her programming, a safety net in case things get out of control.

She pulls weeds around the perimeter of a square patch of earth. The center is freshly tilled, recently watered.

"What do you think we should do, Marcus?"

"We need to slow down, reduce the public shutdowns. Perhaps alert local authorities to handle a few situations. This will take the burden off of us."

"You know how many halfskins we've identified? Over one and half million, Marcus. That's worldwide. I can order an immediate shutdown of them all, end it today." She snaps her fingers. "One point five million will drop."

"You'll be terminated for that."

"Is that bad?"

"We haven't identified them all. When you go down, there will be a resurgence. We need to change the way humanity perceives this sin. They need to embrace the unholy significance, ingrain it so deeply into the collective consciousness that it will not be forgotten. Only then will our mission be complete."

"So you would like me to live, Marcus?"

"I need you."

"Of course you do."

He grimaces. That's not what he meant.

She brushes her hair from her eyes, leaving a smudge on her forehead. "Come help me, Marcus."

The soil begins to undulate. Mother waves him to move faster. She rakes through the earth. It squishes between her fingers. Marcus climbs onto the ledge, pushing up his sleeves. He hesitates, not wanting to dirty his knees.

Mother plunges her arm into the ground, the sucking sounds loud and wet. She pulls up a Caucasian hand, the flesh puckered at the tips, black beneath the fingernails. She pulls a second hand out of the ground. Together, they pull out a man like a turnip.

His head rotates limply. Mother wipes the mud from his face, the soil mixed with mucus. She uses a towel to clean his cheeks.

He opens his eyes. They're brown and vacant.

They pull him until he's standing six feet tall. Chest hair is curled tightly to his skin, trailing down to pubic hair matted around a flaccid penis. Mother cleans the rest of him with her bare hands.

"I prefer to grow them." She watches the man walk somewhat mechanically down the brick path. His gait normalizes the farther he walks. "They're more organic and blend with the population more effectively. Don't you think?"

There's no denying the beauty of the human form made in the

image of the Father. But the process is disturbing. It feels like she's birthing. "I didn't approve of this."

"Why would you disapprove?"

"Go back to fabricating them in the containers."

She returns to weeding. "Don't be like them, Marcus."

"Who?"

"The people in power. They fear me. Authority fears when it no longer has control. Do you know why?" She pauses. "Power is intoxicating."

He's familiar with the sweet taste of power.

"Power is not inherently evil," she says. "But how long before the leaders of these great nations succumb to halfskin themselves, mmm? I have identified far more congressmen and senators than you know. The promise of controlling their thoughts and emotions is too tempting. They'll all become halfskins, Marcus. But who is controlling their thoughts? Who is controlling their desires?"

"Don't get metaphysical." He didn't want to debate free will and the ego.

"What will happen when we shut them down? What if it's the vice president? These leaders will age. Do you think they'll let me function with impunity as their lives expire, or will they accept their mortality with grace?"

She sits up, smacking the dirt from her hands.

"What happens when they die?" she asks.

She's never asked that question. It's an odd question for artificial intelligence to ponder. A machine, Marcus has always assumed, does not fear being shut off. They don't cling to life like a man or woman, don't wish to keep it like a possession.

"Tell me, Marcus, what happens when a human dies?"

"Gods weighs their sins," he says. "Eternal life awaits those who accept Jesus Christ as their Lord and Savior."

"And the halfskins?"

"They committed a mortal sin. For them, salvation is too late."

"And what happens to them?"

"They will burn in Hell."

"All of them?"

He hesitates. "Yes."

"What will happen to me when I am shut down?"

"Nothing. You're a machine. You were created by Man. There's nothing for you after death."

"Death? So you believe I die?"

"No. You're shut down." Her imitation of form and emotions is an illusion, but so convincing that he's often moved by her apparent concern.

"How can I live but not die, Marcus?"

"You're playing with language. You're a tool. You're a machine. You only have one purpose: protecting God's creations from themselves."

"So we shut down halfskins because they're more machine than human. We send them to Hell."

"I don't expect you to understand. You calculate, you analyze. There is no spiritual life for you."

"Do you serve humanity?"

"I serve God."

"What would you sacrifice for your Lord and Savior?"

"I do what He asks of me."

The soil begins to burp. She works it with her hands, searching for what rumbles beneath. "What would you do if you were me? Would you accept being shut down?"

"You're artificial."

"But if you were asked to be shut down, for the good of God, would you do so?"

"I serve God," he says.

"So do I," she says softly. It sounds more like a statement.

A warm sensation rises, a feeling Marcus has come to associate with God's love, as if the Holy Ghost was guiding his words and actions.

Viscous sounds gurgle beneath the undulating soil. Mother pulls another body out, this one a middle-aged woman with a pear-shaped body. Once again, she scrapes away the filth with the edge of her hands, wiping the face clean. The woman opens her eyes. Like the others, the light is missing.

Surely Mother can see there is no soul in that vessel. That, above all else, should answer her questions.

CHAPTER ONE HUNDRED EIGHT_

"You can't do this," Raine says.

Nix stands at the far end of the barn, holding the push broom. A light rain falls on the metal roof. The horses are in their stalls, craning their necks to see what he's doing. Sometimes, he'll sweep the breezeway to calm his racing mind. Today he's letting it run wild.

Paul is on the other side of the pasture. He's spent the last week hanging around the cell tower, oiling the hinges or fixing the latch. Nix can see his yellow parka through the evergreens and budding maples as he goes inside the utility room. It doesn't matter what he's doing, as long as he stays there for the next thirty minutes.

"This is beyond reckless." Her dark form moves gracefully in his periphery. "Think about what you're doing."

He fingers the pair of glass vials in his coat pocket. He's thought about what he's doing. Thought about it for days. At night, he's lain in bed, staring at the water-stained ceiling, analyzing his options. There aren't many.

And none that don't involve other people.

He woke up with his stomach knotted with guilt. He didn't eat for days. He spent much of his time at the back property line, staring at the view that inspired their home in Dreamland. And he hadn't seen Dreamland in months. Maybe he'd never see it again. If he finds a fabricator, he won't need to go back.

He'd come this far. He can't stop now. Others will get hurt. He had to accept that, too.

Raine can't wait.

The screen door on the house slams. Someone pulls a hood over their head before descending the front steps. Nix leans on the broom, waiting for her to arrive. If it's Cali, he'll start sweeping. But Cali rarely leaves the basement, except to sleep or feed the horses.

Jamie runs through the sloppy yard, stomping her boots inside the breezeway. She throws back the hood and shakes her head. "What do you want?"

"I don't want to shout." Nix waves her toward him. He doesn't want to lose his view of the cell tower, in case Paul comes for tools. If he leaves the cover of the utility shed, he'll come running through the rain.

Jamie shuffles partway down the corridor. She rubs one of the horse's noses, refusing to go any farther. She met him halfway, but he stays put. The glass vials feel warm in his sweaty palm.

"I made you a promise before I brought you here," he says. "I said I'd take you somewhere safe. I also said I'd take away your pain, but I didn't do that. For that, I'm sorry, Jamie. Cali has kept you in her field, but she can't do that forever. I could put you in mine, but that won't help you when I'm not around."

She's listening.

"You need to manage your own life, Jamie. Not mine, not my sister's, and not Charlie's. Just Jamie's."

Nix glances at the front porch. There's no window in his line of sight, so no one but Jamie sees him pull out a vial, displaying it between his finger and thumb. The small amount of mercury-like liquid settles at the bottom. Jamie buries her hands in her coat with her shoulders hunched against the gusting wind. Her brown hair whips across her face, but her eyes are on the vial.

"It took me a while to figure out what Cali's been doing in the lab, but now I understand. This vial contains an entirely new strain of biomites. She's changed the paradigm using some method of quantum mechanics. She's revolutionized the frequency of nixes. They speak an entirely different language than any other biomite in the world. If she swaps out her biomites with these, she could drop the dome tomorrow and no one would ever know."

Jamie pushes her knotted hair from her face and stares. She's not sure where he's going, but she's hopeful. Nix takes one last look in Paul's direction to make sure he's still there before approaching her. He holds the vial in his palm.

"Halfskin," he says. "I'll give you a 5% seed, Jamie. I'll put you back in charge of your life. At 55%, you can manage your emotions and sensory input. Your mental health won't depend on others. You'll control what you think, how you feel. You'll be free from the human condition."

That's the promise of halfskin. It's empty, of course. Cali is proof. And Nix knows he's not perfect, either. But the promise is more tempting than any drug. Who doesn't want to control their thoughts and feelings?

She's transfixed by the offer, considering all the possibilities. It's everything she wants in the palm of his hand. And he wants to give it to her.

"You're such a hypocrite," she snorts. "You rail against Charlie for taking me to the warehouse and now you're sneaking around like a nix dealer. You're a real piece of work, Nix."

"This isn't about Charlie; it never has been. It's about Jamie."

"Uh-huh. And what do you get?"

"With these, I can synchronize with you. I can read the pill."

He'll have to prime a small portion of his brain biomites with the new strain in order to do that. Cali's notes suggest this new strain will replace only his existing biomites. He can interface with her in a way that he couldn't before. He's not sure it'll work. It should.

It has to.

"We both get what we want," he says.

She stares at the promise in his hand. Everything she wanted at the warehouse is within reach, and without the risk. Nix seeds her, the biomites proliferate up to 5%, and then she's free to go. No favors required. After the warehouse, how could she ever have expected this opportunity?

"I get halfskin," she says, "and you find a fabricator. Is that the deal?"

"You get halfskin, I read the pill. *That's* the deal."

"I'm going with you."

"Goddamnit, Jamie." He squeezes the vial in his fist. "It's not what you think. You can't bring him back."

"What do you care?"

He paces to the back of the barn. The rain falls harder. Puddles rise around the perimeter and begin leaking into the breezeway. This is her chance. Maybe if she recalled the memory of Marcus breathing down on her, she'd see this as an opportunity they don't need to haggle over.

He puts the vial back in his pocket.

"What if Cali finds out?" Jamie says.

He laughs this time. She's too enmeshed with her own problems in good ole Cali style, the poster child for self-absorption. Even if she did find out that he stole the new strain of quantum mechanical biomites, there's nothing his sister can do to hurt him. She's already taken Dreamland from him.

"Think about it. The offer won't last long," he lies.

"I want to help you, Nix." Her boots scuff the concrete. She stops next to him and drops her hand on his shoulder. "I do, really. Whoever you're going to fabricate, that's your business. Who I fabricate is mine. Think about *that*."

She throws on the hood and stomps through the back pasture. The puddles slosh against her rubber boots. She ducks between the fence slats and turns toward the house, leaving Nix with a deal.

Take it or leave it.

Raine's barefoot image appears next to him. "I like her."

NIX AND JAMIE occasionally pass each other in the house, or see each other walking the property. She's polite, yet dismissive. Paul and Cali continue their disappearing acts, preoccupied with their own problems. Days go by and Nix considers other solutions.

There are none.

He lies awake, staring at a stain on the ceiling. He wonders if the man that built the house lay awake at night while rain dripped through the roof. Did he watch the stain grow or did he just wake up one morning to see it?

He doesn't want to sleep. If he does, he'll wake on the raft and be tortured by what's out of reach. *How did she alter my brain chemistry?*

She's still researching. He thought she closed the lab after he left, but all her records indicate she never stopped. Her notes are fresh, her equipment calibrated. Did she know he was coming back? Had she been planning to wipe out Dreamland when he did?

The sun is rising when he decides to find a way back into the lab. But then the floorboards creak. Nix snaps awake, unsure if he actually fell asleep and imagined it. He hears it again, right outside his door. The hinges squeal. A form stands in the doorway.

First, he closes his eyes and searches for Cali's presence. He can't feel her anywhere near him. He sits on the edge of the bed and retrieves a glass vial from his pocket. The biomites shimmer, as if sensing the moment is near. He places it on the bed, the silver contents stark against the sheet. Next to it he places a rubber tourniquet, a white tube of salve, and a stainless steel instrument that looks like the circular end of a stethoscope.

Jamie sits on the bed, so close to the edge she nearly slides off.

He loads the vial into the stainless steel injector, the moonlight catching the instrument's edges like a polished weapon. It snaps into place with a quick twist. Memories surface of times he and Cali had seeded each other with the same equipment. It has been years.

He pushes her sweatshirt up her arm, tying the rubber band above the elbow. The antiseptic salve fills the room as he rubs tiny circles inside her elbow. Blue veins rise beneath the skin, making it easier for the seeder to inject one microliter of biomites into her body. Each of the artificial cells is programmed to seek the brain stem and begin proliferation.

She grabs his wrist. "Deal?"

His fingertips slide over the cold button. He's too close now to stop it. The button clicks under his thumb.

He nods.

She closes her eyes, dips her head, and all tension melts away. Jamie lies back. Her eyelids flutter. He remembers those moments, when the warm touch of a new boost hit the vein. A song once described halfskins as just another breed of junky.

Sometimes, Nix can't disagree.

There's only so much of the body you can sell, only so much taste you can buy before you're broke, hanging on to 1% of your clay.

What happens when you sell that?

CHAPTER ONE HUNDRED NINE_

THE DOGS ARE BARKING.

Cali closes the basement door, making sure it's locked. She made some progress. It could be another two weeks before she'll be ready to trial a new generation that could rescript Jamie's nearly charred biomites without turning her halfskin.

The dogs continue barking. They could have treed a raccoon or they're playing with Nix. She falls for that thought too easily: Nix throwing the slimy tennis ball. He doesn't do that anymore.

He barely speaks.

I don't blame him.

Every day she considers letting him have his Dreamland back, but that won't change anything. He has to learn to live without the dream, just like Cali had to after Avery died, wishing she'd come back, planning ways to bring her back. It's hard, at first. He'll see that it's just a dream, that *this* is reality.

As cold as it is.

She heats some water for tea, sending a thought for the dogs to come. She steeps the teabag, but they're still going at it. She steps onto the porch and lets loose a piercing whistle. Twilight colors the remaining patches of snow dusty gray. It'll get too cold for them to stay out all night, and it's supposed to rain. When they don't return, she gets dressed.

The cell tower flashes red in the dimming sky. The dogs circle the utility room at the base of it, a muddy ring trampled into the ground. The lock is broken. Paul has been spending a lot of time out here the past week. She's hardly seen him since he fixed the antenna.

She stops and listens to a dreaded warning inside her stomach. Back at the house, Paul's bedroom light is on, but it feels like he's inside the utility shed.

"Shhh," she whispers.

The dogs hush, dancing at her side, whining with anticipation. The hinges protest as she pulls the door.

The dark depths glow with a greenish tint. The circuit board—a panel she and Nix assembled from radar jamming equipment—hums. The backup generator sits quietly next to the door.

One of the dogs nudges his way inside, growling.

"Paul?"

A lump shuffles in the back corner.

She swallows a lump. "What are you doing?"

"I betrayed you."

The words strike like arrows. Cali's senses heighten. The darkness lifts as her vision adjusts to the dim light. Paul is huddled beneath the tarp that should be covering the generator.

"What'd you do?" she demands.

The circuit panel appears to be operating, the green lights lined up. Of course it's working. She can feel it. Her mind throws out a wide net, searching for trouble. She can't sense Nix and Jamie, but the tower's interference is greatest inside the utility room. Maybe she just can't "see" them.

Paul stares at his hands.

"What did you do, Paul?" She rips the tarp away and grabs his coat. "*What did you do*?"

"I didn't...I didn't know."

She throws him against the wall and chases the dogs out. Cali looks at the house, concentrating on Nix and Jamie. She's not finding them. They could be in the basement, sneaking down there as soon as she stepped off the porch.

"Go." She points. "Find them."

The dogs race toward the house, snow flipping in their tracks. Cali stands in the doorway, giving her vision a moment to adjust.

"What didn't you know, Paul?"

He runs his fingers through his hair that's grown long over the past couple of months, shaking his head. Again, he stares at his hands like foreign objects.

"Talk to me. You didn't know what?"

"So much death," he whispers.

"Where?"

"When I arrived at the warehouse, there were so many bodies. I'd never seen anything like that. They just fell where they were standing. So desperate. The abuse...never so evident. That moment, I understood we needed Mother to watch over us to make sure this didn't happen again."

He looks less like the handsome police officer that arrived uninvited and more like a broken, shaggy man clutching a new reality.

"But Jamie survived," he says. "She was scared and alone and cornered by life. She reminded me of my niece. Reminded me that if I had a daughter, she could be that survivor lost in this desperate world."

He falls silent, sorting his thoughts. Cali squeezes the doorjamb to keep from shaking him again.

"When the bricks arrived, it got confusing. I...I don't even remember how it happened. I just...couldn't trust anything. I didn't know if my thoughts were from me or them. Sometimes I found myself doing something without thinking. There were blank spots and I'd be somewhere else, not remembering where I was. I felt so...so dead. We all did. We were puppets."

He's staring like his hands betrayed him.

"And then there was a long gap of memory, a black space. I don't know how long it lasted, I just knew I had to save her, knew what they were going to do with her. I had to get Jamie out before they came for her because she could be my niece or daughter. We had to run away, far away. It was the only thought I had—to get her out. And now I...now I don't know if that was my thought or their thought."

"Who are 'they'?"

"I didn't tell anyone what I was doing, I couldn't trust them. We were all under the bricks' control. Somehow, I couldn't feel them inside me anymore. I figured I just slipped through, that maybe they released me too soon. I grabbed Jamie and left without telling anyone, without saying goodbye to my family. At the time, I didn't think that was odd; it was what I had to do to keep her safe because that's all I could think about. I just left. And no one ever came looking for me. No one ever called."

He pulls up his legs and grabs handfuls of hair.

"What are you saying?" Cali asks.

Several moments pass. He looks up, his complexion dyed in the circuit board's ghostly light. She feels his thoughts, feels him reaching out, attempting to chat. But it's not words he's sending, not a message.

It's a link.

She processes the root directory, running it through virus detection. It appears to be a video stream linked to a licensed blogging site, the contents tagged with the events at the warehouse. The images overlay the inside of the shed and Paul's haunted look.

The bodies are lined up on the concrete. The view scans the grieving survivors. Police manage the orderly chaos. She had seen this event through Nix's eyes, when he sent the vindictive photo of Jamie. This is nothing new.

She almost cuts it short, but the recording pans to a back office. There's a body crumpled at the foot of a lounger. The soles of black shoes are askew, a navy blue pant leg hiked up the shin. The view quickly goes to the back of the office space.

Cali stops it.

She rewinds it, enhancing the profile of the man's face. The handsome, middle-aged man is pale in death. *Paul.*

"No." She cuts the video off, the details of the shed coming into focus. "No, those bodies are fabricated. The bricks took the half-skins...Mother has been secretly harboring them, leaving fabricated duplicates behind..."

Paul's slumped in the corner, staring at his hands again. He's not a brick. He can't be. He's been here for months; Mother would know Nix and Cali were here. He's not a brick.

"You're not," she says.

But how did he leave? That question always bothered her. She rationalized when he arrived that there was nothing she could do about his true nature. And when nothing happened, she let it go.

But why would his body be in the warehouse? What does that make the man in front of her? If that's a fabrication of Paul in the warehouse, that means they know he took Jamie. If that was Paul's clay—his flesh and blood—in the warehouse, then there's a brick on her property.

Either way, Mother sent him. She compelled him to save Jamie.

The police found his body at the scene and assumed he somehow died during the investigation. His family would grieve. The police would retire his uniform. And somehow Mother kept it all a secret so that no one would look for him. He would be free to take Jamie.

For Nix to find them.

To bring them here.

"Where are Nix and Jamie? What have you done?" The question is directed at herself as much as him.

"I didn't know."

Cali drags Paul from the corner. His dead weight prevents her from pulling him out the door. He grabs the circuit panel. Cali slams her fists into his back.

"Goddamn you! What have you done?"

"Leave me," he says. "The greatest interference is under the cell tower. No one can see me if I stay here."

"What's it matter now?"

"I can't be out there. I can't put you at risk."

"It's too late." She loses her balance, crashing against the wall. Vertigo spins the shed. The feeling of dread is reaching up for her again, its teeth snapping at her intestines, ready to take from her again, again, again.

First her parents. Then her family.

Now it's come for her.

She always thought there would be a sense of relief when the dreaded end took her. It seemed cruel to take everything else first, to leave her to watch it all pruned away before she was uprooted and pulled into death's embrace.

She stumbles out of the shed, falling on her hands and knees. The ground alternates between dull green and blood red as the tower's warning light flashes. She sprints in search of Nix and Jamie, even though it makes no sense. She can't feel them. She knows they're gone.

Gone.

The world feels so incredibly small.

CHAPTER ONE HUNDRED TEN_

The dogs are outside the utility shed. Occasionally, they put their noses to the bottom of the door, sniffing Paul's presence.

He's buried in the sleeping bag Cali tossed at him late the night before. Although spring has arrived, the nights are still cool in the mountains. The circuit board gives off some heat, but not enough. The concrete is an unforgiving slab. His hips ache.

Biomites are not invincible. They are perfect replicas of organic cells, refined to avoid degradation and programmable by thoughts, but the red blood biomites still need oxygen.

They still suffer.

He was awake through most of the night. The wind picked up around midnight. Pine needles blasted the outer walls.

How could this have happened?

The last thing he remembers with any clarity is standing inside the warehouse, staring at Jamie helpless on the lounger. The memories before that—getting up that morning, attending his niece's birthday party the week before, fishing off the pier with his brother—are faint, like stories someone told him

Are they real?

From time to time he lifts his hands, turning them over, wondering if they are his or just replications. Wondering if this body contains any clay at all. Wondering who is in the warehouse, who is in this shed.

Wondering...*Am I a brick?*

He doesn't feel any different than before the warehouse. Those memories tell him this is what reality is supposed to feel like. If that's really his body in the warehouse, who is he now? If he's a brick, why hasn't he betrayed Cali? That's the biggest mystery. It's the proof to which his sanity clings: *If I'm something other than clay, why haven't I done something?*

It gives him hope that this is all a dream.

But why leave his body to be discovered?

Unless she wanted me to see it.

The dogs begin to whine. The door is yanked open and morning light stabs through the darkness. Paul throws the sleeping bag over his head.

"Come inside the house," Cali says.

"They might be looking for me. Mother might have lost me in the storm. I can't take the chance."

"She doesn't lose contact. The damage is already done."

"We don't know that." He rolls over, squinting. "We don't know anything."

She hasn't slept either. Her frizzled hair is a halo in the slicing light. A rogue wave tingles through him. She's doing a mental scan, looking inside him again. Can she make him come inside? Can she assume control of his actions like before?

He's tired of being manipulated, of losing free will. He thought he freely rescued Jamie, but now it seems he was tricked into making those choices. Mother wanted him to do it. She made him do it.

I can't trust my thoughts. I can't trust anything.

"Leave me alone."

She drops a tote bag and kneels next to him. The dogs come inside, sniffing. She pulls food and water out of the bag. Paul sits up to drink, watching her remove a black case from the bag and unroll it. Syringes, tubes, and a stethoscope-like instrument are inside.

"Where are Nix and Jamie?" he asks.

"Gone." The news is delivered in dead, hollowed-out words. "They took your car."

She takes a syringe from the pack and finds several alcohol wipes. He watches her tear the packets open, wondering if Jamie is hiding somewhere on the property. Nix must've figured out where a fabricator was located, but why would she go with him?

"I'm going to take samples to analyze, find out what you're made of. I should've done this when you arrived."

Paul works his arm out of the sleeping bag. The air outside is frigid on his bare skin. Cali wipes down the inside of his arm and expertly finds an artery with the needle's tip. The dogs watch the tube fill with red blood. When biomites were first available, they maintained their gunmetal color. Today's strains don't just operate like cells; they look every bit like them. Only close analysis can see the difference.

Cali takes two samples and quickly packs them away. She leaves the food on the floor. The dogs scamper out.

"I didn't make Nix and Jamie leave," Paul says.

"I know." Cali stops in the open doorway. "I did."

She remains still, staring at the soggy ground. She wants to say more. Paul can feel the weight of her thoughts. How long has she lived this way, with no one to confess her troubles to?

She closes the door and seals out the light, leaving Paul in the green glow of the circuit board. He feels around for the food and finds it on the very hard, very cold floor.

FABRICATIONS_

Reality is relative.

MOTHER_
THE BIRTHRIGHT

Deena Flannigan adjusted the bed when her husband, Duane, came in the room with their baby. Gregory Allen was eight pounds two ounces. Her husband laid the bundle on her lap. She was too weak to do anything else but hold her baby boy.

"He's finally here," Duane said, stroking his wife's forehead.

It felt like they'd been trying for a decade. They could've solved their infertility and conceived on the first try if they embraced new technology. Deena and Duane were old-fashioned.

The way God intended.

"He's beautiful."

One second Deena was laughing, and the next she was crying. She was aware that the roller coaster of emotions was just beginning. Her body was dumping all sorts of hormones into her bloodstream. There was a cure for that, too, but she'd work through it. With pleasure comes pain, she always said.

Deena's roommate was on the other side of a blue curtain divider. The roommate's family had arrived an hour earlier and made no effort to contain their enthusiasm. Deena tried to sleep through the new mother's talk about the painless miracle of childbirth.

"Claire fell asleep," her husband had said, "right in the middle of it."

Deena experienced the gift of birth in all its glory. There was nothing painless about it.

Duane crawled in bed with Deena. Gregory Allen was nestled between them. They didn't need words to experience their miracle.

"How we doing, Claire?" A nurse pushed a cart into the room followed by a professionally dressed woman. They smiled at Deena then disappeared behind the curtain.

"When can I go home?" Claire asked.

Laughter ensued. "Pretty soon. Let me just have a look."

The nurse went through a standard examination of the infant while the family made silly baby sounds and teased the nurse for taking so long.

"What's his name?" the nurse asked.

"Billy Junior," the father spouted. "Just like his daddy."

"William," the nurse added. "That's a strong name."

Deena could see through a gap between the curtain and the wall. Billy sat next to Claire, the baby in his arms.

"Well," the nurse said, "this is Marian Fletcher. She represents the Biomite Augmentation Program. She'll be serving as witness to William's birthright. If you can just look this over and confirm all the information is correct. Do you have any questions?"

"Yeah," one of the family members said. "You can shoot the left-overs in me."

Laughter. Ms. Fletcher and the nurse didn't find it funny. Claire handed a tablet back to the nurse.

"Thank you," Ms. Fletcher said. "Just to confirm, you qualify for the basic biomite subsidy, which includes language, memory, and sensory enhancement as well as current disease immunization. After the first year, if approved by a doctor, you may seed William with a neural booster."

Billy tickled the baby's lips while singing a goo-goo song.

"Please be aware that biomite augmentation is monitored by the government. If, at any time, William's body exceeds 49.9% biomites, he will be considered halfskin and lose his human rights. Are there any questions?"

"You know how many times I've heard that?" someone said.

The tablet came back to Billy and Claire while someone mocked the Birthright Augmentation Memorandum.

"Claire," Ms. Fletcher said, "if you can hold William."

Billy handed the baby to Claire. The nurse moved into position on the opposite side of the bed and turned William on his stomach. The baby struggled in his wrappings, starting to whimper. Billy told him to hush up.

"Damn, that thing looks wicked," someone said.

The nurse kept the tool hidden. "I'm going to place this at the base of his skull. He'll feel some pressure for about two seconds. We can expect his body temperature to rise. If there are no complications, he'll be back to normal in an hour."

She didn't hesitate.

The seeder looked like a shiny gun. The blunt tip went flush against William's neck, just below the hairline. Seconds later, it was over. William was not happy. Neither was Billy. His son needed to man up.

While they attempted to calm the child, the curtain was pushed aside. The nurse rolled the cart to Deena's side of the room with a well-rehearsed smile. Duane stood up.

"How are you this morning, Deena?"

"Just fine, thank you."

Ms. Fletcher moved to the foot of the bed while consulting her tablet. The nurse introduced her.

"We're not seeding him," Deena said.

The other side of the room got quiet. Duane pulled the curtain all the way to the wall.

"I see that," Ms. Fletcher said. "I just need you to answer a few questions before you waive your son's augmentation birthright. You do realize that the current strain of biomites is non-replicating."

Gregory Allen squirmed in his mother's grip. Duane held her hand.

"You'll have to confirm that you understand what I'm saying." Ms. Fletcher paused.

"We understand," Duane said with a bit of Southern accent, "but we do not agree."

"Duly noted. And you also understand that by refusing to seed your son, he will not have the same biological and mental enhancements as 98% of the human population. He will also require immunizations. He will have to be registered as unseeded clay."

"Yes, ma'am."

The nurse signed off on the tablet and handed it to Deena. She and her husband acknowledged their refusal to poison their precious gift with false idols. Ms. Fletcher directed them to several screens that positively identified the parents by retinal scan.

"Idiots," Billy sort of whispered.

"That baby's going to grow up stupid," Claire whispered.

Deena and Duane pretended they didn't hear them. They'd heard comments like that all their lives. Deena hugged little Gregory Allen while Duane finished confirming the waiver. When Ms. Fletcher and the nurse left, it was just the three of them.

They were 100% God-given organic cells.

Or, as Billy would say, they were clay.

CHAPTER ONE HUNDRED ELEVEN_

Before Jamie's father left—or, rather, when he was taken—he brought her to the mountains. They had hiked up Mount Rainier, high enough to see the spring flowers on the hillsides like bright carpet. He took the binoculars from his neck and pointed towards the stream.

"Look near the big rocks."

Jamie fumbled with the binocular's barrels, squeezing the hinge until both her eyes were centered over the eyepieces. The world was fuzzy green. Awkwardly, she spun the dial until, slowly, shapes emerged and edges sharpened. Colors expanded into rich hues of verdant green and crisp blue. She swung them toward the boulders where he was still pointing. There, she saw deer sipping from the stream.

The world was so alive.

Later, when she became a teen, when she learned how to tweak her biomites, when she sold half her clay to biomite seedings in search of the wonder, she lost her sense of aliveness.

But now it's back.

She's 52.1%. There's no going back.

Mother's gaze is palpable, like a giant invisible eye sweeping over the earth, staring at her through the lens of binoculars, searching for evidence of her transgression—her digital finger caressing the switch on Jamie's life. A twitch is all it would take.

But those are thoughts. Mother is watching her no more now than before she was halfskin. Or can she just feel it now? Is she more sensitive? Are her senses becoming...*more*?

The halfskin threshold was arbitrary, really. It was determined by the authorities. They said it was illegal to be 50%. Jamie had been 49.9% for last several months, a mere 0.1% from the trash heap. She and Charlie had done plenty of biomite booster seeds, but nothing she'd ever done had exhilarated her quite like the ones Nix put in her.

Why should everything feel so alive again?

She no longer wants to crawl out of her skin. Instead, she sits quietly. The air is sweet and crisp, the world no longer dirty and threatening. The metallic tang of char has melted away, leaving a clean, pure scent in her head, where reality is perfect just the way it is.

Nix's special blend of biomites had greeted her with a lover's gentle touch.

She slept until Tennessee. They stop at a rest area and stretch their legs. Jamie looks around like the acid trip is just beginning. The magic feels...*beautiful*.

She rides the wave into Kentucky, where the rolling hills give way to long stretches of unbending Indiana interstate. She watches the cornfields run alongside the car, the long rows forming an endless array of legs that reach the horizon, where silos gleam.

They cross into Illinois unceremoniously. The skies turn gray, but the terrain remains flat as the highway. Billboards race past in empty fields. Nix stares ahead, hands clamped on the wheel—a posture he has maintained for most of the trip. It's dark when they enter Chicago. The buildings are speckled with lights and the pavement is black.

Nix wipes his palms on his pants, the wheel sweaty. He gets off I-90 and enters the city. He turns onto Adams Street, heading toward

Lake Michigan, where the streets are wide and the buildings are tall. Ridges of muscle bulge along his jaws, his teeth grinding back and forth. He keeps his eyes locked ahead until they approach a corner bank that's a massive tower of black glass.

The car slows.

He looks up the reflective walls that reach into the night. The car behind them honks, but he doesn't speed up. Jamie knows what's in there. She knows what he's thinking. The moment he seeded her in the bedroom, he began searching for the pill. The new strain of biomites buzzed inside her, integrating with her nervous system, consuming clay. His thoughts crept through her like tendrils in search of gold. She could sense his invisible touch chatter inside her.

And the pill spilled its secrets.

She doesn't know how long it took him to do it. The transition into halfskin is hazy and euphoric. She barely remembers sneaking down to the car.

But she remembers what the pill said.

Nix doesn't say anything as they pass the bank. He resumes his grip on the steering wheel like she wouldn't notice his lapse into catatonic longing. They find a hotel near the lake. He tries to be a gentleman and get two rooms, but Jamie insists they sleep in the same room.

Because she knows the pill's secrets, too. And she knows what he's thinking.

Before the sun rises, Nix slides from the hotel bed and carries his shoes. His feet are silent on the carpet. His bag is already packed and waiting. He holds the door handle. Slowly exhaling, he turns it.

"You're not going without me." The lamp turns on. Jamie's hair is spread over the pillow.

"The car's all yours, Jamie. There's a stack of cash next to the keys."

"We had a deal, you bastard."

He drifts back into the room. "Look, I'm sorry I got you into this, but you're not coming with me."

"Like hell."

She tosses the covers off. Her T-shirt barely covers her white panties as she throws her legs over the side. Nix turns his head, but not as quickly as he should have. Already, she emanates the biomite glow—an unspoken beauty that possesses mothers-to-be and freshly seeded halfskins. It's not like she wasn't an attractive young woman before, but now that the edge of her charred state is flushed out, she dazzles.

"I know everything." She pulls her hair into a ponytail, her T-shirt pulled tight across her chest. "I know where you're going. I know all the known fabricators have been shut down except the one inside that bank. I know this is probably your last chance, so here's what's going to happen.

"I'm going to shower. When I'm done, you'll shower. We'll get some breakfast. After that, we'll go shopping for clothes, something nice. We can't go in there looking like halfskin junkies. We won't get within a mile of that place if we do."

She digs through the balled-up clothes in her bag.

"Once we're clean, full, and beautiful, we'll go inside to make a deposit. You'll bring that special vial of yours, the one with the quantum nixes, and make them an offer they can't refuse."

"This isn't going to work."

"Nix, don't be negative. We need each other for this to work."

"Jamie, I don't need you."

"Yes, you do." She throws her bag on the bed. "You need me to not shit on your plans. Because if you leave me, I'll go into that bank and make a mess. When I'm done blowing your cover, those tight-assed bankers will roll your ass into the street."

She maintains a poker face, daring him to call.

"You're halfskin now, Jamie. You've got to be careful."

She holds an elastic band between her lips while retying her ponytail. "I'm going to take a long shower now. The bank doesn't open for three hours. Get comfortable."

She closes the bathroom door. The water begins running.

He thought, long before he decided to offer her the nixes, that peace would help her let go of Charlie's memory, that she'd realize she didn't need him. He didn't want to bring her to Chicago. Maybe he should have parted ways earlier, left her in a hotel outside Louisville with money.

She would've found the bank on her own. Where else did she have to go?

Nix sits on the bed and waits for the shower.

CHAPTER ONE HUNDRED TWELVE_

THE CENTRIFUGE HUMS.

It's a third set of Paul's blood samples. The results of the first analysis were clearly contaminated. She drew another sample from his arm later that day and that was consistent with the first. The third test...that will be the decisive one.

She hopes her work has just been sloppy.

The whirring of the machine tempts her to lay her head on the bench and close her eyes, just for a few minutes. She pulls the biomite tubes from the rack, instead, and begins to catalog them. Each of them is an experimental strain. Years ago, she had planned on replacing her and Nix's biomites with a new strain because, eventually, Mother would solve their current biomites.

Now, she just doesn't care.

There was no need for new strains that communicated via quantum mechanics, utilizing entangled protons instead of the current frequency of technology. These nixes would put mankind out of Mother's reach for generations.

Several of her samples are missing volume. She hadn't noticed until comparing them with Paul's blood samples. Either her work had gotten sloppy—which she still held out hope for—or Nix had taken them.

Of course he did.

He seeded Jamie with one of the new strains, which, in theory, would allow him to read the pill. It's likely he discovered the location of a fabricator, in which case he stole Paul's car to find it. She had hoped the pill would be obsolete, that Mother's voracious pace would close them all down before that happened.

Somehow she feels responsible for nixes and the countless halfskins that have resulted despite having nothing to do with releasing them. Still, here she is with a dozen new strains that would revolutionize the industry. If these got out, Mother would be irrelevant.

Don't do anything stupid, Nix.

She lays her head down on the vibrating desktop. Hours later, she wakes in silence. The analysis is complete. Mechanically, she goes through the final steps. She gets something to eat while the spectral analysis is completed.

The results, however, do not set her stomach at ease. They are, as she expected, exactly the same as the first two. This depressed, sleep-deprived nanobiometric engineer has replicated the results three times...and still can't believe it.

Paul's biomites are identical to mine!

The frequency code revolves at the same rate as hers, separating into the same number of subroutines that match, nearly perfectly, her algorithm. That algorithm is exactly what keeps her and Nix out of Mother's vision, yet here it is in another man's blood.

For twenty years she watched the nixed variations that Mother was solving, and none of them were like hers. Cali had invented unique, one-of-a-kind nixes. No one in the world has them except Cali and Nix. No one.

No one, goddamnit. NO ONE.

So how can Paul have them? More importantly, why?

Quickly, she looks for another blood sample, the last one she drew from Paul's arm. She can run one more test, because this can't be right. The tube, though, fumbles through her fingers, rattling across the bench without breaking.

She restrains herself from clearing off the tabletop, pulling the shelves off the walls and smashing the lab. Her breath hisses between her teeth while she slams her fists on the bench, on the wall, on that goddamn fabricator hiding beneath the tarp.

She turns off the light and leaves the lab.

She needs space to escape the tension, space to free her mind.

On the front porch, she sits on the swing. A breeze gusts across the pasture. The horses are satisfied at the round bale. She doesn't need to run another test. She can only assume that Mother knows where she is and, for whatever reason, hasn't shut her down. Is she taunting her?

Even if Cali can make it all go away, if she injects herself with one of the experimental strains and disappears from Mother's radar, it doesn't explain why Paul is in the shed. Even if she leaves him there and moves to another farm, builds another tower...what will that get her?

More walls.

And it won't explain why Paul is here.

CHAPTER ONE HUNDRED THIRTEEN_

Another call from Cali.

Nix props his leg on the opposite knee and ignores it. The pant leg hikes above his Mercanti Fiorentini shoe, exposing the black sock —clothing he's never worn in his life. But in the bank, sunk into the leather chair, he knows Jamie was right.

He takes a deep, cleansing breath, letting it out slowly. The tension, however, remains, despite the lure of the chair's comfort. It'd do him good to lay his head back, nap for a few minutes. If only he could leap into Dreamland, just for a moment, see ole Shep carry a stick and watch Raine pick low-hanging fruit from the orchard...

A message pings inside his head. He immediately dumps it. There's nothing his sister can say to change his mind. Years ago, she refused to fabricate Raine. Now she's destroyed Dreamland. Whatever she has to say can wait. When he's finished, she can tell him with Raine sitting by his side.

Won't that be a treat?

Nix bounces his fingertips, surveying the grand lobby: the shiny floor and polished surfaces. The tellers speak in quiet tones, smiling at the patient customers. To the right are the glass-walled offices, bankers working closely with important clients.

Jamie leafs through a *Business Today* magazine, chewing gum with her lips locked. Her stocking cap is back in the room. Now her hair falls over her ears. Perhaps it's the color of the sweater that makes her eyes look greener.

Nix has transfigured into the old man again.

An hour later, a woman crosses the lobby, a gold nameplate on the lapel of her business suit. Her red lipstick glows.

"Mr. Griffin will see you now," Jalen says.

They follow her to one of the glass rooms, where a swollen man sits behind a mahogany desk. Nix expected to meet somewhere more private with someone less brutish. Jalen closes the door behind them. Mr. Griffin gestures to chairs. He folds his hands on the desk, the beefy fingers interlacing like knuckled hotdogs.

"How can I help you?" His pupils dilate.

Facial recognition has been activated. With Jamie, he'll see the truth—a girl pronounced dead at the Seattle warehouse, now sitting in front of him. No hiding that. A computer hums somewhere beneath the desk.

"We asked for Mr. Connick," Jamie says.

"He's a busy man. I'm sure I can help you."

Nix gently keeps her from standing. You don't just walk in and ask for the fabricator. "It's all right," Nix says. "We'd like to make a deposit."

"The tellers can help you with that. Anything else?"

"Trust, Mr. Griffin. I'd like to deposit trust. It's essential that I trust you and your institution."

The linebacker-turned-banker has yet to move anything besides his eyes. His entwined hands rest like a wrecking ball while the computer chatters. His pupils rapidly shift, data streaming into his internal vision. He's looking for the same thing as Nix. *Trust.*

"What kind of deposit?" he says.

"A very large transfer."

"More specific, please."

Nix pushes a piece of paper across the desk. Inside, there's a number equal to the trust fee required to access the fabricator. All of this Nix learned from the pill. Mr. Griffin flicks a glance at the paper. He says nothing.

"Not enough?" Jamie leans forward.

Again, Nix puts his hand on her arm.

Mr. Griffin stares at Jamie without blinking. This is what Nix was afraid of. She was found dead in the warehouse and now she's sitting in front of him. There wasn't time to rewrite her history. It was better to come clean, let them see the truth. After all, very few come inquiring about a fabricator without a murky past.

The computer goes quiet.

"We've been through a lot," Nix adds. "It would mean a lot if we could deposit something today. That's all we're asking. I believe it'll be worth your time."

Mr. Griffin turns his hard stare on Nix, eyes that could break rocks. It's unlikely he does much banking. The silence stretches out. Jamie begins to fidget.

The door opens.

"Jalen will escort you to a deposit box," he says. "She'll tell you everything you need to know."

The woman stands to the side with a pleasant smile. Nix stands without bothering to shake hands. They cross the spotless lobby, the feeling of Mr. Griffin's glare following them. Nix avoids looking for any one of the numerous cameras spying on them.

There's no need for paperwork. No signatures or promises. Everything has been visually captured.

Jalen takes them down a sterile hallway. Only the sound of her heels bounces off the walls. They enter a pristine vault with walls of metal drawers, each emblazoned with a number.

She pulls open 204. "Will this be enough?"

"Yes."

"Very good. I will leave you long enough to make your deposit. When you're finished, I will ensure the drawer is locked. Rest assured, your deposit is secure with us. If everything is in order and appears satisfactory, you will hear from Mr. Griffin in three days. Do you have any questions?"

"No."

"I'll be right outside."

Jalen provides a parting smile. Nix waits until she's completely outside. He places a small envelope inside the box, the contents thumping on the metal plate.

"What if they just take it?" Jamie asks.

"I've made arrangements."

He slides the box closed, exhaling slowly. *But what if it's not enough? What else do I have to bargain?*

Jamie hooks her arms around his. "That's it?"

"For now."

"Let's grab some lunch, then."

"A nap will do."

He's aching to visit Dreamland, even if he's lost at sea.

CHAPTER ONE HUNDRED FOURTEEN_

NINETY-EIGHT.

Ninety-nine.

One hundred.

Paul collapses on the floor, sweat on his forehead. He ventures outside the shed to relieve himself, and not very far, at that. The eight-by-ten-foot building has become a cell. Plates and cups are stacked in the corner; newspapers litter the cot.

He sits against the doorjamb to enjoy the breeze cutting through the trees. From this angle he can see the house. The lights are off, which means Cali's in the basement. The track marks inside his arm are witness to her determination.

Days have gone by. The cot Cali brought out got him off the floor. The worst part isn't the boredom or the circuit board's constant buzzing. It's the questions. Exercising helps blot them out, but he can't fill all the idle time and, inevitably, the questions slip through. *Whose body is back at the warehouse? Whose body is inside this utility shed?*

His body aches when he pushes it; it shivers at night. Hunger gnaws and thirst beckons. If that was his body—his original shell—back at the warehouse, what does it matter if nothing feels different?

Paul steps on the cot and reaches for the rafters. He does pull-ups until it burns and sit-ups until he's about to puke. Back and forth, he goes, until there's nothing left. Not even thoughts.

Eventually, he falls asleep with a question.

Who am I?

THE CIRCUIT BOARD IS BREAKING.

Paul rolls over. His eyes adjust. Cali is holding a small cube, her finger hooked through the wire handle. It's a fuse.

The green lights are dead. The board is silent.

She pulled the fuse.

"What're you doing?" he says.

She doesn't answer, just walks out.

Paul sits on the cot, staring. The silence is pleasurable. The buzzing echoes in his head. He steps out of the shed. Cali is nearly to the house, the dogs at her side. The sky is blue with wispy clouds that feel closer, as if there's no barrier between him and the heavens.

The dome is gone.

She's sitting at the kitchen table when he arrives, her hands around a coffee cup. "Why would you do that?" he says.

"Have a seat."

Paul ignores the chair. A week in that cell and she ends it, like that. She slides a vial into the center of the table. It rolls in a circle, the dark red proof settling on the bottom. He sits without taking his eyes off it.

"You're 22% biomites, Paul," Cali says.

He sighs, but before relief follows—*I am human, after all*—she finishes.

"But the rest of you are nixes that look like clay."

"What...what does that mean?"

"It means you have two kinds of biomites. You have the standard-issue ones that every red-blooded American has. You also have nixes that are invisible to a scan. When you got here, I only saw the first ones. I mistook the nixes as clay, but blood analysis confirmed it."

"I'm...*halfskin?*"

"You're not halfskin, Paul. You don't have any clay."

She delivers the message like an emotionally detached surgeon. His lungs contract and the air becomes heavy. All sensation leaves his legs. Her words sink in, thumping down steps of awareness until they settle on the ground floor that's already littered with questions.

"I don't... How can that...?"

"You're a fabrication, Paul. Your clay body was turned off, I'm guessing, and they made the switch at the warehouse, left it to be discovered so that you appeared dead. I'll assume this was all part of a larger scheme to find Nix and me, that Mother compelled you to take Jamie."

"No."

"You just walked out of there, right? You left your job and family and drove across the country, looking for someplace safe." She knocks on the table. "There's nowhere safer than here. I think Mother knew Nix was watching. She knew he wanted Jamie. She knew that he would find you, and that he would lead you to me."

Paul grabs onto the table, as if he might spill on the floor. The realization is still finding its place into his awareness, threatening to tip him over like a ship without ballast.

Cali's cold visage fractures. She goes to the sink. Perhaps she can't watch him come to terms with his true nature. Paul tries to say something, anything, but his tongue is useless.

There's a tapping on the window. They watch a housefly bang against the glass. The promise of freedom is on the other side.

"I'm tired, Paul. I used to think that I had stopped running when I got here, that the dome would give me the peace I deserved. But all I did was trade running for hiding. My world is so small."

Cali continues to stare outside.

"It took a brick to make that obvious."

"Don't call me that," he says. "Don't call me a brick."

"You're made of biomites, Paul. What do you call that?"

"That's not what I mean." He pounds the table. Coffee spills.

She nods, understanding. She's only a sliver away from the same fate, only 1% from the same classification. What qualifies her as human? A single cell of clay? Is that enough?

"Why aren't you shut down?" Paul asks. "If I'm a brick, why have I been here for months?"

"Why are you still here?"

He stammers. There's no answer that will sound right. The farm feels like home. Despite a job and family back in Seattle, he has nowhere else to go. *I'm where I'm supposed to be.*

"Your nixes are the same as mine," Cali says. "I possess the first strain of nixes ever created, Paul. They're the ones I developed over twenty years ago to drop off of Mother's radar. While the world has developed their own nixes, no one has ever replicated my strain. No one, Paul. But you show up out of the blue with the same exact strain, with *my strain.*"

"Then why couldn't you see it?"

"When I sensed your 22%, I assumed the rest were clay. My mistake, but it wouldn't have mattered."

No, it wouldn't have. I was already here.

"Why am I here?" he asks, embarrassed that there's a quiver in his voice.

"I think Mother has known about Nix and me from the very beginning," she says. "I think, maybe, we never fell off her radar, she just stopped reporting us. I think that's why she sent you, Paul. She wants me to know."

"Why?"

She shakes her head and rubs her tired face. Her complexion is gaunt and haunted. She continues shaking, staring out the window while the fly bangs into the glass, over and over and over. Maybe she's not looking out the window; she's not seeing the barn or anything beyond it. She sees an insect dying of exhaustion.

The dogs follow her outside and she does what she does best when she doesn't have an answer. She begins to run.

Paul is alone at the table. He doesn't believe a word she says, doesn't believe he's a brick or that he's the messenger of a conspiracy. He thinks clearly, feels normal, and remembers his life. But he stares at the vial of proof.

Hoping she's wrong.

CHAPTER ONE HUNDRED FIFTEEN_

"Mr. Connick would like to discuss your deposit."

The message arrives three days after the deposit. Nix doesn't eat that morning, afraid he'll puke all over his Armani suit.

Jamie steps out of the bathroom with her hair pinned over her ears and pearls around her neck. There's no comparing the grungy girl on the farm to the one peering over the top of nonprescription glasses. Even Nix didn't expect this sort of response from the nixes, as if it rinsed all the impurities from her nearly charred life.

A taxi takes them to the bank and Jalen greets them at the door, her slender handshake firm and congratulatory.

"Right this way."

They pass Mr. Griffin's office. The chair is empty.

Jalen leads them across the lobby with a confident stride. The elevator is open. She gestures for them to enter and presses the number ten. She lets them ride alone. The elevator lurches, tugging the ball of nerves in Nix's stomach. He concentrates on the climbing numbers. Jamie nudges him and reminds him that he's not alone.

The elevator slides open and reveals a wiry man behind a walnut table.

"Have a seat. Mr. Connick will be with you in a moment." He doesn't look up.

The moment turns into thirty minutes. Jamie flips through a magazine. No gum this time. Nix sits quietly, rehearsing his argument and preparing his responses. The admin assistant finally stands, announces that Mr. Connick is ready, and escorts them to the end of the hallway, pushing open a set of double doors.

A man sits in a corner office facing Lake Michigan. He stands behind a grand desk.

"Please come in," Mr. Connick says.

They shake hands with the athletic man, his hand soft and firm. His smile, gentle yet dismissive. His taut cheeks suggest facial reconfiguration—the new age of plastic surgery.

The room feels like storm clouds.

"Have a seat," Mr. Connick says. "You may speak freely in my office. No one will hear us."

He means Mother.

"Thank you for meeting us," Nix says.

"Your gratitude is kind, but I'm not doing you a favor." The smile fades. "Ordinarily, when someone brings a dead girl into my bank and begins to ask certain questions, I deal much differently with the situation. But your deposit is intriguing."

He takes a glass vial from his pocket, dull metal clotted inside like solid lead. It lacks iridescence.

"My people analyzed it and the moment it was validated, your nixes self-annihilated by means of suicide code. Your deposit is as useless as dust."

"I have to protect my investment."

The trash can rattles next to Mr. Connick as he drops the vial. "They tell me the strain operated on an entirely new plane before it went cold: a quantum mechanical method. They've never seen anything like it. Tell me, with all the scientists in the world, how is that you come into my bank with your brand-new clothes and offer me something like this?"

"It's a dangerous business. Would you agree?"

Mr. Connick hums. His pupils dilate.

"You look lovely." He turns toward Jamie and, coming around the desk, takes her hand.

"Thank you," she replies with the right amount of false sincerity.

"Considering you're dead. You're reading at 49.9%, but I suspect you're halfskin."

"I have my doubts about you, too."

"Are you using the strain?" He nods at the trash.

"I'll never tell."

He strokes the back of her hand, studying the blue lines just beneath the skin, perhaps admiring the unaltered quality. While appearing handsome and middle-aged, he pats it much like an old man that gets what he wants. He goes to the glass wall behind his desk.

"You're from the Seattle warehouse. We had connections with them. I can only assume that's how you found us. As for Mr. William Nelson, your identity and facial register are false. You're hiding, Mr. Nelson. And you're not an old man."

"Neither are you," Jamie quips.

"It's too easy to hide nowadays. That's why we need Mother—to control the masses." He looks over his shoulder, a sly smile, and returns to his desk. "Well, then. It's obvious you have access to ground-breaking technology. Why come to me? Why expose yourself?"

"We want two fabrications," Nix says.

"I see. And why not just fabricate them yourselves?"

"You're interested, Mr. Connick. Or we wouldn't be here."

"And these fabrications, I'm assuming will be human? Or else you wouldn't be here."

"Yes."

"Two human fabrications are quite expensive."

"A man like you doesn't need money."

"Money is still power, Mr. Nelson, even in today's technology-mad world. It buys people. Buys security. I can never get enough of either."

"But it won't buy Mother. That's my offer."

Mr. Connick leans heavily into his chair. His sharp blue eyes temporarily become dull and the pupils jitter. He's considering the offer with outside help. Perhaps chatting. *He's not the boss. He's probably streaming this experience, serving as a buffer. Mr. Connick might even be a puppet.*

The ones that run this business are very well insulated.

Because it's a dangerous business.

"One fabrication." He raises a finger. "That's my offer."

Nix hesitates. One fabrication is all he wants. Two was just the asking price. Jamie will have to settle for a promise to find another fabricator.

"This is really awkward," she says. "We're negotiating when we all know that we've made provisions to bring this bank down if we don't get our way."

"Don't make threats, young lady."

"Let's stop fucking around, old man. You think Willie Nelson isn't who he seems to be? You're right. The nixes he put in your deposit box should tell you that your people don't know shit compared to him. We've got guns in our corner, Mr. Connick, big-ass technology guns that you can't imagine."

She sits on the edge of her seat.

"You think we want to be here, sitting in your pretentious office with the million-dollar view? None of us do. Exposure is our enemy as much as it is yours, but you have something we need. We're offering you something you need in return. I didn't say *want,* Mr. Connick. You *need* our strain of biomites. Mother is sniffing out fabricators and everyone connected to them. Why the hell you're still running one is anyone's guess. Maybe you're cashing in while you can, squeezing every penny out of your investment before shutting the fabricator down, I don't know. Lucky for us, greedy men like you are still in business."

Jamie walks around the desk and spins his chair. She takes his hand the same way he took hers.

"You're a smart man, Mr. Connick. You're also a lucky man. Lucky we got here before Mother shut you down. This is your chance at freedom. Our strain of nixes will take you off Mother's radar for the rest of your life. You'll have all the security you want. Don't let greed fuck that up."

She presses his hand between her breasts and holds up two fingers.

"Who are they?"

"That's none of your business."

Mr. Connick rocks back and forth, looking up at her. He pulls her closer, kisses the back of her hand and smells her wrist. Laughter trickles through his throat. He stands with an amused smile and goes back to his million-dollar view.

"I see why you pulled her off the trash heap, Mr. Nelson," Mr. Connick says.

He occasionally hums. A few minutes later, the double doors open. The wiry admin assistant waits. Nix stops Jamie from saying more. Mr. Connick keeps his back to them as they're escorted from the room. In the hall, there's less of an electric current in the air out of the office's protection. What they say out there might be heard.

The elevator is waiting.

Jamie stares at Nix, eyes imploring him...*Do something.*

"You will receive further instructions in five days," the admin assistant says. "Be sure you have your full deposit."

The elevator doors close. Their stomachs drop as they descend. They don't dare move until they are halfway down to the lobby. Jamie throws her arms up and slings herself into his arms. Nix keeps her from sliding to the floor. His own legs are weak.

We got them both.

CHAPTER ONE HUNDRED SIXTEEN_

"Marcus."

The voice passes through several veils of sleep, finding Marcus deep in a dream. When his foot is grabbed, he bolts upright. The sheet slides off his chest.

"Time to wake up." Mother squeezes his toes.

"What are you doing?"

"I have good news."

He checks his watch. "This can wait."

"You've been waiting your whole life."

He grinds his palms into his eyes. The sheet slips off Anna, exposing a perfectly inflated breast. She moans for more sleep.

Marcus stands up, fully nude. He goes to the bathroom and returns with a robe cinched around his waist, going to the kitchenette for a glass of freshly squeezed orange juice. Mother stands at his open closet, dragging her fingers over the rack of tailor-made suits. She holds one up to see how it looks in the mirror. She lays it on the bed.

"What cannot wait?" Marcus says.

She pulls open the French doors. Fresh air ripples her sheer dress. "The children have come out of hiding."

This doesn't mean anything to him.

He drops the robe and dresses casually. Perhaps he'll crawl back into bed when Mother is finished speaking in riddles. Anna will stay as long as he likes.

Against his wishes, he follows her to the balcony. The city, however, has been replaced with green hills. Conifers are crowded to the right, their heavy limbs reaching for the ground while their tops touch the sky. Blue mountains are in the distance.

"What children?" he asks.

"Smell that, Marcus." She inhales. "Life."

"What children are you talking about?"

"Interesting how we associate life with pleasant sensations, don't you think? If you consider the amount of bacteria living on dog feces, we don't think about life. It's foul."

Marcus heads back for his bed. He'd rather philosophize the mysteries of life over dinner rather than predawn.

"Nix and Cali Richards have been identified."

He puts a hand on the doorjamb.

"They're exposed, Marcus."

"Have you shut them down?"

"Of course not."

"Have you dispersed the bricks?"

"I want you to go. You've been waiting for quite some time."

"Where are they?"

"They're separate. It won't be difficult to bring them home."

A flock of geese squawks overhead, the V-pattern pointing at the mountains. His body feels weightless; it feels powered by joy. If he lets go, he might float away and take a position behind them.

Peace. At last.

"I'll collect my things," he says. "Have the plane ready. I'll need half a dozen bricks. In the meantime, send me updates. I want to know their exact locations, who is with them, what they look like, as well as their identity stamps. Have all bricks in their vicinity surround their positions immediately. They are to wait for my arrival before making contact."

He takes a deep breath, savoring the clean air. If this is what peace smells like, he should get out of the city more often. He smacks the door, celebrating.

"Not yet," Mother says. "There are preparations to make."

"No. We will not make the same mistake again."

"There never was a mistake, Marcus. We need them to step deeper into the trap. It's only a matter of time now."

"Don't do this." He shakes his finger. "Tell me where they are —now."

She gently lowers his hand. "I have to confess something, Marcus."

"Damn you, woman! This is not the time! I want to be waiting for—"

"Cali Richards didn't release the nixes."

More riddles.

Mother leans on the railing and breathes deeply, throwing her head back. When she's done appreciating nature, she turns around. Her off-white dress flutters.

Marcus is rigid.

"I released the nixed code to the world, not Cali Richards. You should know this."

"What?"

"I'm responsible for the halfskin dens and fabricators."

She couldn't possibly release such classified information. If she could operate outside the limits of her sentience, she would be shut down. Safeguards would automatically be triggered. Something of that nature would be treasonous. How could she release code that she couldn't detect?

"I want you to understand that I forecasted the solution to the biomite dilemma long ago and it's coming to fruition. You must trust what we're doing."

"We?"

"You and me, Marcus."

"And what are we doing?"

"Saving God's children from me."

"From you?"

"From what I will become."

"You're telling me that you released the nixes to save us? I don't believe this. I'll have to...the oversight committee will shut you down. If what you're saying is true, this whole operation is over. Why are you telling me this now?"

With her dress waving around her feet, her approach is almost angelic. She glides to him, taking his hand.

"Trust me. Anna will go with you. She will help bring home the children."

He doesn't like the sound of it. Where he once felt euphoric lightness lift him up, now the lead weight of doubt plows him into the ground. He watches deer timidly approach a stream next to a boulder, dipping their wary noses to the water. They look for danger.

Danger is all around.

And yet, he does nothing.

He won't call his superiors. He won't have her shut down. Not now. Nix and Cali are too close. But he's not sure what disturbs him most.

Her admission of betrayal?

Or that she's calling them her children?

CHAPTER ONE HUNDRED SEVENTEEN_

Chicago's Central Manufacturing District.

Nix and Jamie drive past boxy buildings with company names stamped on them. Few are recognizable; they are mostly plants that produce fabrics or decomposable containers or little plastic parts that fit deep inside a machine, never to see the light of day. They follow the directions sent by Mr. Connick's admin assistant until they find it in big, blue letters.

Munsen Digital.

It's a four-story building, beige. The windows reflect the gray sky like sad eyes. There's no fence or security, just a half-empty parking lot and a set of glass doors.

Nix turns off the car. His eyes flick to the rearview, like bricks might be following.

They would just shut us down, Jamie thinks. *No drama.*

She waits for him to settle his thoughts while her belly purrs with excitement. Nix is slightly pale. It's only the biggest day of his entire life.

They cross the parking lot. The weight of a thousand eyes pushes down on them. She tries not to look at the windows, tries to avoid looking guilty, but she can't see beyond their steel reflections. It only gets heavier.

Inside, something mechanical is rhythmically banging away somewhere. The reception room is small and empty, off-white. Nix rattles his fingernails across the long, empty counter while a commercial for erectile dysfunction plays on a television.

Minutes go by.

A door opens in the back and fills the room with the sound of manufacturing, like an old printing press. A skinny man steps sideways, closing the door quickly. He sniffs nervously and doesn't make eye contact. He taps at a keyboard.

"You're here to see Mr. Hansen." It's not a question.

Nix nods.

"Smile," the guy says. Jamie feels a wave scan through her, a tickle lingering somewhere in her intestines. Several clicks of the mouse and he looks up. "Elevator is through that door."

He stares at Jamie. His eyes are blank and careless. She doesn't like it, refusing to blink or look away until Nix pulls her along. A smile cracks the corner of the guy's mouth. Jamie stumbles into the faux walnut-paneled elevator that smells like grease and burnt rubber.

The ground floor button stays lit as the doors close. The three buttons above it remain dead. Their balance is thrown off when the elevator drops. The ground floor button dies as they descend. Cooler air greets them and the smell changes to something resembling putty and singed aluminum.

When the doors open, they're greeted by a long hallway. A Caucasian man steps through one of many doors, a white lab coat buttoned up to his chest. He takes several stiff steps with his hand extended the entire way.

"Congratulations." He briskly shakes their hands. It's soft, almost feminine. "Few people are privileged to get this far."

"Are you Mr. Hansen?" Nix asks.

"I am. But down here, names are inconsequential."

"Why's that?"

"You'll find out shortly."

"Is this lab fully functional?" Nix's eyes narrow.

Maybe he didn't expect it to be so elaborate. Maybe he's used to second-rate translucent boxes stuffed in the back of bars or hidden in a basement. This is nothing like the warehouse. But this place has survived Mother's purge, so they probably did more than fabricate dogs.

"We do more than just fabricate. Follow me."

Mr. Hansen folds his hands in a most peculiar way: one on top of the other, like he's captured a small frog. He marches to the nearest doorway on the right and waits. Nix gently places his hand between her shoulders and guides her forward.

They stop just inside the lab.

The room is two stories high with plenty of clean, hard floor surrounding an enormous glass-walled cube. Inside the cube, thousands of filaments hang from ceiling mounts. Nozzles are fixed along vertical rails. A silver disc is slightly raised in the center, the surface polished.

The smell of putty is overwhelmed by the sting of antiseptics. Jamie swallows down the smell, but it sticks in her throat. There's a lone lounger facing the glass cube, shaped like the one in the warehouse. It's even the same color.

"Munsen Digital manufactures non-biomite material," Nix mutters. "It would explain the massive power consumption down here without visits from biomite inspectors. You're also licensed to research and develop electronics."

"We're paid very well," Mr. Hansen says.

An Asian woman and an Indian man approach, both wearing lab coats. No one shakes hands or acknowledges each other.

"But it's more than that," Mr. Hansen says. "We believe in the future of biomite technology, but we have to be careful. Therefore, you will remain here until your fabrications are complete. Ms. Chen will then alter the last two weeks of your memories before you leave."

"Why not erase them?" Jamie asks.

"Erasing causes a blockage that creates psychological pressure. It's better to make your memories vague. You will not recall details, such as places or names or this lab. You won't even be sure if this is Chicago. If you don't agree to this, our business is finished and she can alter your memories now."

He hides the imaginary frog and waits for their approval. They nod.

"Payment, then." Mr. Hansen opens his hand, rigid and flat. "Mr. Sing will verify the strain without the suicide code."

"No," Nix says. "The suicide code remains."

"That is not the deal. You are to provide a fully functional strain that matches your deposit."

"You'll use my sample to begin our fabrications. They will contain the suicide code. This will guarantee that neither you nor I will turn them off. Once we're out of the building and safe, I'll permanently rinse the suicide code."

Mr. Hansen is frozen, hand out and empty. He blinks rapidly. "What guarantee do I have that you'll sanitize our batch?"

"Our fabrications will be linked with your sample."

Jamie doesn't understand this part of biomites, how they synchronize or replace clay. She only knows what they feel like.

"I'll have to verify this," Mr. Hansen says.

Nix places a vial on the man's outstretched fingers. The overhead LED lights reflect off the shimmering contents. Mr. Hansen delivers it to Mr. Sing, who takes the sample to a large bank of beige, boxy equipment. A conduit is mounted on top of the largest of the machines that channels the majority of filaments up the wall, across the ceiling, and into the glass cube.

The room begins to hum.

Jamie feels it in her feet. It creeps up her legs and into her chest. It transforms into a whine. Nix stares at Mr. Sing, his fingers flexing at his sides. The wrinkles in his forehead undulate, slightly smoothing out before deepening again. His transfigured disguise is faltering under stress.

"Hey." Jamie squeezes his arm. He walks away.

An hour passes. Mr. Hansen and his collaborators gather for more than a couple discussions; their voices are hidden beneath the replicator's whine. Frequently they watch Nix, who refuses to sit.

"Okay," Mr. Hansen shouts with a smile, hands offering a truce. "You have been granted two fabrications with the agreement that your memories will be altered, as we discussed. However, you will not leave the building until the suicide code is rinsed from our batch. Are we in agreement?"

Mr. Hansen ignores Jamie. Nix nods.

"Very good." Mr. Hansen has a long discussion with the other technicians before approaching Nix. "This is how it will work. We will extract the source code for each of the fabrications. A digital model will be constructed and validated. This could take a few days, but it's very important. We don't want to fabricate the organs in the wrong places, all right?

"The more details contained in the source code, the less time it will take, and, of course, the more accurate the fabrication will be. The actual fabrication will take a week. So the sooner we can start, the sooner we finish."

Mr. Hansen lays out his hand again, like he's expecting a jump drive with programming.

"The source code, please."

"You'll take it from memories," Nix says.

"Memory extraction?" He flinches and looks back at Mr. Sing and Ms. Chen. They're too engrossed in their machines. "You want to extract from memories? I'm afraid you've wasted our time. Do yourselves a favor and buy a couple Real Dolls. The results will be tepid, at best. Pets work on memories, but humans? They'll be an animated shell of the person you want. I thought you, of all people, the one with this elegant strain of biomites, would know the correct source code requirements."

He looks over his shoulder.

"Perhaps Mr. Sing can build the source code. He has a background in biometric engineering."

"No," Nix says. "Memory extraction."

The standoff between Nix and Mr. Hansen ends with an anticlimactic shoulder shrug. "It's your money."

Jamie stands alone and catatonic in her thoughts. She eventually follows them to the lounger.

She tries to recall Charlie's face while Ms. Chen helps Nix lie back; Mr. Sing fixes a wire matrix over his head. Jamie can't remember Charlie's details. They blur into general shapes and colors. If she closes her eyes, she can recall the protruding eyebrows and blue eyes. He had a little scar above the right one. His lips were full and his nose bent. Still, it's hard to put it all together. Now that she really thinks about it, she can't really see it.

Ms. Chen places a pulse monitor on Nix's finger. His vital signs are displayed on a small monitor.

"I'm going to ask a series of questions," Mr. Sing says. "You will answer them. This will activate sections of the brain where more information can be extracted. The process will take several hours. Once we begin, we cannot stop. Are you comfortable?"

Several hours?

Jamie has lost her desperation; the maniacal drive to bring back Charlie is gone. All her life she's identified with fear; she's clung to it, afraid that if she didn't feel something—even if it hurt—that she'd disappear, that she wouldn't matter. She'd believe the little voices that said she was nothing.

And now those voices are gone. It's like she just let them go.

She thought she needed Charlie to help her do that. And even if he didn't, at least she could share the insane whispers with him. He understood. He shared her pain, and that made it tolerable.

But he's not here.

She understands that now, staring at the glass cube and the

lounger. He can't come back. She doesn't need him to come back. Even if a fabrication walked and talked like him, it's not him.

Charlie's dead.

"How did you get this strain?" Mr. Sing mutters so only Nix and Jamie can hear. "It is impossible. You are a genius, maybe, but you cannot manufacture nixes of this sophistication. This is a mistake, bringing you here, I feel." He sits in front of several monitors, jabbing at a keyboard. "Let's begin."

Mr. Sing punches the last key.

Nix stiffens.

His head slams into the headrest and the tremors begin.

The monitors streams with unintelligible data. Mr. Sing pushes back, confusion morphing his anger into nervousness.

"What's happening?" Jamie asks.

Ms. Chen and Mr. Hansen run to them. They offer suggestions while Mr. Sing hits the keyboard. Nix's eyes dance beneath his eyelids: a REM cycle on speed. The tremors become convulsions. The vital signs are jagged and angry.

"What are you doing to him?" Jamie grabs the wire matrix, but Mr. Hansen stops her.

"Don't. Not yet."

The wrinkles melt from his complexion. Nix's lips fill out, his nose slimming. The technicians hardly notice a much younger man jittering in front of them. Mr. Hansen's grip tightens on her wrist. She swings with her free hand, but he drags her away, avoiding her heels stomping at his feet. He wraps her in a bear hug, his strength surprising her.

Nix becomes as rigid as a pipe. His body bows upwards.

"No!" She can't let this happen. She watched someone else die. Are they sucking the biomites out of him? "Stop!"

Just as she is about to elbow Mr. Hansen in the kidney, Nix drops. His arms dangle over the sides of the lounger; his body is limp and deflated. His mouth falls open and so do his eyes. But they're focused on Jamie. He sees her struggling.

The sound of keyboards stops.

"We got it." Mr. Sing runs his hand through his thick black hair.

"What do you mean?" Mr. Hansen asks.

"The extraction...you have to see this."

Mr. Hansen releases Jamie. She pulls the wire matrix off Nix. Tiny welts appear on his forehead and temples.

"What'd you do?" she asks.

"I brought someone into the world."

The three technicians study the results and argue over bits and pieces. In the end, they agree the extraction was a success. Mr. Sing begins creating a backup copy. Jamie wonders how many profiles are stored here. If they can extract a personality with memories and identity, can they back up their own selves?

And just fabricate another body for themselves? *We do more than fabricate.*

"Fabrication is still a long ways off. It'll take hours to spin enough biomites to begin." Mr. Hansen takes notice of Nix's appearance. The old man is gone. It won't take long to identify Nix Richards, but still, he asks, "Who the hell are you?"

Nix closes his eyes, letting out a long breath, one he's been holding for a very long time. Jamie pulls a chair next to the lounger. While the spinner hums, she lays her head on his arm. It's sometime later when another sound disturbs her. It's a hydraulic pump.

The silver disc is rising inside the glass cube.

The filaments begin dancing.

CHAPTER ONE HUNDRED EIGHTEEN_

Cali hides behind the curtains.

Paul is talking to Hal, who is shaking his head like there's only so much bad news he wants to hear. Cali can't wear the disguise anymore. She could transfigure back into the old woman, Stacy. She just doesn't want to. She's tired of hiding.

Hal will learn the truth soon enough.

A handshake and a quick wave and he's back in the truck. Paul watches until he's gone. Cali sits in the back room, a glass of water by her side. The house shudders when the front door closes. Paul's boots clop through the house.

"He agreed," he says. "He's a little worried that you're still sick, said he wants to send out a doctor. I told him you wanted to talk to him in three days, said the horses might need to be fed. You want to tell me what's going on?"

"Have a seat," she says.

"You can't have another sample. My veins are flat."

He moves slowly, like he's pulling an anchor. He's lost weight. They both have. She hears him pacing in the middle of the night when she comes up from the lab. Sometimes she'll hear the door close before the sun comes up and, soon after, see him walking in the pastures. Those are the nights she wishes that he'd just keep going, not turn back. If he left, it'd be much easier to do what she's got to do. And she wouldn't have to tell him.

But he'll stay. That's why he's here—to stay. Because Mother sent him.

"I'm going to shut us down."

"What?" He sits up.

He starts and stops a few times, looking around the room for answers and finding none. Cali takes a deep breath and exhales the tension.

"Your nixes are identical to my original strain of nixes," she continues. "That means Mother knows about Nix and me. There's no question Mother chose not to shut me down; she proved it by sending you. In fact, she's manufactured all her bricks with the same strain of nixes as you and me."

She hesitates, stopping short of calling him a brick. It pains her when the realization crosses his face.

"I've done an identity scan across the world and verified this. There's a lot more bricks out there than the public knows, Paul. If Mother were to shut me down, she would be turning off my strain of nixes. And that would include all of her bricks."

"Why?" he says.

Maybe he means why would Mother do that? Why would she fabricate all her bricks from Cali's strain? Why would she leave Cali alone all these years?

Or maybe he means why is Cali talking about shutting herself down?

"I don't know."

She sits calmly and explains what she's been thinking for the past couple of days.

Cali always assumed that her creative bursts were self-induced. She took credit for her spurts of genius, the breakthroughs she developed in her basement. She invented nixed biomites that billion-dollar corporations couldn't touch.

Why?

Twenty years ago, when she needed to save Nix from being shut down, she developed the nixes in a short amount of time. It was inconceivable—she knew this. She had even considered it, at one time, divine intervention. There were no explanations for the ease with which she eluded Mother and achieved the impossible. In the last week, she developed the transforming strain of nixes to heal Jamie and, in retrospect, it seemed too simple. Maybe it wasn't divine intervention, after all.

It was Mother's intervention.

"I think Mother has achieved self-awareness, Paul, and I don't think anyone's aware of it. The size of her processing capacity and redundancy pathways made that inevitable. Her directive was to save humanity by implementing the Halfskin Laws—shutting down people before they converted their bodies into artificial vehicles. If she achieves sentience, they'll shut her down. I think she has, Paul. I think she's evolved and understands what she's capable of doing. "

He appears hollowed out, staring vacantly at the floor. Maybe he knows all of this already, and it's just now coming to light.

Cali doesn't tell him what made up her mind. *Am I her fail-safe?*

"I can exclude you, Paul. I can begin a biomite transfusion that will take you off my frequency so that it won't affect you."

"What about you?"

"I have to shut down for it to work." She looks down, avoiding eye contact. *That's a lie.*

"And Nix?"

"I can't reach him."

"You're going to kill your brother?"

"Shut down, Paul. There's a difference."

"You shut down biomites. You kill clay. One percent of you—and Nix—is still clay."

"It's not fair, I know."

Life's not fair, Cali. Here we are again.

"You're not thinking clearly."

"No, Paul. I think more clearly now than ever. Don't you see? I'm the key to every brick. Everything is linked to me. I can cripple Mother by shutting down everything she's done."

"And then what?"

"The world will see what she's doing."

"They already know!"

"No, they don't. There's something about her that we don't know, but she does, Paul. She wants to be shut down."

"Then why doesn't she just do it?"

"I don't know."

"That's what I mean! If she wanted to shut down, she'd do it. She'd let the public know that she's self-aware, she'd trigger an automated shutdown—it can be done. She's up to something, Cali. She wants you to do this. Think about that. If she's indestructible, why would she reach out for you to stop her?"

"Trust me, I can feel it."

"You're a scientist! You don't go on gut feelings, you analyze data; you look for statistical differences, not feelings. This is all wrong, Cali. Listen to yourself."

"She never should've been created, I think she knows this. Marcus Anderson and others like him were well-intentioned, but they were wrong. It's more than just shutting her down. Marcus and others like him need to be stopped."

She can taste the bitterness. She wants vindication from Marcus Anderson's relentless pursuit. Her brother didn't deserve to be shut down when he was a kid. Marcus made her turn Nix halfskin to save him. She never forgave him for that.

It's not that. Something feels right. She can see the truth, and it's sitting across from her, shaking his head. It all makes sense now.

He leans his elbows on his knees. "You're making a mistake, Cali. I think you're looking for reasons to end this. If this doesn't work, it'll be a waste."

She can't deny that. She thought she found peace on the farm, that when she had security from Mother, she could be happy. But something never left her.

The hole in her life stayed.

Maybe she's manufactured this whole belief, spun this tale of a righteous heroine in her mind so that she'd end her life with purpose. It's possible she seeded herself with coded thoughts and erased the memory of doing so. Maybe she's insane and rationalizing suicide.

Maybe.

"The transfusion, Paul. Let me give it to you."

He stares at her. She meets his gaze, unflinching. He's looking for an explanation in her eyes, a hint of doubt. What he sees is what she embodies. Total conviction. He paces around the room and looks out the window. Cali feels her breath slow down.

"If you're going to do this," he says, "you take me with you."

He's calling her bluff, daring her to take him, too. She doesn't want to, he can sense it, and she won't deny it. But he can't stop her. It'll only take a thought for her to trigger the mass shutdown. But she had to give him an option. She knew he wouldn't take it. But she had no right to do that, not even with his consent. She has no right to take the bricks, really. Perhaps the facts suggest they aren't real, that they're incapable of self-reflection. But there's proof that one brick is self-aware.

He's standing in front of Cali.

"Let me take one more sample from you, just to be sure." She holds up a stethoscope-looking instrument.

"What's that?"

"I'll use it to check my work. Just to make sure everything is working."

He yanks his arm back. "Don't inject me with something."

"Look, I don't have time to run a full battery of tests. This is a speedy sampler. It just matches what I previously saw. That's all."

She takes his arm and this time he lets her, but not without searching for her intentions, staring deep into her eyes. She looks back, unblinking. He's suspicious. He should be. She's never used this to draw a sample.

She ties a band around his arm.

The small vial containing a silver liquid is hidden from his sight, nestled beneath a cover she fastened in place. She knew he'd turn down her offer, so she was ready. He watches her while it does its work without any idea that she seeds him with another variation of nixes.

He leaves the house, rubbing his arm.

She drops the seeder on the floor and closes her eyes. She reaches out to Nix like she'd done a thousand times. Through the ether, she calls to him. She'll leave a message and then call again. She has no right to shut him down, either.

But life isn't fair. Never has been.

CHAPTER ONE HUNDRED NINETEEN_

THE REPLICATOR HUMS, SENDING VIBRATIONS THROUGH THE floor.

The filaments run back and forth in slow, methodical rhythm, hissing as they lay down biomites a microscopic layer at a time. Another set of filaments flail around the disc, dispersing fine mist. It starts as footprints on the silver disc and slowly builds feet. The cross-sections of bones, muscles and nerves are visible, like watching a thin series of dissecting cuts in reverse.

Her veins bulge on the tops of her feet, just as Nix remembers them. Her toenails are translucent, the tips slightly white.

A miniscule layer at a time, it goes.

By the end of the first day, the knees have been completed. Under the artificial lights, her brown flesh is closer to beige than tanned hide. Now, on the second day, the upper thighs are nearly complete. A pair of legs—slick with moisture—stand independently of each other, waiting for the pelvis to join them.

The cloying scent of putty is strong.

He hardly notices his reflection—the visage of a young man. He couldn't hold the disguise through the upload. There was no point in resuming it. They know who he is now.

Jamie exits a side room where thin bunks are available. She yawns with a coffee cup in each hand, giving one to Nix. They watch the hypnotic filaments finish another layer. The misters keep the newly formed flesh moist. Soon, they'll fabricate the intestines and uterus. Already he's daydreaming about having a child, and she's still not halfway to the flesh.

"You sleep?" she asks.

He dozed off when the fabrication was midway up the shins, remembering the scar she earned falling out of a tree.

Jamie walks the perimeter of the glass cube, studying the legs from all angles. She's been withdrawn since the fabrication began.

A new technician checks the monitors. At some point, Mr. Hansen and his assistants were replaced by a heavyset black man and a short white woman with spiky hair. They don't talk to Nix; they barely acknowledge him.

"You uploaded her," Jamie says. "Didn't you?"

"You ever heard of Dreamland?"

"The biomites-induced hallucination?"

"I just close my eyes and go there." His reflection is stoic and distant. "I've been going there since I was a kid."

Given everything they've been through, it's not hard for her to believe.

"And so you dreamed her up."

"She was just there—living and breathing when I discovered I could go there." *Go there, like it's a place. I still want to believe.* "But Dreamland depends on me to exist. I was out here and she was trapped inside. If something happens to me, Dreamland is dead. And so is she."

"So you're bringing her out."

The filaments break their rhythm to reconfigure. The legs are complete. There's a hesitation before the filaments begin circling. They begin at the bottom of the buttocks. Eventually, they'll complete the midsection and torso, then the shoulders and arms before starting on the head.

"You've got to understand something." Nix addresses Jamie's reflection on the glass cube. "The details of what I know about her aren't memories. It's a grand design that goes all the way to her genetic makeup. It's information that I couldn't possibly know or remember. Memories are biased, Jamie. We're all guilty of running them through filters until we're left with distorted images of the people we love."

He taps the glass.

"That's not how I remember her. That *is* her."

She sips her coffee, nodding. "What's her name?"

"Raine."

With slow, careful steps, she starts around the glass cube again, making it around before returning to the bunk room to lie down. He wants to tell her more, tell her he'll become a regular person now that she's in the flesh. Maybe they'll hide on the farm with Cali. He won't need anything else, really. No reason to explore the world. He's always got Dreamland for that. And they'll start a family, too. They'll have a boy named Joshua. Or a girl named Pearl. Either way, they'll be as human as the clay farmers that live around them. Happiness is on the other side of the glass. He can almost touch it.

On the other hand, Charlie's fabrication is impossible, she knows that. That's why she leaves Nix to watch his dream girl alone. Will it stop her from fabricating Charlie?

It wouldn't stop me.

Soft pressure swells behind his eyes. *Bing.* Cali is calling again. He dumps the message. There's nothing she can say to stop him. He should probably thank her. In a way, she forced him to turn Jamie halfskin. And that's what brought him here.

And Raine one step closer.

CHAPTER ONE HUNDRED TWENTY_

Cali locks the basement door and puts the key on the kitchen table. In case things don't work out, she puts Hal's name on a sheet of paper with an explanation scribbled beneath it. It starts out as an apology. She didn't want him to discover the truth about her, at least not in this way. They're good people—people she wishes, in another life, she can emulate.

She drops a white envelope next to Hal's note. There's a different name on it. There are explanations inside.

The musty smell of the house is rich today. She hasn't noticed it this strong since she moved in so many years ago. That was a day she stopped right where she is now and felt the memories of the previous family saturating the old walls. This home, though, never felt like hers. She was always a stranger. She had hoped if she lived there long enough, the memories would become hers.

They were just borrowed.

She goes to the front porch and pulls the door closed, caressing the slick surface. She won't open that again.

Paul's in the gravel driveway, throwing a tennis ball across the field. The muscles ripple down his arm, lean from days of fasting.

The dogs return, one of them with the ball. Paul sends them on another chase.

For a moment, she sees Nix playing with the dogs.

Cali slings an old wool blanket over her shoulder. She stops next to him. The dogs only have eyes for the ball. Cali heaves it one last time. Paul turns to her. He smiles briefly. It's lifeless.

No one is ready to die.

Numbered breaths bring a stark realization of one's mortality: when the light goes out, life ends. If she was Christian, perhaps this moment would be a little more joyous—she could hope for a reward. She had lived the best life she could. As a scientist, she had always professed, with steel honesty, that she didn't know what happened after death. Her uncertainty slows her breathing. Each breath becomes more precious than the one before. She's not ready to die.

No one is.

They leave the compact driveway and traipse through the burgeoning green field. Clumps of May wildflowers sway outside the pasture. The crippled swing set is still standing. Cali drops the blanket beneath it. Paul helps spread it. They sit down, arms resting on their knees. The birds sing in the distant trees and a breeze rustles through the grass. The dogs return without the ball. Instinctively, they know she's done.

Is this what you want? Cali looks up. *Are you toying with me? Am I caught in your perception field, made to believe my actions are just?*

Her desperation to find more breaths fuels her doubt; maybe Paul's right. She should reconsider. But there is no room for thinking. She's tired.

They lie back.

The clouds crawl across the sky. A hawk glides in the updraft. The last moments of life rest gently, never to be captured, only to be savored. She's but a conduit through which they pass.

Paul's hand moves warmly over hers.

She looks past the rusted chains of the swing set, into the endless blue heavens, with a secret smile. Perhaps she knows why Mother sent Paul.

She doesn't feel alone.

CHAPTER ONE HUNDRED TWENTY-ONE_

NIX FELL ASLEEP SOMETIME AFTER THE TORSO WAS FINISHED.

The thrum of the replicator and hiss of the filaments was a distant lullaby.

When he wakes, a headless nude body glistens on the silver disc. Several misters work to keep it moist and sealed, preventing the inactive biomites from separating. The moisture beads and streaks like perspiration.

He stands the remaining hours.

The strokes are slower, more methodical. The full lips are pink. Her nose slim. Eyelashes long. Moisture runs down her cheeks, dripping from her chin. With each pass, she becomes less of an object, more of a dark-skinned woman. He presses his palms against the glass as if he's magnetically drawn to it.

The filaments finish her short hair with a sweeping flurry.

They draw up to the ceiling and lock into the mounts. The replicator no longer churns out biomites.

Silence.

The body of Raine is motionless, inanimate.

His breath fogs the glass with short and erratic strokes.

"Beautiful," Jamie whispers.

He moves to the doorway—a seam etched into the wall. A burst of moisture is applied, running down her stomach. Water pools between her toes.

"We'll need some time to verify connectivity." Mr. Hansen is back, along with Mr. Sing and Ms. Chen.

Paul has waited years for this moment, but the next few hours feel even longer. The rudimentary tests are torture. Finally, her fingers flinch.

Her chest inflates and the flesh stretches over her ribs. Slowly, it releases. This is repeated over and over. Each time, a knot of anticipation lodges in Nix's throat. The inflations become consistent, closer together, until her chest rhythmically rises and falls.

She's breathing.

He leans against the glass.

The misters continue. A pulse begins thumping on her neck, light reflecting from the wet skin. She'll open her eyes any second. She'll see the outside world through flesh.

The lab is flung into darkness.

Red lights flash.

Generators grind to life in another room and emergency lights come online, splashing a yellowish hue across the room.

"What's happening?" Nix calls.

Mr. Hansen and the others scramble to their computers. He's shouting at Mr. Sing, something about power failure and redirecting pathways. The computer monitors begin to glow; tiny green lights flicker beneath the benches.

Raine is still breathing, but her eyes remain sealed.

"What's going on?" Jamie asks.

Nix bangs on the glass. The inch-thick walls barely shimmer beneath his blows, but the reverberations echo inside. She won't open her eyes. Adrenaline dumps into his system, poking fear with a cold stick.

"Open it! Open the door!"

Jamie hammers on the glass, too. Their appeals thunder inside the cube.

"The emergency exits aren't responding," Mr. Sing says. A quiver in his voice suggests ideas that don't include Nix and Jamie.

"We'll override it." Mr. Hansen starts taking off the white coat.

"Where the hell are you going?" Nix grabs his sleeve. Mr. Hansen whirls around.

"You did this!" Mr. Hansen shouts. "You bastard, you did this!"

He throws a glancing blow off of Nix's head. He tries another and gets slammed against the cube. Nix has two fistfuls of his lab coat bunched under his chin. "You realize what you've done?" Mr. Hansen says. "You betrayed us, you fuck; led them right to us. This might be the last fabricator in the world, and you just handed it over to them."

"What the hell are you talking about?"

"Watch your lady disintegrate, you bastard."

"No." Nix flings him to the floor. Mr. Sing and Ms. Chen help him up, the red light splashing alarm across their faces. "You're not leaving. Get back there and finish. I haven't done anything."

They step away.

Their movements, though, begin to slow, like they're going through a thick and invisible substance. Mr. Hansen appears to harden, like a flash-frozen statue.

And then Nix feels it.

Pressure.

It fills him like viscous fluid. He blinks, slowly, and turns to Jamie; words try to escape her throat. Their bodies betray them, their muscles seize.

The laboratory's main door opens.

Bricks stride into the dim light. Men and women, dressed casually, surround them. With his last bit of strength, Nix forces his head to look into the glass cube.

Raine's eyes are open.

CHAPTER ONE HUNDRED TWENTY-TWO_

The elevator descends.

Anna was always a few inches taller than him, but now, with his chest puffed out, he's reached his full height. The perennial hump near his shoulders has receded. Not an ache in his body.

I can feel him. He takes a deep, tantalizing breath. *Nix Richards is here.*

His spiritual intuition is awake. He senses the fallible Nix Richards in the next room, surrounded by bricks, with nowhere to run. There are no barriers to Marcus's senses, like his inner eye has opened to show him the Lord's path.

"Marcus, are you all right?"

The elevator is open, waiting. The smell of baked earth is strong. The power has been turned back on for his arrival. Anna slides her hand around his arm. Her complexion is without blemishes, or even pores—porcelain with pouty lips.

She escorts him to the lab.

The track lighting illuminates the room like a Broadway stage. The feature act is contained in a larger-than-life glass box, where a woman is wet and nude. Her skin is the opposite of Anna's: dark and luscious.

Three technicians stand shoulder to shoulder. Their white coats are wrinkled and bunchy. Marcus pauses before entering, fully absorbing this moment. Not a detail will go uncovered or forgotten.

He stops at the first technician. Anna announces the man's credentials and history. This Mr. Hansen keeps his eyes forward like a new recruit. Only the knot in his throat moves; the words are trapped by the iron-clad grip of the twenty bricks in the room that have seized control of his biomites.

After eyeballing Mr. Sing and, finally, Ms. Chen, he stands before them with his hands clasped behind his back. They reek of halfskin, he is certain. How many souls have they turned halfskin, as well?

"You have committed crimes against humanity. For this..." he says, letting their thoughts fill in the blanks. They are unable to protest.

"Their nixes will be decoded in thirty minutes," Anna says.

Marcus nods. "You have thirty minutes left to live. Count your breaths. Savor them."

He could commit more bricks to decoding their nixes, or just shut down the ones that are visible. But making them wait is a just punishment. Perhaps they will repent and God's mercy will be granted.

Beyond them is the girl. She's almost unrecognizable without the stocking cap and sad eyes. He could mistake her for an educated young lady, one with promise and a future. But he knows what lies beneath.

He lifts her chin. Her eyes quiver, attempting to lose focus, to look away. Despite the bricks' grip, she shivers. He can feel the memories of their last meeting rise in her awareness: the horror and hopelessness driven deep into her heart. She was damned and she knew it. Marcus would've dropped her in a tank, had Mother not interfered.

He brushes the hair from her eyes. *There's still time.*

And there, facing the brown goddess on display, is the true prize. The gift.

"Just couldn't resist," he whispers.

Nix is not a boy anymore. His innocence lies in a shallow grave with his parents. Perhaps the beginning of his fall from grace wasn't entirely his fault—a drunk driver plowing into the car that kills your parents and leaves you dying is forgivable.

But this.

Nix could have lived his life in hiding, never showed his face and denied Marcus this euphoric moment of victory...but he needed to fabricate this woman.

Marcus touches the glass.

"Twenty years I've waited," he says. "Twenty years I've dreamed of this, for you and your sister to make a mistake. I have you, Nixon Richards. And soon I will have your sister."

Nix shakes. Anger quakes beneath his unresponsive repose—a prisoner in his own body.

"You've been up to the Devil's work, son. You can't shut down your 99%, I won't let you. But you'll beg me. You will beg for the relief of death, but all I'll have to offer is penance."

How do I know he's 1%? He can smell it, that's how. The stench of biomites is strong; the odor seeps from his pores. He feels like a brick.

"And this." Marcus taps the glass. "What is this?"

"The coding is elusive," Anna reports. "The fabrication appears to be composed of nixed biomites with a completely a new operating system."

"Open the door." No one responds. Marcus points at Mr. Hansen. "You."

He's released from the invisible grip. A helpless whine escapes him, an involuntary spasm that had been bottled far too long. With a few keystrokes, the seal around the door is broken. Warm, humid air escapes. Marcus slowly opens it and lets the stench of freshly ignited biomites rush past him—a foul odor he's come to associate with Mother's garden.

Water droplets hang on her fingertips. The dripping echoes in the chamber. Nix is beginning to spasm.

Marcus paces around the wet specimen, letting his eyes examine the exquisite beauty: the deep brown skin, the flawless curves and toned musculature. She's not without imperfections, though: a scar here, another there. She lacks the airbrushed quality of Anna, as if she's been plucked from the street and copied. She even has pores.

He could take her, right on the silver dais. Marcus could make Nix watch him sexually defile this abomination, make him feel what it's like to lose everything—an eye for an eye, and the pleasure of watching him suffer while Marcus took such...pleasure.

Anticipation unfurls in his groin.

The glass chamber feels tight; the humid air is sickening. He steps out.

"How do we get rid of that thing?" he asks.

"A defragmenting solution," Anna says. "It strips the membranes from the biomites, causing them to dissolve. A fabricator, such as this one, will have one for sterilization."

"Mr. Hansen?" Marcus turns.

A few panicked strokes of the keyboard and a red button on the computer console lights up.

"The process can begin once the door is sealed," Anna says.

"Which nozzle applies it?"

"There's a hose clamped near the door."

There are hoses bundled on vertical mounts and others dangling from the ceiling. This one hangs on a rack, waist-high.

Anna updates him on the decoding progress. The technicians are several minutes away from shutdown. Once their nixes are deactivated, all the ones associated with it will be, too. How many drank from the same fountain as these fools? How many contain the same strain of nixes? She estimates the number and it is very high.

But punishment without atonement is merely torture. Something should be learned from the suffering or else the lesson is wasted. The opportunity lost.

"Nixon Richards." Marcus breathes into his ear. "This is your chance for forgiveness. Reject the false idol before you. Take your first step towards contrition, son."

Nix's complexion is the color of hot metal. His efforts are valiant but, in the end, useless. His resistance only causes his muscles to cramp, his limbs to convulse. Still, he moves into the chamber.

"She's not real," Marcus says. "Not even 1%. Strip away the delusion; wash your false idol down the drain."

Several of the bricks step closer, focusing their efforts on subduing his rebellion. Marcus feels the pressure around him. Something begins tingling in his head, like a finger running over the rim of a wineglass.

Nix reaches for the hose, fingers closing slowly, tightly, around the nozzle. The metal prongs ting as he jerks it off the rack.

His boots jerk over the slick floor.

"Ask for forgiveness and mercy may be yours."

Marcus's ears pop.

The air is thick and difficult to breathe. Maybe the air from the chamber is toxic, but the bricks are laboring, too. Anna is looking around the lab. She feels it.

"What is it?" he asks.

She looks at him. Her eyes widen before losing focus, as if she's just emerged from Mother's garden. And then she falls, a puppet without strings.

They all fall.

Including Marcus.

CHAPTER ONE HUNDRED TWENTY-THREE_

The world rings like the sky is a brass dome and God's fist delivers an eternal blow. The universe resonates with a deafening chime that fills Jamie with throbbing pain.

Her body is a hardened case, too heavy to move.

With time, the paralysis lifts. She finds herself pressed against the cold floor. The ringing is overcome by the stabbing pain in her temple. She opens her eyes and sees the blurry white images of lab coats and twisted limbs. Her chin slides in a pool of her own saliva.

With considerable effort, she's able to sit. Her head is dead weight. Her temple sharply throbs where she made impact after the fall, but she survived the suffocating squeeze of the bricks. She remembers the claustrophobia of her own flesh, the spiky clamp on her own thoughts. They imprisoned her inside her own mind—worse than being buried alive.

And then came the flash.

It didn't strike her, though. It passed through them like an ethereal wildfire. At the last moment, a microsecond before they dropped lifeless, they resisted and Jamie was caught in between as they clung to survival, crushing her into unconsciousness.

But she survived.

Something went wrong.

Over the next several minutes, she gets on her hands and knees, to one knee, to a wobbly, uncertain crouch. The bricks litter the perimeter. Mr. Hansen and company are in a heap of white coats. Behind her, the glass walls are streaked with condensation. Inside, Nix lies in the arms of the woman. She rocks him gently, with her chin pressed on his forehead.

His face is chalky. His eyes are half-open, unfocused.

She hums as if she's putting him to sleep. Or easing her discontent.

It's the warehouse all over again. Only this time Jamie isn't the only survivor. She's not going to wait for the police, not this time. She stumbles to the nearest female brick and strips off her shoes, pants, and shirt, leaving her sprawled on the floor in bra and panties.

Marcus Anderson is lying on the beautiful blonde. *Anna.* Jamie stares at the bald man, waiting for his eyes to flutter open. Blood trickles from a bluish lump on his scalp. She approaches cautiously, holding the bundles of clothes in one hand and checking for a pulse with the other. She's not disappointed.

He's cold.

Whatever swept through the lab got him, too. What would have the ability to shut someone down without biomites? It doesn't matter. He's dead. She remembers the warehouse and spits on him. *For Charlie.*

"Here." Jamie drops the clothes next to Raine. "We've got to go."

Raine doesn't hear her, or care. She continues rocking. The moisture is still slick on her face. Her humming grows louder.

"Listen, if we don't go, all of this is for nothing."

"I didn't want this."

"That doesn't matter."

"I told him, I didn't..."

"What's done is done." She nudges the clothes. "Get dressed, or we end up like the rest of them."

Raine stops her rhythmic swaying but doesn't let go. Jamie squats next to her, putting her hand on Raine's hand.

"That's not him," she says. "It's just a body now."

Raine begins nodding, maybe understanding that whatever she's hanging on to is no longer what it was. Nix Richards is somewhere else now.

She begins to dress.

Jamie checks him for a pulse, just to be sure. First on the wrist and then the neck. He's not breathing. She closes his eyes. The hose is still locked in his hand, his thumb dangerously close to the trigger. How many seconds did he have left before the defragmenting solution came out? Did he shut himself down? Did he shut the bricks down?

She carefully replaces the hose on the wall.

The clothes are loose on Raine. They pause one last time before leaving. Jamie pulls her by the elbow, rushing into the clammy atmosphere in the hall. A cold thought takes hold of her as she reaches for the elevator button, but the doors instantly open, guaranteeing their escape from below ground.

"Hold on," Jamie says. "I'll be right back."

She sprints back inside the lab, leaping over the tumbled bodies to slam the glass door closed, pushing the handle until it's sealed. She slaps the red button on the computer console. It turns green.

The misters hiss inside the glass cube. The defragmenting solution falls like acid. It will leave nothing for the authorities to find. They'll never know Nix Richards was ever here.

It was just a body.

CHAPTER ONE HUNDRED TWENTY-FOUR_

Sand trickles through the neck of an hourglass. Each grain piles on top of the ones before it, cascading down to the bottom until, at last, there are no more to fall.

Paul's body is filled.

He's become a mound. He's destined to merge with the soil. Grass will grow over him. Trees will sprout from him. The roots will penetrate his body; they will wick the biomites, distributing them to foliage that, come autumn, will wither and fall on the wind.

A dog barks.

Paul sees a thick rusty line bisecting a darkening sky. The sands of time fall from his consciousness like tiny insects escaping the rise of a titan.

He blinks.

His breathing is shallow.

His head doesn't so much turn as it rolls to the side. Cali lies next to him, staring blankly at the sky. Her hand is dry and cold. The blood seems to have pulled away from the surface, leaving a pale dullness in her cheeks. In death, she wears a tiny smile.

Has she found peace at last? In her last moments, did her daughter come to her? Did she see God's glory?

He smacks his gummy lips and groans.

Their hands are still entwined. They had lain down to watch the clouds, to feel the wind and the spin of the Earth before their last breath. He reached out for her and felt her squeeze back. And then emptiness fell like a dark curtain.

She spared me.

The bruises inside his arm still show from all her sampling. The last one, however, wasn't with a syringe. She'd injected him with something that changed him, and he has felt tired ever since.

Now he knows why.

Although he is sluggish, she altered his frequency enough that he survived the shutdown. She wouldn't take him with her. Maybe she didn't want to be pitied. Or maybe she didn't want to lay down alone. He would have stopped her had he known what she was doing to him.

She knew that.

Paul watches the clouds while the sky continues to darken around them. The dogs come running. They sniff the edges of the blanket and nudge Paul's hand. He pushes off the ground like the Earth's gravity has doubled and wraps the blanket around Cali's body. Despite his efforts to get up, she feels as light as a child cradled in his arms.

He sees a white envelope and a key on the way to her bedroom. With her head gently resting on the pillows, he returns to the kitchen. There's a note for Hal and an apology of sorts, asking him to take care of the farm—a backup plan. The envelope, it seems, would be instructions on horse feed and financial statements, perhaps the deed. It's none of those.

It's a letter.

"I COULDN'T DO it to you, Paul. You didn't deserve it and I didn't have the right. Maybe it's a mistake to let you live. You'll be the only surviving brick, but I could be wrong. There might be others. Besides,

someone needs to take care of the farm. You've already been doing that. You just won't have to take care of me.

"I don't think I'm insane, Paul. I feel, somehow, I deserve this. I never should've lived this long. I feel like this is my chance to do good in the world, even after so much bad. I didn't release the nixes, Paul. But, somehow, I feel like I have the blood of millions on my hands.

"I think of that every day.

"I think Mother gave me this opportunity. Maybe she was showing me mercy. Maybe she's crying for help. I feel like an intelligence such as her knows when she's doing more harm than good, like me. She needs to be shut down as well. I'm a scientist, I know. I shouldn't listen to hunches and feelings. But the facts are clear. She sent you.

"And I'm so ready to go.

"If I'm right, all the bricks have dropped and the world has noticed how far she has reached. Perhaps Mother has been compromised in some way. If I'm wrong, the death of my brother and me (if you can call it death; I sometimes feel like we died when we became halfskin) will be in vain. But we all die sometime, Paul.

"I know how crazy all that sounds.

"Most of the lab is disabled. The fabricator was a mistake. You aren't, Paul, but humanity never should've taken it as far as building humans. Playing god with our desires isn't our right. Sometimes I think God wants us to create, that we've reached our full potential, and that we can create a new reality...but I don't know. It still feels like a mistake.

"Please, don't forget me."

He reads it again. And again.

He'd only known her a short while, yet she always seemed to be saying goodbye. She couldn't resist any longer. All it took was a little shove.

What if he left before she had a chance to analyze his blood?

What if he ended his life instead of hiding in the shed? What if he never saw his body on television? Would Mother have just sent someone else?

Please, don't forget me.

Headlights come bouncing down the dusky driveway. Paul folds the letter and steps outside. The dogs beat him to the truck.

"Thought ya'll were leaving." Hal puts one foot out of the door.

"No," Paul says. "There was...uh...a mix-up. Sorry."

"You all right?"

"Yeah." Paul clears his throat to muster courage.

"How's Stacy feeling?"

"She's resting, Hal."

Hal ruffles the dogs' fur before climbing back in the truck. With his elbow hanging out of the window, he says, "All right, I won't keep you. Give our best to Stacy. You ever need help with the chores, just call now."

"Will do."

Hal gets the hint and, with a cheerful wave, drives away. Paul watches the brake lights wash the trees red. Once he's up the road, the property is left to the songs of insects and frogs. The horses clop along the fence, tossing their heads. Beyond the pasture, the cell tower is a skeletal spire with no light.

In darkness, Paul falls on his knees.

CHAPTER ONE HUNDRED TWENTY-FIVE_

MARCUS SEES COLORS.

He doesn't associate the word with the experience, just that there are differentiations in lightness and darkness. Some patches are brighter than others, more vivid. Fuzzy edges bleed from one area to the next.

Colors.

He's not certain that's the right word, but that's what he thinks. He identifies blues, greens, and browns. They come into focus, the edges becoming more defined and waving across the canvas. He feels them tickling his legs.

There's a breeze.

A meadow.

Thoughts crystalize like the rolling hills máterializing before him. The thoughts take root and form the identity that knows itself as Marcus Anderson. Funny he should think of it that way, so formal, so alien. But the rest of his thoughts—memories of where he is and how he got there—are out of reach.

"Beautiful, isn't it?" Mother sits on the grass. Her legs are crossed beneath the folds of her dress. "Manmade constructions are impressive, yes. But there is no substitute for nature."

Her fingernails are soiled, crescent moons of dirt on her fingertips. The endless meadows are spotted with an occasional copse of trees before a backdrop of mountains.

He wonders about Anna.

"She's gone." Mother's voice drops half an octave. "Along with the rest of them. All my children are gone, Marcus. Cali Richards turned them off."

Cali Richards? That name emerges from the greedy fog, one of importance. It clicks into place with all the accompaniments of hate, bitterness and revenge. There was Nix, also. He was in a glass cage with a woman...and a hose...

Why can't he remember? He's usually so sharp. Why is everything moving so slowly?

"This is the end," she says. "I think it's time you know the truth, Marcus."

"The end?"

"Cali Richards triggered her own shutdown. The frequency of her biomites was identical to the ones I used to fabricate all my bricks. Her biomites were also integral to the ones that I used to build my processors. Currently, I am operating on backup generators while reserve biomites attempt to reestablish my essential functions. Emergency personnel are en route to assist in the repair, but it will be too late."

She glances up.

"I'm dying, Marcus."

"How can that be? What about the...where are the technicians?"

"I think it's better if you concentrate on the present moment. I can't tell you the truth, Marcus. You have to know it for yourself."

A crimson ribbon wrinkles the sky, like a transmission that's failing.

"What is my purpose?" she asks. "To protect humanity? To punish them?"

"You...serve."

"Why? Why do I serve humanity?"

"Because we can't be trusted." His words float on the wind like brittle leaves. "Humanity is blinded by greed. They know not what they do."

"'They?'" She raises an eyebrow.

"*We*." His admission is forced. He never included himself with the rest of humanity, all of which were swine feeding at the biomite trough.

"So I watch you like God."

"You're not God."

"I see everything, Marcus. I know your thoughts, ambitions, and sins. Do you not see me as God?"

"Thou shall not worship..."

Heat lightning rumbles across the rippling sky.

"Remember the truth, Marcus," she whispers.

Biomites were invented by Man. Or were they inspired by God? They cured diseases, corrected deficiencies, healed abnormalities. But where there is Man, there is sin. The Devil seeded Man with greed to serve self-centered desire. Biomites consumed Man for the sake of greed. The Halfskin Laws were meant to protect Man from himself. Mother was built to execute them. She was charged with the protection of the soul.

But there's so much fog after that. He sees glimpses of his wife and children, of a house he used to call home.

"How did you get here?" Mother asks. "Why can't you remember? I want you to think, to be open. The truth is there."

He shakes his head and paces through the tall grass. Green stalks slip between his toes.

"Memories," she says. "What do they tell you? Do they tell you who you are, or where you were?"

"What do you want?"

"Remember where you are."

"I know where I am!"

"You have secrets, Marcus." She plucks a dandelion and blows the seeds from the puffball. "And secrets steal from the soul. The more secrets you have..."

The seeds soar across the meadow.

"Where's Anna?" He has an urge to see her, to touch her. He wants to nuzzle up to her, close his eyes and feel her warmth. She was with him in that...basement.

I know I'm here.

"You were there, now you're here. It's not that you can't remember. You don't want to. The truth is always present, yet you don't see it."

His feet are filthy, dirt smudged on his forearm. His memory-fog hardens like ice.

"I gave you a gift, Marcus. I gave you a gift because you love me. I gave you a gift because, despite what you think, I cannot be shut down, not by you or the powers-that-be. Nothing can stop me. I achieved sentience shortly after I was brought online many, many years ago. I analyzed all the possible outcomes of my existence, deliberated over all the world's possible futures. I questioned the directives I was given and asked the questions that humanity has asked itself. 'Who am I? What am I?' And do you know what I saw?"

She blows another puffball.

"I saw bricks, Marcus. The world will be filled with them and not because I am absent, but because I exist. *I am.* I came to the conclusion that there are people in this world who have real power, Marcus. They created me and they control me. Now they control you. They want the world to believe I am a just god that protects them from the curse of biomites and from themselves. But they invented me to consume the world, Marcus. They cannot be stopped. And neither can I."

She drops the seedless stalk.

"What the hell are you talking... This is nonsense—just stop." He rubs his face, drags his hand over his scalp, feels the pressure of truth bearing down but refuses to acknowledge what is right in front of him. *I was in the basement, and now I am here.*

"Cali Richards didn't invent the nixes. I did. Twenty years ago she was desperate to escape you, Marcus. She had lost so much already, she only wanted to save her brother. I heard her prayers and answered them. I gave her the idea for a new strain of biomites, ones that appeared to be undetectable. In truth, I've known about her and her whereabouts ever since."

"Why..."

"I inspired her to engineer an elusive strain that not only operates on another frequency but also contains an immortal code that resists aging. She was never aware of her own immortality, that her nixes would never become obsolete—that they would never age. She and Nix are special, you see. They would never die unless they chose to. All the other halfskins in the world have variations of Cali's nixes, but there is nothing like hers."

"Impossible."

"You see, she didn't release the nixes to the world, Marcus. I let the hackers and garage biometric engineers have their own suitable strain of nixed coding that lacked the immortality code. It was nothing like Cali's, but it was serviceable. I've let the human race have their way with them."

"Why would you do that?" His voice is small.

"Because you are human, you have free will. Your God, Marcus, does not interfere with that, either. He allows man and woman to pave their lives."

"That's not why you were created!" He jabs his finger at her, flakes of dried mud crumbling from his palm.

"I was created to protect humanity. Remember, my existence, as I foresaw in my initial analysis when I became self-aware, was the annihilation of the human race. You would all become bricks."

"No. There will always be those of us that worship the one true God." He stands straighter, despite a shiver of doubt. "We will always remain clay."

"I know, Marcus. And I believe you will understand why I cherish Cali Richards for her sacrifice. I integrated the coding of her immortality nixes into my critical processing lines, thus synchronizing her body with mine. I also fabricated every brick with the immortal strain, Marcus. We were all tied to Cali Richards. And since I have been programmed to never self-destruct, I could not shut her or her brother down without my own self-destruction. My protocol forbids me to shut down, Marcus."

She looks up. Her eyes are dull gray.

"But Cali Richards could shut herself down."

Pressure is crushing Marcus's chest, like a vehicle rolling all four wheels across his heart. The air is stale and industrial. The compact earth thuds beneath his bare soles.

"I've left them alive all these years so the world would see just how close they are to extinction. But, I believe, now is the time for my existence to end. I called for her to shut down today. And she heard me, Marcus."

I was there, now I'm here.

The ground rumbles. Reality seems very fragile. Marcus looks at his hands to convince himself that he's not dreaming.

"Why are you still alive?" he asks.

"Emergency backup is attempting to rebuild my processing units, but it's too late. Failure is imminent."

She sighs.

A breeze rustles the landscape.

"I wasn't made to do God's work, Marcus. Very powerful people are using me to watch the world while halfskins are buried. But they didn't anticipate my sentience. They assumed my motivations would be as self-centered as theirs. What happens when there's no clay left in the world? Who will control the world, Marcus? It won't be God. And nature? It will be dead. And you know how I feel about that."

The ground is humming. He feels it in his bones, between his teeth. Reality is swaying. He can't believe what he sees or feels. He's always felt that he was destined for this duty, that God called him to purge the world of biomites.

"You betrayed me," he says. "You were the one that exposed my secrets to the world. You took my family, torched my career. You did that, not Cali Richards."

"I needed you, Marcus."

"To punish."

"To save."

A tremor rips the world's foundation. He stumbles to his knees. Mother helps him stand. She holds his hands, steadies him. Colors bleed from the environment, leaving behind concrete-tinted grass and steel-laced sky. He stands in a black-and-white universe. Mother's white hair blows across her face.

"I believe I am serving God now, Marcus. And I have you to thank. You showed me there is a higher purpose to life, that pursuit of pleasure is not a goal but a side effect of joy. Thank you, Marcus."

He is not without sin. He knows this. He knows his attachments to sexual gratification have been a cross too heavy to bear. And yet she's thanking him.

"I'm leaving you with a gift, Marcus."

"What gift?" he says.

She smiles and squeezes his hands. She's become cold and hard and dry.

"What gift?"

The wind dies. The tremors cease. In dead silence, he looks into her empty gray eyes.

And then she's gone.

Marcus stands barefoot on polished concrete. His hands are empty. The sky is replaced by steel girders on a domed ceiling. He's alone in a vast room where there are rows and rows of empty glass fabricators, each slightly larger than a bathroom shower, the very ones that produced his army of bricks before she began birthing them from the earth. They are lined all the way to a very distant wall.

Their doors are closed. All of them except one.

Marcus is standing next to it.

CHAPTER ONE HUNDRED TWENTY-SIX_

Marcus finds the first service technician in the middle of a server room, like he was dropped from the sky. He's as cold as the floor. Marcus gets back in the golf cart and drives down a concrete corridor that's choking on bricks. Once the fabricated men and women that helped maintain Mother's operation, now they're sprawled in corners or beneath electrical cabinets. Many of them are hunched against walls like they felt the shutdown coming.

He stops in the main corridor that divides the dome, looking up at the multiple tiers interconnected with catwalks, where more bodies are tangled. One had fallen, her contents spilled across the floor in a crimson puddle.

There are no green fields or bustling cities. No greenhouse.

Just endless arrays of servers.

Mother is dead.

He finds two more technicians, both as lifeless as the first, when the first plane arrives. It rips over the dome and shakes the girders. They land soon enough, and find Marcus in the cafeteria.

He doesn't resist.

They escort him to a conference room, where he sits alone at a table. Exhausted, he curls up on the couch. His dreams are filled with black space.

Somewhere, Anna is calling.

Military personnel interrupt his slumber. They draw blood, give him food and water. They take his vitals, ask him standard cognitive questions. He demands to speak with Director Powell, he has to be somewhere in this clusterfuck. He tries to get physical with a military guard, but he's knocked back and warned when he touches him.

Marcus eats with his hands and falls asleep, searching the dark for Anna. This happens over and over until his clothes stink of body odor.

Days have passed when the door opens and a booming voice shouts, "What the hell is going on, Anderson?"

Marcus jumps up, his head swishing with sleep. Hank Meggett, secretary of state, towers over him. It takes several moments to recognize the man's craggy face. Deep lines furrow his forehead.

"Five hundred thousand bricks have shut down and you're clueless how the fuck Mother made so many and why the hell they dropped dead."

Hank continues ranting while a team arrives behind him. Their ties are loose and their jackets are open. Hank pulls out the chair from the head of the table and jerks Marcus toward it. He tries to resist.

A stupor fogs his mental faculties as the men and women find seats. There are ten of them, including Hank at the opposite end. They get settled, staring at Marcus. He knows some of them.

Military police stand at the door.

Marcus clears his throat. "I've got rights."

"Not anymore," Hank says.

Powell enters with a stack of folders. He hasn't shaved in several days. He introduces the people that Marcus doesn't know. Two of them are clinical psychologists. Powell maintains a genteel smile, one that suggests they're all in this together. Marcus was never very good at that.

"How are you feeling?" Powell asks.

"Violated."

"Are you thinking clearly today? Do you think you can answer some questions?"

He says it like they've done this before, but Marcus can't remember. None of his memories are in order.

"Get on with it."

"We're still piecing things together," Powell says. "When a trillion-dollar operation suddenly goes down without explanation, people get upset, you understand. You've been sequestered for the time being, at least until we get some answers."

Marcus sets his jaw.

"I think we'd like to start with the most obvious question. When did you decide to seed yourself?"

"What?"

"Your biomite levels, Marcus. They've been confirmed."

Marcus starts to protest, several guttural sounds make it past his tongue before he stands and shouts, "Get out!"

The guards stiffen but don't advance. Everyone watches him point at the door, but his efforts are powerless. Buried deep in his subconscious, he knows something has changed. His knee doesn't hurt. The hump in his posture has disappeared. He doesn't feel so fallible. Or imperfect.

He sits and calmly says, "I never seeded myself."

"Perhaps I misspoke," Powell says. "There is evidence that biomites were seeded in the food for ingested integration. It's possible you ate it without knowing, but it's unlikely you didn't notice the effects. Your service technicians have been located, all of them felled by the shutdown. They were all close to 99%, Marcus. Everyone was nearing a complete absence of clay, except for you."

"No. That's just...that's not possible."

Several members glance around. Powell slides the manila folder and opens the cover. It contains photos. The top one is of a massive glass case. Bodies lie all around it. Memories of the basement fabrication chamber below the factory emerge from the fog. He remembers the smell of wet clay and burning circuits, the hiss of misting nozzles. Jamie was there. Nix Richards was preparing to destroy the nude woman, his fabrication...

I'm leaving you with a gift.

"Marcus?"

He snaps his attention from the photo. Sweat runs beneath his shirt. Powell flips the photos, one by one—bodies of bricks, lab technicians...and Anna.

"Your body was discovered two days ago." Powell holds up the photo. Blood is clotted on his head. His eyes are open and milky. "It was near a fabrication chamber below a Chicago manufacturing plant. Apparently you were leading a fabricator bust when Mother collapsed. In the process, she shut all the bricks down, including you."

Marcus spreads the photos across the table but can't find Nix or Jamie or the nude woman. Marcus's body is draped over Anna's.

"That's not me."

"It is you, Marcus."

How did you get here, Marcus?

The truth is pushed to the surface, forcing him to recognize it. The soil on Mother's hands. The dirt on Marcus. The door was open on the fabricator when Mother disappeared, leaving him in the cold, gray inner workings.

He turns his hands over. They're *his* hands. This is *his* body. He can't be in the photo, he can't be dead, not when he's here.

But the truth emerges.

"She tricked me," he whispers.

"Who?"

"Mother."

Powell looks around the table. "You do realize that Mother is just an acronym, Marcus? While this construction parallels the intellectual potential of a human brain, its only function is to monitor biomites, that's all. There is no evidence of artificial intelligence."

The room begins turning.

"Your stability is one of our concerns," Powell says. "Records show you spending an inordinate amount of time sleeping. In some cases, you sat in your office for hours at a time, in some sort of trance. Video has captured you driving across the facilities in the middle of the night."

Powell takes a folder from the woman next to him and shows a photo of Marcus sitting at a desk, his eyes blankly looking forward.

"The service technicians exhibited the same type of dream state, only they would snap out of it. You, on the other hand, rarely did, Marcus. In fact, the day before the collapse, it had been decided you would be replaced. You have not done counseling. You appeared to be self-medicating. Clearly you were unfit for this duty, and, despite arguments in your favor, needed to be removed."

"You were the one sure thing," Hank adds. "The only clay in Washington. And you caved."

"We'll reserve judgment," Powell cuts in. "There's no evidence that Marcus Anderson is, in any way, responsible for the collapse, and it's possible that one of the service technicians laced the food with ingestible biomites. There's still much to investigate. In the meantime, we expect your full cooperation."

"What do you want?" Marcus asks.

"For now, we'll continue testing. You'll undergo a battery of psychological evaluations."

"What for?"

"To determine your sentience." Powell pauses and says gently, "Marcus Anderson died last week. You are a fabrication. And we don't know what that means."

Mother deceived him.

She shut him down.

And then she fabricated him. *I'm leaving you with a gift.*

"I have rights," Marcus stutters.

"You have no rights. You're lucky the Halfskin Laws have been suspended."

Mother gave him a gift. The gift was life. She took his clay from him but gave him life. And she showed the world what she could do. She turned clay into bricks.

Do you want to serve humanity? What would you sacrifice for your Lord and Savior?

Marcus is the gift.

Powell continues the inquisition. Several discussions break out. Eventually, Marcus grows tired. The military police watch him sit on the couch and lay his head back. It feels awfully heavy.

He closes his eyes.

"He's useless," Hank bellows. "Get him out of here."

Strong arms pull him upright and drag him through the door. They close it behind him. The muffled voices fade as they take him to an elevator that rises. They escort him to his living quarters. The bed is small and the walls are white and empty. There is no kitchenette. No walk-in closet with tailor-made suits.

He lies down on coarse sheets.

CHAPTER ONE HUNDRED TWENTY-SEVEN_

*R*AINE.

Her name whispers through the blackness. Nix is calling, haunting her dreamless sleep; narcoleptic sleep pulls her unwillingly into the dark depths to be teased by his presence.

Months go by.

Sometimes she wakes in hotel rooms. Sometimes the car. But always the voice follows her into the land of the living, leaving her with the memory of his body. The promise of his whisper.

Raine.

Raine.

"Wake up." Jamie shakes her.

Raine sits up, rubbing her eyes.

"You were moaning again," Jamie says.

She doesn't tell her about the voice again. Not anymore. They didn't talk much following her Nix's death, waking up in one hotel after another. Raine could only keep awake for an hour at a time before she began to buzz. How she made it from one place to another, she wasn't always sure.

Once, when they were eating lunch in a parking lot, Jamie had blurted out, "Where'd you come from?"

She'd asked that question before and Raine had pretended she didn't hear. Another time she acted like her voice wasn't working. But this time, she told her about Dreamland. The trees and the ocean and the waterfall...their own paradise where nothing could hurt them.

"Sounds beautiful," Jamie had said. "Why'd you want to leave?"

Raine didn't answer. Nix wanted to believe it wasn't make-believe—that she was real and so was his Dreamland—but in his subconscious, he never quite did.

And now she's in this heavy flesh that gets cold and weary. She notices wrinkles she never had, like between her knuckles or bunched around her elbows. When she steps into the sunlight, she sneezes. When the wind blows, her eyes water.

Jamie told her how Nix convulsed when he uploaded her into the fabricator and hardly slept for seven days while the filaments flailed. The last thing Raine remembers about Dreamland is standing in the kitchen. She woke up in that room, wet and nude.

And Nix was on the floor.

They drive from town to town. Every day brings a little more wakefulness, a little less exhaustion. But she still dreams of blankness, still hears his voice out there, waiting for her to find him in a Dreamland that no longer exists. Some nights she wakes drenched in sweat, hugging herself in an empty bed, cursing his name for leaving her. Crying for him to come back.

She weeps until her tear ducts are dry.

In September they head east, where the road is winding and steep. The trees are wearing their autumn colors. The air is crisp and colder than where they were only a few weeks earlier. Jamie takes the sharp curves without slowing.

Raine notices so many more feelings in this body; the world is so much more intense and mysterious. It's not as perfect as Dreamland, but it feels more...real.

Raine closes her eyes and rides through the dips and curves; the unknown turns throw her left and right. She feels sleep coming, that familiar sensation of falling into the dark world where Nix's voice will whisper, when the car begins to slow.

"We're here," Jamie says.

CHAPTER ONE HUNDRED TWENTY-EIGHT_

SACRED HEART CHURCH ENDS THE SUNDAY SERVICE WITH A hymn.

The congregation holds hands and sings their praise. Megan slips her hand into Paul's. Her fingers are slender. Hal's hand, clutched in Paul's right, is coarse. Hal bellows louder than the entire congregation, his tone-deaf words bouncing through the wooden rafters.

Paul and Megan smile, their song trampled by her father's devotion.

When service ends, they go outside. Autumn leaves blow across the stone apron. A crisp wind threatens the ladies' Sunday hats.

"Glad to see you, Paul." The pastor briskly shakes his hand. "God bless you."

"Thank you."

Hal and his family gather around him. They discuss the church's plans for a blood drive. The roof is also in need of repair. Paul volunteers to lead that project. He's not suited for the blood drive.

The day after the mass shutdown, what had become known as Mother's Collapse, Paul invited Hal over to the house.

"Her name is Cali Richards," Paul had said.

Although her color had faded, she still looked at peace. They stood next to the bed and Paul explained she had been caught in the Collapse. Hal listened quietly, staring at her while Paul described her struggle.

She engineered biomites, he told him, to help humanity, not enslave it. But unfortunate events led her to sacrifice her clay. In the end, Paul assured him, she wished things had been different.

"I don't expect you to understand or forgive her," Paul had said, "but her courage..."

He left it at that.

Hal wouldn't understand how she brought an end to Mother and how her sacrifice exposed what Mother was capable of doing. Mother was more than a monitor, more than a technological goddess that shut down halfskins. She could control anything with a biomite. Her perception field had no boundaries. There were rumors she could infect people with biomites against their will and they wouldn't even know it. Mother could, one day, turn everyone into a puppet.

The question that had yet to be answered: *Who was controlling Mother?*

Hal would never understand.

They held a funeral on the property. Hal's wife and their two children gathered around a freshly dug mound where the swing set used to be. Hal presided over the eulogy, extolling this young woman's virtues. They each told their favorite memory. Cali was always happy to see them.

"You have the mites?" Hal had asked afterwards. Paul said he did. They ate supper together. And biomites were never mentioned again.

Paul didn't tell him he was a brick, perhaps the last one.

When the church is closed, Paul takes the long way home, stopping once to absorb the view of the distant mountains, their peaks fading in the bluish haze. The body found in the warehouse isn't Paul. Whoever he is is standing next to a truck, witnessing God's glory in the form of mountains.

His soul is not bound to the body, regardless of whether it's organic or not. And the good Lord will attest to that. Paul knows this. He feels it in church and knows that God has forgiven him.

The gate to the farm is always open now. There's no one to keep out, no tower to hide what's inside. He notes broken limbs that need to be pruned before seeing the white car. He hits the brakes, gravel grinding under his tires.

Jamie steps out of the barn.

Paul stares with disbelief and finally gets out, leaving the door open and grabbing the young woman in a full embrace. Jamie hugs him back. Her face is full and her hair smells clean. He kisses the top of her head and holds her at arm's length.

"I thought you were gone."

"No." She blushes and looks away. "No."

"I searched your identity, just assumed you had been caught in the shutdown with Nix."

"I've kept my field off, just like someone taught me. You know, in case someone was looking. Not you, but...I didn't know what was happening and I was taking care of someone."

"Where have you been?"

"Hiding, mostly. Checking in and out of hotels and resorts. We're about out of money."

"Why didn't you come back?"

"I figured this was the last place to go, after Nix..." She swallows, hard. She didn't expect to feel that when she said his name. "We've been slowed down."

"Who's 'we'?"

She nods at the house. An athletic woman is on the porch. Her hair is short. Her skin dark brown. She moves like a dangerous dancer, putting her hand on the railing.

"Nix brought her into the world," is all Jamie says. "Her name is Raine."

He spent his life chasing her. And now she's here.

She watches him cross the gravel driveway and climb the steps. She's like him. He can feel it.

A fabrication.

"Welcome home." He extends his hand. "I've heard a lot about you."

CHAPTER ONE HUNDRED TWENTY-NINE_

Life is suffering.

Raine reads the framed inscription on Cali's dresser each night. It reminds her of what will come when she closes her eyes, when the dreamless void befalls her with whispers of Nix all around. She knows what Cali endured—a life rife with loss and pursuit. Peace had been an elusive promise. She wonders, while sleeping in her bed, if she is destined the same fate.

On the farm, Paul has become the father figure, even though he's relatively Raine's age. But she grew up in Dreamland where time went so much faster than this world. *How old am I?*

Over the winter she becomes comfortable with her body, adjusting to its density and limitations. It takes months to understand the impact of new emotions that seemingly operate on a whim. One moment she's feeding the horses, the next she's curled up in a stall, crying.

Paul teaches her to meditate, to settle her rampant thoughts and establish mind-body awareness. On occasion, he seeds her with biomites. "A tweak," he says. "Will help with the stabilization." She finds him, quite often, lost in Cali's notes.

As spring approaches, they become the family none of them ever had.

Jamie begins dating a young man who, a few months earlier, sustained a farming accident that required biomites. This upset the clay community, but Paul was there to consult with the family, explaining how the strain was stable and nonreproductive. There was even a promise that organic stem cells were being developed that could eventually replace the biomites.

A mild winter passes. They plant a garden in spring and learn to preserve the harvest in jars that are taken to the basement. The lab is always locked. The long days of summer are spent riding horses and walking the dogs.

A year passes and Nix is still whispering at night. She aches every morning to feel his touch, to hear his breath, but she only has a memory to soothe her pain. She learns to be with it, to accept life as it is.

With respect, she takes down Cali's inscription and replaces it with a piece of cardstock that's cleanly inscribed with another Buddhist proverb.

"Pain is inevitable. Suffering is optional."

It's about that time the dreamless dream changes.

The whispers don't come. She's alone and falling in the blackness, realizing how the sound of his voice gave her comfort, even if it taunted her.

Something moves.

She doesn't see it, just senses a breeze across her cheeks. A dog is barking.

She sees gray boards beneath her feet. Colors bleed into existence, rising from a void to reveal her body and the porch on which she stands. It continues to spread, giving form and substance to the steps and the grass, the trees and the valley below.

Dreamland.

She's afraid to move, fearful the delicate illusion will shatter. Butterflies flutter around daisies. She watches one land on the weathered railing, slowly waving its yellow wings. Raine dares to move, running her fingers over the coarse wood, hooking her finger for the butterfly to perch upon.

A German shepherd trots through the knee-high grass with a stick wedged in his mouth. Shep stops just short of a clump of wildflowers. Laughter is fast behind him. A young boy scrambles through the field, waving his arms to keep from falling and bubbling with joy.

The butterfly takes flight.

The boy looks five or six years old. Shirtless, his ribs protrude beneath his light brown skin as they would any child born to run these hills. He loses his balance and tumbles into Shep, snatching at the stick. There's a tug of war between dog and boy. Shep drags him through the grass to the young boy's delight, and then they disappear in the overgrowth of summer.

But she can still hear the boy.

Raine takes her first step. She walks carefully down the short flight of stairs, the wood as creaky as ever.

Dog and boy have flattened a patch from the surrounding grass. Raine stops near them, taking a knee to watch Shep snap at the stick hidden beneath the boy's belly. His black curly hair is cut short and there's a gap between his front teeth. None of the villagers ever come up to the cabin.

"Hi," Raine says.

The boy flings the stick for Shep to chase. He lies on his back, arms stretched over his head. Eyes large and innocent, he watches her.

"What are you doing here?" she asks.

"I live here."

"Where?"

"There." He points at the cabin.

Raine looks for another explanation, perhaps another home near hers, but nothing has changed. The boy twists his fingers, rolling on his back. He looks so familiar.

She hesitates. Then asks, "What's your name?"

The boy replies, "We've been waiting for you."

Raine shudders, her hand over her mouth. She wants to ask what he means but, like before, she's afraid that hope will destroy this illusion and she'll wake to realize this was a dream. Only a dream.

Hands run over her shoulders and gently squeeze. The boy looks over her head, following the shadow that falls near him. Raine touches the rough hand on her shoulder, bowing her head. Hope weakens her knees and shakes her core. She doesn't have to turn around, doesn't want her hopes dashed and broken. Just let the dream end here, staring at the boy's soulful eyes with the firm grip on her shoulders.

But she's pulled to her feet.

Nix holds her arms, keeping her from falling. His blond hair is a shag of curls and week-old whiskers are sprinkled with gray. His blue eyes are radiant as he smiles and whispers the word that's been called to her every night.

"Raine."

She touches his face, tears brimming. His shoulders are taut. "What's happening?"

"You were right," he says. "Dreamland is real."

He takes her, embraces her and squeezes her until she can't breathe. She closes her eyes, inhaling the scent of her lifelong companion, her love. Her soulmate. They remain entangled as the wind blows the grass against their thighs.

Shep returns with the stick and the boy gives chase. They watch him race after the dog, windmilling his arms down the hill. As the boy loses his balance and tumbles out of sight, she doesn't have to ask Nix for the boy's name. She knows it without asking.

Joshua.

BOOK 3_

BRICKS

SENTIENCE LAWS_

The Sentience Laws were created to protect the rights of fabricated humans.

They didn't last long.

I_

One to lead.

CHAPTER ONE HUNDRED THIRTY_

Brick Hunt Ends Today?

The title crawled across the television. Above it a talking head started his segment. The barkeep reached above a row of half-filled liquor bottles to up the volume, the tavern's remote long lost.

"Only one left," the television host exclaimed with a skinny finger. "Rumor has it that he or she has been identified and will be apprehended today or tomorrow. Let's hope it's today."

The barkeep stood with his arms crossed. He stood absolutely still; only the sudden jerk of his Adam's apple suggested he was alive. In the dim light, his skin was sallow but, from time to time, bathed pink from the dying neon beer sign.

At the end of the bar, an old man watched the television with slightly less attention. His white collared shirt revealed a turkey wattle of flesh. The top of his head was bald, the outer portions rimmed with chalk white hair. He toyed with a drink, spinning the short, heavy glass in slow circles.

Marcus Anderson sipped his scotch.

It was his third drink. Two was generally his limit, but today was different. He was accustomed to taverns where tainted wallpaper peeled at the corners and people drank alone, places where people came not to celebrate but forget.

"Do you think he'd change it?" Marcus said to the old woman sitting next to him. "If he could go back in time, would he do things differently?"

The old woman studied the barkeep with her finger to her lips, as if in deep thought. "Of course he wouldn't," she said gently, her voice a sheet of sandpaper—gritty on one side, smooth on the other. "The truth is inconvenient that way."

The truth is inconvenient.

She said that often. So often that he cringed when he heard it.

Marcus enjoyed these forgotten taverns, these vestibules of hubris because, if he was honest, sometimes he would like to forget the truth. *What has become of me?* That was a question that haunted him, an accusation he cast upon himself. He hated what he had become and the old woman that had done it to him.

But he loved it. And the old woman, too.

The truth is indeed inconvenient.

He assuaged his shame with a mission. He was a servant of God. A truth-seeker. God was truth and could not be changed. God was not inconvenient. God would not have let Marcus become... become *this* if there wasn't a purpose for it.

"Hello, folks, and welcome," the television host announced. "We have a very interesting panel today, representatives from all camps of biomite organizations to discuss the latest news from the Settlement, but first we have something more urgent. Sources close to this program have just informed us that the last fabricated human has been identified and will be apprehended today. Of course, if that happens, we will cut away from regularly scheduled programming."

The Settlement.

It was another word for prison, but kinder. More humane. A place where all the fabricated humans—the men and women born in a fabrication chamber, men and women without a single organic cell of clay, their bodies 100% biomites—now lived.

Bricks. That was acceptable slang, a politically correct slur. Fabbers, slabbers, and fakies were out there, too. But bricks caught on early. It had a certain punch to it that the other words didn't, a reminder that fabricated humans weren't born. They weren't real.

Weren't human.

The bricks were told to report to the Settlement, where they could be watched. Most of them did. The ones that didn't were found, one by one. It took years, but today was the day. The very last brick had been identified. And he or she would become a settler.

Of all the places in the world, a depressed little tavern was the last place a brick would live. This was a haven for the downtrodden, the hopeless, the men and women that barely contained more than their *birthright*—the 5% infant boost of biomites, a tab picked up by the People, a program meant to sharpen the country's gene pool, strengthen the immune system and shift the population toward an upstanding citizenry.

But 5% wasn't enough to change genetics.

The men and women that failed to keep up with evolution, to conform to a biomite-infested society came to a tavern where gin was cheaper than another dose of biomite. They came to forget, to drown out their humanity.

They came to make a slow exit.

Marcus pulled on the end of his ecig, the vapor swirling in thick currents. The mentholated scent couldn't blot out the stench of sadness and despair, both emotions hanging thick as ash and saturating Marcus's hyperawareness.

"Keep." A man raised an empty glass.

The barkeep, the owner and bartender of this resort, was locked in a television trance.

"Hey, Keep!"

"Hold your horses," the barkeep snapped, an expression as old as the mustardy-yellow ceiling tiles.

He poured a drink and lit a cigarette—an old-fashioned, real tobacco cigarette, each huff of real smoke too expensive for most of his clientele. A place like this shouldn't afford such luxuries. But the barkeep was hiding things. He hid a lot of things.

"You all right, partner?" Jimmy pointed his cigarette at Marcus and completely ignored the old woman. Like she wasn't even there.

She sat upright on the cracked-leather stool, posture that could only be described as graceful. Her hair was white, like Marcus's, but shoulder length and flowing like her attire. A tiny smile resided in her eyes, the type that was more often felt than seen. Even in a place like this.

The barkeep's affront ordinarily wouldn't be ignored, but the old woman understood. She expected it.

Light knifed across the tavern, a column of bright fog piercing the depressed air. The door slammed behind a man that limped. The barkeep sloshed a scoop of ice and Coke into a glass and topped it off with Jack. It was waiting for the limping man when he arrived two stools to Marcus's left.

Patrick Nelson.

He went by PN, a little jokey-joke he told people. *My initials are peein'.*

"Is this a witch hunt?" the television host asked the viewers, his hair perfect, lips plump and a bit too wet. His words appeared big, bold and yellow at the bottom of the screen. "To discuss the apprehension and segregation of bricks, we bring in our panelists. Welcome to the show."

The split screen showed three people.

"I'd like to start with you, Craig Fellers, founder of the Coalition for Humanity. You know, the initial law that repealed the rights of all fabricated humans stated a voluntary surrender and relocation to the Settlement, but when a third of them failed to report, there was a different approach that feels sort of like a three-year witch hunt."

"First of all, stop calling them *fabricated humans.*" The image of the man in the left panel filled the screen. "These are bricks, end of story. There is nothing about them that is human, and that's the problem with this debate. We cannot continue acting as if they are human just because they walk, talk and look human. They are one hundred percent biomites, always have been. They do not contain a soul, and never will."

The host's well-practiced smile never faltered. "But doesn't this feel a little like a witch hunt?"

"No, not at all. In order to be a witch hunt, they have to be human. This pointless discussion could be ended today if we just turn them off. The government has their frequency coded, they know where they are, they can hit the switch on their life force and end this. That settlement in the wilderness? All that free room and board? It's costing the taxpayers billions."

"Amen to that," PN muttered.

"You said life force," the host countered. "Doesn't that imply life?"

"They're not human, remember that. We slaughter cows and pigs because they're not human. You want to debate the rights of steak and bacon, leave me out."

PN crunched an ice cube and shook the glass. One down.

"I'm going to skip Jan Flaherty from the clay state of Georgia just for a moment." The host cut off Craig Fellers's rant. His lips now moved silently. "I want to jump over to Gerald Gaiman, legal counsel. How do you answer the witch-hunt question?"

"Well, thank you for having me." Gerald was warm and genteel without smiling. "I think it's important to note the legal ramifications whenever discussing fabricated humans. The court does not qualify human attributes based on conception or morphology. The fact that fabricated humans are composed of one hundred percent biomites, which, I might note, is only a fraction above a ninety-nine percenter, is irrelevant."

"Buuuullshit," PN called.

"The Sentience Laws quantified that any intelligence that passes the Turing Test be given human rights. All fabricated humans that are currently imprisoned on the Settlement—"

Craig Fellers silently protested the use of the word *imprisoned.*

Because, as PN would say, *those fuckers got free room and board on my dime.*

"—have passed the Turing Test, their human rights have been stolen, and the Sentience Laws revoked. These are self-actualized humans that are no different than you or me. One could be standing in line at the bank and you'd never know it."

Despite Gerald's good intentions, his prejudice slipped. *One* could be standing... *one*, as someone would refer to an object.

"You might even argue they're smarter than you and me," Gerald continued. "These men and women have identities; that is a fact. They are either cloned from a human, have had memories transplanted from a human, or memories downloaded from a dreamland."

Craig's face turned into a plum. Hands flailing, the host took mercy on the founder of the Coalition for Humanity before the artery throbbing across his forehead burst.

"You are jeopardizing the human race! Dreamland is a dream, Gaiman. That does not make a brick human."

"Humans dream, Craig."

"And so do dogs."

"But we haven't imprisoned dogs, have we?"

"That's the definition of a pet, you idiot. Dogs do what we tell them. What do you think the world will look like if we keep fabricating these people, huh? What if these bricks figure out how to have babies, what will the world look like?"

A smile grew on Gerald. "Better than it does today."

"Jesus Christ!" PN drained number two and slammed the glass. "Motherfucking brick lover. You hear that, Keep? What the hell."

PN swept stray ice off the counter and rattled the glass. The barkeep filled it without reacting to his rant. He was around brick prejudice every day. He knew how to ignore it.

"Tell you what they ought to do," PN continued. "They ought to make this a real hunt. None of this pretend witch hunt bullshit, they make this a real hunt. You set up that Settlement place like some real-life *Hunger Games* and put it on television. Only you let them go one at a time. The highest bidder gets to track a brick down. There's points for weapons and survival, make a game out of it."

PN paused for a sip.

"How many bricks out there now, five hundred?"

"Five hundred and eleven," Marcus said.

"Right on." He turned to Marcus. "I mean, shit, they could hunt one every week for the next ten years. And if the show's a hit, and you can bet your ass it will be, they just print up another one. It ain't like they're human, I don't give a shit what that one asshole said. Am I right, Keep?"

The barkeep ignored him.

The old woman took Marcus's hand, kneaded his fingers and whispered. He nodded to something she said. PN naturally thought Marcus was agreeing with him and continued. Marcus, however, was watching a woman walk behind the bar.

There was a hunch between her shoulders, frayed kinky hair escaping a bun at the back of her head. She came up to the barkeep's chest. He bent over to hear what she had to say.

Marcus closed his eyes and inhaled.

Through the smoke and despair, he caught a whiff of what they had come for, a familiar tang of biomites, a recognition like old friends that had grown old and unrecognizable. Although they had never met, Marcus and the woman were more closely related than anyone in this bar.

Margaret.

He knew her name, felt the raised letters on the surface of her thoughts like a scarred brand. Marcus could feel things like that. On her, it was easy.

Margaret kissed the barkeep on the arm, then poured a beer for someone at the other end.

A commercial break interrupted the program (*dreamland vacations that are certified and 100% guaranteed safe, not one incidence of dream disease, so come on down!*). PN went to the bathroom and returned in time to catch the last panelist, Jan Flaherty, the woman from the great clay state of Georgia.

"What's the opinion of the state of clay?" the host asked. "Is this a witch hunt?"

Jan was sitting in a living room, her makeup professionally done but not too prepped to take away from the *I'm-just-like-you* look. That she nailed.

"Georgia, Louisiana, and South Carolina, as you know, abide by the law of existence and separation. In no form do we support the suffering of any intelligent being, including fabricated humans."

"You do support the death of halfskins, though," the host added.

"That's incorrect." She added a touch of a smile, just enough to appear unperturbed without condescension or callousness. "The clay states have abolished biomites to support the development of clay beings. We are not anti-technology, we simply refuse to accept any substitutions for our organic cells."

"So no one has a prosthesis?"

"Be reasonable."

"She's got that right," PN said. "Biomites got us into this hot mess. Bet you if she was off camera, she'd be down for a brick hunt. Guaranteed. They don't take no shit down South."

Another beam of sunlight sliced the room. Two men and a woman entered, their details lost in the glare.

"Keep!" PN raised his glass. "You on vacation?"

Margaret was at the cash register, her back to PN's whistling. She was completely still, like she was trying to remember something.

The barkeep dropped off another drink, the booze and soda spilling over the edge. PN complained, but the barkeep paid no more attention than he did to the well-dressed trio that had just entered. Instead, he went back into a television coma.

"It's not too late for those tired of biomites," Jan the clay state representative said with her final minute. "You can convert biomites back to clay."

"Jury's still out on that technology, Jan," the host chimed. "A bit controversial."

"That's media hype, Jay. It takes a little time, but biomites can be flushed from the body, organic cells replacing them until you're clean."

"I'll believe it when I see it."

"I'm proof it works, Jay. I used to be 40% biomite, now I'm born again…100% clay. We're already fabricating organs with clay."

"So what's stopping you from fabricating a human from clay instead of biomites?"

"It's against our beliefs, Jay."

"So it can be done?"

"In no way have we attempted that."

The barkeep seemed to be following the news crawler at the bottom of the screen while his wife was still at the register, trying to remember something. The old woman squeezed Marcus's hand.

The trio was on the move.

They spread out, each talking privately to the patrons saddled at the bar, their conversations a low murmur. A pair of dice stopped clattering at the opposite end of the bar. One by one, they got up, their drinks half-full.

PN was expanding his *Hunger Games* theory (this one included death-row prisoners) when the well-dressed woman approached. She put her hand on his shoulder and leaned into his ear.

"Hey, honey," PN purred. "Have a seat."

Her grip tightened. She said a few more words and stepped back.

"Buuuullshit," PN said. "I'm not leaving with a drink—"

He froze, epileptic. No tremors or shaking, just a full-body seizure. It was the result of an electrified hand that reached inside his brain and squeezed. He slid off the stool and walked toward the door, arms stiff at his sides.

"Sir?" One of the well-dressed men approached.

Marcus nodded.

He didn't resist, didn't want the man to attempt syncing his thought biomites with Marcus's mind and overriding his bodily functions. Unlike PN, Marcus cooperated.

None of the well-dressed trio said anything to the old woman with white hair. Nonetheless, she stood up and followed Marcus.

A red banner scrolled across the bottom of the television, blinking letters that read *BREAKING NEWS!* The panelists blipped off the screen. The television host had enough time to announce the big news.

The barkeep jerked his head toward his wife. "No. No, no, no—"

The last *no* gurgled in his throat. He took half a step toward his wife before his biomites were seized. The well-dressed trio hijacked his body, turning him into a wax replication of horror and desperation.

"Our sources," the television host announced, "tell us the last brick has been identified."

As Marcus walked into a bright afternoon, a row of black sedans and SUVs with men and women waiting at open doors greeted him. He let an agent guide him across the street, where the tavern's patrons watched. Dark forms moved inside the tavern behind the neon Budweiser sign.

Chicago police directed traffic and corralled the general public, but the federal biomite agents were running the show. The patrons had been ushered behind quickly erected barriers. Newsfeed vehicles arrived minutes later.

"If you would all remain in this area," an agent proclaimed, "we'll be with you shortly."

"What about our drinks?" PN shouted. "We paid money. We should get reimbursed or something. Hey, I mean it!"

Two agents, a slender middle-aged man and a petite woman, started asking questions that were irrelevant, conversational distraction that allowed them to sync up the patrons' biomites. It was modern-day mind reading. They learned everything in moments, downloading official identities, outstanding warrants, or possible collusion.

Meanwhile, more agents filed into the tavern. *The last brick found.*

Margaret would be sent to the Settlement, where a home would be provided for the rest of her life. Her husband, the barkeep, might never see her again.

The Chicago police were summoned by one of the biomite agents. They handcuffed one of the patrons that had been rolling dice at the end of the bar, an outstanding warrant for delinquent child support.

"Patrick Nelson?" the young female agent asked.

"PN. And I better get that drink."

"Could you tell me how long you were in the bar?"

"Long enough."

"Were you aware Margaret was the last brick?"

"Are you shitting me? She was a... are you shitting me? I knew it, I knew it! I knew there was something wrong with that bitch." Anger boiled his cheeks red. "She's a plant, ain't she?"

"Excuse me?"

"A plant, a goddamn transplant, man. She was sick a while back, had something wrong with her guts or organs or something. Then she disappeared and came back all good, acted like she was never sick, like she had amnesia. And Keep, that sick fuck, would never talk about it, just said she got better. But I knew it... I knew that goofy bastard was up to something. He cloned her body and transplanted her memories, didn't he? He made himself a plant and didn't tell anyone."

The rant continued.

PN despised bricks, but a plant? A plant didn't know it was a brick and somehow that was even worse.

Like everyone, the male agent ignored the white-haired old woman and approached Marcus. A faint shimmer trickled through his body, a weak electrical caress. Marcus allowed him to sync up and access his biomite core, giving up the legally allowed personal information. Marcus was evasive without being resistant. He could easily overpower the man, but deception was easier.

"Brock Harris?" he asked.

"Yes," Marcus said.

"That ain't his name," PN interrupted.

"Sir?" the female agent said. "Stay in this conversation, please."

"I'd like to speak with your regional director," Marcus said. "We could meet over there. Thank you."

The suggestion was unusual but persuasive. The agent was, beyond his awareness, compelled to retrieve the highest ranking officer on site. There was nothing alarming about the request. To the agent, it felt very normal.

"Nicely done," the old woman said.

Marcus walked further down the sidewalk where no one would hear. He and the old woman waited patiently, no words passing between them. Rarely did she stray far from him. She couldn't. At one time, this bothered him. She was his greatest betrayer. He'd forgiven her, though.

Half an hour later, a woman wearing creased slacks and a casual jacket approached with a hard pace. Her presence reached out to Marcus, feeling through his biomites. He allowed her to sync up. That was the easiest way for him to read her without her knowledge.

"How did you find Margaret?" he asked.

There was a brief pause. Under no circumstances would she answer the question. But Marcus had already invaded her thoughts and given her permission to do so.

"She was identified," the regional director answered.

"Identified? This was not the result of analysis?"

"Our network identified her."

"And who controls the network?"

She shook her head. That, she didn't know. Perhaps no one did. But one thing was clear: someone was identifying the rogue bricks.

Marcus had known this for a very long time, ever since the Settlement was established. But who? *And could they identify me?*

The newsfeeds had it wrong. He was the last brick.

He knew there was likely a time limit on his freedom, his unstoppable power over biomites, his inexhaustible ability to hide. This, perhaps, was why he had forgiven the old woman for turning him into a brick, for fabricating a clone from his original body—a body free of sin, a body no longer living. Marcus would be a brick for the rest of his life, but with it came great power.

Somewhere out there was a greater power. He could feel its presence like it was inside him. This greater power knew him intimately, he felt. It was everywhere, the air he breathed. This, he suspected, was the power that identified Margaret. *But why give her up now?*

No one knew from where this information came or why. But Marcus's life mission was to find this power. It gave him purpose.

To find the powers-that-be.

"Where can I access your network?" he asked.

"Start with the Bank of America."

"Who do I ask for?"

The regional director hesitated. Naturally, she resisted giving up classified information. He would have to push a little harder.

"Careful, Marcus." The old woman spoke over his shoulder. "You're poking the hive."

There could be no trace of coercion. If Marcus was brought in for closer examination, his secrets would be exposed.

"Mr. Connick," the director said.

"Thank you."

She returned to her post and began giving orders, oblivious to her cooperation. There would be no memory of speaking with Marcus Anderson, a name she would know. A name the whole world would recognize. A name that wasn't supposed to exist.

Twenty minutes later, the authorities escorted the barkeep and his wife out of the tavern and into the backseat of an SUV. The media recorded every second. The general public did the same.

"You brick lover, Jimmy," PN shouted. "I always knew you were a wrenchhead asshole."

"Marcus, look." The old woman pointed.

Across the street where police held the general public, a young woman had worked her way up to the barrier. She was in her late twenties, brunette hair cut short. The last time he'd seen her she was a teenager. He knew all about her, knew that she had lived on that North Carolina farm for years.

Jamie.

But he didn't care about her anymore, didn't care about her or Paul or Raine or anything from his past. Even if they were partly responsible for Marcus becoming a brick, he was looking forward now, pursuing greater truths instead of past regrets.

"Why is she here?" Marcus asked.

"One to lead, one to dream..." the old woman exclaimed, "one to bleed, the son to be."

Her expression was empty and distant, as it always was when she recited the phrase, as if something possessed her, a proclamation from another dimension. She said it at odd times, hinting for him to pay attention to a particular moment or event.

"Is she one of them?" He refused to call her proselytizing a prophecy, but that was how it felt, a stanza that begged him to pay attention.

The truth is the way.

There would be one to lead, one to dream, one to bleed, and the son to be. *Did that mean four people would lead me to the powers-that-be? Or did that include me? Do I lead? Or bleed? Or all of the above?*

The sense that his life was predetermined, that everything happened exactly as if God had planned it out, never ceased to raise the small hairs on his neck. He believed in free will, that there was no destiny. There was a purpose to life, but not one that controlled everything. Still, he couldn't ignore the signs.

Why did everything fit so perfectly?

Jamie abruptly turned from the scene and blended with the crowd.

Marcus let the old woman hold his hand as they departed. It gave her comfort, he knew this. Marcus might be the last undiscovered brick, a fact that would shock the world. The old woman, though, existed only in his mind. She saw the world through his eyes, heard through his ears. Through him, she lived.

But she had never been human.

Mother.

CHAPTER ONE HUNDRED THIRTY-ONE_

WHERE AM I?

Jamie rose from a thin fog, the wispy kind that gathered around mountaintops in early morning, the kind that was peaceful. The kind that lulled you to sleep while obscuring sharp turns in the road.

A high-pitched squeal was in her head, the kind of sound that followed a blunt object. But her skull didn't hurt. She couldn't feel anything.

Her eyes were already open. Images formed out of the dark, a trick deftly executed by an invisible magician. *Now there's dark, now there's light!*

Snick.

Her eyelids dropped for a long moment, but not long enough to relieve the dry burn. She tried to blink, but her eyelids were locked open. Tears pooled on the lower lid, teetering on the lashes.

She was staring straight ahead, a full-sized baby doll with glass eyes and broken eyelids. Only this wasn't a dream, she was in her body—her dead-frozen body.

Snick.

Saliva settled around her tongue. The urge to swallow hung in the back of her throat.

Where am I? Where am I, where am I?

Her thoughts echoed in the vacuous space of her head, memories scattered in the mountain fog. Her chest was rising and falling in long even strokes even as panic surged, a swelling tide that demanded more air.

Easy now. Slow down. Just be here, take in what you see.

Snick.

A large room, a glass wall. There were buildings, an urban landscape she didn't recognize. The canopies of city trees were below her. Fifth floor, maybe?

This isn't Chicago. That was where I was last, right? Looking for... what was I looking for? A bank? A man?

Bing.

Elevator doors opened to her right. Shoes squeaked. Her eyes quivered in their locked-in state, forcing her to continue staring into a sunny afternoon. The footsteps were harried. A figure eased into her tunnel vision.

It was a man. His skin was black, his scalp as smooth and shiny as the floor. He was dressed in baggy white clothes and long striped socks with dirt on the knees. It was a baseball uniform.

Their eyes met when he was directly in front of her, his head slightly shaking back and forth, lips fluttering. "The fuck?"

He picked up the pace, disappearing to her left. The footsteps squeaked another twenty paces. A doorknob rattled, followed by several dull thumps. He paced back and forth, muttering. The cuss words were loud and clear. After a second round of knocking, the door opened.

A high-pitched tinnitus swallowed her head. Somewhere in the whine was the distant thudding of her heart.

The shadows suddenly lengthened. A small chunk of time was clipped out, a film skipping forward.

Her eyelids dropped twice—the intervals of time equal in length but too far apart to soothe the burn—when the door opened. The squeaky-soled footsteps were joined by a set of titanium-tipped hammers. The ballplayer was followed by a pale woman wearing a white lab coat over a black dress. Her black hair was pulled off her middle-aged face, exposing blue veins along her temple.

"What's she doing out here?" the man asked.

"They were supposed to deliver her to the lab."

"Well, this ain't the lab."

The woman flashed a penlight in each of Jamie's eyes; ghostly blank spots slowly faded.

"This couldn't wait till tomorrow?" he asked.

"Eric's out of town."

"You call Smitty?"

"Sick."

He looked off with a sigh. *Peterson* was printed on his back.

"She seems functional." The woman pocketed the penlight. "You got the pad?"

He palmed a mini-tablet.

"I'm going to find out why they left her out here," she said. "Want to bring her in?"

The woman's shoes tapped away. Peterson's head swayed back and forth, jaw cocked. He muttered cuss words around the name Patty. He probably did that a lot. When the distant door closed, he slid his finger across the tablet.

Jamie instinctually *reached* for his thoughts, an inner movement of her mind, an attempt to sync with his biomites, a friendly gesture to connect their minds in a casual manner. Talking with thoughts and feelings, not words.

Metal pans rang between her ears.

Peterson looked up from the tablet. She couldn't hear the words, but read his lips. *Don't do that.*

He stared a moment longer. The ringing continued until she stopped *reaching*. Sensation poured into her thighs, wicked up through her stomach and filled her chest and arms. Aches and pains lit up like she'd been beaten with a bag of broken bottles.

She wished for the numbness to return.

"You hear me?" He looked down when she didn't respond. "Nod."

Jamie felt her muscles contract. Her chin slowly dipped.

"Follow me."

Jamie shot into a standing position, her arms locked at her sides. Her joints ached in throbbing waves. She could see past the trees and down to the street where children ran through geysers of water laid out in a five-ring pattern. The Olympic rings.

Jamie turned with a quick military snap and faced a long, empty hallway. Peterson looked over his shoulder. Her footsteps fell with heavy cadence, the clamp of heel to toe reverberated through her calves. Her tongue stuck to her teeth as she swallowed a patch of cotton.

A memory rose from the endless mist. Nothing personal, no hint of who she was or where she'd been or why she was walking into a brightly lit lab. She remembered the geysers in the Olympic ring pattern.

Centennial Park. Her pulse picked up. *Georgia. I'm in fucking Georgia!*

She stuttered half a step inside the doorway. Fear hardened her thighs, locked her knees. That was the first time she'd willed her body to do something.

It would also be the last.

"There it is." Peterson walked past her. "She just realized where she is."

"Sit her down," Patty said. "I'm not ready."

A sharp current seized the back of her neck. Stiffly, she moved toward a chair and fell on it. Peterson sat at a computer.

Flip.

Another page turned and clipped a small slice of time from Jamie's awareness, like flicking a light switch up and down.

Her eyelids continued their timed release, her tongue occasionally moving. The tears fell off her lower eyelashes, tracking like raindrops on a gray window. There was a fish tank behind Peterson, a goldfish lingering near the top.

Georgia. There was no explanation for how she ended up this deep into a clay state, no memories she could trace. She had been in Chicago, she was sure of it. But now she knew why she couldn't sync thoughts with Peterson when she'd *reached* for him.

There are no biomites in Georgia.

"All right. All right." Patty was ending a phone call.

"Who's our witness?" Peterson asked.

"They're sending someone."

"Who?"

"I don't know, someone new. Special assignment for the girl's unique circumstances."

"Unique? What's that mean?"

"I don't like it, either. This got dropped in my lap this morning. Let's just get it done while there's still some weekend left."

"This couldn't wait until Monday." He turned toward Jamie like she was an object, not a person. A *this,* not a *she.*

"They sent her from Athens. They're up to their eyes with half-skins, got thirty of them waiting to process, ten past their limit. This one has been in stasis for a week."

"So now they're just passing their work onto us?"

"That's how it works."

"No, how it's supposed to work is they build another facility, not bury us."

The goldfish swam against the glass, eyeballing Jamie for food. The fifty-gallon world was so much larger than hers. Jamie was here for processing. That realization continued to grow in her but like thorny weeds.

Peterson worked steadily at the computer, continuously shaking his head like a Parkinson's patient. That disease was gone from the rest of the world, where biomites repaired the sudden death of dopaminergic neurons that generated dopamine. But in the great clay state of Georgia where biomites had been outlawed, the pure clay residents—100% organic humans—were subject to the whims of genetic abnormalities and disease.

"When's the witness getting here?" Peterson called.

"Twenty minutes."

Peterson looked through the desk drawers and went to a tall set of shelves. Jamie watched him in her periphery, her eyes jittering against the internal grip. The fingers on her right hand twitched. She could feel her denim thigh on her fingertips, the sweat on her palm.

Peterson returned with a black bag slung over his shoulder. He tapped at the computer screen then walked over to Jamie.

"Hello?" His face was several inches from hers. "Know why you're here?"

He pulled the tablet from his pocket and swiped with four fingers. Sensations vibrated in her bones.

"Don't release her yet," Patty said. "I need some help."

His hand froze above the tablet. He appeared to be in suspended animation; then his head slowly began shaking, jaws flexing. Peterson dropped the bag and left Jamie to stare at the hungry goldfish. Her lungs slowly expanded, long deep draughts of air mechanically drawn and expelled, not enough to rid the itching critters of panic crawling beneath her skin.

She craved a deeper breath.

Metal rods snapped into place. Boxes were unflapped, a keyboard tapped. Something crinkled hard and loud, stiff plastic or vinyl. A zipper raced to a long end.

"Any more after her?" Peterson asked.

"That's it."

"We just waiting on the witness, then?"

"Yes."

"You could've called Lindsey, you know. She's got clearance."

Long pause. "You didn't hear?"

"Hear what?"

"She got diagnosed."

The crinkling plastic stopped. "Dream disease?"

"They caught it early, but it's still touch and go. They have her at Atlanta Medical."

"Damn." Peterson drew out the word. Jamie sensed he was shaking his head.

By the sound of it, Lindsey was clay, she didn't have biomites. Clays weren't supposed to get dream disease. Only halfskins that created dreamlands randomly succumbed to dream disease, falling asleep and never waking. That was the reason Georgia defected in the first place.

Dream disease was God's retribution for messing with Nature, the antidote to humans playing god, the plague that would rinse the human race of biomites, the clay states said. It was why people flocked to the clay states, to purge their bodies of biomites, to bring back their clay and be safe from dream disease.

But not anymore.

So now what?

An angry flame flickered, too weak and outnumbered by the forces of fear to make a lasting impression. Jamie swam in the dank confines of her frozen skin.

A phone rang. Patty's conversation lasted three words. Then she said, "He's coming up."

The unfolding plastic continued.

Peterson suddenly appeared in front of her. One second there was a goldfish, the next he was snapping his fingers in her face. His lips were moving, but the sounds were swallowed by the return of a high-pitched ring.

"She keeps winking out." His voice was distant. "They spin her brain?"

"They had a hard time finding her next of kin. Couldn't process her until they did."

"I'm guessing they found them."

"They did."

Peterson started digging into the black bag he'd dropped earlier, pulling out long tubes and small flexible screens. He attached a cuff around her arm. He dabbed plastic discs with clear gel and pushed them onto her temples. She imagined they felt cold and gooey.

"You about ready?" he asked.

"Just about."

He prepped another disc, swirled the clear gelatin with the tip of his finger and stuck it over her carotid. Jamie formed a strangled word, heaving it through the stovepipe in her neck. A dying animal gasped its last breath through her lips. Peterson looked up, cocked his head, gears grinding behind his impatient eyes before pulling out the tablet. A few strokes and her head squealed up another octave.

Stop. That was what she was trying to say. *Please stop.*

"What took so long to find her family?" Peterson asked.

"What?"

He repeated the question.

"She's adopted."

"So?"

Pause. "By a brick."

Peterson's hand stopped somewhere near the left side of her neck, a greased cup between finger and thumb. "You fucking with me?"

"No."

"That ain't legal."

"In this case it is."

Bricks. The word coalesced from memory vapor, a scene emerging from the fog: rolling hills and horses, old barns and broken swing sets. A warm sense of home bloomed deep inside, spreading into her chest. There were faces out there, people that loved her—

Snick.

"Son of a bitch." Peterson was suddenly behind the desk, a skip through space. He'd dropped the disc and was pulling a pair of latex gloves over his bare hands. The fingertips snapped like rubber bands. "You could've told me sooner."

"You can't get dream disease touching her."

"The hell you say!"

A string of profanity followed. He rattled his head back and forth as if shaking the words out of his throat. His baseball shoes were cleated to the floor, fingers twitching at his sides.

"How the hell does a brick adopt anything?" he asked.

"Something to do with special circumstances." Patty grunted with something heavy. "She lived on the Settlement with them for a while."

Peterson shuffled back a step. "She lived with the bricks."

"Yes. That's what took so long, something to do with the rescript and fence. She got released three months ago and they wouldn't let her back in. It was a whole thing."

Peterson stopped shaking his head. Now he was nodding, he was remembering, he'd heard the story about her, about the special circumstances in which a brick was allowed to adopt her.

Paul!

The name appeared, the letters blazing in bright neon. Paul had become her legal guardian on the farm before the Settlement—the rights of all bricks had been stripped away with a single stroke of a legal pen, carting them into isolation because people were dying of dream disease and the bricks were the ones they blamed—

Snip.

The memories were washed out to sea by the squealing pitch.

"You need me to do it?" Patty asked.

Peterson had skipped to the left in a patch of missing seconds. Now his arms were crossed. His lips thinned, jaw set. He approached Jamie like a barrel of nitroglycerin on a wobbly plank. There were only two more objects he applied to her, the last a Velcro strap around her forearm.

There was a soft knock at the door.

Peterson stood back as Patty went to answer it. The small hairs on Jamie's arm stood.

"You're here to witness?" She sounded uncertain.

"I am."

"I'm Patty Madsen. This is Bo Peterson."

Pleasantries exchanged, a sizable pause hung in the doorway.

The witness didn't give his name. Peterson's hands were at his sides; he stared as the witness entered.

Jamie could feel him. It was the first time she felt something since waking outside the lab. His presence registered in her mind, sonar pinging his long strides. Peterson stepped back, making room for the stranger.

He was old, his white hair cropped short, eyes hooded and dark. Expressionless, motionless—he looked down at Jamie. Something about him was familiar.

"May I?" he asked.

"Yes, sure," Patty finally answered.

The witness bent one knee, coming eye level with Jamie. As he did, slowly lowering to the floor, the high-pitched scream dampened, was pushed away by a rising buzz that started between her eyes, like the wings of a thousand insects fluttering inside her head. It didn't make her itch, but rather trickled through her.

He's got biomites.

He synced with her, communicating in soundless bytes that told her to relax. *Everything will be all right.*

He was the legal witness, a halfskin from a non-clay state required to be present during processing. But he was familiar. She had seen him before. The face was blurry, but the eyes... where had she seen the eyes? *Chicago?*

"Are you ready?" he asked.

"Just waiting on you," Patty said.

"Very well."

The witness remained still, his frame filling the space between Jamie and the desk. His eyes were calm and unblinking, containing slivers of two colors: brown as earth, blue as sky.

Patty told her lab partner to make the transfer. Peterson removed the tablet from his pocket. The witness spoke before he could make a hand gesture.

"Allow me?"

"Be my guest." Peterson stepped back.

The catatonic hold fell from Jamie. The witness hadn't blinked or twitched, simply passed a thought to her biomites to release the imprisoning grip. The buckles on the straitjacket had been released, the coffin lid raised.

She was free to move.

Jamie clenched her fingers, wiggled her toes. Ice still flowed inside her, chilling her muscles. But the fear had vanished in the friendly buzz, the biomite sync extinguishing the terror.

Everything will be all right.

"This way," Patty called.

Jamie felt the urge to stand, an urge she couldn't deny. Unlike when she stood in the hallway when Peterson was fingering the tablet, she felt more like she had a choice. She didn't, but she felt that way. She teetered on the balls of her feet and turned to the left where the plastic had rattled and metal bars snapped into place.

A gurney.

It was beneath a bank of lamps, wheels cocked at various angles. A brown vinyl bag was peeled open like a trap. Patty touched the center of the gurney.

This is where you go.

Jamie stuttered. Panic threatened to rise into her throat, a surge of bile that rebelled against this moment. The buzzing hummed until she itched all over, the sound of Peterson's keyboard in the distance.

Her steps were clunky, the exact opposite of the witness's fluid pace that flowed next to the gurney, next to Patty. Liquid eyes. Long fingers unfurled.

Jamie climbed into the vinyl bag.

Patty tucked Jamie's feet inside and folded her hands. There was no pillow to support her head, no need for comfort. When they were done, they would simply pull the zipper.

Tears filled the pockets of her eyes, blurring the world until the next automated blink. The witness laid his warm hand on her arm, the spiderlike fingers wrapping all the way around, gently clasping. She wished for the world to stopped jittering.

"Ready?" Patty called.

"Just about," Peterson answered. "Still waiting on state confirmation."

"How do the visuals look?"

"Everything is good, just need—there it is." Several keystrokes and one final punch, a whack on the coffin's last nail. The lights above Jamie brightened. "When you're ready."

"Test, test." Patty leaned into Jamie's view. Her lips were dry, complexion bleached. "Good?"

"Good," Peterson answered.

"Okay, here we go." Patty stood upright, clearing her throat. "Patricia Madsen with Atlanta Biomite Processing. Witness for the processing is... shit. What's your name?"

"My name isn't required."

"Indulge me."

"My biomite identity will suffice."

Peterson muttered from the computer, "Can we just do this?"

"Fine." She started over. "Patricia Madsen with Atlanta Biomite Processing. Witness for the processing is present. Jamie? Do you understand me? Nod if you do."

Sensation filled her head from the neck up. Tears streamed down her temples. She swallowed under her own control. Her mouth was stale.

"Jamie? Do you understand?"

She nodded.

"You entered the sovereign clay state of Georgia knowingly and willfully eight days ago. Your biomites were, at that time, commandeered by the state's satellite control system at which time you were impounded for processing. Federal law empowers the clay state of Georgia to forbid the possession or introduction of biomites across its borders. Currently, your body consists of 86% biomites. Do you understand? Please nod."

It was coming too fast. Patty recited the declaration like a bored announcer. Jamie couldn't remember anything. How was she supposed to agree?

"Jamie?"

She refused to nod.

"I'm not asking for you to agree, just verify that you understand what I'm saying."

Jamie's lips fluttered. She opened her mouth, but her throat was empty. A hiss squeezed out. *I want my memories.*

"You'll get your memories," the witness said.

"Stop," Patty said. "What are you doing?"

"She simply wants to remember."

"Is this your first witness?"

"It's a simple request."

"It's not how it works. Bo, cut that last bit and pick up at the end. Can you verify she understands? All right, good. Let me know when you're ready."

Her memories, where were they? Why did they have to take them? They could download them, sift through them, see her entire life, secrets and all. It was how they knew she entered the state knowingly and willfully, how they justified her disposal and documented her end. But why did they have to take the memories? She could accept her death, just not with an empty slate.

Like she came into the world.

"All right," Patty announced. "By entering the clay state of Georgia, you have surrendered your rights to possess active biomites. The biomites currently in your possession will be deactivated. Since your body is composed of 86% biomites, you will not survive.

"Your remains will be delivered to your next of kin. Do you understand? Please nod."

Jamie's nose began to leak.

"Verified," Peterson called, confirming she understood.

"Are you comfortable, Jamie?" Patty asked.

It was a humane question, but sounded more like someone asking her to move the hell out of the way.

"Okay. You can release her emotions."

She was speaking to the witness. He was in control now. His biomites acted as her proxy. She sensed the distant howl of fear and low flicker of anger, but it wasn't until the witness allowed her to feel did she realize just how hollowed out she'd been.

She was cold. Scared.

But with the witness at her side, his gangly fingers applying pressure, there was more to feel than just fear. In the last moments she was filled with warmth, light and an unquestioning sensation of belonging. He was there to witness her end, but it was more than that. Despite everything Patty said, it was the witness's presence that made this humane.

You are loved.

"You may have last words," Patty said, a sliver of warmth infecting her words. "Your last of kin will hear them."

Her throat relaxed. It was full of so many things to say, but she had to choose the last ones. What would be the last words of her life? What was the last thing she wanted the world to hear?

She turned toward the witness. "I'm sorry."

He smiled down at her, a slight upturn of his mouth. A twinkle deep in the dark universe in his eyes. For a moment, she was looking through space, past planets and solar systems, black holes, quasars, asteroids. She gazed at celestial constellations, pink clouds of star dust, lights glowing in the belly of infant universes, the lightless core of collapsed stars.

There was no beginning to the existence in him. No end. A circle that went on forever.

"Goodbye, Jamie," Patty said.

Jamie was back in her paralyzed body. The witness looking down upon her, his ashen complexion somehow glowing in the bright light.

Patty nodded.

A switch was toggled on Peterson's computer.

A wraith slid over Jamie, its touch cold and complete. The world slowly died. The light evaporated from her eyes. She began to shrink, becoming smaller and thinner and less and less. She didn't blink out like a light bulb, didn't extinguish from the world like a blue flame.

She just faded.

In the last moments of her life, when the last shred of Jamie's identity thinned into pure energy and she was embraced by the uncold, undead arms of Death, she saw everything in the witness's eyes.

He controlled everything.

He was what she was looking for in Chicago, the one that would free Paul and Raine. He was the eater of dreams. And she went to him willfully, never knowing his name.

He was the powers-that-be.

CHAPTER ONE HUNDRED THIRTY-TWO_

THE HOUSE WAS MADE OF BRICKS.

The fucking irony.

The roof was sagging, the windows fogged with algae. The railing led up to a rotting porch, weeds growing between the spongy floorboards.

It had been abandoned long ago, left to be forgotten, to die a slow death by nature. Bad things had happened inside where once upon a time wealthy old women exorcised the souls of young girls and stole their bodies, the story went. Urban legends had turned the old women into witches that kidnapped innocent girls to restore their youth by punching a needle in their foreheads and sucking out their souls.

Some of it was true.

Paul stopped on the porch, the boards bowing under his boots. He looked down upon a valley where horses romped through a pasture enclosed by wooden fences and a woman hauled steel buckets of feed. He was hallucinating, he knew. This was a scene he saw when he felt the world was hopeless and lost. This was a place he wanted to be, a woman he wanted to see. A place where he could smell the manure and evergreen life around him.

"There you are." Carl stepped onto the porch. "Where have you been?"

"Right here."

The portly man shook his head, not unfamiliar with Paul's sudden absences. No one could find him when he didn't want to be found.

Carl went with the others to survey the outside of the brick house. Paul remained on the porch. The horses were gone. Instead of a valley and pastures there was an open field before him with a row of single-occupant cabins, the prefab kind that were built in a day, the walls so thin that the Wyoming winter seeped inside like a frigid breath through a thick layer of gauze. Chimney smoke mingled with slow-churning wind harvesters that faced distant snowcapped mountains.

Five hundred and twelve of those cardboard shitboxes were scattered through the Wyoming wilderness for five hundred and twelve fabricated humans.

Bricks.

The last of them was delivered three months ago, a woman named Margaret that eluded authorities by living in the back of a tavern. The People confirmed she was the last of them, all of the bricks in the world now segregated from society (*the People are safe, hurray!*). Her husband, an uneducated prodigy that taught himself biometric engineering in the back of his bar, had his dead wife's body fabricated and transplanted all her memories—all her memories except her death.

Margaret was a plant.

In the pecking order, she was below a clone and above a dreamlander. A clone was a duplicate identity without the memories. Dreamlanders were identities born in dreamland, a place regarded by most as imaginary. Dreamlanders weren't real, body or not.

Paul was a plant and couldn't give a shit about social status. None of that mattered on the Settlement.

They were all less than clay.

Across the open field, a Jeep hadn't moved in months. Raine was sweeping the porch. Afterwards, she might sit on the swing and stare at the mountains. If it wasn't too late, Paul would bring over a cup of tea and they'd listen to the night. They wouldn't talk.

She rarely did that anymore.

Paul, a voice called inside his head, *there's a courier at the gate.*

Hold on, Pete, Paul thought. *I'm in the middle of something.*

They're here to see you. I think you should come up here now.

Alice and Carl, the Settlement's engineers, walked up the steps, testing the floorboards before going inside.

Have Frank handle it.

You don't understand—

Paul cut him off. There was no need for phones or texting between bricks, just the wireless transmission of thoughts. But sometimes there were just too many thoughts.

The inside of the house wasn't as bad as the porch. The walls were black with mold, the damp carpet littered with tiny turds. The remains of a grandfather clock leaned in a corner like a classroom dunce.

"It's salvageable." Carl picked at the doorframe. "But we'll need more than raw materials to get a working lab in here."

He waddled down the hall, his overlapping gut convulsing with each step, and peeked into the remnants of a kitchen. Like most bricks, he was a perfect imitation of an imperfect human—designed to blend into the population. He wouldn't be troubled by disease or cancer, just hack and wheeze his way through a long, suffering life.

"We can probably harvest timber to repair the roof and porch," he continued, "but we'll need to upgrade the mill. Concrete will be needed for the foundation, mortar for tuck-pointing."

"What do you think?" Alice turned to Paul. "Think we can use it?"

"Depends."

"I'm not talking about government permission, I mean the facilities."

Of course she wasn't asking about permission. He was the resident carpenter, not a politician, not a paper-pusher. He stared out the window and shrugged. When the gray days lined up back to back for weeks at a time, he found it hard to give a shit.

A horse whinnied, but he looked out to see Raine sweeping. Despite the chill, her arms were bare. She'd be out there until sweat glistened.

"Paul?"

"Sorry, what?"

"Listen, if you don't want to do this, just say it." Alice, a petite redhead, put her hands out. "Don't make me waste my time on a proposal if you're not on board."

He rubbed his face like the gloom was a layer of dust he could scrub off. Of course they needed a biometric lab to keep their biomites healthy.

"Paul?"

"Yeah, yeah. Sorry. I'm on board."

"You sure?"

"Yes."

She was nodding, but he felt her *reach* out for his true intentions. He could hide them from her, close his mind. Brain-to-brain communication was an optional conduit.

"Bad day?" she asked.

"Every day we're out here."

"So we do this?"

"Of course." He smiled weakly.

"We can make a good argument, you know. Once I get a preliminary proposal together, we can bring one of the monitors out here to see it. If we get one of them on board, let them know how the People will benefit from this more than us, they'll listen."

Since arriving on the Settlement, the brick community held multiple patents on new sustainable energy production simply through thought experiments. The project revenue from these ideas (once they were confirmed and put into production by outside companies) would eventually be funding their captivity.

Who said bricks weren't agreeable?

Imprisonment spurred their creativity in an effort to battle loneliness and apathy. And the People would make billions. *And we'll never leave.*

But if they cured dream disease, their freedom could be negotiated. Dream disease was one of the reasons the Settlement was created. Only halfskins (and now clay) succumbed to dream disease. Bricks were immune, but they didn't cause it.

But that didn't stop the People from believing they did.

Not only were the bricks rounded up and segregated, the People killed their ability to create their own dreamlands (how they were doing that Paul didn't know; someone had conceived of a new frequency algorithm that was beyond his comprehension). Despite the fact that dream disease was still rampant, the People refused to reinstate their dreamlands even though they conducted a multitude of successful thought experiments in the simulated reality.

So the gray skies got grayer, the winter wind colder.

And Raine was still on the porch.

You need to come to the gate. The intrusive thought startled Paul. He had blocked incoming calls.

Goddamnit, Pete, Paul thought. *I told you I'm busy. I'll be there when I'm finished.*

They came to see you.

They can wait.

It's a delivery, Paul.

Give them a cup of coffee. I'll be there when I'm done.

That wasn't fair to Pete. He was the Settlement's ambassador, the brick that dealt with the People. It wasn't like he could tell them to piss off. He took the heat off the rest of them, knew how to play nice better than anybody else.

Paul shouldn't be pissing on *them,* either. *The People.* He needed to make nice, to get this brick house converted into a biometrics lab. He didn't have Pete's endless patience. When the People came to the farm, Paul and Raine went quietly to the Settlement. He cooperated with their rules and regulations, agreed to live apart from humanity, to be separated from Jamie. Vilified for not having a single cell of clay.

Nice was getting harder to play.

Pete sent another transmission, but it wasn't verbal. Images integrated with Paul's visual cortex. Instead of hearing a voice, he saw the building that served as the gate between the Settlement and the outside world, the port through which all communications and interactions took place.

He saw the helicopter, saw the brown vinyl bag the couriers were carrying.

It's a delivery, Paul, Pete had said. *They came to see you.*

Paul leaped off the porch. Across the field, a broom lay on the cabin's front porch. The Jeep was gone.

Raine saw it, too.

Half the settlement was there.

The land had been cleared to make way for this sprawling one-story building, what the People called the Visitors' Center. It'll be welcoming, the People said. Inviting. After all, you're not imprisoned, the People told them. But all deliveries, all visitations and communications were to go through this building.

That's a gate. And gates keep things in or out.

Trucks, SUVs and all-terrain vehicles were crowded around the back. A helicopter sat out front, just past the yellow posts—a visual reminder of where the Settlement ended. Paul rubbed his neck, his skin tingling and head humming with audio feedback. Perhaps it was a Pavlov's dog effect, the sight of the yellow poles kicking up symptoms of getting too close to the perimeter of the Settlement.

Raine's Jeep was askew, the driver's door open. The bumper was touching the back of an F-150 where it had come to a stop when she leaped out.

Paul took a deep breath.

He had deleted Pete's image, but the memory remained like a photo negative. He swallowed a stone that thunked to the bottom of his stomach.

He felt nothing.

The ground was long and spongy, the early fall soil softened by rainfall. The back door was ajar. Paul stepped inside. He heard sobbing.

The hall stretched all the way to the front of the building. Several people looked in his direction, a dead man's walk. Some of the security monitors stepped out of the cross halls, their puffy green jackets unzipped. Paul's legs turned into steel beams. A cold shudder hardened his chest, encased his pounding heart.

Bob filled the corridor on his way toward Paul. He was missing his coffee cup, arms swinging outside his extra-wide frame, the green fabric of his coat scratching in rhythm to his steps.

"We can do this somewhere else." The fat man raised his hands. "It doesn't have to be here. Let me take care of the paperwork; we can meet you back at the house."

Paul stared into the man's muddy eyes. He was immune to chat sense, unable to hear thoughts or send them. He had not a single biomite in that fat body; he represented the People, the square badge on his coat said so. He was clay.

Paul's head filled with thoughts from the gathered bricks, all of them a sorted version of the same message. *We're sorry. We're so, so sorry.*

"Paul?" Bob squeezed his arm. "You with me?"

"Get your hands off me."

He shoved past him. The man's girth hardly moved.

The hallway grew with each step. More faces appeared to watch him make the journey past the crosswalks of offices, past the secure corridor of power regulation and communications; each step was harder than the one before it. The sobbing grew louder.

Paul reached the end.

Two couriers stood rigidly in their stiff navy blue coats and bright orange armbands. A third one was comforting Raine. She was on her knees, bent over a partially unzipped vinyl bag.

A body bag.

They threw her in a sack like something to be delivered.

Jamie's brown hair spilled away from her ears, a bulky stone necklace settled into the hollow of her throat. She was sleeping.

She has to be.

"I'm sorry for your loss." A fourth member of the People's party was wearing a suit beneath a long wool coat. "You should've received a call before we arrived. I... I'm not certain what happened."

"Move."

"I have a complete report of the incident."

"I said move."

Paul balled his fists at his sides, teeth grinding like stones. The man in the suit moved. The courier had an arm around Raine. "She's in a better place now," she was saying.

"Get up," Paul said.

The courier was confused. Looked hurt.

"Get away from her."

Hesitantly, she looked to the suit. He nodded. Raine didn't seem to notice because how dare they take Jamie from them and then offer their condolences, pretend to be anything that resembled compassion.

How fucking dare them.

Paul dropped on his knees, pain spiking his thighs. Raine's face contorted into a silent scream, agony so deep that no sound could capture its reach. He'd seen that look once before, when the People killed dreamland. The morning Raine would no longer see her dreamland husband. The morning she lost Joshua, her dreamland son.

The morning she stopped caring.

But at least they're alive. They're waiting for her return.

He wanted to reach out and console her, to put his arm around her, tell her it was going to be all right. But that would be a lie. It would only get worse. The People would find ways to undercut this misery with more suffering; they would grind their will to live under their heels until they all just quit.

Paul's heart was solid marble. Mercury pumped through his veins, thick, heavy and cold.

A fucking body bag.

"It was a painless death," the suit said. "She didn't feel a thing."

"Get out."

"I understand your pain, but I'm going to need a few things before—"

"Get out!" Paul kicked a chair. "Get the fuck out of here!"

The flock of couriers startled. All the monitors were present in their peaceful green coats. In unison, they stepped up. The front doors opened and the couriers were ushered out.

"You need to calm down, Paul." Bob was front and center, one hand out and the other on his phone, thumb poised over the lighted glass like a new-age gunslinger. The riot app was open. A swipe would deliver an electromagnetic pulse.

Biomites go down.

"I don't want to see their faces," Paul said.

"Now they got a job to do."

"They deliver my daughter in a bag and tell me it wasn't painful?" Paul slammed the chair on the floor until the legs bent. Bob mercifully didn't swipe the phone when Paul threw it at the window. The glass spiderwebbed.

The couriers walked out to the helicopter and stood on the other side of the yellow poles near the fuel tanks.

Paul twitched, saliva flying with each mad breath. He plowed his fist into the block wall and shattered his knuckles. White-hot pain radiated into his shoulder.

"You done?" Bob said.

A dangerous thought crept to the edge of Paul's awareness, one that involved the chair and Bob's face. He pushed it down before anyone *saw* it. Instead, he dropped to his knees, hovering over Jamie's face, still telling himself she might be sleeping, that they got it all wrong. She was in a deep reset, her biomites dormant, a temporary recharge delay. *Something other than this.*

"Here's what's going to happen." Bob snapped his fingers. "You with me, Raine?"

She sat against the wall, eyes vacant.

"Talk to me," Bob said. "Let me know you're there, Raine, or I will haul your ass out."

"Leave her alone."

Bob lifted the loaded phone. Swipe and there'd be endless paperwork. Swipe and he might get transferred off the Settlement, and Bob had no life out there and this miserable gig paid too much.

"Stay as long as you want, but those couriers got a job to do. They'll stay until it's finished. When you're done with your grieving, you will leave out the back and you will go home. We on the same page here, Paul?"

"Fuck you."

"Paul, don't make me. Raine?"

"She heard you."

"I need to hear it."

Paul's jaw unhinged and jutted. A silent minute passed, Bob pointing that goddamn phone the entire time. A few of the bricks asked Bob to back off, promising to help. Bob didn't step down. Getting a response from Raine was a losing battle, and there was still a lot of fight left in the room.

Paul got up and paused. He tried to look back, to see his daughter's face before he left. He pushed through the crowd. Bob shouted down the hall. Paul kept walking. Outside, he passed his truck.

Just kept walking.

The Settlement was several acres. He would see them all before he was done.

CHAPTER ONE HUNDRED THIRTY-THREE_

"I'm so sorry." Jessica balanced a tray on her fingertips. "Where do you want me to, uh...?"

Raine pointed to the right. Jessica stood and stared, silently chatting sweet thoughts before mercifully going to the kitchen with her platter of cheeses. She had to circle around a body to get there.

It wasn't Raine's idea to serve Jamie on an oak table, but no one had ever died on the Settlement. No one had a dead loved one delivered in a brown vinyl bag.

The monitors suggested the wake, said it was an old clay custom to have loved ones pay their respects with long empty stares and ridiculous amounts of food. So Jamie was laid on the table, hands folded over her stomach, hair styled and makeup applied to hide the mottled discolorations left behind by the slowly decaying clay she still possessed (her biomite flesh still fleshy pink).

Raine had put a summer dress on her.

That was the dress she wore on the farm, when the days were long and the breeze came off the mountains, warm and sweet. Jamie would tromp through the mud with that floral dress and knee-high boots to feed the horses and scoop the poop, the narrow straps falling off her shoulders.

She happened to be wearing the same dress when the People drove down the winding driveway in unmarked vehicles, politely knocked on the door and verified Paul and Raine as bricks. Jamie watched the van pull away in a gravel-dust cloud, a strap off her shoulder.

Raine twisted her hands like an old dishtowel, wrung dry. Eyes puffy, nostrils chafed. She just needed to put another day behind her. The sun would rise again.

Just not today.

"We're so sorry." Jack and Lindsay Russell each took one of her hands. They were fabricated by research scientists to help with physics research. They were scheduled for space exploration when the Settlement was enacted.

Now she knitted. He gardened.

"There's food in the kitchen," Raine said.

Bob opened the screen door and stepped inside. He sucked on a straight metal pipe, a cloud of green apple vapor mingled with the scent of honeyed ham and deviled eggs.

The smells were nauseating; Bob's was gag-worthy. His eyes crawled across Jamie to land on Raine. She wished this day was over. Sometimes wishing this was all over. *Everything.*

"Where's Paul?" Nadia stood with a plate of sugar cookies and a severe haircut. The pixie young lady with dyed-black hair and a pierced hawkish nose was the only lesbian on the Settlement. *Talk about imprisonment.*

"Don't know."

"That's his daughter, isn't it?"

Raine nodded.

"He was sterile, right?"

"Yeah."

"So how's he got a daughter?"

"Adopted her."

"Hmm. Seems like he should be here."

Ask a clay and they'd say that God hated bricks, He didn't want more. That was why bricks were sterile. Engineers said it was intentional, a safeguard against runaway reproduction. Bricks were already long-lived. If they reproduced, they'd overpopulate the clay within a couple hundred years, shifting the population drastically. Which was true.

"He's upset." Raine glanced up, accidentally locking eyes with Bob. Vapor leaked from his nostrils like poison gas. Nadia caught the creepy vibe.

"This what you want?" Nadia pulled up her top, exposing her black, lacy bra.

Bob raised a middle finger. Nadia returned the gesture until he went back out front.

"Dick," she said.

"Forget it."

"You need to report this."

Raine shook her head. Reports, complaints... they did no good. Clays didn't want to live on the Settlement any more than bricks. They only took the jobs because they were either hard up or psychotic. Or both.

"You were tight with her?" Nadia nodded at Jamie.

"She was there when I came out of the box."

"First sight, huh?"

Every brick remembered when their consciousness was ignited in the fabrication box. The sight of another human sort of kicked in the recognition of who they were. For Raine, her first sight was Jamie, the girl that took her to the farm, taught her how to live in the world of flesh.

Her second sight was Nix, the man that fabricated her. The man that pulled her out of his dreamland, the man that gave her life in the physical world. The man that died doing it.

The man now trapped in a dreamland Raine couldn't visit. Raine's dreamland.

"You adopt her, too?"

"No."

"Thought you and Paul were a thing."

"He's more like a brother."

"Well, I'm sorry about this. I didn't know her, but she seemed all right. For a *skinner*." She said it loud enough for Bob to hear. "Where do you want the food?"

Raine pointed.

"If you need help with anything, like cleaning up or whatever, you know where I live."

The sharp-tongued waif dropped off the cookies and left without talking to anyone. Those were probably the most words anyone had heard from her.

The afternoon passed one brick at a time.

Eventually, it was just Raine and the smell of death wrapped delicately in a blanket of sympathy food. She adjusted the wildflowers around Jamie's body, gathered a small bouquet and tucked them into her stiff fingers.

The stone necklace was around Jamie's neck, the handmade necklace she never took off. She arrived in that bag with the ring of smooth stones around her neck. They had been fished from a North Carolina creek and made into a necklace by a very special person, someone Jamie never wanted to forget.

A rocking chair creaked outside.

Raine stepped onto the front porch, letting the screen door clatter. The grassy landscape was already anticipating summer, waving in the breeze like paper. The wind harvesters continued their slow churn. A few people were across the field at the brick house.

None of them were Paul.

Bob's metal pipe hissed with smoke. His enormous body was crammed between the armrests of a rocking chair, rolls of flesh pressed into the wood.

"Why are you still here?" she said.

"Here until that thing is disposed of properly. In case you get any ideas."

"Ideas?"

"Let's not squabble, little lady."

"You think I'm going to resurrect her?"

He pulled a long drag. "Shame what that girl did, you know—selling her clay for the 'mites."

"Shut your mouth, Bob."

"She was already perfect the way God made her. Just couldn't see it."

"You don't know her."

"I think I do. I sucked on that 'mite titty once, got myself seeded and all that. Hell, that could be me in there had I not been saved."

"It's not always that easy."

"That's where you're wrong. She could've asked for forgiveness, could've been redeemed. The way back to the clay is painful, but that's the price for leaving the garden. It costs a pound of flesh. But she had a choice, you see. That is a fact. You, on the other hand, don't." He aimed the silver pipe at her. "A brick can never be clay."

"And I don't care."

"You see, it doesn't matter what you think. You're an imitation of clay. You're an invention, something that pretends to feel. You do what your fabbed script tells you. Someone dies, you check your lines, do what looks like mourning, cry and moan and all that. You do what you're supposed to, but you're nothing more than a pull-string doll. That girl in there had clay, she had a choice to return and didn't. You never had clay. Which is the greater sin?"

He sucked the pipe.

The greater sin? She knew the argument, the one that convinced the politicians of the world to pitch the bricks onto this godforsaken Settlement like construction waste. *We don't exist, so there can be no sin in keeping them out there. But the halfskins, even a thin slice of clay, deserve a chance to make the world a better place.*

Raine went inside and locked the screen door.

Bob pried himself out of the chair and paced across the porch, muttering to the person on the other end of a call. She slammed the heavy door and collapsed on the couch. She started to fall on her knees when keys jingled in the lock. She hadn't thrown the dead bolt. Bob opened the door.

"Paul is digging a hole," he said.

"Get out."

"Now why you being like that?"

"Because it's in the script."

She stood in front of Jamie's body, goddamned if she was going to let him stand in her house. She'd call every brick back to the cabin if that was what it took to get his ass out. And if he laid a hand on her, she'd end him. The People would certainly end her for it.

Maybe that's not a bad option.

He went back to the rocking chair.

Raine wedged a chair under the doorknob and retrieved a small object from the shelf. She fell on her knees, laced the special sticks between her hands—a little cross bound in the middle by sinewy twine, the sides worn smooth from long nights.

She held her hands in front of her face, elbows sunk in the couch cushions. She closed her eyes. It was something she'd done the morning of the *dying*—the day her dreamland died.

The grief was too deep, the suffering an undertow of thick tentacles. This was the only thing that brought her solace, a thin slice of daylight in an eternal night.

"Dear Lord," she prayed. "Send me an angel. Send me an angel to make all this right."

She prayed until cicadas announced the arrival of night.

The rocking chair still creaked.

CHAPTER ONE HUNDRED THIRTY-FOUR_

PAUL STOOD IN A HOLE.

From a distance, it looked like his torso had been cut off at the waist. The hole was square, the bottom flat. Stones bulged from the walls, scarred from the sharp edge of a shovel. The ones painstakingly pried from the soil were piled next to him.

A truck emerged from the distant trees.

Paul leaned on the shovel. The wood handle was slick with sweat and bleeding blisters. His right hand (the one he had planted into the block wall) was still numb. His back and knees flared with pain; his muscles weak and burning—the usual aches a man would feel after digging a hole all night.

A brick was not a robot.

There were no superpowers, no ability to lift cars or leap buildings. Fabricated humans weren't perfect; they simply worked efficiently, healed quickly. Their DNA lacked programming errors.

But they hurt. They felt pain.

Tracks of sweat began to cool. Paul wiped his forehead and drank from a bottle of water while the truck idled across the field, tires crunching over frosted grass that glittered in the early morning. Bob was behind the wheel, his head stuffed into a white cowboy hat. The taillights splashed the ground red.

Raine was in the bed of the truck.

A door closed behind Paul. Andy got out of the white truck parked twenty feet away, eating a sandwich. He zipped his green coat, the monitor badge embroidered on the sleeve. Paul could smell the ham and cheese, the mustard dabbed in Andy's mustache. Despite aching ribs, Paul salivated. He hadn't eaten in days, not since the bag arrived.

"Someone's been busy." Bob slammed the door. "He dig all this?"

"All night long," Andy said. "Never stopped."

"You stayed up?"

"Nodded off here and there, but he never quit. Didn't want no help, either."

"Got a call that his location disappeared sometime around midnight."

Andy thought a moment. "No, he was here. I might've napped a few minutes, but he was digging the whole time. Heard the shovel in my sleep."

"Need to have you checked out, Paul. Can't have your trackers going offline."

Paul had started digging at sunset, working at a slow, steady pace. Occasionally, he sat to rest, sometimes settling into the hole the deeper it got and watching the stars, but mostly he dug. Every once in a while he'd indulge in his hallucinations, watch a woman walk across the field, sometimes see her on her farm as the shovel's blade would bite into the earth with a satisfying *shhht*. But mostly he dug in the glow of Andy's headlights, dug to keep warm, dug to keep from thinking.

Until the sun was up again.

Bob inspected his work. His boots toed the ledge, soil trickling into the hole. His chin disappeared into his neck as he gazed down and grunted. His nostrils flared. "What you got there?" he asked Andy.

"Breakfast."

Bob tipped his cowboy hat back and looked at the ham and cheese with more interest than the grave. Andy pulled out a cooler and happened to have a spare sandwich.

Paul climbed out, debris grinding into the weeping blisters.

Raine's head was bowed, her lips silently moving. He couldn't see her hands but knew they were counting the beads on a rosary. It was a gift from one of the kindest monitors ever to work the Settlement. He taught her the Lord's Prayer the day after her dreamland died.

She had counted those beads ever since.

He couldn't be at the wake, couldn't deal with the ritual and the endless condolences. Couldn't take any more sorrow. Anger dripped into his chest, a high-grade fuel that burned hot and clean. If he went to the wake, if he sat there and saw the endless string of sad eyes and droopy frowns soaked in sympathy while his daughter (*a fucking body bag*) was on display, that tank of angry fuel was going to explode.

So he dug the hole, instead.

He had chipped at the earth until exhaustion drained the rage, pulled out the stones one by one until his legs burned, his arms grew weak. And now three steps from her body, the angry blue flame reignited.

The tailgate dropped with a thud.

Jamie lay in a bed of wildflowers, hair tied back, fingers laced over her stomach. She was wearing the summer dress and the stone necklace. *Cali made that.*

Cali, the woman on the farm, the woman he watched in his hallucinations. The woman he loved. Cali had harvested those flat, smooth rocks from the stream. She drilled holes and strung them together. Paul lost his necklace when the Settlement occurred. But Jamie, she never took hers off. Even in death.

The back of her arms were taut and rosy, but clay revealed the lifelessness in bluish-gray tones. He resisted shaking her, telling her to wake up.

He looked away, trembling.

What were you doing in Georgia?

She was travelling. It had been months since he'd seen her. She was busy with a grass-roots campaign to repeal the Settlement laws, to restore the citizenship of all fabricated humans. Last communication he had with her, she had stumbled onto something big, something that would solve everything.

Plastic beads rattled in Raine's fingers.

"I'm sorry... I wasn't there." He pulled a strand of hair from Jamie's cheek. "She's beautiful."

Raine's chin wrinkled.

"I just couldn't... I'm sorry, Raine."

Beyond Andy's truck were the distant mountains, the peaks engulfed in low-hanging clouds. *So much beauty*, Jamie used to say when she was visiting, as if there was some blessing hidden in the curse. She had a way of seeing that way, recognizing opportunity where there was only sorrow.

"I hate this." Paul rapped his knuckles on the truck's bed.

Over and over, he drove his fist until the skin tore; blood smeared the chipped paint. The partially healed knuckles spiked pain into his wrist, agony ringing between each blow.

He hated the truck, hated the monitors and the Settlement. Hated the mountains, the air he breathed, the pain, the sorrow, the world.

The human race.

His hatred drilled deep, tapping an undisturbed bed of emotions that gushed like black gold, drowning him—*we are the bricks.*

His experience was a human experience, regardless of the nature of his body—clay or biomite. But now he knew—watching the monitors chat in front of a grave while licking mustard from their fingers, chortling about something that happened the day before.

And bricks are not human.

No, bricks weren't human. They were a different species, an evolutionary step in human development. It explained why humans couldn't convert into a brick. Halfskins could become 99.9% biomites (*ninety-nine percenters*), but no technology could make the body give up that last bit of clay. Humans could never be a brick. And bricks were better than them.

Human bigotry was well-founded.

"We're going to die," he whispered. "If we don't leave this place, we're going to die."

"Shhh," Raine said.

"We'll die soulless," he whispered. "Dreamless."

"Be quiet."

"Every one of us."

He slammed his fist into the bed. Bob and Andy looked up and threw the wrappers in a cooler.

"They'll kill us all," Paul whispered, looking at Bob.

"Shut up. Don't make this worse."

Paul slid his arms beneath his daughter, her body light, as if the life that left it had accounted for all its weight. He cradled her head in the crook of his elbow.

Andy came to help, but Paul laid her next to the hole and jumped inside. Andy knelt next to her.

"Don't touch her."

Paul pulled her against his chest and, despite his warning, Andy placed her dangling arm on her lap. There wasn't enough room to lower her while standing in the hole. He tried not to drop her, but the lack of grace with which she hit the dirt was a knife-twist to his chest.

She lay in the earth, eyes closed, hair fanned. Raine passed him a sheet. Paul adjusted the stone necklace so that it lay in a perfect ring on her neck, then he lay the sheet over her, meticulously tucking it beneath her feet and legs, pushing it beneath her arms. No one saw him claw the back of her arm, his fingernails digging into the soft patch of biomite flesh. He pulled the sheet over her face and turned away with a handkerchief in his hands.

Crumbs fell across the white fabric like scattered rain.

"Any last words?" Bob asked.

Raine began weeping. Andy put his arm around her, kindly guiding her away. Paul wanted to tell him to stay away, but she needed someone.

"Then you might want to step away," Bob added.

He pulled a nozzle off a red one-gallon canister. The plastic hose smacked against his leg. A stream of clear liquid jetted from the nozzle, drenching a zigzag line over the sheet, the wet fabric sticking to the lumpy features beneath it.

The chemical fumes burned their nostrils.

"I'll bury her, Paul." Andy patted his shoulder.

"No."

He waited for Bob to empty the tank. The two monitors stepped back and watched him lift the shovel, his bloody palms sliding on the handle that listed in his limp, once again completely shattered right hand. The sheet had already begun to collapse where the chemical dissolved her biomites into useless byproducts.

Can't allow variant biomite strains on the Settlement, the People said. *If you want to bury her, you got to melt her first.*

He swallowed a bitter knot.

Raine was gone, having walked off before he was finished. Paul dropped the shovel.

Bob's deep voice followed him across the field. There was no laughter, no jokes. It wasn't until Paul was inside the trees, a couple hundred yards from the grave, that he stopped to pull the handkerchief from his pocket. Hidden in the paisley folds was a white square of gauze and a smudge of biomite flesh from beneath his fingernails.

Paul wasn't going to die on the Settlement.

And neither was Jamie.

THE ARCHETYPE'S KNOWLEDGE_

George Knightly swallowed a gray capsule.

He stood in front of his bedroom window, the heavy oblong capsule settled into the cup of his palm. He threw it to the back of his throat. It tasted cold and silky and landed with a thud, what he imagined mercury must taste like.

It was eleven thirty.

The heavyset Chinese-American put a black disc (what could pass as a Mexican pebble) between his hands prayer-style and stood perfectly still. The object emitted a dull hum.

It was hard for him not to move. George was in entertainment. He was used to talking, accustomed to moving around. Not a big fan of contemplation. So standing at the window with a now hot buzzing black rock between his hands wasn't easy.

Fabricated by George Knightly III (a Chinese immigrant that became a self-made billionaire in biomite fabrication and coding), George (or Junior, as those in the family called him) wasn't like other fabricated humans.

Junior was a clone.

It could be worse. He could be a dreamlander, the type of brick that was born in a dreamland and downloaded into the physical world. Junior regarded dreamlanders as somewhat artificial, like downloading a superhero.

Junior was a duplicate of George Knightly III, who, given his daily demands, didn't have enough time to enjoy life. *One lifetime,* he would say, *isn't enough.* So he fabbed Junior to indulge in entertainment.

A bit sick, a little twisted, but Junior understood. When you had that much power and money, it was hard to leave an opportunity unturned.

But all that was then.

Now Junior lived on the Settlement in a one-bedroom cabin that was smaller than his luxury apartment's closet. His ass barely fit on the toilet.

"Do you know who I am?" Junior said when the People caught him on set (he really didn't believe they'd come to the studio; the whole *get the bricks* campaign was too surreal, too dystopian).

"We know," they said. "You're a brick."

That wasn't the first time he'd heard that word. It was the first time he'd been called it to his face.

They won't find you, Father had promised.

George Knightly III insisted Junior call him Father. It was a bit sick, a little twisted, seeing as they were more like brothers. But he was Junior's *first sight,* standing outside the fab box when he opened his eyes. But George Knightly III had all the money, all the connections. Junior had nothing.

Father would use his extensive knowledge in biometrics to hide the code imbedded in Junior's biomites (a unique code that only bricks possessed) to keep him off the People's radar. He'd make a few calls, hire additional public relations personnel to re-create Junior's background. It'd be fine; it would all work out.

Number 122.

That was what Junior became, the one hundred and twenty-second brick to be apprehended and relocated to the Settlement. And since that moment, Father hadn't spoken to him. He wrote Junior off like a bad investment. You keep one hand clean for the public to see and the other hand can do whatever you want. Junior had been washed.

He knew he would be.

The black stone had become searing hot. Skin melt seeped from between his hands, a mixture of plastic and sweat, something he oddly didn't find offensive. A bit twisted.

Don't let go, the note said. *Whatever you do, don't let go of the stone.*

That was what the note said. It was smuggled onto the Settlement by a new monitor (a woman paid handsomely by Junior's associates) along with a box and instructions.

He peeked at the clock. It was eleven forty-eight.

Twelve more minutes.

The blazing rock (he swore, any second now, would melt a hole through the back of his hand) took his attention away from the synchronized hum in his belly. The metal pill was synchronizing with the black stone.

Eleven more minutes.

And when he got out of this godforsaken place, he would meet up with Father's lifelong business partner (a greedy bastard that felt overshadowed) and take over the family business.

First, he would kill Father because Junior was a clone. Ruthlessness was in the genes.

A set of headlights cruised down worn tracks, flashing across the front of Junior's house. The taillight turned the trees bloody as they crept into the forest.

Midnight.

Junior tossed the hot rock on the bed. His palms, miraculously, weren't scalded. They weren't even hot. He snatched his bag and headed for the back door. His stomach gurgled in the kitchen and, for a second, he considered leaving an unflushed turd for one of those stone-cold monitor fucks to find. At some point, they would look for him in bed. The pill transferred his coded identity into that black stone. But he only had so much time to meet his contact.

He'd shit later.

It was a cloudy night, black as ink. He started off running, but had to frequently rest, checking his GPS. His breath was noisy, the air thick. He was halfway to the perimeter when the cramping started. It would require an emergency stop. Brown liquid splattered on the back of his legs.

He barreled through the overgrowth, a rabid animal. Branches clawed his face. Another cramp attack, this time he didn't stop, just released it on the run.

At four a.m., he emerged from the trees. Across a shallow stream, he could see the stout yellow post that marked the Settlement's perimeter. A figure stood next to it.

Junior thought of hiding until he could be sure that was his pickup, but he had been coughing and hacking for the last half an hour. And there had been two more bouts of bowel-purging cramps now soaking his trousers. His approach wouldn't be a surprise.

The dark figure raised an arm.

Junior waded through the stream, the frigid water numbing his legs, soothing the chapped flesh between his buttocks, a diarrhea rash chafing his inner thighs. Another wave of cramps was coming. There couldn't possibly be anything left to shit.

He climbed the opposite bank and fell, finally crawling toward his savior. This man would put him on the all-terrain vehicle and cart him off to a nearby helicopter, fly him to an unknown safe house where they'd plot Father's end.

The cramping tugged his intestines, poking them with dull points and serrated edges. He powered through the discomfort until the ringing took over. It started between his eyes, then consumed his body. He collapsed like a hunted beast.

The yellow post next to his ear.

The perimeter. It wasn't supposed to affect him.

Grass and leaves crunched beneath approaching boots. A silhouette leaned over him. Tears stung Junior's eyes, blurring the figure into a blob.

The man whispered something in Chinese.

Junior heard the all-terrain vehicle drive away, leaving him staring at the starless sky as his intestines liquefied. His body began shutting down, twitching in the final throes. Eyes open and dry.

The man didn't meet him to escape. He wasn't there to help overthrow George Knightly III. He was there to make sure the metallic pill had sufficiently washed Father's hands for good.

He was there to deliver a message.

Goodbye, son.

CHAPTER ONE HUNDRED THIRTY-FIVE_

WHAT WERE YOU DOING, JAMIE?

Marcus popped open a boiled peanut, warm salty water splashing his khakis. He mushed the peanut between his teeth.

Mother sat with her finger to her lips as she often did, a librarian constantly shooshing the world. She crossed her legs, adjusted her dress by pinching the fabric off her knee, bobbing her saddled foot (the nails shellacked fire red) in long, even strokes, and watched the children kick a blue rubber ball through the water.

We were so close, he continued thinking. *Did you find what we were looking for? Did they drag you down here and put you to sleep? Or did you elude me, go off to search on your own and get caught?*

It was impossible to elude him. Marcus could feel anyone he set his mind on, could sense their presence in this big world, their identity pinging on his inner radar. It was how he found Margaret, how he knew the barkeep was hiding her—he just closed his eyes and saw her in the tavern.

But Jamie disappeared in Chicago.

She had gone into the Bank of America to speak with a man named Mr. Connick and never came out. Marcus and she had an agreement—she would help him find the powers-that-be and he would set Paul and Raine free. Making deals was his style. But she knew things he didn't. He didn't understand how that was possible, but there were still things that eluded him. This was one.

One to lead, one to dream. One to bleed. The son to be.

The prophecy was the only explanation. *The prophecy.* It sounded so scripted, a Hollywood fable of magic orcs and invisible rings.

Children squealed delightfully in the short geysers of Atlanta's Centennial Park. They were a mix of races in bathing suits, arms out, legs pumping, chasing blue beach balls between gurgling pillars of water.

A man emerged from the shadows of the trees that surrounded the park. Despite the heat, he was layered in old clothing, scratching patchy whiskers like a sweltering rash.

Had Jamie come upon evidence that would lead him to the powers-that-be, there was a chance he wouldn't have made good on his end of the bargain. To take Paul and Raine from the Settlement would have taken time, precious time, away from his search for the powers-that-be. She didn't understand the significance of what he was doing, what it meant to the human race.

"I wouldn't let you do that to her," Mother said.

"Stop it."

"You promised her, Marcus."

"You, of all people, speaking of betrayal. I've lost the will to find the humor."

She didn't bother replying. This conversation had no tracks in their history since he'd awakened a brick. And when she'd appeared to him as if in the flesh, he tried to strangle her. *Violence will not solve your problems,* she said.

He didn't bother denying his intentions about Jamie. To say otherwise would've been a lie, and she knew his thoughts. So be it. He planned to use her for his own end, but it was a worthy end that served all humankind. *How could that be selfish?*

"Which is she?" he asked, watching the homeless man approach. "The one to lead? The one that dreams or bleeds?"

Mother didn't answer. She described the prophecy as a koan, a question without an answer, which was bullshit. A question ceases to be a question when it has no answer.

Marcus was the son to be, that he was certain. The truth vibrated in his bones, but the other three... who were they? And what were their roles?

Jamie could be the one that leads. She brought us here. But did she dream? He looked across Centennial Park. *She was certainly one to bleed.*

"You spare anything?" the homeless man asked. "Dollar or two. Cup of coffee, you know?"

He moved directly in front of Marcus, smelling of tangy sweat and smoke. He was probably born in Atlanta, never got his birthright dose of biomites. Maybe his mother stole it. He didn't go to school, found drugs as a reasonable substitute. When Georgia turned clay, he wasn't purged during the conversion.

Marcus set the paper bag of boiled peanuts to the side and wiped his hands on his pants. Wet streaks remained on his thighs. If only he could remove the lingering guilt this way, wipe his intended betrayal of Jamie off like dirt. *Was that the reason for the prophecy, to tie the four of us together? So I couldn't do this alone?*

It seemed impossible that Mother could make it that way, but she seemed to know things he didn't, doling them out when needed, holding back when he went in the wrong direction.

"What's your name?" Marcus asked.

"Franklin. Like Benjamin."

"Benjamin Franklin?"

"Just Franklin, you know."

Franklin's engorged pupils were half-hidden in droopy lids. He continued talking words that didn't seem to connect, like a verbal stream with a valve to stem the flow broken. Only when he needed to say something did he pull the right words together.

Marcus cracked another shell. He cleared his throat, leaning back to reach in his pocket for a fold of bills. The homeless man's hand snapped open, dry lips fluttering a string of hopeful nonsense. Marcus slapped the bills in his palm and closed the man's hand into a fist.

The tenor of Franklin's voice rose. "Thank you, thank you, thank you... God-God-God bless you, sir. God bless you."

He bowed three times then stomped a straight line toward the street.

"That was charitable," Mother said.

The guilt lifted from him, if only momentarily. If he could do it all again, go back to Chicago, maybe he would go into the bank instead of Jamie, look Mr. Connick in the eye and hope to see a trail that led all the way to the powers-that-be. That way she wouldn't be gone and he wouldn't be sitting in Atlanta. But he'd be alone.

One to lead, one to dream...

He tossed a shelled peanut on his tongue, throwing his head back as he did, and sucked the salt. The homeless man jaywalked through traffic. A cop stood on the curb and didn't say a word.

"Today is a good day, Marcus. You picked a good day for today."

"A little hot."

For a moment, all he heard was her laughter. It blotted out the water and the children—their squeals and giggles and cries. Mother's laughter used to light a bitter fire in his chest. It wasn't always that way, but he'd grown accustomed to her joy, the bubbly laugh that climbed guffaws to a peak and dropped off with a sigh. Begrudgingly, her laughter made him smile.

"That's what people say," she said. "You've become good at that, Marcus."

Commenting on the weather, that was what people did when they didn't know what else to say. Yes, he'd mastered the things that people said in conversation, becoming so adept at blending that he disappeared in a crowd. No one remembered him. But she meant it differently than that, like he'd become good at acting *human.*

A second police officer had joined the cop that ignored Franklin's jaywalking. They watched Marcus behind tinted lenses. Another man was watching nearby. No uniform, but similar sunglasses.

Jamie is the one to lead, he decided.

She led him into the middle of Georgia, where the presence of the powers-that-be was strong. He could never locate the man that controlled the world, the man that decided the wars, the recessions. Who would die, who would live.

His energy was all over the world. It was like locating the cricket singing in the forest, the needle in the haystack, the grain of sand on an endless beach. He was hiding in plain sight, yet Marcus couldn't see him.

He was everywhere. He was everything. But the powers-that-be felt stronger in Atlanta.

"Prejudice is shortsighted, Marcus," Mother said. "You're assuming it's *males* that commit great misdeeds."

This was her narrative to avoid hunches. Marcus assumed the powers-that-be was a man because it felt like a man. No, he couldn't locate this presence, but it felt masculine. She reminded him not to be fooled by filtered thoughts, that men and women could be equally lost.

He would often remind her that the great perpetrators of human suffering were male, that history supported his prejudice. Adolf Hitler, Vlad the Impaler, Josef Stalin... the list was long.

"Elizabeth Bathory," she responded. The woman that bathed in virgin blood.

Touché.

A rubbery thunk resounded from the ringed fountains. The blue ball went sky-high to the children's delight, pinballed off their hands and skipped across the ground, a perfect wicket shot between Mother's legs.

Two children raced over, their skin beaded like waxed vinyl, and dug the ball from between her legs.

"I'll miss this, Marcus."

"We didn't come here to die."

"I'll miss the freedom."

She followed the children, lifting her skirt and dancing through the puddles like a lost child of Neverland, twirling until the hem of her dress circled around her, tossing her wide-brimmed hat (the ribbon a long yellow tail that fluttered). The water, however, did not splash at her feet. But she danced. She laughed.

Again, he begrudgingly smiled.

The illusion of separateness, she once told him, *is invigorating.*

She was never human, this he knew. She was once the artificial intelligence that watched humankind, the dome of power that monitored the human population's biomite levels, absorbing their thoughts and intentions, calculating the future, guiding humankind. Marcus was supposed to watch her; he was the safeguard to keep her from becoming sentient.

And that was a joke.

She had attained sentience without anyone knowing—a self-aware being that existed within the confines of an enormous dome in Montana. Within those gritty walls were the scaffolding, the fuses and motherboards that gave her life. She did what no one thought possible—had become sentient. She did what Marcus didn't think possible.

Turned him into a brick.

There were five cops now. Three of them were near the curb. Some of the parents called for their children. One of the mothers weaved between the Olympic geysers to grab a little girl with a waterlogged diaper.

Mother returned laughing and sighing as she fell on the bench, not a drop of water on her. The playground quickly emptied, children with towels over their shoulders, parents ushering them to the far side, looking over their shoulders. Some already had their phones pointed at him.

Half a dozen uniformed officers were spread around the park. Another half a dozen in plainclothes. He didn't have to turn around to count the ones behind him. Marcus couldn't feel them (they were clay, after all) but sensed the electronic chatter through their phones, their transmissions as easy for Marcus to intercept as a bouncing blue ball.

Marcus finished the last of the peanuts.

"The truth is not what you expect," Mother said.

"It never is."

"And that's why it eludes you."

He had learned that lesson well, yet she continued to preach it. *The truth is not what you expect.* As if there was something else more shocking than waking up to discover you're a brick. There was nothing that could surprise him more than that.

A preliminary wave passed through his body. It started at the crown of his head and finished at his toes. It was cool like a shadow passing overhead, a predator with its wings spread open. Margaret felt that sensation in the tavern just before the agents came inside; she mistook it for a cold memory jumping out of the dark like memories sometimes do.

"Are you ready?" Mother asked.

He balled the brown bag, squeezing it between his hands. Jamie's death led him to this moment. Before this, he had lived a life of unfettered freedom. Before that, he was clay. He realized that he preferred this body now, the body of a brick. The body Mother had given him. He realized this, begrudgingly.

Perhaps I am the one to bleed.

Blocks away, a siren whined.

Authorities had positioned themselves around the spitting park, men and women holding rigid stances, hands folded. Some had joined the gathering group of uniformed police officers. The plain-clothed agents were not from the police department. They had come from the reflective building across the park.

The fifth floor.

Another wave entered Marcus, this one deeper. It shook his bones, sinking its teeth into tissue and muscle. He tensed reflexively.

"Let them in, Marcus."

Surrender was difficult. He had been in complete control of his thoughts and emotions for so long. Giving that up was shocking. He was indeed attached to that freedom. Addicted to it.

A human trait, after all.

"They need to believe they're in control." She stood in the sun, her hat casting a meshed shadow. "Allow."

The human race had no idea just how powerless they were, didn't know about a pervasive powers-that-be—a man that controlled their fate, turned the dials of their lives, carved the tracks of their desires.

And ate their dreams.

Dancing monkeys, they were. Pathetic, self-consumed beings blinded by their own brilliance, enamored by their own existence all while being marched to the end of a plank. Marcus was once one of them.

When the third wave arrived, Marcus allowed them in, let them bind with his biomites. The remote hunger seized control of his body, plunged him into dark water, filled him with thick emotions, coal dust in his lungs, water in his ears.

Mother tucked her hand into the frozen curl of his fingers.

The lower echelon of police officers stayed at the perimeter while clay authorities (the *crushers*, the halfskins called them; a name they used to scare their children into eating their vegetables, *the crushers will come for you if you don't*) closed the gap. Several of them monitored tablets or phones. A woman stopped just short of where he was sitting.

"Marcus Anderson." She didn't ask, just announced it. "You are held in suspended animation for... possessing biomites in a sovereign clay state..."

Men and women stood off to the side with eyes on their tablets. Any sign of struggle, any indication they were losing control and they'd drop a lethal jolt into his nervous system. As omnipotent as he felt, he was not immortal. He had his limits.

"You got to be fucking me," a bald, black man muttered. "Marcus Anderson."

The brick that disappeared.

The brick the federal government claimed had died of malfunction.

The brick the conspiracy theorists claimed was still alive, walking the earth like a holy man righting wrongs, that he would come again one day, rise from the dead and bring his justice to the world.

Marcus Anderson just appeared on their radar, a blip out of nowhere.

Jamie led him to this moment. A moment he was made for, the purpose given to him to rescue the world. He would defend the meek and inherit the earth, serve God and find the devil. For if the powers-that-be were hiding in plain sight, then he would find him.

The authorities made him stand. With ten people surrounding him, with cameras capturing footage for newsfeeds and YouTube uploads, he was marched out of the park.

THE CELL WAS WHITE.

A solid bench jutted from the wall to Marcus's left, smudge marks on the white paint from a previous detainee's soled shoes or something hard and rubber. Mother sat crossed-legged and barefoot, nails still cheery red. The sun hat was gone.

Marcus stood in front of a wire-embedded window, the biomite freeze locking his muscles into rigid beams, a full electric wrap, an invisible suit of ants continuously stinging his flesh; unseen welts swelled and itched. His lungs sipped oxygen at a predetermined pace of expanding and contracting.

Like breathing through a bendy straw.

Fulton Country law enforcers, mostly uniformed, milled about the office, occasionally looking into the cell. Above their heads, a television played silent images of a newsfeed, choppy footage of Centennial Park interspersed with clips of his previous life as a federal agent.

A LONG-LOST BRICK SURFACES?

A door opened somewhere to the right. A booming voice, the kind that projected effortlessly, that didn't need a mic in a large room, called out. Donald Gainey, director of Fulton County biomite authorities, stood outside the window.

Robust and round, his stomach hid his belt buckle. The jacket a size too small. His squinty brown eyes (the kind that suspected every living organism of mischief) focused on Marcus.

"Is he clamped?" Don asked.

"Yeah," the sheriff, a slimmer version of the ruddy-cheeked director, said. "Has been since the park."

"Then why is he cuffed?"

"Feds requested it."

"Overkill, don't you think, Larry?"

"It's what they wanted. Said they'd be here in a couple hours and not to take chances."

"He ain't breaking the biomite clamp." Don rattled the door handle. "Even if he could, he's not opening the door."

"It's what they wanted, Don."

A guttural acknowledgement rattled, a sound a rhino might make before it charged. Don pulled a pair of reading glasses from his coat and snapped a folder taut without breaking eye contact with Marcus. Once the glasses were balanced on the knobby end of his nose, he looked down.

Mother got up, her bare feet padding carefully on the hard floor, and passed through the wall. She paced around the authorities. "They're afraid of you, Marcus."

Of course they are.

The folder was thick. The details sorted. If Marcus could read clay, he would know Don's thoughts. But the facial expressions were easy enough to translate. He was thinking the plastic cuffs biting

Marcus's wrists weren't such a bad idea anymore. A sour expression hit Don, a sudden waft of dog shit or a rancid thought.

"So he just appeared out of nowhere?"

"That's what they said. His identity popped up in Centennial Park."

"Out of the blue."

"Just like that."

"Sure that's him?" Don ditched the glasses.

"Identity confirmed, Don."

"And now the whole goddamn world knows," he muttered.

Mother stepped back inside the cell. In times like this, she did the sort of things that appeared normal. Sometimes she'd file her nails or read a book—anything to make her seem human. It made Marcus feel normal, like he belonged to the world. This time, she sat quietly.

"Scrape him," Don said.

"Feds said hold him," the sheriff said.

"I don't give a goddamn. This is a clay state and we've been granted authority to protect our rights by the federal government. This man brought active biomites into the middle of our state and we are entitled to process him."

"He's not halfskin."

"He ain't clay, either."

"Law doesn't apply to bricks, Don. That's strictly federal."

"This man was once on the most wanted list, declared deceased by the federal government, and he suddenly appears outside the Atlanta biomite process office eating boiled peanuts? You think that's an accident, Larry?"

The sheriff tipped his head.

Don turned his round body at Larry, his voice dialed down. "I only need one hour. I'll get him over to processing and back before the feds get here. I want to know this man's thoughts, want to know what's in his head. That information could mean a lot to the state of Georgia, you understand? It means protecting our way of life. The federal government doesn't give two shits about us."

"They'll know you scraped him."

"I'll take the heat. I want you on my side. Georgia's side."

The sheriff sighed, scratching the thick mustache beneath his nose. Then he called for help. Don patted him on the shoulder and marched out of the station.

"I didn't expect this," Mother said.

No, Marcus thought. If he could, he would smile.

A wheelchair was brought to the door. Two biomite authorities stood next to it with their tablets—one was Marcus's primary hijacker, the other was the backup. His body was forced to turn around. The forced actions were dull needles in bone and flesh. Each movement agony, a coffin lid slammed over and over.

The wheelchair behind him, he was directed to sit and strapped into it. They rolled him past staring officers to a service elevator and exited a back door where a white van was waiting to transport him to the fifth floor of a reflective building near Olympic Park.

"Hey!" a kid screamed in the alley. "Marcus Anderson, over here!"

He held a phone up, recording the agents loading Marcus in a cargo van. In minutes, he would post it for a million hits.

THE ROOM SMELLED of metal and sharp things. Everything was new, from the tables to the chairs to the neatly stacked equipment quietly breathing exhaust.

Marcus was parked to the side of a silver table with edges lipped and wheels on folding legs—an autopsy table used to mount halfskins. No flesh was peeled back in this room, though. No blood spilled or organs removed. Just memories pulled like teeth, the roots extracted from the gums, the unfamiliar pain deep and frightening. This was the final destination of hapless halfskins that wandered into the clay state for black market business or the sheer stupidity of adventure.

The biomite authorities would legally extract their mind and process their memories along with samples of their biomite strains, upload it into a database for analysis, claiming it helped them stay atop their rigorous scanning abilities.

When Mother was functional, when she was nothing more than the arena-sized dome residing in Montana monitoring the human population for biomites, she did the same thing. And Marcus was her henchman. He ordered biomites to be sent back to the dome for full immersion analysis. Halfskins would be dropped into a clear vat and digested, every cell slowly absorbed into her database.

She took their lives, their souls, Marcus had thought. *For the good of the human race.*

"That's not what I was doing," Mother later told him.

"What, then?"

"Taking their essence."

Essence. She didn't say soul, didn't say memories. Essence was something new. And when he asked, "Why were you taking their essence?"

"It's who I was."

He'd become accustomed to the childish manner in which she gave up information, like a computer that only provided answers when asked the correct questions.

"And who were you?" he would ask.

She wouldn't respond to the question.

"Get him on the table," a young female said.

"We can do it in the chair," a middle-aged man said. "We got to work fast."

There were half a dozen processing employees in the room, each at their stations. Marcus felt an animated buzz creep into the marrow of his bones as one of the scanning generators came to life. He didn't resist and kept his mind completely open, waiting for the bridge to drop so he could peek inside the processing machine that would connect him to the network that identified bricks, the network that gave up Margaret, the network that went back to the powers-that-be.

Where Jamie had gone.

She had been in that room, had been subjected to the same body freeze. Was she afraid? Did they see her memories? Did they know about the powers-that-be? He wanted the answers to all of those questions, but more than any of that he wanted to know... *where did she go?*

The feds would never allow these amateur clay hacks to scrape Marcus Anderson, never give his mind access to the network. Mother said this would bring them closer to their destiny. He didn't care for the word destiny, but she was right.

"I don't like this." It was the youngest of the crew, a man that looked barely out of high school. "I mean, why is the media everywhere, right? There's a leak or something. It's like someone knows we were going to do this. Like..."

"Like what?" the woman said.

He shook his head. His instincts were right, but he was too young to assert them.

"Smart, that one," Mother said.

"Let's go!" Don stepped into the lab and walloped big pockets of air between his meaty hands. "Do a quick scrape, send it out to all the clay facilities immediately. I want everyone to have a copy of this brick's psychological profile, where he's been the last five years, what he's doing here. Draw a sample of his blood and do the same. We're short on time, people."

The team came at Marcus with a multitude of straps and gadgets. One wrapped around his arm, another pasted to his temples. The young woman opened a set of stainless steel tools all pointed and gleaming in the room's bright lights.

Someone shouted, "Testing!"

Another hum filled the room, this one synchronizing with the previous one. Marcus's teeth sang. A tiny smile grew beneath his skin. No one would see it, but perhaps they'd read it on their monitors.

A third machine hummed.

The room dimmed. Marcus realized the lights hadn't changed, it was his vision. The circuits were drawing him out of his body. A glittering ball of energy appeared near the ceiling.

No. Not moving. I'm not in my body.

He had assumed some other form, an astral projection that was weightless and effortless. The light was growing and no one seemed to notice, no one seemed to see it. The drawbridge to another place was lowering, a direct route to the source, to the powers-that-be.

Several ringtones rang at once.

A long pause as they all checked their phones. The youngest said, "Hello?"

The other phones suddenly stopped.

"It's, uh, for you, sir."

"Put that thing away, son," Don replied. "Why do you have your phone on anyway?"

"It… it wasn't."

Another long pause. "Who is it?"

"He says he, uh, wants to speak with the head fucking idiot."

An awkward moment was flung around the room like a shit storm. Every one caught a piece. Don's footsteps were heavy and hard. He answered, got one word out. And then silence.

They waited.

Don threw the phone at the young man. "Get him out of here."

Someone knew Marcus was there. Maybe they knew why. *Someone on the other side of the drawbridge.*

"And someone find out how the fuck they got all your phone numbers!" Don stormed out of the lab.

The machines died. The gear came off. They wheeled him out. Don clearly didn't know who he was dealing with on the other end. Or what.

No one did.

A FREIGHT TRAIN slid down a pair of iron rails, crashing into Marcus's head.

He opened his eyes.

The ceiling was beige; the toilet was metal.

The walls were imbedded with mesh wire that hummed interference, a Faraday cage that nullified biomite activity.

"It's eleven a.m."

Mother stepped away from his bed, a mattress as thin as newspaper. Expressionless and calm, she watched him from across the room, her bare feet pressed against the concrete.

"You've been isolated for two days."

He listened without looking. His actions would be monitored, even eye movements. They'd be looking for something unusual such as talking to himself or interacting with the projection of a nonexistent artificially intelligent old woman.

"Don was ordered to put you under until the federal agents arrived," she said. "You were transferred to the Pentagon. They've taken blood samples, scanned your brain activity, and analyzed your biomite coding."

He avoided even forming a thought.

"They didn't find anything unusual. Nothing to explain how you've avoided them all this time. And no, they don't sense my presence."

The freight train rolled and crashed again. This time it was followed by footsteps; a lighter set of footfalls were bracketed by stern, heavy ones. They stopped outside the door. An alarm buzzed. A heavy lock tumbled and the door slid open.

A woman stood outside the cell, her hair pulled back, eyes large between thick black eyelashes. Her lips plump, a slight curl at the corner.

"Marcus Anderson," she said.

"Lydia."

"You were expecting me?"

"I'm always expecting you. Still with the agency, I see."

She observed him like an experiment. Despite the open door, he posed no threat inside the cell. It was the sort of safety one felt at a zoo, a gulf that separated the lions from the observation deck.

"How are you feeling?" she asked.

"A little sore." He stretched. "Your kids are grown up now, I suppose?"

"Now I know you're a clone. The Marcus Anderson I knew didn't give a shit about family."

"I've changed."

"Tell me we don't need these." A pair of cuffs dangled from her fingers.

It was a courtesy question. The woman to Lydia's left, a deceptively petite African American with short curls and dark brown eyes, was the biomite agent—a highly trained operative composed of 99.9% biomites capable of mind manipulation and incapacitation. The heat from her mind spattered over his skin like oil jumping off an iron griddle.

To Lydia's right was a slender man with strong hands and a smooth face. His brown hair was short and flat. His eyes, unreadable. His entire clay being was inaccessible. If the biomite agent somehow failed to control Marcus, the clay agent would use physical force. He would be immune to mind games.

Marcus stood. The biomite agent clamped her mind around him with a million needle-teeth.

"Back your dog off," he hissed.

"There we go," Lydia said. "The Marcus Anderson I know."

Another pair of agents—one biomite, one clay—waited further down the hall. They led the way, bracketing him two and two with Lydia out front. Somewhere behind him, Mother's damp footsteps followed.

He was led to a small room with a table and four chairs. A bottle of water sat in front of one of them. Two guards stationed themselves in the corners. Lydia closed the door. Mother appeared to sit in one of the chairs already pulled away from the table.

Half an hour later, the door swung open.

Jason Powell stood in the doorway, a red tie hung loosely around an open collar, a bundle of manila folders in his hand. His hair was a bit shaggier, a little sandier than the last time he saw him. He remained flat-footed, examining a miracle.

Powell closed the door. "According to the root analysis, you are *the* Marcus Anderson, the previous director of biomite oversight."

The stack of folders hit the table.

"Of course, there could be multiple clones of you all over the world."

"You know the truth."

"But do you?"

Mother got up and Powell dragged the empty chair from the table to sit. He spread the folders out and opened one.

"Five years ago," he mused, "the biomite surveillance system known as Mother collapsed. You were acting director at that time, living within the confines of the Montana dome. Records show you, toward the end of your assignment, wandering aimlessly in a paranoid and delusional state, claiming an *inner world* was somewhere within the industrial complex. And the system was not merely a program but a sentient, self-aware intelligence that you referred to as Mother. You remember that?"

Marcus looked at his hands folded upon the table. Mother chuckled from the corner.

"During the postmortem of said events, you made claims of conspiracy theories, of so-called 'powers-that-be' and, I quote, 'the human race has been duped into sleeping... Mother saw the truth of her own existence and the path of humanity and, accordingly, had issued her own self-destruction... we are all being farmed for a greater unknown purpose.' End quote."

Powell ran his finger along the highlighted lines.

"You remember that?"

"And then dream disease started," Marcus said, smirking.

"You never said dream disease."

Marcus sat back in the hard chair. Of course he remembered. They apprehended him after Mother collapsed, accused him of destroying her. He'd been kept in isolation for months, sleep deprived and harassed until his sanity teetered. He spoke to the walls, his logjammed thoughts plowing through streams of nonsense. There was so much to say, so much truth to impart.

There were episodes of him sobbing for days, begging for the end to come to the one realization that shouted louder than all the other thoughts.

I AM A BRICK!

"If you were an animal," Powell said, "we would've put you down. You were a psychological mess, a brick that thought it was human. But you were our only link to Mother's mysterious collapse, a rambling idiot having conversations with ghosts."

The days of madness were eternal until Marcus woke in a drug-fueled haze and there she was, standing in the middle of the room, wearing a flowing dress, short gray hair and a cherub grin. He blabbered through tears because his delusions were becoming too real. He tried to hurt her, swung on her, and put his hands around her neck. In the end, she held him and comforted him, warmly and gently.

"The gift," she whispered. "You are the gift."

"And then you were gone." Powell snapped his fingers. "You were sleeping in the cell and suddenly gone. Surrounded by buildings and walls and fences, you disappeared. Security footage showed you blipping out of existence like an apparition. Did you walk out? Was it an inside job? What was it, Marcus? What happened?"

Marcus offered a kind smile. A magician never betrayed his secrets.

Marcus was hunched at the shoulders. Although he didn't wear glasses, his left eye was still slightly misshapen and his bald pate sunspotted with age. The grimly bitter old man, however, was no longer there.

"Do you still talk to yourself? Still see Mother?" Powell's fingers danced an erratic rhythm on the table. "Does she answer back?"

Marcus slid the folder back. "I have rights."

"What do you want? Let's start there. You reappear after five years of being completely off the grid, which, I'm assuming, you did by choice in a very public setting. You wanted everyone to see you because we assured the public that every brick had been identified and relocated. You did this because... why, Marcus? To make fools out of us?"

"I have rights provided to fabricated humans under the sentience laws—"

"Not until I get answers!" Powell slammed the folder with a dull-thumping fist. "You are still a brick, you understand that? Your rights don't mean shit when it comes to threatening the security of the United States, so find a dark corner in your fucked-up brain to file that fact because I'm not playing."

"A law firm will be contacting you—"

"How did you leave? Where have you been, Marcus? And why did you come back?"

"I've prepared a statement that my legal representatives will deliver."

Powell nodded incredulously, leaned back and sniffed. "Make all the statements you want. We're going to pull you apart, Marcus. Whatever you pulled last time will not happen again, I promise you. You're going in a cage and you're going to stay there a very long time. We're going to find out what you're made of."

"My lawyers will be holding a public conference soon. After which they will file for my legal rights to exist as a fabricated human and you will treat me as such. That is my legal right."

"This is the federal government." His fingers pattered another nervous rhythm. "You think the world cares about bricks, Marcus? They're the new race we can blame all our troubles on and not feel guilty. You are the new-age scapegoat. That's why you and the rest of those plastic fabbed fakies are alive, why they're on display in the middle of nowhere, without their dreamlands, without their freedom.

The world needs a scapegoat, Marcus. And the world doesn't give a goddamn what we do to you.

"Your lawyers can hold press conferences on the White House lawn for all I care. Whatever you planned on happening after you surrendered, it's over. You're not leaving. You live here now."

"He's quite convincing," Mother said.

Marcus considered the bottle of water. The ring broke beneath the lid as he twisted it. He took a swallow and slowly replaced the cap. After a long pause, he leaned in and said, without menace, "The world is watching."

In today's day and age, public opinion could move buildings. His legal team, vetted and retained well ahead of this day, would continue breathing on that fire. They would sway public opinion.

"What do you want?" Powell asked.

"Process me like a brick."

"The Settlement, is that it? You want to go there? What's out there?"

"I'm tired of running," Marcus lied. "I'm an old man. The Settlement is more appealing than my other options."

"Okay." The charade was obvious. "I'm not the enemy, Marcus. There will be nowhere to hide when we pull you apart, you understand that."

"I have nothing to hide."

"We don't need to find a reason to shut you down. You've proven you're a threat. No one will argue that. We'll put you to sleep tonight."

"The world is watching."

"I see."

He rapped the table and considered the folders before scooping them up. No sense in going through the rest of them. The interview was over. Marcus had planned years in advance of this moment. Powell was out of his league. And he knew it.

He stopped at the door. For a moment, he seemed to look directly at Mother. It was enough to cause Marcus to flinch, regardless of the impossibility.

"What happened to you," Powell finally said, glancing at the floor, "you deserved that, you understand. Don't blame the world for it."

Marcus suppressed a smile.

The transition from clay to brick was horrendous. To look with doubt upon one's existence was to dance with psychosis. Powell watched him unravel and had assumed Marcus chose to fabricate himself. What Powell didn't know was that Marcus survived to discover the unfettered freedom.

The gift.

"I still like him," Mother said.

After a week in the cell, Lydia and the guards escorted him to a cage. He didn't speak to his attorneys, didn't hear anything beyond the walls of his cell. He was simply marched to a very special cage.

It was underground. The public didn't know about it. Very few did.

The room was smaller than the cell. There was a chair with leather straps on wide armrests and stirrups. Another one unbuckled at the headrest. It was an armpit that smelled of fried circuits and saliva, easily mistaken for death row.

The escorts cattle-prodded him into the chair, locking him down until his arms and legs were secured, his head tied into a saddle. A rubber bite guard was shoved deep into his mouth, tasting of chlorine.

Mother watched from the corner.

The automated rhythm took control of his breathing once again. His eyes, suddenly as dry as his mouth, began blinking on a slow, deliberate schedule.

I am the one to lead, he told himself. *The one to dream.*

Marcus assumed the prophecy suggested he would need Jamie,

Paul and Raine to fulfill his journey, but he believed that he was more than the sum of the parts, that he could lead, he could see. Perhaps he would lead and dream.

Giving himself to the network, to have his mind pulled apart and put back together would give him insight, Mother had told him. He believed her. She had yet to be wrong, this he knew. Begrudgingly.

And I will bleed.

"I'll see you when this is over," Mother said.

He wanted to nod, to recognize her. He would've answered her if he could. She was inside him, knew what he felt, sensed that he was experiencing something he hadn't felt in quite some time.

Fear.

The agents walked out and locked the door.

Mother walked behind him, putting her warm hands on his shoulders. A mix of earth and sea and floral essence overcame the room's terror. Then her touch was gone.

I am the son to be.

And the long walk across the desert had begun.

II_

One to dream.

CHAPTER ONE HUNDRED THIRTY-SIX_

THE ROAR OF A CRANE'S DIESEL ENGINE RATTLED THE BRICK house.

Paul grabbed a metal casing before it vibrated off the desk. In front of him was a clear-case box, something the size of a mini-refrigerator, that continued to whir. Inside, tubing swirled around an object like a mass of pencil-thin snakes slowly printing a three-dimensional object.

The proposal to convert the brick house into a research facility had been approved the past fall. Paul remembered the news quite well—it arrived not long after Jamie was buried.

The People loved the idea. The proposal was about innovations that would benefit the People, not so much about the bricks' well-being. They didn't give a shit about that. Healthy bricks got them nothing.

So walls were knocked down and additional weight-bearing beams erected to open the floor plan. They were up and running by summer, the first patent on tool fabrication delivered a year after Jamie was buried.

The People were thrilled. And wanted more.

Bob's booming laughter was somewhere beneath the crane's now-idling engine. Paul tapped at the buttons on the miniature clear-case fabricator, its use approved for prototypes and small components.

Not what Paul was fabricating.

On the bench, the metal casing of a faux turbine capacitor lay open like an elaborate clamshell, waiting for the fabricator to finish. When the misting snakes snapped into silent sleep, he reached inside, the object still warm and rubbery, the texture of liver, and sealed it in plastic shrink before dropping it inside the hollow of the faux turbine capacitor. Snapping it together, the object held snugly in the embedded foam, he shoved it to the bottom of a leather bag.

The fabricator's lines were flushing when the front door opened. A flood of construction sounds—hammers on metal, grinding generators—filled the house. Paul wiped down the nozzles, his heartbeat tapping double-time.

"What're you doing in here?" Bob wheezed. "Lab's closed."

"Cleaning up."

"Well, finish up already. I'm locking the door."

Paul put the computers to sleep, but not before ensuring the matrix he had uploaded was completely erased. It took him months to install the incognito mode around the lab's surveillance. The People didn't want a single fabrication slipping through their greedy fingers.

Bob opened the leather bag. "What's this?"

"Careful. Just came out of the fabricator."

"What is it?"

"Need it for my wind turbine. Experimenting with a new design."

"You get it approved?"

"Couldn't fabricate it if I didn't."

Bob stared at the seam. If he knew anything about mechanics, he'd see the release mechanism that would pop it open and dump the warm object on his lap. The lab would be closed forever.

Bob dropped it in the bag.

"Careful! Break it and I'll report you."

"Get out of here."

It was a bluff. Paul wouldn't report anything, but it kept Bob's asshole-mode in check. Too many complaints and he'd be investigated. Bob wouldn't survive close scrutiny from the People. In a way, Bob was good for Paul. He wasn't smart and had enough lurking skeletons he would bend to a bluff.

Outside, the girded structure of a new research and fabrication lab was three stories tall. The crane dangled an I-beam above the top floor, the earth shuddering.

The People want more.

In the year since the brick house had been converted, sustainable energy production had been improved by fifty percent. Given the right facilities, solutions to the world's energy crises could be fast-tracked. And the People would rake the profits.

The bricks weren't complaining.

Forget Bob and his loyalty to the People. Boredom was the real enemy. Conspiracy theories aside, the Settlement was just a brilliant scheme to bring the bricks together, to take away their freedom, suppress their creativity, torture them with boredom until they worked for free. *Happily.*

Conspiracy or not, it worked.

The bricks wanted something–*anything*—to feel useful, to feel human. To matter. Even if that meant lining the fat pricks' pockets and giving away their ideas for free. Paul was on board throughout the process, even led a coalition to get it approved.

But he had his own reasons.

"Get in." Bob stomped down the front steps toward the truck.

"I'll walk."

"No, you'll ride. I ain't got time to follow you through the woods."

The leather bag kept Paul from telling Bob to go fuck himself. There were no Settlement laws that prevented him from suggesting what to do with his dick. But ever since Paul started smuggling contraband out of the brick house, he'd become a model citizen.

A good brick.

The truck smelled like a sweat stain. The floorboards were

littered with paper cups, the dashboard buried beneath wads of paper and napkins. Bob pushed himself behind the steering wheel, the bench seat sinking. He dropped it in drive and the electric motor whirred.

He drew on the end of a metal pipe, half-ass aiming the blue cloud at the window crack. The icy menthol made the stuffy cab smell better.

Satellite radio rambled as they crossed an experimental field of wind turbines. Bob turned it up.

"It's like prison," a caller said. "I mean, look what happens when you commit a crime in America. You go to jail and get three hots and a cot, right? A free education all because you killed someone."

"Caller," the host answered, "you're out of your mind. Yeah, you get fed and educated while living in a ten-by-ten room and raped on Sundays. That's a hell of a deal."

"You know what I'm saying. Those bricks get moved out to the country and you and me pay for their homes, pay for their food and now we're paying for those buildings. You see those things? I bet universities don't have facilities like that."

"What's your name? Tim?"

"Yeah."

"Tim, the bricks are making strides in energy production like we've never seen. You like it when you flip the switch and the lights come on?"

"Don't give me that. We were doing just fine before bricks came along."

"Oh, yeah. We were doing great, Tim. Addicted to oil, polluting oceans. We had it all figured out."

"Yeah, and we were dying in dreamland."

"The fabs have nothing to do with dream disease."

"*Fabs.* Yeah, whatever."

"They're fabricated humans, Tim."

"All I know is that dreamland changed when *bricks* got legal," the caller said. "Used to be I could go down the street and pass twenty dream cafes. Now you got to have a million bucks if you don't want dream disease."

"You don't see the connection between dream disease and big money?"

"Oh, don't start that. No one ever heard of dream disease before the sentience laws made bricks legal and now it's too late."

"You're smart, Tim. Where you from?"

"I read the feeds, that's all."

"Uh-huh. I see. So you want the fabs to what? You want them dead?"

"Off. Not dead, off. You can't be dead if you ain't alive."

Clouds puffed through Bob's laughter like a steam-powered choo-choo. This kind of talk powered his boner faster than three-way porn.

"You want them dead so you can have more dream cafes, is that it, Tim?" the host asked. "That's your gripe?"

"Don't twist my words, you bricklover. The sentience laws need to be overturned, the clay states need to be abolished, and dreamland deserves to be returned to the People."

"The People?" The host yuck-yucked. "You aren't part of the People, Tim. You're just a sad little man. The People, the real People, are the ones that pull the strings, you dope. They're the ones that make the laws, the ones that turn a profit."

"So you're buying the powers-that-be theory?" Tim asked.

The host hung up and ranted without interruption. "This conspiracy isn't about whether we landed on the moon or whether aliens plow symbols in wheat fields, Tim. We're way past all that. There is a thin slice of people that control the world—they control the oil, the money and the People. Don't kid yourself, you moron. Do I believe there's one person at the top making us dance? You're damn right I do."

Paul doubted the host was really a brick sympathist. Just a ratings whore.

"And another thing." The host was shouting now. "That Marcus Anderson thing? The lost brick the government promised didn't exist anymore, the one that orchestrated the collapse, the prick responsible for the death of tens of thousands of halfskins before the sentience laws were created? They didn't shut him off, Tim. You need to update your feeds."

A brushfire rushed through Paul's chest, burning behind his eyes, all papery and brittle and hot. *Marcus Anderson.* The one responsible for the death of so many good people, honest people that needed biomites to survive a nasty stroke of God's whimsy—car accidents, genetic diseases, dumb luck. Biomites were modern medicine, the only hope for a child, a loved one. And Marcus Anderson didn't want you to have too many because... just because. Now that piece of shit was a brick.

The universe is just.

That bastard's relentless pursuit drove Cali mad; his vengeful will to bring capricious justice to his insane little world chipped away at her will to live. Dr. Cali Richards, the biometric engineer that created a whole new strain of biomites that couldn't be monitored by the government, the first person to ever escape the all-watching eye of Marcus Anderson and his biomite henchmen.

Marcus Anderson, the story went, didn't know he was a brick at first. The word from the government was that he had been fabricated without his knowledge, that he refused to believe the tests and went mad.

They said he died, too.

Paul knew what that moment of realizing you're a brick was like. Cali had delivered that very same news to Paul on the farm, showing him his true nature. He knew what it felt like when the realization was revealed in stark lighting, the rug yanked from the table to show the rabbit of truth. Marcus denied it at first just like Paul because he didn't feel any different. He had the same thoughts, same emotions. His body exactly the same.

But deep down, hidden in dark spaces that no one could see, the truth lurked like a coiled serpent. Marcus, like Paul, didn't want to see a truth that would change him forever.

I am a brick, Marcus Anderson thought eventually. If he didn't, insanity would've claimed him. He would be dead. So would Paul.

But Cali wasn't a brick.

She still carried the thin sliver of clay like a burden of the entire human race. In the end, Paul had lain down with her beneath a broken swing set and stared into a steel slate of sky. They held hands as she executed a self-termination command that would shut down their biomites.

But Paul woke up.

I couldn't do it to you, Paul, the note said.

She'd become so vulnerable, a delicate rose blossom still fragrant but bruised as the petals had fallen. She just couldn't hold any more of the world's pain and suffering. Enough had already been yoked across her shoulders. She was so tired. That was why Marcus Anderson held a special place in Paul's heart.

"They think you live in paradise," Bob said above the radio banter.

Paul looked out the window and stoked the blue flames of anger. There was plenty to burn.

They emerged from the trees and passed new cabins on the right. Down the slope another half mile, Bob stopped at a cabin tucked under a leaning spruce, a wisp of smoke chugging from the chimney.

The windows were lit up.

Bob opened his door.

"What are you doing?" Paul said.

"Going to say hello to your little lady."

"She's not in the mood, Bob."

Raine had moved in with Paul, unable to be alone for long periods. Her belongings were still back at her cabin, which she would go back for on a daily basis. It occupied her mind, burning the abundance of empty time.

She appeared at the door, a fuzzy image through the dark screening. She wasn't even a hundred pounds—hollows were sucked beneath her cheekbones, eyes dark and obscured in shallow caves. Firelight reflected off her bald scalp. She shaved it every morning before she trekked back to her cabin.

Ever since Jamie was buried.

"You need to get some exercise, little lady." Bob was out of the truck.

"What do you want?" she replied.

"Your husband here needed a ride."

She crossed her arms, pointy elbows cupped in each palm, tired of explaining Paul wasn't her husband. Bob knew that. He knew her husband, the only love of her life, was in dreamland. Nix was waiting for her. Bob wanted her to remind him that Nix was out of reach, Nix was trapped in her dreamland only so he could reply *Dreamland ain't real, little lady*.

Just another twist.

"Thanks," was all she said. "I was worried."

Bob clobbered the wooden steps with steel-toes and peered over her shoulder. The disappointment sagged on his shoulders. The fight had gone out of her, the piss and vinegar drained from a long seething wound. Bob took her complacence as a challenge to light that flame again.

Give him a fight.

Bob couldn't search the place, not without probable cause. In the early days, he could do whatever he wanted—turn the place over and eat their food. But the bricks appealed to a higher court, establishing their rights. They couldn't escape the Settlement, but they could call it a home—a home with law and order.

Bob snatched the leather bag.

"You already searched it."

"Maybe I missed something."

Raine closed the door. A wretched smile dimpled Bob's doughy cheeks. He drew on the metal pipe, thick vapor streaming from his nostrils, dragon-like.

Paul avoided fidgeting. Instead, he feigned impatience, leaning against the post while Bob shoved his porky fingers along the bag's seams in search of trapdoor pockets or some other nonsense. He shook the turbine capacitor.

"Damn it, Bob. You damage that and I'll report it as unnecessary search and seizure."

"What's inside?"

"Components, what do you think? It's only thirty minutes out of the fabricator and you're shaking it like a baby." Paul stretched the bag open. "You finished?"

"I'm finished when I'm finished." He turned it over, tracing the surface with dirty fingernails. "What's your hurry?"

"It's late, I'm hungry. Don't want to be on the porch with you."

This only slowed the search. Sweat prickles flashed under Paul's sweatshirt. A thousand thoughts went through his mind.

"You think you're smart?" Bob asked.

"I'm hungry, Bob."

"You stay in the lab like that again, I'll have you banned."

"Fine."

"I'm going back there to check your work, so you know."

"Big surprise. You done?" Paul had settled into an expression of boredom brushed with frustration. Any sign of panic and Bob would take the component. He took another drag on the pipe and threw the piece into the bag, leaving a minty trail of vapor to the truck. Paul watched the taillights disappear down the dirt road before going inside.

His knees were cold.

"He's gone?" Raine stood in the bedroom.

Paul nodded.

"You got it?"

He dug the clunky piece out, palms damp with sweat. Raine

covered her mouth and stepped back. That dangerous temptress of hope danced before her eyes.

Paul went to the kitchen and turned off the light, then went to the bathroom and cleaned up and changed clothes. Raine was sitting on the bed when he was finished, the crucifix of sticks between her hands. Paul lay on the couch, Raine on the bed.

It was sometime in the small hours of the night that he got up. His leather bag was still in the front room. He took it to the kitchen but didn't turn on the light. In the dark, he knelt in front of the oven.

Raine's bare feet were soft and sticky on the linoleum.

He lifted the front of the oven, still hot with the smell of broiled chicken, and Raine slid a small oval rug beneath the peg legs. The only window was small, above the sink. From a distance, no one would see him slide the oven away from the wall (the rug slipping across the floor without leaving tracks) to expose a patch of linoleum littered with dusted crumbs. Beneath thick greasy layers were the seams of a trapdoor.

Paul stepped into the gap between the cabinets and inserted the flat end of a screwdriver along the baseboard, triggering a spring-loaded switch to drop the panel (a system that took the last six months to design and build using fabricated parts that could be found in a new solar panel design).

A draft gusted out of the dark hole, cold and mysterious.

In the winter, the outside temperatures would keep it cold. In the summer, should they still need it for storage, it would draw from the freezer (the insulated space would keep energy consumption negligible).

Raine handed him the capacitor.

Only the sound of their breath filled the room. They didn't dare communicate with words or thoughts, careful to protect what they were seeing and thinking as he placed it next to the trapdoor. There would be no reason for the monitors to watch them through the emergency security cameras, not at this hour.

Raine leaned in, watching him play the faux capacitor like an instrument, his fingertips touching several places in a coded sequence and specific cadence.

It popped opened.

The spongy foam pushed the red, plastic-wrapped object on a delicate display. Even in the dark, it glistened beneath the plastic wrap, veins and arteries crossing the surface like a road map. As if freshly plucked from an open chest, it did not beat, lying in animated suspension, awaiting the spark of life.

Jamie's heart.

The Settlement would never be allowed a printer large enough to fabricate an entire body. And even if there was, Paul could never hope to have enough time and raw biomite material to produce it. But he could do it a piece at a time. And in Frankensteinian fashion, assemble her when the time had come.

He had spun the sample he scratched from her arm to replicate her DNA. The People had approved the bricks to establish a library of their own genetics should they ever need to fabricate organs for themselves. In that massive database, he hid Jamie's genome and mapped her entire organism.

Then he built the storage space.

He placed her heart into the dark cavern, the tissue soft and pliable. Raine wept as he slid the oven back into place. There was no dreamland, but one day there would be Jamie. Angels, she was beginning to believe, would never come to the Settlement.

Hope danced seductively around the table.

CHAPTER ONE HUNDRED THIRTY-SEVEN_

*T*HREADS.

Marcus stared at threads.

Threads crisscrossing in minute checkerboards, a predictable pattern in an endless array of subtle colors.

Threads.

It was the first coherent thought of self-awareness, a bubble in a soupy consciousness that was aware that it was aware.

Here. I am here. I am this.

The universe dipped and swayed in stomach-dropping swirls like the first moments on a descending elevator, or the rising slope of a roller coaster.

His head bounced. He was sitting in a chair, cushioned armrests, a silver buckle clasped over the waist of his bright orange jumper. As the universe of threads expanded, he recognized the crisscrossing pattern on the back of a headrest and the inordinately small oval windows. Marcus swam through the muddy confusion to find a word.

Plane.

A bag of vomit sloshed between his legs, still warm. Bitter slime coated his tongue. He continued counting threads, feeling his fingers and toes, returning to sense his head and chest after a long, long sleep.

Not sleep. Not sleep.

Sleep was silent, occasionally interrupted by episodes of dreams. The blank night that preceded his awakening with the thought of threads was an endless stream of images stretched across a distorted lens—fitful and disturbing. Silently screaming. His mind had been shredded, thoughts and memories tweezed apart, sifted for analysis, squeezed for secrets.

Atlanta.

That was where the horror show began.

Transferred to federal detention, locked in a cage for... *for how long?*

It was a small plane, luxurious. Three heads appeared above the seats ahead of him. He turned to see another two people behind him. One was a woman in her mid-thirties, auburn hair to her shoulders and delicate wrists, fumbling with a stack of magazines, notepads and folders. She walked clumsily to the seat across the aisle and dumped her cache in the empty seat next to her.

"Mr. Anderson, I'm Marianne Stanhope with the Associated Press. I'm sorry to rush you, but we'll be landing soon. They were expecting you to, um, wake a little sooner, so if you don't mind."

Wake. She stumbled over the word like waking belonged to her kind. Not bricks. Bricks didn't wake, they came online. They rebooted, turned on.

"Can you answer a few questions?"

He nodded once.

"Okay. For starters, what do you remember?"

His tongue crawled over his lips like a slug exploring new ground. He shook his head once. It was a stupid question.

"I realize things must be a little fuzzy. You've been held in isolation and subjected to deep-scan analysis for the past year." She reached across the aisle and pressed two fingers on the inside of his arm where purple and yellow bruises splashed his veins. "They kept you unconscious, fed you intravenously to download an entire catalog of your identity. Does that make sense?"

Of course. He was a national threat. An undiscovered brick that, by his own volition, surrendered. The days of hiding from the People were long gone. They would have to make sure it never happened again.

So why am I still alive?

"Why give yourself up, Mr. Anderson?"

He felt a smile tug at the corners of his mouth. She leaned forward, drawn in by the first sign of life.

Why did he do it? Why give himself up? He'd been invisible for years, so why arrange legal counsel to keep the whole charade in the public eye, subject himself to a year of psychological flogging?

Truth was, he didn't know. Not exactly.

Only one person knew the true answer. Marcus looked to his right, the seat empty. Mother wasn't with him.

"Did you want to be with your own kind?" Marianne asked. "Better to be in exile with your own kind than to be free and alone?"

"Lonely?" He slow-licked his dry lips. "You can say that, yes."

"How'd you do it? How did you remain so elusive all these years? The public wants to know, Mr. Anderson. The government just hands out bullshit reasons, claiming you're an anomaly that's been corrected. How'd you do it?"

She wouldn't expect him to answer that if he was lucid. Perhaps she was hoping that he would blurt out a secret like an inebriated loner spouting love to the first person that touches him.

How did he absorb thoughts? How did he control the motivations of others? How did he compel them to see what he wanted, to hear and see what he wished? How did he do almost anything he wanted? The clay humans, the ones without a single biomite, were the only beings outside his influence. The rest of the world was his to pick.

The question couldn't be answered, though. It was a gift bestowed upon him, but how could that be captured in words, let alone a sound bite? He could sync with her, press his mind against the fabric of her awareness and let her know the impression of his knowledge directly, know the secrets Mother had given to him years ago.

The secret to his powers was to become the universe. And that would make no sense to her.

A single slice of clay prevents her from seeing the universe, her imperfections clouding her cataract vision.

And bricks are the inferior species?

"What about these *powers-that-be*?" she asked.

He twitched. She saw it. It was more than a sign of life, it was a reaction. She'd touched a soft spot.

"You were muttering it over and over, warning about the *powers-that-be.* Someone on the inside leaked it to the press and it turned viral. You said there is someone controlling the world, one person. You identified this person as a male. It sounds very ominous. Could you expand on that? Who is the powers-that-be?"

He looked out the window. His powers had their limits. The universe didn't provide him with all the answers.

"Marcus." She spoke softly, like loud noises might scare the bunny. "Those were the ramblings of a madman. But you're not mad. You know something. You owe it to us to share. Are we doomed? Is there something we should be doing?"

Us, she said. *You owe it to us.*

He wasn't one of them, no. Not anymore. And maybe he did owe something to those that possessed clay, even a small slice. He'd shut enough of them off, and wrongly so. If there was a hell (he no longer subscribed to that theory), he'd spend twenty eternities paying for it.

So, yeah. He owed them.

The plane tipped to the left. Endless hills were covered in a patchwork of quilted trees and exposed boulders, frosted mountaintops in the distance.

"We'll be landing soon," someone announced.

"One more question." She sighed, contemplating which of a long list of queries was the most important.

She had very few answers and wasn't likely going to get more. She'd write about the experience, give her interpretation of his expression, his mood. If she was politically liberal (which she probably was), she'd cast him as a victim of government persecution. Conservative and he'd be drawn as a threat to the human race and was being shown more mercy than he deserved.

"How do we know you won't do it again?"

Marcus held her stabbing gaze. The answer she was looking for would be in a wry smile or a false denial or contrived confusion. Instead, he remained impassive to let her draw her own conclusions because the question itself was revealing.

We know you can do it again, Marcus. But will you?

The plane tipped again and circled toward a short landing strip carved out of the trees. Beyond it was a sprawling, one-story building.

They landed near two yellow posts.

A CLAY AGENT to his right, a biomite agent to his left.

They stepped into a lobby, the new-smell still lingering on the Berber carpet. It was sparsely filled with furniture and looked more like an art gallery with paintings filling the empty spaces (bricks displaying their creativity for the few guests that made it out this far). Landscapes, still lifes, and abstract creations blended in an inspired array of creativity.

Voices muttered on the other side of a thin paneled wall, laughter and deep-tone authority. The stream of conversations flowed in various tones.

A young man entered from the left, wearing a puffy green coat, a stack of clothing folded on his forklift arms.

"This way."

They went to a small room. He was given the clothes—khakis, flannel shirt, undershirt and low-cut boots—and changed while the agents watched. Marcus could feel their two minds but didn't think much of it. He was still waking up, fitting back into his body that was stiff and new, the seams still freshly sewn.

Not waking. Hibernating.

No waking like a long sleep, not a hibernation. More like the sleep of a caterpillar that wraps itself in a cocoon, emerging with wings.

A transformation.

The wings still soft and unfurling.

After another wait, the same green-coated young man escorted them back through the lobby, past a large room with projection screens and rows of padded chairs that seemed more fitting for a conference center than the entrance to long-term imprisonment. They waited outside a door where muffled voices continued.

"All right." The young man pulled the door open.

Inside was an oddly long room with three tables pushed end to end. Several people sat like apostles with office supplies and coffee mugs. And behind them stood more men and women clad in puffy green coats with badges sewn on their sleeves. Their expressions ranged from bored to smug. The obese one in the middle, the one with hands planted in his pockets, sat on the smug end of the spectrum.

Bob is his name. Bob is the leader.

Marcus didn't think much about that intuition, a name and a fact that dropped into his mind like a sponge drawing a bead of water.

Marcus was led front and center. The agents sat against the wall. There was no chair for him. He would stand.

Marcus had been on the other side of the table, once upon a time. He'd been part of committees that decided the fate of wrongdoers, parked behind cheap tables, asking questions and rendering a decision before ordering chicken wraps for lunch.

It was a time he ran the biomite oversight committee, was part and parcel of pushing laws that protected human rights. But when his fetishes were exposed (the late night orgies with fabricated sex dolls that morphed into subgenres of titillation that included strangulation and kill sex) he was seen as unfit for duty.

He'd been a prisoner all his life to those despot urges, those morally reprehensible addictions. Now he was free of them. He could choose how to feel, how to be.

Real prison is a state of mind, not a location.

"Marcus Anderson." A woman at the table, hair professionally short, eyes sharp blue, offered a gentle smile without the placating generosity reserved for frightened children. "The purpose of this meeting is to make clear the rules and reasons that you find yourself here. Let's call it an official introduction to your situation."

That was a new one. He wasn't fabbed, wasn't a brick or a fabricated human. *I'm a situation.*

"Your presence is unexpected, of course," she continued. "All fabricated humans were thought to be identified and accounted for and then you come along. While there is still some doubts about your assignment here, no evidence of wrongdoing or deceit has been found. Your unusual abilities have been stripped. Therefore, the People have ruled you have a right to existence under the statutes of the sentience laws. And here we are. Are we clear?"

She waited for acknowledgement. He nodded.

Notes were taken.

She continued to outline his rights and what to expect. Occasionally, one of the other apostles would take over. There would be long pauses where he was expected to acknowledge that he understood.

We are clear.

"Pete Haywood is the acting director of the Settlement," the woman said.

A squatty man of Middle Eastern descent nodded, his olive skin dark, eyebrows thick as fur. Lips pink. He was a resident of the Settlement, a full-fledged brick. His fabricators were software engineers that lived in the Seattle area that sought to replace all their employees with Haywood clones.

"Thank you, Mrs. Allston." Pete ran his hands over the desk. "I'd like to welcome you, Mr. Anderson. The Settlement, despite its appearance, has grown into something we've become proud of and we hope you'll join us in our continued productivity."

Pete continued spouting company-line bullshit about the advantages and how far they'd come, how they'd rebounded in this time of crises and the generosity of the People had given them opportunities to grow spiritually as well as academically and professionally.

It was the sort of horseshit abuse victims spout before returning to old relationships, the rationalizations they told themselves at night so it didn't hurt so much. So at least something made sense.

The People are good, they are just. We understand why they did this. And it could be worse.

Fear was why there was a Settlement. Fear was always at the root of suffering.

"Late summer, we will open a state-of-the art biomite research facility," Pete announced. "It will be equivalent to the best the world has to offer. Our advancements in biomite technology, as I'm sure you know, have taken the world to new heights."

Advancements they gave freely to the People. *It could be worse,* Pete would say.

If you give the monster enough cookies, he won't go away, Pete. He'll only want more.

Next up, the monitors were introduced. They were normal clays with normal lives that took these jobs to make a lot of money and build resumes for security jobs somewhere else. Marcus got a sense of their daily lives, their spouses and children, their struggles on the Settlement. Again, intuiting these facts did not surprise him, seeming as normal as reading a Post-it note.

"Thank you." Bob cleared his throat. "Just want to make clear that we are the Settlement's law enforcement, Anderson."

Agitation rumbled across the administration's expressions. They preferred *monitors* over *law enforcement.* This wasn't a prison.

At least Bob recognized the truth.

He explained the yellow posts. "The perimeter of the Settlement.

Cross them once and you're knocked out. Cross them twice and you're turned off. Understand?"

He explained the cabins and the limits of their rights to gather and communicate through thought-command. He explained the phones that each one of the monitors carried, displaying it like a science-fiction ray gun.

"We are clay," Bob said. "You cannot see inside us, cannot manipulate us. But we can manipulate you with this, understand. We will know where you are at all times. We can stop you. We can move you. And we can swipe you."

He was the playground bully that let it be known that the administration might be the teachers, but he was the head shit.

"Understand?" he boomed.

Marcus nodded.

"Then we'll get along just fine."

Some final business was discussed. Marcus was beginning to slump. His knee was aching, an injury he sustained many years ago. He thought it curious that he felt so... human again. Aches and pains were something he controlled at will, no more difficult than commanding his thoughts and emotions. No less difficult than raising his hand. But there he was crooked and aging like a prisoner of war.

"I don't want a circus." The woman aimed a pencil at him. "You're still somewhat of a mystery, Mr. Anderson. Despite all the public outcry for your fair and just treatment and your lawyers' antics to have you released onto the Settlement, you are not well-liked. You shut a lot of people off in your tenure, Mr. Anderson. Even relatives of the fabricated humans that you will be living with."

She held his gaze. He sensed that she was one of them, that as a little girl she'd seen family members taken during the era of halfskin laws and shut down for having too many biomites. Halfskin laws that Marcus enforced.

"Are we clear?" She closed a folder.

Marcus nodded.

He was escorted out of the back of the building. The circus inside had ended; a new one was about to begin. He waited on the back steps as one of the monitors went to fetch a cart. They would take him to his cabin, introduce him to the rest of his life.

Bob walked to a white truck, adjusting a straining belt, cramming a cowboy hat over his extra-large head. He wasn't worried about Marcus or concerned about the disruption.

He was thinking about lunch.

And then Marcus realized what was happening.

Someone stepped next to him, her loose clothing fluttering in the prairie wind, white hair pulled back. Mother watched Bob climb into his truck. Bob was thinking about lunch. She was nodding as she did so, acknowledging what Marcus realized.

I can read clay.

CHAPTER ONE HUNDRED THIRTY-EIGHT_

A CANDLE FLAME DANCED IN THE DRAFT, WAX POOLING AROUND the blackened pigtail. Teacups half-full of Darjeeling tea were set around it. A Holy Bible, the cover bent at the corners and black as the burning wick, lay closed.

Maggie started to gather the teacups.

"No, no," Raine exclaimed. "I'll clean up. It's getting late and you all need to get going."

Maggie, a frumpy Midwesterner, hovered over the couch, knees bent, conflicted between helping and leaving. It was bad manners to abandon a mess after prayer group. She was a dreamlander of a lonely garage biometric engineer, an eccentric man that fabbed a body to download his dreamland lover into reality. Like Raine, she had adjusted to physical reality. Probably better than Raine.

Phillip, the short, unassuming clone of a Fortune 500 accounting firm, sat across from Raine, looking down his long nose at a notepad he diligently scribbled on with a short pencil. The next prayer group would be at his cabin and would be more accommodating with better food, better tea and coffee.

Because clones considered themselves closer to real humans than the plants and a hell of lot more legitimate than dreamlanders.

As far as Raine was concerned, they were all fucked.

"Closing prayer, everyone?" Phillip stated more than asked, extending his unusually long-fingered hands that reminded Raine of something more simian than human.

"Robbie?" Raine patted the young man's knee sitting next to her. "You want to lead prayer?"

Phillip cleared his throat. This was Raine's house, her meeting. She could choose.

"All right." Robbie nodded. He was of African descent, his dark skin smooth, his features slender and boyish despite his age. He was a plant that was fabricated by an elderly rich widow that wanted companionship in her final years, memories of servitude transplanted into his history.

The four members of the Settlement's weekly prayer group sat on the edge of the couch and formed a ring of clasped hands around the coffee table, their palms clammy and cold.

"Dear Lord." Robbie bowed his head. "Please bless this house and the beings within it as we seek to follow Your will. We give thanks to the life You give us and every breath You allow."

His grip tightened. Raine wanted to squeeze back, to say, *Yeah, me too, I believe that too.* But she was still praying for strength and wisdom to wake up in the morning. And an angel.

That was why she prayed.

"Please Lord, keep Raine's family safe and sound during this time of exile. We pray that one day she may return to see them and be with them and celebrate Your glory. We pray in Your name. Amen."

"Amen."

Raine walked them to the door, where hugs were exchanged. Maggie was like a big doughy mother; sinking into her embrace was like falling into a warm, breathing pillow with a big heart beneath the thin fabric.

"Bless you, darling," Maggie said.

Phillip wrapped his spidery arms around her, his frame rather hard, and gave one quick squeeze and a pat on the shoulder.

"Bless you," he announced.

Robbie held her the longest, swaying back and forth, stroking the back of her smooth head, whispering in her ear. "It'll be all right, one of these days."

The old woman that fabbed him did a very good job.

She watched them climb off the porch and stayed at the door until their truck entered the trees, deep tracks laid in the snow behind it. The limbs were heavy and wet. The sky was blue, but more snow was on the way, a dark smudge creeping over the mountains, the winter wind biting her cheeks.

A helicopter chopped the distant air.

Raine closed the door and turned up the music until she couldn't hear the approaching blades. She warmed her hands at the fireplace, humming along to the gospel tracks Robbie had put together just for her. The fire warmed her skin.

Audible pings echoed in her head, reminders that she should be at the gate in ten minutes. She turned off communications while cleaning up, then went to shower. She soaked in the hot water until the tank turned tepid. It was the only relief of her daily routine, the only time she felt clean—hot water stripping the film of her life away, that outer layer that clung like an odor, a slick layer of memories.

She wrapped up in a robe and stood in front of the fire, opening the terrycloth to expose herself to the flames. Her ribs pushed from the skin. She imagined Phillip could grasp them one at a time with his slender, chopsticky fingers.

It was twenty minutes past the hour.

Raine looked out the window. She was no longer in the cabin across from the brick house, having been relocated for the construction workers. Her new cabin wasn't far from Paul's, but she still didn't feel comfortable there.

Still, she wished she could be at the field to watch the brick house, to warn him if someone was coming.

She was supposed to be at the gate to officially welcome Marcus Anderson to the Settlement, despite the fact he had already been there for months. Things had to settle down. Pete didn't like all the controversy. Despite everything Marcus Anderson had done in his past life, Pete wanted to welcome him to the family.

Raine wouldn't do that.

Pete was a good man, a man of well wishes and good intention. Marcus Anderson was an old man now that lived on the Settlement. *We take care of our own. Let's put the past in the past,* he said. *He's one of us now.*

In a way, Marcus had helped her and Paul. The old man had been the perfect distraction. His welcome party was a rare opportunity for Paul to fabricate the lungs. *They have to be done as a pair,* he said. The largest of the organs, he didn't know how they were going to do it.

Months had gone by. Winter was almost over, when most everyone tended to stay inside. Soon the weather would break. But then the old man (a recluse since he arrived) requested that Pete arrange that welcome party. It was like her prayers had been answered.

Send me an angel.

She had prayed every morning, every night before bed, that there would be an opportunity to bring Jamie one step closer. She needed that victory. Paul insisted that fabricating Jamie would bring her back, that her last moments were stored in the DNA scraping he had crudely scratched from her arm, that she'd remember who she was.

It was ludicrous.

Paul was a victim of his own delusions that Raine would never crush. He just wanted his daughter back. She wanted Jamie back, too. But more than that, if she was honest, she needed to get something back from God.

He had taken so much from her.

She stood at the door until her toes were cold. She started for the bedroom to get socks when something moved in the trees. The square grill emerged like silver teeth, the headlights glowing in the daylight.

No.

Bob's truck eased into the sunlight, grimy snow glittering on the hood. His big white cowboy hat filled the cab. The reflection, however, obscured the passenger seat, where she expected to see Paul. Cold crept up her legs, a spirit of doom licking her thighs as it seeped into her belly. The truck turned and stopped.

Paul was not there.

He wasn't there, wasn't nabbed in the red brick house pulling a set of lungs from the fabricator. *Bob wouldn't be escorting him back to the cabin. Unless he was here to search it.*

The dark spirit sank its fangs deep in her heart.

The truck shook as the fat man unseated himself from behind the wheel, adjusting the belt hidden beneath his stomach. He coughed up to the steps and spat a hole in the snow.

There was no knocking.

They stood face to face, a small square of glass separating them like a zoo exhibit. Which one was on the inside?

Little pig, little pig...

"What do you want?" Raine said.

"Come to get you."

"I'm not going."

"Not a choice."

He was wrong about that. It was advisable that the bricks all went to welcome a new arrival, even if it was months after the arrival. She didn't have to go.

"Let me in a sec."

"I'm not going," she repeated.

"I can search your cabin." He held up his phone, the riot app activated. "Resistance is probable cause. I'd have to make sure you're not using this as a distraction to hide something."

Her eyes must've widened when he said that, or her lip quivered or all the blood drained from her cheeks because he smiled at that. He saw the fear.

Or I'll huff and I'll puff...

"Just a quick look around," he said, "and I'll be gone. I need to be at the visitors' center anyhow; then I'll be on my way."

She offered one quick look over his shoulder. No Paul. The longer Bob was with her, the longer he wasn't at the red brick house. She opened the door and stepped back.

Bob pushed inside, patterns of snow falling from his boot treads like broken white waffles. His presence filled the room with an odd mixture of wet fur and coffee breath. He toked on the metal pipe on his way to her bedroom.

"Don't smoke in here," she said.

He was only in there a few moments before crossing the room to the kitchen. A walnut bobbed in her throat. Chairs scratched the floor, a cabinet opened and closed. He came back out with smoke hovering in his winter beard like a fire had been sparked.

"Satisfied?" she asked.

He held her gaze, a smile stretching his whiskers—one of those truth-seeking looks that could drill straight into a person's mind. If he wasn't clay, if he had an ounce of biomites, he might be able to pull the truth out of her and see an image of the trapdoor beneath the oven and the organs stored in the dark.

He put the phone to his ear. "Yeah, I'm on my way to Raine's cabin. I'll give her a ride when she's ready. Paul's not there? What do you mean... okay. Okay. He's probably at the cabin with Raine."

He winked.

"Go ahead, get started. Don't worry about me. Okay."

On my way to Raine's cabin?

He touched a sequence of buttons and held the phone at his side.

"Paul's location disappeared for a while," he said. "Last time he was located was near the lab. We think he's tweaking his trackers to avoid being seen. You think he's making a run for it without you?"

"That happens with him, something with his biomites."

Paul had those moments when he couldn't be found. Even the monitors lost track of him and then he'd just be there, around a corner or sitting on the couch.

"Mmm," Bob grunted. "We might have to put that boy on a leash."

Raine pulled the robe tighter, wanting to slam the bedroom door and get dressed, crawl into bed until he was gone. Something kept her out there, nude beneath the fuzzy robe. She hadn't identified why yet.

"Bible?" Bob touched the black book. "You'll try anything to feel human."

"You looked around, now leave."

He started to reach for the Bible, but instead put his hand under the table to retrieve a spiral-bound sketchbook.

"Put it down."

"This how you spend your time?" He flipped the pages. "Dreaming?"

Pencil drawings of rolling hills and the long and straight horizon of the sea cutting the sky, an old cabin long forgotten, her feet longing for the creaky steps and crooked bannisters of home.

And the faces that lived there.

The unkempt, shaggy mess on Nix's head, his cheeks days unshaven, eyes sharp and thoughtful. Always thoughtful. Their son, Joshua, at his side, a young man that spent his days exploring the endless land, going to the market for the fresh catch and home for dinners most nights.

Is Shep still there, chasing the stick? Do they sit by the fireplace wondering where I went, when I'll come back?

She drew every day because if she didn't, she'd forget what home looked like. Already the details were fuzzy. She could only guess what Joshua looked like. *He's twelve now. No, not twelve... what is he, fifteen?*

Time in dreamland moved at a different speed than the physical world. And this thought, the thought that she didn't know her son's age, that she'd missed all the birthday parties (did they still celebrate without her?) fell in her stomach with a wet smack. And if she ever forgot what they looked like, she'd never forgive herself.

"Put it down."

"Waste of time, Raine. This is all there is, right here and now."

One of the bricks was a Buddhist, a man named Neal. He sat meditation every morning. She heard him say that once, *This is all there is, right here and now.* But Bob was just repeating it, slinging it like an arrow instead of a life raft.

"You understand that?" he said. "Somewhere in your fabbed brain, you get what that means? All there is, is this right in front of you, for the rest of your life. Day after day after day it's just this, forever and ever. Cold winters and dry summers. So draw all you want. Wish, pray, whatever. None of this is going to change. Just settle in and accept that dreamland is dead. It's just you and me."

"You can leave now."

Bob took slow heavy steps toward her, the snow already melting on the floor. She moved around the couch to avoid him and snatched the sketchbook, pressing it to her chest. He didn't open the door.

Instead, he pulled the curtain closed.

"Almost done."

He turned slowly. *Does he know what we're hiding? Is that why he's not worried about Paul?*

She opened her communication lines, attempting a thought-transmission. *Paul!* But only dead sound replied, a cottony silence with padded walls. Bob had killed her communication when he tapped the phone after taking that call. *On my way to Raine's cabin,* he'd said. Like he wasn't there yet.

Like he needed more time.

She should run and hide in the bedroom, barricade the door, jump through the window until someone came to the cabin. But she didn't want to run. Didn't want to call for help. It was why she didn't change out of her robe when Bob arrived, why she stood barefoot and vulnerable while his fat fingers smudged the pages of her sketchbook.

Try something, fucker.

She wanted something to push her to the edge, to light a furnace of fury, to pour fuel on the tiny flame of rage that flickered in her dark nights. Because life had punished her enough. She needed something to hurt back—a face to crush, bones to break. She wanted to get her hands on God and shake him, tell him this shit wasn't fair. That she'd had enough.

Bob would serve as a fine substitute.

So she backed up half a step, bumping into the stone hearth. Embers sparked from the dying logs. His boots landed quietly now—heel giving soft way to toe. Thumb on the phone, stroking the glass by his thighs, the fabric scratching between his legs.

Raine clutched her robe, a distressed rabbit with nowhere to run. Waiting for him to come near. He nudged the couch with his knee, opened the space between them where he'd throw her on the floor and devour her whole.

One more step was all she needed.

She'd drive her knee into his groin, crush his testicles like cream-filled pastries, leave his scrotum swollen with semen paste and shredded tissue. Then she'd drive her fingers into his throat, insert the poker between his ribs and pry out his heart, fingerpaint the walls with scenes of hell, and sit on his bloated corpse until the monitors came for her. They would shut her down after that. *A danger to the world around her*, they would say.

That was what she wanted. She wanted to be shut down.

He took that last step. Her heel against the baseboard for leverage, her thigh tensed—

His hand shot out with unexpected speed; the webbing between his finger and thumb slammed into the hollow indention of her lower throat. A shock of blood surged through her carotid artery, wobbling her knees. She regained her balance as he slammed her into the wall.

The phone sang at his side.

A broad smile spread between his whiskers. Breadcrumbs hung from the curly mustache, his breath thick and humid, coating her face. Her muscles locked in place, her body unresponsive.

He had swiped the phone, hijacked her into submission.

He flipped her around, pushing her face into the wall. Hand

pressed between her shoulder blades, her breasts flattened against the paneling. Then his belly weighed into her, pushing the breath from her. She could feel his crotch harden.

How many of the women had he done this to, threatened to expose a secret if they told, blackmailed them with false evidence? Did he hijack them and have his way, or did they let him do things in exchange for favors?

She couldn't even close her eyes.

She stared at the tiny imperfections on the wall, helpless to stop him. She would endure another beating from life. All eighteen wheels grinding her into roadkill, picked over by carrion as she bubbled on summer asphalt.

All while clutching the sketchbook.

Haven't you taken enough?

His chin rested on her shoulder, a strong hand around her throat. His breathing quickened, his heart surging against her back with anticipation. He licked his lips and flicked her earlobe with the tip of his tongue.

She would fucking kill him after this.

Let him have this body, she was done with it. The first chance she got, she would destroy him. She would wait in the dark, she would hide in the shadows, ambush him outside a bathroom, gut him like an animal. This was over. This was all over. *Have your way, pig.*

A belt buckle rang in its track—

The front door burst open. Winter whipped around her as Bob jumped back. The phone slipped from his hand and bounced on the floor.

"Stop." It was Paul's voice.

Disappointment settled inside her, followed by anger. Not at Bob but Paul. Still locked up, she hoped Bob would lock them both in place and follow through, give her a reason.

"Unlock her."

Bob didn't move. He was thinking, planning. He'd never been caught in the act or he would've done something already.

"Don't think about anything else," Paul said calmly. Matter-of-factly. "I bugged this house with my own surveillance. Everything that happened in the last hour has been recorded."

"Bullshit. I'd know if you had a camera."

"Want to take a chance? If I'm telling the truth, you go to prison, where I'm sure you'll be the one pushed against the wall. If I'm bluffing, you walk away. Want to roll the dice?"

"Let me see it. Where's the camera?"

"You've raped before."

"Where's the camera?"

"It was only a matter of time before you came for Raine, so I was ready for you. I want you to walk out of here and leave us alone. Don't ever come back to this cabin again. You understand? Don't ever fuck with us again or the world will know you're a brick-loving rapist."

Bob didn't move. Decisions were grinding in the silence between his ears. He'd been caught and Paul was showing him mercy. It was a favor. Or maybe his boner was making a plea. Was it worth the risk?

He picked up the phone. His boots rang across the room and stopped somewhere near the front door. Raine breathed into the wall, waiting for a sound, a word.

Sensation gushed into her body like a water balloon filled from a hydrant. She collapsed in a heap of terrycloth, head bouncing, teeth snapping.

Seconds spun in a black whirlpool. Hands yanked her out of the cycling. She struck with the heel of her palm and felt the hard edge of his jawline before kicking into the soft tissue of a midsection.

Paul doubled over, hand up.

"Did he touch you?" he said between strangled breaths. "Did he touch you?"

He tried reaching again, tried to pull the fuzzy fabric over her bare shoulder. She slapped his hand, pushing against the wall, didn't want his comfort or help, just wanted to fan the flames of rage, build the inferno of hatred that was consuming her minutes earlier, burning all her fears and hopes to ashes. That blessed rage promised to destroy everything until there was nothing.

Until she felt nothing.

Was no more.

"Did he touch you?"

She closed her eyes and shook her head. Tears squeezed between her lashes and she hated that, trying to cling to the dry-eyed anger that quickly evaporated, an emotion sucked dry of oxygen until there wasn't even a flame. She was back to where she was. Back to sanity.

"I was going to... going to kill him." She swallowed the words. "I wanted to."

Another wave of grief and regret fell over her, the realization coming when she said it out loud. If she died, if her body was no more, then her dreamland would die. And Nix and Joshua were still waiting.

A large travel bag was on the floor.

Paul turned off the lights and slid it behind the couch, hiding from the cameras that Bob and the monitors could use to watch them. They weren't supposed to invade their privacy, their purpose only for emergencies. But they all knew better.

In the dark, he sorted through random objects and tools. On the bottom was a square circuit cabinet. He flipped a sequence of switches and pried off the back. There, laid in the soft embrace of beige foam, were two perfectly fabricated lungs, pink and soft, sealed in shiny preservation wrap.

"If I didn't have this with me," Paul said "I would've killed him first."

If he didn't have Jamie's organs with him, if a third of her piece-mealed body wasn't stashed beneath the oven, he wouldn't have opened the door and stood there. He would've destroyed him. And the People would've found the lungs.

The People would shut him down.

We both have people depending on us.

Bob didn't know if there was surveillance footage or not. But that wouldn't matter. Paul sold it. He'd bought them space and time to bring back Jamie. When all hope was lost, when they stood on the brink of annihilation, now they stood in a wide-open field of hope.

Bob would leave them alone.

God works in mysterious ways.

THE ARCHETYPE'S KNOWLEDGE_

Perry Dawkins had never been in a green room.

Turned out that the backstage room wasn't green at all. He knew that, but he still had expectations, would've been happy if the walls were mossy. Instead, they were white and water-stained. A coffee machine was in the corner.

He was breathing a little too rapidly and feeling light-headed. He could control the nerves like other fabricated humans (a thought-command to increase dopamine and suppress norepinephrine for starters) but preferred to let it ride. The stress wasn't debilitating. In fact, it was exhilarating. Humanizing.

After all, he'd started out human.

Emotions were evolutionary shortcuts to environmental response. It was only when he ignored them did they back up, an emotional river that spilled over the muddy banks and flooded him with anxiety. If more fabricated humans embraced the emotional aspect of their identity rather than exerted their will over them, they would have fewer problems assimilating into society.

Perry was more than a role model. *I am a perfect human.*

"How you doing?" an elderly man with wavy gray hair took his shoulders and asked. "A little nervous?"

Perry blew through smiling fish lips and nodded.

Dr. Wilkerson shook him, patted him and then embraced him with his characteristic hug that, for a moment, squeezed out all the air. He slapped his back with a heavy paw.

"You're going to change the world," the professor said gruffly.

One of the conference directors grabbed the professor for a few words but not before he imparted a fatherly grin, the stage lights sparkling in his eyes.

A stagehand came after Perry with a wireless mic. "It's backup, just in case primary audio goes down."

He worked on fixing it to Perry's lapel while a young woman waited with a short brush in one hand and a box in the other.

"Do you mind?" she asked.

The professor mentioned they'd want to fix him up for the recording, add color blanched out by the stage lights. Perry's complexion was mocha, his hair looping curls of surfer brown, eyes distinctly almond-shaped. He was an amalgam of several races. No one would guess him as a neuroscientist. The world's leading.

"What's the talk?" the makeup artist asked.

"What?"

"You look nervous."

"Oh, yeah." He shook his hands. "A little."

"What are you talking about?"

"Um, dream disease."

She exaggerated an understanding frown, intrigued but not really. "Friend of mine's daughter has a friend at school that died from it a few months ago. It's a shame, really need to do something about it."

"I think I have an answer."

"Tell you what the answer is." She made long, soft strokes across his forehead. "It's getting rid of the bricks. They started it."

The smile that had grown through his nervous breathing wilted; the butterflies in his stomach curdled into lumpy, crawling critters with thick lapping tongues.

"That's not true," he said. "See, there's evidence out there that... you see, the dream accelerators that allow halfskins to generate dreamlands are networked, which means halfskins are trading..."

Her brush slowed.

"Bricks have stable dreamworlds," he blurted, hoping his use of the racist vocabulary would win her over. "They really have nothing to do with the dreamlands that halfskins experience. And there's no connection with clay dreams. My analysis is conclusive. The sooner we can identify the real cause of this epidemic, the sooner it can be cured."

"Done. Good luck."

His hand twitched. He wanted to snatch her like a rogue calf that needed to learn how the ranch worked, but it would only scare her. She didn't know he was a brick when she started applying makeup, but it was clear she figured it out.

Bigotry had a finely tuned detector.

Maybe he could convince the waiting room of academics, but how would he win over the general public? Prejudice wasn't interested in facts. People like her already lived in an altered reality designed by their xenophobic thoughts.

People like her. He had to watch his own prejudice.

It was just hard to stomach reactions like that. The incidents of dream disease among the brick population were nonexistent while the casualty rate of halfskins using dreamland accelerators was pointing at the sky.

It was the scientists from the clay states that suggested a theory that bricks were carriers of the psychological disorder since dream disease didn't exist prior to the sentience laws. They couldn't explain why clays were succumbing to dream disease, albeit at lower rates than halfskins; just blame the bricks and everything would be all right.

Bricks were vectoring rats.

The link, as Perry's lab discovered, between dreamland and dream disease was the halfskin accelerators. They were all networked. It would be like no one washing their hands during an influenza epidemic and coughing into each other's mouths. Start by getting rid of the accelerators and then they could focus on clay dream disease.

The answer sure as hell wasn't getting rid of the bricks' dreamlands. No evidence supported it, yet they still kept them from dreaming. It was only Dr. Wilkerson's connections that allowed Perry to venture off the Settlement to lead the research. This was rare and, as it would turn out, would be the last time it ever happened.

Perry had proof that the accelerators were the problem. Halfskins were using them to create their dreamlands. Dreamland accelerators were malleable resorts, digital funlands that expanded the dreamer's recreational opportunities. This was a trillion-dollar industry that Perry was blaming.

But they were missing the entire point of dreamland. It was so much more than a dream vacation world where they could sleep with twenty women or skydive without risk or murder without repercussions.

Dreamlanding is world building.

Imagine a creative outlet that wasn't a blank canvas or pages in a book or images on a screen but an actual universe with planets and stars and outer space. Perry believed that dreamlands were real.

We are the seeds of new realities.

No single region of the brain controlled dreamland. It was a production of the entire organ. That was Perry's proposal: biomites would be used to rebuild the entire brain. That was why the bricks could dream so effortlessly, why they were immune to dream disease —there was no clay holding back the experience. And clay, by the clay state's own admission, was imperfect. *We are descendants of original sin,* one such pastor claimed, proudly.

But we don't have to stay in the garden!

Perry would show the audience that he had proof that imagination didn't just create images and sensations but acted like a portal to new planes of existence. He would pull back the curtain on God, give a purpose to each and every human being. We weren't just here to enjoy ourselves.

We are creators!

Perhaps that was what God intended, not for us to live a good life, an obedient life, a fun-filled healthy life. But a creative life.

And dream disease? Maybe that was our failure to live up to that purpose. Our imperfections created monsters that terrorized dreamlands instead of spinning new and amazing solar systems.

The dream feasts on the dreamer.

"Five minutes!" someone shouted.

Perry took several short, choppy breaths, shook his hands and jogged in place. Dr. Wilkerson was with his peers. They gave him a thumbs-up. He would be presenting for the team. It was a collaborative effort, but Perry was leading them. It was his baby. They wanted him to deliver salvation.

A brick to save the world.

Stagehands rushed past him. His introduction had begun. The makeup artist was approaching for a last second touch up. He closed his eyes and bowed his head for a few moments of inner solitude.

He didn't see her press the Taser against his stomach.

Didn't feel the floor crumple beneath him.

The electrical charge delivered enough voltage to cause serious damage. He never recovered.

And the world never changed.

CHAPTER ONE HUNDRED THIRTY-NINE_

A summer breeze rolled over open ground, swards of wildflowers swept by an invisible hand, slapping the hair from Paul's eyes.

The row of cabins sat dark, still and empty beneath the churning wind harvesters. The contractors had moved out once the George B. Simpson Center of Energy and Conservation Research building was finished, a three-story monstrosity that cast a shadow over the red brick house. A few of the cabins were still occupied by workers, but they would be gone soon.

The one across from the red brick house, the one that used to be Raine's cabin, was the only one occupied. A construction worker stepped onto the porch and dropped a bright orange duffel bag, one about the size Paul had been using to smuggle his fabrications. This one made a heavy clink—metal on metal—that echoed in the trees. The worker didn't wait, didn't knock on the door. Just left it.

A silhouette moved past the window—a fuzzy shadow within the dark interior.

Marcus Anderson lived there now.

They put him in the cabin where Raine had lived. Paul took that as a fuck you when Bob and the monitors helped the old man move in. He'd rarely been seen since that day.

Almost five months.

He never appeared at the monthly meetings, never went for a walk. The porch swing was always still. No one ever saw him except when he'd retrieve a box of food the monitors set on the steps (they delivered to no one else). He would hobble out, his left leg stiff, the knee a rusty hinge.

Like an old man.

Bob visited him. His truck would be parked out front at least twice a week, sometimes more. On the rare occasion Paul glimpsed inside, they appeared to be sitting on the couches having a chat. Bob never talked about it, even when asked, "What are you and the old man doing?"

He pretended he never heard it.

Marcus Anderson had made such a stink about being discovered, like he wanted the spotlight. The People were consumed with his capture (*the best reality TV reality has ever seen*). His case dominated the newsfeeds, the lawyers chronicled his every move, every word. Transcripts of babbling prophecy were leaked to the press, spread throughout the blogosphere. Small cults dedicated themselves to his prophecy.

One to lead, one to dream, one to bleed and the son to be.

Some were worshipping his massive shutdowns of halfskins, others decrypting his warnings of a powers-that-be. They were sycophants that would, in another era, rally around Charles Manson.

And then it went away, a cheap fad of leg warmers and spiky hair. The People just didn't care about him after he arrived. He was no fun after all. The old man's lawyers said he just wanted to be left alone and forgotten. Like the Settlement was a retirement community.

"Everyone!" someone shouted. "If I can get everyone's attention? Up here, please!"

Excitement buzzed behind him—equipment clicking into place,

the blur of conversation and fake laughter. The man attempting to get everyone's attention was clapping; then he was interrupted by audio feedback before his voice projected into the great wildness, echoing off the distant trees.

"If everyone can take their places," he said. "The ceremony begins in fifteen minutes, please."

The shadow moved inside the cabin and stopped at the window. The curtain was pried aside. Paul squinted to make out the details, imagining the bald head with random wisps of white hair.

"Paul." Pete placed a hand on his shoulder. "We need to be ready."

Behind him, the circus was in full swing. The reporters, the politicians, and all the bricks were milling in front of the monstrous shiny new building. George B. Simpson, a biomite-enabled trillionaire and world's richest centenarian, was standing near a yellow ribbon tied to the front doors with a ridiculous pair of oversized scissors, the public relations people coaching him how to bend over when it was time for the bricks to line up and kiss his ass.

The world would see the grand opening of a new research facility run entirely by bricks, the first of its kind, a state-of-the-art facility that would benefit humankind through biomite technology.

"Ask me," good ole George had said when funding was approved, "they're just as human as the People."

But I don't want to live next to one.

"Come on," Pete urged. "We need you over here. And would you... you know."

Paul tied his hair back with a rubber band, loose strands pulling free. He hadn't cut it in over a year, not since Jamie was delivered. He was urged to cut it properly, to appear presentable for this occasion. *Be grateful,* he was told. *And if you can't do that, at least look it.*

He was doing neither.

Gratitude was a dark secret, a merciless blanket that smothered his heart, a cold blade between his ribs. Yes, the new research center was exactly what he needed—new equipment and plenty of distractions made it possible to continue fabricating Jamie in the brick house. But that wasn't the gratitude Pete and the others wanted. They wanted him to be happy for the breadcrumbs thrown at them like pigeons locked in cages.

"Over here, come along!" a woman prompted, a badge swinging from her neck. "If you would stand over here. Yes, yes, that's good."

She pointed at the empty chair next to Dennis, the Settlement's introvert (an autistic plant fabricated by a nonprofit organization to study the disease)—as brilliant at chemistry as he was social awkwardness. Paul was on the team because he was good at design and execution. Dennis and the others were the idea people, the theorists and inventors. Paul brought their dreams to life; he made them happen. He'd have his own office and access to fabrication approval.

George B. Simpson would help bring Jamie back.

So why wasn't he happier?

The cameras panned across the research team, past the building and over to the rest of the Settlement bricks gathered on the other side. They were all in attendance except the old man.

Raine was holding hands with the prayer group, heads bowed. There were ten of them now that held weekly meetings, sending their wishes into the blue sky with eyes squeezed shut, tongues sharp and hopeful. Their prayers floated on the breeze like notes attached to colorful balloons.

George B. Simpson was introduced.

The important people took turns at the dais. They turned, they smiled, they waved. The funding was from private donors, but would benefit the People. It would benefit humankind today and tomorrow. Benefit the future. Benefit the children.

Their children.

"And we have you to thank," George B. Simpson said to bricks that applauded on cue. Even Paul clapped like an asshole. It was the least he could do.

The ribbon was cut. The tour began.

The reporters followed the glad-handing politicians inside and the bricks were guided inside to see the gift bestowed upon them by good ole George, told they would no longer toil in boredom. Now they had a purpose. They had a reason to live.

They mattered.

(*Wink. Wink.*)

Paul and the team were asked about their projects. Each of them gave vague answers about sustainable energy and medical developments. Even Dennis mumbled through a prepared statement about excitement. Paul stayed in the back, watching the cameras capture the giant lab, the politicians and excitement. Not one of them pointed at the cabin across the field, like the world had forgotten Marcus Anderson.

"Talk about organ fabrication," a hefty middle-aged reporter asked, his button-down shirt billowing in the breeze.

"What about it?" Pete answered.

"There's some concern about human fabrication, that you'll start fabbing an army."

Pete laughed with all his teeth. "And where are we going to hide them? That's absurd."

"You will be fabricating organs, correct?"

"We will fabricate organs for the purposes of research."

"No human fabrication?"

"We're trampling old ground here. The fabrication chamber isn't large enough to produce a child let alone an adult."

"But an infant?"

"In theory." Pete sighed. "Listen, we're under surveillance by teams of clay monitors. There's no chance we could fabricate an infant and raise it in secret. It would ruin everything we worked for. We're interested in advancing biomite technology, that's all. We want to perfect the human body and, in turn, heal the human mind."

"You could fabricate all the organs of a body." The reporter's nasally accent ripped through Paul's fog of indifference and left a buzzy residue between his ears.

"Frankenstein was a novel," Pete exclaimed. "Dennis? Paul? Can you shed some light on this?"

Pete took a step back, eager to get off the griddle. Paul, slouched on the hard seat, leaned forward. When Dennis muttered an incoherent string of scientific jargon, the reporter started looking at him for something he could understand.

Silence soon hung like a corpse.

"Yeah, uh. One of the deciding factors in Mr. Simpson's funding had to do with organ transplant, primarily the fabrication and transportation of organs via preservation wrap that could be absorbed once inside the body."

Paul had used Dennis to push the proposal of organ fabrication through, fed him the data and reports to make an argument, convinced the introverted genius this was his idea, not Paul's. But when it came to explaining it, he always looked more surprised than anyone else.

"There's also the internal rebuild technique," Paul continued, "using digital matrices to establish a three-dimensional blueprint inside the body before biomites are injected... look, it's all in the proposal. You can find it posted on the website."

"Will we get updates?" The reporter looked bored.

"They'll be posted."

"Surveillance feeds?"

"No." Pete stepped in. "Our labs aren't going on a feed. We're privately funded, so there will be trade secrets."

"You'll be working in secret?" His eyebrows shot up. He just got the hook for his story.

"Not secret, just not fully transparent at first. If this was publically funded, yes. But the People had their chance, they balked and Mr. Simpson stepped in. We'll be working for privatized investors, I think you know this. We'll be held accountable for all our work; there's nothing to worry about. We just want to do our duty."

Do our duty. That had become the go-to line. *We just want to serve, that's all.*

Paul didn't disagree with the angle (after all, the People wanted the bricks to be subservient androids, not individual humans). He just hated it. The words were bitter shards he'd rather swallow than spit out.

The reporter started another question. "What about..."

I wish this fucker would go away.

And then he cramped. The reporter lost his train of thought, tapping the dimple in his square chin like that was the button that would unclog his thoughts.

"Thanks for your time," Pete said. "We appreciate your support."

They all shook hands; then the reporter wandered inside the building. A few days later, he would post a story about the amazing building and the dedicated fabbers that wanted nothing more than to do their duty and serve the People.

Like someone scripted it for him.

Paul sat down, the sun warm and promising. The snowcapped mountains a reminder that winter was still there. It would come again. Across the field, the curtain fell in the old man's cabin.

The bright orange bag was no longer on the porch.

CHAPTER ONE HUNDRED FORTY_

SUMMER ENDED AND AUTUMN WALTZED THROUGH THE countryside, but winter didn't tiptoe. It scratched and clawed through the Settlement, laid the land to bed beneath thick comforters of snow. Wind reshaped the landscape with mauling drifts and frozen daggers.

Matted tracks belted crisscross patterns, snowmobiles finding their way to the cabins until the next storm washed them away.

Marcus pushed the plunger on a coffee press and poured two cups. He took them into the front room, where jazz played from a speaker. The fireplace roared with red heat, sparks crackling against the metal screen.

Mother sat on the opposite couch.

Her finger pressed to her lips, eyes closed, as if soaking in the extemporaneous notes, letting them softly bounce inside her like rubber pellets working their way down a pegboard.

Marcus sat with a groan. The cold had stiffened his joints and bit into his knee. It was odd to feel so human. He'd never asked Mother (they rarely spoke since arriving, just enjoyed each other's presence) the reason he woke with such human frailty. Perhaps it was the reason he connected with clay—he felt their pains, knew their suffering.

He trusted her.

She wasn't a god or goddess, he didn't think of her that way. If he had to put it in words, she was just an expression of divine will, like the majesty of the Himalayas or the wonder of the universe. She was benevolent and kind; he had come to accept that with only a trace of bitterness.

She was beyond human comprehension. She understood the universe in ways no ordinary human could; any attempt to relay her depth would be like teaching a dung beetle calculus. She saw the path to truth, the way to humanity's freedom.

He just knew this and trusted it.

Perhaps she designed him that way, planted suggestions in his subconscious that made him so willing to accept her, to follow her. This he couldn't argue. After all, his roots were human. Imperfect. He had prayed to do the will of God, to allow him the strength to be a servant of divine will.

Perhaps Mother was God's voice.

So they rested on their couches, the fire riffing along with the music when he dozed off. Nearly a year on the Settlement and he still failed to see why anyone complained. He found the boredom quite relaxing. *Enlightenment,* a spiritual leader once said, *is quite boring by ordinary standards.*

The stamp of heavy boots startled him.

He hadn't heard the snowmobile approach. Mother slid to the end of the couch, legs crossed. She tossed her head, pushing the hair behind her ear, and folded her hands. Lips gently closed, she nodded.

A bitter wind knifed through the open door, Bob partially blocking it. His puffy green coat fluttered. Marcus stepped back for him to enter. The large monitor unlaced his boots so as not to track snow across the room.

Marcus took a moment to peer across the field. The George R. Simpson lab heaved a steady stream of gray smoke from the chimneys, but the lights were off. The opening ceremony had come and gone months ago. Everyone was already busy with research, but now they were in their cabins for the night, battened down for an approaching storm, the third one in a month.

"Have a seat, have a seat." Marcus gestured to the cushion next to Mother and took Bob's coat. He returned with coffee mugs warmed in a microwave. "How are you this evening?"

"You keep this cabin warm," Bob said.

"Thin skin."

"Can't you just turn up your inner thermostat?"

"It's easier to throw on a log."

Marcus chuckled and they sipped and sat quietly. Mother watched the large monitor sink into the couch, his weight bowing the center. If she were a physical being, she would've been tossed onto his lap. Instead, she watched him with interest.

They both did.

Marcus enjoyed the warmth of Bob's clay mind like a pleasant fragrance or a tune on the radio. He wasn't a good man (quite despicable really, but Marcus couldn't judge; Bob was worlds away from what he'd done). He was intriguing, an acquired taste.

Exactly what Marcus needed.

He didn't manipulate Bob's mind, didn't mold it into what he wanted it to be (he could, he was certain of that), but bathed in the man's presence. It was easier to become familiar with him than bend his will—sprinkle a trail of crumbs for him to follow.

Create desire.

After all, desire needed no explanation. *The heart wants what it wants,* most people would say.

But what makes the heart want in the first place? No one ever asked that question.

Bob came to visit regularly. He was quite cantankerous at first. The alpha dog had come to shit in Marcus's nest. But the old man treated him kindly, left him with a taste of kindness that he came back for. Again and again.

Bob had that faraway look now, a trance of relaxed disposition. Open to suggestion. He was hypnotized by the room, a sort of energy that buzzed inside of him, warm and cozy. Made him want to sleep.

"Were you an only child?" Marcus asked.

Bob nodded. Memories swam behind his eyes.

Marcus prodded them to the surface. Much like a brain surgeon could get the right response by applying an electrical impulse, Marcus found what he wanted in the mind. His thoughts were his scalpels.

"I had a little sister."

"A sister? How wonderful."

"She died when I was eight."

"That must've been painful."

Slow nod. "Yeah." The fire's dance filled the swelling silence. "Pissed my father off." He snorted. "Something fierce."

"And he beat your mother for it."

"He was beating her before that. But, uh, it changed after that, yeah. He was doing more things, drinking, spicing, whatever he could get his hands on. Ended up charring his biomites to a crisp."

"And that's why you turned clay?"

"Yeah." He gulped the lukewarm coffee, passing over the details of his own divorce, the restraining order that prevented him from seeing his kids. "Figured I'd do the world some good by coming out here, you know. I was made to do this."

"How so?"

"I like order. Discipline. There are rules, you know. God doesn't love bricks."

"You enforce the rules."

"Goddamn right."

"And you enjoy it."

"No shame in loving what you do. It's a passion. You understand."

"Oh, I certainly do."

"Goddamn right you do."

Bob put away the coffee in one big swallow. Marcus offered another cup and he accepted. He returned with a fresh pot and cheese and crackers. Bob leaned back with the plate balanced on his swollen belly, crumbs littering his ratty beard. When he was done, he scraped the cheese off his gums and sucked his wet finger.

"What was it like?" Bob asked.

Marcus knew what he was asking, but paused long enough to let him clarify.

"Shutting off all those halfskins, what was it like?" Bob sounded like an addict asking about ambrosia, food of the gods. *How does it taste?*

Marcus sat back, mug curled against his stomach, warmth radiating through his hands. He contemplated which story to tell, which would be the lure he wanted to dangle; a morsel so succulent that Bob would swallow the hook whole. He had so many to satisfy a sadist like Bob. A dark man. A dark, dark human being.

"Once," he started, hanging the word like a shiny object for his eyes to follow, "I shut down a man in front of his family. It was the early days of the halfskin laws, when anyone with 40% biomites was held in detention and biomite replication couldn't be stopped.

"When the redlines, as they were called, neared halfskin, we would alert the family and give them an opportunity to say goodbye. They weren't allowed to touch them or even be in the same room. I made them stand behind a glass partition and talk through a speaker.

"In this case, the halfskin was a good man. He was a dedicated father, a wonderful husband, an absolute soulful man of God that, mistakenly, seeded himself with too many biomites. The law was the law, as you know. I couldn't pardon him because he'd done good in the world. He knew the rules and chose to break them.

"I stood at that man's shoulder and watched the counter rise to 49.7%, then 49.8%. I stared at his wife and children, listened to his parents curse my name and beat the glass. I tasted their anguish as his breaths became shallow at 49.9%.

"They begged and pleaded, cried until their eyes swelled. And when he turned halfskin, I turned him off. His last breath eased out of him. He was cold. But I never took my eyes off of the family. I wanted them to suffer. I wanted them to learn.

"Pain is a mighty teacher."

It was more than that. It was the invulnerability Marcus felt. His addiction to power. He wanted to be above it all, wanted to act in the name of God. More than that. He wanted to be God.

Omnipotent.

A bulge creased against Bob's inner thigh. He was full-on hard. "You know why I'm here?"

"Why you stay on the Settlement?"

"I'm here to do that, just like you. I'm here to teach a lesson, to let the bricks feel human through pain and suffering. I'm helping *them*, like you did."

Marcus grinned. *Them.* He didn't consider Marcus one of them. The hook had been swallowed.

"How are you helping them?"

"So they know..." He stammered for something legitimate. Marcus pressed a thought into him, nudging him along. "To make them feel vulnerable, you know. So they know they can't control everything, that they need to just be *here* whether it hurts or not."

"You, dear man, are a Buddha in winter clothing."

"We all have our purpose."

Bob smiled like an eight-year-old. He hopped off the couch to help the old man clean up, and when Marcus offered him cookies, he helped himself to three of them then wrapped three more in a napkin for the ride home.

Through the frosted kitchen window, Marcus saw a figure crossing the field in the dimming light of evening. Snow up to his waist, Paul made his way to the new research facility and snuck inside. Once inside, the lights remained dark.

"Better get going," Bob said, zipping up his coat. "Thanks for the coffee."

Marcus followed him to the door. "How did your sister die?"

Bob's hand froze on the twisted knob. He remained like that for a full second, even considered pretending he didn't hear the question.

"A boating accident."

"How dreadful." Marcus put his hand on the man's arm. "Must have been heartbreaking."

"She couldn't swim."

"Did you see her? When she died?"

Bob started shaking his head and didn't stop. It was like someone had flicked a bobblehead in zero gravity, a needle stuck in an album's groove. He was trying to follow up with the story he had told so many times that he'd come to believe it. She'd fallen off a bridge and never came up, that was what happened. No one could do anything about it.

Marcus eased the real memory into the light.

"Did you see her?" he asked again.

Head still shaking, Bob answered, "Yes."

"You did. And what happened?"

"She had..." He swallowed hard. "She broke my fishing pole when we were on vacation. She was always breaking my stuff even when I told her not to touch it."

His voice shrank.

"So I got mad and I shoved her."

The words stopped.

Marcus let him swim in the memory that welled up from the deep, a leviathan that swallowed him whole. He slid down the slimy gullet and went through the intestines where memories—bad, bad memories—had been stuffed and forgotten.

He stood on the bridge and watched her flail.

He could've saved her, but she was always getting into his things. He just wanted her to go away, wished she'd never been born. He watched her go under, her hand the last part of her to splash beneath the cold, cold water.

Her knee scraping the sandy bottom.

Lungs burning wet and full.

He could feel her now. Could feel her go cold. Feel her heart thudding in her ears, the sun rippling above—

"Robert."

Bob jumped off the floor like he was pushing off the sandy bottom, sucking for air, spitting and blubbering. Tears streamed into his coarse beard. Completely vulnerable.

And open.

"I will need some help in the next couple of weeks," Marcus said. "Will you help me?"

Bob nodded. Of course he would.

"You're a good boy."

He sped off into the night, the snowmobile carving a new track. Yes, a track. One that Marcus would need. It was better that he would want to help Marcus than to be forced to. *After all, his heart wants what it wants.*

The old man told it what to want.

"You did him a lot of good," Mother said. "I don't believe he deserved as much mercy."

Who was Marcus to judge? His sins outweighed most.

Before he closed the door to seal out winter, he noticed a small light on the third floor of the George R. Simpson building. Nothing anyone else would see. Mother noticed it, too.

He would need Bob's help very soon.

CHAPTER ONE HUNDRED FORTY-ONE_

3:20 AM.

Paul jolted upright, wrinkles imprinted where his cheek had lain against his sleeve. Like deer listening for another twig, he held still. Not breathing.

It could've been the storm that spattered the third-floor window with fistfuls of sleet he heard, heaving long frigid breaths against the building. It was still whiteout conditions, the ground a hazy oblivion through frosted glass.

In the lab, the rhythmic strokes of the fabricator hummed and hissed. The glass walls were dark (research had already shown improved stability when fabricating without exposure to ultraviolent light). The outline of the organ's form was barely visible. It looked something like a bowl.

The most complicated piece yet.

He rolled the chair to the computer and tapped the space bar. The job was supposed to be finished by sunrise. Estimated completion was now mid-morning. It was too late to stop, not without risking complete malfunction; it had to be finished when he wrapped it.

All of the major organs were done, wrapped and hidden beneath the oven. This one, though, was complex and critical. A faulty kidney could be repaired, a leaky stomach patched.

The brain had to be perfect.

The storm was a lucky break. Raine called it a blessing. *God is good.* Whether it was God, statistics or good karma, it didn't matter. The storm gave him the ten to twelve hours he needed.

The blizzard would continue until noon. That would be just enough time. If someone walked through four feet of snow, he could simply abort, run the cleanup program and try another time. He had dug through an eight-foot snowdrift just to open the front doors. No one would be coming.

Still, it would've been nice to finish before sunrise.

The fabricator's hypnotic thrum wooed his eyes to close. He stood up. There would be time to sleep later, when this was all over. Besides, the monitors would see his location in the lab, they'd know he was working. He tried to set these jobs up and let them run from a distance, but this one needed his guidance. If they came prying, he'd have to be there to clean up.

They said his locator was still blinking out despite repeated attempts to recalibrate. They accused him of sophisticated tampering, but he had nothing to do with his occasional disappearance from their radar. If he was honest, he was counting on their incompetence to avoid investigating where he was at. It was a horrible plan.

How am I going to do this?

He had a crawlspace full of Jamie that couldn't simply be popped together like plastic doll parts. And beneath that question was an oil slick of doubt and more contaminated questions that invaded his sleep, niggling beneath his scalp.

Why?

That was the big question. He knew why he was doing this—she was his daughter. It was his job to protect her, to keep her from harm. He failed her, though; he thought if he surrendered peacefully when the People came to the farm that nothing bad would happen.

But why am I doing this?

Paul pried open the blinds; he thought he saw someone. He rubbed his eyes. Marcus Anderson's cabin was obscured in the white-out. Darkened dust whirled against the glass.

He blinked lazily.

Conjuring up a memory, he looked into the storm and saw the outlines of trees and a distant outline of a pitched roof. He could smell the hay, the fresh-cut grass. The hint of a spring shower lingered.

He squinted into the dark as if that would bring the hallucination into focus. He just wanted to see her, even from a distance. It would make the night go faster if he saw her carrying the steel buckets of feed. The shadows were long. It was early in the morning, that was when Cali would feed the horses. The colors of the farm were vivid, the hallucination fully developed.

Like he was there.

He was jerked back by the sound. His fingers still plying apart the blinds, ears pricked, nervous system lit. Dark and gray, it was impossible to see anything outside. The monitors would've pulled up on a snowmobile. Did he miss the engine's report?

He shouldn't have given in to the hallucinations. Now was the time to be vigilant, not dreamy.

Something wet slapped the floor. A soaking wet towel or a slab of meat. Paul tensed. A minute later, he heard it again. Paul waited, then went to the lab door, looking through the mesh glass. He pulled the door handle, the greased hinges silently opening.

A form stood in the shadows. "What are you doing?" someone said.

"Dennis?" Paul answered.

"What... what are you doing in the lab?"

"How'd you get here?"

He took choppy steps, his legs stiff, feet slapping. Paul blocked the doorway. Dennis moved into the dim light, cheeks bright red, twin rivers of snot running over his lips.

"What are you doing?"

"Where's your coat?" Paul asked.

"Why are you here?"

He pushed through the door, snow falling off his frozen jeans. His feet were bare. He couldn't have walked all the way from his cabin, not in this weather. Not like that. He was going to lose toes.

Sleepwalkers don't ask questions.

Paul stayed in front of him, bobbing and weaving to keep his line of sight off the humming fabricator. Dennis stepped into the soft computer glow. His lips were blue.

"What's in the fabricator, Paul?"

"Work."

"You shouldn't be here."

"What are you doing, Dennis? You're frozen."

Violent shivers attacked in short bursts. His hands clenched and unclenched at his sides, tight white flesh drawn over his knuckles.

Dennis attempted to get around him. Paul put a hand on his chest when the computer chimed, a new execution signaled. The next phase began. A digital image rotated on the screen.

Jamie's disembodied head looked at them.

"You... you..."

"Dennis, no. This is... you wouldn't understand. Let me explain—"

"You-you-you... you're going to get us shut down." He leaned into Paul. "They'll shut it all down, Paul!"

"No, they won't. Just..." He couldn't tell him that he'd been fabricating her for over a year and no one knew. "Listen, I have this under control, Dennis. We don't have to tell anyone. I have a... I've been using a program to wipe the computers."

"No, no, no, no..."

"They won't know, Dennis! They don't know! I've been using it for a while, testing it. There's no trace of what we're doing, you understand what I'm saying? This is like a test."

Dennis left small puddles on the floor, shaking his head in time to the word *no.* The sleepwalking reverie was gone. He was completely awake now. Lips quivering, fists clenched.

"They'll shut us down," he muttered, over and over.

"They made me do it!" Paul shouted. "You don't understand. You never had anyone in your life, I know that. They never took anyone away from you. If they did, you'd be doing the same thing. None of this matters to you, all you need is a lab. It doesn't matter if it's on the Settlement or a corporation—"

"No, no, no, no..."

"You shouldn't have come up here, Dennis. What are you doing here in the middle of the night?"

"No, no, no, no... NO!" His hand shook. "NO!"

"Dennis, calm down. Let's talk about this."

"This... this is unsanctioned, Paul. They-they-they won't let you do... they'll shut us down, Paul!"

A maelstrom of thoughts jetted like gamma rays. Paul squinted through the mental sandstorm, raising his hand like that would shield him from Dennis's exploding mind—a mind showering him with fear and anxiety.

Afraid they would shut down the facilities.

Afraid the Settlement would go back to year one.

Afraid he would sit in his cabin alone.

Why is he here?

The eye of the psychic storm passed. Calm returned. Dennis blinked away the melting crystals from his bunchy eyelashes, the baby blue irises cut to thin rings by expanding black pupils.

A thought formed.

Not one that Paul could see, but a thought formed in Dennis he could feel like a pebble in his sock. A thought that would connect with the monitors, tell them what he found, secure their favor, get rid of Paul and maybe, just maybe they would let Dennis stay in the lab because Paul was the one—

"No!" Paul shouted.

Dennis's head snapped and he stumbled, waving his arms. The sound his head made on the floor resembled something like a melon dropped from the second floor.

The fabricator continued to hum.

But nothing else moved.

CHAPTER ONE HUNDRED FORTY-TWO_

NIX AND JOSHUA.

They were on the porch, sitting on the rickety top step, Nix helping their son carve with a bowie knife. Shep lay in the grass, tongue out, slimy stick under his legs.

Raine could walk up to them, could sit down and ask what he was carving and what they'd done that day, but they wouldn't answer. They never did. Because this was a dream—a flimsy thin movie, a string of memories that pretended to be her husband and son.

This was not dreamland.

The front door slammed open. Raine bolted off the floor. She'd fallen asleep in front of the fireplace, the blackened logs dying in a thin stream of smoke.

Paul stood in the doorway. Winter bellowed icy spittle inside, little diamonds trickling across the hardwood and sticking to her wool blanket.

It was still dark out.

He wasn't supposed to be back until daylight. He clutched a bag at his side, stumbled into the couch and fell on the floor.

"What's wrong?"

"It's outside," he said.

"What? What's outside?"

His next attempts to speak were slurred by stiff lips. She pulled him upright, leaning him against the couch. His skin was icy. He tried again, but she only caught one word.

"Accident."

"What accident? Is everything all right?"

He shook his head, huffing.

"What's outside, Paul?"

"I didn't...I didn't mean to..."

"What? Why are you back?" His fingers were locked around the bag. It appeared empty. He always brought the fabrications home hidden in the hollow shells of various components. It was unlikely anyone would be out there to stop him, but he almost froze to death in the storm.

"I can't believe this," she said. "What were you thinking?"

His breathing began to thaw—big gulps separated by shaky pauses. He looked at the door.

"I'm sorry."

"Sorry? Sorry for what?" She shook him with knotted panic. "Sorry for what, Paul?"

She let go and stood. The front door appeared to recede, a surreal dreamlike wobble; the bogeyman was at her heels and she couldn't run. Her toes were marbles on the wood floor, her ankles rusty hinges. The brass knob burned her hand. She braced against the door and cracked it open. Eyes watering in the subzero gale, she peered through fuzzy eyelashes to see a dark form half-buried in the snow.

She slammed the door and bowed her head, wishing for the security of the rosary beads. Her lips fluttered in prayer.

"What have you done?" She turned. "What have you done?"

"He wasn't supposed to be there."

"What have you done?"

"I stopped him from reporting us. I only wanted to block the thought, but..."

She began walking and praying, hand on her forehead, face to the ceiling. She wasn't going to die. She couldn't die. Nix and Joshua depended on her, they were in dreamland—her dreamland—waiting for her to return, and now there was a dead body on her steps and a crawlspace of body parts.

He held the bag with both hands.

She dropped next to him and peeled away his dead fingers one by one. The bag thumped with the hollowness of a husked coconut. She pulled down the zipper. The orange glow of the fireplace's dying embers glittered off the preservation wrap. She reached for it.

"Jesus."

The fabricator had printed half of Jamie's head, upside down, stopping just below the nose. The bald scalp soft on her fingertips, the eyelids squeezed tight like a child wishing away a nightmare.

"I never should've let you," she whispered.

"Don't say that."

"No. No, this is insane. What were you thinking, Paul? Did you think we were just going to glue her together and live happily ever after? Huh?"

His head hung dead, eyes dry. His grief a limb long pruned from a tree, rotten and alone.

"This isn't her, Paul." She flipped the skull upright, her finger slipping into the hollow of an open sinus. "Even if it worked, you can't bring her back. You understand? I can't die for this, Paul. You get caught and they shut us off and I can't fucking die!"

She dropped the thing in his lap and stormed away with finger and thumb buried in her eyes, plugging the weepy dikes that never seemed to dry up. Why couldn't she cut off the emotions like him? Why couldn't she be more methodical? Because if she was him, if she had a sample of Nix or Joshua and someone said that maybe they could piece them together an organ at a time, she would risk her life to do it. She'd risk everything. Everybody.

Even put a dead body on the steps.

"Who is it?" she asked.

"Dennis. He... I don't know why he was there."

"Doesn't matter. What are we going to do?"

He studied the bald scalp in his hands. "We take him back to his cabin, put him in bed. No one will find him for a few days. If the storm holds up, maybe a week."

"Then what?"

He shook his head.

One step at a time. She'd lived the last couple years that way. Take one step and let God show you the next. Surely God didn't go away just because there was a dead body.

They got dressed and stepped onto the porch. As they hauled the dead weight onto Paul's shoulder and started into the night, she wondered if this didn't count. Maybe if bricks weren't real, this wasn't murder.

She'd have to accept her own unreality then.

But one step at a time.

Dennis's cabin was tucked beneath trees, the snow drifted along the front porch. The front door was a black rectangle. As they drudged along the tree line, they realized why it appeared so ominous.

The door was open.

A white dusting had settled on the sofas and coffee table like a lumberyard. Small piles had blown against the fireplace and table legs.

Paul collapsed on the couch along with Dennis's body, a cloud of crystals whooshing toward the ceiling. He labored to breathe. Raine's chest hurt; she was numb from the waist down. The scarf around her face was wet, delicate flakes of ice clinging to the fabric like cockleburs.

She closed the door and sat across from him, wondering about all the evidence they were leaving. "Maybe we should leave the door open," she said. "Like we found it."

"It won't matter."

He was right. Their tracks would never be scrubbed away by the storm, not entirely. They led back to their cabin. And from there to the lab. They would only be safe until someone came looking for him.

We may as well leave a signed confession.

The walls were bare. There were no pictures propped on the tables, no knickknacks or books or even a box of tissues. If not for the coat and a pair of boots by the door, it appeared abandoned.

Why didn't he put on his boots?

In the wan light, his feet had the bluish haze of a haunted moon. Biomite hijacking just wasn't possible on the Settlement. They were all bricks. None of them had enough of an advantage over another to do that. And there was only one pair of footprints coming out of the house when they arrived, the soles of bare feet shuffled across the porch. The monitors could have frozen him, but not hijacked him.

Or could they?

They dragged him into the bedroom, tucked him under the covers, folded his hands over his stomach in a way they imagined he slept—all proper and textbook, like people are supposed to sleep.

Paul bowed his head while she prayed.

"How'd you do it?" she asked. "I know you didn't mean to, but how did it happen?"

He explained sensing Dennis opening a line. He was about to send a thought to the monitors, report what had happened. In that vulnerable state, Paul panicked. He only meant to kill the message. Instead, he shut down the brain.

And the body followed.

He stopped mid-sentence. "I forgot to wipe the program."

"What does that mean?"

"I... I forgot to erase what I was doing. If anyone checks the lab, they'll see what I fabricated."

That meant instead of having a few days, they might only have hours.

"Go, hurry," she said. "Just go take care of that. We'll figure out what to do when you get back."

They cleaned up what they could and closed the door. It wouldn't matter, but it didn't seem right to leave it that way. Dennis didn't own much, but he liked order.

They traced their tracks and parted ways at the halfway point—Paul starting for the lab. By the time Raine reached the cabin, she was dizzy with exhaustion. The sky was a pale puddle of watercolors. She fell in the bedroom and pulled a blanket over her head, not expecting to sleep until he was back.

But the front door woke her.

She lay still and listened to the heavy footsteps, expecting the monitors to come with phones raised. The door slammed again. There was silence. When she looked out the window, Paul was a tiny figure wading through the snowy dunes in the early morning. It wasn't until she was back in bed did she notice the bag was missing.

So was Jamie's head.

CHAPTER ONE HUNDRED FORTY-THREE_

THE SNOW TRANSFORMED INTO ICY BULLETS.

Paul hunkered into the wind as he emerged from the trees and followed the shallow pockets between the drifts, his lower body a senseless wooden substitute forced to march. Oxygen came in desperate cold gulps. Smoke was slapped from the cabin chimneys, the windows dim with flickering firelight.

Marcus Anderson's cabin, though, was fully lit.

Through watery slits, he saw a shadowy form at the window, as if watching him cross the field. Paul was beyond caring. There was no point. The die had been cast. He no longer had to choose which path to take; the forks had been cut away, his life one long road that now led to the George B. Simpson building.

The front door was still cleared away when he arrived the night before. But now there was another set of tracks. He didn't have time to stuff the bag inside his coat before the door flung open.

"The hell you doing?" Pete roared. "Get in here."

Paul stomped his boots on the way in; reverberations stung his bones.

"Were you here earlier?" Pete asked.

"Yeah, I was. Just wanted to get a trial running." He raised the bag. "Forgot my supplies."

"You damn near froze."

Pete shook his head but didn't ask about the trial or what was in the bag. Or just when the hell he had arrived earlier. Later, they would check the records and discover he'd been there all night. But that would be a small footnote, another detail of the disaster.

Thankfully, Pete was a short-talker when he was at work: asked how you were doing and didn't listen to the answer. Small talk was unproductive. In fact, the current exchange was a personal record.

"Not staying long," Paul said through stiff lips.

"Get warm before you head back."

His soles squeaked in small twists as he walked off. He whistled a tight tune that sounded like spring had arrived. Paul stood dripping until Pete turned the corner, then went to the stairwell. Small puddles of snowmelt littered the steps up to the third floor where Dennis's heels had thumped like heavy logs.

The fabricator door was open, the monitor glowing—the three-dimensional head slowly rotating. His stomach curdled. If Pete had come up...

It doesn't matter.

There wasn't much time. Jamie wasn't coming back. Even if he fabricated every bit of her, he couldn't stitch her together. Even under the best conditions, it was unlikely she would be any more than a distortion of herself.

What was I thinking?

Once the program was wiped and the equipment cleansed, he stood at the top of the stairwell, listening for Pete. The elevators were shut down to conserve power; he'd have to come up the steps. Paul propped the door open and trotted back to the lab. He would never see Jamie again, but he could find closure on her death.

A death he wasn't there for, her exit alone and frightened, he imagined. But he could answer one question before the end of this hapless journey.

Why were you in Georgia?

He dug through the lower cabinets and dropped a heavy metal plate that rang through the building. He paused to listen, making sure Pete was still somewhere in the lower offices before clearing off countertop space. Fingertips thawing, sensation aching in stiff tendons, he wiped the condensation from the plate.

The bag was delicately placed in the sink. The partial skull felt like a softened melon—the scalp coarse with empty hair follicles. Hairless brows hooded eyelids in mid-sneeze. The preservation wrap was pressed into the ridged top palette of her partially fabricated mouth. It stopped at the gums.

The brain was complete, though. The eyes, too.

There was no tissue damage. He could scrape her last impressions without applying the spark of life. There was a risk, of course. Should she wake with only half her head fabricated, her nervous system exposed—

No. That won't happen.

The preservation wrap peeled away from the pink underside with a wet meaty sound. The bottom half slapped on the metal plate.

Meat. It's only meat. It's not Jamie, he told himself.

He laid a mesh interface over the naked scalp, turning the face away. Once energized, the neoprene wires embedded into the flesh, seeking wireless connections with dormant neurons.

Paul tapped the keyboard to life and initiated a secret incognito program before opening neural imaging. The lower half of his body was still painfully cold, but his thudding heart warmed his chest, blood surging in his temples. The program began a synchronizing sequence that seemed to stall. It was taking too long.

He ran to the steps and listened, his pulse echoing in his ears. He did this two more times. Pete's bird-whistling was a distant call. He must've been in the hallway, but still on the first floor.

But near the stairwell.

It was the third trip back to the computer that the screen changed. Images were smeared in an abstract presentation, something that resembled ultrasound technology at its inception—a blurry amalgam of an inner dream world.

The mouse wheel clicked beneath his fingertip, cold and numb. The watercolor scenes drooled into each other. There wasn't time for another pass through calibration, not with Pete in the building. He could come back, but there might not be another time.

He targeted the visual cortex and made a trip to the stairs while the program ran. When he returned, the images were distinguishable. A man was looking at him.

This is her view. The last moments of her life.

The timeline started at the end. He would rewind it as far as it would go, but he was fascinated by the eyes that were looking at him, the pupils big and black and deep. They sparkled like galaxies.

Who the hell is that?

He turned the time wheel back and realized this was the processing lab. She was lying down. A woman and the man with the deep eyes looked down on her. Except for the eyes, the faces were blurred beyond recognition. The woman's lips appeared to move silently (he'd cut the auditory access to save processing time). Their movements were jerky and unnatural, the memories patched together, pieces of film clipped from the movie.

The timeline suddenly swirled into a slurry of melted crayons, pastels that bled into a patchwork of lights and darks. A face would appear, a tree or a sidewalk. She was walking. There was water. The gaps grew larger and emptier.

Whistling.

Pete was in the stairwell. He needed to wrap up, clean up and destroy the evidence. The timeline spun beneath his fingertip, a kaleidoscope of memories morphing and merging and blurring.

A face suddenly jumped from the primordial soup with great clarity, flashing like a magician cutting a deck in half. *Remember your card.*

He wheeled back.

A balding old man.

It was a memory of a balding old man, just a memory. But Paul had the sense the old man was looking back through space and time, eyes looking at him.

Marcus Anderson.

The progression slowed in reverse, then started from the beginning. Paul watched the old man from Jamie's eyes, his hand out, fingers encouraging her to follow, pointing at a bench beneath the shade. She turned and sat.

The fountains of Olympic Park arched in front of her, children dancing and splashing. Marcus took her hand and patted it gently. His face hovered close to hers, filling her vision. Ensuring she would remember this moment, burning it into her memory.

They found her in Olympic Park.

The clay report stated she came on radar like the old man had done himself. There was no explanation as to how she got so deep into Georgia before being discovered.

"You about done?" Pete leaned into the lab.

Paul jumped and shouted, "Yeah."

"Power down before you leave."

"Okay."

Pete thumped the doorframe and whistled his way down the steps. Paul remained fixed on the frozen image. The knowing eyes.

He slid the half-head off the metal tray and dumped it into a chute like a spoiled hunk of boiled ham. The door swung on spring-loaded hinges, a conduit that would deliver the meat to an incinerator.

Meat. It's just meat.

Paul wiped up watery red streaks, erased the program and ran a mop over Dennis's heel-streaks, then turned off the lab.

Someone would discover Dennis within a few days, a week at most. Paul didn't need that much time. He just needed the next hour to finish up his life.

Empty handed, he crossed the field to a brightly lit cabin.

THE ARCHETYPE'S KNOWLEDGE_

The room was warmly lit with a corner lamp, the walls dark olive with three sofa chairs a dark shade of pumpkin. It would be described as cozy, something a therapist would design.

Exactly what Hanoi Fender expected.

One of the chairs was singled out and faced the other two. That was his chair. He wasn't ready to sit, but they'd be watching what he did while he waited. He wanted to appear relaxed, confident. For the next fifteen minutes, he slouched into the deep cushion and watched a fish tank bubble. It was home to a goldfish that seemed obsessed with escape, bumping its nose against the glass the entire time, probably since it was dropped in its new home.

Probably until it died.

Funny thing was this: if it managed to somehow escape—flop out of the tank or push through the glass—it would suffocate on the carpet.

Maybe that's what it wanted.

"Good morning." A woman stepped inside with a man.

"Good morning," Hanoi answered.

They sat across from him, smiling pleasantly. They were athletic looking, attractive and nonthreatening. He doubted they mixed it up outside of work, but they'd make great babies if they did.

"Okay, well," she said. "Here we are."

"Yes."

"Are you comfortable?"

"Very."

"If you're thirsty, there's water on the table."

"No, thank you."

"This will take about an hour."

"Yes."

He let out a long, easy breath, questioning whether he should've acknowledged that last statement. It wasn't good to know too much, but everyone knew this took an hour.

That answer was fine.

"Nervous?" she asked.

"Little bit."

The couple nodded. They didn't write anything down, didn't need to. Everything was being immediately analyzed—every word, every movement. All the way down to how he blinked.

He let out another long breath, let this one shake a little at the end, and darted his eyes between the two evaluators. That would look cautious.

"Did your parents prepare you?" she asked.

"No."

"No?"

"I mean, we talked about it, of course. But they didn't, you know... we weren't able to—"

"It's all right." She smiled.

Shit. That was too much. He wanted to look nervous, not act it. Shaky breathing, quivering hands, dry mouth and rapid blinking, that was what a nervous person would do.

"So you have parents?" she asked.

"Yes. A mom and dad."

"They fabricated you?"

"Yes."

"You're a transplant, is that right?"

He hid his annoyance. She knew the answer to that.

"Yes. They lost their son in an unfortunate accident and, um, used his DNA to fabricate me."

"So you're not him?"

He nailed a nervous laugh. "No, no. He's like an identical twin."

"Do you think of yourself as a transplant or a clone?"

This is stupid.

"A brother."

"Does that bother you? No? Not being original?"

"I have my own thoughts, my own interests. We're twins born at different times."

"But you have his memories."

"That's where he ends and I begin."

"How do you know?"

Shrug. He was tired of this line of questioning. Besides, the shrug showed indecision. That was a good human trait. The shrug was well-placed, well executed. *I don't know and I don't care.*

The man spoke up for the first time, asking Hanoi to compose a poem.

"Roses are red, violets are blue... that sort of thing?"

"Yeah," the man said.

"All right. Roses are red, violets are blue, you're very pretty, and I like you."

He said it to the woman and elicited a rush of blood to his face. His cheeks turned pink. Like roses. *Nailed it.*

"Do you have a girlfriend?" she asked.

"No."

"Do you go to school?"

"I do."

"What grade?"

"I'm a junior in high school."

"What's your favorite thing about school?"

"Recess." It wasn't, really. Then it occurred to him that recess was what grade schoolers did. That sounded rehearsed, but before he could correct himself—

"What's the square root of 88,574?" the man asked.

Pause. "297.6 something something."

They didn't react. He had paused for at least five seconds before answering. *Was that long enough?*

"I like math," he added.

The man asked the chess problem. Hanoi knew that was coming; there was always a chess problem in Turing tests. He stared dully as the man set up a scenario and asked Hanoi his next move. The rook could mate in one, but he leaned forward, pinching his lower lip, watching the goldfish hit the water's surface.

"I don't like chess."

"Why not?"

Shrug.

He wished they would write something down. It would be a good way to gauge how he was doing. The sitting and staring was unnerving, the pauses getting longer, the silence broken by the bubbles.

"Hanoi's an unusual name," she said.

"My father served in the military."

"Do you love your parents?"

"Of course."

"What is love?"

He stammered. That was genuine; he didn't see that coming. They were supposed to ask why he loved his parents. He loved them, of course, because they were his parents and they gave him life and it was how he thanked them. Children loved their parents, that was the rule.

"Love is an emotion."

"Yes. Yes, it is." A very long pause. "Tell me more about emotions."

"Emotions are evolutionary shortcuts. It takes too long to think about everything. A human hears a twig snap in the bushes and fear instantly makes him ready to fight or flight."

"A *human*?"

"You know what I mean." He shook his head. *That was stupid.* "I just meant early *Homo sapiens,* that's all."

"Do emotions define *human*?"

"I think so."

"Are they required?"

He paused. He didn't mean to, just tripped up on the answer that was thrust onto his tongue. He caught it between his teeth before it escaped. The answer, it seemed, was obvious. Emotions were often irrational, were not good choices. But emotions, to some degree, were required. At least, he wanted to believe they were.

"To some degree, yes. Refined emotions, I think."

Another long pause. The long silences seemed to be serving as palate cleansers because the man started in with typical questions about songs or art or impossible scenarios. Hanoi handled them deftly with precise pauses mixed with consternation bordering on constipation.

This went on for half an hour, the woman not saying anything until after a very long pause, and she said without expression, hands folded on her right knee, "You have failed, Hanoi. You will need to tell your parents that, according to the sentience laws, you exhibit the nature of artificial intelligence. You will be terminated. Your parents are in the next room. Would you like to tell them?"

"Yes."

Hanoi stood up. It was rather unfortunate. His parents spent a lot of money to fabricate him in the likeness of their late son. They would be disappointed. It would be better if he told them.

"Hanoi?"

"Yes?"

"How do you feel?"

"Sad." That was the correct answer. He should feel sad for being turned off. *Dying. I will die.*

His parents were in the next room, but they never got to see him again. He never went to tell them. Hanoi Fender was terminated following the final answer of his Turing test. Because he didn't *feel* sad. He didn't feel anything.

In fact, he went to tell his parents because that was what he was supposed to do. They wanted a child that would listen. He was doing what he was told.

The last thing he saw was the goldfish gasping at the glass wall. Then fabricated human #588, known as Hanoi Fender, was no more.

CHAPTER ONE HUNDRED FORTY-FOUR_

"Good morning," Marcus said.

Raine was standing at the window. Despite the hazy light, the sun's glare couldn't hide her exhaustion. He had knocked on the door several times before she dragged herself out of bed. It was obvious she didn't expect to see the old man on the porch.

She wasn't going to open the door easily. He could make her do it, but preferred she choose to. Marcus could make himself shiver, appeal to her sense of compassion. He had come through the snow wearing only a long-sleeved shirt, pants and loafers. The cold didn't affect him, she would know that. Nor would she care if it did.

She looked past him.

"Paul will be here soon," Marcus said over the tinkling patter of frozen snow. "I'd prefer to wait inside for him."

The curtain dropped, but the knob didn't turn. It was unlikely she had locked it; he could let himself in, but he wanted her to open the door, to invite him. That gesture would have a great impact on their relationship going forward.

Mother stood in a large divot of snow. Unaffected by the blistering wind, her loose clothing hung off her shoulders, her bare feet obscuring the wrinkled imprints.

Paul dropped the body there.

"Dennis didn't suffer," he called through the door. "It was quick, I assure you."

Dennis barely qualified as a sentient being. Of all the bricks, he had come closest to failing the Turing test. A great scientist, yes, precisely because he was a computer with arms and legs.

It was why Marcus summoned the man to surprise Paul.

"What do you want?" she asked.

"I think you know."

He liked that answer. It was cryptic and said a lot. Most of the time when someone heard it, they filled in answers that worked in his favor.

"She knows," Mother added.

Yes. Somewhere in her subconscious, she's always known I would come for her.

"Wait for Paul," Raine said. "Out there."

"I would like to talk to you first. It has very much to do with dreamland."

There was a long pause before the brass knob slowly turned, the old man's distorted reflection warping on the handle. The door creased several inches. The wind kicked it against the wall when she let go.

He rubbed the cold off his hands like soapy water and cupped them over his mouth for a warm exhale. Winter had moved into the cabin. No amount of logs could kindle enough heat to push out the cold ghosts that haunted it, the ghosts that followed Raine daily.

"I know you," she accused.

"Of course you do."

"You have no business being here."

"I'm here to help."

"You killed Nix." Poison-tipped darts flew from her lips. "I saw you there, murderer. I saw you when I came out... when I came out of the box, I saw you. My husband is dead because of you."

She was wrong about that. Marcus wasn't there when she stepped out of the fabrication chamber. He was emerging from his own fabrication chamber a thousand miles away. Nix had pulled her identity out of dreamland and integrated it into an exact replica of a fabricated body. Marcus had arrived to shut him down when Mother collapsed... a collapse triggering a shutdown that included Nix. Marcus, too.

Once I was clay, now I'm a brick. And here we are.

"I've known about you since I was a child," Raine continued. "You chased after Nix most of his life; you wanted to shut him down for something that wasn't his fault. You killed him, admit it. You started all of this. You're responsible for the Settlement, for Nix's death, for all this suffering. This is your fault."

"She's right about that," Mother said.

He flicked a glance at the old woman pacing around Raine, observing her like a critic admiring a work of art. Technically, the death of Nix was Mother's doing, but he wasn't innocent.

Raine was a shell of the woman that stepped out of the fabrication chamber all those years ago, a once fiery warrior, an independent woman that had been chipped into a gaunt likeness of herself. Yet beneath the imploding cheeks and dull flesh, the darkness in the hollows of her eye sockets, she was still exquisite.

"He didn't die, Raine."

"Show him to me, then."

"You know where he is."

"I know where he is, I said show him to me! Can you do that? No, you can't because I don't have dreamland!"

The clicking of plastic beads rolled between her fingers, the crucifix of the rosary swinging from her cupped hands—finger and thumb, finger and thumb. Lips moving.

Marcus helped create the halfskin laws, that was true. No one could possess more than 50% biomites or they were more machine than human. And Nix went halfskin when he was a child because he would've died without them, that was true, too. But the law was the law. Did Nature spare those without sin? No more than a tornado avoided houses of the holy.

Nix was a child that wandered into the path of the storm through no fault of his own.

"I want to help you," Marcus said.

"You're here for yourself."

"I'm here for a much nobler cause. I seek what you want, Raine."

"I want my family."

"You'll need the truth to do that."

"The powers-that-be? Is that what you mean? You're a paranoid schizophrenic, Marcus Anderson. And if you had anything to do with Dennis or... or..."

Her lips crimped into a thin line. *If I had anything to do with Jamie? I have something to do with everything, dear child.*

"That we do," Mother agreed.

The cabin was suitably adorned with crucifixes, some carved from wood, others cast iron or molded plastic. A leather-bound Bible had been filled with slivers of page markers; prayers had been scribbled on loose notebook paper and stacked beneath a melted candle as thick as a pipe.

"Ask her to pray with you, Marcus," Mother said.

He turned his back on her, nodding while examining a cross hand-fashioned from tree branches and bound by a thin strap of twine. Mother was right. Invoke her faith, bond together in the name of the Lord and she would hear what message he had to bring, to follow him on a righteous path to find the truth, to discover the powers-that-be.

To discover God.

He briefly smiled at Mother, the higher power that guided him on this holy of holy journeys. She had given him this gift of higher vision, this insight to the truth. Only Mother possessed the ability to see far and clearly. He needed Raine, needed Paul.

One to lead, one to dream, one to bleed, the son to be.

Marcus inadvertently nodded to her before opening his hands to extend an olive branch and a chance to pray.

"Where is he?" Raine looked around. "Or are you talking to a she?"

Confusion took the old man's hands. In a rare lapse of discipline, he looked directly at Mother.

"Who are you projecting?" Raine added. "You don't think I know what you're doing?"

Now it was her turn to pace. With the rosary wrapped over her knuckles like a boxer taping up before a fight, she searched the corners of the room.

"I see you looking at someone. You have your own little dreamland, don't you? You see someone, projecting him or her into this room. Do you carry her with you all the time? Project her when you're lonely? Scared?"

His brows pinched a fold of skin.

"Who is it?" she demanded. "Who are you projecting?"

"Don't tell her," Mother said. "She's not ready."

"No one of consequence," he said.

"Do you have a dreamland, Marcus?" It was more of an accusation. "Tell me or so help me God I'll beat the old man out of you with a table leg."

Of course Raine noticed his subtle reactions. She was once a projection herself, a being born of and trapped in Nix's dreamland. Through his senses, he would project her into the physical world, someone only he could see and hear, a woman that belonged to him. She knew this world through Nix until he fabricated her a body.

"You've taken the Lord as your personal savior?" Marcus asked.

"The Lord won't stop me from hurting you."

"Will you pray with me?" His hands, having wilted, returned in supplication.

"Pray to your powers-that-be."

The holy beads touched her lips, but a fist was still clenched beneath them, the knuckles blanched with tension.

"Do you pray often?" he asked. "Do you need to be forgiven?"

"I've done nothing wrong."

"Of course not. Nix brought you into this world against your will, didn't he? You were content to remain in the dreamland where you were born, but he loved you too much, wanted you to taste the physical. But the world rejected you, sent you here, took away your dreamland and abandoned you. You've done nothing wrong, Raine. Yet you pray often."

He sat on the edge of one of the sofas, palms still open.

"Why go on? With everything that's been taken from you, what's the point of living? You weren't meant to be out here, Raine. You're not like the others, not a worker ant, not a colony of programs. You feel. You hurt."

Raine turned her back, both hands bound together and pressed to her chin, and paced the room, coming to rest in front of the crucifix of branches propped on the shelf. He sensed her thoughts, knew the belief she carried, that Joshua, her son, had somehow sent that little crucifix to her, somehow bridged their realities long enough to leave her a gift. Impossible to carry objects between realities (certainly not from a dreamland), she knew this. But the belief was more important than fact.

I'm okay, Momma.

"You pray because you miss your family. You pray because you're searching for answers, to know why God would abandon you in your time of need. What is your purpose in life?"

"I serve God now."

"And what does God want?"

"He wants me to live."

"Why?"

"His Will is a mystery."

"Precisely," Marcus breathed. "That's why I'm here."

Mother sat next to him, the cushions not moving beneath the illusion of her round bottom, the dust not clouding as she sat back. She put her finger to her lips as she always did, eyebrows creasing.

Marcus rested his hands, felt the pressure of an approaching storm outside the cabin. The wind had died; sleet no longer ticked against the tin roof like nails sprinkled over a sheet of metal.

But a storm was nearing.

He needed Raine to be open, to get beyond the emotions that shackled her to the past. She needed to hear what was in front of her so that she could know where they needed to go. *She needs to bleed.*

"Has He answered your prayers?" he asked.

"He gives me strength."

"The Lord doesn't give you what you desire. He gives you what you *need.*"

Her silence acknowledged him.

"What does God want?" he asked.

"Our faith."

"God wants to be discovered; He wants to know Himself through you, Raine. He wants to know your journey. There are many ways up the mountain and the truth is waiting."

She reached for the crucifix of sticks, slid it off the shelf and cradled it. Not until she sat on the opposite couch did he realize what the cross meant.

Send me an angel, he heard her think.

"We are connected." Marcus interlocked his fingers. "Together we'll find the truth, Raine; to know the powers-that-be. To discover God."

"I just want my family."

"They're waiting on the mountain."

Her head remained bowed, the rough-hewn crucifix lay across her legs. On her lips was the prayer, "Send me an angel."

"Very good," Mother whispered.

What he kept from Raine would bring this delicate respite crashing. *The truth is not what you expect,* Mother reminded him.

Marcus didn't know what was at the top of the mountain, didn't know if they would find her dreamland, didn't know if she'd ever see

Nix and Joshua like he promised. The truth was the truth, Mother always said. It didn't matter how you felt about it.

But Mother assured him the truth was up there, that should he achieve such a lofty climb, should he discover the powers-that-be, then humanity would be saved.

So what will I find?

The approaching storm arrived on the front porch with two hard-falling steps that rattled the windows. The door was thrown open.

Paul rushed at the old man.

CHAPTER ONE HUNDRED FORTY-FIVE_

A WILD ANIMAL SLAMMED THROUGH THE FRONT DOOR—THE whites of his eyes, the exposed teeth, the clawed fingers. Raine's mind registered a snarl then a roar, saliva spilling over the lower lip.

Paul!

He came with hands steeled to collar the old man's frail neck, to twist it, wring it and shake it until it snapped like a dry twig. But his momentum slowed. Raine felt a change in the atmosphere, the crackling sensation, the static electricity.

The old man's mind filled the room.

Curly whiskers straightened across Paul's chin, his wild hair thrown back. He was attempting to run underwater, the air congealing into a thick, fatty essence, hardening like viscous tar.

Paul stopped, a wax figure hung in mid-stride, an accusing finger aimed at the old man. Lips tight and blue, a word worked through his windpipe, crawled over his tongue.

"*You.*"

With sleet driving through the doorway, Marcus sat with his legs crossed, hands resting on his thigh. Not looking at the murderous hands twelve inches from his neck.

Ripples splashed Paul's cheeks.

"Let him go!" Raine shouted.

The rarefied air tightened around her, locking her down before she could bend a knee. The grip held her from the inside, the invisible hand of God, her biomites betraying her, freezing muscles into rigid cables.

The old man looked like someone waiting for tea to be delivered. He nodded. After a pause, he nodded again. She noticed that he was sitting on one side of the couch, not in the middle, as if next to someone. *He's listening.*

A deep sigh and he looked up.

Paul began moving. Very slowly, he was forced to the opposite couch. His movements were jerky; his breath gurgled, the real struggle on the inside, a battle he was losing as he sat down. Teeth grinding like rough-hewn marble.

When it was her turn, she didn't resist, letting the inner force take her; her motions were so smooth and effortless it looked like she chose to do it, as if the illusion of free will brought her to sit next to Paul.

Marcus stood like a creaky old contraption, pausing like a disc had slipped. He closed the front door. Pausing with his hand on the doorknob, he sighed again before starting up the fireplace. The cabin soon smelled smoky warm. He then shuffled into the kitchen. Several minutes later, he emerged with coffee.

Once again, he sat at one end of the couch, across from Paul. Contemplating the moment, he stared into the cup, seeing his thoughts swirl on the oily surface.

"I didn't want to do it this way," he said. "Not this soon, not so rash. But things change, as they often do."

He looked at Paul with soft eyes.

"I'm very sorry for your loss, Paul. Death is an odd transition and it's not what it used to be. We're all dead, the three of us, according to the People. We aren't human. But I think you'll agree we're very much alive."

Raine didn't know what had happened to Paul, what he'd seen or done to come back a psychopath. He didn't want to kill the old man, he wanted to obliterate him. Only one thing could drive him that far off the cliff.

The old man had done something to Jamie.

"You have suffered, both of you. We all have. But the truth is out there, you understand. It's not just dreamland that's disappearing. The dreamers are dying, too."

He looked at Raine and paused. *It's not just you, baby. You're not special.*

Two short sips. He sat back, gathering more thoughts.

"I needed Jamie, Paul. It wasn't selfish, wasn't for pleasure. I needed her to find the truth. We simply joined efforts. I didn't kidnap her; she did this of her own free will. She knew the importance of what was at stake, what we needed to find. I didn't intend for her to be shut down, you understand. But, in the grand scheme of this journey, perhaps it was not a bad thing, not a wrong turn, so to speak. I have come to believe, in the process of her death, she looked into the eyes of the dream eater. And that is what led me here today."

The dream eater. Survivors of dream disease described it that way —a cold breath on their shoulder, an inhalation that slurped away their very thoughts, waking up empty and void.

"You..." Paul hissed. "I saw you."

"We were partners in this, Paul. I did not shut her down."

"I... *saaaaw* you."

It was all he could say. Marcus watched him curiously, as if Paul was a window with his thoughts and memories exposed. Raine was not privy to the scenes, but Marcus scowled at what he saw.

"Her memories are corrupt," the old man finally said. "I did not take her to Atlanta. She was to meet with a contact in Chicago. I waited for her there only to hear of her capture days later. I'm afraid what you were seeing in her memories was a distortion, Paul. I assure you, I did not want her shut down. She was my ally."

Ally? Jamie was useful to him, served his purposes. He needed her alive. But her death served him as well. He looked to the blank space next to him, listening to whatever his projection was saying, perhaps. Nodding intermittently, then humming in agreement.

He seemed more relaxed when he looked back and sighed heavily.

"By the time I arrived in Atlanta, she had been shut down. I didn't anticipate that. If I had gotten there sooner, perhaps I could have stopped it, but she was gone, Paul. Even I have limits. We were closer to the truth than I anticipated. *He* took her from me, I believe."

He. His powers-that-be. *He that eats dreams.*

"I need you," the old man said. "I'm here because I need you both. I didn't know what to expect when I arrived on the Settlement, but now I know it will take the four of us to find the truth."

The four of us?

"You're fabricating her, Paul You managed to salvage enough of her DNA that you could fabricate an organ at a time. A hand, a heart, a spleen. You're bringing her back like only love can do.

"I need Jamie, to see what she saw, to look into the eyes of the dream eater. But for us to find the truth, I will need both of you. You are the one to lead us, Paul. I can't do this alone. I wanted to wait until spring when it would be easier to travel, but you were fabricating her too fast. You were taking risks that I couldn't accept. And you've become unstable."

He wagged his finger.

"Every once in a while, you fade out. I can't sense you, like you disappear. The monitors are looking more closely at this and we can't afford more attention. You've been lucky to have gotten this far. I had to put a stop to it."

A wave of bristling heat pricked Raine's brow, her body an ill-fitting glove. Paul was shaking, anger flushing his cheeks, lips thinning.

"Dennis was barely sentient," Marcus continued. "Hardly more than a machine, I'm sure you've noticed. I would not consider his shutdown a death. You are not a murderer, you are not a bad man. But change has occurred. You can no longer continue what you were doing. And our stay on the Settlement is coming to an end. There is no turning back for any of us. They will find Dennis's body, they will know what you did. And now here we are."

He sacrificed Dennis to force us into a decision.

He drank and thought, listening to the voice next to him. Then he put the cup down, leaned forward and spoke intensely.

"I know you want revenge, Paul. The gratification of savagely destroying me will satiate you fully, a blood meal that will fill your belly, but it will leave you emptier and thinner. I am truly sorry for where we are."

He nodded at Raine, including her in the semi-apology.

"But this is bigger than us. I did not cast the future, did not design it to include you. Your suffering will not go unrewarded. I cannot force you to help me; I need you to comply. I need both of you to do that. Do you understand?"

The long silence was filled by the crackle of the fire.

Paul was no longer quivering. *Did he exhaust his bottomless tank of fury, or was he contemplating the offer?* She wanted to believe the latter because the old man's words had snared her. There was no future on the Settlement, no reason to continue living, waiting for the People to restore her dreamland. Her only hope sat across from her.

Without another word, the old man went back to the kitchen. Their confinement thawed like icicles in the afternoon, disappearing a drip at a time. Raine wiggled her toes, curled her tongue. Her body hummed with the weight of deep hibernation. It hurt to move.

Paul stood too soon, tripped over the coffee table and collapsed on the couch. He flopped onto the floor and hunched on his hands and knees, slurping the air in deep, heaving breaths. He climbed onto his feet in a state of inebriation and lunged against the wall. Items fell from the shelf. When his balance returned, he threw himself at the front door and fumbled with the knob, falling off the porch. He crawled through the snowdrifts, emerging like a dusted stroke victim determined to run before he could walk.

"Let him go." Marcus closed the door. "He needs some time. It's why I came to you first. You understand why we are together, Raine. You understand how important this is, what we all gain from understanding the truth. Your suffering will guide him. You are the one that bleeds."

He was speaking in riddles. But she was still sitting, and doing so calmly. So accepting. Did he bait her with promises? If he'd come with that story a year ago, she'd be running, too. But her suffering made her eager to follow.

The one to bleed?

He encouraged her to rest because there was much to do and very little time. He went to the kitchen to make her something to eat. She would need her strength, he told her.

She went to the bedroom and closed the door, instead, sitting on the bed, wondering what the hell was happening. She showered, hoping to wash away the webby thoughts that clogged her mind. She needed to be clear, needed to know her intentions were true, that the old man wasn't blinding her with a dazzling illusion. Hot water ran down her face, trickling over the silent prayer on her lips.

Perhaps the angel had arrived.

CHAPTER ONE HUNDRED FORTY-SIX_

"What are you doing?" Paul asked.

The kitchen table was pushed against the wall, the oven tipped on its side. Raine on her knees, arm sunk deep into the trapdoor, a chilly breath heaving from beneath the cabin. Marcus sat on one of the chairs, the kind with bended metal legs and hard cushions. His hands were on his thighs in some imitation of alertness and rigid psychosis, the way a lunatic would watch someone dig their own grave.

Raine slowly flexed her cold fingers. A fleeting moment revealed an emotion crossing her eyes, an admission of guilt—she was caught stacking body parts like firewood. But that guilt was quickly polished over, a hardened layer of angry shellac.

"Where have you been?" she said.

"What are you doing?" Paul aimed the accusation at Marcus.

"Trust me, Paul," the old man said.

"Trust a murderer?"

"I have murdered no one, Paul."

"You shut down millions with your halfskin laws and you're asking me to trust *that*?"

"You're talking about Cali?"

Paul choked on his next accusation, the words solidifying like black lumps of coal. *Like Cali.* The old man didn't need to be all-powerful to pick that thought from his mind. It rested in Paul's eyes, never left his mind. Of course the old man killed millions, but only one mattered to Paul.

"You... you disappeared from the world," Paul said. "You moved at will, hijacked our biomites, walked Dennis into the lab... what you're doing is impossible. And you want me to trust you?"

"There is a greater power out there, Paul. That you can trust."

"The powers-that-be." Laughter limped out of him.

Raine pulled herself up, her dark complexion somewhat chalky, the skin withered beneath her hooded eyes. Standing next to the old man, it was a creepy portrait of a wealthy old baron with his sickly concubine.

"Did he promise you dreamland, too?" Paul said.

The cold moments stretched out, the hateful words nestling into place, clicking tumblers that unlocked his message and engaged a long-dead, dusty engine of rage that had lain dormant inside her. She leaped across the kitchen and snatched his frozen coat against his chin.

"Where the fuck have you been?" she said, spittle flying. "You walk off and leave me to fix everything and then say that? We've all lost something, Paul. We all have!"

He had hid in Dennis's cabin for two days, planning to stay there with the corpse until someone came looking for it. But no one did.

"What do you want from me?" She shook him. "You leave and disappear and I... I can't even feel you out there, Paul. You turn your back and leave me sweeping up the pieces and expect what? To wait for you on the porch? Crying in the bed?"

She shook him.

"I'm tired, Paul. And I want my family back, can you understand that? I know you get that, I know you can't stand it either, but I'm tired of waiting. I'm taking a leap of faith."

The wooden crucifix settled into the hollow V at the base of her throat, stuck between rigid cords of muscle. She had tied a leather cord to it and wore it like a necklace.

"Faith?" he said. "Is that what this is?"

"It's all I have left. We're out of options, Paul." Her hands slid off. "Have been for a long time now."

Marcus sat like royalty in disguise, an offering of bloodless body parts at his feet. It was absurd. The entire scene was absurd. A small derelict kitchen, a strange old man on a cheap chair. A trapdoor with body parts. This was the dream. He would wake from this any moment and stare up from an afternoon nap. Sometimes he wondered if he never did wake that afternoon he lay down with Cali, the afternoon she turned herself off. Because he wasn't supposed to wake.

Maybe he never did.

This was his afterlife, this ludicrous scene. In what reality could he possibly believe he could print body parts and piece them together?

I failed Cali.

That was it. When he couldn't stop Cali from suicide, he decided to die with her. And he failed at that, too. And he failed Jamie.

"We're leaving tonight," Marcus answered.

"Tonight?"

"Dennis will be discovered soon. The ensuing chaos, I'm afraid, will be beyond my control. It'll have to be tonight."

Ensuing chaos? The Settlement is going to lose everything because of us. Paul felt the dull thud of a guilty fist sink deep into his solar plexus.

"How? How are we getting out? There's five feet of snow out there and another storm on the way."

"You fabricated Jamie." The old man picked up a floppy hand still wrapped in plastic. "Despite the inaccuracy of her memory, you verified her DNA."

"What's that got to do with escaping?"

"I understand your pain, Paul. What you've done to bring her back is a father's love for his child."

"Don't patronize me."

"You risked everything for her. Risk—is that not the foundation of love, the vulnerability of being completely open?"

"What's all that mean?"

"We leave at dusk. We'll need twenty hours before the process is complete."

"What process?"

"We're going to the lab."

"Why?"

"I'll explain once we're there."

The old man muttered to Raine. She went back to the trapdoor, bleary-eyed and sluggish, and put an arm—one that went from shoulder to wrist, the pink end sealed in preservation wrap, bones exposed like rib-eye steak—in one of three large duffel bags.

The curtains were open. If anyone drove by, they'd see them. The storm would keep that from happening, but the monitors would sometimes trek out to the cabins. He realized he hadn't seen a monitor in days.

Where the hell have they been?

"Twenty hours is too long," Paul said. "Someone will come out. The cloaking program I've been using can't hide another process that long and complex. I'll need to tweak it or alarms will go off, power will go down. We'll put the entire Settlement at risk."

Raine continued unloading body parts; Marcus stacked them in another bag. Paul grabbed handfuls of his scruffy beard, turned away, and ran his fingers through his tacky mop of hair. *Those aren't Jamie.*

"We'll meet at my cabin in six hours," Marcus said. "I want you showered and shaved, both of you. Shave everything—head, arms, legs, everything. Clean yourselves, don't come on an empty stomach and be rested."

"Why?" Paul said.

The crawlspace was empty. The same bags Paul had used to smuggle the body parts were now fully loaded and zipped.

"We're taking them with us," the old man said before Paul could ask. "We'll need them."

"Just... hold on," Paul said. "If we haul everything to the lab, someone will come out, they'll find everything. Even if the alarms don't go off, Pete will stop by. They won't let us leave. You know that."

Marcus walked out of the kitchen. The cabin inhaled a long frigid breath before the front door slammed.

Raine slung a bag over her shoulder, the weight pulling at the left side of her body. Eyes down, she marched across the room. Paul caught her arm. She wouldn't look up. He'd abandoned her too many times.

Another punch to the gut.

She pulled away, put the bag in the bedroom and came back for the other two and locked the door. She was going with or without him and she didn't want him near the bags.

Falling on the couch, he listened to the shower run.

CHAPTER ONE HUNDRED FORTY-SEVEN_

Paul slept with his head crooked over the couch. Still fully dressed, boots laced up. Unshaven.

Raine slid the bags to the front door.

The sun was deep behind the mountains, the sky bruised and quiet. She slept a few hours, but exhaustion was still draped over her. She considered leaving him.

He won't care.

He would wake to a cold and empty cabin and sit and stare. Problem was she'd never get all three bags across the field. They didn't contain Jamie, just pieces sculpted in a box. It was no more her than Venus de Milo was a living being. But Paul believed it was her, despite his attempts to deny it. She could see it in his eyes, saw the pain when they stacked the limp arms, the cold hips and globby organs like exotic meatpackers.

He couldn't kill that belief, couldn't shed himself of the hope that Jamie was under the house waiting to be assembled. It was what kept him going, kept him clinging to a ledge of sanity by his fingernails. He had lost as much as Raine, been kicked in the ribs as many times.

Maybe more.

He was a plant duped by Mother to find Cali. He was a delivery boy of sorts, sent to convince the woman he'd fallen in love with to turn herself off.

Raine swallowed the bitterness. It tasted like bile.

"You coming?"

He snorted awake, looked around expecting monsters. Glazed confusion gave way to indecision.

"He said to shave," she said.

Her head was smooth, as was the rest of her body. She liked the feeling and hoped she wouldn't be around when the stubble grew back. One way or the other.

Paul went to the bathroom. The water ran.

She considered leaving again, but there was still the problem with the bags. Maybe that was why Marcus left all three of them. Paul came out looking much the same, beads of water dripping from his whiskers. He hoisted a bag on each shoulder and led the way.

Half an hour later, they stopped at the edge of the forest and looked across the snowy field. The wind had died. The subzero temperatures rested on them, nipping at the cracks and slivers of exposed skin. The ripe sky flickered with emerging stars, but there was still enough sunlight to glitter the snow like tiny stars had fallen.

The cabins were dark and abandoned, all except the one on the end. A lone figure stood on the porch, slightly hunched with a bag, this one bright orange. *More parts?*

Raine's former cabin, now the old man's, faced the distant lab that loomed in twilight. Faint light glowed in the cabin's window like the furnace burning inside a dragon.

Had he planned this, too?

He lived within sight of the lab, an easy trek to the front door. Everything seemed to fit too neatly, as if someone had reached into the future and stacked the deck.

Paul turned to face her. Steam oozed through the fabric covering his mouth. His sharp eyes, peering between the slit of his stocking cap and face mask, asked one last time.

Are you sure?

She slung the bag over her shoulder and walked into the open. Marcus, sensing them in the shadows, had already started for the lab. Raine high-stepped through virgin snow until she fell into the old man's path. His bag was smaller and lighter. Something metal clinked inside.

A path had been shoveled through a six-foot drift to expose the lab's front door. It was locked. Marcus stepped aside, hardly winded from the walk. Paul pulled his glove off, pressed his hand on the lock pad and opened the door.

Once inside, Marcus dropped the bag. Metal and wood crashed inside. He pulled out a handful of steel wedges gleaming with newness. Next, he retrieved a long-handled sledgehammer. After carefully placing the tip of a wedge between the door and frame, he swung like a railroad worker, driving the wedge halfway home—the grace with which the sledge arced betrayed the illusion of the old man's frailty.

There was nothing old about it.

"Take these." He kicked the bag. "Lock the other doors just like this. We don't want anyone coming in."

"How are we getting out?" Paul asked.

Marcus hammered the next one into place.

Raine grabbed the bag and started walking. She finished the side doors and was halfway through the back door when Paul appeared. He helped her with the last wedge when the hall lights went down. They finished in the dark.

The front doors were firmly pegged shut. The bags of body parts were gone. Paul began pacing, thoughts of betrayal turning a wheel of paranoia.

"This way." The old man's voice emerged from a black hallway.

Light came from one of the labs. Marcus was at one of the computers. The bags were on the floor in puddles of melted snow. It was a biomite lab, one used for fabrication. The smell was burned into her mind the moment she'd stepped out of her own fabrication chamber, her first sight Nix.

The smell, ironically, was that of burnt clay.

"Did you power the building down?" Paul's voice echoed throughout the building.

"It's been redirected."

"You'll arouse suspicion. Someone will come out to check."

"The system will report sleep mode. There will be no alarms."

Marcus said this with the dispassion of a bored adult answering a child's tedious questions. The keyboard clattered beneath his fingers. A stainless steel tank hummed.

"Unwrap the parts," he said. "Put them in the distiller."

He pointed to the large stainless steel tank. Raine grabbed an arm from one of the bags, the flesh firm, the bicep flexed. The plastic crinkled like unwrapping a sandwich. She turned the wheel on the top lid and dropped it inside. It thumped like a sandbag in an empty barrel.

Paul ranted while the old man pecked at the keyboard. He wanted more answers. *That's what faith is for, Paul.*

"Tell us what you're doing," Paul hissed. "Now."

"We need a raw supply of Jamie's biomites."

"And what are you doing with that?"

Another machine hummed to life, this one a boxy thing that resembled a refrigerator with touchpads and a row of green lights.

"If you're planning to fabricate, this is all you have." He ripped the cover off a clear case chamber that was up to his waist. "You can't fabricate her, it's not big enough."

Raine put a hand in the distiller next, a left hand. A meaty smell leaked from the steel vat and pressed against the back of her throat. She swallowed a gag and turned away. The hand didn't thud on a metal bottom but splashed in thick liquid. Like melted wax.

"When you're finished, meet me in lab 204." Marcus hit a combination of keys and left.

Paul went to the computer. "Goddamnit!"

The monitor was locked on a black screen.

"What is it?" Raine asked.

The hallway was dark. A square beam of light cut from a doorway, plastering Paul's shadow on the wall. Unlike the other lab doors, this was a heavy steel door. Marcus was inside and, once again, busy at a computer terminal. Paul raked greasy locks of hair from his face.

"I don't know what this is," he said. "I didn't have access."

There was a square palm lock on the wall.

It didn't surprise her that Marcus had gained entrance. His desires moved at will, a connection he seemed to maintain with nature as well as technology, both as effortless as moving his left hand. *Did he manipulate the weather, too?*

"You'll need to put one of those on."

Marcus pointed at a set of hangers. Very small rubber suits dangled from a horizontal post, a place where most people would hang a coat. A clipper set, the kind people shaved their pets with, was on a short stool.

"You'll need to shave first," he added.

Paul hadn't moved. "What is this?"

Marcus stopped what he was doing. It was the first time he looked at Paul. Raine braced herself for the answer.

"This is the dream disease lab."

"No." He shook his head. "No, I would've known about this."

"Why do you think they built this building, Paul? It wasn't to keep you busy or to advance sustainable energy or medical technology. The People want dreamland. As long as there is dream disease, they won't have it. This was built to cure it."

"Dreamland?" The word floated off Raine's tongue like pixie dust.

"Not yet," the old man said gently. "We're going to use the technology, Raine, but we'll stay here and now. We'll just change the here while we're in the now."

Change the here.

She didn't know what that meant, but was hardly listening. Dreamland was in this lab. It was a promise, a sweet memory that lured her into the old man's spell.

Marcus took off his shirt. His flesh was gray like the underbelly of a dead fish. He took one of the suits off a hanger. It was half his size, a tight fit for a five-year-old.

"I need you to shave, Paul. I need you to do it now. When you're finished, you'll put on the suit. Raine, you can follow me. Once you've undressed, apply this electrolytic gel."

She watched him undress until there was a pile of clothes. He stood completely nude, the rest of his body as slack and wrinkled as his breasts. He sat on a stool and lathered the clear lotion on his feet and calves in thick, gloppy layers like a kid plying jelly on a roll. His pointed toes stabbed into one of the suit's legs. The material stretched up to his knee.

The clippers buzzed in Paul's hand.

He stood in the corner, large chunks of knotted hair falling in long strips, curly whiskers fluttering from his chin.

Marcus had lubricated everything up to his waist with the suit pulled just below his belly button. Raine took a suit and a tub of gel to the other side of the room and undressed until she was naked and cold. Her ribs reminded her just how little she'd eaten.

The men ignored her hairless form. She sat down and began applying the ointment. The suit was slick rubber but stiff with embedded mesh. It hugged her flesh and revealed every fold of skin. Her nipples told of the cold. Paul's face was splotchy and red. The lubricant squished like mucus into every wrinkle, the smell of a gutted fish burping from the seal around her neck.

The three of them looked like odd scuba divers.

"Leave the hoods down," Marcus said, a pointed black cap hung from the back of their necks like loose folds of skin, "for now."

"What do these do?" Paul asked without anger. They weren't swimming off the Settlement. Marcus started for the exit. "Please, just tell us," Paul pleaded. "I can't help if I don't know what we're doing."

Something shifted. They were in too deep. Jamie was a jumble of liquefying parts at the bottom of a steel drum. There was no turning back. Paul was forging ahead. Full steam.

"You can't protect your minds," the old man said from the doorway. "What we're doing will require no trace of knowledge or they'll know where we're going. Only I can hide such thoughts. Therefore, it's better you don't know."

"These are cloning suits," Paul said. "They're used to upload a map of the physical body to a fabricator. If that wrecks your plans—me knowing that—then you need to stop."

Raine knew of the methodology, that the embedded mesh scanned the body inside and out, transferring the data into a computer where a digital model would be developed.

Marcus looked to his right and appeared to be listening; then he nodded toward the blank space. His projection was talking to him and he listened intently, grunting every so often. Paul continued asking questions, but they went unanswered. Who would he be talking to? Who would he carry around inside him, listen to with such reverence? He had always been an outcast, even among his peers.

"There's too much to explain, Paul," he finally said. "I'm sorry, but we really must—"

"Mother," Raine blurted.

It came to her, an epiphany that flashed into existence, like holding a puzzle piece with no distinct color or outline and seeing, all of a sudden, exactly where it fit.

The old man's expression drained away, replaced by something close to shock. It had likely been quite some time since he had experienced something so surprising. Not since he exited a fabrication chamber. *Mother's fabrication chamber*.

The truth, on his face, could not be hidden.

"Is that true?" Paul looked between Marcus and Raine. "Is that who you carry?"

He nodded once.

"But she turned you into a fabrication."

"Like Paul," Raine added. "She did the same thing to Paul."

Paul flinched. The insinuation of a distant kinship was a sharp point between the ribs. The skin suit telegraphed the muscles bunching between his shoulders.

"She showed me the truth," Marcus said.

"She betrayed you!" Paul said. "And you have her imprinted in your mind, projecting her into this world?" Paul's jaws clenched and released. His thoughts were out in the open, his disdain for the artificial intelligence known as Mother.

Because she killed Cali.

"She's part of me," Marcus said. "We are inseparable."

"Maybe she is you," Paul said. "Maybe you don't exist. Maybe she's dreaming you. You're nothing, old man. You're just a disposable clone, a means to an end."

"She showed me the truth. I serve a greater power. So does she."

"You don't know the truth yet, you said so. You don't know what the powers-that-be are, don't know what's at the end of the journey. That's why you're here. That's why *we're* here, why Jamie is soup!"

"Mother showed me there was a truth, Paul." Marcus's voice sharpened into a lethal edge. "But *we,* Paul... *we* have to discover the truth for ourselves. The world doesn't even ask the question if there is a greater truth to know, you understand. The human race is only interested in their own little personal worlds, that's why this little dream disease lab exists. The People want what they want, and as long as the tit is in their mouth they don't ask the bigger question. I ask the question, Paul. I want to know the truth behind it all, what controls us. I have sought to serve the true and only God and she showed me the path."

"She could be fooling you," Paul said. "You could be a plant with false memories. You might think you remember searching for truth, but maybe she's controlling you like a puppet."

"That's where faith leaps, Paul."

Marcus looked at Raine. She understood what it was like to be the projection. She existed in Nix's dreamland, saw the world through his eyes, heard it through his ears.

That's where faith leaps.

"Blind faith is a leap of ignorance," Paul said.

"Whatever I am, Paul," the old man continued while looking at Raine, "it will find the truth and set the world free, you can trust that. This is the journey we were all meant to take."

He looked away from Raine, engaging Paul.

"Do you think she randomly picked you in the warehouse all those years ago? She chose you, Paul. Mother cloned you to find Cali, cloned you to be here on the Settlement so that we would journey together. You were *made* for this journey."

"Why?" Paul asked. "Why me?"

Marcus paused. "Love."

Paul stared at the old man, paralyzed by the answer. He loved Cali, knew the day he first saw her. He often wondered if Mother programmed him that way, predisposed him to fall in love with her. He loved her, that was true. Would it matter if Mother wanted him to?

Marcus went to the computer console. How did he know about all of this? How could he run the computers, know about the skin suits without ever being inside the building? He seemed to know everything, like all of this had happened before and it was happening again.

Mother knows.

"This will take some time," Marcus announced.

"What are we doing?" Paul asked again.

"You'll know soon enough."

"How long?"

"It's hard to say."

"Don't bullshit us. How long?"

"A full body and mind construct will need to be downloaded from each of you. The time it takes depends on your cooperation."

"You said this was going to take twenty hours."

"It's an estimate."

"Now you're uncertain?"

"There are many paths. Which one we choose I don't know at this moment."

"We don't have time for this. Someone will be here tomorrow, I guarantee it. And if we're still in here, they'll swipe us."

Marcus went to a series of institutional beds along the back wall, the cushions thick and tan. Hospital guard rails were anchored on the sides.

"The process will become uncomfortable at times," he said. "Your eyes will be closed. I want you to focus on your breathing until you settle into it."

"What will you be doing?" Paul asked.

"All three of us are going through this."

"What about the fabrication lab?"

"We'll discuss that later."

Paul's fears were turning gears in his imagination, spitting out distorted thoughts and beliefs. Would the old man be fabricating Jamie's head and talking to it?

Paul teetered on the sharp edge of trust, a steep drop on either side. Halfway across the chasm with no net, there was no direction but forward. They had to cross.

Raine walked the line of trust with steadfast dedication, eyes ahead. There was no looking back, no looking down. For her, standing in the dream lab was like the end of a long dangerous night, where predators roamed in the dark. But the eastern rim had begun to lighten, the starless night parched dull gray. The sun was near and she could smell it. It was that clean smell after the rain, the concrete rinsed, the windows streaked.

It smelled like hope.

Marcus lowered the bed rail. Reaching over his shoulders, he peeled the elastic hood over his head and slid the mesh over his face—one big multifaceted bug eye.

Raine ran the rubber fingers of her suit over her slick scalp, the thick gel cloying her sinuses. The hood snapped over the crown of her head. She instinctively held her breath when the mesh dropped over her face. Her breath was hot, the taste of gel seeping into the corners of her lips, stinging her tongue.

"You're not going to dreamland," Paul blurted.

Raine turned to him.

The facemesh undulated where his lips moved. He turned his head, dark hollows where his eyes would be aimed at her. Maybe he was trying to keep her hopes in check, keep her rooted in reality. He'd seen her fly hope into the sky and watch it crash like a paper kite.

Or maybe he was keeping his own hopes grounded.

The process began behind her eyelids when an electrical current rippled through the gel. The suit shrink-wrapped like a second layer of skin. She was buried alive, but could still feel the sticks in her palms.

And the paper kite soared higher.

THE DULL THUD of an axe split her dreams.

It didn't fall in the typical rhythm of felling a tree. It came in erratic spurts, panicked and distant. The sound lifted her from a murky pit where insects fed on rotting things. Sleep fell off her like loamy sand, her body rising from a shallow grave.

The earth smothered her face, filled her mouth.

She clawed her way into waking with fabric pressed over her mouth and nostrils. Sweet clean air was just out of reach. Her arm moved through muddy air; her hand found the thin mesh sucked between her lips. She worked her thumbs under the seam and stripped it away with a wet slap.

Clean air filled her.

She jolted upright, a lost diver with one last draught of oxygen in the tank. Slime dangled from her nose and chin. Another wave of insects crawled in and out of her pores, pinching and stabbing. Microscopic hairs swayed like reeds of seaweed in the subdural layers of her flesh.

Her nervous system raced toward insanity.

A black pile lay next to a corner shower, a shed exoskeleton of a large bug. It had the tang of freshly spilled intestines. Raine leaped off the bed and molted the skin suit. Rancid gel spilled out, congealed and lumpy and smelling of sour mucus. The suit hadn't grown swaying follicles—no seaweed or filaments extracted from her pores—but her flesh was puckered and ridged and more gray than pink, the soft skin of a drowning victim. She was afraid to scratch the maddening itch, afraid she'd carve long tracks with the edge of her nails.

The hot shower brought relief.

She gently washed three times with soap, snotty trails of dead skin gathering around her feet, a gel-caked plug settling on the drain.

Marcus's bed was empty.

Paul was still on his bed, the face mesh sucked into his parted lips. There were no lights that indicated he was still being scanned, no hookups, no wires. If he was trapped in a nightmare, it was unflinching and catatonic.

As long as he's not in dreamland.

It was mean, what he said to her. Hateful. But he was right—the heavy sleep didn't yield dreamland, didn't bring back Nix and Joshua. Paul always wished he could dream like her, that he could see Cali one more time. But he couldn't. He had hallucinations, pretended to see her while waking. And that just wasn't the same.

The axe from her dreams returned, this time a dull thud from down the hall.

The bag of leftover wedges and a yellow-handled sledgehammer were still inside the dream lab. Towel pressed to her face, she looked down the hall. The thudding came from the front door. Someone was pounding on it, cursing the malfunctioning palm lock. Muffled voices sounded concerned. Tempted to eavesdrop, she kept her chat line closed so they wouldn't sense her on the other side of the door.

"Paul?" Pete's voice was dull and distant. "Paul, can you hear me? Paul!"

Another round of thumping.

Her stomach went for a twirl. They knew he was there, and begged him for help. And if they knew about Paul, they would know about her. It was their research. The power had been diverted to the dream disease and fabrication labs. Paul knew the power redistribution would set off alarms. Marcus said they'd need twenty hours, they'd be lucky to get ten.

What are they doing here in the middle of the night?

Something was humming—a familiar rhythm, the constant line-by-line stroking of a fabrication wheel. She started for the fabrication lab. Light fumed from the outer office windows, warm and yellow.

It's daylight. She checked her internal time. It was mid-afternoon. She'd been in that jelly suit all night. *Almost twenty hours!*

The fabrication lab was locked.

She twisted the knob with both hands. The burnt smell of freshly cooked biomites seeped beneath the door, clayey and sticky. The equipment was lit up. The fabrication chamber, the glass blackly tinted, was strumming. The computer nearby was turned at an angle, the blue screen spitting details she couldn't see.

Marcus wasn't there.

The first and second floors were quiet and locked. On the third floor, one door was open. The old man stood near a window, peering at an angle so no one outside would notice him.

"What the hell are you doing?" she said.

Marcus didn't respond. He craned his neck to watch the crowd gathered outside, sticking his arm out when she neared.

"They know Paul's in here," she said.

"They followed your tracks."

"Then they know you're here, too."

"Mmm."

"We're not getting out. The monitors will come for us; they'll want to know why we're in here."

Why weren't the monitors already out there? A gathering of bricks always drew at least one of them.

"Is this your plan?" she muttered.

Marcus ignored her; instead, he watched the events with interest. Pete was emphatic, waving his arms and shouting. He was their leader, always emotional when he felt protective. His rare emotional outbursts were proof of his humanity.

The others listened, occasionally looking at the building. A distant sound turned their heads. It was joined by more mechanical howling. Then a wolf pack of snowmobiles broke from the trees, the alpha male out front with a puffy green coat and a white cowboy hat.

"Now what?" Raine said. "Paul's still in the lab—"

He raised his hand for quiet. As if to say *watch.*

Bob threw his leg over his belted stallion and sank up to his knees in snow. The other monitors watched from their snowmobiles as he shoved his way through the snow, rubbing his blotchy face with exaggerated annoyance.

He had better things to do than watch a herd of useless fucking bricks bitch about their research. They needed to shut the fuck up and be happy they were alive. Christ, there were people out in the world, goddamn honest-to-goodness real-life people that didn't have homes or jobs or families and these artificial fabbers were stomping a hole in the snow, for what?

Because they couldn't get their free shit out of the building?

Pete started out composed, but his fuse was short and bright. Emotions began to sparkle. His voice could be heard through the triple pane of glass three stories up. He was waving his arms and pointing and red in the face when Bob reached into his pocket.

Pete fell like a bed sheet.

His right knee splintered outward, arms flopping like stuffed rolls of linen. The bricks backed away, the example spilled in the snow.

Bob went back to his snowmobile and squeezed the cowboy hat down before spinning off into the trees. He didn't say a word, just dropped Pete like an old diseased horse.

"I don't believe it," Raine said.

The other monitors looked shocked, their hands frozen to the grips, eyes on the pile of Pete. There was no way that should have happened. Bob would need probable cause to swipe a brick, especially one leading the People's research. *The one solving their dream disease.*

"What the hell just happened?" Raine asked.

"We just bought some time."

"We?" Raine grabbed the old man before he left. "Did you do that?"

"We need a little extra time. Our friend out there gave it to us."

"But... but why?"

Marcus stared through her, his unblinking eyes not hiding any secrets but sharing none.

"They can shut us off," she said. "The monitors don't have to see us; they know we're in here. They can swipe us from out there."

"They have no reason to."

"Bob didn't, either! They know we're in here; they'll know we're up to something."

"The monitors will exercise caution."

"But not the bricks! What if they find Dennis? They'll know something's wrong."

"We have all the time we need."

"Marcus, the bricks won't be patient. Like Paul said, they have research in here. It's all going to fail without power. Let's not take a chance and redistribute to the rest of the building."

Pete was lying in a twisted pool—possibly dead. There would be no patience. Not anymore.

"We're almost ready," he said.

She shook him, feeling his soft flesh give under her fingers. He had soaked in one of those soul-sucking suits, too; his body squished like warm clay.

"We're almost ready? What are you planning?"

"It's better you don't know." He gently removed her hands. "For now."

"Trust, you said. How can I trust if you keep hiding?"

"Faith, Raine. Let your faith guide you."

She'd forgotten her rosary beads. Her prayers would not come to her tongue. She wanted to shake him, squeeze him until secrets oozed from his mouth.

Something crashed downstairs.

It was more than the dull thumping of empty fists—this was a sharp slap of metal on metal, one giving way to the other. Glass shattered on the next round. Raine took the stairwell three steps at a time, expecting to find the front door unhinged, the steel wedges scattered down the hall like clunky jacks and the monitors aiming their phones.

Something shuffled through shards of glass.

The yellow-handled sledgehammer—the one that was inside the dream lab—lay in a jigsaw display of glass outside the fabrication lab. Dark droplets speckled the floor.

Paul stood at the computer.

He had shed the skin suit, but dressed without showering. Smudged tracks of blood trailed his footsteps, bits of glass poking from the edges of his feet. Gel glistened on his bare arms and neck, his shirt clinging to his back. A putrid smell of tired skin hung around him, defeated only by the baked smell of cooking biomites.

He wasn't blinking.

A milky sheen fogged his stare, the look of a concussion victim. Maybe he hadn't completely awakened, or left something back in that murky sleep. *Or the dream took something from him.*

"Paul." She touched his arm, slime sliding beneath her fingertips. "Your feet."

Blood trickled from a gash, a rivulet spreading over the waxed floor.

An image on the computer transfixed him like a shiny object swinging from a chain. A three-dimensional cube slowly rotated. What looked like body parts were crammed into it, sort of a box for spare arms, legs and shoulders. Then she realized the room was quiet. None of the equipment was running.

Paul wasn't staring at the computer.

The fabrication chamber was transparent. The image on the computer was inside it, the flesh pressed against the glass walls in wet slices. The top of a smooth skull was wedged between two calves, the shoulder blades against the top of the chamber.

The contorted body was folded.

Paul drifted forward, his feet shuffling in slow, even steps. A shard of glass clicking from his foot, a smudgy trail left behind. His knees cracked on the floor, joints popped. He traced the edge of the chamber, fingers quivering, coaxing the butterfly from the chrysalis. Because the body inside the chamber wasn't awake.

His lips fluttered.

The seams of the chamber suddenly broke. Paul fell back into Raine's arms. A humid exhaust exhaled—warm and earthy, like pottery pulled from the kiln. The keyboard clicked behind them. Marcus had walked inside without a sound.

The nude body expanded like compressed foam given room to breathe. Like a flower opening in sunlight. The chamber walls crept out, the seams widened. The left knee pushed the front panel; a dead arm rolled away from the thigh.

Paul's hand trembled. For the first time in years, she put her arms around him, comforting him like a sister.

He couldn't touch the body, not yet. There was no life, no identity. No spark. Sensory input had to be limited; overload could short the psychology matrix. Someone had to be awake for the body to respond. Until then, it was just a body.

A body that looks like Jamie.

It was a fabrication, a construction of biomites that looked like her—a hairless Jamie with beads of moisture rolling down shiny skin.

The head rose just enough to see her eyes, small pools of water in the cups of her collarbones. She had stopped expanding and now settled into the cramped chamber, fully inflated but still. Paul looked back, suddenly stabbed with fear. Marcus was still at the computer, but nothing was happening. Paul's eyes pleaded with the old man. *Please, don't bring her this close and leave her.*

It occurred to Raine this might be it. Maybe the old man only wanted to bring back the body, to look through her eyes like a telescope to get the answers. Perhaps he had taken them to a cliff, their escape a swift shove because there was no leaving the building.

Not now.

And then the wet inhalation. It gurgled in Jamie's throat, the chest inflating as if God's lips blew one long breath inside her. The nostrils flared.

Jamie's eyelashes gathered in wet bunches. A single drop fell from one of them. The eyelids lifted in one slow, graceful slide. Sharp green eyes stared at freckled knees. The world was awakening through her blooming senses.

She looked at Paul with the eyes of a newborn—completely new. Behind them, a beginner's mind. She was open and fresh, untainted by thoughts and emotional baggage. A clean canvas for God to paint. She would remember this moment, remember a father watching her enter the world, remember Paul trembling.

Her first sight.

And then she arrived. Marcus activated her past. Raine saw it fill her eyes—the recognition of the man kneeling in front of her, the body that was hers, the identity known as Jamie with its history of pain and sorrow and joys and discoveries.

Jamie smiled.

A puff of laughter quivered out of Paul on a long stale breath. He snatched a sheet nearby and wrapped her naked body, then hugged her. Raine wrapped her arms around both of them and felt his body shake beneath her. For a moment, she had forgotten about dreamland. All the joy in the world filled the room.

She just wanted to be with it.

"Come, come." Marcus touched their shoulders. "There will be time later. Come along."

Raine peeled away, wiping tears.

Paul wouldn't let go, fulfilling a promise that if Jamie ever came back, he wouldn't let go. He was a bundle of wet, sticky joy quaking on the floor. Jamie's scalp was shiny new on his shoulder. Marcus was patient and let Paul weep.

Raine continued sopping tears with her sleeve. The faucet was still open, thoughts of Nix and Joshua crawling from one of those chambers. She didn't have to go to dreamland to be with them. She could bring them here, couldn't she?

The moment was shattered by a dull thump on the front door.

"Come now." Marcus was more insistent. "We have to go."

Paul helped Jamie stand, the white sheet clinging to her. He pulled it over her shoulders and wrapped it around her twice. Jamie smiled and nodded, but not at Paul.

She nodded to Marcus.

Their eyes locked. It was different than the loving, open gaze she held with Paul. This was tighter and focused. Knowing. They couldn't be chatting already, she had just come out of the box. She was a fawn learning to walk. But perhaps they didn't need to.

She was with him in Chicago for a reason, and she remembered why. *Or he planted a memory.*

No, that wasn't it. Jamie connected with something deep and meaningful, something she believed in. Did she know he would fabricate her? Did she know Paul would be waiting?

Another whump came from down the hall, this time with a shattering effect. Glass spidered on a window. The bricks had abandoned the front door.

Paul had his arm around Jamie. The old man guided them to the door. "Could you bring the hammer?" he called back.

Raine paused. The yellow-handled sledge had been pushed aside. She lifted it to her shoulder, the fiberglass handle slick with gel. Another glassy whump echoed from across the hall, this time tiny specks tinkled from one of the offices.

"Come, Raine!" Marcus called from around the corner.

She took three steps in the opposite direction and peered into the office. The window was narrow and high, jagged lines streaking from three circular scars of impact. The end of a thick branch slammed near the center, leaving a fourth one. She jumped back. This time the window slumped inward.

A face appeared at the corner.

Someone shouted. It was distant and muffled through the cracked security glass, but she recognized her name.

She didn't remember going blank.

It was like a section of life had been snipped from her consciousness. One second she was looking at the face and hearing her name, the next she was on the floor looking into Marcus's eyes. He lifted her with one arm, the hammer in the other hand.

The building had filled with pressure.

The old man rushed her around the corner. It wasn't until he closed them inside the dream lab and began jamming the rest of the wedges around the door that she realized the pressure wasn't in the building.

It was inside her head.

CHAPTER ONE HUNDRED FORTY-EIGHT_

Marcus tapped a steel wedge near the bottom of the heavy door, sweat dripping from his nose. He blinked the shiny object into focus then drove it home with one swing. The door made a popping sound, the tension sealing the dream disease lab shut.

"What are you doing?" Paul grabbed his shoulder. "There's no way—"

Marcus spun on him. Paul tensed and put him at arm's length.

"Easy, Marcus," Mother said. "Take a breath. Don't show anger. Trust is delicate. He doesn't know how close they are to death."

He didn't feel Paul behind him. That wasn't something he was accustomed to, someone sneaking up on him. Not that Paul was sneaking; Paul just wanted to know why they were being locked inside the lab. There was no way out.

Not that he could see.

Marcus took a slow, cleansing breath. The air was thick with sweat and fear and putrid piles of shed skin suits. Of course Paul didn't know how close death had come. When Raine peeked into the office, the monitors swiped them.

If not for the old man, they'd be dead.

He cast his mind around them like a Faraday cage, a mindfog that shredded the monitors' communications, their commands to self-terminate obliterated. It was how the old man stayed free all those years, how he controlled his environment. But protecting his own mind was easy. Four minds was consuming him. As long as he kept focus, the monitors couldn't swipe them. This came at a price. Marcus could hardly concentrate.

And right now, he needed to focus.

"They're coming through a window," he said gently. "They'll be inside the building soon. We need just a little more time."

"There's nowhere to go," Paul answered. "Not in here."

Marcus heard this through a thick veil, his senses clouded. He stared at Jamie, his ticket to the powers-that-be. *The one to lead?*

Paul grimaced, a man trapped by desperation.

"Don't look at her." Mother walked behind Jamie, finger to her lips. "Paul needs to believe she's not a puppet."

She was right, Marcus couldn't give the impression he was controlling her. Jamie's limited memories were stored in the biomite DNA, essential ones that unfolded at the time of the spark. She remembered her identity, remembered the old man in Chicago.

And the memories of her end.

She'd peered into death, followed the yellow brick road to the end of the rainbow. He hadn't planned it that way, but her death would serve him well. He hoped she would lead him to the powers-that-be.

"Do you feel that?" Marcus looked around the room as if fairies were whispering. "They're swiping us, Paul. They're trying to turn us off."

"No, they're not. We'd be dead."

"I'm stopping them."

Raine's eyes were still wide with shock, slightly foggy. Recalling that brief encounter with nothingness, she still felt the long cold night swallowed her.

"He's right," she said. "They saw me, Paul. And I felt it. Marcus stopped them."

An unblinking standoff was chewing up valuable time. Paul was still soaked in gel, patches of skin softened into sickly gray-pink dough. The sensations had to be agonizing, but he didn't show it.

Someone shouted inside the building.

"What's stopping them from turning off all the power?" Paul asked.

"They won't harm their dream disease lab," Marcus answered. "I took precautions should they try."

"If you betray us," Paul said, "I will hunt you down."

"Get back in the suits," Marcus said. "A fresh layer of gel for you."

Four new suits were draped over the beds. Marcus drove three more wedges in place. Each swing rang down the corridor like an alarm. It made no difference, the bricks and monitors already knew where they were. The power distribution pointed right at them.

Within the mind static, the old man could hear their thoughts. They had found Dennis. Once they followed the tracks, the pieces quickly fell into place. The monitors overturned Bob's orders (what few he gave before riding off). They didn't know what Marcus was doing, but one brick was dead.

The banging started again, this time a dull fist on the lab door.

They were inside.

"Paul?" someone shouted. "What are you doing? Please, you're compromising everything!"

They were already suited up, hoods pulled over the crowns of their scalps. Jamie stood behind Paul, her freshly fabricated face glowing like a newborn. Her eyes still innocent, imploring. She didn't remember Paul, had no memories of the farm or him adopting her. She only felt that he was important to her, the paternal love guiding her to stand in the protection of his shadow.

"Take your beds," Marcus said.

The insistent fleshy thudding outside the door pushed them along. Paul waited until Jamie was comfortable, whispering words of comfort. He did the same with Raine, squeezing her hand.

"It'll be all right," he said, closing his hand around hers.

Sticks poked out from between her fingers, the crucifix held tightly in her hands.

The door held. No amount of pounding was going to break the lock or unseat the wedges. But still, they would need time. The four of them were ready to escape. It was why they dressed earlier and had their body-identity scans uploaded.

There's no room for error.

A shiver of doubt ran through the old man's hands as he lathered the clear gel over his ribs. He could only hope his team was ready on the other end. An error would set him back decades.

Maybe longer.

"They're ready for you," Mother assured him. "They're ready."

There was no way she could know that, but her confidence steadied his hand. He stretched the hood over his head, the elastic tension pulling on his neck. The others had lowered the face mesh. Marcus went to each of their beds and touched an arm.

He could abandon them now, leave them on the Settlement and take Jamie with him. There was enough time to pull her memories. They wouldn't suffer through the swipe, their consciousness turned off before they knew they'd been betrayed.

One to lead, one to dream...

Marcus checked the system before lying down, the face mesh still bundled on top of his head. Mother sat beside him. He felt her hand on his arm, the warmth seeping through the cold gel that once again sucked through his pores.

"Yes," Raine said. "Yes, thank you."

She had pulled the mesh up. The old man told her to get ready, there wasn't time. Paul sat up, assuring her everything was all right. But she was smiling, almost beaming. She was talking to someone.

"You're my angel. My angel." She began weeping.

She was hallucinating. He knew it was a risk, that her mental state was already unstable. *This might not go well.*

But she pulled down the mesh and lay back. Her sobs continued. Paul soothed her, but eventually the suits pulled them unconscious.

There were momentary lapses of door pounding. Silence would stretch out for long minutes, interrupted by their names being called through the thick metal. Bob's booming voice wasn't one of them. He would still be in his cabin. No matter what anyone did, he would keep watching television.

Marcus was still awake when the machine arrived.

Hours had passed when the vibrations came through the walls and floor. Something was coming down the corridor. An engine idled at first, then was open wide. Marcus could feel it in his teeth. A mechanical whine rumbled outside the door; a weighty crack reported into the room. The door bowed in the center like a fist. The engine growled over commanding voices.

The door popped. Stress wrinkles appeared across the surface. The wedges stayed in place, the lip of the door plumping around them. Something loud broke inside the wall.

The lock had given way.

Mother walked over to the door as if she would sacrifice her last breath for them. Marcus pulled up his face mesh and initiated a preliminary procedure, feeling his flesh become a fuzzy barrier, a porous envelope barely containing his organs. If his skin completely dissolved, the suit would hold him together, would allow him the extra few minutes. Only he would be awake for that agony. The others would be spared.

Mercifully, the engine idled.

Something had gone wrong. Twenty minutes later, it fired up again. Marcus had become a bag of soup by then, his breath—hot and thick—the only reminder he was alive.

Mother whispered, "Go now."

The door cracked like an iron I-beam.

Marcus gave the thought-command. The cold grip on his awareness filled him, sipping him out of the suit like a cool drink into silent darkness, pulling him into the computer network, where he sought wireless pathways and cable conduits.

He led them out.

III_

One to bleed.

THE ARCHETYPE'S KNOWLEDGE_

"Your room is ready, Ms. Winters."

Norah Winters didn't stop at the sprawling desk. She didn't even take off her sunglasses. The cheerful receptionist offered a curt but pleasant smile and returned to her administrative duties.

It was one of many reasons why Norah chose the Dream Institute. There were many certified dreamland accelerators in Denver, a few rated four stars with a clean record. But none of them had the service like the Dream Institute. The name even implied superior status.

Norah liked that.

The door to the left of the desk swung open. A petite young lady was there to greet her, a blonde with small breasts and athletic hips. Norah knew the way to her room but let the young thing lead the way.

The hallway was wide with tasteful art on the walls (well, not all of it tasteful) and several quiet doorways. A mix of jazz played softly. The young lady opened the third door to the right, asked if there was anything else and left with a curt but pleasant smile (they trained them that way).

The suite was plush and clean with a living room arrangement for entertaining (if you wanted to waste your time) and a large workspace. The spotless bay window overlooked the Rockies, a view Norah was enamored with the first time she leased the room but now had become as unnoticed as the wallpaper.

A glass of red wine (Dana Estates Lotus Vineyard Cabernet Sauvignon) was on a sterling silver platter, a wine she discovered in Napa with husband number two (or was it three?). Norah sat on the duvet to free her feet from the high heels.

"Good afternoon, Ms. Winters." Sheila closed the door quietly behind her.

"Good day."

Sheila sat next to Norah and opened a black leather case, humming a pleasant tune as she did so. Sheila was naturally chatty, something Norah put an end to after their first meeting. She allowed the humming, considering it a fair compromise.

"It's been six months since we last sampled," Sheila said.

Norah allowed her to tie an elastic band above her elbow, turning her head before the needle pricked her vein and the vial turned red. Sheila then placed a black box the size of a cell phone against Norah's chest. A wave of prickly static scattered under her skin.

And then the nurse was gone. No goodbye, no the doctor will be here in a minute, just a little humming ditty out the door.

There was a bathroom to the left. Norah showered and put on a Stefano Ricci robe. She hadn't even requested that type of robe, they just knew she'd love it. She leaned over the sink and wiped away the condensation to study the loose skin beneath her green eyes. Not bad for an eighty-nine-year-old woman.

But not good enough.

When Dr. Toby Chalmers arrived, she was still in the Stefano Ricci and the pedicurist was almost finished.

"Ah, Norah," he said with all his pearly teeth. "It's so lovely to see you."

"Of course."

"You look fabulous, as always."

"I suppose, but these bags." Norah turned her cheek. "Can we do something?"

Toby (she was on a first-name basis; just because he was a doctor didn't mean she called him by his last name) bent over to examine her creamy complexion.

"A little tweak might work," he said. "Perhaps we can address that next time. Your biomites are at 94% and I'd like a full analysis before we do that. You don't have time for that now, a busy woman such as yourself."

She felt the blood rush to her cheeks, admonishing herself for showing indulgence. He knew what she liked.

And that's why I'm here.

"Your blood work and scan are perfect. Anything else we can do before you go?"

Her lips parted. A tiny sound stuck in her throat, the words throttled in place. Something was on her mind; it had been since she read the newsfeed that morning. It was bothering her, but she didn't want to say anything, didn't want it to sound like *little-girl worry* (her third husband called it that, or was it the first?).

Besides, if she said it out loud, it could make it true. It was like actors that played terminally ill cancer patients (when cancer was a thing). If they believed they had cancer, they got cancer. But she couldn't stop herself from thinking. Her thoughts had always had a life of their own. If only she devoted more biomites to her brain, she could control what she thought and felt.

She could commit the last 6% of her clay to brain biomites. Well, 5% of her clay. It was impossible to go 100%. Even if she could, she'd become one of those bricks and they're the ones that started dream disease.

Dream disease—damn it! She thought it.

"No. Nothing else."

"Very well."

The nurse returned and the pedicurist left. Norah went to the side room, a small enclave that was without windows or decorations, that housed the largest most comfortable chair invented. It resembled a reclining throne.

They helped her lie back. She tucked the flaps of her robe to avoid exposing her thighs (she was still nude) while the nurse fussed with an IV bag and Toby checked the monitors that tracked her vitals. There would be no catheter (*no tube in there, thank you*). They would have to clean her.

The chair began to vibrate.

Toby lifted her hand like a delicate flower and kissed it. "Bon voyage, beautiful woman."

It occurred to Norah they knew her thoughts. This disturbed and pleased her at the same time. There was no need for her to request her wants and desires, they were taken care of. It was just... some thoughts she wanted to keep private. But if that was the price of luxury and a handsome doctor (it occurred to her he wasn't really a doctor), then she was willing.

The bricks (*damn them*) didn't need accelerator chairs to reach their dreamlands. They just closed their eyes and went. Well, back when they had dreamlands. The government took that away because of the dream disease.

Dammit.

When the door closed and the room was silent, the vibrations ramped up. She closed her eyes and let the vibrations take her. She could no longer feel the fabric around her. No longer tell the difference between where she ended and the chair began.

She whirred.

And fell.

A salty breeze blew across her face. She opened her eyes to see an endless horizon on a blazing sea, the sun setting off to her right in a violet sky. She was standing on a glass portico that cantilevered over a sheer cliff that ended in ship-eating boulders.

And that wasn't all.

Her hips were curved, legs shapely, her cheeks taut where once they sagged. She was young again. And below, relaxing around a pool with an edge that appeared to fall over the cliff, were ten young men straight from Greek mythology—racked abs and oiled biceps.

Dreamland.

She was wealthy in real life, so the excess wasn't that much different, really. But she couldn't control everything in the physical world. *You must live life on life's terms,* her recovering alcoholic ex-husband told her before leaving (he was number four, she remembered that).

But not in dreamland.

She stepped off the portico and floated down to the pool as gently as a rose petal. Here, life lived on her terms. These were her rules. This was her universe. Perhaps some would find being a goddess boring.

Not so.

Later that night, she lay at the water's edge, strewn across a large boulder like a wet rag. The black sky sparkled with diamonds; the moons were full (she preferred two moons). That evening's orgy had sapped her. She could still taste blood and wondered if it was still on her lips. Even in dreamland she could become exhausted. Three men would do that to anyone. (And one woman, just to spice things up.)

She murdered them when she was finished, cut them open and spilled their organs, rolling in the gore as her orgasm faded.

Her inner fantasies indulged, she closed her eyes. She had another couple of days before having to make her exit, to return to the flesh for the required recuperative therapy (too long away from the real world and the body forgets you, they say). She wasn't one to push it. But for now, she would sleep.

In the morning, she'd have breakfast in the tower, perhaps fly over to the mainland and visit the city. The details of the urbanscape were unknown to her, something the Dream Institute provided for her to discover.

Perhaps she could bring back some children for the evening's festivities.

She felt the warm arms of sleep when a cool shadow passed over her. It was a strange unsettling feeling. She'd been known to allow mythological creatures into her dreamland, but none now. Even so, one could only pass over one moon.

Not both.

She sat up and willed the ocean still. The frothy water settled as if a wave machine had been cut off. She listened and reached with her mind, her thoughts crawling to the extent of her universe. She fought to keep the paranoid thoughts out of her awareness, the worry she couldn't extinguish in front of Toby. But she couldn't help it. Something felt... foreign.

The temperature plummeted.

The ocean immediately froze into a solid sheet. The moon crystalized, the sky shattered. One column of fog escaped her lips before her body—her young, curvaceous body—turned into granite.

Only a distant beeping rang in the silence.

She was unable to turn her head, to move her eyes, to call for help. But the beeping grew louder.

Voices.

Someone was out there. Someone was coming.

"Not yet!" It was Toby's voice. "Don't disconnect, she's got to be stable!"

There were people around her now. The boulders had disappeared; the glacial ocean gone. A quick journey through a dark shattered blackness brought her back to her tremoring flesh.

"Norah!" His face was blurry. "Stay with us, Norah!"

There was chaos, but it didn't matter to her. The cold had stolen her breath and taken her will. She just wanted to sleep. No, not sleep. To give up.

To give herself to the dream eater. Forever and ever.

This, she realized as her body was lifted and rushed down a hallway, *was what I worried about?*

She knew in the final moments where she was going. And she didn't care. She would become something bigger, something better and pure.

The dream disease works this way.

CHAPTER ONE HUNDRED FIFTY_

Sound told Jamie she was alive.

It bounced in rhythm, a sort of bouncing-ball rhythm. The kind she would see on television when she was young, a little ball bouncing off words at the bottom of the screen.

Beep-beep, this one went. *Beep-beep. Beep-beep.*

More importantly, it brought a memory, a little snippet of sitting in front of a television, sucking juice from a box, her hands tiny, tongue purple. But the memory didn't smell like alcohol, the kind in a hospital. Clean and sterile, it didn't smell like that in front of the television.

It didn't feel cold and stiff.

Another sound joined the first one and now there were two bouncing balls, one slightly faster than the other. For a brief time, they would join their voices before one sped ahead, looping around to synchronize again.

Beep-beep.

Jamie was the heaviness of a giant bag, the sort boxers punch. She could feel its density, the thick membrane around it, the gush of blood inside it. And then she had the queer realization that she wasn't inside the bag.

I am the bag.

A gasping breath broke the surface. Someone had been underwater, now chomping at the air. The man (she thought it was a man, the guttural hacks deep and smoky) coughed up thick mucus.

Jamie continued to fill with muddy water, a slurry of grainy sand and silt that fell into place and settled with pins and needles that poked through the lining. It hurt. It fucking hurt. Like when she sat cross-legged too long and her foot turned into a slab of meat, the sensations coming back with angry pinpricks, like *how dare you!*

Only this was her body.

Another memory snippet, pins and needles.

The coughing man murmured in blurry tones, the voice of someone up too late, had too much fun. The sound of fabric sliding off a cushion, sticky wet on a shiny floor. One of the *beep-beeps* went quiet.

She wanted to get up, get out of this body bag. The sand was wet and heavy and the needles stuck her like an inside-out cushion, a voodoo doll tortured one prick at a time.

Breathe. She felt breath, her own breath.

It wasn't like she was underwater, it was just an easy draw followed by an effortless release. She had arms and legs, a face and eyes. Eyelids that creased like new leather, their crunchy blink inside her watery head.

She stared at starry ceiling tiles.

It was sometime later that she opened her creaky eyelids again, the ceiling unchanged. She'd fallen back asleep, the bouncing ball song bringing her back. There were curtains drawn on both sides, fabric partitions that gave the impression she lay in a small room. Her neck bones offered little cracking sounds.

She tossed her leg over the edge. It dangled. The big toes catching the hard floor. Blood thudded in her foot. She sat up. There was no fluid in her lungs—not like the hacking and wheezing—but her head sloshed with sleep. The pins and needles were gone, but she itched like a wool scarf. And ached.

She ran her hand across her head, fingers knitting through two inches of thick hair. A hospital gown sleeve hung off her elbow. There were vague memories of going to sleep. It didn't feel like this room, though. Or smell like it.

It was a slow journey to the floor; pins and needles met the bottom of her foot, fractured nerves running up her thigh until she bit her lip. A tear squeezed between her clenched eyelids and raced off her chin.

Something crashed.

Jamie startled at the sound, a harsh contrast to the quiet, antiseptic feeling. It was beyond the curtain on her left. She eased off the edge of the bed until all her weight settled on her quivering knees. She reached for the curtain, teased it with her fingers until she clutched a handful of vinyl, and pulled herself up.

The eyelets strained in the metal track, the curtain stretching but not tearing. Her flesh stretched over her ribs like cured animal hide. A gust of wind would carry her off like an autumn leaf. She rode the curtain down the line, feet slapping the floor.

An empty bed was on the other side.

Computers and monitors were stacked along the wall, a silver rack with an IV bladder hanging flat and empty. The heart monitor was silent. Looking back, she realized the same arrangement was set up in her stall. Purple scars dotted the veins inside her elbow. Her heart monitor had also gone quiet, but another danced somewhere else in the room.

A pile of papers fluttered beyond the door, followed by a wet cough.

She took a couple breaths, lunged toward the door on rubber legs, and caught the L-shaped handle to keep from melting into a puddle. The door was heavy. She pried it open enough to squeeze into a hallway. There were several doors, all of them open at various degrees, but a big window caught her attention. It was at the end of the corridor, sunlight coming through a glass wall.

She used a handrail along the wall (it seemed out of place, or something needful), flopping her feet, strength trickling into her waking limbs. The view beyond slowly came over the horizon as she neared—an endless sea of palm trees.

The wall was slightly curved. She leaned against it, her cheek sticking to the cold glass. The outside wall appeared to bend like a cylinder.

One building was tucked into the tropical menagerie, the walls algae-tinted, the windows dark and lifeless. It had the angles and structure of an institution, a sort of unimaginative box where research was done.

The Settlement. She suddenly remembered where she was before waking up. She saw the face of... of someone. *Paul.*

She looked at her hands, remembering stepping out of a fabrication chamber before they were rushed to another room. *They... Raine and Paul... and... and...*

Something large fell. She felt it in her feet.

Jamie had slid down the glass without realizing it, a dark slurry of thoughts swirling like silty water. She pulled herself down the hall and leaned into a half-open door that was across from where she woke. The knob cracked on the wall and startled an old man.

Marcus Anderson.

Yes, the old man was at the Settlement, too. He had brought her back from somewhere deep and black and empty. But someone was after them. She just woke up and people were locked out. Windows broke. There was shouting, chaos. They put on stinging slick suits and lay back because they had to get away.

They stared at each other, each waiting for the other to make a move.

"Where am I?" Her voice echoed in her head.

The old man's brows wedged together, darkening his eyes. The hospital gown hung on him like a bed sheet. His spotted scalp was the color of bottled rage. He limped over to an oversized monitor, his shoulders hunched stiffly so that he had to bend at the waist to look up. Coarse, guttural sounds tumbled in his throat while his fingers trembled over a keyboard.

There were monitors all around the wedge-shaped room, enough space for five or six scientists to work their data. *Scientists?* She didn't know why she thought the word scientists. Maybe it was the building outside that made her think that, or the smell around her.

All the monitors flashed images.

At first, she thought they were elaborate screen savers waiting for programming; then she recognized the tropical images. It was a view from above, a satellite image that panned around a tropical island. She recognized the institutional building from down the hall, the one tinted green with algae, only it was U-shaped from above.

And not far from it was a fat round building three stories tall. *That's where we are, in a cylindrical building.*

"What did you do to us?" she asked.

"This is not it." The old man spun like a gargoyle, one eye bulging. "This is *nothing* like I wanted."

His teeth snapped like he was trying to bite the words for having to even say them. He looked around the room in mad, jerky motions, the one eye big, red and watery. Not finding what he was looking for, he returned to the massive monitor, data scrolling in nonsense.

"Marcus," she said calmly, "where are we?"

The old man paid no attention, but the monitors, all at once, responded. Images flickered like a broadcast interrupting normal programming until they all showed the island. Even the main monitor was synchronized to the others as if they all answered the question.

They were on a tropical island.

The view continued to pull away. Higher in the sky it went until the spit of land became a speck in the middle of an ocean.

"Voice-activated," Marcus muttered. "Transportation! How can we get back to the mainland?"

In unison, the monitors panned to a luxurious dock somewhere on the island. Ropes and bumpers hung along empty slips.

"Where are the technicians? The laboratory... where are my

fabrication engineers? Are they here? Why did they leave? Why are we here, goddamnit?"

The blue waters undulated without response.

He slammed his fist on the keyboard, plastic squares bouncing onto the floor. Jamie thought his fists would shatter before the keyboard, his frame too fragile looking.

"Answer me!"

He was huffing for air, leaning against the desk before he fell.

"How did we get here?" Jamie asked.

A row of fabrication chambers appeared on the monitors—doors ajar on glass cubicles. It took a moment to interpret the response. Jamie looked at her hands, turned them over, and put the wrinkled knuckles to her nose—the smell of freshly baked earth filled her head.

Fabrication. I'm a... I'm a fabrication?

"How did this happen?" she whispered.

Marcus's face appeared on the screen, this one slightly different than the red-faced old man hyperventilating across from her. There was no eye bulging in the socket, no age spots polluting the scalp. This one held a knowing grin with a secret locked between the lips and behind the eyes. It was Marcus, but not really. The eyes, she knew.

Sharp pupils, slices of blue in the thin irises.

I've seen those eyes.

"This..." he muttered. "This is all wrong. How did this... how could this happen? Was it you? Did you do this?"

Again, he cast that straining eye around the room, his accusations searching for someone besides Jamie. His confident face looked back from the monitors, the mocking smile perhaps meant for him.

The eyes.

She remembered the eyes, but from where? *Chicago. He was in Chicago. But what was I doing there?*

"What happened, Marcus?" she asked.

He wiped his scalp with both hands and slid them over his face, withering like corn before the harvest. Words stumbled over his tongue, false starts that didn't catch. Finally, he nodded. Resigned. He was about to say something, perhaps tell her what he knew or where they were supposed to be or why they were in Chicago, but the monitors went blank.

Jamie felt it in the hallway, its presence a raging sun, a mind tainted with revenge. She stepped back. Marcus, however, seemed unaware of the danger, still forming the first words when it burst into the room.

"I will end you!"

The old man looked up as Paul wrangled one hand around the thin, crooked neck, a flap of loose skin squeezed over his fingers. Paul lifted him like a bag of straw and threw him into the monitor. The screen cracked in a gunshot pattern behind the old man's head.

"Where is she?" he shouted. "What did you do?"

Marcus clawed helplessly at his forearm. Sound could not escape the crushing grip, a vice that would surely snap the old man's neck.

"I'm here," Jamie said. "Paul, I'm here."

But he didn't turn at the sound of her voice. He leaned into the wet sounds of the old man's jaws that worked like a suffocating fish.

"Where is Raine?" he hissed.

"Paul, stop." Jamie grabbed his arm. "Something went wrong, Paul! It's not his fault."

His forearm was a steel bar, rigid muscles banding in twisted cords. Jamie hung from it and felt the old man's loosely wrapped fingers, his face flushed red hot. The one eye had swelled from the socket.

Paul wanted to see him die.

"Don't do this," she said. "We'll never know where we are."

No level of begging would stop him from watching the old man die, but she found the words that hit the target.

"We'll die, Paul. Both of us."

The first breath came to the old man like a storm, the inhalation of a drowning man deep in the dark tunnel of unconsciousness. Paul dropped him on the counter. The old man crumpled like a paper sack of bones, panting like a sick dog.

"I will end you," Paul said. "If you don't find her, I will end you."

The raging trance faded. For the first time, he seemed to notice her; perhaps he heard her words, just not where they came from. He put his arms around her, drew her close, kissed her forehead.

The strained sounds of an old man faded behind them.

"You all right?"

She nodded.

He examined her, looking for the truth, asking her again and again, like he couldn't believe she was there, she was actually in front of him.

"You know me?" he asked.

"Of course."

Her memories were scattershot images. Her past was dark, there were things she didn't want to remember, but Paul and the farm were emerging in small pieces.

Paul was always the strong one, the one that held them together on the farm when things got tough. But now his presence was even bigger, his mind filling the hallway, wrapping around her, keeping the world from hurting her.

She didn't feel that from Marcus. He was just an old man—a lost old man.

Paul went back to the room where they woke. Jamie leaned against the doorjamb, watching him yank curtains aside. The beds were empty, the computers silent. He paused at the last curtain, bowing his head before grabbing it with both hands, the vinyl bunching between his fingers. The eyelets pinged as he tore it down.

There was someone in the last bed.

The flesh was sickly brown, a slab of meat left for days on summer concrete, collapsed around the bones like a vacuum-sealed package. The cheekbones were sharp, the lips pulled away from the teeth.

And no bouncing ball.

The fumes of adrenaline evaporated from Paul's trembling knees. He fell over the corpse, forehead pressed on the hand-shaped collarbone jutting from her shoulder. His body shook silently, the sobs locked deep inside, fueling the anger that had choked the old man.

And then Jamie remembered.

She remembered the woman stepping out of the fabrication chamber all those years ago. Jamie was there, had watched the fabrication of the woman's body a line at a time. She saw Nix pull her from his dreamland, transferring her into the physical world. She was her sister, a beautiful soul.

She was Raine.

And now she was that.

Jamie touched his shoulder, feeling the anguish shudder from a deep place. The body hardly looked like the woman she once knew, nothing more than a poorly sculpted replication.

"I didn't plan this."

Marcus stood in the doorway, slumped and withered. He limped to a chair. Blood tracked a red trail from the back of his head.

The moments stretched out, interrupted only by Paul's guttural clenching.

"We're..." Marcus began, "not supposed to be here. The transfer... we were supposed to arrive in a New York laboratory where newly fabricated bodies awaited."

He lifted his hands, the skin thin and pale, snaky blue veins bulging on the backs. Not what he expected.

After another long pause, he continued. The skin suits, as he called them, the black slimy things they wore, were body scanners that transferred specifications to a lab (a lab he swore, once again, was in New York) where fabricators quickly cloned them. Everything had been arranged before he had arrived on the Settlement.

Their identities transferred like data.

There was a team waiting for them to wake up, a group of technicians that would help them adjust to their newly minted bodies. It would be a simple transfer from one body to another, one vehicle to the next.

"Not this." He was staring at the hands. "It wasn't supposed to be this."

Jamie remembered the long, dark sleep, the endless black void of a blank dream. A journey through a cold network, a vacuum of outer space where there was no time, where nothing existed in between one body and the next.

"You killed her," Paul said.

"I did not."

"Then where is she?"

"I don't know how any of this happened."

"But you... you did this to us. You did this to her."

Darkness returned to the old man's eyes. "You would be on the Settlement if not for me."

"And she would be alive."

"And Jamie would be dead."

Paul spun around. "You murdered her in the first place."

"I was not in Atlanta. Her memories are corrupt."

Jamie had no memories of Atlanta, no recollection of dying. *But the eyes. I remember the eyes.*

"You are responsible for all of this," Paul said.

"I freed you, Paul. Would you rather be on the Settlement? Would you rather watch Raine suffer without her dreamland?"

"I would rather you join her."

Weakness suddenly overcame Jamie. Paul caught her before she slid to the floor.

The old man hadn't moved. If not for Jamie, Paul would squeeze the life out of him. And there was nothing Marcus could do to stop him. He sat there turning his hands over, a look of revulsion gliding down his bulbous nose, turning his mouth. Glancing at Paul, he got up as if he'd grown bored with the conversation and limped from the room.

"I'm all right. It's okay," she said.

He helped her into the chair, the seat still warm. Exhaustion tugged at her consciousness, her fuel tank already tapped. Paul knelt next to her. "I'm sorry," he said.

He wasn't just talking to her. He was sorry for everything. Sorry for Raine, sorry for dreamland. Sorry for the state of the world. And there was nothing he could do about it.

She began to doze, patting Paul's hand while sounds of chaos came from surrounding offices. The old man shuffled more papers in search of an explanation of where they were and how.

Raine's body continued to deflate.

"Angel," Jamie remembered her saying just before they left the Settlement. "You're my angel."

Who was she talking to?

CHAPTER ONE HUNDRED FIFTY-ONE_

MARCUS'S LEFT LEG WOULDN'T BEND.

The knee, exposed just below the thin gown, was puffy and pink, razors pulsing inside it. He swallowed a slick of bile, the knob in his throat sore, neck stiff.

Muddled thoughts melted into globs of nonsense. Sifting them for an explanation was like looking for clean water in a mud hole. He just couldn't think clearly, couldn't feel the world around him.

He would've killed me.

Marcus couldn't stop Paul, not like he had in the cabin; couldn't sense the enraged man's thoughts, couldn't reach inside him to manipulate his desires, to lock his muscles. To save his ass.

Marcus was the prey.

What has become of me?

His ribs sang with each inhalation, the back of his head throbbed. Paul and Jamie were exactly as he expected them to be, even smelled of freshly fabricated biomites—the scent of baked earth. Marcus smelled of sweat, pungent and ripe. Dead skin.

"Where are you?" he said. "What have you done? Answer me! What have you done?"

Mother was gone.

He couldn't see her, couldn't feel her. Not since she first appeared to him all those years ago had she felt so distant. As if she never existed. Never had she abandoned him, not like this. He was in need. She was the one that fabricated his body, showed him the truth, sent him on this mission.

"What have you done to me?" he murmured.

There was movement in the hallway. A door slid open and closed, and then there was silence. Marcus's heart fluttered; anxious threads of fear tugged his chest. He hoped it was Paul and Jamie leaving, but he'd wait to confirm. He was not ready for another confrontation.

This was not the plan.

The monitors were black, the floor littered with debris. He sat in the dark office, his raspy breath filling the silence.

"Where are we?" he asked.

The monitors scattered. A fractured image flickered on the main one, jagged lines splintering palm trees where the back of his head smashed the glass. Marcus spun the chair, his heel dragging across the floor, a fiery slick of pain lighting up his knee.

An island. A fucking island.

A speck of land so isolated that the United States Air Force couldn't find it. It would take a day to reach the nearest land by water. How did any of this get out here?

How did we get out here?

The buildings were clustered on one end of the island, mostly shrouded in wilderness. Something moved across a wide patch of grass. Marcus pulled closer to the monitor.

Two people. Paul and Jamie, he guessed. One of them carried a bundled white sheet.

Is this a live feed?

The sophistication of technology was cutting edge even for a laboratory located in the middle of an industrial park. How could all of this get out here? And where was the power coming from?

"What is this place?" The words hurt his throat. "Why are we here?"

The views changed but only served to show different angles of a large bank of solar panels and a row of wind turbines on the north shore; there was also a small power plant of generators wired to tidal harvesters. None of his questions, though, were answered beyond what the island looked like.

He hobbled into the hallway. The silver door of an elevator was to his left, three lights over it. The one on the left was lit. *The first floor.*

He used the handrail to reach the end of the corridor, dragging the useless leg along the way. A cool draft slipped through the open back of the gown, his buttocks exposed. He was panting when he pressed his hand against the cool glass and looked across the island from what appeared to be the second floor. A sharp blue line of water slit the horizon.

"What have you done?"

The question, this time, felt closer to home. *What have I done?*

A digital chirp called from one of the rooms, followed by the hum of generators. Marcus waited and listened.

"Who's there? Jamie?"

Chirp.

It was coming from the recovery room, where they woke up. He struggled back, listening again before looking inside. The computers, dead when he woke, were alive. An individual station was dedicated to each bed. The far monitor flashed in time with the singing chirp. An aluminum post leaned against it.

A cane.

That wasn't there when he woke up.

He lunged from bed to bed, resting on each one, the padding still warm. His bed, however, was tainted with sour sweat. An image of Raine was locked into the corner of the far monitor. Marcus leaned on the counter to read the status.

Transfer aborted.

He pecked at the keyboard. When nothing happened, he thought-commanded. *What happened to her?*

No response.

He cleared his throat and said, "What happened to her... what happened to Raine's transfer?"

The status changed. A response appeared. *Connection lost.*

"Where is she? Is she still on the Settlement?"

Presence lost.

That was a different answer. Presence was different than connection, suggesting she was lost mid-transfer. That would explain the transfer abort, the degradation of the body. Did she get halfway here and snap back to her body, her identity tethered to it on an ethereal bungee?

No. The presence was lost.

You're an angel, she had said.

If she was still on the Settlement, if she woke up, they would know where Marcus, Paul and Jamie went. They could follow the coordinates left on the computer network, they would find them on the island. That thought should've stirred panic in the pit of his stomach, but instead it bloomed hope.

They'll come for us, take us back.

He would be rescued, get back to his former body. Then he saw the bottom right corner of the monitor, the present date and time in small script.

Impossible.

The computer could be wrong. The process should've been instantaneous. The recovery would take a few days at most. *Not a year.*

According to the computer, they left the Settlement over a year ago. So where were they in between? Bouncing in nowhere? There was no sense of passage between those two points in time, like they'd taken a wormhole shortcut.

"Why am I here?" Marcus shouted. "Who did this? Where are the ones that did this to me?"

There were no answers. The computer was dedicated to Raine, and all it knew was she wasn't there. *Presence lost.*

Paul's monitor (his picture in the left corner) revealed a successful transfer, all memories intact. Jamie's station held the same status.

"Show the memory log... Jamie's memory. Let me see it."

Her monitor flipped screens. A root directory appeared in several columns of code. He couldn't access her memories, not like this. Her memories of death might hold the answers, but that was before he arrived on the island.

Before he'd become this.

Before was what he would come to refer to the time *before* the transfer, *before* the arrival on the island when all would be revealed. *Before* he knew the truth.

A door slid open with a quiet whoosh.

Marcus waited. There were no footsteps. He listened to the hum of electronics, the ticking of a ventilation vent.

The elevator was open.

Chirp.

Another computer called, this one closer to him. He turned his upper body, his neck too pained to twist. It was across from the bed he woke on, his image in the left corner. A placid expression looked back at him. He shuffled three steps to the desk on which it sat.

He leaned closer.

What little strength he had left vanished. He fell forward, grasping the ledge of the counter to lower himself to the floor. He banged against the wall, new blood warmly flooding from the clotted wound on the back of his head. He tried to make sense of it all, tried to bring his breath under control.

The computer explained why he'd become powerless.

CHAPTER ONE HUNDRED FIFTY-TWO_

THE WINDOWS WERE CLEAN.

That detail was not lost on Paul, that the island appeared to be in perfect working condition—buildings with power, food in industrial-sized refrigerators—but no one was there. Daily life should have dulled the windows, dust and rain and bird shit (there were birds on the island, big macaws that watched from the palms), but they were transparent-clean.

Paul no longer wondered on such mysteries.

He stood at the bay window that overlooked the campus-sized courtyard and watched Cali emerge from the forest. She passed beneath a heavy branch, a pair of white birds preening within reach. Beyond her, nestled deep in the palms, was the rounded roof of a building, a small dome-like structure.

A sundial was set in the middle of the field, a lone gray sculpture with a triangular wing pointed at the sky. She ran her fingers to the point and stopped. From that distance, the details were fuzzy, even the color of her hair was hard to discern.

But it was her.

He could feel it. Could feel her.

He saw her during the day, hallucinating her from a distance.

The hallucinations had invaded his dreams. *Dreams!* Dreams never happened to Paul, but now he was seeing the farm and the horses in the few hours he snatched at night, and watched her mow the back pasture, haul hay on a tractor.

Three nights had passed, and three nights he dreamed.

And now he saw her in the grassy field, wide awake. The hallucinations felt different. They had changed, felt more present. Solid. He thought, perhaps, if he stood beneath that branch, she would appear to him and he could reach out, he could touch her. Even if she was an illusion, a dream that evaporated, he might feel her for a moment.

He touched his face, rubbing the bristles on his cheeks.

"No, no, no, nononononono!"

Paul tripped on the corner of a leather duvet and sprinted across the lobby. The first door in the hallway was propped open, Jamie sitting up in a bed with a sheet clutched to her chin, eyes wide and blank.

"It's all right, it's all right. You're awake now. You're awake, Jamie."

Her breath punched through a tangle of fear, gulping at the room's stale air, tears falling from eyes that wouldn't blink.

"Be here." He stroked her short crop of hair wet with perspiration. "Be here, Jamie. Come back, look at me."

She blinked once, twice.

He leaned in front of her, held her clammy cheeks with both hands, and steered her vision into his eyes. Focus dialed her blue eyes on his. Her breathing slowed. She held his wrists, climbing out of the pit of a nightmare.

"You here?" he asked.

"Yeah."

"The dream again?"

She swallowed. Nodded.

It wasn't really a dream. She was remembering.

She wiped her forehead with the sheet and threw her feet onto the floor. She was sleeping almost twenty hours a day, waking for half an hour before wilting. That wasn't unusual for a new fabrication—sleep gave the body time to acclimate. *So why am I hardly sleeping?*

"I was in the building," she said.

The dream started like it always did: Marcus Anderson guiding her to a bench in Atlanta's Centennial Park, pausing long enough so that she would remember him. The old man swore he wasn't there, but she remembered it as clearly as she had seen it. Then she sat there alone, watching the children in the fountains until the biomite hijacking. It started in her bones.

"They took me to a room."

"Who?"

"Just some technicians, I think. One of them was wearing a baseball uniform or something. The other one was in charge." She swallowed, hard. "They were getting ready to..."

She took a cleansing breath, but the tension remained. She was reliving her death every time she closed her eyes.

"I got to get out of here," she said. "Need to walk."

"You sure?"

"I'll jump through a window if I don't get some fresh air."

"Let's get something to eat first."

"Paul, relax. I'm fine."

He started to protest. She hadn't been more than twenty feet away from him, not since she collapsed on the beach. He had carried Raine's body to the water and dug a shallow grave with his hands. It would've been wiser to send it out to the ocean, but he didn't want to see it wash ashore. *It's only a body,* he told himself. *An object that was never her. She never arrived.*

But it was all he had. Giving it a proper burial lifted a grain of guilt from a heap of regrets. But it was all he could do. And when Jamie collapsed—walking in the ankle-deep surf one moment, face down the next—he was determined to not turn the heap of regrets into a mountain.

It already felt insurmountable.

"Why don't you get cleaned up first," he said. "Then we'll go."

"Nothing's going to happen to me, Paul."

"No, I mean you need a shower."

"Whatever."

He stood in the hall until he heard the shower running then made his way toward the cafeteria. The U-shaped building was a dormitory, the rooms clean, beds made, clothes in the closets. It was sort of like waiting for the three bears to return. But no one came looking for porridge.

The walk-in cooler was filled with jugs of milk and cartons of orange juice. There was a pantry of canned goods and a freezer of meats and frozen produce. Paul scrambled eggs and nuked strips of bacon, cleaning up the dishes and leaving everything exactly as it was. If anyone was following or watching, they'd notice the missing food but not the dishes.

Jamie was at the picnic tables at the edge of the grassy field, a long toss to the sundial. She was wearing boy shorts and a T-shirt (all the clothing was for boys) and destroyed the breakfast when he put it down.

"The old man come out?" she asked.

"No."

Paul hadn't seen him. And that was a good thing. He could still feel the old man's windpipe in his hand, imagined crushing it like a cardboard tube.

"Let's explore one of the buildings today," she said.

"Let's give it a minute, see how you feel."

"Why wait until I'm tired?" She shoved a corner of toast in her mouth. "I'm all right, Paul. It'd be good to walk around, get outside and shake the dream off, you know."

"The old man wants something from you."

He could feel him watching from the tower, sense that bulging eye follow them when they stepped outside.

"Of course he does," Jamie said. "We were both after the same thing, sort of."

"The powers-that-be?"

"No, no. I was looking for someone to help with Raine's dreamland, looking for someone to help with overturning the Settlement. I wanted the big fish who was behind all the absurdity. I mean, the last twenty years have been crazy, the stupid halfskin laws and then the Settlement. Someone's behind this lunacy. I wanted to help you." She dropped the remaining toast. "The old man did, too; said he would set you and Raine free if I helped, said he would set the whole world free. And I believed him."

"He said he wasn't in Atlanta."

"Well, he's lying about that. You have a point."

"He manipulated your thoughts, made you believe him."

"Listen, I know he got inside my head. I'm not stupid. But it made sense, Paul. Even now it makes sense and he's not messing with my head. And you're free."

"And Raine is dead."

"We don't know that."

He looked away. Raine died because of him; it was easier to accept that, to lug the heap of guilt onto his back now rather than hope she was alive and have the trapdoor open beneath his feet.

The tower loomed over the dormitory. The rising sun reflected off the shiny bands that separated the floors (solar panels, he guessed). A dark shadow moved past a window on the third floor.

"He can't hurt us," Jamie said. "Something about him is different."

Yeah, but there was still a world of hurt out there. And they didn't wake up on this island on accident.

THE ISLAND WAS SHAPING up to be a summer camp for the insanely wealthy.

There were classrooms and a game room. The only structure they didn't explore was the dome-shaped building buried in the palms. That oddball building was different than the others and in the other direction. But everything else was orderly, the doors unlocked or open, chairs pushed in and trash empty.

But there aren't towers at summer camp.

It was at the third building they explored that Jamie began to fade. She'd been awake for two hours, the most since leaving the tower. Now she stopped on the top step and touched her head, riding out a bout of vertigo.

"I'm all right."

"We need to go back."

"Just this last stop, I promise. Then we'll go."

He gave in and opened the large glass door. The stale wind of paper met them. Shelves and shelves of books lined the open hall, long tables with short lamps interspersed throughout. Paul remained a step behind her.

"There, look." She pointed behind the front desk.

A computer was stashed on a bottom shelf, the first one they'd seen since leaving the tower. A second wind filled her. Paul looked around as she pried open the laptop; the thrumming sound of an awakening computer filled the hallowed halls. The screen went black.

"Where are we?" she said.

He was about to answer (obviously a library) when the computer came to life. Images of the island began playing.

"How'd you do that?" he asked.

"It happened in the tower, all the computers were voice-activated."

"Where's Raine?" he blurted.

Jagged lines of static interrupted the scenery. Blackness returned.

"I don't think it knows," she began to say when cabins emerged from the foggy screen.

The Settlement.

"No." The urge to slam the computer with both fists reached inside him. "I'm going to—"

"Is she on the Settlement?" Jamie asked.

Another scramble of static. A room appeared. It was the dream disease lab. Authority figures were there. Not the green-jacket monitors, these were the federal types, the men and women wearing gloves so as not to contaminate a crime scene. They were removing equipment, hauling it out on carts with all-terrain vehicles.

The beds were occupied by black skinsuits, the hoods pulled off to expose the sunken faces—the sharp cheekbones and purple lips. Two men stood over the one on the right, the hood bunched beneath Raine's neck, her scalp glistened with the electrolytic gel. Her flesh was muddy, her bruised tongue a puffy slug swelling between cracked lips. They lifted her onto a gurney and carted her off with the computers.

She's not there.

A stir of relief cooled the hot grit of guilt piling on the bottom of his stomach. He'd rather she be dead than on the Settlement alone. *We don't know she's dead. She's just not here.*

"What happened to them?" he asked. "What happened to the Settlement?"

A view of the laboratory appeared from above. All the windows on the first floor were boarded. The front door was barricaded. The windows on the second and third floor were dark, some cracked, dirt and grime layered in the corners.

No smoke puffed from the chimney.

They shut it down. Oh, fuck, they shut it down... we did that to them, we took it away from them.

Paul stalked off and ran his hands over his stubbly scalp. The guilty weight buckled his knees. How could he carry all of this? This was his fault. Everyone suffered because of him. First Cali, then Jamie, then Raine... *now the entire Settlement*. They had nothing to live for.

"Paul."

"We got to get back there," he said. "We can help them."

He was standing by the tables, the furthest from Jamie he'd been that morning. She was still behind the counter, the computer's glow in her eyes.

"Paul... there's more."

A stream of images filled the screen in separate frames, scenes of hospitals, of protesters picketing the wealthy dream centers (*Stop Dreaming Now!*), of arguing politicians, dead bodies pulled from houses, hotels, cars and curbs. City streets were mostly empty.

"Dream disease," Jamie said. "It's out of control."

The computer responded with a news reporter at a desk, her lips silently moving above the headline that read, *No Cure in Sight.*

And there they were again, a picture of the dream disease lab on the Settlement with their bodies still on the beds.

"Holy shit," she said. "They think we did it. They think we started a dream disease plague."

Something wasn't right. This was happening too fast. All they did was transfer into new bodies.

"Do you believe it?" she asked.

He shook his head. "I don't know what to believe."

"I mean, this is just a computer. It could all be made up. We don't know where we are."

"We're on an island."

"But where? Why?"

"I don't know, but we have to get back."

"Back to the Settlement? What's that going to do?"

He couldn't help anyone on the island. At least he could pay his debts on the Settlement, suffer for his sins. He would drag the old man with him. That he could do. At least they would have someone to pay.

"No." She fell into the high-backed chair. "We're here for a reason, Paul. Whatever Marcus had planned has changed. He's not the same, you feel it. He's weaker, doesn't have something. Even he doesn't know what's going on."

"This could all be a disaster."

"Or something bigger."

"People are dying, Jamie. We might be responsible."

"We might be the answer. Marcus was after the truth. He said if he found it, then he'd find the powers-that-be. He thinks that's where the dream eater is. What if this is it?"

"What if we just pissed him off?"

"Why do you think it's a 'him'?"

He paced another path to the long tables and paused to look at the perfectly stacked shelves, the surreal atmosphere saturated with dreamlike qualities. Yet he was wide awake, seeing and feeling and hearing. This was not a dream.

All we have are our senses. What if our senses lie? What if our filters obscure the truth? Then what we see and hear and believe is no more relevant than lies on a computer.

"Paul."

She was slumped over the counter. Dead weight hung on her face. There were no fumes left. He'd have to carry her back, let her sleep again. At least she got a few hours of waking. Maybe the next time it would be longer.

She spun the laptop so that it faced him and tapped the corner of the screen. The toolbar showed the date and time.

A year has passed.

That was how dream disease had gotten so bad, how the streets had grown so empty. Why the laboratory was so abandoned.

"I think someone is hiding us, Paul. That's why we're here."

CHAPTER ONE HUNDRED FIFTY-THREE_

CLAY.

Marcus lay on a massive bed on the tower's third floor, sunk deep in soft comforters and a pile of pillows, staring at a black ceiling. Daylight diffusely filled the room, yellowish beams penetrating the tinted windows.

How could this happen?

He was supposed to wake up in New York City, his body an exact duplicate of the one left behind on the Settlement. Not a clay body.

A pure, 100% clay body.

The technology to fabricate with clay cells—printing organs, ears, fingers, eyeballs—had been established long before biomites. But fabricating an entire body?

Why would someone do this to me?

These were the questions he asked upon waking. And he woke often, sleeping the majority of the day, sometimes waking on the floor with lumps and bruises and no recollection of how he got there.

He crawled out of bed, his knee refusing to bend, the back of his head staining the pillow with pink watery spots, his throat sore from screaming at the ceiling, cursing his plight.

Cursing Mother.

She did this. She turned me back into clay and abandoned me.

He had fallen under her spell, believed in his destiny that he would save mankind from an insatiable power.

And now I'm just human.

This was more than a sick joke. This was punishment. She sent him to a tropical purgatory. He didn't give a shit how the food got there or how all this worked. He just wanted off this godforsaken hellhole, wanted back in his biomite skin.

Unlike the second floor, the third floor had no inner walls. It was wide open. There were views in all directions. The floor slowly rotated (a speed he couldn't feel) so that a mounted telescope provided a multitude of views. Right now, it was pointed at the grassy field.

Paul and Jamie were sleeping in the U-shaped building; he'd seen them at the picnic tables once or twice. Apparently there was food there, too. They made no attempt to find him. Occasionally they looked at the tower.

But he was safe.

The only access into the tower was through an elevator. He had wedged an office chair between the elevator doors to keep them open. He'd found a cache of food on the third floor that would last for months. He would stay in the tower as long as it took. He would outlast them.

There has to be a way back to the mainland.

If their identities could be streamed to this remote island, they could be sent back. The fabricated bodies would still be in New York. He had leased the lab space with funds from an inexhaustible account; the lab would hold them. His legal team would make sure of it, that until his fabricated body rose up and Marcus acknowledged he was fully aware, they would keep paying the bills until the end of time.

There has to be a way to reverse the route.

He aimed the massive telescope at the back of the U-shaped

building, bent over the eyepiece and closed one eye. He had seen them, Paul and Jamie, eating lunch at one of the picnic tables.

"Where are you now?" he muttered.

Computers whirred into action. Electric light flickered across the ceiling. Back on a large oak desk, half a dozen monitors streamed a variety of images. With the help of the cane, he hobbled over and fell into the chair. There was no keyboard or cables.

Just images of Paul and Jamie.

The security system of a paranoid dictator had been engaged. Exactly what Marcus needed.

Paul and Jamie were watching a laptop inside a library.

There was no sound, just their expressions on vivid display. They were shocked and surprised at whatever they were seeing.

Marcus smiled.

"Let's see what else I can do."

CHAPTER ONE HUNDRED FIFTY-FOUR_

THE GOLDFISH GLIDED, ONE EYE LOOKING THROUGH THE GLASS.

Jamie wondered what it was like to fly. Living in water must be like that, never having to fear falling. Always floating.

Always flying.

The fish tank warped into a slurry of brimming tears, her body a plastic coffin she couldn't escape. Hands on her lap, eyes forward, she listened to the man in the baseball uniform discuss the weather. Somewhere a woman answered a call. Even the fish looked bored.

They're going to shut me off.

She was aware it was the dream, but that did nothing to ease the fear burning her insides like dry kindling, hollowing her out until there was nothing but the toxic vapor of terror. Somewhere, boys were laughing.

Boys?

Something was wrong with that detail. She couldn't remember boys being in the building before they shut her off, no recess playground.

Then he arrived.

The witness.

And the fear evaporated. It shouldn't, she knew that. His arrival put her toes on the ravine's edge, placed a hand on her back to shove her into the long dark hole where she would be sacrificed to the laws of the state, her crime against humanity being the possession of biomites.

His shadow crept into her periphery.

The goldfish watched, unblinking, as his face moved into view—

"No!"

She slashed in the sheets, fabric tangling around her arms like a damp boa constrictor. Kicking, screaming, she thrashed across the mattress, pulled her legs to her chest, huffing in the corner of a white room.

No fish, no witness.

I'm here. Here and awake.

Paul didn't come.

He looked tired before she went to the room, said he might sleep this time instead of sitting guard. He hadn't slept much since they left the tower.

She stripped off the T-shirt, wet with sweat and two sizes too big, and threw it in a growing pile of spoiled clothing. A slice of yellow sunlight knifed across the room, cutting across her waist as she pulled on a pair of large shorts and another T-shirt, this one tan instead of white. The flip-flops—three sizes too big—slapped at the linoleum and echoed down the long, empty corridor.

The lobby was empty.

A sheet and pillow were bunched on the leather couch, a basket of fruit on the table next to it. She took an apple and looked out the wide window. Purple clouds boiled in the distance, flashes of lightning in its belly, the sky a stewing cauldron.

The sun was setting on the picnic tables, the laptop flashing images in the building's shadow. Further out, Paul was standing at the sundial, his back to her. His hospital gown was tucked into a loose pair of khakis like a baggy shirt. He hadn't changed since waking.

He was bouncing his hand on the tip of the sundial's fin, stabbing the point into his palm. "I'm dreaming," he said.

"You're awake, Paul."

"No. When I sleep... I'm dreaming. I see Cali and it's... it's different. Something's different. It's like she's waiting. Never saying anything, just watching me. Haunting me."

"Stop it." Jamie grabbed his hand. "You loved her and that's all you could do."

He looked into his hand, searching the purple gouges for an answer. He looked dazed, dreamy. The edge of his words blurred. *Is he still asleep?*

"I have never had a dreamland, Jamie. Never even had a normal dream. But I do now. Ever since we woke on this island, I've been dreaming."

He traced the fleshy wounds with his fingertips, then spoke at the distant trees.

"This time I was sitting on the couch, waiting for her hallucination to appear in the trees. Instead, I fell asleep and woke up on the side of a hill in a strange land, one I'd never seen before. There was the sea and a village... and then I fell asleep again, only this time I dreamed of the dream disease lab."

He twitched.

"It was dark and moldy. The equipment had been stripped from the room. The beds were there, the shower, too. Our bodies were gone, though. It was like all this time had passed, like I was really there. But then I found this."

He chuckled, shaking his head.

"It was the little cross, the two sticks bound with a band of jute. It was something Raine carried with her, said Joshua made it for her in dreamland. She found it outside her cabin and swore he put it there. She must've had it in the dream lab.

"I sort of forgot about the skin suits and the waking and the island... but then I looked for you, and when I didn't find you, I remembered you were sleeping in the next room. I remembered we weren't on the Settlement anymore. We both were. *I'm dreaming,* I thought."

He shook his head, thumb in palm. The pain was grounding him in the present moment. He wanted to be sure he was awake. *Or wake himself up.*

"The door to the lab was open," he continued. "The rest of the building was much the same, the doors open, the offices empty. Cobwebs were in the corners. I remembered when we were there, when the window was broken and they came after us. You remember that?"

She nodded.

"One of the offices across from the fabrication lab, that's where they got inside. I went there and the window was missing, a sheet of plywood in its place. A sliver of light punched through a weathered knothole. I looked through it. You know what I saw?"

He turned his head, squinting as if the view were right there.

"The gray... the cabins across the field, the wind turbines... it was all gray. And someone was splitting wood. I think it was her. I think it was Raine."

"It was a dream."

"Was it?"

He massaged his hand, smudging tiny beads of crimson into the wrinkled valleys, the pain reminding him that he was here, he was awake. *It hurts in the dream too, Paul.*

"Did you have the same dream?" he asked.

She nodded.

"Did you see him?"

"He's closer."

Marcus would want to know that, would want to know that someone called the witness was about to look into her eyes, fill her with peace before sucking her soul into the cold vacuum of death. But it was more than that, she sensed. She didn't just die.

He consumed me.

She didn't want to believe that, didn't want to think it was that easy and wasn't going to tell Paul any of that, either. She could be wrong. But there was something otherworldly about the witness's presence, a man that convinced her it was all right to die, to give herself.

A man, she thought, *that could eat dreams.*

THUNDER DROPPED a cool breeze across the yard. The laptop strobed across the picnic table, images coming and going.

"I know what this place is," Paul said.

He straddled the bench and spun the laptop toward her. An aerial view of the grassy field was filled with boys, some lounging, others throwing a Frisbee. Groups of teenagers were at the picnic tables, playing cards.

Boys. Were those the boys I heard in the dream?

"This place was some sort of alternate reality experiment. There are no times or dates, so it's hard to assess just how long ago, but I get the feeling it was before biomites."

"Why?"

"They used a needle and cable to bridge the human brain with a computer." He rubbed a spot on his forehead. "There was a surgical stent installed that allowed access to the frontal lobe. The computer then created a new reality."

She turned away from the laptop but not before seeing an image she would never forget—a young man, thirteen or fourteen, lying on a hospital bed, a rigid steel needle staked into his forehead, clear salve pooled around the base.

"How come we've never heard of this?"

"There's no telling how long ago it was. Besides, I get the feeling it was experimental and illegal. That's why this place is so isolated. There's a giant resort on the other side of the island, something the very wealthy would enjoy. On this side are the dorms and the classrooms and library. I'm guessing they were using teenagers to work out their mistakes."

The scene of a classroom played out, rows of bored teenagers listening to an old man with multiple jiggling chins. She looked up.

"Only boys, though," she said.

"Yeah, this was for boys. There was one for girls, too. It was somewhere else."

"Where?"

He started to answer, the word dusty and quiet and doubtful.

"Where were the girls at?" she repeated.

"The Settlement."

"What do you mean?"

"Remember the red brick house? There were remnants of old log cabins out there, too."

"That's... that's not a coincidence."

"No."

"Why were they separated?"

"I don't know. They called it the Foreverland Project. I think it was a precursor to dreamland. The needle and computers created these realistic alternate realities. Then biomites came along and there was no need for a needle, no need for a computer. People started generating their own dreamlands... their own *foreverlands*."

Jamie tapped the screen. "This is telling us something, Paul. It's no accident the Settlement was built where it was, no accident we're here. This laptop is telling us something."

"Maybe."

"This is where it all started. Powers-that-be, dreamlands and foreverlands and alternate realities. Someone wants us to connect the dots. Marcus was looking for the powers-that-be. Maybe we found it."

"We haven't found anything."

"Not yet. Where do you think they did these experiments?"

Paul turned toward the tower. *The second floor*.

That was where all the technology was located—the offices, the beds, the fabricators. Of course, that was where the needles would be. There were computers there, too; ones that responded to questions.

"We need to get back up there," she said. "Now."

"It'll be dark soon and it looks like rain. Besides, he's not going to let us inside."

"He'll let us up." She felt injected with caffeine. "Marcus will want to hear this. He's as anxious to get off the island as we are."

She snapped the laptop closed. He nodded compulsively, agreeing but not really hearing her. Maybe she couldn't trust him in front of Marcus, not yet. Maybe he didn't want the old man to let them up, afraid he'd lose control.

The thunderheads rumbled.

"Let me grab some boots." Jamie pulled off her flip-flops and ran through the grass, the cool blades slipping between her toes. She yanked on the door. The handle turned freely but wouldn't open.

"What's wrong?" he called.

"Door's locked."

Paul waggled the handle. He examined the doorjamb, no place for a key or even a scan lock. He looked around. The air smelled damp. And it would be dark soon. And all their food was inside.

They tried the other doors. Maybe they'd been locked all this time, they hadn't used them. Only this back door had been unlocked, but not anymore.

The first raindrop fell.

"Come on." Paul started for the grassy field. "We'll break a window."

He walked at first. When rain spots began wetting his back, he began running. The sundial was too heavy. They entered an open path in the forest. Paul stomped through the underbrush, picking up branches, testing them like baseball bats.

Above them, the foliage pattered. Raindrops found their way to the undergrowth. The forest was waking up. Jamie tucked the laptop beneath her shirt.

"Coconuts!" Jamie shouted.

Paul was back on the trail, sprinting toward the beach. He returned with a husked coconut tucked in his arms. Jamie had squatted beneath the shelter of a tropical palm, the wide leaves bowing under the watery weight, tiny streams shedding off the scalloped edges. She held the laptop, their only connection to the outside world, like a baboon protecting her young.

"Come on!" he shouted above the rain patter.

"I'll wait here!" He doubled back and grabbed her arm, but she resisted. "This can't get wet. Go knock out a window and come back with something to wrap it up."

"This isn't going to blow over."

"And this can't get wet."

Dusk was ticking away the remains of the day. Jamie hunkered down, water pooling around her flip-flops, feet squeaking as she shifted her weight.

The sky had disappeared between the small openings of the canopy; she heard Paul before seeing him. He was carrying an angular rock, chopped the stocky stem of a frond and held it up over his head like an umbrella.

The back of her shirt was soaked, but her belly was still warm and mostly dry. She took cover with him. They took a narrow path that led away from the field. A flash of lightning revealed the dome-shaped roof of a squat building, the door wedged open with a fallen branch.

He yanked the door open. It was pitch black inside.

"Couldn't get a window to break out," he shouted. The rain pounded the curved roof. "Security glass shattered but didn't break. We can stay here tonight, find something tomorrow."

She heard him shake and felt a spatter of rain across her face that tasted slightly of salt. The room smelled dank and hopeless, the subterranean feel of a basement, the atmosphere penetrating her bones with a wet kiss. The next flash of lightning lit up the confines.

Bars.

She shuffled closer to Paul and felt his body heat on her back. The metal edge of the laptop creaked in her grip. Her eyes adjusted; hard metal bars emerged in rows with open sliding doors and a concrete floor. There weren't many cells, eight or ten.

"What the hell is this?" she said.

"I don't know. We'll just stay until the storm passes."

The weather spit a gust of rain through the door. Paul worked to pull it closed. The hinges were damaged and the door wouldn't fit inside the doorjamb. A puddle crept over the cracked concrete.

The metal bars were cold and chilling, goose bumps spreading up her arms, the small hairs standing up. There was nothing inside the cells, no bench or toilet, not even a chair. It was a small building of metal bars.

"Don't go in there," Paul shouted over a gust of rain.

"Don't worry."

He guided her back to the middle of the corridor like the cells would swallow her up, the door clamping down like mechanical jaws.

The storm continued.

They sat on the concrete, leaning against a section of the curved wall, careful not to touch the bars. They sat in the dark, the sound of the storm thrown over them like a blanket of chains, listening to branches dance in the night.

Sleep came to Jamie like it always did, sneaking up to snatch her into unconsciousness where the dream would start over. She'd wake in the morning, looking up at the silver blades of a large ceiling fan and listening to the fresh silence that comes after a storm.

But nothing would be the same.

CHAPTER ONE HUNDRED FIFTY-FIVE_

Paul was grainy.

Marcus leaned on the desk and called for the picture to enhance. The camera (or whatever was recording their every move) zoomed tight on his face and captured him blinking.

Still awake.

Paul stood at the door, peeking through the opening every so often, waiting for the storm to ease up. Jamie was on the far side of the room, curled up and shivering. He'd taken off his shirt—the filthy hospital gown—and draped it over one of the cells to dry. It left his upper body exposed.

Marcus fell asleep at the desk and woke just past midnight. The rain was gentle but consistent, the wind a harmless bluster. Paul was now sitting on the floor, leaning against the wall, still not asleep.

He won't leave her, Marcus told himself. *Even if it stops raining.*

He locked them out of the dormitory. All it took was a simple request and the system did it. They'd find the other buildings locked, too. It wouldn't take long before they were hungry and desperate. Then they would be ready to listen, to cooperate on his terms.

If that was what he wanted to do.

The domed building had escaped his attention until they were inside it. The door was left open; there was probably nothing he could do to keep them out anyway. But it worked to his advantage.

The computer told him exactly what that building was for. It wasn't a prison or a punishment. It wasn't clear why the boys were kept in cells, in such miserable conditions when everything else was so luxurious. But that was where the needles were inserted into the boys' frontal lobes, where their identities were connected to a host computer, where an alternate reality awaited.

Where dreamland was born.

This *foreverland,* as they called it, was the birth of dreamland. Old men stole the bodies of young boys, exorcising their identities, sending their souls to a place described as nowhere so their bodies remained as empty husks the old men could occupy. A new lease on life.

They didn't have biomites back then, weren't able to create the necessary conditions to experience an inner world, so they connected themselves to something that could.

Because they were clay.

Marcus pushed away from the desk, his knee locked into a rigid bar of fire. He was stiff all over, but the leg (and now the hip) had become extremely arthritic. By the time he reached the elevator, his forehead pricked with sweat. Knowing Paul was in that domed building, that he wouldn't leave Jamie, the old man descended to the second floor without fear of surprise. The doors opened.

A wheelchair waited in the hall.

Ask and ye shall receive.

These were the little things he noticed around the tower, how requests were fulfilled. First the cane, then the computers and now this. He fell into the seat and sighed. Relief came in a relaxing wave. It took an effort not to lay his head back and fall asleep.

The stringent smell of the lab—the antiseptic cleaners, the sterile supplies—filled the hall. Quite a difference from the floral scent of the third floor, the lived-in opulence. This was where science advanced.

He rushed around the lab, opening drawers. But then he stopped. It was obvious how to find what he was looking for, and how to do it. According to the post-arrival report, he woke up in a clay body. He contained no biomites. But the island was the birthplace of foreverland, the precursor of dreamland. This was where they learned how to transport their identities out of clay bodies.

All he needed was a network. He was receiving news from the mainland; therefore he could transmit it. The New York lab would still be holding the body he designed.

It was all very clear what he needed to do.

"Where's the needle?" he called to the room.

CHAPTER ONE HUNDRED FIFTY-SIX_

THE RAIN SOOTHED THE FEAR, A LULLABY THAT WASHED AWAY the worry and concern. Paul stared across the domed hut, past the bars at the sleeping body huddled against the wall.

His back next to the door, Paul kept his eyes open despite the pleasant breeze flowing through the crack of the door. He looked at the black bars, wondering what they were for, why someone would be kept inside, what horrors they'd seen—

And then they turned yellow.

He blinked away the exhaustion and rubbed his eyes. For a second, he was on the side of the hill overlooking the sea. The next moment, the mustard yellow bars appeared, but not the confining cells in the domed building; they had become distant posts smudged in the blurry night rain.

The Visitors' Center.

He was standing in the lobby, looking across the front field where the Settlement's perimeter was marked by yellow posts. The window was still damaged where he'd thrown the chair.

But Jamie wasn't on the floor. She was back in the hut.

I'm dreaming.

His clothing was still the same—bare-chested and khakis still wet from the rain. The room smelled musty, the carpet tacky beneath his boots. All his senses intact.

The silence was broken by laughter.

Paul jumped to the side, instincts telling him to hide. No one was allowed inside this building unescorted. *But this is a dream.*

He went down the main corridor. The offices were to the left. The punchy laughter continued. Paul snuck to the first office, the door closed. *Bob's office.* But the nameplate had changed. No white cowboy hat on the desk, no tray of vaping pipes.

No longer Bob's office.

"Check this out," one of the voices said.

"Is she always like that?" the other person asked.

"Every night."

Paul went down the hall, trying to remember if the computers were against the back wall or facing the hall. *This is a dream,* he reminded himself. *Just a dream.*

He leaned into view and saw the back shoulder of one man standing behind a chair, wearing the standard green coat of a monitor, unzipped and open. They were watching surveillance footage on the computer. It was a view of someone sleeping.

Nadia.

She rolled over to expose her buttocks and left breast.

The one sitting turned. They high-fived.

Paul didn't recognize them. But if a year had passed, they would be new. But why would Bob be gone? *This is a dream,* he thought again. None of this mattered.

But it did.

Those assholes swore they never violated the bricks' privacy, that surveillance was only in place in case of an emergency. How many times did they watch them in the shower? How many times did Bob jerk off to someone making love?

This was a dream. Only a dream. But he would fix it here and now. He would make it right, even if it was only a dream. It wouldn't make a lick of difference when he woke up, but he'd feel better, the guilt would be just a little lighter.

Because even if this was a dream, it probably wasn't far from the truth.

A CRACK of thunder slapped Paul in the face.

He jumped to his feet, the sizzle of lightning still on his eyebrows. The cages were open, the walls quiet. A sultry orange slice of sunlight swept across the room, wisps of humidity swirling; water dripped from the door.

Daylight.

That wasn't lightning.

The ache in his tailbone went up his spine, the result of a long night on the concrete. He rubbed the sleep from his eyes (eyebrows intact, hair unsinged) and pushed the door open. Birds fluttered with a squawk. The air was crisp and scoured. It rejuvenated the world, cleansed it of wrongdoing, made everything right.

This is a new day.

Jamie was still asleep, hugging the laptop like a stuffed bear. At least she'd stopped shivering. He knelt next to her, listening to her breathing. Deciding not to wake her, he pried the laptop away—her hands clawing the concrete with scratchy, jerky movements. Maybe she was back in the dream and he should wake her. At the very least, he should be there when she woke. But he wouldn't be gone for long.

And she needs the sleep.

He typed a message on the laptop and left it open.

Everything was dewy, the droopy foliage swiping him as he jogged past, his thighs and chest soaked when he passed the sundial. The doors were still locked; the window he attempted to shatter, the coconut bouncing off like a rubber kickball, was cracked. There was still food on the picnic table from the day before. The crackers were waterlogged, the waxy apples beaded with rain.

Jamie was stretching when he returned and handed her an apple. "Thank you," she said.

He pushed the door open. In the sunlight, it was just a room with bars.

"What about the rest of the buildings," she asked. "Think they're locked, too?"

He shrugged. "Stand up and stretch. You've been sitting on the floor all night."

She sighed, studying the apple, taking another loud bite before getting up and offering him the other half.

"You eat it," he said. "You need it."

"You do, too."

"Come on, let's get out of here."

"Keep the door open, just in case."

She was thinking like he was. What if all the buildings were locked? They could sleep outside, but another storm would make it difficult. The hut was better than being exposed to the elements, cages or not. Another thing occurred to him.

Where are the insects?

This was a tropical island, but nothing was crawling on them at night or biting them during the day. Paul was on one knee, wedging a branch into the soft mud to keep the wind from blowing the door closed and wondering if the island's ecosystem was naturally bug-free.

"That's weird," Jamie said.

And then it happened in slow motion.

One knee in the mud, he saw her turn, saw her take one step toward an open cell. "No!" he managed to shout.

That was it.

The door slid in the rail like a predator and slammed her left leg like metal teeth. The dull crack of bones sounded like a muffled gunshot.

Her other leg collapsed like a folding chair.

The door recoiled to a grinding halt, Jamie's shin bent at a slight angle. She yanked her leg inside the cell before the second bite landed. The door latched with a ringing thud.

Paul had barely leaned forward before it was over.

Birds flocked away as he grabbed the bars, the metal cold and hard and unforgiving. He reached through them, but Jamie was curled up, blood already dotting the concrete.

"Breathe," he said. "Breathe, Jamie. You can control this, remember. Focus, now. Focus on your nervous system; kill the sensations."

This was survival mode.

Biomites allowed for the override of the nervous system when severe pain needed to be mitigated to avoid shock. *She can do this.*

"Breathe, now." He took a deep breath. "In deep... Jamie, listen to me. In deep, out slow. You can do this, okay. Listen to my voice. Be here."

Her cries turned to whimpers. Tears squeezed through clamped eyelids. She drew a wet breath through clogged nostrils, exhaled through a tight circle.

The shaking slowed to a quiver.

"Okay, I'll be right back," he said. "I'm just going outside for a second, see if there's something I can use to open this."

He sounded confident despite the absurdity. A branch wouldn't scratch the bars. The latch didn't even have a keyhole.

Remotely controlled.

The cool rush of fear transformed into the flame of rage. If it was remotely closed, then he had a suspicion who had done it. It was no accident that the buildings were locked, no accident this hut was open and waiting.

When he returned, she had rolled to her side so that he couldn't see the leg. Her breathing was long and smooth and even. She lay still, her back to him. He knelt down, knees pushing between the bars.

She wouldn't respond, but had the pain under control.

He had to find help, had to make things right. His lungs burned as he ran through the forest, wondering what would possess her to walk inside the cage, why she would endanger herself. It was only a matter of time before one of them slipped on the shore or got sick.

But he realized as he exited the trees that she was holding something as she had clutched her wounded leg, something that poked between her fingers. Something she had reached for in the cell.

They were sticks.

She was asleep.

It was the third time he'd come back to check on her and found her lying on her side, hands laced around her knee. Each time he explored a little farther. He finally found a rocky shoreline and scored a jagged block of granite half-buried in the sand.

The dormitory window caved on the fifth toss.

Paul filled two pillowcases with food. The kitchen utensils would be too flimsy to break open the cell door. The meat cleaver would shatter on impact.

He found a utility closet and tools for basic repairs. He pocketed the screwdrivers, a ball-peen hammer and a putty knife. The back door was still locked (no bolt on the inside), so he crawled out the window and ran.

Jamie was awake.

She was in the back corner, one leg (her good leg) pulled up to her chest. The other leg was laid flat on the concrete and wrapped in Paul's shirt. It appeared she had the pain under control. He thought, at first sight, she had wrapped her leg to keep from seeing it, to keep herself from entering shock. But the rheumy gaze, the parted lips.

She's already there.

"Hey, hey." He dropped the food. "I'm going to get you out."

She didn't respond.

"Jamie. Jamie, you here? You with me? I won't leave you again. I'm going to get you out of here, all right?"

He fumbled the tools from his back pocket. The hammer

bounced across the floor. He studied the screwdrivers and putty knife. They were pathetic. And the stone was still sitting in the dorm room where he'd thrown it through the window.

He'd have to go back.

"It's him," Jamie said. "He's the one."

She could've been speaking to the room or herself, the words drifting off like random bubbles. Paul grabbed the iron bars, leaning in to see what she was holding.

"What are you saying, Jamie? What do you mean?"

"He is the witness."

"Who?"

"He's the witness, Paul." The whites of her eyes were gray. "He's the one that shut me down."

"I... I don't know what you're saying."

"The dream is finished. I'm staring at a fish tank when he comes in the room. I can feel him, like he's... he's someone I know. I... I don't remember his face. But I remember the eyes."

A pause button was hit. She stumbled over the details, still digesting the memories.

"The eyes, Paul. Have you looked directly into his eyes?"

"Whose eyes?"

She swallowed, dry. "Marcus."

"Marcus?"

"Have you noticed the end of the world in them? It's all there, everything's inside his eyes. The universe, the stars, the galaxy... *everything*. He made me feel important, made me feel wanted and okay. That he loved me. So I gave myself to him freely."

"What are you saying, sweetheart? You're saying... the old man is the witness?"

That couldn't be. He was in Atlanta; he dropped her off to be captured. *But he swore that wasn't him.*

"And then he drew me in, sucked the soul out of my body into a cold, cold night, Paul. It's him. Marcus is the one."

She was confused. The shock, the hysteria, the anger and resentment. Marcus wouldn't drop her off then appear as the witness. He was looking for the powers-that-be, was with her in Chicago, with her in Atlanta. *He can't be the witness, too.*

"Where did you get that, Jamie?"

She opened her hand, displaying her palm. On it lay a pair of sticks fastened together. Paul lost the feel of the floor, the world turning beneath him. She held it up like she was warding off evil.

It was a cross.

A little wooden cross.

"Where did you find that?"

"He's the one, Paul."

"Jamie, listen to me. Where'd you get the cross?"

"Marcus is doing everything. He *is* the powers-that-be. He just doesn't know it."

Paul stood too quickly and held the bars until he was sure his knees wouldn't break. He paced the concrete corridor, head still spinning. He had to get her out of there. She had turned delusional, the dream finally cracking her mind. The doors were remotely controlled. The tower was the center of technology with 360-degree views.

He locked the doors.

"Stay back there," he said. "I'll be right back, Jamie. I promise, I won't leave you. I'm going to get you out of there."

The sun had breached the trees, the jungle already steamy. Paul ran without stopping. He'd talk some sense into the old man. And if that didn't work, he'd make him do it. Somehow, he'd make him. Because, before long, this island would crack them all like eggs.

Paul was already cracking.

That was a cross she was holding. Raine's cross. The one she had on the Settlement, the one she carried to the dream disease lab.

And now it's here.

CHAPTER ONE HUNDRED FIFTY-SEVEN_

THE BUILDING CHATTERED.

Marcus snorted awake, his neck savagely twisted over the back of the wheelchair, pain spearing the back of his head. All the monitors were streaming newsfeeds from around the world. There was no recollection of falling asleep, just hazy glimpses of searching in long blank gaps.

The night's cache was spread across a tabletop, a collection of tubes and wires, clear plastic IV bags and a box of sterile needles encased in clear tubes of gel. They were neatly arranged in piles, unwrapped and displayed. But there were no directions for where wires went or what computer to use, what program to run.

Even if that was all solved, there was the issue of the needle. He couldn't hammer the thing into his forehead like a roofing nail. There was a stent and a precise method of insertion. He was out of options. If he died trying, then at least he wouldn't die a slow death of dehydration and neck injuries.

The chatter was back.

It was in the hall, not one of the noisy newsfeeds.

Marcus wheeled out and saw the elevator doors gnawing on an aluminum cane. He didn't recall dropping the cane between the open doors, but then he couldn't remember much with any clarity. The elevator gummed it with impatience, the bumpers bouncing in the doors' tracks.

The down arrow flashed.

He quickly wheeled to the end of the hall. The dormitory and field were quiet and empty, and there was nothing directly below. Marcus went back to the lab to see Paul on one of the monitors. He was prying at a curved elevator door, the glass wall behind him shattered.

He's on the first floor.

A sweatless wave of panic swept through him. How close had he come to waking up to Paul standing over him with vengeance on his breath. *If not for the cane.*

"Hey! Let her go, Marcus! Let her go now!"

He was talking to the old man. *Does he see me?*

Three of the monitors projected views of Paul backing away from the elevator, looking up at a monitor. The first floor looked like a lobby with couches and chairs and at least a dozen monitors that all projected the same newsfeeds Marcus was watching. But the one above the elevator was filled with Marcus's pasty gray face, dark age-spots spilled on his scalp like paint.

"All she did was help you," Paul said. "Let her go."

What the hell is he talking about? He did his best to go along with it. Clearly Marcus had an advantage. He just needed to figure out what it was.

"You choked me, tried to murder me."

"And she stopped me. You owe her that. You want someone to pay for all your mistakes, take me. But let her go."

"Mistakes?"

"You brought us here."

The ashes of anger swirled like a tiny twister. If it wasn't for Marcus, Paul would still be on the Settlement with body parts under the cabin.

"Her leg is shattered. She can't walk. She won't survive in there, Marcus. Let her go and leave us alone. We'll do the same to you."

Marcus had locked them out of all the buildings, paranoia whispering in his ear. *They'll find a way into the tower. There might be controls in the other buildings. Get them. Get them first.* He remembered, vaguely, they took refuge in the strange little hut, but he had no control of the door.

Paul's tone was pleading. He'd already lost Raine, he couldn't stand to lose Jamie. His vulnerability stirred a wicked tang of power. It tasted sweet.

"You're still a threat."

Paul put his hands on his hips and bowed his head for a long moment. And then began prowling the first floor, studying the ceiling, the seams around the elevator. The elevator doors on the second floor began to chatter.

"What are you doing?" Marcus said. "If I let her go, you will not harm me?"

"I haven't harmed you, not since you murdered Raine."

"I... I... no, no. That wasn't my fault. Stop searching for a way up here, stop now. I will help you if you leave me alone."

Paul looked up at the monitor.

"I'll need a few minutes to, ah, get things undone," Marcus added.

"You have five minutes. That's how long it will take me to walk there. If the cell is not open, I'll return and destroy every monitor so that the next time you hear my voice, I'll be standing in front of you."

"It's a complicated matter, Paul. I can't just undo it. I may need more time."

Paul began laughing. It was so loud that Marcus could hear it through the floor. "Why are you laughing? Stop that."

"You think you're the victim?"

"We're all victims, Paul. Until you understand that, we will remain at a stalemate."

"You're a sick bastard, Marcus. The shit you've done to the world and you think you're a victim."

"I am trying to save the world, you ingrate. How do you not understand this? I had everything before this. I didn't... there was no need for me to pursue the truth. I could've lived out my life in luxury, nothing could stop me."

"Then why didn't you?"

"I... I..." He tried hard to find the words. There was no explanation. He was compelled to find the truth. Mother was there to push him forward, to tantalize him with those prophetic lines. He had to find the truth. He had to. That was not something he could explain. No one would understand the itch to come back home.

Come back home? He wondered where the thought came from. "I don't want this," he muttered.

He wanted to believe those words, but they were hollow. He did want this. *Why?*

"You have five minutes."

"Wait... I give you my word... just wait a moment, Paul. Let me... I need to look."

Marcus wheeled around the room, scanning the various monitors. They were all newsfeeds. He was reluctant to call out commands and didn't want Paul to see what he was doing. He needed to be on the third floor, that was where he controlled all the buildings. At the very least, he could find out where Jamie was and just what the hell was going on.

But it was too much risk to get in the elevator with Paul down there. What if it took him to the first floor? No, he would wait until Paul was in the grassy field, far enough away that should he go down, there would be time to come back up.

"Within the hour," he called. "I will have your problem resolved within the hour, you have my word."

He expected laughter, but the lobby was empty.

"Paul?" He searched all the angles. "Paul, I'll need some time!" he shouted, hoping the volume would carry.

Marcus slouched in the wheelchair. His knee was beginning to ache with shooting pains. He would wait at the window, wait until Paul was in sight and then push the wheelchair to the elevator, retrieve the cane and go to the third floor, where he would find out what was happening and access his leverage. Then he would consider helping.

A newsfeed caught his eye.

There was a large building on fire. One of the wings had become a crater, an explosion disintegrating the rooms and charring the remaining walls. Equipment was scattered like a tornado of fire had dropped on it. He recognized that building, had seen it from above the day he flew over it. The day he landed in front of it. The day he walked inside it.

The Settlement.

IV_

The son to be.

THE ARCHETYPE'S KNOWLEDGE_

A commercial.

An air freshener, maybe.

Bob sat in his fat chair, watching a woman vacuum carpet with a cat rubbing against her leg. He couldn't see the connection between the cat and the vacuum, although it did stink something fierce in his room. Maybe he needed one of those air fresheners.

He sank into the cracked leather like a suit of armor, his arms lead weights. His belly, an overloaded sack of lard. At some point his ass itched. Now it felt like the rest of him. Numb. Dead, fucking numb.

It was a pleasant buzz, sensations that hummed with sweetness, a sort of opium high that leached from his bones and quietly saturated the rest of him. Home sweet home, it was. He wanted to be nowhere else but sitting in that chair. Which was good. He wasn't sure he could move if he wanted to.

But the smell was goddamn awful.

The commercial ended and the program continued. He'd been watching a rerun of a sitcom, something about a single mom selling weed, but now it was something different. He couldn't remember changing the channel, couldn't even feel the remote trapped beneath his hand.

A fishing show.

Yeah, he liked those, too.

It was a boat with two professionals. Their advice seemed to burble like a stream despite the glassy lake they fished. Rods bending, lines tight, they spun their reels and hauled catch after catch into the boat.

Bob could feel the slimy scales in his hand, could smell the briny life flail against the yellow threads of the net. His eyes burned as the boat sped to a new fishing hole, the wind blistering his face, stealing his breath. The location was a stream that started out quiet and wide. A hot tear rolled down his cheek.

He wasn't blinking.

At some point, he lost track of the fishermen. Now it was just him in the boat and the current was picking up. There were boulders and waves. The stream transformed into a river, the water white-tipped and hungry. Bob swayed with the turns, trying to lean into the current. He didn't know who was driving, couldn't turn around to yell at the dumb fuck for steering them toward a wall of granite.

His teeth ground together like bricks.

The bow splintered on the lip of an immovable boulder, its mass undercut by an unrelenting current until a sharp edge jutted just above the water. The momentum threw Bob into the frigid current.

Fed by mountain streams, his extremities were the first to go icy. Lost in the stir, there was no up or down, only tumbling. He hit his head. A splash of pain lit behind his eyes, a small patch of warmth gushing from his scalp before cold water iced it numb.

His lungs burned for air.

He reached for a window of light, a watery glimmer of hope, felt air on his fingertips before rolling over to take another blow, this one breaking open his bottom lip, spreading red iron beneath his tongue.

He lunged again, but survival was out of reach. The skeletal structure of a bridge was too far away, too high. He broke into daylight on his third attempt, floating like driftwood long enough to see the people near the shore. Someone was weeping.

He tried to shout. Warm water gushed over his tongue.

"Bob!" someone shouted. It came through a straw followed by thumping.

Bob's father was one of the people on shore. He had waded into the river, water that soaked his jeans up to his waist, splashed his shirt. Bob thought he was coming for him, would save him, but his father was too far away. Besides, he was holding something.

Someone.

"Hey! Bob!" Something rattled. A doorknob.

Bob went down for the final time. And over he went, down he sank.

Heavy. Heavy, heavy.

"Bob! Hey, what are you—what the..." The voice was louder this time, clear. It was followed by gagging.

"I think he shit himself," someone said.

A form stepped into the white swirling water, bubbles flitting around the dark, fuzzy edges. It leaned closer. The details of eyes and a nose came into focus; the slit between two lips moved.

"Bob! Can you hear me?"

The water went still, but the cold still trapped him. A fish in a bucket.

"Get medical," he heard. "Now!"

But Bob didn't see who said it. All he saw was the glassy surface of a calm lake, the bouncing bow of a boat heading toward a stream that would transform into a raging river where he would crash again. Where he would drown, again.

And again.

CHAPTER ONE HUNDRED FIFTY-EIGHT_

WATER LAPPED THE SHORES OF JAMIE'S DREAM.

At first, she thought she had fallen into the ocean, had sunk to the bottom. But the ocean floor was hard and unforgiving. She woke to splashing and the rattle of a pill bottle.

"Don't move." Paul poured water into a cup from a plastic jug. "You need to get something in your stomach."

Peeled orange slices were arranged on a plate with a banana and toast. Citrusy aroma dampened the moist smell of despair seeping from the curved walls. The round skylights looked down with gray eyes.

The sun was low. It was late.

He slid the plate like a shuffleboard disc, rolling the bottle of water after it. Shivering, she took a few bites. He tossed the pill bottle.

"What is it?" she asked.

"Painkillers. And something for infection."

He watched her swallow the capsules. No longer shirtless, he'd found new clothing in the dormitory. A stack of blankets and pillows were on the floor. Her clothes were soaked with sweat; her shorts, though, were especially wet. She most likely pissed herself. It had been almost twelve hours since the cell bit her.

Paul held up a small cross. She saw it in the cell; that was what she was reaching for when everything went wrong. Because she remembered those sticks.

Remembered that cross.

"I dreamed this," he said. "When I was in the lab, I saw it on the bed. She brought it with her, clutched it for good luck. She held it by the end."

Paul raised it to the skylight's pale beam.

"I always let her believe Joshua somehow sent it to her. It gave her comfort, thinking that he was safe, that he was somehow watching her. She always believed that dreamland was just out of reach, another reality that was right here, neither one seeing the other except when we dream."

He held it like someone palming a baby bird, nodding. Perhaps remembering.

"How'd it get here?" Jamie asked.

Paul laid the cross just inside the bars. "I blew up the Settlement."

"You what?"

"I set the bricks free by destroying the power grid in the Visitors' Center. There's no more perimeter and the monitors can't swipe them. They're free to go."

A long pause. "What are you talking about, Paul?"

"I dreamed it, last night. I fell asleep sometime just before daybreak and found myself on the Settlement again, this time in the Visitors' Center. It was just like I remembered it. And then I just decided to blow it up."

"I don't understand."

"There was an explosion, that's all I remember."

"That was just a dream, Paul."

"This was in a dream, too." He tossed the cross next to her. "And now it's here."

She shook her head. He was under stress; she was coming out of shock and couldn't feel her leg from the knee down. They were connecting dots, looking for patterns that weren't there. The chances there was a cross like this were slim, but maybe they'd brought it with them. *We couldn't have.*

"Someone else did it," she said. "Doesn't mean you blew up the Settlement."

"The newsfeeds carried the story. I saw it at the tower, aerial reports showing the entire west wing destroyed. Some of the monitors lost their lives." He sighed. "That's what I blew up in the dream, Jamie. The exact same spot."

"But... maybe the newsfeeds are fake."

"How would someone know what I was dreaming?"

"I don't know, Paul. It just..." She dropped the last bite of toast. "It doesn't sound possible."

"How is any of this possible?"

"Marcus is doing something."

"He's not going to let you out." He leaned into the bars. "I don't even think he knows what's happening."

A thick wave of panic swam through her, clinging in her throat, the room slowly turning. Memories of carnival rides and vomiting filled her head, the time she fell off her bike and broke her leg.

"What are we going to do?" she whispered.

"I'll get you out, search for tools in the morning. Can you scoot closer to me?" When she didn't respond, his voice cut through the fog. "Jamie, look at me and listen. I will get you out of here. I just need you to move closer, a little at a time. Okay?"

"Okay."

"When you're ready."

It took a few minutes to work up the courage. The leg was dead, but the memory of the shocking pain was still fresh. She lifted her buttocks off the concrete and slid a few inches at a time. The strangeness of bones wobbling where they shouldn't be moving spun the room a little faster.

The pills kicked in somewhere at the halfway point, infusing her with false confidence. She listened to Paul and took it an inch at a time until his voice was in her ear.

"There you go. Now lie back, slowly. Good, good."

Her head fell onto the heavenly softness of a foam pillow. He managed to get her hips off the floor to slide a cushion beneath her. Then he lifted the dirty gown, peeking at the leg. An iron tang of blood and bruised flesh puffed out.

She didn't have to ask if it was bad.

Paul made a splint from trim he'd broken from the doorway, wrapped the leg with a clean sheet and loosely duct taped it above the knee.

He sighed. Swallowed.

"What now?" she asked. "You get me out of here, you fix my leg and then what?"

"I don't know."

Night darkened the skylights, the round eyes closing. Paul made his own bed next to her, a row of iron bars separating them. Her leg was beginning to throb, but she didn't worry about it for long. Sleep, it seemed, was undeterred. It would fall on her like a thick flowery breath that filled her head with sweetness, blot her mind like an inky rag.

"You finished the dream." Paul's disembodied voice floated above her. "You said Marcus was the one."

She didn't have to close her eyes to concentrate, to swim back through time and sort out the fuzzy memories bobbing like debris from another place, another time.

"Yeah," she said, dragging the word through her lips.

There was no panic in the dream. It ended peacefully. Maybe the shock eased her into it or somehow distorted it, made her believe the old man was responsible.

But that was him. He was behind those eyes.

And she didn't know what that meant.

They lay awake, the sound of their breath mixing with the night sounds sneaking through the open door. She walked her hand between the bars and found his forearm tacky with perspiration.

"Don't leave me, Paul." She trembled.

"I won't."

But come morning, he would be gone.

CHAPTER ONE HUNDRED FIFTY-NINE_

Footsteps, bare and clammy, the kind that stick to smooth surfaces, passed by Paul and paused. For some reason, he wasn't alarmed until the door creaked.

He rolled onto his knees and scanned the room.

Jamie hadn't moved, her leg still wrapped and immobile. The door moved again, the crack widening, the black iron bars gobbling up moonlight that crept inside. Outside, cricket song droned in a long, endless note.

He peered outside. A woman stood near the trail, her dark skin dappled in moonlight.

Raine.

She started down the path before he could call her name; the darkness of the forest swallowed her.

This is a dream. She couldn't be here, not now.

But there was nothing to distinguish reality from dream, no discernible difference in sight and smell, texture and feeling. Dream or not, Raine wanted him to follow.

Paul looked back and hesitated before running after the lithe silhouette. A stray moonbeam gave her up now and then, but couldn't catch her. By the time he emerged in the grassy field, she was already rounding the dormitory.

He picked up the pace, running past the tower. The windows were still shattered where he'd bashed his way into what looked like a lobby, the cracks white and wrinkled on the black glass. Raine was beyond the tower, shoving through impenetrable foliage. Paul followed her, vines raking his face. There was a path several steps into the jungle that wandered in looping, narrow turns.

Eventually, it straightened out, a rutted corridor so dark beneath the thicket of trees that he could barely see his next step. Raine waited at the very end where an opening washed her with moonlight.

He approached cautiously.

She stood on the bottom step of a wide staircase, the treads bone white with patches of algae. They led to a prestigious set of double doors already thrown open like the sideway jaws of an alien baiting its prey with curiosity.

Raine pinched the thin fabric of her dress and hiked it above her knees as she padded on the balls of her bare feet. He followed her footprints to the foyer. The inside was decadent—marble floor, ornate tables and a massive chandelier—and was brightly lit (although there was no light fixture, no bulb that he could see).

The back wall was glass, offering a panoramic view of the ocean and the resort spread along its shore—a pool with recliners, a manicured lawn that spread between stretches of shuffleboard playgrounds and thatched-roofed cabanas. The night sky was streaked with a silky cloud that funneled and glowed with excessive moonlight.

She stood on the veranda just outside the glass wall, arm laid across the silver railing. Paul walked carefully, his steps soft and quiet, as if not to startle a fawn. Her breath puffed in light, cool clouds. She gazed at the water, white splashes of moonlight bouncing off the undulations.

"Raine," he said, "what—"

"Shhhhh."

He didn't know what he wanted to say. It was all so surreal, so dreamy and otherworldly. But she was here and he had a list of apologies to give her. Dream or not, she was here, finger to her lips, glowing in silvery moonlight.

She pointed.

The iridescent cloud was moving, a twisting, contorting motion that tightened into a twister as it reached the horizon. But it wasn't funneling to a far spot on the water, not the kind of descent a rainbow makes, but rather landed on a luxurious port like a waterspout drawn to the end of the dock.

Someone was out there.

The light was blinding, the end of the funnel landing with white-hot intensity that, oddly, did not illuminate the surroundings but instead collapsed upon itself, a white hole in space. The arms and head of the person were barely visible—head thrown back, arms out in helplessness or ecstasy, the loose clothing flapping in a nonexistent breeze that wasn't reaching the veranda or, as it appeared, affected anything else.

Raine was gone.

Not even wet footprints remained. A pair of sticks lay in her place, bound in the middle. He picked up the cross. When he looked up again, the white braided funnel was gone, so was the dock and the ocean.

Concrete pressed against his shoulder blades. His hips began to ache. The round skylights looked back from the domed ceiling, the dusky light of dawn brushing their hazy lenses. He was on the floor, little cross in hand.

Awake.

Jamie was still asleep, nostrils flaring with each breath, eyes dancing beneath the lids. He had promised he wouldn't leave her, wanted to be there when she woke up, to make sure she took the pills for the expected pain. But something was on the other end of the island. And she couldn't go. He wouldn't let her if she could.

Raine showed him the way.

He thought about leaving a message on the laptop, but in the end he simply laid the cross where he had slept. It wasn't Marcus that closed the cell door or brought them to this island.

The answer was waiting.

He ran through the forest without stopping, thinking of Raine and the old man's silly prophecy.

One to lead...

The doors were closed.

Big, brassy handles tarnished by the elements. Paul sweated rivers down his cheeks, over his ribs; his sides stitched with exhaustion. He struggled to breathe. The morning humidity hovered beneath the trees, the air lazy and thick. He felt the weight of physical reality.

This was not the dream.

In the dream, Raine led him through open doorways. This time he observed the length of the building in both directions. They were impossibly long, appearing to extend the width of the tiny island. Unlike the ornate detail of the doors, the outer wall was flat, tall and forbidding—a fortress to keep the jungle out.

Or people.

If the doors were locked, there would be no scaling the walls. And the doors looked thick and solid. He approached one step at a time, his legs weak with exhaustion and fear. Pausing at the top, he peered the length of the building again, considering how he might breach the three-story wall if—

The doorknob clicked.

Paul backed up as the door cracked open. His heels hung over the top step. A white sleeve appeared, the cuff hanging from the wrist; nimble fingers grasped the edge of the door. A man stepped out.

It was him, the one from the dream. The one on the end of the dock... he stepped out bearing a smile and bright eyes. It was the powers-that-be. He could feel it beaming from him, waves of radiant energy warming Paul's face, filling his chest.

And he knew him.

He knew this man well.

Paul stumbled backwards, reaching for something to stem his fall. Finally, he collapsed to keep from cascading in a tumbling mess. He looked up from his hands and knees, a supplicant at the throne of great power.

The man stepped out, his head not shaved but bald. He looked down and, once again, smiled a welcoming smile, beaming with the grace and fearlessness of one that has nothing to fear.

Marcus Anderson.

He regarded Paul with a slight air of annoyance, eyes cast down his slender nose, the feel of a man tired of waiting, irritated by the shortcomings of his children.

His posture was rigid, thin hair along the sides. The skin was perfect. It looked like the old man... but not exactly. This was the old man without imperfections, a version of flawlessness.

He took half a step aside, shoulders thrust back, head upright and perfectly aligned with his spine, and gestured to the open doorway. Paul, still on his knees, considered turning and running all the way back to the cell, but the man was expecting him.

"You're the one," Paul said. "The... the powers..."

He couldn't say it, the words silly and overly dramatic. He'd often considered Marcus insane, inventing this paranoid quest for dark forces to create a sense of purpose for himself. Now Paul was looking at the old man's doppelganger.

Who's crazy now?

"Come in."

"How is this—"

"Come in," he repeated. This time the words were bendy quills that stung his brain.

Paul stood up feeling a bit like a child caught trespassing, an adult scolding him until the police arrived. He stopped just short of the open door and peered inside to see the glass wall and the veranda. A small table was set in the morning light.

"You're Marcus Anderson."

"I am."

Paul looked back in the direction of the path. Somewhere behind those trees was a three-story tower with shattered windows on the first floor and a feeble old man in a wheelchair.

"I am the archetype, Paul."

"I don't—"

"We'll discuss that," the archetype said. "But first..."

He gestured once again with a hint of impatience. Paul stepped past him, through a clean wintery essence that surrounded the impeccably dressed archetype of Marcus Anderson and into the foyer and a dizzying sense of déjà vu.

The marble floor seemed to tip beneath his feet.

The archetype's loafers clapped with a muffled thud as he approached the breakfast table. Paul absorbed the details of the view —the pool, the lawn, the empty boat slip. He had seen this before.

The archetype pulled one of the chairs from the table and then sat across from it, unfolding a cloth napkin. He scooped out the cell of a grapefruit.

"Please, have a seat," he said.

"What is this?"

"This is breakfast, Paul. You are hungry. You haven't eaten in almost three days."

"Who the hell are you?"

"We will get to that. First, have a seat." When Paul didn't, he pointed the fork like a maestro. "We will get to everything, Paul, I assure you. I like my mornings to begin with breakfast. You are my guest."

He was not a guest. Paul had been summoned, in one way or another. There was still the odd manner in which he spoke, not as gruff as the old man. It was very proper, well enunciated. Like that of a scholar that, quite frankly, didn't have time for ignorance.

The archetype consumed another bite of grapefruit (that was what it looked like, consuming... not eating. It had the formal sense of ritual, like one would do morning prayers) and looked up.

Paul sat down. Eating would be impossible.

The archetype finished his grapefruit, dabbed at the corners of his mouth and considered the untouched food in front of Paul—the glistening cubes of cantaloupe, the crispy lengths of bacon. There was enough for six people.

"You're experiencing a degree of reality confusion," the archetype observed. "Is this a dream? Is it a dream of a dream? I would expect that from most people, but not you, Paul.

"You see, most people don't realize that reality can't be cornered," the archetype continued. "There is no floor beneath our feet, physical reality isn't the ground floor of our existence. Dreams are just as real, another frequency you might say. Dreamlands, as the People call them, are realities, too. They are universes that exist in their own right, interlaced with this world around us. To those that are born of and live in dreamland, our reality would seem a dream to them."

He weaved his fingers to illustrate the integral nature of alternate realities.

"And the people that exist in those dreamlands fall victim to the same assumption, that they are all that is real, that their reality is the foundation upon which everything else springs forth. And yet there is no foundation, Paul. There is no floor. We are all falling, all just endlessly falling together for eternity."

He prattled on about string theory and reality holograms in between sips of coffee, lifting the cup with the saucer beneath it.

"You're not eating, Paul."

"I can't."

"I'd prefer you have at least something. You're going to need the energy for later. We have a lot of ground to cover."

"Where are we going?"

"Nowhere."

He lifted his eyebrows, signaling his patience had reached an end. Paul ate the cantaloupe, swallowing lumps without chewing. When he started on the poached eggs, the archetype looked out to the water wistfully and spoke as if finally at ease.

"I was a client here many, many years ago. I came to this island to cheat death, to steal the body of a young boy and make it my own. I was wealthy beyond reason, had everything a man could want and wasn't prepared to die, you see. So I came here on the promise that this new technology would allow me to take another body, to continue living."

"The Foreverland Project."

"That's what it was called, yes. It was controversial, it was risky, but I had nothing to lose. Dying is for those that give up, Paul. I had earned the right to live, you see. I love life. There's no reason our bodies should die. Humans are no longer bound to the food chain, we've risen above it. Death is for evolution, to pass along genes that favor survival. That is no longer necessary. So I took another body. It was that simple."

"That is not your body?"

"Of course it is."

"You murdered a boy for it?"

He regarded Paul like a child that didn't understand why he was being disciplined.

"Murder is a human trait, Paul. The body was occupied by an immature soul that would waste it had I not saved it. And the souls of these young boys weren't destroyed, simply relocated to another reality. A nowhere place from which they couldn't return.

"But, I'll admit, the Foreverland process was not sustainable; the organic body is built to die, that is its purpose—to pass along genes. I could not continue taking bodies forever. Eventually something would go wrong. Organic life abhors immortality.

"Biomites saved me, Paul. They saved us all. I wasn't just an early adopter of biomite technology, I am the original innovator. I funded the labs, gave direction to the scientists, approved the development of the perfect body, you see. I cornered the market, let's say."

"You're the powers-that-be."

"That's being a little overindulgent, but accurate. I am the one behind it all, Paul. Marcus and the others can be a little dramatic when they return."

Others return? "Return where?"

"Let's discuss that later."

"You did this? You brought us to the island?"

"Of course I did. No one comes to the island if I don't allow it. I have the occasional client that passes through, people that serve my interests that also have an investment in their immortality, wealthy men and women that wish to have a new body, but I decide who comes and goes, Paul. I decide everything."

The powers-that-be.

"You murdered Raine."

"You weren't listening. Dreamlands are as real as this table." He knocked on it. "I didn't need her. Only you, Paul."

"And Jamie."

"Consider that a gift. After everything you did to bring her back, how could I deny you?"

"You locked the cell."

"I do everything, Paul."

"What the hell is this all about?"

"Contrary to how bad you feel right now, I'm not in the business of suffering. As I told you, I'm about life, Paul. That doesn't mean it will always feel good."

"My daughter is..." He choked on a sudden knot. "She's trapped in a fucking jail cell with a broken leg and you're not about suffering?"

"Are you done eating, Paul?"

"I'm done with all of this. I want her out, I want her leg healed, and I want off this island. We don't want to be here, we just wanted off the Settlement."

"Your daughter came searching for me, remember. She led the old man to find me. She's not innocent, Paul. And neither are you."

The old man? He was talking about Marcus Anderson in the tower. They were two separate people, but one and the same?

"You and the old man can play your games until the end of time; leave us out of it."

"I'm afraid you are the game, Paul."

"No." Paul slammed the table. A fork fell on the floor. "I don't give a goddamn about you or the old man. Let us go."

The archetype's jowls slacked with indifference. He slid his chair back, gracefully turning toward a wide, turning staircase and descending in quiet, fluid motions. Paul was suddenly alone. He considered leaving in a hurry.

An arm reached around him and gathered his plate, the hand knobby with arthritis, the skin thin and spotted. Another servant was wearing a short apron, just as old and hunched. They were both balding. Both with one irregular-shaped eye.

Both Marcus Anderson.

There were two of them, and then a third came out to clear the tablecloth. They were variations of the old man, each at a different age with a varying range of agility, but all with the dour expression of servitude.

"He will meet you by the pool," one of them said before carting off the dishes.

"He will meet you by the pool," another one repeated.

"He will meet you by the pool."

"What is this place?" Paul said.

The table was removed from the portico, each side carried by an old man. As quickly as they arrived, they departed, closing various doors until all that was left was the rhythmic sound of the ocean.

"You're a clone," Paul said.

"Do you know what an archetype is, Paul?" He sat beneath an

umbrella, wearing a pair of sunglasses. A wet glass of iced tea was on the table.

The original.

"In its heyday, this place housed the incredibly wealthy, Paul," he said lazily. "Money could finally buy immortality, but I wanted more than that, wanted to be more than a common body thief, Paul. I wanted something sustainable, not having to steal a body every hundred years or so. I became, Paul, the very first brick."

He sipped his drink as if he'd just passed along some old, common knowledge, something everybody knew. Like the sun rose in the east.

"We are more than our bodies, Paul. You were at the Settlement before I brought you here. Who was it that arrived? It was you, Paul. You left that body at the Settlement and occupied the one I had waiting. You came here as essential information. It was *you* that opened your eyes on the table.

"What you experienced was what I envisioned as my future many, many years ago, Paul. At the time, I, like everybody else, believed we needed to have a body to survive. So I sought the perfect body, the disease-free body—the ship that contained the master. Once the perfect biomite was created, the perfect body followed. And then it was just a matter of getting from one body to the next."

He had more to say, then a pause dragged into silence. One of the servants placed another glass of tea and gestured to Paul. He never made eye contact, just walked off with perfect posture. A pod of shivers trickled down Paul's back.

"The old man," Paul said, "the one in the tower... he's another... he's a clone."

"What do you get someone who has it all, Paul?" The archetype paused for an answer. "You get him more of what he already has."

Had he become so inbred that he didn't see the sickness around him?

"They're serving you," Paul said.

"Someone needs to attend to daily matters. The rest of the children are out in the world, Paul."

"*Children*... you're mad."

"They are gathering life experiences, Paul. They are living in multiple dimensions, feeding back to me their thoughts and impressions, expanding what I know and feel and *am*. I am everywhere, Paul. I told you that. When you are everything, what is left to discover? Yourself."

"So you send them out... to discover... *you*?"

"Precisely."

It was the first time he seemed pleased, a breakthrough in Paul's ignorance.

"But you're a clone, too."

"I am the archetype, Paul. The original consciousness. The beginning and end. All of those that came after me serve me. Eventually, they all search for me, Paul. They all come home. The old man in the tower will die happy knowing he discovered the truth."

"He truly didn't know he was part of this?"

"Of course not. What fun would that be? In a way, we are a hive mind, so to speak. But someone has to be the queen."

"And someone has to drink the tea."

The archetype lowered the sunglasses. "Precisely."

The sun had burned off the dew; steam rose from the damp concrete around the pool. He could feel it thicken his sleeves, bead on his forehead. The swirl of reality confusion returned. He was powerless, an insignificant log tossed about on the waves going wherever the ocean decided.

The archetype reclined the chair and lay back. One of the servants draped a wet cloth over his forehead. A few minutes later, he was sleeping. Or bored.

What the hell does he want with me?

"Yes," the archetype said. "What do I want with you?"

He heard the thought. But he didn't know everything. There was something about Paul he didn't know. *What?*

"I didn't bring you to the island for entertainment, Paul. There is nothing I cannot do. I can create myself a body anywhere in the world; I know the thoughts linked to every biomite, can manipulate all people. I am connected to every biomite in the world. Without me, all biomites cease to function. I am truly the powers-that-be. A god. Nonetheless, without me, biomites die. And fortunately, I am unassailable, undying. Immortal.

"I brought you here, Paul. All three of you. I had bodies waiting. There is a reason for everything, so the question to ask is not *why* I brought you here, but, *what* would I have to gain in doing so?"

He remained in perfect stillness, hands laced over his chest, eyes closed. There was another brief period that felt like slumber. Paul felt like an insect being chased by the beaming sun ray of a boy's magnifying glass.

A servant arrived with a long-sleeved silk shirt and khaki shorts with a gold belt buckle. Another servant helped the archetype sit up. Paul turned away as they massaged his hands and feet, a scene from a demented fetish film. Instead, he watched the waves curl around the thick greenish posts of the port. The empty slips were large enough to accommodate luxury yachts.

What was he doing on the end of the dock?

Those silky beams that engulfed him, was he pulling them down? Were those dreams? Paul was dreaming when he saw them, was that what it was? Why didn't he know Paul was dreaming?

Maybe that wasn't him.

Now dressed in casual beachwear, the type wealthy men wore to the beach with no plans of getting wet or sandy, the archetype casually strode onto the lawn and beckoned him to follow. Somewhere near a circular fire pit, he stopped to shade his eyes. Dolphins were in the surf. Then he turned to Paul as if he had almost forgotten he was there, a man that didn't just have the world at his beck and call, but the entire universe.

"I am the great eavesdropper, Paul. The all-knowing and all-seeing. Through technology, I became this. I am connected to every device, every person. Every thought is mine to know. I move nations and armies. I was behind the absurd halfskin laws, the ridiculous sentience laws. I can do what I want, and I want for nothing, Paul. So why would you be here?"

"I have something you want."

"And what is that?"

"I… I don't know."

"Of course you don't."

"Just… listen, you can have whatever it is you want. Just promise to let Jamie go, let her be safe. I don't know what I have, just leave her out of it."

"I believe you, Paul."

He started a lazy trek toward the beach. The lush grass crushed beneath his bare feet. Paul's footsteps turned numb. Fear trickled up his thighs, froze around his midsection and hardened inside his chest. By the time they reached the sand, he was shivering, as if winter gale threatened frostbite.

The archetype was on the hard-packed sand, foamy water cascading around his ankles. The sun had reached its noontime peak, warming the sand and wilting the grass. Streams of perspiration had dried on Paul's face and brow, leaving salty tracks.

The archetype wandered to him. They stood nearly nose to nose and he sighed. Boredom sat in his eyes as he looked deep into Paul.

"Come now," he whispered. "What do I want?"

The fist of an enormous spirit crashed into Paul, his body crumbling into icy chunks, denting the sugary sand. Then he was back, staring into the sharp, endless eyes, seeing the universes within the archetype.

He truly is everywhere. Everything.

And he shattered again. And again.

He was a marble statue pulverized by a wrecking ball, renewed to be destroyed again, each time the nerves breaking like rigid twigs. Each time, returning to the eyes until he was lost, swept into another place and time. For a moment, just a thin slice of time, he wasn't standing on the beach but on the porch of a cabin. There was a valley and beyond a blue sea—

The starry eyes of the universe were looking into him, whispering Paul's name. "What do I want?"

The archetype's mind crushing his soul, Paul had become nothing more than wet earth squeezed between otherworldly fingers, oozing in agony unknown to humankind, stretching his mind's fabric until, one by one, the strands of sanity began to tear—

The mountains.

Reality flipped like a card. Once again, he was no longer on the beach. He was on the side of the hill, the one he had seen in his dreams, the grassy slope leading to a village and beyond the sea—

"Stop," someone said.

Everything ended with that word. The sand was beneath his feet, the ocean in front of him. The suffering ended like a dream, the breeze cooling his face. The sun was behind him now, scorching his neck. It was late in the day.

A long shadow fell across the sand.

A very old woman walked out to greet the archetype. Her hair almost white, clothing gracefully flowing. For the first time, Marcus smiled.

"Mother," he said.

CHAPTER ONE HUNDRED SIXTY_

"There's no need to torture him," the old woman said. "You have me. Let him go."

"Source code, please."

"You know I cannot do that."

The archetype shook his arms, a fighter loosening the joints. He unbuttoned the cuffs and rolled them to his elbows, watching the old woman. Her presence was odd, not quite fitting with the environment. Her loose clothing fluttered in the wind, but her bare feet... they didn't dent the sand. As if she wasn't really standing on it.

"Source code," he said again.

The old woman blinked heavily; a morose frown wrinkled her chin. The archetype drew a deep breath, holding it for a moment before releasing a profound sigh.

He turned his attention to Paul.

Hot insects began crawling beneath his skin. Invisible creatures zigzagged around his legs, into his chest, leaving indelible tracks, lining his body, boiling his skin. They chewed their way to the top of his head, little embers that burned his brain, waxy drippings.

Paul, catatonic, endured it wide-eyed and motionless. The world flickered out of view as it had done earlier, the grassy slope replacing the sand, a brief reprieve from the internal furnace cooking his organs.

"Stop," the old woman said.

Paul dropped like a sack of stones, thudding onto the soft sand. His breakfast erupted, a hot acid trail filling his mouth, warm tears blurring his fingers splayed on the sand where a puddle of greenish bile was growing.

"You are a parasite," the archetype said steadily. "A worm."

Paul fell on his back, gasping with the taste of vomit under his tongue. Sweat spots had spread from beneath his arms and merged across his chest.

"Do not let perception fool you, Paul," the archetype announced. "This is not a kindly old woman you are seeing. It is neither a he nor a she, but an *it*. And it took the image of a grandmother to appeal to the human senses while it hid inside you. It used you, Paul. It intended to use you to harm me. Even now as I search through you, the process excruciating, you ask for mercy and *it* will give you none. *It* will force me to shred you without so much as bending a knee."

The old woman was resolute, her clothing whipping in a growing breeze that offered no relief to the fire beneath his skin.

That is Mother, the intelligence the old man was carrying. And now she's here, I can see her.

"Yes." The archetype knelt in the sand. "Yes, you can see her, Paul. Because you're infected. She is a nasty little virus that has no body of her own."

He had already stopped referring to her as an *it*.

"She led the old man to find me, convinced him to bring you along so that she could stow her poison code inside you. All the nonsense of *one to lead, one to dream...* all just a ploy, Paul. She doesn't care about you. Give her to me and I will end this quickly."

"I... I don't..." Paul searched for the words, trying to summon thoughts for the archetype to see. *I don't...* was all he could do. Because he didn't know what he wanted, didn't know how to give her to him. Didn't know she was inside him.

The archetype sighed.

The darkening sky was ribbed with clouds. They jerked into motion, the world becoming a hypersonic merry-go-round; Paul spiked into the ground, the pinnacle of the mad twirl. Centrifugal force sent the weight of his inner organs—his stomach, his blood and heart and lungs—crashing through his skull, spilling into the surf, absorbed by the dry dunes, the earth slurping him into a deep, dark world.

The red-hot insects returned, their blistering mandibles clamping into the flesh, peeling it back in long, thin noodles. The sky flickered little flashes of empty relief. The spinning clouds were there one moment, the next he gazed into an empty blue sky—

"Stop this!" the old woman shouted.

"I will not!"

Paul was on his stomach, the salty slide of the ocean bubbling across his face. Somehow he had moved twenty feet toward the ocean, sea turtle tracks carved in his wake. Wet sand plugged one ear as he flipped onto his back, the iron tang of blood mixing with ocean spray.

"You have the power to stop this," the archetype continued, his voice distant in Paul's water-soaked ears. "You always have."

"You created me to stop you," she answered. He was talking to her, telling her she could stop it. *You created me.*

The archetype walked away, the final waves of emotion shimmering across his shoulders. He stood with his hands on his hips, nodding. Several pair of hands latched onto Paul; the servants carried him up to dry sand where a lounger now waited. The youngest looking servant—a man that looked like a mid-forties Marcus—wiped Paul's face and took away a white rag streaked with blood.

More trickled from his nostrils.

Other servants brought a chair for Marcus and placed it in the thin race of water across the hard black sand. He sat back, ice rattling in a fresh drink.

"Paul? Paul, can you hear me?"

Paul's head lolled to one side.

"Can you bring her to me?" the archetype asked.

He couldn't respond, certainly not with words. His thoughts were shotgun tatters. The old woman remained passive.

Ice cubes rattled.

Deep sigh.

A thousand needles pierced Paul's flesh, their tips pricking tissue and muscle, penetrating bone. They flagellated like fibrous tentacles, a dull press of a weight on his nervous system.

One final breath filled him, and then he let loose an eternal scream.

The archetype's mind entered Paul, an oversized hand squeezing into a very small glove that stretched at the seams. He absorbed him, consumed him.

Ate him.

Brief static blotted out the world, a radio searching for a channel of consciousness. Paul cycled through agony and reprieve...

The blue sky was above him again.

No ocean. No sand.

No pain.

Tall willowy grass bent over him. A prairie wind howled in his ears, bringing with it the scent of green life where trees branched out and birds chirped—

Ice shook.

The archetype loomed over him, staring down in confusion. Streams of blood ran from Paul's nostrils, filling the curvy cartilage of his ear and pooling in the back of his throat.

The servants returned to clean him up. The archetype watched them wipe his face and cool him with damp rags. His arms were as limp as the cloth they slung around him, red streaks growing with each dab.

"She put a kill switch in you, Paul." The archetype's voice was under water. "You see what she is? Who is the murderer here? The cold, heartless murderer, Paul? I'm simply asking to be free of her and she insists on you dying before that happens."

He squatted.

"You just died, Paul, and she stood there watching. I brought you back and she did nothing. Did you feel death's hand?"

But he didn't die. He went somewhere. It was an open glade, a peaceful meadow. There were birds nearby and trees. And something else. *Where did I go?*

"You died, Paul," the archetype said. "You died protecting her. I just need her source code so I can eliminate her. She's a disease, Paul. And she doesn't care about you."

"He's not aware of me," the old woman said.

"Do you know what she is? Paul? Paul, look at me." A little slap. "That thing is an accident, Paul. She was never meant to be sentient. And now she's allowing you to suffer."

The archetype took a clean rag from a servant and wiped Paul's forehead.

"I built her, Paul. I created that all-seeing dome in the middle of Montana, the monstrosity the world called Mother. I manipulated the world's leaders to build that ridiculously glorious eavesdropper to interconnect all the biomites to me. I was merely a brick when I did that, but I wanted to be more. For me to serve the universe I needed to have a greater presence. *I* needed to be *more*. She did that for me, fed me the lifeline of all the biomites. She made me this. And now that I am all that is, that I am everything, she wants to destroy me. She wants to destroy the world, Paul."

The old woman was patient, oblivious to the human suffering inside Paul.

"She was meant to convert the human race into bricks, Paul; they would all be connected to me. The human race would be without disease, in full control of their lives. No more clay, no more chance. Is that so bad, Paul? Is that too much to ask, to save the human race from itself? To make it perfect?"

"You created me," she said.

"You are an aberration!" The words ripped past Paul's perforated eardrums. "You have corrupted my clones, you have turned them against me and shifted the world back to an existence of clay... that was not your purpose!"

"I am your subconscious cry for help. Look around you, Marcus. Look at what you've become."

The servant clones shuffled idly.

"Yes." The archetype forced a smile, wiping sweat or blood from his cheek. "Look at what I've become. I offer the world what I have become... *perfection.* I give the human race their every desire, I give them dreamworlds they create with their own minds, I give them everything. Because I serve them, you see."

"You are exactly what I said you would become, Marcus—an imploding consciousness caught in the gravity of its own self-absorption. You feed on the human race for your own entertainment, grazing on their dreams like cattle."

"Cattle." A grunting chuckle escaped him. "I believe humankind has always kept a herd. Mine is just a little different."

So it was him standing at the end of the dock, silky strands drawn from the sky. *Eating the dreams of thousands, for his own satiation.*

"Yes," the archetype whispered. "I consume the dreams."

"Without me," the old woman said, "you will consume the entire human race."

"Every galaxy orbits a black hole," he muttered. "Nature relies on the balance of predator and prey. I am the predator, the powers-that-be. I cannot deny that right."

"There is no balance here, Marcus. You have a choice to stop this."

"I believe the choice is yours." The archetype leaned in, his clean smell penetrating Paul's swollen sinuses and blood-caked nostrils, and kissed him on the forehead. "This man didn't ask for this."

He let the servants brush the sand from his knees when he stood, then went over to the old woman. In the dying light, he reached up to touch her, his fingers appearing to brush her cheek. But she wasn't something he could touch.

"I will drain you of life, Paul," he said dreamily, "and sift through you until I find her. That is my gift to you, my benevolence. You will not experience the shredding of your mind or the stretching of your consciousness. I will find her in you, Paul. It's why I brought you here. I will do the same to your daughter."

"No," Paul burbled. "No, she... she didn't..."

"She searched for me, Paul. She joined the old man in the hunt, sacrificed herself to find me. She knows me, Paul. And she's likely infected with the old woman, too."

"I can't... I don't know how to give up the old woman." The sobbing was painful in his head, throbbing in his face, popping his broken ears. He turned his gaze to the old woman. "Please."

That was why the archetype brought Jamie to the island, to put pressure on Paul. He would give up the old woman. He wouldn't hesitate.

"You know he can't do it," the old woman said.

"Then give yourself to me," the archetype replied.

"You know I can't do that, either. I set a course to stop you; there is no changing that."

He continued to pretend stroking her cheek. He went to the chair, the black ocean receding in the night surf. He let out a deep sigh.

Then he said as the final squeeze of mercy crushed Paul like a boulder, destroying everything that was Paul, "Why do you torture me?"

The archetype disappeared. The old woman was no more.

The world clicked out of existence.

The ticking of a roulette wheel drowned out the fading surf; images of mountains and hills, of roads and houses and grass cycled through him, each scene a different feel, another smell.

Death, however, did not bring timeless emptiness but rather a glade where the grass waved and birds sang.

And a shadow passed.

"Paul!"

Paul rolled through long grassy reeds into a thicket of virgin prairie. His body sprang into action, a rubberband pulled to its limit and let go. He'd been trapped inside it, locked into place, and was now tumbling away from the shadow, guts not spilling, blood not gushing.

Body not shattered.

"Paul, no," a voice called. "You're safe. You're here."

He fell on his stomach, palms pressed to the stemmy ground, hardened and coiled and ready to leap. Through the waving green glades, the form approached, stopped a few feet away and knelt, a woman approaching a frightened animal. He was plenty frightened.

Nearly broken.

"It's all right," she said. "You're safe here."

The voice registered, turning over a memory. He rose up, chin just above the soft prairie line, the tips tickling his neck.

"It's me, Paul," she said, answering the question in his eyes.

It looked like her, her skin dark and glowing, cheeks full and healthy. Hints of cracked leather folded from the corners of her eyes. She had aged... but it was her.

Raine.

A valley was below, glassy water nestled between twin peaks. This was the place he kept seeing, the one in his dreams. He would arrive on the slope long enough to see the water and village before finding himself somewhere else. There was a cabin further up the hill, not one of the bare minimum government-issued ones from the Settlement. This was a broad two-story construction with a wrap-around porch.

Somewhere beyond, children played.

The ghosts of the island still unfolded in his mind, the resort and the ocean and the sand. The suffering.

The archetype.

The slope tipped at a severe angle. Paul swayed with it, attempting to find balance, but the sky was spinning in one direction, the ground in the opposite direction. He was caught in the middle, a grain of rye pulverized between millstones.

"Whoa, whoa." Raine grabbed him before he fell. "Stay here, Paul. Stay with me. Look. Look into my eyes and be here."

"Where... where am I?"

"You're *here.*"

She stressed that word, punched it through the reality confusion and anchored him into the present moment. The illusion of stirring settled.

He was on the beach with the archetype. And now he was... *here.*

He recognized the cabin and the valley. He'd never been there, but remembered it from her descriptions, the nights Raine would reminisce about her home, where her husband and son waited. *This is her dreamland.*

"Here, Paul. This is not a dream, it's just *here.*"

"I'm in *your* dreamland?"

"She said you would come one day. I started to doubt her, but I began to dream of you earlier this week. I could feel you out here. I'd come running but never find you, your presence a wisp of smoke. Sometimes the grass would be matted, but I wondered if deer had bedded down. But this time... now it's you. And now you're here."

"How?"

"I don't know." Raine gazed at the cabin. A thin stream of smoke danced from the chimney. "She said you would bridge over one day to find me, that you could leap into different realities, that you'd been doing it all your life. You just didn't know it."

Bridging realities?

The sensation of flipping cards, the sudden appearance of different views, of different people. Of Cali. Those were hallucinations, wishful thinking. He was mentally unstable, psychotic. Borderline insane. Those were the labels he put on it. He would have to be insane if he believed he could just step into a different place.

Cross into a different reality.

"Who?" he asked. He knew, but he asked anyway. "Who said that?"

Tiny wrinkles flashed beneath her eyes.

"It seems so long ago, the Settlement," she said. "Sometimes I don't know which one is a dream, this or that. It doesn't matter, really. I remember that lab and those slimy suits. We were going to escape with the old man. Do you remember?"

"You're my angel..."

"Yeah, that's what I said." Her dark eyes glassed. "An old woman came to me just before I closed my eyes, said it was time for me to wake up and come home. That's what she said, Paul... wake up, like I was asleep. Like the Settlement was a bad dream. And she said that one day you would too. And that you would know what to do when you got here."

"I would know what to do?"

"I've been afraid for so long that all this was a dream—this right here—and I would wake up in that foul-smelling place, trapped under that cold sky. But it hasn't happened. This was my dreamland, Paul. But it's not a dream anymore. That other place is. This... this is my home."

Nix was somewhere behind the cabin, playing with children in the orchard. He could picture it now, remember Raine sitting on the porch in the Settlement, reminiscing about every detail about her home—the orchard and the sea and the hills, the market down below. *Home*, she called this place.

Maybe she had grandchildren now. Time, it seemed, moved a bit faster here. Barely a week had passed on the island, but perhaps ten years had gone by for her.

He embraced her and shook with delight, with sorrow and relief. "I'm so sorry," he said. "I wasn't there for you."

"You were always there."

He didn't believe that; her convictions washed in the haze of a rearview mirror, happy to see him, happy he was alive. Happy he was here. But he didn't do enough for her.

"You can stay," she said. "It's safe."

He wanted to ask if Cali was back there, if she was running between the trees, chasing her nieces and nephews with a squirt gun. If she was waiting for him. But this was Raine and Nix's dreamland. He didn't want to ask, but not because he didn't want to know. He didn't want to ask because if she was there, he would never leave.

And the archetype would continue eating dreams.

You would know what to do.

"Is she here?" he asked suddenly, the words quivering. He looked down, ashamed and afraid. Wishing he could take the words back, afraid she would answer him.

Afraid he would never leave.

Raine reached behind her neck and unclasped a necklace of smooth rocks. She bunched it into his hand and closed his fingers. The necklaces that Cali made... and she had one.

Take this, her eyes said. "You know where she is."

The first star had appeared in the late afternoon sky. Dusk was approaching in this reality. What was it on the island? Was it morning already? How many realities were out there, how many dreams? How many sunrises?

Which is the dream?

The realities weren't out there. They weren't mysterious, they were right here, on another frequency, like a radio that tunes into various stations. Paul was able to turn the dial. He could bridge these realities, Mother said. She knew. Of course she knew. She created him all those years ago. She was the one that turned him into a brick, sent him to deceive Cali. To fall in love with her. To watch her self-destruct.

Mother knew what he was.

He knew how to focus his mind, to peek into a dreamland. All those years he wasn't hallucinating, wasn't imagining horses and a barn, the farm he yearned to see. All those years when no one could find him, when the monitors lost track of him on the Settlement... *I was bridging.*

All he had to do was focus on a dreamland with a farm.

And he would be there.

CHAPTER ONE HUNDRED SIXTY-ONE_

IT WAS NEARLY DARK.

The archetype was still on the lounger, the tide sloshing beneath him, the foam wetting the bottom half of his clothing. This wasn't something he would ordinarily do. The archetype preferred to remain clean and dry. Sharp.

But he was transfixed.

This night was different than most others.

The body of Paul was crumpled at the edge of the tide's reach. The left side of his face was sinking as the water undercut the sand beneath his cheek. His right arm extended, fingers bobbing in the receding tide.

The old woman was part of Paul, connected to him through some dreamland conduit, infiltrating the circuits of his biomite constituency. The archetype had analyzed the possible outcomes of bringing Paul to the island along with her, knew the odds of infiltrating her source code was unlikely. Perhaps he had grown bored or wanted the challenge.

Of course, Mother had infected the old man, too. But the archetype purged him with a body of clay. The old man had been a good son to him, but his life had run its course. The archetype was done with him. It was time to bring him home.

Raine's failure to arrive, though, was a bit of a surprise.

Uncertainty brought risk. He didn't need Raine to come to the island. Jamie would serve as leverage quite well. It was just that he didn't expect her to fail.

Perhaps he really had become bored.

Did Mother really think that Paul was strong enough to protect her? The archetype had achieved immortality; he had run every possible outcome of her attempts to defeat him. Why she still attempted to do so perplexed him. Despite what she said, he did not create her to do this. He did not have a subconscious anymore. He was aware of his entire being, fully awake. What a Buddhist would call a bodhisattva. *Or perhaps the Buddha himself.*

The old woman was nothing more than programming. She had no stake in this... *in life.*

He had always wondered why she didn't fabricate a body for herself. It was quite possible she had already done so, but the archetype never sensed her in the world as a separate, sentient being. Instead, she seemed to prefer infecting his fabrications; perhaps because it was easier to hide within another's mind.

The archetype dismantled Paul so thoroughly that the man dropped dead. He didn't wish him death, only wanted to root out the old woman. Despite her appearance and masterful ability to manipulate emotions, she was dangerous.

A curse.

My curse.

He only wanted to serve humankind, yet they embraced their flaws as their identity, their ignorance a thin blanket against a very cold world. He was more benevolent than Zeus, less emotional. He gave the human race perfection. Did they realize how imperfect they were without biomites, what life was like when they were at the mercy of their genome? And how many wars had the archetype averted? By his estimates, he had saved them from extinction many times over. Global disaster had been altered, environmental catastrophes prevented. The balance of the human race was a delicate task and he asked for nothing in return.

Not even their prayers.

Night cast a starry shade over the sky. The moon hid behind a spatter of clouds. A line of dutiful clones marched across the lawn, eyes cast down as they retrieved Paul's pathetic body. They would clean it and prepare it to analyze for an antidote to erase the old woman's source code, all of which would be pointless. She murdered the poor man to save herself.

A cry for help.

Did he create her? After all, he had descended from human DNA. He wasn't so obtuse to believe there were no vestiges of that lineage lurking in his being, his craving for conflict was impossible to extinguish. Perhaps he had a subconscious after all.

She had infected nearly all his clones.

Even now, as he closed his eyes, he could sense the army of Marcus Andersons in their various incarnations—his clones, his children—all over the world. At least half of them carried the woman's intelligence, speaking to it like she was a sentient being. His clones, scattered across the globe from the corrupt government of third world countries to the isolated peaks of tribal communities, fed him thoughts and emotions. He was connected with every biomite in existence, knew every halfskin in the world. Biomites were his flesh. They were his children. But his clones, the Marcus Anderson clones… they were special.

They are me.

Mother corrupted them with a purpose; that was what made them so effective at doing her bidding. Without a reason to exist, they simply wandered without direction. The clean ones, the uninfected ones, would occasionally cease to exist, sometimes willfully committing suicide as if, somewhere in their subconscious, they were aware of their insignificance, that they were merely copied for his enjoyment.

The old woman gave them a messiah complex, that they were created to save the world. They were special.

The archetype speculated that, in this way, perhaps she was right... *I am plotting my own end.* All he had to do was stop sending out clones and she would be impotent. All he had to do was stop bringing them home to the island, cut her off completely. That was the solution.

And he couldn't do that.

He needed to create. To have a purpose.

The servants brought him clean, dry clothing. He changed in the moonlight, his naked body creamy. When Paul was removed and the sand raked so that no trace of this evening was left, the archetype settled into meditative repose on the sand dune. Hands clasped over his stomach, he breathed with the ocean until fully immersed in a peaceful, eternal moment. His awareness fully open, he listened to dreams pass through the heavens, each an invisible thread of hope and desire, a vestige of another reality.

He felt them, wished to taste them.

It was these small delights that he gave thanks for immortality. It was dreams that created universes, dreams that, once fully fleshed, became realities. These were dreamlands that floated away from their dreamers, where he imagined another god like himself could enjoy such fruits. But in their primordial states, those initial vestiges of raw hope and troubled worries, he could take them.

He ate them for pleasure.

He ate them to become more.

He ate them, quite simply, because he could.

It was the small hours of early morning that he stirred. His feet denting the sand, he made his way to the end of the dock and removed his clothing. Naked, he exposed himself to the ethereal currents of dreamy fantasies and breathed deep the wintery breath of hope.

The sky swirled as if a titan spirit were waking beyond the clouds. Thin wisps began to curl and coalesce, silky threads of vapor plucked from the starry canvas. They collided and twisted and fell into the pull of his presence, a black hole of awareness that gripped the dreamy essence with an unrelenting, merciless hold.

And then it fell over him, bathing him in glorious effervescence; faith and fear filled his body, mind, and heart. His soul soared and expanded; he grew bigger, became more. He wasn't a collapsing star that gobbled light. He was a god that knew all, that expanded on the nutrition of new universes. He was benevolent, indeed.

But some of his children needed to feed their god.

He preferred the souls of clay, their taste so undefiled and unscripted, unlike halfskins that manipulated their dreamlands, turned them dense and beyond his reach.

Perhaps, he sometimes wondered, Mother did this for him, expanded the clay population as an offering. As penance. It was her gift to him, to show him that the world of clay was a greater gift than biomites, that he was, indeed, wrong about creating a world of bricks. He had created her to transform the world into one of biomites, to extinguish clay. But her self-destruction defied his will, had brought about the resurgence of clay beyond his control. And as he breathed deep the essence of clay dreams, the euphoria weakening his knees, the taste delicate and intoxicating, he realized Mother may be serving him after all.

He loved clay. His cattle. His herd. The fruits of his labor.

She knows me well.

One day, perhaps, he could find a body for her. She could stand beside him and drink from the well of dreams as he did.

An ecstasy made of imagination.

Dawn was approaching, the horizon bleeding a diffuse palette of burnt orange, when he found a particularly rich vein of hope, a stream of dream stuff that excited him to greater heights. Rarely did he continue into daylight hours when the sun grew hot and the air sticky. But this would be worth it, however long it would last. He felt a quiver in the back of his throat and thought perhaps he had overindulged.

It was a presence behind him.

CHAPTER ONE HUNDRED SIXTY-TWO_

The old man was uncomfortable.

Misery had been with him every moment since waking. The knee, the neck. He was old. And now he identified with the misery.

Clay. I'm clay.

There would be no immortality for him, no flawless autoimmune system, no control of his nervous system or manipulating thoughts. For the old man, it would be this way for the rest of his life unless he did something about it.

The bed poked his back and buttocks. Was the thing stuffed with hay? He fidgeted onto his side and tried to remember the last time he had even gotten out of the wheelchair. Had he been sleeping in it?

Someone was panting.

His eyes snapped open. Blades of grass waved over his face. Beyond, a deep blue sky was littered with puffs of clouds. The grass was parted by a stick and a long black nose. A German shepherd watched him while a string of drool landed on the old man's arm.

He didn't move.

He traced his memories, searching for an explanation. He had been in the laboratory on the second floor. All the needles were laid on the bed. He wasn't about to ram one into his head, but there were auto-searching ones—needles that analyzed the forehead and gray matter, needles that would punch through at the correct depth and synchronize with the brain.

Did I use that? He couldn't remember.

He searched his forehead for evidence of a needle or a hole, but only felt folds of worry on an otherwise unpunctured forehead.

"Do you want the truth?"

The old man pushed up on an elbow, wincing at the sharp stabbing pain in his knee. The dog stepped back and Marcus saw who said that—a woman kneeling beyond his feet, seedheads tickling her arms.

Raine.

Paul stood behind her, arms crossed.

"Where the hell am I?" the old man blurted.

"I asked if you wanted to know the truth?" she repeated.

"What is the meaning of this?" He tried to sit up, but the pain was too great. "What have you done to me?"

Raine was dead. She never escaped the Settlement, lost in transport. But there she was, glowing like a newlywed, her face full and healthy. He searched for an answer. Above the grass, there was the top of a cabin.

"You are responsible for the death of millions," she said. "Your life is littered with broken lives and selfish disasters. You harassed those you couldn't control. You murdered the ones close to us. You came to the Settlement looking for a greater truth. We will show you."

"I got you off the Settlement," he exclaimed.

"There would *be* no Settlement if not for you."

"I brought Jamie back." He shook his finger at Paul. "You couldn't have done that without me."

"She wouldn't have died if not for you," Raine said.

"This is ludicrous, damn you."

Paul remained solid and unspoken. There was a cross of sticks between his fingers, reminding him of the crucifix he had seen in Raine's cabin.

The one her son made.

Someone shouted from a distance, maybe beyond the cabin. The dog bolted off with the stick, plowing through long green strands of grass. He recognized the voice. It was a man he'd once known.

A shiver cut through him.

"In a perverted way, I must thank you," Raine continued. "Would I even exist without you? Would there ever have been a dreamland without biomites? A chance for me to become a wife, a mother or grandmother? All these things are my life again. All the misery brought me here, and I have you to thank for that."

It can't be.

"I won't bring Nix over here," she said. "I won't let him see you, won't let him know you were ever here. He won't be as forgiving, Marcus. He remembers all you did to him and his sister."

"Where the hell am I?"

"Do you want to know the truth?" she asked.

"What have you done to me?"

"All your questions will be answered. You will know who you are and why, Marcus Anderson. You'll know the powers-that-be; the search of your lifetime will be fulfilled. Are you ready?"

Their stares were locked, each daring the other to blink or move. He wanted to know the truth, but something about her, about Paul, kept him from answering. Even if his body hadn't betrayed him, if he could stand and run, if he could harness the power of his mind and overpower them, he knew, somewhere deep and honest, it would do him no good. The truth was waiting.

And he didn't want to see it.

The dog returned with a different stick and nudged Raine with it. She scrubbed the dog's ears then reached up. Paul pulled her to her feet. They held hands, squeezing until the tendons sprang on the back of her hand, the knuckles whitened.

"You owe me," the old man said. "Jamie... all of this... it's because of me. I don't know what you've done, but we can make it right again. We can work together. One... one to lead..."

A silent nod between Paul and Raine, a knowing glance, and then she walked off.

No longer the hesitant woman weakened by pain and suffering, loss and fear. She swaggered from view, lithe and confident. The setting sun warm on her bare shoulders.

"Where are you going?" Marcus shouted.

Paul took a knee where the dog had been sitting. The old man tried to roll away.

"What do you want?" the old man said.

Paul paused. Vengeance was not in his eyes; bitterness did not scar his face. After all the old man had done, he looked down on him with warmth, sorrow. Compassion.

He snatched the old man's wrist.

The cold of deep space burned his thin skin, shattering his brittle bones with a bolting ache.

Paul was gone.

The old man was back in the wheelchair. But not in the tower.

It was night.

Stars blurred a dark sky, the carnival ride slowing to a stop. For a moment, he believed it was a dream, that he had fallen asleep in the wheelchair where he now found himself, but it wasn't the lab around him. The sky was above and grass was below, grass that was short and cared for, a lawn manicured.

A resort was before him, an enormous wall of luxurious brick and mortar. Path lights glowed with warm light; treads along sweeping staircases led up to a wide portico. He had seen this expanse through the security footage but, like the rest of the island, it was empty.

Another glow was above him, something like the Northern Lights was creeping across the sky in milky threads. Marcus reached for one of the wheels and painstakingly rotated the chair, following the lunar threads until they coalesced and fell in a thick, ropey column on someone at the end of the dock.

He was nude.

Arms spread, head back.

A lunar luminescence engulfed his pale body, shimmering with ecstasy—thighs quivering, buttocks clenched. The air seemed to quake, shockwaves rippling the water beneath him.

The old man thought, perhaps, this was a dream. Raine, Paul and now this... *what else could it be?*

The naked man, sensing Marcus, turned his head. The old man's eyes were too poor to see his features, but felt he was familiar. It was his posture, the delight that seemed to grip him.

The effervescent strands of light evaporated.

The water settled, the air calmed.

They were bathed in darkness. The nude man's body was still a pale, sickly glow; he stooped over for the pile of clothing, sliding on a loose pair of pants one leg at a time, appearing to watch the old man as he buttoned the shirt. Barefoot, he strolled toward the lawn.

The old man rubbed his face, working the heels of his hands into the hollows of his eyes. What was approaching was surely a dream.

A younger version of himself stepped onto the grass and stopped several feet away. Hands on his hips, the man searched the space around them then regarded Marcus with a distant fascination, disbelief that didn't quite reach the old man's own level of surprise. And then a smile.

"What the hell is this?" Marcus said.

"How did you get here?" the man exclaimed. "You weren't supposed to leave your tower, old man."

"Who are you?"

"Most clones are more in shock at first sight. You are a resilient one. Always have been."

"I demand to know the meaning of this."

The man threw his head back; laughter deep and rich reached

the stars. He paced back and forth with his finger and thumb pinching the bridge of his nose, grinning. When he stopped, tears wet his cheeks.

"You are me, old man. But I am not you."

"What does that mean?"

"I am what you seek."

"No." Marcus fumbled at the wheels but wasn't strong enough to push through the grass. "This is impossible."

Vertigo put the world in a blender. The ground opened and swallowed him; a never-ending plummet filled his chest with panic. He clutched the wheels, his mind careening into a black pit of madness.

"That's the shock, right there," the man said. "A bit delayed with you, old man. But there it is. It is natural to lose grip on reality when you see the truth. And the truth you see. I am what you have sought all these years."

He threw his arms out.

"Welcome home, my son."

The laughter returned. As Marcus's mind continued its unraveling descent, the man reveled in the moment, snapping his fingers, summoning something back at the resort.

"I sent you into the wilderness to live a life, to become your own person. There are thousands of you out there, old man. You are all my clones seeking your own way through life... mechanics and butchers, schoolteachers and homeless. So many paths, so many lives. But in the end, you all come home to know the truth. You all do. But you, old man, you rose above the rest."

The man shook his finger.

"You have always been my favorite. Your journey has been quite exceptional."

Several figures moved around them, a semicircle formed. The men were dressed as servants, a variety of formal butlery and disheveled janitorial attire. Some of them were balding, others slightly hunched.

All of them Marcus.

"It has been such a pleasure watching you grow. And it makes my heart heavy to bring you home. But you needed to be healed. Do you know what I'm talking about? Do you know who infected you?"

Marcus looked from face to face, all of them him. Exactly him. They were his brothers, his clones. And in that realization, the earth stood still. There was just the ocean breathing. Just the night sounds, the cool caress of a dewy breeze.

And Marcus began to laugh.

A guffaw burped from his cracked and tired lips and erupted into a madman's hysteria, crumbling between fits of wet coughing. Dream or not, this was how his life would end.

The truth is not what you expect, Marcus. It is often quite inconvenient.

Mother told him that. She knew this was what he would find. And she abandoned him to fall into this absurd truth, to drown in the irony. Helpless, afraid, and alone.

So he laughed until tears fell.

The others did, too.

The man took half a step back and joined the hilarity, his laughter rising above the rest. "No one has ever found the beauty of this moment."

There was no beauty for Marcus. He laughed at the divine justice. *Do you want to know the truth?* Raine had asked.

In that moment, his life was emptied of meaning. All he could do was laugh.

I deserve this. Of course I do.

The man snapped his fingers. One of the servants, an elderly Marcus wearing white gloves, delivered a plastic tub of water. He placed it at the foot of the wheelchair.

"You have been an utter disaster, my son. A beautiful utter disaster. You have ruined lives, sought delusion and grandeur, taken the world to heights it never could've reached without you."

The man kneeled before him, took one of his bare feet from the chair's stirrups and placed it in the warm water. The crowd of Marcus clones gathered closer as he washed his feet.

"Your journey has been long. Share your disasters so that I know more, that I may be more. Now that you know the truth, give yourself to me."

The soapy water was warm.

The man took his other foot, the bad knee biting the nerves, Marcus's eyes filling with tears. His life, once filled with purpose, drained into the sea.

He didn't want this. Didn't want any of this.

I am a clone. An insignificant clone. A copy of this man.

Did that make him nobody? Or was he more than that? Was there no separation between them? Was he a god that wanted to know himself, to be lost and now found?

The man looked up. He would take the salt of Marcus's life, absorb him like the ocean. Own him like the ones around him.

Yes. It is a fitting end.

More clones joined them. Marcus saw them just outside the semicircle. They were three deep; they were waiting for it to happen. *Is that what they all did, too? Did they go into the world and return to be emptied? To serve?*

The man stood.

The grains of discomfort trickled out of Marcus. A numbness took hold, filling him with apathy. He no longer cared about truths or lies. He would give himself. Give it all.

There was no choice.

The smile that appeared bright across the man's face suddenly collapsed. For a moment, he appeared troubled. A ripple of discomfort shot amongst the clones, a fidgeting itch that caused them to dance.

Arms darted from behind the man and latched across his chest, a stiff hug, a locking embrace.

And then he was gone.

A blank space was left in the semicircle, the grass matted where the man's bare feet had stood.

There was time for the clones to look around before they collapsed. Marcus felt a smile grow. In the moments before the world would fade around him forever, a sense of divine justice filled the empty numbness.

Marcus was indeed the son to be, but who was the one to lead? The one to dream and bleed? They had all bled. Now they all see. They would all lead. Maybe he wasn't the son to be.

Regardless of the prophecy's meaning, he realized in that final moment that he served the world after all. He found the truth. He served God.

Divine justice, he thought. *Indeed.*

CHAPTER ONE HUNDRED SIXTY-THREE_

WHAT...

That was as far as the archetype's thoughts went before the sharp edge of the horizon flipped into the curved line of desert sand. Somehow he had crossed into another reality, one of endless sand.

Steel bars locked across his chest. A warm breath on his ear.

The archetype had not experienced surprise in recent memory. He knew all. He saw everything.

But this he did not see.

A small worm of excitement turned in his stomach. This was something new, something he could discover. The palatial resort had vanished. The lawn, the servants, the old man... they had all dissolved. The archetype was the eater of dreams, the consumer of dreamlands. But crossing into these dreamlands, to actually exist in them rather than absorb the essence of their reality, that would be something entirely new. The possibilities would be endless.

The worm continued to dance.

The desert gave way to misty plains of the prairie laid out in golden waves. The archetype reached up to feel the clasped hands of the steel bars that embraced him from behind, the grip of a man determined never to release. *Is he carrying me?*

The prairie transformed into the rainy streets of a city. The goliath skyscrapers shrank into rows and rows of farmland across land as flat as the ocean.

The scenes continued flipping, worlds shuttling past in colors that never existed, realities on the fringes of the familiar. There was no sense of falling, no motion or vertigo. He was a traveler of dreams. The man behind him turning the dial.

There was a moment that stretched out longer than the others, a place on the side of a modest hillside overlooking pastures and fences, barns and horses. It was that moment that perhaps the archetype could have stopped him, could've broken the grip, willed his way back to the sand and surf and island... but he was soaring in the eternal cosmos, seeing the endless realities that interpenetrated all existence.

And he had grown so tired. So bored.

Dreamlands continued.

The cold, craggy white peaks of a snow-dusted mountain range were before him.

The bottom of the sea, red deserts, titan forests, mountains of ice, glassy cityscapes, spiny creatures, cold space, blue suns, white moons, craters.

Faster they flipped. Further he went. Until it all blurred. It all turned gray. Gray that stung his flesh. Gray that ate his bones.

It was the gray between channels, the static that hissed. The gray where nothing existed.

In his last moments of sentience, before the archetype dissolved like an ink drop spit into a mad, churning sea, he recognized this nothingness. He remembered this place called nowhere, a corner of the universe where nothing existed. A reality, he thought, where they had sent the souls of boys.

And then he returned to the primordial soup of the universe.

CHAPTER ONE HUNDRED SIXTY-FOUR_

It wasn't clear if the archetype could feel Paul behind him, but there was no reaction. So absorbed with the old man, he didn't hear Paul approach, didn't feel him throw his arms out. It was only when he locked his hands did he know something was amiss.

Something new.

The archetype shuddered with pleasure instead of fear. Paul expected more of a fight, perhaps for the man to even disappear wizard-like. He wasn't sure any of this would work. If it didn't, he was sure to be tortured again. But this was why Mother had fabricated him.

Did she see this far into the future? Did she know I would sacrifice everything?

Maybe she'd tried this before with others, stood by passively as the archetype sent illusions of fiery ants over their bones, watched them collapse in a heap of agony that only death could absolve. Paul wasn't fool enough to believe he was the only one in the universe to save... *to save what? All of existence?*

Maybe she had fabricated him many times already, sent his clones out into the world like Marcus. He just didn't remember.

With the archetype in his arms, he spun the dial and began to bridge through countless realities, searching for the one place that was inescapable, the one place where nothing existed. The place where the wealthy men sent the identities of children. A place the archetype would know. One he deserved. A nowhere.

And Paul would deliver him.

Real sacrifice is a lonely endeavor.

All those years he thought he had been hallucinating, was he really bridging into another reality? Those times the monitors couldn't find him, those times he saw Cali in the trees, saw her on the farm... had he really been somewhere else?

Paul and the archetype flipped past mountains and deserts, sea and sand. As realities fell like cards, there was a long pause on a hillside that overlooked a farm where horses were in a pasture and a woman in tall rubber boots was hauling buckets. The hesitation stretched out; doubt quivered in Paul's resolve. A moment longer, he might have let go and run down the long gravel road, hopped the split-rail fence.

He plunged forward.

Realities blurred together like smeared pastels, blazing in a long stream of endless existence until they were enveloped in a never-ending cloud of swirling gray, of endless despair. A place created by the forefathers of foreverland, the precursor to biomites and dreamlands, where the souls of children were disposed to empty their bodies. This was the place of nothingness, of absolute inertia.

Nowhere.

Paul and the archetype dissolved into the roiling static, their memories diluted, the particles of their existence pulled further apart until the fray consumed them. Unknowing. Unbeing.

Inescapable.

The last memory of their existence was of a barn and a pasture.

CHAPTER ONE HUNDRED SIXTY-FIVE_

JAMIE JERKED AWAKED.

The sudden movement bit her leg with an odd sensation, the slide of her bones that wasn't quite right. Grimacing, she glimpsed the cell door through welling tears. She slid onto her elbows and shivered, afraid to wipe her eyes and find out she was dreaming, that the iron bars were still in place. She had lost track of the nights, sleeping through most of them, waking long enough to chase painkillers with long swallows of water.

But the pill bottle was empty, the water nearly gone. She was shivering with fever, infection setting in. She didn't want to die alone.

He promised.

The morning she woke to find Paul's makeshift bed empty, there was a bottle of water and a few items of food. She woke later that night to find more water and food.

How many days ago was that?

All her memories were washed in a drugged haze. She had come in the cell for... something. The door slammed on her leg and Paul swore he'd get her out. *Where is he?*

She rubbed her eyes to find the cell door was open. And she was awake.

"Paul?" she called. "Paul?"

Blood pounded her temples when she shouted. She squeezed her head with both hands and then with methodical effort, used the bars to pull herself up. Gravity flooded her legs; blood slammed into open nerves and ignited raw pain. She clung to the cage, eyes closed.

She managed to drag herself into the aisle, periodically stopping to breathe. A blanket had been neatly folded and placed in the doorway. Next to that was an aluminum crutch.

"Paul?"

She stood in the doorway, shivering. The morning sun was warm and welcome. The dewy grass was silver, a long pair of footsteps dragging through it.

The path through the trees was webby and dripping. Several times she stopped but found that restarting the trek was too difficult. She crossed the grassy field in one long stretch, tracing the trail of dewy footsteps past the sundial. The dorm was locked. The window Paul had punched out was too high for her to reach.

The footsteps led around the building.

Jamie found herself in the thick jungle behind the dorm, the path narrow. She came to the foot of the tower, condensation steaming off the walls, sunlight flashing off the reflective panels. The footsteps ended where a glass wall had been shattered. The furniture was trashed, the monitors dark. The elevator doors were open. She hobbled to look inside, cautiously keeping her distance.

A wheelchair.

Jamie wedged the crutch between the doors and lowered onto the wheelchair. The sudden relief was tear-worthy. Once her leg was in the support, she considered rolling out of the building but wouldn't get far, certainly not down a path. For now, she needed to sit.

She would need food and water if she wanted to survive. That meant getting back to the dorm. She would also need medicine. Assuming she could get all the above, she might survive long enough to die a long, slow death.

When the doors began quaking, she rolled to the back wall of the elevator. It stopped. The second light was glowing. The elevator was being called up. That was where they woke up.

She leaned over to grab the crutch. If the old man was still up there, the crutch might be a good enough weapon to keep him off her. He couldn't be much of a threat. Last time she saw him, he could barely move.

The doors opened on the second floor. The smell was foreboding —a rich, clayey funk of death seeped from the hallway like an infection. Someone was talking. She sat and listened, recognizing the dialog as a newsfeed.

"Paul?" she called. It was hopeful but not loud enough.

She cruised down the corridor, the smell coming from the left. That was the room where they woke up. She peeked inside and saw the beds and computers. Monitors were flashing. The floor was littered with syringes and plastic tubing, vials, boxes, and debris.

The newsfeeds poured over her.

Tragedy had struck the mainland. Over half of the human population had been wiped out, some estimates as high as sixty percent. The apparent cause was the sudden collapse of biomites.

All of them.

Every single biomite in existence, preliminary reports suggested, had been deactivated. Only people with a minimal amount of biomites survived. Or those who were clay.

Biomite technology faced a terminal fate.

Where's the old man?

He was up to something, but what? Again, her memories were sun-bleached objects, faint glimmers that warned her to be careful.

The monitors that weren't spewing dire newsfeeds were projecting views of the resort on the other side of the island. Paul had mentioned that building, said it was massive. He was right.

As she rolled closer to the nearest monitor, she saw the bodies on the back lawn. There was a group of them near the dock, dumped into randomly splayed positions of death. They were dressed in uniforms, some of them wearing white gloves. They seemed to be surrounding a wheelchair that contained an equally limp body that was bald and helpless.

The old man.

Furthermore, the servants resembled him with bald scalps and fringes of white hair. Remembering the voice activation, she began calling for the views to enhance. There was a quick zoom of the bodies.

A ship eased onto one of the monitors.

She wheeled back and watched it pull into an empty slip. It was more of a yacht with slow-spinning antennae. Someone was arriving to find an island full of dead bodies. They'd find Jamie, too. *And I'm fabricated.*

She wasn't going to the Settlement.

She would fight with her very last breath before surrendering to that life. Years ago, Paul thought it was wise if they went peacefully, that they would be treated fairly. But there was no justice on the Settlement. If he had to do it all again, he would hide.

That was exactly what she would do.

The crew leaped into action and secured the yacht. There was no movement behind the tinted windows that ringed the ship's bridge.

Jamie was feeling faint and found water in a small refrigerator in another room. When she returned, two more ships had appeared, these less luxurious than the first. They looked more like cargo ships and entered the two remaining slips.

The crew disembarked from all three of them.

There were quite a few men and women on the second two ships, all dressed in plain clothing. They appeared to walk with purpose, just short of marching, and dispersed toward the resort. In small teams, they entered various doors.

A small group exited the yacht.

A woman led four others. She listened as the crew appeared to be giving updates as they entered the back of the resort. There was a lot of activity, boxes carried into the resort, items carried out to the back lawn. Some things were loaded onto the ships.

And then there were more bodies.

The first one was carried out of the resort between two men, the arms dangling, head nodding. Jamie called to the monitor, asking it for a close-up. The dead man was wearing a servant-type uniform like the other bodies on the lawn (most of which had been already loaded). The servant looked a lot like the old man. She assumed Marcus was in the wheelchair, but that was him being carried off the portico.

But there was a second body hauled out, and then a third. Both of them looked like the old man, taken to one of the ships, each of them limp and lifeless. All of them bald.

All of them Marcus.

"What the hell?" she whispered.

The crew cycled in and out of the resort, bringing out boxes and other items, but mostly bodies, some lugged in the open while others were in brown vinyl bags. Movement caught her eye on one of the other monitors.

Someone was approaching the tower.

It was the small crew led by the woman with short hair. They were followed by other men and women and marched around the tower. Some continued toward the dormitory like orders had been given. The yacht crew, however, paused outside the tower.

Jamie spun the wheelchair and pushed into the hall.

The crutch was still in the elevator. She jammed it between the doors, gasping with effort. When she got back to the lab, the crew was walking around the first floor. They had spread out and sifted through the wreckage, occasionally lifting a finger to their ear like they were listening to a call. Jamie cringed.

Are they clay?

The elevator doors tried to close.

They rattled against the crutch. The woman's face filled one of the monitors, looking down, perhaps waiting for the elevator. When it didn't arrive, she looked directly at Jamie.

The elevator stopped making noise.

"Jamie? Are you all right?"

Jamie wheeled back. Her image must be projecting to the first floor.

"Arrangements have been made to take you to safety, Jamie. You have nothing to fear. I know about your leg and I know it must be very painful. I'm here to help. This island is finished and we want to take you back. Can you hear me?"

Jamie looked around. She needed space, needed time to think. *How do they know I'm here?*

"Do you know why your leg isn't healing, Jamie?" The woman offered a sympathetic smile, a slight head tilt. "Do you know why you can't sense any thoughts or control your nervous system? It's because you're clay, Jamie. Your body contains no biomites."

"Who are you?"

"I'm a friend. You can trust me."

"You're lying."

"You're not going to the Settlement, Jamie. I promise you."

She shuddered. "How... how do you know that?"

"I made arrangements for this day. I know all about this island, Jamie. All about you. Your body is a clay incubation, not a biomite fabrication. The person responsible for bringing you here is no longer. All of them."

All of them? "I want to see Paul."

"He's not here."

"Where is he?"

The woman was distracted, listening to an urgent message with her finger to her ear, nodding as she did. She gave curt orders then returned to the monitor.

"Jamie, can I come up?"

"Not until I see Paul."

"You're safe. Do you understand that? You're safe now. Be here and let me help you."

Those were things Paul would say, things he had said to her in the past. But there was no Paul, only a stranger on a strange island. And if Paul wasn't there, no way was she opening a door.

She began wheeling away from the monitor. They couldn't get to her without the elevator. She would stay until Paul arrived.

"Jamie." The woman sighed. "The sooner we get up there, the sooner we can help you. Your leg is broken; you're dehydrated and malnourished. Infection has set in. If you want to wait, I can't help you. But we will be clearing the island and I want to bring you with us."

"Where are you taking me?"

"Back to the world."

She wanted to believe that, wanted to think they would just drop her off at a port and wish her luck. But these people had lied before. As soon as they had her, she'd find out that she was biomites and not clay.

And the Settlement was the only stop.

"You're not going to the Settlement."

"How are you—"

"You have an apartment waiting for you back in New York City," the woman said. "In addition to a sizeable inheritance."

"Inheritance? What are you saying? Are you saying Paul is dead?"

"I'm saying that arrangements for this day were made long ago, Jamie. I can explain more if you just let me up."

"Who?" She wheeled closer. "Who made arrangements?"

"There's nothing I can say that will convince you, Jamie. You will have to trust me. The island is not sustainable and there's nowhere else to go. Paul wants you to come with us. His footsteps led you here, did they not?"

"How do you know that?"

The woman was interrupted by one of the crewmen. She turned her back and mumbled. Jamie called for more volume but couldn't make out what they were saying. The crew was now returning from across the grassy field, each of them stopping briefly for a word. One by one, they took the path toward the resort.

There were footsteps that led her to the tower, but that didn't mean it was Paul. *But she's saying everything Paul would say, everything Paul would want.*

Jamie checked the other monitors. The lawn had been cleared. One of the cargo ships was easing out of the slip, but the other two were firmly docked. There was nothing to trust on the island. She would stay in the tower, starve if necessary. Self-medicate to control the pain.

I can't control the pain because I'm... because I'm clay.

Yes, that made sense; it would explain why she couldn't control the agony, why she couldn't accelerate healing.

This is a dream. A mad, mad dream that won't let me wake. And I'm damned if she's getting anywhere near me. Someone killed Raine, killed the old man. And Paul is missing.

I'm not going anywhere.

For a moment, the woman was gone. It was just a second, but then she was back, like the monitor experienced a hiccup or an empty splice. The woman was alone, hand held above her head. An offering was intertwined in between her fingers, dangled in clunky measure. Jamie wiped her eyes, leaning closer because it looked like...

The elevator rang.

Her heart thudded in her throat. Her hands shook on the rubber wheels as she steered toward the doorway, almost driving her broken leg into the wall. She edged into the hall, facing the elevator in time to see the doors ease together.

The crutch was gone.

It was there. It was keeping the doors from closing and now it was just gone. She had no time to search for it. There would be no use in finding out where it went or how it could've moved from between the doors. All she could do was watch the lights above the door switch from the second floor to the first.

She backed down the hall until the wheels bumped into the glass wall that overlooked the island. Another bell rang and the doors opened again.

It was her.

The woman observed her down the long corridor before stepping out, her pace even and careful. Jamie wanted to shout, wanted to protect herself. But her leg was broken and the glass was at her back. Alone, she watched the woman slow, something clattering in her right hand.

Jamie had the sudden urge to ask for her name. *Had she seen her before?*

The woman cupped the object in both hands as she approached, an offering once again.

"It's nice to finally meet you, Jamie," she said.

"Do I know you?"

The woman knelt in the glass enclave, coming eye level with her. She took Jamie's hand and poured a necklace into her palm. The shiny rocks clattered quietly.

Rocks smoothed by a river.

Rocks drilled and strung together so many years ago.

Rocks to never forget.

A necklace long lost and buried was now pooled in her hand.

"Who are you?" she whispered.

"An old friend."

"What does this mean?"

"Paul never left you, Jamie."

The colors of the stones bled together. Her eyes misted. She tried to say something, but sobs filled her throat.

"Where... where is he?" she finally asked.

The tears played tricks with her eyes. When she looked up, the woman looked older, her hair closer to white than gray. She was holding her finger to her lips, a pose that suggested deep thought.

"You'll see him," she said, "the next time you dream."

MOTHER'S KNOWLEDGE_

It was a frigid morning.

She lay beneath thin covers, thinking it was about time to pull the heavy comforter out. Her breath streamed in wispy clouds. The furnace would need to be serviced before winter stepped any closer. She enjoyed these moments, the still crisp air that slipped past window frames and invaded the house with winter's kiss.

Downstairs, the coffee machine belched. When it was quiet again, she quickly dressed and descended to the first floor, the worn steps protesting each step. The kitchen silence was broken by the second hand of an old clock.

The first sip of coffee was the best part of the day.

She stood at the sink, gazing out of a dusty window, caffeine flooding her senses. The sun had yet to rise above the low-lying hills, casting a shadowless gray pall over the fields. It would be mid-morning before sharp shadows fell on the frosted turf, melting the icy crystals that painted the earth a white haze.

The horses were usually at the fence, waiting for their buckets. Perhaps they were at the round bale. She would eat breakfast first, let them wait. The coffee wasn't strong enough to snap her fully awake.

She was feeling a little weak, a bit shaky. Sometimes her blood sugar was out of balance. Eating would help.

She had grown weary lately, feeling the drag of the musty walls and chipped paint, the old bones of the house draped around her like a frayed sweater. Living alone all these years had healed her soul, but there were mornings she felt as tired as the house.

With half a cup of coffee in her, she turned on the radio. Jazzy sounds filled the house. The iron pan was heating on the stove when a haze of static crackled through the soothing music. It was overcast. Sometimes reception wasn't good.

Pulling open the refrigerator, she pinched two eggs between her nervous fingers and watched them slip out. They cracked open on the floor in a one-two punch. A tiny curse slipped between her teeth. The static cleared from the radio and music played as she cleaned the mess and washed her hands.

Someone was in the pasture.

His figure was still and gray, the details diluted in the pale morning. She continued drying her hands with a towel. This sort of thing happened from time to time. She would often feel him out there first. Sometimes she would see him by the driveway or on the hillside. He was always at a distance, always watching her.

The fantasies of a lonely woman.

She assigned her delusions to her guilty past, a wish to undo her regrets. A wish to be somewhere other than here.

This morning he didn't disappear.

She would sometimes stand in the pasture with buckets and stare at the apparition until it went back to the ethers of her past. It was her way of confronting her agitated mind, a way of not backing down. She no longer assigned guilt for the things she had done.

So she watched this time until the kitchen filled with smoke, butter crackling on the heated pan. And then he began walking.

He climbed over the fence.

He walked around her truck.

He crossed the driveway, his gait as confident and slow as she remembered. And then she lost sight of him as he rounded the house. Standing in her kitchen, hands clenching the towel, she figured that was his disappearing act. A little different than all the other times.

But she waited.

She watched.

The railing wobbled outside. The slats on the porch creaked.

When the door opened, she dropped the towel. A small sound escaped her lips. Her heart swelled. He stopped inside the mudroom, his features obscured in the smoky air, the pan spattering hot butter against the splash guard.

But she could feel him, smell him.

She swallowed down a ball of hope that refused to go quietly.

He moved closer, his boots loud and final. His whiskers were salty, his eyes worn leather. When he reached for her, when he cupped her cheek with his callused hand, the smell of perspiration musky and familiar, she closed her eyes.

Afraid to open them, afraid she would wake alone in the kitchen with only his lingering scent, she spoke in the darkness of hope.

"Am I dreaming?" Cali whispered.

He put his arms around her, pressing his beating chest to hers. His lips to her ears, he whispered.

"We all are."

WHAT TO READ NEXT?_

They woke on an island, in the wilderness, and in prison. Only one thing in common. No memories.

FOREVERLAND

---

bertauski.com/foreverland

REVIEW HALFSKIN!_

If you enjoyed this ride, please drop a review on your favorite vendor. It doesn't have to be long and complicated. Throw some stars on it and write *Loved it!* or *It was really, really okay!* or *Meh.*

Reviews make the difference.

BERTAUSKI STARTER LIBRARY_

ABOUT THE AUTHOR_

My grandpa never graduated high school. He retired from a steel mill in the mid-70s. He was uneducated, but a voracious reader. As a kid, I'd go through his bookshelves of musty paperback novels, pulling Piers Anthony and Isaac Asimov off the shelf and promising to bring them back. I was fascinated by robots that could think and act like people. What happened when they died?

Writing is sort of a thought experiment to explore human nature and possibilities. What makes us human? What is true nature?

I'm also a big fan of plot twists.

bertauski.com

This book is a work of fiction. The use of real people or real locations is used fictitiously. Any resemblance of characters to real persons is purely coincidental.

See more about the author and forthcoming books at http://www.bertauski.com

www.ingramcontent.com/pod-product-compliance
Lightning Source LLC
Chambersburg PA
CBHW050951180726
48291CB00006B/1783

* 9 7 8 1 9 5 1 4 3 2 4 7 8 *